PRAISE FOR JAMES DASHNER AND THE MAZE RUNNER SERIES

More Than 10 Million Copies In Print!

A #1 *NEW YORK TIMES* BESTSELLER
A *USA TODAY* BESTSELLER
A *KIRKUS REVIEWS* BEST TEEN BOOK OF THE YEAR
AN ALA-YALSA BEST FICTION FOR YOUNG ADULTS BOOK
AN ALA-YALSA QUICK PICK

"[A] mysterious survival saga that passionate fans describe as a fusion of *Lord of the Flies, The Hunger Games,* and *Lost.*" —EW.com

"[A] nail-biting must-read." —Seventeen.com

"Wonderful action writing—fast-paced . . . but smart and well observed."
—*Newsday*

"Breathless, cinematic action." —*Publishers Weekly*

"Heart-pounding to the very last moment." —*Kirkus Reviews*

"Exclamation-worthy." —*Romantic Times*

★ "James Dashner's illuminating prequel [*The Kill Order*] will thrill fans of this Maze Runner [series] and prove just as exciting for readers new to the series." —*Shelf Awareness,* Starred

"Take a deep breath before you start any James Dashner book."
—*Deseret News*

BOOKS BY JAMES DASHNER

The Mortality Doctrine Series

The Eye of Minds

The Rule of Thoughts

The Maze Runner Series

The Maze Runner

The Scorch Trials

The Death Cure

The Kill Order

The 13th Reality Series

The Journal of Curious Letters

The Hunt for Dark Infinity

The Blade of Shattered Hope

The Void of Mist and Thunder

CONTENTS

BOOK 1 IN THE #1 *NEW YORK TIMES* BESTSELLING SERIES BY

JAMES DASHNER

THE MAZE RUNNER

NOW A MAJOR MOTION PICTURE

The Maze Runner dedication:
For Lynette. This book was a three-year journey, and you never doubted.

The Scorch Trials dedication:
For Wesley, Bryson, Kayla, and Dallin. Best kids ever.

Visit us on the Web! randomhouseteens.com

Educators and librarians, for a variety of teaching tools, visit us at RHTeachersLibrarians.com

Library of Congress Cataloging-in-Publication Data is available upon request.

ISBN 978-0-553-53824-3 (hc) — ISBN 978-1-110-93212-4 (ebook)

Printed in the United States of America

10 9 8 7 6 5 4 3 2 1

THE MAZE RUNNER

CHAPTER 1

He began his new life standing up, surrounded by cold darkness and stale, dusty air.

Metal ground against metal; a lurching shudder shook the floor beneath him. He fell down at the sudden movement and shuffled backward on his hands and feet, drops of sweat beading on his forehead despite the cool air. His back struck a hard metal wall; he slid along it until he hit the corner of the room. Sinking to the floor, he pulled his legs up tight against his body, hoping his eyes would soon adjust to the darkness.

With another jolt, the room jerked upward like an old lift in a mine shaft.

Harsh sounds of chains and pulleys, like the workings of an ancient steel factory, echoed through the room, bouncing off the walls with a hollow, tinny whine. The lightless elevator swayed back and forth as it ascended, turning the boy's stomach sour with nausea; a smell like burnt oil invaded his senses, making him feel worse. He wanted to cry, but no tears came; he could only sit there, alone, waiting.

My name is Thomas, he thought.

That . . . that was the only thing he could remember about his life.

He didn't understand how this could be possible. His mind functioned without flaw, trying to calculate his surroundings and predicament. Knowledge flooded his thoughts, facts and images, memories and details of the world and how it works. He pictured snow on trees, running down a leaf-strewn road, eating a hamburger, the moon casting a pale glow on a grassy meadow, swimming in a lake, a busy city square with hundreds of people bustling about their business.

And yet he didn't know where he came from, or how he'd gotten inside the dark lift, or who his parents were. He didn't even know his last name. Images of people flashed across his mind, but there was no recognition, their faces replaced with haunted smears of color. He couldn't think of one person he knew, or recall a single conversation.

The room continued its ascent, swaying; Thomas grew immune to the ceaseless rattling of the chains that pulled him upward. A long time passed. Minutes stretched into hours, although it was impossible to know for sure because every second seemed an eternity. No. He was smarter than that. Trusting his instincts, he knew he'd been moving for roughly *half* an hour.

Strangely enough, he felt his fear whisked away like a swarm of gnats caught in the wind, replaced by an intense curiosity. He wanted to know where he was and what was happening.

With a groan and then a clonk, the rising room halted; the sudden change jolted Thomas from his huddled position and threw him across the hard floor. As he scrambled to his feet, he felt the room sway less and less until it finally stilled. Everything fell silent.

A minute passed. Two. He looked in every direction but saw only darkness; he felt along the walls again, searching for a way out. But there was nothing, only the cool metal. He groaned in frustration; his echo amplified through the air, like the haunted moan of death. It faded, and silence returned. He screamed, called for help, pounded on the walls with his fists.

Nothing.

Thomas backed into the corner once again, folded his arms and shivered, and the fear returned. He felt a worrying shudder in his chest, as if his heart wanted to escape, to flee his body.

"Someone . . . help . . . me!" he screamed; each word ripped his throat raw.

A loud clank rang out above him and he sucked in a startled breath as he looked up. A straight line of light appeared across the ceiling of the room, and Thomas watched as it expanded. A heavy grating sound revealed double sliding doors being forced open. After so long in darkness, the light stabbed his eyes; he looked away, covering his face with both hands.

He heard noises above—voices—and fear squeezed his chest.

"Look at that shank."

"How old is he?"

"Looks like a klunk in a T-shirt."

"You're the klunk, shuck-face."

"Dude, it smells like *feet* down there!"

"Hope you enjoyed the one-way trip, Greenie."

"Ain't no ticket back, bro."

Thomas was hit with a wave of confusion, blistered with panic. The voices were odd, tinged with echo; some of the words were completely foreign—others felt familiar. He willed his eyes to adjust as he squinted toward the light and those speaking. At first he could see only shifting shadows, but they soon turned into the shapes of bodies—people bending over the hole in the ceiling, looking down at him, pointing.

And then, as if the lens of a camera had sharpened its focus, the faces cleared. They were boys, all of them—some young, some older. Thomas didn't know what he'd expected, but seeing those faces puzzled him. They were just teenagers. Kids. Some of his fear melted away, but not enough to calm his racing heart.

Someone lowered a rope from above, the end of it tied into a big loop. Thomas hesitated, then stepped into it with his right foot and clutched the rope as he was yanked toward the sky. Hands reached down, lots of hands, grabbing him by his clothes, pulling him up. The world seemed to spin, a swirling mist of faces and color and light. A storm of emotions wrenched his gut, twisted and pulled; he wanted to scream, cry, throw up. The chorus of voices had grown silent, but someone spoke as they yanked him over the sharp edge of the dark box. And Thomas knew he'd never forget the words.

"Nice to meet ya, shank," the boy said. "Welcome to the Glade."

CHAPTER 2

The helping hands didn't stop swarming around him until Thomas stood up straight and had the dust brushed from his shirt and pants. Still dazzled by the light, he staggered a bit. He was consumed with curiosity but still felt too ill to look closely at his surroundings. His new companions said nothing as he swiveled his head around, trying to take it all in.

As he rotated in a slow circle, the other kids snickered and stared; some reached out and poked him with a finger. There had to be at least fifty of them, their clothes smudged and sweaty as if they'd been hard at work, all shapes and sizes and races, their hair of varying lengths. Thomas suddenly felt dizzy, his eyes flickering between the boys and the bizarre place in which he'd found himself.

They stood in a vast courtyard several times the size of a football field, surrounded by four enormous walls made of gray stone and covered in spots with thick ivy. The walls had to be hundreds of feet high and formed a perfect square around them, each side split in the exact middle by an opening as tall as the walls themselves that, from what Thomas could see, led to passages and long corridors beyond.

"Look at the Greenbean," a scratchy voice said; Thomas couldn't see who it came from. "Gonna break his shuck neck checkin' out the new digs." Several boys laughed.

"Shut your hole, Gally," a deeper voice responded.

Thomas focused back in on the dozens of strangers around him. He knew he must look out of it—he felt like he'd been drugged. A tall kid with blond hair and a square jaw sniffed at him, his face devoid of expression. A short, pudgy boy fidgeted back and forth on his feet, looking up at Thomas with wide eyes. A thick, heavily muscled Asian kid folded his arms as he studied Thomas, his tight shirtsleeves rolled up to show off his biceps. A dark-skinned boy frowned—the same one who'd welcomed him. Countless others stared.

"Where am I?" Thomas asked, surprised at hearing his voice for the first time in his salvageable memory. It didn't sound quite right—higher than he would've imagined.

"Nowhere good." This came from the dark-skinned boy. "Just slim yourself nice and calm."

"Which Keeper he gonna get?" someone shouted from the back of the crowd.

"I told ya, shuck-face," a shrill voice responded. "He's a klunk, so he'll be a Slopper—no doubt about it." The kid giggled like he'd just said the funniest thing in history.

Thomas once again felt a pressing ache of confusion—hearing so many words and phrases that didn't make sense. *Shank. Shuck. Keeper. Slopper.* They popped out of the boys' mouths so naturally it seemed odd for him not to understand. It was as if his memory loss had stolen a chunk of his language—it was disorienting.

Different emotions battled for dominance in his mind and heart. Confusion. Curiosity. Panic. Fear. But laced through it all was the dark feeling of utter hopelessness, like the world had ended for him, had been wiped from his memory and replaced with something awful. He wanted to run and hide from these people.

The scratchy-voiced boy was talking. "—even do that much, bet my liver on it." Thomas still couldn't see his face.

"I said shut your holes!" the dark boy yelled. "Keep yapping and next break'll be cut in half!"

That must be their leader, Thomas realized. Hating how everyone gawked at him, he concentrated on studying the place the boy had called the Glade.

The floor of the courtyard looked like it was made of huge stone blocks, many of them cracked and filled with long grasses and weeds. An odd, dilapidated wooden building near one of the corners of the square contrasted greatly with the gray stone. A few trees surrounded it, their roots like gnarled hands digging into the rock floor for food. Another corner of the compound held gardens—from where he was standing Thomas recognized corn, tomato plants, fruit trees.

Across the courtyard from there stood wooden pens holding sheep and pigs and cows. A large grove of trees filled the final corner; the closest ones looked crippled and close to dying. The sky overhead was cloudless and blue, but Thomas could see no sign of the sun despite the brightness of the day. The creeping shadows of the walls didn't reveal the time or direction—it could be early morning or late afternoon. As he breathed in deeply, trying to settle his nerves, a mixture of smells bombarded him. Freshly turned dirt, manure, pine, something rotten and something sweet. Somehow he knew that these were the smells of a farm.

Thomas looked back at his captors, feeling awkward but desperate to ask questions. *Captors,* he thought. Then, *Why did that word pop into my head?* He scanned their faces, taking in each expression, judging them. One boy's eyes, flared with hatred, stopped him cold. He looked so angry, Thomas wouldn't have been surprised if the kid came at him with a knife. He had black hair, and when they made eye contact, the boy shook his head and turned away, walking toward a greasy iron pole with a wooden bench next to it. A multicolored flag hung limply at the top of the pole, no wind to reveal its pattern.

Shaken, Thomas stared at the boy's back until he turned and took a seat. Thomas quickly looked away.

Suddenly the leader of the group—perhaps he was seventeen—took a step forward. He wore normal clothes: black T-shirt, jeans, tennis shoes, a digital watch. For some reason the clothing here surprised Thomas; it seemed like everyone should be wearing something more menacing—like prison garb. The dark-skinned boy had short-cropped hair, his face clean shaven. But other than the permanent scowl, there was nothing scary about him at all.

"It's a long story, shank," the boy said. "Piece by piece, you'll learn—I'll be takin' you on the Tour tomorrow. Till then . . . just don't break anything." He held a hand out. "Name's Alby." He waited, clearly wanting to shake hands.

Thomas refused. Some instinct took over his actions and without saying anything he turned away from Alby and walked to a nearby tree, where he plopped down to sit with his back against the rough bark. Panic swelled inside him once again, almost too much to bear. But he took a deep breath and forced himself to try to accept the situation. *Just go with it*, he thought. *You won't figure out anything if you give in to fear.*

"Then tell me," Thomas called out, struggling to keep his voice even. "Tell me the long story."

Alby glanced at the friends closest to him, rolling his eyes, and Thomas studied the crowd again. His original estimate had been close—there were probably fifty to sixty of them, ranging from boys in their midteens to young adults like Alby, who seemed to be one of the oldest. At that moment, Thomas realized with a sickening lurch that he had no idea how old *he* was. His heart sank at the thought—he was so lost he didn't even know his own age.

"Seriously," he said, giving up on the show of courage. "Where am I?"

Alby walked over to him and sat down cross-legged; the crowd of boys followed and packed in behind. Heads popped up here and there, kids leaning in every direction to get a better look.

"If you ain't scared," Alby said, "you ain't human. Act any different and I'd throw you off the Cliff because it'd mean you're a psycho."

"The Cliff?" Thomas asked, blood draining from his face.

"Shuck it," Alby said, rubbing his eyes. "Ain't no way to start these conversations, you get me? We don't kill shanks like you here, I promise. Just try and avoid *being* killed, survive, whatever."

He paused, and Thomas realized his face must've whitened even more when he heard that last part.

"Man," Alby said, then ran his hands over his short hair as he let out a long sigh. "I ain't good at this—you're the first Greenbean since Nick was killed."

Thomas's eyes widened, and another boy stepped up and playfully slapped Alby across the head. "Wait for the bloody Tour, Alby," he said, his voice thick with an odd accent. "Kid's gonna have a buggin' heart attack, nothin' even been heard yet." He bent down and extended his hand toward Thomas. "Name's Newt, Greenie, and we'd all be right cheery if ya'd forgive our klunk-for-brains new leader, here."

Thomas reached out and shook the boy's hand—he seemed a lot nicer than Alby. Newt was taller than Alby too, but looked to be a year or so younger. His hair was blond and cut long, cascading over his T-shirt. Veins stuck out of his muscled arms.

"Pipe it, shuck-face," Alby grunted, pulling Newt down to sit next to him. "At least he can understand *half* my words." There were a few scattered laughs, and then everyone gathered behind Alby and Newt, packing in even tighter, waiting to hear what they said.

Alby spread his arms out, palms up. "This place is called the Glade, all right? It's where we live, where we eat, where we sleep—we call ourselves the Gladers. That's all you—"

"Who sent me here?" Thomas demanded, fear finally giving way to anger. "How'd—"

But Alby's hand shot out before he could finish, grabbing Thomas by the shirt as he leaned forward on his knees. "Get up, shank, get up!" Alby stood, pulling Thomas with him.

Thomas finally got his feet under him, scared all over again. He backed against the tree, trying to get away from Alby, who stayed right in his face.

"No interruptions, boy!" Alby shouted. "Whacker, if we told you everything, you'd die on the spot, right after you klunked your pants. Baggers'd drag you off, and you ain't no good to us then, are ya?"

"I don't even know what you're talking about," Thomas said slowly, shocked at how steady his voice sounded.

Newt reached out and grabbed Alby by the shoulders. "Alby, lay off a bit. You're hurtin' more than helpin', ya know?"

Alby let go of Thomas's shirt and stepped back, his chest heaving with breaths. "Ain't got time to be nice, Greenbean. Old life's over, new life's begun. Learn the rules quick, listen, don't talk. You get me?"

Thomas looked over at Newt, hoping for help. Everything inside him churned and hurt; the tears that had yet to come burned his eyes.

Newt nodded. "Greenie, you get him, right?" He nodded again.

Thomas fumed, wanted to punch somebody. But he simply said, "Yeah."

"Good that," Alby said. "First Day. That's what today is for you, shank. Night's comin', Runners'll be back soon. The Box came late today, ain't got time for the Tour. Tomorrow morning, right after the wake-up." He turned toward Newt. "Get him a bed, get him to sleep."

"Good that," Newt said.

Alby's eyes returned to Thomas, narrowing. "A few weeks, you'll be happy, shank. You'll be happy and helpin'. None of us knew jack on First Day, you neither. New life begins tomorrow."

Alby turned and pushed his way through the crowd, then headed for the slanted wooden building in the corner. Most of the kids wandered away then, each one giving Thomas a lingering look before they walked off.

Thomas folded his arms, closed his eyes, took a deep breath. Emptiness ate away at his insides, quickly replaced by a sadness that hurt his heart. It was all too much—where was he? What was this place? Was it some kind of prison? If so, why had he been sent here, and for how long? The language was odd, and none of the boys seemed to care whether he lived or died. Tears threatened again to fill his eyes, but he refused to let them come.

"What did I do?" he whispered, not really meaning for anyone to hear him. "What did I do—why'd they send me here?"

Newt clapped him on the shoulder. "Greenie, what you're feelin', we've all felt it. We've all had First Day, come out of that dark box. Things are bad, they are, and they'll get much worse for ya soon, that's the truth. But down the road a piece, you'll be fightin' true and good. I can tell you're not a bloody sissy."

"Is this a prison?" Thomas asked; he dug in the darkness of his thoughts, trying to find a crack to his past.

"Done asked four questions, haven't ya?" Newt replied. "No good answers for ya, not yet, anyway. Best be quiet now, accept the change—morn comes tomorrow."

Thomas said nothing, his head sunk, his eyes staring at the cracked, rocky ground. A line of small-leafed weeds ran along the edge of one of the stone blocks, tiny yellow flowers peeping through as if searching for the sun, long disappeared behind the enormous walls of the Glade.

"Chuck'll be a good fit for ya," Newt said. "Wee little fat shank, but nice sap when all's said and done. Stay here, I'll be back."

Newt had barely finished his sentence when a sudden, piercing scream ripped through the air. High and shrill, the barely human shriek echoed across the stone courtyard; every kid in sight turned to look toward the source. Thomas felt his blood turn to icy slush as he realized that the horrible sound came from the wooden building.

Even Newt had jumped as if startled, his forehead creasing in concern.

"Shuck it," he said. "Can't the bloody Med-jacks handle that boy for ten minutes without needin' my help?" He shook his head and lightly kicked Thomas on the foot. "Find Chuckie, tell him he's in charge of your sleepin' arrangements." And then he turned and headed in the direction of the building, running.

Thomas slid down the rough face of the tree until he sat on the ground again; he shrank back against the bark and closed his eyes, wishing he could wake up from this terrible, terrible dream.

CHAPTER 3

Thomas sat there for several moments, too overwhelmed to move. He finally forced himself to look over at the haggard building. A group of boys milled around outside, glancing anxiously at the upper windows as if expecting a hideous beast to leap out in an explosion of glass and wood.

A metallic clicking sound from the branches above grabbed his attention, made him look up; a flash of silver and red light caught his eyes just before disappearing around the trunk to the other side. He scrambled to his feet and walked around the tree, craning his neck for a sign of whatever he'd heard, but he saw only bare branches, gray and brown, forking out like skeleton fingers—and looking just as alive.

"That was one of them beetle blades," someone said.

Thomas turned to his right to see a kid standing nearby, short and pudgy, staring at him. He was young—probably the youngest of any in the group he'd seen so far, maybe twelve or thirteen years old. His brown hair hung down over his ears and neck, scraping the tops of his shoulders. Blue eyes shone through an otherwise pitiful face, flabby and flushed.

Thomas nodded at him. "A beetle what?"

"Beetle blade," the boy said, pointing to the top of the tree. "Won't hurt ya unless you're stupid enough to touch one of them." He paused. "Shank." He didn't sound comfortable saying the last word, as if he hadn't quite grasped the slang of the Glade.

Another scream, this one long and nerve-grinding, tore through the air and Thomas's heart lurched. The fear was like icy dew on his skin. "What's going on over there?" he asked, pointing at the building.

"Don't know," the chubby boy replied; his voice still carried the high pitch of childhood. "Ben's in there, sicker than a dog. *They* got him."

"They?" Thomas didn't like the malicious way the boy had said the word.

"Yeah."

"Who are *They*?"

"Better hope you never find out," the kid answered, looking far too comfortable for the situation. He held out his hand. "My name's Chuck. I was the Greenbean until you showed up."

This is my guide for the night? Thomas thought. He couldn't shake his extreme discomfort, and now annoyance crept in as well. Nothing made sense; his head hurt.

"Why is everyone calling me Greenbean?" he asked, shaking Chuck's hand quickly, then letting go.

"Cuz you're the newest Newbie." Chuck pointed at Thomas and laughed. Another scream came from the house, a sound like a starving animal being tortured.

"How can you be laughing?" Thomas asked, horrified by the noise. "It sounds like someone's dying in there."

"He'll be okay. No one dies if they make it back in time to get the Serum. It's all or nothing. Dead or not dead. Just hurts a lot."

This gave Thomas pause. "What hurts a lot?"

Chuck's eyes wandered as if he wasn't sure what to say. "Um, gettin' stung by the Grievers."

"Grievers?" Thomas was only getting more and more confused. *Stung. Grievers.* The words had a heavy weight of dread to them, and he suddenly wasn't so sure he wanted to know what Chuck was talking about.

Chuck shrugged, then looked away, eyes rolling.

Thomas sighed in frustration and leaned back against the tree. "Looks like you barely know more than I do," he said, but he knew it wasn't true. His memory loss was strange. He mostly remembered the workings of the world—but emptied of specifics, faces, names. Like a book completely intact but missing one word in every dozen, making it a miserable and confusing read. He didn't even know his age.

"Chuck, how . . . old do you think I am?"

The boy scanned him up and down. "I'd say you're sixteen. And in case you were wondering, five foot nine . . . brown hair. Oh, and ugly as fried liver on a stick." He snorted a laugh.

Thomas was so stunned he'd barely heard the last part. Sixteen? He was *sixteen*? He felt much older than that.

"Are you serious?" He paused, searching for words. "How . . ." He didn't even know what to ask.

"Don't worry. You'll be all whacked for a few days, but then you'll get used to this place. I have. We live here, this is it. Better than living in a pile of klunk." He squinted, maybe anticipating Thomas's question. "*Klunk*'s another word for poo. Poo makes a klunk sound when it falls in our pee pots."

Thomas looked at Chuck, unable to believe he was having this conversation. "That's nice" was all he could manage. He stood up and walked past Chuck toward the old building; *shack* was a better word for the place. It looked three or four stories high and about to fall down at any minute—a crazy assortment of logs and boards and thick twine and windows seemingly thrown together at random, the massive, ivy-strewn stone walls rising up behind it. As he moved across the courtyard, the distinct smell of firewood and some kind of meat cooking made his stomach grumble. Knowing now that it was just a sick kid doing the screaming made Thomas feel better. Until he thought about what had caused it . . .

"What's your name?" Chuck asked from behind, running to catch up.

"What?"

"Your *name*? You still haven't told us—and I know you remember that much."

"Thomas." He barely heard himself say it—his thoughts had spun in a new direction. If Chuck was right, he'd just discovered a link to the rest of the boys. A common pattern to their memory losses. They all remembered their names. Why not their parents' names? Why not a friend's name? Why not their *last* names?

"Nice to meet you, Thomas," Chuck said. "Don't you worry, I'll take care of you. I've been here a whole month, and I know the place inside and out. You can count on Chuck, okay?"

Thomas had almost reached the front door of the shack and the small group of boys congregating there when he was hit by a sudden and surprise rush of anger. He turned to face Chuck. "You can't even *tell* me anything. I wouldn't call that taking care of me." He turned back toward the door, intent on going inside to find some answers. Where this sudden courage and resolve came from, he had no idea.

Chuck shrugged. "Nothin' I say'll do you any good," he said. "I'm basically still a Newbie, too. But I can be your friend—"

"I don't need friends," Thomas interrupted.

He'd reached the door, an ugly slab of sun-faded wood, and he pulled it open to see several stoic-faced boys standing at the foot of a crooked staircase, the steps and railings twisted and angled in all directions. Dark wallpaper covered the walls of the foyer and hallway, half of it peeling off. The only decorations in sight were a dusty vase on a three-legged table and a black-and-white picture of an ancient woman dressed in an old-fashioned white dress. It reminded Thomas of a haunted house from a movie or something. There were even planks of wood missing from the floor.

The place reeked of dust and mildew—a big contrast to the pleasant smells outside. Flickering fluorescent lights shone from the ceiling. He hadn't thought of it yet, but he had to wonder where the electricity came from in a place like the Glade. He stared at the old woman in the picture. Had she lived here once? Taken care of these people?

"Hey, look, it's the Greenbean," one of the older boys called out. With a start, Thomas realized it was the black-haired guy who'd given him the look of death earlier. He looked like he was fifteen or so, tall and skinny. His nose was the size of a small fist and resembled a deformed potato. "This shank probably klunked his pants when he heard old Benny baby scream like a girl. Need a new diaper, shuck-face?"

"My name's Thomas." He had to get away from this guy. Without another word, he made for the stairs, only because they were close, only because he had no idea what to do or say. But the bully stepped in front of him, holding a hand up.

"Hold on there, Greenie." He jerked a thumb in the direction of the upper floor. "Newbies aren't allowed to see someone who's been . . . *taken*. Newt and Alby won't allow it."

"What's your problem?" Thomas asked, trying to keep the fear out of his voice, trying not to think what the kid had meant by *taken*. "I don't even know where I am. All I want is some help."

"Listen to me, Greenbean." The boy wrinkled up his face, folded his arms. "I've seen you before. Something's fishy about you showing up here, and I'm gonna find out what."

A surge of heat pulsed through Thomas's veins. "I've never seen you before in my life. I have no idea who you are, and I couldn't care less," he spat. But really, how would he know? And how could this kid remember *him*?

The bully snickered, a short burst of laughter mixed with a phlegm-filled snort. Then his face grew serious, his eyebrows slanting inward. "I've . . . *seen* you, shank. Not too many in these parts can say they've been stung." He pointed up the stairs. "I have. I know what old Benny baby's going through. I've been there. And I saw *you* during the Changing."

He reached out and poked Thomas in the chest. "And I bet your first meal from Frypan that Benny'll say he's seen ya, too."

Thomas refused to break eye contact but decided to say nothing. Panic ate at him once again. Would things ever stop getting worse?

"Griever got ya wettin' yourself?" the boy said through a sneer. "A little scared now? Don't wanna get *stung,* do ya?"

There was that word again. *Stung*. Thomas tried not to think about it and pointed up the stairs, from where the moans of the sick kid echoed through the building. "If Newt went up there, then I wanna talk to him."

The boy said nothing, stared at Thomas for several seconds. Then he shook his head. "You know what? You're right, Tommy—I shouldn't be so mean to Newbies. Go on upstairs and I'm sure Alby and Newt'll fill you in. Seriously, go on. I'm sorry."

He lightly slapped Thomas's shoulder, then stepped back, gesturing up the stairs. But Thomas knew the kid was up to something. Losing parts of your memory didn't make you an idiot.

"What's your name?" Thomas asked, stalling for time while he tried to decide if he should go up after all.

"Gally. And don't let anyone fool you. I'm the real leader here, not the two geezer shanks upstairs. Me. You can call me Captain Gally if you want." He smiled for the first time; his teeth matched his disgusting nose. Two or three were missing, and not a single one approached anything close to the color white. His breath escaped just enough for Thomas to get a whiff, reminding him of some horrible memory that was just out of reach. It made his stomach turn.

"Okay," he said, so sick of the guy he wanted to scream, punch him in the face. "Captain Gally it is." He exaggerated a salute, feeling a rush of adrenaline, as he knew he'd just crossed a line.

A few snickers escaped the crowd, and Gally looked around, his face bright red. He peered back at Thomas, hatred furrowing his brow and crinkling his monstrous nose.

"Just go up the stairs," Gally said. "And stay away from me, you little slinthead." He pointed up again but didn't take his eyes off Thomas.

"Fine." Thomas looked around one more time, embarrassed, confused, angry. He felt the heat of blood in his face. No one made a move to stop him from doing as Gally asked, except for Chuck, who stood at the front door, shaking his head.

"You're not supposed to," the younger boy said. "You're a Newbie—you can't go up there."

"Go," said Gally with a sneer. "Go on up."

Thomas regretted having come inside in the first place—but he *did* want to talk to that Newt guy.

He started up the stairs. Each step groaned and creaked under his weight; he might've stopped for fear of falling through the old wood if he weren't leaving such an awkward situation below. Up he went, wincing at every splintered sound. The stairs reached a landing, turned left, then came upon a railed hallway leading to several rooms. Only one door had a light coming through the crack at the bottom.

"The Changing!" Gally shouted from below. "Look forward to it, shuck-face!"

As if the taunting gave Thomas a sudden burst of courage, he walked over to the lit door, ignoring the creaking floorboards and laughter downstairs—ignoring the onslaught of words he didn't understand, suppressing the dreadful feelings they induced. He reached down, turned the brass handle, and opened the door.

Inside the room, Newt and Alby crouched over someone lying on a bed.

Thomas leaned in closer to see what the fuss was all about, but when he got a clear look at the condition of the patient, his heart went cold. He had to fight the bile that surged up his throat.

The look was fast—only a few seconds—but it was enough to haunt him forever. A twisted, pale figure writhing in agony, chest bare and hideous. Tight, rigid cords of sickly green veins webbed across the boy's body and limbs, like ropes under his skin. Purplish bruises covered the kid, red hives, bloody scratches. His bloodshot eyes bulged, darting back and forth. The image had already burned into Thomas's mind before Alby jumped up, blocking the view but not the moans and screams, pushing Thomas out of the room, then slamming the door shut behind them.

"What're you doing up here, Greenie!" Alby yelled, his lips taut with anger, eyes on fire.

Thomas felt weak. "I . . . uh . . . want some answers," he murmured, but he couldn't put any strength in his words—felt himself give up inside. What was wrong with that kid? Thomas slouched against the railing in the hallway and stared at the floor, not sure what to do next.

"Get your runtcheeks down those stairs, right now," Alby ordered. "Chuck'll help you. If I see you again before tomorrow morning, you ain't reachin' another one alive. I'll throw you off the Cliff myself, you get me?"

Thomas was humiliated and scared. He felt like he'd shrunk to the size of a small rat. Without saying a word, he pushed past Alby and headed down the creaky steps, going as fast as he dared. Ignoring the gaping stares of everyone at the bottom—especially Gally—he walked out the door, pulling Chuck by the arm as he did so.

Thomas hated these people. He hated all of them. Except Chuck. "Get me away from these guys," Thomas said. He realized that Chuck might actually be his only friend in the world.

"You got it," Chuck replied, his voice chipper, as if thrilled to be needed. "But first we should get you some food from Frypan."

"I don't know if I can ever eat again." Not after what he'd just seen.

Chuck nodded. "Yeah, you will. I'll meet you at the same tree as before. Ten minutes."

Thomas was more than happy to get away from the house, and headed back toward the tree. He'd only known what it was like to be alive here for a short while and he already wanted it to end. He wished for all the world he could remember something about his previous life. Anything. His mom, his dad, a friend, his school, a hobby. A girl.

He blinked hard several times, trying to get the image of what he'd just seen in the shack out of his mind.

The Changing. Gally had called it the Changing.

It wasn't cold, but Thomas shuddered once again.

CHAPTER 4

Thomas leaned against the tree as he waited for Chuck. He scanned the compound of the Glade, this new place of nightmares where he seemed destined to live. The shadows from the walls had lengthened considerably, already creeping up the sides of the ivy-covered stone faces on the other side.

At least this helped Thomas know directions—the wooden building crouched in the northwest corner, wedged in a darkening patch of shadow, the grove of trees in the southwest. The farm area, where a few workers were still picking their way through the fields, spread across the entire northeast quarter of the Glade. The animals were in the southeast corner, mooing and crowing and baying.

In the exact middle of the courtyard, the still-gaping hole of the Box lay open, as if inviting him to jump back in and go home. Near that, maybe twenty feet to the south, stood a squat building made of rough concrete blocks, a menacing iron door its only entrance—there were no windows. A large round handle resembling a steel steering wheel marked the only way to open the door, just like something within a submarine. Despite what he'd just seen, Thomas didn't know which he felt more strongly—curiosity to know what was inside, or dread at finding out.

Thomas had just moved his attention to the four vast openings in the middle of the main walls of the Glade when Chuck arrived, a couple of sandwiches cradled in his arms, along with apples and two metal cups of water. The sense of relief that flooded through Thomas surprised him—he wasn't *completely* alone in this place.

"Frypan wasn't too happy about me invading his kitchen before suppertime," Chuck said, sitting down next to the tree, motioning to Thomas to do the same. He did, grabbed the sandwich, but hesitated, the writhing, monstrous image of what he'd seen in the shack popping back into his mind. Soon, though, his hunger won out and he took a huge bite. The wonderful tastes of ham and cheese and mayonnaise filled his mouth.

"Ah, man," Thomas mumbled through a mouthful. "I was starving."

"Told ya." Chuck chomped into his own sandwich.

After another couple of bites, Thomas finally asked the question that had been bothering him. "What's actually *wrong* with that Ben guy? He doesn't even look human anymore."

Chuck glanced over at the house. "Don't really know," he muttered absently. "I didn't see him."

Thomas could tell the boy was being less than honest but decided not to press him. "Well, you don't want to see him, trust me." He continued to eat, munching on the apples as he studied the huge breaks in the walls. Though it was hard to make out from where he sat, there was something odd about the stone edges of the exits to the outside corridors. He felt an uncomfortable sense of vertigo looking at the towering walls, as if he hovered above them instead of sitting at their base.

"What's out there?" he asked, finally breaking the silence. "Is this part of a huge castle or something?"

Chuck hesitated. Looked uncomfortable. "Um, I've never been outside the Glade."

Thomas paused. "You're hiding something," he finally replied, finishing off his last bite and taking a long swig of water. The frustration at getting no answers from anyone was starting to grind his nerves. It only made it worse to think that even if he *did* get answers, he wouldn't know if he'd be getting the truth. "Why are you guys so secretive?"

"That's just the way it is. Things are really weird around here, and most of us don't know everything. *Half* of everything."

It bothered Thomas that Chuck didn't seem to care about what he'd just said. That he seemed indifferent to having his life taken away from him. What was wrong with these people? Thomas got to his feet and started walking toward the eastern opening. "Well, no one said I couldn't look around." He needed to learn something or he was going to lose his mind.

"Whoa, wait!" Chuck cried, running to catch up. "Be careful, those puppies are about to close." He already sounded out of breath.

"Close?" Thomas repeated. "What are you talking about?"

"The Doors, you shank."

"Doors? I don't see any doors." Thomas knew Chuck wasn't just making stuff up—he knew he was missing something obvious. He grew uneasy and realized he'd slowed his pace, not so eager to reach the walls anymore.

"What do you call those big openings?" Chuck pointed up at the enormously tall gaps in the walls. They were only thirty feet away now.

"I'd call them *big openings*," Thomas said, trying to counter his discomfort with sarcasm and disappointed that it wasn't working.

"Well, they're *doors*. And they close up every night."

Thomas stopped, thinking Chuck had to have said something wrong. He looked up, looked side to side, examined the massive slabs of stone as the uneasy feeling blossomed into outright dread. "What do you mean, they *close*?"

"Just see for yourself in a minute. The Runners'll be back soon; then those big walls are going to *move* until the gaps are closed."

"You're jacked in the head," Thomas muttered. He couldn't see how the mammoth walls could possibly be mobile—felt so sure of it he relaxed, thinking Chuck was just playing a trick on him.

They reached the huge split that led outside to more stone pathways. Thomas gaped, his mind emptying of thought as he saw it all firsthand.

"This is called the East Door," Chuck said, as if proudly revealing a piece of art he'd created.

Thomas barely heard him, shocked by how much bigger it was up close. At least twenty feet across, the break in the wall went all the way to the top, far above. The edges that bordered the vast opening were smooth, except for one odd, repeating pattern on both sides. On the left side of the East Door, deep holes several inches in diameter and spaced a foot apart were bored into the rock, beginning near the ground and continuing all the way up.

On the right side of the Door, foot-long rods jutted out from the wall edge, also several inches in diameter, in the same pattern as the holes facing them on the other side. The purpose was obvious.

"Are you kidding?" Thomas asked, the dread slamming back into his gut. "You weren't playing with me? The walls really *move*?"

"What else would I have meant?"

Thomas had a hard time wrapping his mind around the possibility. "I don't know. I figured there was a door that swung shut or a little mini-wall that slid out of the big one. How could these walls move? They're huge, and they look like they've been standing here for a thousand years." And the idea of those walls closing and trapping him inside this place they called the Glade was downright terrifying.

Chuck threw his arms up, clearly frustrated. "I don't know, they just move. Makes one heck of a grinding noise. Same thing happens out in the Maze—those walls shift every night, too."

Thomas, his attention suddenly snapped up by a new detail, turned to face the younger boy. "What did you just say?"

"Huh?"

"You just called it a maze—you said, 'same thing happens out in the *maze*.' "

Chuck's face reddened. "I'm done with you. I'm done." He walked back toward the tree they'd just left.

Thomas ignored him, more interested than ever in the outside of the Glade. A *maze*? In front of him, through the East Door, he could make out passages leading to the left, to the right, and straight ahead. And the walls of the corridors were similar to those that surrounded the Glade, the ground made of the same massive stone blocks as in the courtyard. The ivy seemed even thicker out there. In the distance, more breaks in the walls led to other paths, and farther down, maybe a hundred yards or so away, the straight passage came to a dead end.

"Looks like a maze," Thomas whispered, almost laughing to himself. As if things couldn't have gotten any stranger. They'd wiped his memory and put him inside a gigantic maze. It was all so crazy it really did seem funny.

His heart skipped a beat when a boy unexpectedly appeared around a corner up ahead, entering the main passage from one of the offshoots to the right, running toward him and the Glade. Covered in sweat, his face red, clothes sticking to his body, the boy didn't slow, hardly glancing at Thomas as he went past. He headed straight for the squat concrete building located near the Box.

Thomas turned as he passed, his eyes riveted to the exhausted runner, unsure why this new development surprised him so much. Why *wouldn't* people go out and search the maze? Then he realized others were entering through the remaining three Glade openings, all of them running and looking as ragged as the guy who'd just whisked by him. There couldn't be much good about the maze if these guys came back looking so weary and worn.

He watched, curious, as they met at the big iron door of the small building; one of the boys turned the rusty wheel handle, grunting with the effort. Chuck had said something about runners earlier. What had they been doing out there?

The big door finally popped open, and with a deafening squeal of metal against metal, the boys swung it wide. They disappeared inside, pulling it shut behind them with a loud clonk. Thomas stared, his mind churning to come up with any possible explanation for what he'd just witnessed. Nothing developed, but something about that creepy old building gave him goose bumps, a disquieting chill.

Someone tugged on his sleeve, breaking him from his thoughts; Chuck had come back.

Before Thomas had a chance to think, questions were rushing out of his mouth. "Who are those guys and what were they doing? What's in that building?" He wheeled around and pointed out the East Door. "And why do you live inside a freaking maze?" He felt a rattling pressure of uncertainty, making his head splinter with pain.

"I'm not saying another word," Chuck replied, a new authority filling his voice. "I think you should get to bed early—you'll need your sleep. Ah"—he stopped, held up a finger, pricking up his right ear—"it's about to happen."

"What?" Thomas asked, thinking it kind of strange that Chuck was suddenly acting like an adult instead of the little kid desperate for a friend he'd been only moments earlier.

A loud boom exploded through the air, making Thomas jump. It was followed by a horrible crunching, grinding sound. He stumbled backward, fell to the ground. It felt as if the whole earth shook; he looked around, panicked. The walls were closing. The walls were *really* closing—trapping him inside the Glade. An onrushing sense of claustrophobia stifled him, compressed his lungs, as if water filled their cavities.

"Calm down, Greenie," Chuck yelled over the noise. "It's just the walls!"

Thomas barely heard him, too fascinated, too shaken by the closing of the Doors. He scrambled to his feet and took a few trembling steps back for a better view, finding it hard to believe what his eyes were seeing.

The enormous stone wall to the right of them seemed to defy every known law of physics as it slid along the ground, throwing sparks and dust as it moved, rock against rock. The crunching sound rattled his bones. Thomas realized that only *that* wall was moving, heading for its neighbor to the left, ready to seal shut with its protruding rods slipping into the drilled holes across from it. He looked around at the other openings. It felt like his head was spinning faster than his body, and his stomach flipped over with the dizziness. On all four sides of the Glade, only the right walls were moving, toward the left, closing the gap of the Doors.

Impossible, he thought. *How can they* do *that?* He fought the urge to run out there, slip past the moving slabs of rock before they shut, flee the Glade. Common sense won out—the maze held even more unknowns than his situation inside.

He tried to picture in his mind how the structure of it all worked. Massive stone walls, hundreds of feet high, moving like sliding glass doors—an image from his past life that flashed through his thoughts. He tried to grasp the memory, hold on to it, complete the picture with faces, names, a place, but it faded into obscurity. A pang of sadness pricked through his other swirling emotions.

He watched as the right wall reached the end of its journey, its connecting rods finding their mark and entering without a glitch. An echoing boom rumbled across the Glade as all four Doors sealed shut for the night. Thomas felt one final moment of trepidation, a quick slice of fear through his body, and then it vanished.

A surprising sense of calm eased his nerves; he let out a long sigh of relief. "Wow," he said, feeling dumb at such a monumental understatement.

"Ain't nothin', as Alby would say," Chuck murmured. "You kind of get used to it after a while."

Thomas looked around one more time, the *feel* of the place completely different now that all the walls were solid with no way out. He tried to imagine the purpose of such a thing, and he didn't know which guess was worse—that they were being sealed *in* or that they were being protected from something *out there.* The thought ended his brief moment of calm, stirring in his mind a million possibilities of what might live in the maze outside, all of them terrifying. Fear gripped him once again.

"Come *on*," Chuck said, pulling at Thomas's sleeve a second time. "Trust me, when nighttime strikes, you want to be in *bed*."

Thomas knew he had no other choice. He did his best to suppress everything he was feeling and followed.

CHAPTER 5

They ended up near the back of the Homestead—that was what Chuck called the leaning structure of wood and windows—in a dark shadow between the building and the stone wall behind it.

"Where are we going?" Thomas asked, still feeling the weight of seeing those walls close, thinking about the maze, the confusion, the fear. He told himself to stop or he'd drive himself crazy. Trying to grasp a sense of normalcy, he made a weak attempt at a joke. "If you're looking for a goodnight kiss, forget it."

Chuck didn't miss a beat. "Just shut up and stay close."

Thomas let out a big breath and shrugged before following the younger boy along the back of the building. They tiptoed until they came upon a small, dusty window, a soft beam of light shining through onto the stone and ivy. Thomas heard someone moving around inside.

"The bathroom," Chuck whispered.

"So?" A thread of unease stitched along Thomas's skin.

"I love doing this to people. Gives me great pleasure before bedtime."

"Doing what?" Something told Thomas Chuck was up to no good. "Maybe I should—"

"Just shut your mouth and watch." Chuck quietly stepped up onto a big wooden box that sat right under the window. He crouched so that his head was positioned just below where the person on the inside would be able to see him. Then he reached up with his hand and lightly tapped on the glass.

"This is stupid," Thomas whispered. There couldn't possibly be a worse time to play a joke—Newt or Alby could be in there. "I don't wanna get in trouble—I just got here!"

Chuck suppressed a laugh by putting his hand over his mouth. Ignoring Thomas, he reached up and tapped the window again.

A shadow crossed the light; then the window slid open. Thomas jumped to hide, pressing himself against the back of the building as hard as he could. He just couldn't believe he'd been suckered into playing a practical joke on somebody. The angle of vision from the window protected him for the moment, but he knew he and Chuck would be seen if whoever was in there pushed his head outside to get a better look.

"Who's that!" yelled the boy from the bathroom, his voice scratchy and laced with anger. Thomas had to hold in a gasp when he realized it was Gally—he *knew* that voice already.

Without warning, Chuck suddenly popped his head up toward the window and screamed at the top of his lungs. A loud crash from inside revealed that the trick had worked—and the litany of swearwords following it let them know Gally was none too happy about it. Thomas was struck with an odd mix of horror and embarrassment.

"I'm gonna kill you, shuck-face!" Gally yelled, but Chuck was already off the box and running toward the open Glade. Thomas froze as he heard Gally open the door inside and run out of the bathroom.

Thomas finally snapped out of his daze and took off after his new—and only—friend. He'd just rounded the corner when Gally came screaming out of the Homestead, looking like a ferocious beast on the loose.

He immediately pointed at Thomas. "Come here!" he yelled.

Thomas's heart sank in surrender. Everything seemed to indicate that he'd be getting a fist in the face. "It wasn't me, I swear," he said, though as he stood there, he sized the boy up and realized he shouldn't be so terrified after all. Gally wasn't that big—Thomas could actually take him if he had to.

"Wasn't you?" Gally snarled. He ambled up to Thomas slowly and stopped right in front of him. "Then how do you know there was something you didn't do?"

Thomas didn't say anything. He was definitely uncomfortable but not nearly as scared as a few moments earlier.

"I'm not a dong, Greenie," Gally spat. "I saw Chuck's fat face in the window." He pointed again, this time right at Thomas's chest. "But you better decide right quick who you want as your friends and enemies, hear me? One more trick like that—I don't care if it's your sissy idea or not—there'll be blood spilled. You got that, Newbie?" But before Thomas could answer Gally'd already turned to walk away.

Thomas just wanted this episode over. "Sorry," he muttered, wincing at how stupid it sounded.

"I know you," Gally added without looking back. "I saw you in the Changing, and I'm gonna figure out who you are."

Thomas watched as the bully disappeared back into the Homestead. He couldn't remember much, but something told him he'd never disliked someone so strongly. He was surprised by how much he truly hated the guy. He really, really hated him. He turned to see Chuck standing there, staring at the ground, clearly embarassed. "Thanks a lot, *buddy*."

"Sorry—if I'd known it was Gally, I never would've done it, I swear."

Surprising himself, Thomas laughed. An hour ago, he'd thought he'd never hear such a sound come out of his mouth again.

Chuck looked closely at Thomas and slowly broke into an uneasy grin. "What?"

Thomas shook his head. "Don't be sorry. The . . . shank deserved it, and I don't even know what a shank is. That was awesome." He felt much better.

A couple of hours later, Thomas was lying in a soft sleeping bag next to Chuck on a bed of grass near the gardens. It was a wide lawn that he hadn't noticed before, and quite a few of the group chose it as their bedtime spot. Thomas thought that was strange, but apparently there wasn't enough room inside the Homestead. At least it was warm. Which made him wonder for the millionth time *where* they were. His mind had a hard time grasping names of places, or remembering countries or rulers, how the world was organized. And none of the kids in the Glade had a clue, either—at least, they weren't sharing if they did.

He lay in silence for the longest time, looking at the stars and listening to the soft murmurs of various conversations drifting across the Glade. Sleep felt miles away, and he couldn't shake the despair and hopelessness that coursed through his body and mind—the temporary joy of Chuck's trick on Gally had long since faded away. It'd been one endless—and strange—day.

It was just so . . . weird. He remembered lots of little things about life—eating, clothes, studying, playing, general images of the makeup of the world. But any detail that would fill in the picture to create a true and complete memory had been erased somehow. It was like looking at an image through a foot of muddy water. More than anything else, perhaps, he felt . . . *sad.*

Chuck interrupted his thoughts. "Well, Greenie, you survived First Day."

"Barely." *Not now, Chuck*, he wanted to say. *I'm not in the mood.*

Chuck pulled himself up to lean on an elbow, looking at Thomas. "You'll learn a lot in the next couple of days, start getting used to things. Good that?"

"Um, yeah, good that, I guess. Where'd all these weird words and phrases come from, anyway?" It seemed like they'd taken some other language and melded it with his own.

Chuck flopped back down with a heavy flump. "I don't know—I've only been here a month, remember?"

Thomas wondered about Chuck, whether he knew more than he let on. He was a quirky kid, funny, and he seemed innocent, but who was to say? Really he was just as mysterious as everything else in the Glade.

A few minutes passed, and Thomas felt the long day finally catch up to him, the leaded edge of sleep crossing over his mind. But—like a fist had shoved it in his brain and let go—a thought popped into his head. One that he didn't expect, and he wasn't sure from where it came.

Suddenly, the Glade, the walls, the Maze—it all seemed . . . familiar. Comfortable. A warmth of calmness spread through his chest, and for the first time since he'd found himself there, he didn't feel like the Glade was the worst place in the universe. He stilled, felt his eyes widen, his breathing stop for a long moment. *What just happened?* he thought. *What changed?* Ironically, the feeling that things would be okay made him slightly uneasy.

Not quite understanding how, he knew what he needed to do. He didn't get it. The feeling—the epiphany—was a strange one, foreign and familiar at the same time. But it felt . . . right.

"I want to be one of those guys that goes out there," he said aloud, not knowing if Chuck was still awake. "Inside the Maze."

"Huh?" was the response from Chuck. Thomas could hear a tinge of annoyance in his voice.

"Runners," Thomas said, wishing he knew where this was coming from. "Whatever they're doing out there, I want in."

"You don't even know what you're talking about," Chuck grumbled, and rolled over. "Go to sleep."

Thomas felt a new surge of confidence, even though he truly *didn't* know what he was talking about. "I want to be a Runner."

Chuck turned back and got up on his elbow. "You can forget that little thought right now."

Thomas wondered at Chuck's reaction, but pressed on. "Don't try to—"

"Thomas. Newbie. My new friend. Forget it."

"I'll tell Alby tomorrow." *A Runner,* Thomas thought. *I don't even know what that* means. *Have I gone completely insane?*

Chuck lay down with a laugh. "You're a piece of klunk. Go to sleep."

But Thomas couldn't quit. "Something out there—it feels familiar."

"Go . . . to . . . sleep."

Then it hit Thomas—he felt like several pieces of a puzzle had been put together. He didn't know what the ultimate picture would be, but his next words almost felt like they were coming from someone else. "Chuck, I . . . I think I've *been* here before."

He heard his friend sit up, heard the intake of breath. But Thomas rolled over and refused to say another word, worried he'd mess up this new sense of being encouraged, eradicate the reassuring calm that filled his heart.

Sleep came much more easily than he'd expected.

CHAPTER 6

Someone shook Thomas awake. His eyes snapped open to see a too-close face staring down at him, everything around them still shadowed by the darkness of early morning. He opened his mouth to speak but a cold hand clamped down on it, gripping it shut. Panic flared until he saw who it was.

"Shh, Greenie. Don't wanna be wakin' Chuckie, now, do we?"

It was Newt—the guy who seemed to be second in command; the air reeked of his morning breath.

Though Thomas was surprised, any alarm melted away immediately. He couldn't help being curious, wondering what this boy wanted with him. Thomas nodded, doing his best to say yes with his eyes, until Newt finally took his hand away, then leaned back on his heels.

"Come on, Greenie," the tall boy whispered as he stood. He reached down and helped Thomas to his feet—he was so strong it felt like he could rip Thomas's arm off. "Supposed to show ya somethin' before the wake-up."

Any lingering haze of sleep had already vanished from Thomas's mind. "Okay," he said simply, ready to follow. He knew he should hold *some* suspicion, having no reason to trust anyone yet, but the curiosity won out. He quickly leaned over and slipped on his shoes. "Where are we going?"

"Just follow me. And stay close."

They snuck their way through the tightly strewn pack of sleeping bodies, Thomas almost tripping several times. He stepped on someone's hand, earning a sharp cry of pain in return, then a punch on the calf.

"Sorry," he whispered, ignoring a dirty look from Newt.

Once they left the lawn area and stepped onto the hard gray stone of the courtyard floor, Newt broke into a run, heading for the western wall. Thomas hesitated at first, wondering why he needed to run, but snapped out of it quickly and followed at the same pace.

The light was dim, but any obstructions loomed as darker shadows and he was able to make his way quickly along. He stopped when Newt did, right next to the massive wall towering above them like a skyscraper—another random image that floated in the murky pool of his memory wipe. Thomas noticed small red lights flashing here and there along the wall's face, moving about, stopping, turning off and on.

"What are those?" he whispered as loudly as he dared, wondering if his voice sounded as shaky as he felt. The twinkling red glow of the lights held an undercurrent of warning.

Newt stood just a couple of feet in front of the thick curtain of ivy on the wall. "When you bloody need to know, you'll know, Greenie."

"Well, it's kind of stupid to send me to a place where nothing makes sense and not answer my questions." Thomas paused, surprised at himself. *"Shank,"* he added, throwing all the sarcasm he could into the syllable.

Newt broke out in a laugh, but quickly cut it off. "I like you, Greenie. Now shut it and let me show ya somethin'."

Newt stepped forward and dug his hands into the thick ivy, spreading several vines away from the wall to reveal a dust-frosted window, a square about two feet wide. It was dark at the moment, as if it had been painted black.

"What're we looking for?" Thomas whispered.

"Hold your undies, boy. One'll be comin' along soon enough."

A minute passed, then two. Several more. Thomas fidgeted on his feet, wondering how Newt could stand there, perfectly patient and still, staring into nothing but darkness.

Then it changed.

Glimmers of an eerie light shone through the window; it cast a wavering spectrum of colors on Newt's body and face, as if he stood next to a lighted swimming pool. Thomas grew perfectly still, squinting, trying to make out what was on the other side. A thick lump grew in his throat. *What* is *that?* he thought.

"Out there's the Maze," Newt whispered, eyes wide as if in a trance. "Everything we do—our whole life, Greenie—revolves around the Maze. Every lovin' second of every lovin' day we spend in honor of the Maze, tryin' to solve somethin' that's not shown us it has a bloody solution, ya know? And we want to show ya why it's not to be messed with. Show ya why them buggin' walls close shut every night. Show ya why you should never, never find your butt out there."

Newt stepped back, still holding on to the ivy vines. He gestured for Thomas to take his place and look through the window.

Thomas did, leaning forward until his nose touched the cool surface of the glass. It took a second for his eyes to focus on the moving object on the other side, to look past the grime and dust and see what Newt wanted him to see. And when he did, he felt his breath catch in his throat, like an icy wind had blown down there and frozen the air solid.

A large, bulbous creature the size of a cow but with no distinct shape twisted and seethed along the ground in the corridor outside. It climbed the opposite wall, then leaped at the thick-glassed window with a loud thump. Thomas shrieked before he could stop himself, jerked away from the window—but the thing bounced backward, leaving the glass undamaged.

Thomas sucked in two huge breaths and leaned in once again. It was too dark to make out clearly, but odd lights flashed from an unknown source, revealing blurs of silver spikes and glistening flesh. Wicked instrument-tipped appendages protruded from its body like arms: a saw blade, a set of shears, long rods whose purpose could only be guessed.

The creature was a horrific mix of animal and machine, and seemed to realize it was being observed, seemed to know what lay inside the walls of the Glade, seemed to want to get inside and feast on human flesh. Thomas felt an icy terror blossom in his chest, expand like a tumor, making it hard to breathe. Even with the memory wipe, he felt sure he'd never seen something so truly awful.

He stepped back, the courage he'd felt the previous evening melting away.

"What is that thing?" he asked. Something shivered in his gut, and he wondered if he'd ever be able to eat again.

"Grievers, we call 'em," Newt answered. "Nasty bugger, eh? Just be glad the Grievers only come *out* at night. Be thankful for these walls."

Thomas swallowed, wondering how he could ever go out there. His desire to become a Runner had taken a major blow. But he had to do it. Somehow he *knew* he had to do it. It was such an odd thing to feel, especially after what he'd just seen.

Newt looked at the window absently. "Now you know what bloody lurks in the Maze, my friend. Now you know this isn't joke time. You've been sent to the Glade, Greenie, and we'll be expectin' ya to survive and help us do what we've been sent here to do."

"And what's that?" Thomas asked, even though he was terrified to hear the answer.

Newt turned to look him dead in the eye. The first traces of dawn had crept up on them, and Thomas could see every detail of Newt's face, his skin tight, his brow creased.

"Find our way out, Greenie," Newt said. "Solve the buggin' Maze and find our way home."

A couple of hours later, the doors having reopened, rumbling and grumbling and shaking the ground until they were finished, Thomas sat at a worn, tilted picnic table outside the Homestead. All he could think about was the Grievers, what their purpose could be, what they did out there during the night. What it would be like to be attacked by something so terrible.

He tried to get the image out of his head, move on to something else. The Runners. They'd just left without saying a word to anybody, bolting into the Maze at full speed and disappearing around corners. He pictured them in his mind as he picked at his eggs and bacon with a fork, speaking to no one, not even Chuck, who ate silently next to him. The poor guy had exhausted himself trying to start a conversation with Thomas, who'd refused to respond. All he wanted was to be left alone.

He just didn't get it; his brain was on overload trying to compute the sheer impossibility of the situation. How could a maze, with walls so massive and tall, be so big that dozens of kids hadn't been able to solve it after who knew how long trying? How could such a structure exist? And more importantly, *why?* What could possibly be the purpose of such a thing? Why were they all there? How *long* had they been there?

Try as he might to avoid it, his mind still kept wandering back to the image of the vicious Griever. Its phantom brother seemed to leap at him every time he blinked or rubbed his eyes.

Thomas knew he was a smart kid—he somehow felt it in his bones. But nothing about this place made any sense. Except for one thing. He was supposed to be a Runner. Why did he feel that so strongly? And even now, after seeing what lived in the maze?

A tap on his shoulder jarred him from his thoughts; he looked up to see Alby standing behind him, arms folded.

"Ain't you lookin' fresh?" Alby said. "Get a nice view out the window this morning?"

Thomas stood, hoping the time for answers had come—or maybe hoping for a distraction from his gloomy thoughts. "Enough to make me want to learn about this place," he said, hoping to avoid provoking the temper he'd seen flare in this guy the day before.

Alby nodded. "Me and you, shank. The Tour begins now." He started to move but then stopped, holding up a finger. "Ain't no questions till the end, you get me? Ain't got time to jaw with you all day."

"But . . ." Thomas stopped when Alby's eyebrows shot up. Why did the guy have to be such a jerk? "But tell me everything—I wanna know everything." He'd decided the night before not to tell anyone else how strangely familiar the place seemed, the odd feeling that he'd been there before—that he could *remember* things about it. Sharing that seemed like a very bad idea.

"I'll tell ya what I wanna tell ya, Greenie. Let's go."

"Can I come?" Chuck asked from the table.

Alby reached down and tweaked the boy's ear.

"Ow!" Chuck shrieked.

"Ain't you got a job, slinthead?" Alby asked. "Lots of sloppin' to do?"

Chuck rolled his eyes, then looked at Thomas. "Have fun."

"I'll try." He suddenly felt sorry for Chuck, wished people would treat the kid better. But there was nothing he could do about it—it was time to go.

He walked away with Alby, hoping the Tour had officially begun.

CHAPTER 7

They started at the Box, which was closed at the moment—double doors of metal lying flat on the ground, covered in white paint, faded and cracked. The day had brightened considerably, the shadows stretching in the opposite direction from what Thomas had seen yesterday. He still hadn't spotted the sun, but it looked like it was about to pop over the eastern wall at any minute.

Alby pointed down at the doors. "This here's the Box. Once a month, we get a Newbie like you, never fails. Once a *week,* we get supplies, clothes, some food. Ain't needin' a lot—pretty much run ourselves in the Glade."

Thomas nodded, his whole body itching with the desire to ask questions. *I need some tape to put over my mouth,* he thought.

"We don't know jack about the Box, you get me?" Alby continued. "Where it came from, how it gets here, who's in charge. The shanks that sent us here ain't told us nothin'. We got all the electricity we need, grow and raise most of our food, get clothes and such. Tried to send a slinthead Greenie back in the Box one time—thing wouldn't move till we took him out."

Thomas wondered what lay under the doors when the Box wasn't there, but held his tongue. He felt such a mixture of emotions—curiosity, frustration, wonder—all laced with the lingering horror of seeing the Griever that morning.

Alby kept talking, never bothering to look Thomas in the eye. "Glade's cut into four sections." He held up his fingers as he counted off the next four words. "Gardens, Blood House, Homestead, Deadheads. You got that?"

Thomas hesitated, then shook his head, confused.

Alby's eyelids fluttered briefly as he continued; he looked like he could think of a thousand things he'd rather be doing right then. He pointed to the northeast corner, where the fields and fruit trees were located. "Gardens—where we grow the crops. Water's pumped in through pipes in the ground—always has been, or we'd have starved to death a long time ago. Never rains here. Never." He pointed to the southeast corner, at the animal pens and barn. "Blood House—where we raise and slaughter animals." He pointed at the pitiful living quarters. "Homestead—stupid place is twice as big than when the first of us got here because we keep addin' to it when they send us wood and klunk. Ain't pretty, but it works. Most of us sleep outside anyway."

Thomas felt dizzy. So many questions splintered his mind he couldn't keep them straight.

Alby pointed to the southwest corner, the forest area fronted with several sickly trees and benches. "Call that the Deadheads. Graveyard's back in that corner, in the thicker woods. Ain't much else. You can go there to sit and rest, hang out, whatever." He cleared his throat, as if wanting to change subjects. "You'll spend the next two weeks working one day apiece for our different job Keepers—until we know what you're best at. Slopper, Bricknick, Bagger, Track-hoe—somethin'll stick, always does. Come on."

Alby walked toward the South Door, located between what he'd called the Deadheads and the Blood House. Thomas followed, wrinkling his nose up at the sudden smell of dirt and manure coming from the animal pens. *Graveyard?* he thought. *Why do they need a graveyard in a place full of teenagers?* That disturbed him even more than not knowing some of the words Alby kept saying—words like *Slopper* and *Bagger*—that didn't sound so good. He came as close to interrupting Alby as he'd done so far, but willed his mouth shut.

Frustrated, he turned his attention to the pens in the Blood House area.

Several cows nibbled and chewed at a trough full of greenish hay. Pigs lounged in a muddy pit, an occasionally flickering tail the only sign they were alive. Another pen held sheep, and there were chicken coops and turkey cages as well. Workers bustled about the area, looking as if they'd spent their whole lives on a farm.

Why do I remember these animals? Thomas wondered. Nothing about them seemed new or interesting—he knew what they were called, what they normally ate, what they looked like. Why was stuff like that still lodged in his memory, but not *where* he'd seen animals before, or with whom? His memory loss was baffling in its complexity.

Alby pointed to the large barn in the back corner, its red paint long faded to a dull rust color. "Back there's where the Slicers work. Nasty stuff, that. Nasty. If you like blood, you can be a Slicer."

Thomas shook his head. Slicer didn't sound good at all. As they kept walking, he focused his attention on the other side of the Glade, the section Alby had called the Deadheads. The trees grew thicker and denser the farther back in the corner they went, more alive and full of leaves. Dark shadows filled the depths of the wooded area, despite the time of day. Thomas looked up, squinting to see that the sun was finally visible, though it looked odd—more orange than it should be. It hit him that this was yet another example of the odd selective memory in his mind.

He returned his gaze to the Deadheads, a glowing disk still floating in his vision. Blinking to clear it away, he suddenly caught the red lights again, flickering and skittering about deep in the darkness of the woods. *What* are *those things?* he wondered, irritated that Alby hadn't answered him earlier. The secrecy was very annoying.

Alby stopped walking, and Thomas was surprised to see they'd reached the South Door; the two walls bracketing the exit towered above them. The thick slabs of gray stone were cracked and covered in ivy, as ancient as anything Thomas could imagine. He craned his neck to see the top of the walls far above; his mind spun with the odd sensation that he was looking *down,* not up. He staggered back a step, awed once again by the structure of his new home, then finally returned his attention to Alby, who had his back to the exit.

"Out there's the Maze." Alby jabbed a thumb over his shoulder, then paused. Thomas stared in that direction, through the gap in the walls that served as an exit from the Glade. The corridors out there looked much the same as the ones he'd seen from the window by the East Door early that morning. This thought gave him a chill, made him wonder if a Griever might come charging toward them at any minute. He took a step backward before realizing what he was doing. *Calm down,* he chided himself, embarrassed.

Alby continued. "Two years, I've been here. Ain't none been here longer. The few before me are already dead." Thomas felt his eyes widen, his heart quicken. "Two years we've tried to solve this thing, no luck. Shuckin' walls move out there at night just as much as these here doors. Mappin' it out ain't easy, ain't easy nohow." He nodded toward the concrete-blocked building into which the Runners had disappeared the night before.

Another stab of pain sliced through Thomas's head—there were too many things to compute at once. They'd been here two years? The walls moved out in the Maze? How many had died? He stepped forward, wanting to see the Maze for himself, as if the answers were printed on the walls out there.

Alby held out a hand and pushed Thomas in the chest, sent him stumbling backward. "Ain't no goin' out there, shank."

Thomas had to suppress his pride. "Why not?"

"You think I sent Newt to ya before the wake-up just for kicks? Freak, that's the Number One Rule, the only one you'll never be forgiven for breaking. Ain't nobody—*nobody*—allowed in the Maze except the Runners. Break that rule, and if you ain't killed by the Grievers, we'll kill you ourselves, you get me?"

Thomas nodded, grumbling inside, sure that Alby was exaggerating. Hoping that he was. Either way, if he'd had any doubt about what he'd told Chuck the night before, it had now completely vanished. He wanted to be a Runner. He *would* be a Runner. Deep inside he knew he had to go out there, into the Maze. Despite everything he'd learned and witnessed firsthand, it called to him as much as hunger or thirst.

A movement up on the left wall of the South Door caught his attention. Startled, he reacted quickly, looking just in time to see a flash of silver. A patch of ivy shook as the thing disappeared into it.

Thomas pointed up at the wall. "What was that?" he asked before he could be shut down again.

Alby didn't bother looking. "No questions till the end, shank. How many times I gotta tell ya?" He paused, then let out a sigh. "Beetle blades—it's how the Creators watch us. You better not—"

He was cut off by a booming, ringing alarm that sounded from all directions. Thomas clamped his hands to his ears, looking around as the siren blared, his heart about to thump its way out of his chest. But when he focused back on Alby, he stopped.

Alby wasn't acting scared—he appeared . . . confused. Surprised. The alarm clanged through the air.

"What's going on?" Thomas asked. Relief flooded his chest that his tour guide didn't seem to think the world was about to end—but even so, Thomas was getting tired of being hit by waves of panic.

"That's weird" was all Alby said as he scanned the Glade, squinting. Thomas noticed people in the Blood House pens glancing around, apparently just as confused. One shouted to Alby, a short, skinny kid drenched in mud.

"What's up with that?" the boy asked, looking to Thomas for some reason.

"I don't know," Alby murmured back in a distant voice.

But Thomas couldn't stand it anymore. "Alby! What's going on?"

"The Box, shuck-face, the Box!" was all Alby said before he set off for the middle of the Glade at a brisk pace that almost looked to Thomas like panic.

"What about it?" Thomas demanded, hurrying to catch up. *Talk to me!* he wanted to scream at him.

But Alby didn't answer or slow down, and as they got closer to the box Thomas could see that dozens of kids were running around the courtyard. He spotted Newt and called to him, trying to suppress his rising fear, telling himself things would be okay, that there had to be a reasonable explanation.

"Newt, what's going on!" he yelled.

Newt glanced over at him, then nodded and walked over, strangely calm in the middle of the chaos. He swatted Thomas on the back. "Means a bloody Newbie's comin' up in the Box." He paused as if expecting Thomas to be impressed. "Right *now*."

"So?" As Thomas looked more closely at Newt, he realized that what he'd mistaken for calm was actually disbelief—maybe even excitement.

"So?" Newt replied, his jaw dropping slightly. "Greenie, we've never had two Newbies show up in the same *month,* much less two days in a row."

And with that, he ran off toward the Homestead.

CHAPTER 8

The alarm finally stopped after blaring for a full two minutes. A crowd was gathered in the middle of the courtyard around the steel doors through which Thomas was startled to realize he'd arrived just yesterday. *Yesterday?* he thought. *Was that really just* yesterday*?*

Someone tapped him on the elbow; he looked over to see Chuck by his side again.

"How goes it, Greenbean?" Chuck asked.

"Fine," he replied, even though nothing could've been further from the truth. He pointed toward the doors of the Box. "Why is everyone freaking out? Isn't this how you all got here?"

Chuck shrugged. "I don't know—guess it's always been real regular-like. One a month, every month, same day. Maybe whoever's in charge realized you were nothing but a big mistake, sent someone to replace you." He giggled as he elbowed Thomas in the ribs, a high-pitched snicker that inexplicably made Thomas like him more.

Thomas shot his new friend a fake glare. "You're annoying. Seriously."

"Yeah, but we're buddies, now, right?" Chuck fully laughed this time, a squeaky sort of snort.

"Looks like you're not giving me much choice on that one." But truth was, he needed a friend, and Chuck would do just fine.

The kid folded his arms, looking very satisfied. "Glad that's settled, Greenie. Everyone needs a buddy in this place."

Thomas grabbed Chuck by the collar, joking around. "Okay, *buddy*, then call me by my name. Thomas. Or I'll throw you down the hole after the Box leaves." That triggered a thought in his head as he released Chuck. "Wait a minute, have you guys ever—"

"Tried it," Chuck interrupted before Thomas could finish.

"Tried what?"

"Going down in the Box after it makes a delivery," Chuck answered. "It won't do it. Won't go down until it's completely empty."

Thomas remembered Alby telling him that very thing. "I already knew that, but what about—"

"Tried it."

Thomas had to suppress a groan—this was getting irritating. "Man you're hard to talk to. Tried what?"

"Going through the hole *after* the Box goes down. Can't. Doors will open, but there's just emptiness, blackness, nothing. No ropes, nada. Can't do it."

How could that be possible? "Did you—"

"Tried it."

Thomas did groan this time. "Okay, what?"

"We threw some things into the hole. Never heard them land. It goes on for a long time."

Thomas paused before he replied, not wanting to be cut off again. "What are you, a mind reader or something?" He threw as much sarcasm as he could into the comment.

"Just brilliant, that's all." Chuck winked.

"Chuck, never wink at me again." Thomas said it with a smile. Chuck *was* a little annoying, but there was something about him that made things seem less terrible. Thomas took a deep breath and looked back toward the crowd around the hole. "So, how long until the delivery gets here?"

"Usually takes about half an hour after the alarm."

Thomas thought for a second. There *had* to be something they hadn't tried. "You're sure about the hole? Have you ever . . ." He paused, waiting for the interruption, but none came. "Have you ever tried making a rope?"

"Yeah, they did. With the ivy. Longest one they could possibly make. Let's just say that little experiment didn't go so well."

"What do you mean?" *What now?* Thomas thought.

"I wasn't here, but I heard the kid who volunteered to do it had only gone down about ten feet when something swooshed through the air and cut him clean in half."

"What?" Thomas laughed. "I don't believe that for a second."

"Oh, yeah, smart guy? I've seen the sucker's bones. Cut in half like a knife through whipped cream. They keep him in a box to remind future kids not to be so stupid."

Thomas waited for Chuck to laugh or smile, thinking it had to be a joke—who ever heard of someone being cut in half? But it never came. "You're serious?"

Chuck just stared back at him. "I don't lie, Gree—uh, Thomas. Come on, let's go over and see who's coming up. I can't believe you only have to be the Greenbean for one day. Klunkhead."

As they walked over, Thomas asked the one question he hadn't posed yet. "How do you know it's not just supplies or whatever?"

"The alarm doesn't go off when that happens," Chuck answered, simply. "The supplies come up at the same time every week. Hey, look." Chuck stopped and pointed to someone in the crowd. It was Gally, staring dead at them.

"Shuck it," Chuck said. "He does *not* like you, man."

"Yeah," Thomas muttered. "Figured that out already." And the feeling was mutual.

Chuck nudged Thomas with his elbow and the boys resumed their walk to the edge of the crowd, then waited in silence; any questions Thomas had were forgotten. He'd lost the urge to talk after seeing Gally.

Chuck apparently hadn't. "Why don't you go ask him what his problem is?" he asked, trying to sound tough.

Thomas wanted to think he was brave enough, but that currently sounded like the worst idea in history. "Well, for one, he has a lot more allies than I do. Not a good person to pick a fight with."

"Yeah, but you're smarter. And I bet you're quicker. You could take him and all his buddies."

One of the boys standing in front of them looked back over his shoulder, annoyance crossing his face.

Must be a friend of Gally's, Thomas thought. "Would you shut it?" he hissed at Chuck.

A door closed behind them; Thomas turned to see Alby and Newt heading over from the Homestead. They both looked exhausted.

Seeing them brought Ben back to his mind—along with the horrific image of him writhing in bed. "Chuck, man, you gotta tell me what this whole Changing business is. What have they been *doing* in there with that poor Ben kid?"

Chuck shrugged. "Don't know the details. The Grievers do bad things to you, make your whole body go through something awful. When it's over, you're . . . different."

Thomas sensed a chance to finally have a solid answer. "Different? What do you mean? And what does it have to do with the Grievers? Is that what Gally meant by 'being stung'?"

"Shh." Chuck held a finger to his mouth.

Thomas almost screamed in frustration, but he kept quiet. He resolved to make Chuck tell him later, whether the guy wanted to or not.

Alby and Newt had reached the crowd and pushed themselves to the front, standing right over the doors that led to the Box. Everyone quieted, and for the first time, Thomas noted the grinds and rattles of the rising lift, reminding him of his own nightmarish trip the day before. Sadness washed over him, almost as if he were reliving those few terrible minutes of awakening in darkness to the memory loss. He felt sorry for whoever this new kid was, going through the same things.

A muffled boom announced that the bizarre elevator had arrived.

Thomas watched in anticipation as Newt and Alby took positions on opposite sides of the shaft doors—a crack split the metal square right down the middle. Simple hook-handles were attached on both sides, and together they yanked them apart. With a metallic scrape the doors were opened, and a puff of dust from the surrounding stone rose into the air.

Complete silence settled over the Gladers. As Newt leaned over to get a better look into the Box, the faint bleating of a goat in the distance echoed across the courtyard. Thomas leaned forward as far as he possibly could, hoping to get a glance at the newcomer.

With a sudden jerk, Newt pushed himself back into an upright position, his face scrunched up in confusion. "Holy . . . ," he breathed, looking around at nothing in particular.

By this time, Alby had gotten a good look as well, with a similar reaction. "No way," he murmured, almost in a trance.

A chorus of questions filled the air as everyone began pushing forward to get a look into the small opening. *What do they see down there?* Thomas wondered. *What do they see!* He felt a sliver of muted fear, similar to what he'd experienced that morning when he stepped toward the window to see the Griever.

"Hold on!" Alby yelled, silencing everyone. "Just hold on!"

"Well, what's wrong?" someone yelled back.

Alby stood up. "Two Newbies in two days," he said, almost in a whisper. "Now this. Two years, nothing different, now this." Then, for some reason, he looked straight at Thomas. "What's goin' on here, Greenie?"

Thomas stared back, confused, his face turning bright red, his gut clenching. "How am I supposed to know?"

"Why don't you just tell us what the shuck is down there, Alby?" Gally called out. There were more murmurs and another surge forward.

"You shanks shut up!" Alby yelled. "Tell 'em, Newt."

Newt looked down in the Box one more time, then faced the crowd, gravely.

"It's a girl," he said.

Everyone started talking at once; Thomas only caught pieces here and there.

"A *girl*?"

"I got dibs!"

"What's she look like?"

"How old is she?"

Thomas was drowning in a sea of confusion. A *girl*? He hadn't even thought about why the Glade only had boys, no girls. Hadn't even had the chance to notice, really. *Who is she?* he wondered. *Why—*

Newt shushed them again. "That's not bloody half of it," he said, then pointed down into the Box. "I think she's dead."

A couple of boys grabbed some ropes made from ivy vines and lowered Alby and Newt into the Box so they could retrieve the girl's body. A mood of reserved shock had come over most of the Gladers, who were milling about with solemn faces, kicking loose rocks and not saying much at all. No one dared admit they couldn't wait to see the girl, but Thomas assumed they were all just as curious as he was.

Gally was one of the boys holding on to the ropes, ready to hoist her, Alby, and Newt out of the Box. Thomas watched him closely. His eyes were laced with something dark—almost a sick fascination. A gleam that made Thomas suddenly more scared of him than he'd been minutes earlier.

From deep in the shaft came Alby's voice shouting that they were ready, and Gally and a couple of others started pulling up on the rope. A few grunts later and the girl's lifeless body was dragged out, across the edge of the door and onto one of the stone blocks making up the ground of the Glade. Everyone immediately ran forward, forming a packed crowd around her, a palpable excitement hovering in the air. But Thomas stayed back. The eerie silence gave him the creeps, as if they'd just opened up a recently laid tomb.

Despite his own curiosity, Thomas didn't bother trying to force his way through to get a look—the bodies were too tightly squeezed together. But he *had* caught a glimpse of her before being blocked off. She was thin, but not too small. Maybe five and a half feet tall, from what he could tell. She looked like she could be fifteen or sixteen years old, and her hair was tar black. But the thing that had really stood out to him was her skin: pale, white as pearls.

Newt and Alby scrambled out of the Box after her, then forced their way through to the girl's lifeless body, the crowd re-forming behind to cut them off from Thomas's view. Only a few seconds later, the group parted again, and Newt was pointing straight at Thomas.

"Greenie, get over here," he said, not bothering to be polite about it.

Thomas's heart jumped into his throat; his hands started to sweat. What did they want him for? Things just kept getting worse and worse. He forced himself to walk forward, trying to seem innocent without acting like someone who was guilty who was trying to act innocent. *Oh, calm it,* he told himself. *You haven't done anything wrong.* But he had a strange feeling that maybe he had without realizing it.

The boys lining the path to Newt and the girl glared at him as he walked past, as if he were responsible for the entire mess of the Maze and the Glade and the Grievers. Thomas refused to make eye contact with any of them, afraid of looking guilty.

He approached Newt and Alby, who both knelt beside the girl. Thomas, not wanting to meet their stares, concentrated on the girl; despite her paleness, she was really pretty. More than pretty. Beautiful. Silky hair, flawless skin, perfect lips, long legs. It made him sick to think that way about a dead girl, but he couldn't look away. *Won't be that way for long,* he thought with a queasy twist in his stomach. *She'll start rotting soon.* He was surprised at having such a morbid thought.

"You know this girl, shank?" Alby asked, sounding ticked off.

Thomas was shocked by the question. "*Know* her? Of course I don't know her. I don't know anyone. Except for you guys."

"That's not . . . ," Alby began, then stopped with a frustrated sigh. "I meant does she look *familiar* at all? Any kind of feelin' you've seen her before?"

"No. Nothing." Thomas shifted, looked down at his feet, then back at the girl.

Alby's forehead creased. "You're sure?" He looked like he didn't believe a word Thomas said, seemed almost angry.

What could he possibly think I have to do with this? Thomas thought. He met Alby's glare evenly and answered the only way he knew how. "*Yes*. Why?"

"Shuck it," Alby muttered, looking back down at the girl. "Can't be a coincidence. Two days, two Greenies, one alive, one dead."

Then Alby's words started to make sense and panic flared in Thomas. "You don't think I . . ." He couldn't even finish the sentence.

"Slim it, Greenie," Newt said. "We're not sayin' you bloody killed the girl."

Thomas's mind was spinning. He was sure he'd never seen her before—but then the slightest hint of doubt crept into his mind. "I swear she doesn't look familiar at all," he said anyway. He'd had enough accusations.

"Are you—"

Before Newt could finish, the girl shot up into a sitting position. As she sucked in a huge breath, her eyes snapped open and she blinked, looking around at the crowd surrounding her. Alby cried out and fell backward. Newt gasped and jumped up, stumbling away from her. Thomas didn't move, his gaze locked on the girl, frozen in fear.

Burning blue eyes darted back and forth as she took deep breaths. Her pink lips trembled as she mumbled something over and over, indecipherable. Then she spoke one sentence—her voice hollow and haunted, but clear.

"Everything is going to change."

Thomas stared in wonder as her eyes rolled up into her head and she fell back to the ground. Her right fist shot into the air as she landed, staying rigid after she grew still, pointing toward the sky. Clutched in her hand was a wadded piece of paper.

Thomas tried to swallow but his mouth was too dry. Newt ran forward and pulled her fingers apart, grabbing the paper. With shaking hands he unfolded it, then dropped to his knees, spreading out the note on the ground. Thomas moved up behind him to get a look.

Scrawled across the paper in thick black letters were five words:

She's the last one.

Ever.

CHAPTER 9

An odd moment of complete silence hung over the Glade. It was as if a supernatural wind had swept through the place and sucked out all sound. Newt had read the message aloud for those who couldn't see the paper, but instead of erupting in confusion, the Gladers all stood dumbfounded.

Thomas would've expected shouts and questions, arguments. But no one said a word; all eyes were glued to the girl, now lying there as if asleep, her chest rising and falling with shallow breaths. Contrary to their original conclusion, she was very much alive.

Newt stood, and Thomas hoped for an explanation, a voice of reason, a calming presence. But all he did was crumple the note in his fist, veins popping from his skin as he squeezed it, and Thomas's heart sank. He wasn't sure why, but the situation made him very uneasy.

Alby cupped his hands around his mouth. "Med-jacks!"

Thomas wondered what that word meant—he knew he'd heard it before—but then he was abruptly knocked aside. Two older boys were pushing their way through the crowd—one was tall with a buzz cut, his nose the size of a fat lemon. The other was short and actually had gray hair already conquering the black on the sides of his head. Thomas could only hope they'd make some sense of everything.

"So what do we do with her?" the taller one asked, his voice much higher pitched than Thomas expected.

"How should I know?" Alby said. "You two shanks are the Med-jacks—figure it out."

Med-jacks, Thomas repeated in his head, a light going off. *They must be the closest thing they have to doctors.* The short one was already on the ground, kneeling beside the girl, feeling for her pulse and leaning over to listen to her heartbeat.

"Who said Clint had first shot at her?" someone yelled from the crowd. There were several barks of laughter. "I'm next!"

How can they joke around? Thomas thought. *The girl's half dead.* He felt sick inside.

Alby's eyes narrowed; his mouth pulled into a tight grin that didn't look like it had anything to do with humor. "If anybody touches this girl," Alby said, "you're gonna spend the night sleepin' with the Grievers in the Maze. Banished, no questions." He paused, turning in a slow circle as if he wanted every person to see his face. "Ain't nobody better touch her! Nobody!"

It was the first time Thomas had actually liked hearing something come out of Alby's mouth.

The short guy who'd been referred to as a Med-jack—*Clint,* if the spectator had been correct—stood up from his examination. "She seems fine. Breathing okay, normal heartbeat. Though it's a bit slow. Your guess is as good as mine, but I'd say she's in a coma. Jeff, let's take her to the Homestead."

His partner, Jeff, stepped over to grab her by the arms while Clint took hold of her feet. Thomas wished he could do more than watch—with every passing second, he doubted more and more that what he'd said earlier was true. She *did* seem familiar; he felt a connection to her, though it was impossible to grasp in his mind. The idea made him nervous, and he looked around, as if someone might've heard his thoughts.

"On the count of three," Jeff, the taller Med-jack, was saying, his tall frame looking ridiculous bent in half, like a praying mantis. "One . . . two . . . three!"

They lifted her with a quick jerk, almost throwing her up in the air—she was obviously a lot lighter than they'd thought—and Thomas almost shouted at them to be more careful.

"Guess we'll have to see what she does," Jeff said to no one in particular. "We can feed her soupy stuff if she doesn't wake up soon."

"Just watch her closely," Newt said. "Must be something special about her or they wouldn't have sent her here."

Thomas's gut clenched. He knew that he and the girl were connected somehow. They'd come a day apart, she seemed familiar, he had a consuming urge to become a Runner despite learning so many terrible things. . . . What did it all mean?

Alby leaned over to look in her face once more before they carried her off. "Put her next to Ben's room, and keep a watch on her day and night. Nothin' better happen without me knowing about it. I don't care if she talks in her sleep or takes a klunk—you come tell me."

"Yeah," Jeff muttered; then he and Clint shuffled off to the Homestead, the girl's body bouncing as they went, and the other Gladers finally started to talk about it, scattering as theories bubbled through the air.

Thomas watched all this in mute contemplation. This strange connection he felt wasn't his alone. The not-so-veiled accusations thrown at him only a few minutes before proved that the others suspected something, too, but what? He was already completely confused—being blamed for things only made him feel worse. As if reading his thoughts, Alby walked over and grabbed him by the shoulder.

"You ain't never seen her before?" he asked.

Thomas hesitated before he answered. "Not . . . no, not that I remember." He hoped his shaky voice didn't betray his doubts. What if he *did* know her somehow? What would that mean?

"You're sure?" Newt prodded, standing right behind Alby.

"I . . . no, I don't think so. Why are you grilling me like this?" All Thomas wanted right then was for night to fall, so he could be alone, go to sleep.

Alby shook his head, then turned back to Newt, releasing his grip on Thomas's shoulder. "Something's whacked. Call a Gathering."

He said it quietly enough that Thomas didn't think anyone else heard, but it sounded ominous. Then the leader and Newt walked off, and Thomas was relieved to see Chuck coming his way.

"Chuck, what's a Gathering?"

He looked proud to know the answer. "It's when the Keepers meet—they only call one when something weird or terrible happens."

"Well, I guess today fits both of those categories pretty well." Thomas's stomach rumbled, interrupting his thoughts. "I didn't finish my breakfast—can we get something somewhere? I'm starving."

Chuck looked up at him, his eyebrows raised. "Seeing that chick wig out made you hungry? You must be more psycho than I thought."

Thomas sighed. "Just get me some food."

The kitchen was small but had everything one needed to make a hearty meal. A big oven, a microwave, a dishwasher, a couple of tables. It seemed old and run-down but clean. Seeing the appliances and the familiar layout made Thomas feel as if memories—real, solid memories—were right on the edge of his mind. But again, the essential parts were missing—names, faces, places, events. It was maddening.

"Take a seat," Chuck said. "I'll get you something—but I swear this is the last time. Just be glad Frypan isn't around—he hates it when we raid his fridge."

Thomas was relieved they were alone. As Chuck fumbled about with dishes and things from the fridge, Thomas pulled out a wooden chair from a small plastic table and sat down. "This is crazy. How can this be for real? Somebody sent us here. Somebody evil."

Chuck paused. "Quit complaining. Just accept it and don't think about it."

"Yeah, right." Thomas looked out a window. This seemed a good time to bring up one of the million questions bouncing through his brain. "So where does the electricity come from?"

"Who cares? I'll take it."

What a surprise, Thomas thought. *No answer.*

Chuck brought two plates with sandwiches and carrots over to the table. The bread was thick and white, the carrots a sparkling, bright orange. Thomas's stomach begged him to hurry; he picked up his sandwich and started devouring it.

"Oh, man," he mumbled with a full mouth. "At least the food is good."

Thomas was able to eat the rest of his meal without another word from Chuck. And he was lucky that the kid didn't feel like talking, because despite the complete weirdness of everything that had happened within Thomas's known reach of memory, he felt calm again. His stomach full, his energy replenished, his mind thankful for a few moments of silence, he decided that from then on he'd quit whining and deal with things.

After his last bite, Thomas sat back in his chair. "So, Chuck," he said as he wiped his mouth with a napkin. "What do I have to do to become a Runner?"

"Not that again." Chuck looked up from his plate, where he'd been picking at the crumbs. He let out a low, gurgly burp that made Thomas cringe.

"Alby said I'd start my trials soon with the different Keepers. So, when do I get a shot with the Runners?" Thomas waited patiently to get some sort of actual information from Chuck.

Chuck rolled his eyes dramatically, leaving no doubt as to how stupid an idea he thought that would be. "They should be back in a few hours. Why don't you ask *them*?"

Thomas ignored the sarcasm, digging deeper. "What do they do when they get back every night? What's up with the concrete building?"

"Maps. They meet right when they get back, before they forget anything."

Maps? Thomas was confused. "But if they're trying to make a map, don't they have paper to write on while they're out there?" Maps. This intrigued him more than anything else he'd heard in a while. It was the first thing suggesting a potential solution to their predicament.

"Of course they do, but there's still stuff they need to talk about and discuss and analyze and all that klunk. Plus"—the boy rolled his eyes—"they spend most of their time running, not writing. That's why they're called *Runners*."

Thomas thought about the Runners and the maps. Could the Maze really be so massively huge that even after two years they still hadn't found a way out? It seemed impossible. But then, he remembered what Alby said about the moving walls. What if all of them were sentenced to live here until they died?

Sentenced. The word made him feel a rush of panic, and the spark of hope the meal had brought him fizzled with a silent hiss.

"Chuck, what if we're all criminals? I mean—what if we're murderers or something?"

"Huh?" Chuck looked up at him as if he were a crazy person. "Where did that happy thought come from?"

"Think about it. Our memories are wiped. We live inside a place that seems to have no way out, surrounded by bloodthirsty monster-guards. Doesn't that sound like a prison to you?" As he said it out loud, it sounded more and more possible. Nausea trickled into his chest.

"I'm probably twelve years old, dude." Chuck pointed to his chest. "At the most, thirteen. You really think I did something that would send me to prison for the rest of my life?"

"I don't care what you did or didn't do. Either way, you *have* been sent to a prison. Does this seem like a vacation to you?" *Oh, man,* Thomas thought. *Please let me be wrong.*

Chuck thought for a moment. "I don't know. It's better than—"

"Yeah, I know, living in pile of klunk." Thomas stood up and pushed his chair back under the table. He liked Chuck, but trying to have an intelligent conversation with him was impossible. Not to mention frustrating and irritating. "Go make yourself another sandwich—I'm going exploring. See ya tonight."

He stepped out of the kitchen and into the courtyard before Chuck could offer to join him. The Glade had gone back to business as usual—people working the jobs, the doors of the Box closed, sun shining down. Any signs of a crazed girl bearing notes of doom had disappeared.

Having had his tour cut short, he decided to take a walk around the Glade on his own and get a better look and feel for the place. He headed out for the northeast corner, toward the big rows of tall green cornstalks that looked ready to harvest. There was other stuff, too: tomatoes, lettuce, peas, a lot more that Thomas didn't recognize.

He took a deep breath, loving the fresh whiff of dirt and growing plants. He was almost positive the smell would bring back some sort of pleasant memory, but nothing came. As he got closer, he saw that several boys were weeding and picking in the small fields. One waved at him with a smile. An actual smile.

Maybe this place won't be so bad after all, Thomas thought. *Not everyone here could be a jerk.* He took another deep breath of the pleasant air and pulled himself out of his thoughts—there was a lot more he wanted to see.

Next was the southeast corner, where shabbily built wooden fences held in several cows, goats, sheep, and pigs. No horses, though. *That sucks,* Thomas thought. *Riders* would definitely be faster than *Runners.* As he approached, he figured he must've dealt with animals in his life before the Glade. Their smell, their sound—they seemed very familiar to him.

The smell wasn't quite as nice as the crops, but still, he imagined it could've been a lot worse. As he explored the area, he realized more and more how well the Gladers kept up the place, how clean it was. He was impressed by how organized they must be, how hard they all must work. He could only imagine how truly horrific a place like this could be if everyone went lazy and stupid.

Finally, he made it to the southwest quarter, near the forest.

He was approaching the sparse, skeletal trees in front of the denser woods when he was startled by a blur of movement at his feet, followed by a hurried set of clacking sounds. He looked down just in time to see the sun flash off something metallic—a toy rat—scurrying past him and toward the small forest. The thing was already ten feet away by the time he realized it wasn't a rat at all—it was more like a lizard, with at least six legs scuttling the long silver torso along.

A beetle blade. *It's how they watch us*, Alby had said.

He caught a gleam of red light sweeping the ground in front of the creature as if it came from its eyes. Logic told him it had to be his mind playing tricks on him, but he swore he saw the word *WICKED* scrawled down its rounded back in large green letters. Something so strange had to be investigated.

Thomas sprinted after the scurrying spy, and in a matter of seconds he entered the thick copse of trees and the world became dark.

CHAPTER 10

He couldn't believe how quickly the light disappeared. From the Glade proper, the forest didn't look that big, maybe a couple of acres. Yet the trees were tall with sturdy trunks, packed tightly together, the canopy up above thick with leaves. The air around him had a greenish, muted hue, as if only several minutes of twilight remained in the day.

It was somehow beautiful and creepy, all at once.

Moving as fast as he could, Thomas crashed through the heavy foliage, thin branches slapping at his face. He ducked to avoid a low-hanging limb, almost falling. Reaching out, he caught hold of a branch and swung himself forward to regain his balance. A thick bed of leaves and fallen twigs crunched underneath him.

All the while, his eyes stayed riveted on the beetle blade scuttling across the forest floor. Deeper it went, its red light glowing brighter as the surroundings darkened.

Thomas had charged thirty or forty feet into the woods, dodging and ducking and losing ground with every second, when the beetle blade jumped onto a particularly large tree and scooted up its trunk. But by the time Thomas reached the tree, any sign of the creature had vanished. It had disappeared deep within the foliage—almost as if it had never existed.

He'd lost the sucker.

"Shuck it," Thomas whispered, almost as a joke. Almost. As strange as it seemed, the word felt natural on his lips, like he was already morphing into a Glader.

A twig snapped somewhere to his right and he jerked his head in that direction. He stilled his breath, listened.

Another snap, this time louder, almost like someone had broken a stick over their knee.

"Who's there?" Thomas yelled out, a tingle of fear shooting across his shoulders. His voice bounced off the canopy of leaves above him, echoing through the air. He stayed frozen, rooted to the spot as all grew silent, except for the whistling song of a few birds in the distance. But no one answered his call. Nor did he hear any more sounds from that direction.

Without really thinking it through, Thomas headed toward the noise he'd heard. Not bothering to hide his progress, he pushed aside branches as he walked, letting them whip back to position when he passed. He squinted, willed his eyes to work in the growing darkness, wishing he had a flashlight. He thought about flashlights and his memory. Once again, he remembered a tangible thing from his past, but couldn't assign it to any specific time or place, couldn't associate it with any other person or event. Frustrating.

"Anybody there?" he asked again, feeling a little calmer since the noise hadn't repeated. It was probably just an animal, maybe another beetle blade. Just in case, he called out, "It's me, Thomas. The new guy. Well, second-newest guy."

He winced and shook his head, hoping now that no one *was* there. He sounded like a complete idiot.

Again, no reply.

He stepped around a large oak and pulled up short. An icy shiver ran down his back. He'd reached the graveyard.

The clearing was small, maybe thirty square feet, and covered with a thick layer of leafy weeds growing close to the ground. Thomas could see several clumsily prepared wooden crosses poking through this growth, their horizontal pieces lashed to the upright ones with a splintery twine. The grave markers had been painted white, but by someone in an obvious hurry—gelled globs covered them and bare streaks of wood showed through. Names had been carved into the wood.

Thomas stepped up, hesitantly, to the closest one and knelt down to get a look. The light was so dull now that he almost felt as if he were looking through black mist. Even the birds had quieted, like they'd gone to bed for the night, and the sound of insects was barely noticeable, or at least much less than normal. For the first time, Thomas realized how humid it was in the woods, the damp air already beading sweat on his forehead, the backs of his hands.

He leaned closer to the first cross. It looked fresh and bore the name Stephen—the *n* extra small and right at the edge because the carver hadn't estimated well how much room he'd need.

Stephen, Thomas thought, feeling an unexpected but detached sorrow. *What's your story? Chuck annoy you to death?*

He stood and walked over to another cross, this one almost completely overgrown with weeds, the ground firm at its base. Whoever it was, he must've been one of the first to die, because his grave looked the oldest. The name was George.

Thomas looked around and saw there were a dozen or so other graves. A couple of them appeared to be just as fresh as the first one he'd examined. A silvery glint caught his attention. It was different from the scuttling beetle that had led him to the forest, but just as odd. He moved through the markers until he got to a grave covered with a sheet of grimy plastic or glass, its edges slimed with filth. He squinted, trying to make out what was on the other side, then gasped when it came into focus. It was a window into another grave—one that had the dusty remnants of a rotting body.

Completely creeped out, Thomas leaned closer to get a better look anyway, curious. The tomb was smaller than usual—only the top *half* of the deceased person lay inside. He remembered Chuck's story about the boy who'd tried to rappel down the dark hole of the Box after it had descended, only to be cut in two by something slicing through the air. Words were etched on the glass; Thomas could barely read them:

Let this half-shank be a warning to all:
You can't escape through the Box Hole.

Thomas felt the odd urge to snicker—it seemed too ridiculous to be true. But he was also disgusted with himself for being so shallow and glib. Shaking his head, he had stepped aside to read more names of the dead when another twig broke, this time straight in front of him, right behind the trees on the other side of the graveyard.

Then another snap. Then another. Coming closer. And the darkness was thick.

"Who's out there?" he called, his voice shaky and hollow—it sounded as if he were speaking inside an insulated tunnel. "Seriously, this is stupid." He hated to admit to himself just how terrified he was.

Instead of answering, the person gave up all pretense of stealth and started running, crashing through the forest line around the clearing of the graveyard, circling toward the spot where Thomas stood. He froze, panic overtaking him. Now only a few feet away, the visitor grew louder and louder until Thomas caught a shadowed glimpse of a skinny boy limping along in a strange, lilting run.

"Who the he—"

The boy burst through the trees before Thomas could finish. He saw only a flash of pale skin and enormous eyes—the haunted image of an apparition—and cried out, tried to run, but it was too late. The figure leaped into the air and was on top of him, slamming into his shoulders, gripping him with strong hands. Thomas crashed to the ground; he felt a grave marker dig into his back before it snapped in two, burning a deep scratch along his flesh.

He pushed and swatted at his attacker, a relentless jumble of skin and bones cavorting on top of him as he tried to gain purchase. It seemed like a monster, a horror from a nightmare, but Thomas knew it had to be a Glader, someone who'd completely lost his mind. He heard teeth snapping open and closed, a horrific clack, clack, clack. Then he felt the jarring dagger of pain as the boy's mouth found a home, bit deeply into Thomas's shoulder.

Thomas screamed, the pain like a burst of adrenaline through his blood. He planted the palms of his hands against his attacker's chest and pushed, straightening his arms until his muscles strained against the struggling figure above him. Finally the kid fell back; a sharp crack filled the air as another grave marker met its demise.

Thomas squirmed away on his hands and feet, sucking in breaths of air, and got his first good look at the crazed attacker.

It was the sick boy.

It was Ben.

CHAPTER 11

It looked as if Ben had recovered only slightly since Thomas had seen him in the Homestead. He wore nothing but shorts, his whiter-than-white skin stretched across his bones like a sheet wrapped tightly around a bundle of sticks. Ropelike veins ran along his body, pulsing and green—but less pronounced than the day before. His bloodshot eyes fell upon Thomas as if he were seeing his next meal.

Ben crouched, ready to spring for another attack. At some point a knife had made an appearance, gripped in his right hand. Thomas was filled with a queasy fear, disbelief that this was happening at all.

"Ben!"

Thomas looked toward the voice, surprised to see Alby standing at the edge of the graveyard, a mere phantom in the fading light. Relief flooded Thomas's body—Alby held a large bow, an arrow cocked for the kill, pointed straight at Ben.

"Ben," Alby repeated. "Stop right now, or you ain't gonna see tomorrow."

Thomas looked back at Ben, who stared viciously at Alby, his tongue darting between his lips to wet them. *What could possibly be wrong with that kid?* Thomas thought. The boy had turned into a monster. Why?

"If you kill me," Ben shrieked, spittle flying from his mouth, far enough to hit Thomas in the face, "you'll get the wrong guy." He snapped his gaze back to Thomas. "He's the shank you wanna kill." His voice was full of madness.

"Don't be stupid, Ben," Alby said, his voice calm as he continued to aim the arrow. "Thomas just got here—ain't nothing to worry about. You're still buggin' from the Changing. You should've never left your bed."

"He's not one of us!" Ben shouted. "I saw him—he's . . . he's bad. We have to kill him! Let me gut him!"

Thomas took an involuntary step backward, horrified by what Ben had said. What did he mean, he'd seen him? Why did he think Thomas was bad?

Alby hadn't moved his weapon an inch, still aiming for Ben. "You leave that to me and the Keepers to figure out, shuck-face." His hands were perfectly steady as he held the bow, almost as if he had propped it against a branch for support. "Right now, back your scrawny butt down and get to the Homestead."

"He'll wanna take us home," Ben said. "He'll wanna get us out of the Maze. Better we all jumped off the Cliff! Better we tore each other's guts out!"

"What are you talking—" Thomas began.

"Shut your face!" Ben screamed. "Shut your ugly, traitorous face!"

"Ben," Alby said calmly. "I'm gonna count to three."

"He's bad, he's bad, he's bad . . . ," Ben was whispering now, almost chanting. He swayed back and forth, switching the knife from hand to hand, eyes glued on Thomas.

"One."

"Bad, bad, bad, bad, bad . . ." Ben smiled; his teeth seemed to glow, greenish in the pale light.

Thomas wanted to look away, get out of there. But he couldn't move; he was too mesmerized, too scared.

"Two." Alby's voice was louder, filled with warning.

"Ben," Thomas said, trying to make sense of it all. "I'm not . . . I don't even know what—"

Ben screamed, a strangled gurgle of madness, and leaped into the air, slashing out with his blade.

"Three!" Alby shouted.

There was the sound of snapping wire. The *whoosh* of an object slicing through the air. The sickening, wet *thunk* of it finding a home.

Ben's head snapped violently to the left, twisting his body until he landed on his stomach, his feet pointed toward Thomas. He made no sound.

Thomas jumped to his feet and stumbled forward. The long shaft of the arrow stuck from Ben's cheek, the blood surprisingly less than Thomas had expected, but seeping out all the same. Black in the darkness, like oil. The only movement was Ben's right pinky finger, twitching. Thomas fought the urge to puke. Was Ben dead because of him? Was it his fault?

"Come on," Alby said. "Baggers'll take care of him tomorrow."

What just happened here? Thomas thought, the world tilting around him as he stared at the lifeless body. *What did I ever do to this kid?*

He looked up, wanting answers, but Alby was already gone, a trembling branch the only sign he'd ever stood there in the first place.

Thomas squeezed his eyes against the blinding light of the sun as he emerged from the woods. He was limping, his ankle screaming in pain, though he had no memory of hurting it. He held one hand carefully over the area where he'd been bitten; the other clutched his stomach as if that would prevent what Thomas now felt was an inevitable barf. The image of Ben's head popped into his mind, cocked at an unnatural angle, blood running down the shaft of the arrow until it collected, dripped, splattered on the ground. . . .

The image of it was the last straw.

He fell to his knees by one of the scraggly trees on the outskirts of the forest and threw up, retching as he coughed and spat out every last morsel of the acidic, nasty bile from his stomach. His whole body shook, and it seemed like the vomiting would never end.

And then, as if his brain were mocking him, trying to make it worse, he had a thought.

He'd now been at the Glade for roughly twenty-four hours. One full day. That was it. And look at all the things that had happened. All the terrible things.

Surely it could only get better.

That night, Thomas lay staring at the sparkling sky, wondering if he'd ever sleep again. Every time he closed his eyes, the monstrous image of Ben leaping at him, the boy's face set in lunacy, filled his mind. Eyes opened or not, he could swear he kept hearing the moist thunk of the arrow slamming into Ben's cheek.

Thomas knew he'd never forget those few terrible minutes in the graveyard.

"Say something," Chuck said for the fifth time since they'd set out their sleeping bags.

"No," Thomas replied, just as he had before.

"Everyone knows what happened. It's happened once or twice—some Griever-stung shank flipped out and attacked somebody. Don't think you're special."

For the first time, Thomas thought Chuck's personality had gone from mildly irritating to intolerable. "Chuck, be glad I'm not holding Alby's bow right about now."

"I'm just play—"

"Shut up, Chuck. Go to sleep." Thomas just couldn't handle it right then.

Eventually, his "buddy" did doze off, and based on the rumble of snores across the Glade, so did everyone else. Hours later, deep in the night, Thomas was still the only one awake. He wanted to cry, but didn't. He wanted to find Alby and punch him, for no reason whatsoever, but didn't. He wanted to scream and kick and spit and open up the Box and jump into the blackness below. But he didn't.

He closed his eyes and forced the thoughts and dark images away and at some point he fell asleep.

Chuck had to drag Thomas out of his sleeping bag in the morning, drag him to the showers, and drag him to the dressing rooms. The whole time, Thomas felt mopey and indifferent, his head aching, his body wanting more sleep. Breakfast was a blur, and an hour after it was over, Thomas couldn't remember what he'd eaten. He was so tired, his brain felt like someone had gone in and stapled it to his skull in a dozen places. Heartburn ravaged his chest.

But from what he could tell, naps were frowned upon in the giant working farm of the Glade.

He stood with Newt in front of the barn of the Blood House, getting ready for his first training session with a Keeper. Despite the rough morning, he was actually excited to learn more, and for the chance to get his mind off Ben and the graveyard. Cows mooed, sheep bleated, pigs squealed all around him. Somewhere close by, a dog barked, making Thomas hope Frypan didn't bring new meaning to the word *hot dog. Hot dog,* he thought. *When's the last time I had a hot dog? Who did I eat it with?*

"Tommy, are you even listening to me?"

Thomas snapped out of his daze and focused on Newt, who'd been talking for who knew how long; Thomas hadn't heard a word of it. "Yeah, sorry. Couldn't sleep last night."

Newt attempted a pathetic smile. "Can't blame ya there. Went through the buggin' ringer, you did. Probably think I'm a slinthead shank for gettin' you ready to work your butt off today after an episode the likes of that."

Thomas shrugged. "Work's probably the best thing I could do. Anything to get my mind off it."

Newt nodded, and his smile became more genuine. "You're as smart as you look, Tommy. That's one of the reasons we run this place all nice and busylike. You get lazy, you get sad. Start givin' up. Plain and simple."

Thomas nodded, absently kicking a loose rock across the dusty, cracked stone floor of the Glade. "So what's the latest on that girl from yesterday?" If anything had penetrated the haze of his long morning, it had been thoughts of her. He wanted to know more about her, understand the odd connection he felt to her.

"Still in a coma, sleepin'. Med-jacks are spoon-feeding her whatever soups Frypan can cook up, checking her vitals and such. She seems okay, just dead to the world for now."

"That was just plain weird." If it hadn't been for the whole Ben-in-the-graveyard incident, Thomas was sure she would've been all he'd thought about last night. Maybe he wouldn't have been able to sleep for an entirely different reason. He wanted to know who she was and if he really did know her somehow.

"Yeah," Newt said. "*Weird*'s as good a word as any, I 'spect."

Thomas looked over Newt's shoulder at the big faded-red barn, pushing thoughts of the girl aside. "So what's first? Milk cows or slaughter some poor little pigs?"

Newt laughed, a sound Thomas realized he hadn't heard much since he'd arrived. "We always make the Newbies start with the bloody Slicers. Don't worry, cuttin' up Frypan's victuals ain't but a part. Slicers do anything and everything dealin' with the beasties."

"Too bad I can't remember my whole life. Maybe I love killing animals." He was just joking, but Newt didn't seem to get it.

Newt nodded toward the barn. "Oh, you'll know good and well by the time sun sets tonight. Let's go meet Winston—he's the Keeper."

Winston was an acne-covered kid, short but muscular, and it seemed to Thomas the Keeper liked his job way too much. *Maybe he was sent here for being a serial killer,* he thought.

Winston showed Thomas around for the first hour, pointing out which pens held which animals, where the chicken and turkey coops were, what went where in the barn. The dog, a pesky black Lab named Bark, took quickly to Thomas, hanging at his feet the entire tour. Wondering where the dog came from, Thomas asked Winston, who said Bark had just always been there. Luckily, he seemed to have gotten his name as a joke, because he was pretty quiet.

The second hour was spent actually working with the farm animals—feeding, cleaning, fixing a fence, scraping up klunk. *Klunk.* Thomas found himself using the Glader terms more and more.

The third hour was the hardest for Thomas. He had to watch as Winston slaughtered a hog and began preparing its many parts for future eating. Thomas swore two things to himself as he walked away for lunch break. First, his career would not be with the animals; second, he'd never again eat something that came out of a pig.

Winston had said for him to go on alone, that he'd hang around the

Blood House, which was fine with Thomas. As he walked toward the East Door, he couldn't stop picturing Winston in a dark corner of the barn, gnawing on raw pigs' feet. The guy gave him the willies.

Thomas was just passing the Box when he was surprised to see someone enter the Glade from the Maze, through the West Door, to his left—an Asian kid with strong arms and short black hair, who looked a little older than Thomas. The Runner stopped three steps in, then bent over and put his hands on his knees, gasping for breath. He looked like he'd just run twenty miles, face red, skin covered in sweat, clothes soaked.

Thomas stared, overcome with curiosity—he'd yet to see a Runner up close or talk to one. Plus, based on the last couple of days, the Runner was home hours early. Thomas stepped forward, eager to meet him and ask questions.

But before he could form a sentence, the boy collapsed to the ground.

CHAPTER 12

Thomas didn't move for a few seconds. The boy lay in a crumpled heap, barely moving, but Thomas was frozen by indecision, afraid to get involved. What if something was seriously wrong with this guy? What if he'd been . . . *stung*? What if—

Thomas snapped out of it—the Runner obviously needed help.

"Alby!" he shouted. "Newt! Somebody get them!"

Thomas sprinted to the older boy and knelt down beside him. "Hey—you okay?" The Runner's head rested on outstretched arms as he panted, his chest heaving. He was conscious, but Thomas had never seen someone so exhausted.

"I'm . . . fine," he said between breaths, then looked up. "Who the klunk are you?"

"I'm new here." It hit Thomas then that the Runners were out in the Maze during the day and hadn't witnessed any of the recent events firsthand. Did this guy even know about the girl? Probably—surely someone had told him. "I'm Thomas—been here just a couple of days."

The Runner pushed himself up into a sitting position, his black hair matted to his skull with sweat. "Oh, yeah, Thomas," he huffed. "Newbie. You and the chick."

Alby jogged up then, clearly upset. "What're you doin' back, Minho? What happened?"

"Calm your wad, Alby," the Runner replied, seeming to gain

strength by the second. "Make yourself useful and get me some water—I dropped my pack out there somewhere."

But Alby didn't move. He kicked Minho in the leg—too hard to be playful. "What *happened*?"

"I can barely talk, shuck-face!" Minho yelled, his voice raw. "Get me some water!"

Alby looked over at Thomas, who was shocked to see the slightest hint of a smile flash across his face before vanishing in a scowl. "Minho's the only shank who can talk to me like that without getting his butt kicked off the Cliff."

Then, surprising Thomas even more, Alby turned and ran off, presumably to get Minho some water.

Thomas turned toward Minho. "He lets you boss him around?"

Minho shrugged, then wiped fresh beads of sweat off his forehead. "You scared of that pip-squeak? Dude, you got a lot to learn. Freakin' Newbies."

The rebuke hurt Thomas far more than it should have, considering he'd known this guy all of three minutes. "Isn't he the leader?"

"Leader?" Minho barked a grunt that was probably supposed to be a laugh. "Yeah, call him leader all you want. Maybe we should call him El Presidente. Nah, nah—Admiral Alby. There you go." He rubbed his eyes, snickering as he did so.

Thomas didn't know what to make of the conversation—it was hard to tell when Minho was joking. "So who *is* the leader if he isn't?"

"Greenie, just shut it before you confuse yourself more." Minho sighed as if bored, then muttered, almost to himself, "Why do you shanks always come in here asking stupid questions? It's really annoying."

"What do you expect us to do?" Thomas felt a flush of anger. *Like you were any different when you first came,* he wanted to say.

"Do what you're told, keep your mouth shut. That's what I expect."

Minho had looked him square in the face for the first time with that last sentence, and Thomas scooted back a few inches before he could stop himself. He realized immediately he'd just made a mistake—he couldn't let this guy think he could talk to him like that.

He pushed himself back up onto his knees so he was looking down at the older boy. "Yeah, I'm sure that's exactly what you did as a Newbie."

Minho looked at Thomas carefully. Then, again staring straight in his eyes, said, "I was one of the first Gladers, slinthead. Shut your hole till you know what you're talking about."

Thomas, now slightly scared of the guy but mostly fed up with his attitude, moved to get up. Minho's hand snapped out and grabbed his arm.

"Dude, sit down. I'm just playin' with your head. It's too much fun—you'll see when the next Newbie . . ." He trailed off, a perplexed look wrinkling his eyebrows. "Guess there won't *be* another Newbie, huh?"

Thomas relaxed, returned to a sitting position, surprised at how easily he'd been put back at ease. He thought of the girl and the note saying she was the last one ever. "Guess not."

Minho squinted slightly, as if he was studying Thomas. "You saw the chick, right? Everybody says you probably know her or something."

Thomas felt himself grow defensive. "I saw her. Doesn't really look familiar at all." He felt immediately guilty for lying—even if it was just a little lie.

"She hot?"

Thomas paused, not having thought of her in that way since she'd freaked out and delivered the note and her one-liner—*Everything is going to change*. But he remembered how beautiful she was. "Yeah, I guess she's hot."

Minho leaned back until he lay flat, eyes closed. "Yeah, you guess. If you got a thing for chicks in comas, right?" He snickered again.

"Right." Thomas was having the hardest time figuring out if he liked Minho or not—his personality seemed to change every minute. After a long pause, Thomas decided to take a chance. "So . . . ," he asked cautiously, "did you find anything today?"

Minho's eyes opened wide; he focused on Thomas. "You know what, Greenie? That's usually the dumbest shuck-faced thing you could ask a Runner." He closed his eyes again. "But not today."

"What do you mean?" Thomas dared to hope for information. *An answer,* he thought. *Please just give me an answer!*

"Just wait till the fancy admiral gets back. I don't like saying stuff twice. Plus, he might not want you to hear it anyway."

Thomas sighed. He wasn't in the least bit surprised at the non-answer. "Well, at least tell me why you look so tired. Don't you run out there every day?"

Minho groaned as he pulled himself up and crossed his legs under him. "Yeah, Greenie, I run out there every day. Let's just say I got a little excited and ran extra fast to get my bee-hind back here."

"Why?" Thomas desperately wanted to hear about what happened out in the Maze.

Minho threw his hands up. "Dude. I told you. Patience. Wait for General Alby."

Something in his voice lessened the blow, and Thomas made his decision. He liked Minho. "Okay, I'll shut up. Just make sure Alby lets me hear the news, too."

Minho studied him for a second. "Okay, Greenie. You da boss."

Alby walked up a moment later with a big plastic cup full of water and handed it to Minho, who gulped down the whole thing without stopping once for breath.

"Okay," Alby said, "out with it. What happened?"

Minho raised his eyebrows and nodded toward Thomas.

"He's fine," Alby replied. "I don't care what this shank hears. Just talk!"

Thomas sat quietly in anticipation as Minho struggled to stand up, wincing with every move, his whole demeanor just *screaming* exhaustion. The Runner balanced himself against the wall, gave both of them a cold look. "I found a dead one."

"Huh?" Alby asked. "A dead what?"

Minho smiled. "A dead Griever."

CHAPTER 13

Thomas was fascinated at the mention of a Griever. The nasty creature was terrifying to think about, but he wondered why finding a dead one was such a big deal. Had it never happened before?

Alby looked like someone had just told him he could grow wings and fly. "Ain't a good time for jokes," he said.

"Look," Minho answered, "I wouldn't believe me if I were you, either. But trust me, I did. Big fat nasty one."

It's definitely never happened before, Thomas thought.

"You found a *dead* Griever," Alby repeated.

"*Yes,* Alby," Minho said, his words laced with annoyance. "A couple of miles from here, out near the Cliff."

Alby looked out at the Maze, then back at Minho. "Well . . . why didn't you bring it back with you?"

Minho laughed again, a half-grunt, half-giggle. "You been drinkin' Frypan's saucy-sauce? Those things must weigh half a ton, dude. Plus, I wouldn't touch one if you gave me a free trip out of this place."

Alby persisted with the questions. "What did it look like? Were the metal spikes in or out of its body? Did it move at all—was its skin still moist?"

Thomas was bursting with questions—*Metal spikes? Moist skin? What in the world?*—but held his tongue, not wanting to remind them he was there. And that maybe they should talk in private.

"Slim it, man," Minho said. "You gotta see it for yourself. It's . . . weird."

"Weird?" Alby looked confused.

"Dude, I'm exhausted, starving, and sun-sick. But if you wanna haul it right now, we could probably make it there and back before the walls shut."

Alby looked at his watch. "Better wait till the wake-up tomorrow."

"Smartest thing you've said in a week." Minho righted himself from leaning on the wall, hit Alby on the arm, then started walking toward the Homestead with a slight limp. He spoke over his shoulder as he shuffled away—it looked like his whole body was in pain. "I should go back out there, but screw it. I'm gonna go eat some of Frypan's nasty casserole."

Thomas felt a wash of disappointment. He had to admit Minho did look like he deserved a rest and a bite to eat, but he wanted to learn more.

Then Alby turned to Thomas, surprising him. "If you know something and ain't tellin' me . . ."

Thomas was sick of being accused of knowing things. Wasn't that the problem in the first place? He *didn't* know anything. He looked at the boy square in the face and asked, simply, "Why do you hate me so much?"

The look that came over Alby's face was indescribable—part confusion, part anger, part shock. "*Hate* you? Boy, you ain't learned nothin' since showing up in that Box. This ain't got nothin' to do with no hate or like or love or friends or anything. All we care about is surviving. Drop your sissy side and start using that shuck brain if you got one."

Thomas felt like he'd been slapped. "But . . . why do you keep accusing—"

"Cuz it can't be a coincidence, slinthead! You pop in here, then we get us a girl Newbie the next *day,* a crazy note, Ben tryin' to bite ya, dead Grievers. Something's goin' on and I ain't restin' till I figure it out."

"I don't *know* anything, Alby." It felt good to put some heat into his words. "I don't even know where I *was* three days ago, much less why this Minho guy would find a dead thing called a Griever. So back off!"

Alby leaned back slightly, stared absently at Thomas for several seconds. Then he said, "Slim it, Greenie. Grow up and start thinkin'. Ain't got nothin' to do with accusing nobody of nothin'. But if you remember anything, if something even *seems* familiar, you better start talking. Promise me."

Not until I have a solid memory, Thomas thought. *Not unless I want to share.* "Yeah, I guess, but—"

"Just promise!"

Thomas paused, sick of Alby and his attitude. "Whatever," he finally said. "I promise."

At that Alby turned and walked away, not saying another word.

Thomas found a tree in the Deadheads, one of the nicer ones on the edge of the forest with plenty of shade. He dreaded going back to work with Winston the Butcher and knew he needed to eat lunch, but he didn't want to be near anybody for as long as he could get away with it. Leaning back against the thick trunk, he wished for a breeze but didn't get one.

He'd just felt his eyelids droop when Chuck ruined his peace and quiet.

"Thomas! Thomas!" the boy shrieked as he ran toward him, pumping his arms, his face lit up with excitement.

Thomas rubbed his eyes and groaned; he wanted nothing in the world more than a half-hour nap. It wasn't until Chuck stopped right in front of him, panting to catch his breath, that he finally looked up. "What?"

Words slowly fell from Chuck, in between his gasps for breath. "Ben . . . Ben . . . he isn't . . . dead."

All signs of fatigue catapulted out of Thomas's system. He jumped up to stand nose to nose with Chuck. *"What?"*

"He . . . isn't dead. Baggers went to get him . . . arrow missed his brain . . . Med-jacks patched him up."

Thomas turned away to stare into the forest where the sick boy had attacked him just the night before. "You gotta be kidding. I saw him. . . ." He wasn't dead? Thomas didn't know what he felt most strongly: confusion, relief, fear that he'd be attacked again . . .

"Well, so did I," Chuck said. "He's locked up in the Slammer, a huge bandage covering half his head."

Thomas spun to face Chuck again. "The Slammer? What do you mean?"

"The Slammer. It's our jail on the north side of the Homestead." Chuck pointed in that direction. "They threw him in it so fast, the Med-jacks had to patch him up in there."

Thomas rubbed his eyes. Guilt consumed him when he realized how he truly felt—he'd been relieved that Ben was dead, that he didn't have to worry about facing him again. "So what are they gonna do with him?"

"Already had a Gathering of the Keepers this morning—made a unanimous decision by the sounds of it. Looks like Ben'll be wishing that arrow had found a home inside his shuck brain after all."

Thomas squinted, confused by what Chuck had said. "What are you talking about?"

"He's being Banished. Tonight, for trying to kill you."

"Banished? What does *that* mean?" Thomas had to ask, though he knew it couldn't be good if Chuck thought it was worse than being dead.

And then Thomas saw perhaps the most disturbing thing he'd seen since he'd arrived at the Glade. Chuck didn't answer; he only smiled. *Smiled,* despite it all, despite the sinister sound of what he'd just announced. Then he turned and ran, maybe to tell someone else the exciting news.

That night, Newt and Alby gathered every last Glader at the East Door about a half hour before it closed, the first traces of twilight's dimness creeping across the sky. The Runners had just returned and entered the mysterious Map Room, clanging the iron door shut; Minho had already gone in earlier. Alby told the Runners to hurry about their business—he wanted them back out in twenty minutes.

It still bothered Thomas how Chuck had smiled when breaking the news about Ben being Banished. Though he didn't know exactly what it meant, it certainly didn't sound like a good thing. Especially since they were all standing so close to the Maze. *Are they going to put him out there?* he wondered. *With the Grievers?*

The other Gladers murmured their conversations in hushed tones, an intense feeling of dreadful anticipation hanging over them like a patch of thick fog. But Thomas said nothing, standing with arms folded, waiting for the show. He stood quietly until the Runners finally came out of their building, all of them looking exhausted, their faces pinched from deep thinking. Minho had been the first to exit, which made Thomas wonder if he was the Keeper of the Runners.

"Bring him out!" Alby shouted, startling Thomas out of his thoughts.

His arms fell to his sides as he turned, looking around the Glade for a sign of Ben, trepidation building within him as he wondered what the boy would do when he saw him.

From around the far side of the Homestead, three of the bigger boys appeared, literally dragging Ben along the ground. His clothes were tattered, barely hanging on; a bloody, thick bandage covered half his head and face. Refusing to put his feet down or help the progress in any way, he seemed as dead as the last time Thomas had seen him. Except for one thing.

His eyes were open, and they were wide with terror.

"Newt," Alby said in a much quieter voice; Thomas wouldn't have heard him if he hadn't been standing just a few feet away. "Bring out the Pole."

Newt nodded, already on the move toward a small tool shed used for the Gardens; he'd clearly been waiting for the order.

Thomas turned his focus back to Ben and the guards. The pale, miserable boy still made no effort to resist, letting them drag him across the dusty stone of the courtyard. When they reached the crowd, they pulled Ben to his feet in front of Alby, their leader, where Ben hung his head, refusing to make eye contact with anyone.

"You brought this on yourself, Ben," Alby said. Then he shook his head and looked toward the shack to which Newt had gone.

Thomas followed his gaze just in time to see Newt walk though the slanted door. He was holding several aluminum poles, connecting the ends to make a shaft maybe twenty feet long. When he was finished, he grabbed something odd-shaped on one of the ends and dragged the whole thing along toward the group. A shiver ran up Thomas's spine at the metallic scrape of the pole on the stone ground as Newt walked.

Thomas was horrified by the whole affair—he couldn't help feeling responsible even though he'd never done anything to provoke Ben.

How was any of this his fault? No answer came to him, but he felt the guilt all the same, like a disease in his blood.

Finally, Newt stepped up to Alby and handed over the end of the pole he was holding. Thomas could see the strange attachment now. A loop of rough leather, fastened to the metal with a massive staple. A large button snap revealed that the loop could be opened and closed, and its purpose became obvious.

It was a collar.

CHAPTER 14

Thomas watched as Alby unbuttoned the collar, then wrapped it around Ben's neck; Ben finally looked up just as the loop of leather snapped closed with a loud pop. Tears glistened in his eyes; dribbles of snot oozed from his nostrils. The Gladers looked on, not a word from any of them.

"Please, Alby," Ben pleaded, his shaky voice so pathetic that Thomas couldn't believe it was the same guy who'd tried to bite his throat off the day before. "I swear I was just sick in the head from the Changing. I never would've killed him—just lost my mind for a second. Please, Alby, *please*."

Every word from the kid was like a fist punching Thomas in the gut, making him feel more guilty and confused.

Alby didn't respond to Ben; he pulled on the collar to make sure it was both firmly snapped and solidly attached to the long pole. He walked past Ben and along the pole, picking it up off the ground as he slid its length through his palm and fingers. When he reached the end, he gripped it tightly and turned to face the crowd. Eyes bloodshot, face wrinkled in anger, breathing heavily—to Thomas, he suddenly looked evil.

And it was an odd sight on the other side: Ben, trembling, crying, a roughly cut collar of old leather wrapped around his pale, scrawny neck, attached to a long pole that stretched from him to Alby, twenty feet away. The shaft of aluminum bowed in the middle, but only a little. Even from where Thomas was standing, it looked surprisingly strong.

Alby spoke in a loud, almost ceremonious voice, looking at no one and everyone at the same time. "Ben of the Builders, you've been sentenced to Banishment for the attempted murder of Thomas the Newbie. The Keepers have spoken, and their word ain't changing. And you ain't coming back. Ever." A long pause. "Keepers, take your place on the Banishment Pole."

Thomas hated that his link to Ben was being made public—hated the responsibility he felt. Being the center of attention again could only bring more suspicion about him. His guilt transformed into anger and blame. More than anything, he just wanted Ben gone, wanted it all to be over.

One by one, boys were stepping out of the crowd and walking over to the long pole; they grabbed it with both hands, gripped it as if readying for a tug-of-war match. Newt was one of them, as was Minho, confirming Thomas's guess that he was the Keeper of the Runners. Winston the Butcher also took up a position.

Once they were all in place—ten Keepers spaced evenly apart between Alby and Ben—the air grew still and silent. The only sounds were the muffled sobs of Ben, who kept wiping at his nose and eyes. He was looking left and right, though the collar around his neck prevented him from seeing the pole and Keepers behind him.

Thomas's feelings changed again. Something was obviously wrong with Ben. Why did he deserve this fate? Couldn't something be done for him? Would Thomas spend the rest of his days feeling responsible? *Just end,* he screamed in his head. *Just be over!*

"Please," Ben said, his voice rising in desperation. *"Pllllleeeeeeeeease!* Somebody, help me! You can't do this to me!"

"Shut up!" Alby roared from behind.

But Ben ignored him, pleading for help as he started to pull on the leather looped around his neck. "Someone stop them! Help me!

Please!" He glanced from boy to boy, begging with his eyes. Without fail, everyone looked away. Thomas quickly stepped behind a taller boy to avoid his own confrontation with Ben. *I can't look into those eyes again,* he thought.

"If we let shanks like you get away with that stuff," Alby said, "we never would've survived this long. Keepers, get ready."

"No, no, no, no, no," Ben was saying, half under his breath. "I swear I'll do anything! I swear I'll never do it again! *Pllllleeeeeee—*"

His shrill cry was cut off by the rumbling crack of the East Door beginning to close. Sparks flew from the stone as the massive right wall slid to the left, groaning thunderously as it made its journey to close off the Glade from the Maze for the night. The ground shook beneath them, and Thomas didn't know if he could watch what he knew was going to happen next.

"Keepers, *now*!" Alby shouted.

Ben's head snapped back as he was jerked forward, the Keepers pushing the pole toward the Maze outside the Glade. A strangling cry erupted from Ben's throat, louder than the sounds of the closing Door. He fell to his knees, only to be jerked back to his feet by the Keeper in front, a thick guy with black hair and a snarl on his face.

"Nooooooooo!" Ben screamed, spit flying from his mouth as he thrashed about, tearing at the collar with his hands. But the combined strength of the Keepers was way too much, forcing the condemned boy closer and closer to the edge of the Glade, just as the right wall was almost there. *"Noooo!"* he screamed again, and then again.

He tried to plant his feet at the threshold, but it only lasted for a split second; the pole sent him into the Maze with a lurch. Soon he was fully four feet outside the Glade, jerking his body from side to side as he tried to escape his collar. The walls of the Door were only seconds from sealing shut.

With one last violent effort, Ben was finally able to twist his neck in the circle of leather so that his whole body turned to face the Gladers. Thomas couldn't believe he was still looking upon a human being—the madness in Ben's eyes, the phlegm flying from his mouth, the pale skin stretched taut across his veins and bones. He looked as alien as anything Thomas could imagine.

"Hold!" Alby shouted.

Ben screamed then, without pause, a sound so piercing that Thomas covered his ears. It was a bestial, lunatic cry, surely ripping the boy's vocal cords to shreds. At the last second, the front Keeper somehow loosened the larger pole from the piece attached to Ben and yanked it back into the Glade, leaving the boy to his Banishment. Ben's final screams were cut off when the walls closed with a terrible boom.

Thomas squeezed his eyes shut and was surprised to feel tears trickling down his cheeks.

CHAPTER 15

For the second night in a row, Thomas went to bed with the haunted image of Ben's face burned into his mind, tormenting him. How different would things be right now if it weren't for that one boy? Thomas could almost convince himself he'd be completely content, happy and excited to learn his new life, aim for his goal of being a Runner. Almost. Deep down he knew that Ben was only part of his many problems.

But now he was gone, Banished to the world of the Grievers, taken to wherever they took their prey, victim to whatever was done there. Though he had plenty of reasons to despise Ben, he mostly felt sorry for him.

Thomas couldn't imagine going out that way, but based on Ben's last moments, psychotically thrashing and spitting and screaming, he no longer doubted the importance of the Glade rule that no one should enter the Maze except Runners, and then only during the day. Somehow Ben had already been stung once, which meant he knew better than perhaps anyone just exactly what lay in store for him.

That poor guy, he thought. *That poor, poor guy.*

Thomas shuddered and rolled over on his side. The more he thought about it, being a Runner didn't sound like such a great idea. But, inexplicably, it still called to him.

The next morning, dawn had barely touched the sky before the working sounds of the Glade wakened Thomas from the deepest slumber since he'd arrived. He sat up, rubbing his eyes, trying to shake the heavy grogginess. Giving up, he lay back down, hoping no one would bother him.

It didn't last a minute.

Someone tapped his shoulder and he opened his eyes to see Newt staring down at him. *What now?* he thought.

"Get up, ya lug."

"Yeah, good morning to you, too. What time is it?"

"Seven o'clock, Greenie," Newt said with a mocking smile. "Figured I'd let ya sleep in after such a rough couple days."

Thomas rolled into a sitting position, hating that he couldn't just lie there for another few hours. "Sleep in? What are you guys, a bunch of farmers?" Farmers—how did he remember so much about them? Once again his memory wipe baffled him.

"Uh . . . yeah, now that ya mention it." Newt plopped down beside Thomas and folded his legs up under himself. He sat quietly for a few moments, looking out at all the hustle-bustle starting to whip up across the Glade. "Gonna put ya with the Track-hoes today, Greenie. See if that suits your fancy more than slicin' up bloody piggies and such."

Thomas was sick of being treated like a baby. "Aren't you supposed to quit calling me that?"

"What, bloody piggies?"

Thomas forced a laugh and shook his head. "No, *Greenie*. I'm not really the newest Newbie anymore, right? The girl in the coma is. Call *her* Greenie—my name's Thomas." Thoughts of the girl crashed around his mind, made him remember the connection he felt. A sadness washed over him, as if he missed her, wanted to see her. *That doesn't make sense,* he thought. *I don't even know her name.*

Newt leaned back, eyebrows raised. "Burn me—you grew some right nice-sized eggs over night, now didn't ya?"

Thomas ignored him and moved on. "What's a Track-hoe?"

"It's what we call the guys workin' their butts off in the Gardens—tilling, weeding, planting and such."

Thomas nodded in that direction. "Who's the Keeper?"

"Zart. Nice guy, s'long as you don't sluff on the job, that is. He's the big one that stood in front last night."

Thomas didn't say anything to that, hoping that somehow he could go through the entire day without talking about Ben and the Banishment. The subject only made him sick and guilty, so he moved on to something else. "So why'd you come wake me up?"

"What, don't like seein' my face first thing on the wake-up?"

"Not especially. So—" But before he could finish his sentence the rumble of the walls opening for the day cut him off. He looked toward the East Door, almost expecting to see Ben standing there on the other side. Instead, he saw Minho stretching. Then Thomas watched as he walked over and picked something up.

It was the section of pole with the leather collar attached to it. Minho seemed to think nothing of it, throwing it to one of the other Runners, who went and put it back in the tool shed near the Gardens.

Thomas turned back to Newt, confused. How could Minho act so nonchalant about it all? "What the—"

"Only seen three Banishments, Tommy. All as nasty as the one you peeped on last night. But every buggin' time, the Grievers leave the collar on our doorstep. Gives me the willies like nothin' else."

Thomas had to agree. "What do they *do* with people when they catch them?" Did he really want to know?

Newt just shrugged, his indifference not very convincing. More likely he didn't want to talk about it.

"So tell me about the Runners," Thomas said suddenly. The words seemed to pop out of nowhere. But he remained still, despite an odd urge to apologize and change the subject; he wanted to know everything about them. Even after what he'd seen last night, even after witnessing the Griever through the window, he wanted to know. The *pull* to know was strong, and he didn't quite understand why. Becoming a Runner just felt like something he was born to do.

Newt had paused, looking confused. "The Runners? Why?"

"Just wondering."

Newt gave him a suspicious look. "Best of the best, those guys. Have to be. Everything depends on them." He picked up a loose rock and tossed it, watching it absently as it bounced to a stop.

"Why aren't you one?"

Newt's gaze returned to Thomas, sharply. "Was till I hurt my leg few months back. Hasn't been the bloody same since." He reached down and rubbed his right ankle absently, a brief look of pain flashing across his face. The look made Thomas think it was more from the memory, not any actual physical pain he still felt.

"How'd you do it?" Thomas asked, thinking the more he could get Newt to talk, the more he'd learn.

"Runnin' from the buggin' Grievers, what else? Almost got me." He paused. "Still gives me the chills thinkin' I might have gone through the Changing."

The Changing. It was the one topic that Thomas thought might lead him to answers more than anything else. "What *is* that, anyway? What changes? Does everyone go psycho like Ben and start trying to kill people?"

"Ben was way worse than most. But I thought you wanted to talk about the Runners." Newt's tone warned that the conversation about the Changing was over.

This made Thomas even more curious, though he was just fine going back to the subject of Runners. "Okay, I'm listening."

"Like I said, best of the best."

"So what do you do? Test everybody to see how fast they are?"

Newt gave Thomas a disgusted look, then groaned. "Show me some smarts, Greenie, Tommy, whatever ya like. How fast you can bloody run is only part of it. A very small part, actually."

This piqued Thomas's interest. "What do you mean?"

"When I say best of the best, I mean at everything. To survive the buggin' Maze, you gotta be smart, quick, strong. Gotta be a decision maker, know the right amount of risk to take. Can't be reckless, can't be timid, either." Newt straightened his legs and leaned back on his hands. "It's bloody awful out there, ya know? I don't miss it."

"I thought the Grievers only came out at night." Destiny or not, Thomas didn't want to run into one of those things.

"Yeah, usually."

"Then why is it so terrible out there?" What *else* didn't he know about?

Newt sighed. "Pressure. Stress. Maze pattern different every day, tryin' to picture things in your mind, tryin' to get us out of here. Worryin' about the bloody Maps. Worst part, you're always scared you might not make it back. A normal maze'd be hard enough—but when it *changes* every night, couple of mental mistakes and you're spendin' the night with vicious beasts. No room or time for dummies or brats."

Thomas frowned, not quite understanding the drive inside him, urging him on. Especially after last night. But he still felt it. Felt it all over.

"Why all the interest?" Newt asked.

Thomas hesitated, thinking, scared to say it out loud again. "I want to be a Runner."

Newt turned and looked him in the eye. "Haven't been here a week, shank. Little early for death wishes, don't ya think?"

"I'm serious." It barely made sense even to Thomas, but he felt it deeply. In fact, the desire to become a Runner was the only thing driving him on, helping him accept his predicament.

Newt didn't break his gaze. "So am I. Forget it. No one's ever become a Runner in their first month, much less their first week. Got a lot of provin' to do before we'll recommend you to the Keeper."

Thomas stood and started folding up his sleeping gear. "Newt, I mean it. I can't pull weeds all day—I'll go nuts. I don't have a clue what I did before they shipped me here in that metal box, but my gut tells me that being a Runner is what I'm supposed to do. I can do it."

Newt still sat there, staring up at Thomas, not offering to help. "No one said you couldn't. But give it a rest for now."

Thomas felt a surge of impatience. "But—"

"Listen, trust me on this, Tommy. Start stompin' around this place yappin' about how you're too good to work like a peasant, how you're all nice and ready to be a Runner—you'll make plenty of enemies. Drop it for now."

Making enemies was the last thing Thomas wanted, but still. He decided on another direction. "Fine, I'll talk to Minho about it."

"Good try, ya buggin' shank. The Gathering elects Runners, and if you think *I'm* tough, they'd laugh in your face."

"For all you guys know, I could be really good at it. It's a waste of time to make me wait."

Newt stood to join Thomas and jabbed a finger in his face. "You listen to me, Greenie. You listenin' all nice and pretty?"

Thomas surprisingly didn't feel that intimidated. He rolled his eyes, but then nodded.

"You better stop this nonsense, before others hear about it. That's not how it works around here, and our whole existence depends on things *working*."

He paused, but Thomas said nothing, dreading the lecture he knew was coming.

"Order," Newt continued. "Order. You say that bloody word over and over in your shuck head. Reason we're all sane around here is 'cause we work our butts off and maintain order. Order's the reason we put Ben out—can't very well have loonies runnin' around tryin' to kill people, now can we? *Order.* Last thing we need is you screwin' that up."

The stubbornness washed out of Thomas. He knew it was time to shut up. "Yeah" was all he said.

Newt slapped him on the back. "Let's make a deal."

"What?" Thomas felt his hopes rise.

"You keep your mouth shut about it, and I'll put you on the list of potential trainees as soon as you show some clout. *Don't* keep your trap shut, and I'll bloody make sure ya never see it happen. Deal?"

Thomas hated the idea of waiting, not knowing how long it might be. "That's a sucky deal."

Newt raised his eyebrows.

Thomas finally nodded. "Deal."

"Come on, let's get us some grub from Frypan. And hope we don't bloody choke."

That morning, Thomas finally met the infamous Frypan, if only from a distance. The guy was too busy trying to feed breakfast to an army of starving Gladers. He couldn't have been more than sixteen years old, but he had a full beard and hair sticking out all over the rest of his body, as if each follicle were trying to escape the confines of his food-smeared clothes. Didn't seem like the most sanitary guy in the world to oversee all the cooking, Thomas thought. He made a mental note to watch out for nasty black hairs in his meals.

He and Newt had just joined Chuck for breakfast at a picnic table right outside the Kitchen when a large group of Gladers got up and ran toward the West Door, talking excitedly about something.

"What's going on?" Thomas asked, surprising himself at how nonchalantly he said it. New developments in the Glade had just become a part of life.

Newt shrugged as he dug into his eggs. "Just seein' off Minho and Alby—they're going to look at the buggin' dead Griever."

"Hey," Chuck said. A small piece of bacon flew out of his mouth when he spoke. "I've got a question about that."

"Yeah, Chuckie?" Newt asked, somewhat sarcastically. "And what's your bloody question?"

Chuck seemed deep in thought. "Well, they found a dead Griever, right?"

"Yeah," Newt replied. "Thanks for that bit of news."

Chuck absently tapped his fork against the table for a few seconds. "Well, then who *killed* the stupid thing?"

Excellent question, Thomas thought. He waited for Newt to answer, but nothing came. He obviously didn't have a clue.

CHAPTER 16

Thomas spent the morning with the Keeper of the Gardens, "working his butt off," as Newt would've said. Zart was the tall, black-haired kid who'd stood at the front of the pole during Ben's Banishment, and who for some odd reason smelled like sour milk. He didn't say much, but showed Thomas the ropes until he could start working on his own. Weeding, pruning an apricot tree, planting squash and zucchini seeds, picking veggies. He didn't love it, and mostly ignored the other boys working alongside him, but he didn't hate it nearly as much as what he'd done for Winston at the Blood House.

Thomas and Zart were weeding a long row of young corn when Thomas decided it was a good time to start asking questions. This Keeper seemed a lot more approachable.

"So, Zart," he said.

The Keeper glanced up at him, then resumed his work. The kid had droopy eyes and a long face—for some reason he looked as bored as humanly possible. "Yeah, Greenie, what you want?"

"How many Keepers total are there?" Thomas asked, trying to act casual. "And what are the job options?"

"Well, you got the Builders, the Sloppers, Baggers, Cooks, Map-makers, Med-jacks, Track-Hoes, Blood Housers. The Runners, of course. I don't know, a few more, maybe. Pretty much keep to myself and my own stuff."

Most of the words were self-explanatory, but Thomas wondered about a couple of them. "What's a Slopper?" He knew that was what Chuck did, but the boy never wanted to talk about it. Refused to talk about it.

"That's what the shanks do that can't do nothin' else. Clean toilets, clean the showers, clean the kitchen, clean up the Blood House after a slaughter, everything. Spend one day with them suckers—that'll cure any thoughts of goin' that direction, I can tell ya that."

Thomas felt a pang of guilt over Chuck—felt sorry for him. The kid tried so hard to be everyone's friend, but no one seemed to like him or even pay attention to him. Yeah, he was a little excitable and talked too much, but Thomas was glad enough to have him around.

"What about the Track-hoes?" Thomas asked as he yanked out a huge weed, clumps of dirt swaying on the roots.

Zart cleared his throat and kept on working as he answered. "They're the ones take care of all the heavy stuff for the Gardens. Trenching and whatnot. During off times they do other stuff round the Glade. Actually, a lot of Gladers have more than one job. Anyone tell you that?"

Thomas ignored the question and moved on, determined to get as many answers as possible. "What about the Baggers? I know they take care of dead people, but it can't happen *that* often, can it?"

"Those are the creepy fellas. They act as guards and poh-lice, too. Everyone just likes to call 'em Baggers. Have fun that day, brother." He snickered, the first time Thomas had heard him do so—there was something very likable about it.

Thomas had more questions. Lots more. Chuck and everyone else around the Glade never wanted to give him the answers to anything. And here was Zart, who seemed perfectly willing. But suddenly Thomas didn't feel like talking anymore. For some reason the girl had popped into his head again, out of the blue, and then thoughts of Ben, and the dead Griever, which should have been a good thing but everyone acted as if it were anything but.

His new life pretty much sucked.

He drew a deep, long breath. *Just work,* he thought. And he did.

By the time midafternoon arrived, Thomas was ready to collapse from exhaustion—all that bending over and crawling around on your knees in the dirt was the pits. Blood House, Gardens. Two strikes.

Runner, he thought as he went on break. *Just let me be a Runner.* Once again he thought about how absurd it was that he wanted it so badly. But even though he didn't understand it, or where it came from, the desire was undeniable. Just as strong were thoughts of the girl, but he pushed them aside as much as possible.

Tired and sore, he headed to the Kitchen for a snack and some water. He could've eaten a full-blown meal despite having had lunch just two hours earlier. Even pig was starting to sound good again.

He bit into an apple, then plopped on the ground beside Chuck. Newt was there, too, but sat alone, ignoring everybody. His eyes were bloodshot, his forehead creased with heavy lines. Thomas watched as Newt chewed his fingernails, something he hadn't seen the older boy do before.

Chuck noticed and asked the question that was on Thomas's mind. "What's wrong with him?" the boy whispered. "Looks like you did when you popped out of the Box."

"I don't know," Thomas replied. "Why don't you go ask him."

"I can hear every bloody word you guys are saying," Newt called in a loud voice. "No wonder people hate sleepin' next to you shanks."

Thomas felt like he'd been caught stealing, but he was genuinely concerned—Newt was one of the few people in the Glade he actually liked.

"What *is* wrong with you?" Chuck asked. "No offense, but you look like klunk."

"Every lovin' thing in the universe," he replied, then fell silent as he stared off into space for a long moment. Thomas almost pushed him with another question, but Newt finally continued. "The girl from the Box. Keeps groanin' and saying all kinds of weird stuff, but won't wake up. Med-jacks're doing their best to feed her, but she's eatin' less each time. I'm tellin' ya, something's very bad about that whole bloody thing."

Thomas looked down at his apple, then took a bite. It tasted sour now—he realized he was worried about the girl. Concerned for her welfare. As if he knew her.

Newt let out a long sigh. "Shuck it. But that's not what really has me buggin'."

"Then what does?" Chuck asked.

Thomas leaned forward, so curious he was able to put the girl out of his mind.

Newt's eyes narrowed as he looked out toward one of the entrances to the Maze. "Alby and Minho," he muttered. "They should've come back hours ago."

Before Thomas knew it he was back at work, pulling up weeds again, counting down the minutes until he'd be done with the Gardens. He glanced constantly at the West Door, looking for any sign of Alby and Minho, Newt's concern having rubbed off on him.

Newt had said they were supposed to have come back by noon, just enough time for them to get to the dead Griever, explore for an hour or two, then return. No wonder he'd looked so upset. When Chuck offered up that maybe they were just exploring and having some fun, Newt had given him a stare so harsh Thomas thought Chuck might spontaneously combust.

He'd never forget the next look that had come over Newt's face. When Thomas asked why Newt and some others didn't just go into the Maze and search for their friends, Newt's expression had changed to outright horror—his cheeks had *shrunk* into his face, becoming sallow and dark. It gradually passed, and he'd explained that sending out search parties was forbidden, lest even more people be lost, but there was no mistaking the fear that had crossed his face.

Newt was terrified of the Maze.

Whatever had happened to him out there—maybe even related to his lingering ankle injury—had been truly awful.

Thomas tried not to think about it as he put his focus back on yanking weeds.

That night dinner proved to be a somber affair, and it had nothing to do with the food. Frypan and his cooks served up a grand meal of steak, mashed potatoes, green beans and hot rolls. Thomas was quickly learning that jokes about Frypan's cooking were just that—jokes. Everyone gobbled up his food and usually begged for more. But tonight, the Gladers ate like dead men resurrected for one last meal before being sent to live with the devil.

The Runners had returned at their normal time, and Thomas had grown more and more upset as he watched Newt run from Door to Door as they entered the Glade, not bothering to hide his panic. But Alby and Minho never showed up. Newt forced the Gladers to go on and get some of Frypan's hard-earned dinner, but he insisted on standing watch for the missing duo. No one said it, but Thomas knew it wouldn't be long before the Doors closed.

Thomas reluctantly followed orders like the rest of the boys and was sharing a picnic table on the south side of the Homestead with

Chuck and Winston. He'd only been able to eat a few bites when he couldn't take it anymore.

"I can't stand sitting here while they're out there missing," he said as he dropped his fork on the plate. "I'm going over to watch the Doors with Newt." He stood up and headed out to look.

Not surprisingly, Chuck was right behind him.

They found Newt at the West Door, pacing, running his hands through his hair. He looked up as Thomas and Chuck approached.

"Where *are* they?" Newt said, his voice thin and strained.

Thomas was touched that Newt cared so much about Alby and Minho—as if they were his own kin. "Why don't we send out a search party?" he suggested again. It seemed so stupid to sit here and worry themselves to death when they could go out there and *find* them.

"Bloody he—" Newt started before stopping himself; he closed his eyes for a second and took a deep breath. "We can't. Okay? Don't say it again. One hundred percent against the rules. Especially with the buggin' Doors about to close."

"But why?" Thomas persisted, in disbelief at Newt's stubbornness. "Won't the Grievers get them if they stay out there? Shouldn't we do something?"

Newt turned on him, his face flushed red, his eyes flamed with fury.

"Shut your hole, Greenie!" he yelled. "Not a bloody week you've been here! You think I wouldn't risk my life in a second to save those lugs?"

"No . . . I . . . Sorry. I didn't mean . . ." Thomas didn't know what to say—he was just trying to help.

Newt's face softened. "You don't get it yet, Tommy. Going out there at night is beggin' for death. We'd just be throwin' more lives away. If those shanks don't make it back . . ." He paused, seeming hesitant to say what everyone was thinking. "Both of 'em swore an oath, just like I did. Like we all did. You, too, when you go to your first Gathering and get chosen by a Keeper. Never go out at night. No matter what. Never."

Thomas looked over at Chuck, who seemed as pale-faced as Newt.

"Newt won't say it," the boy said, "so I will. If they're not back, it means they're dead. Minho's too smart to get lost. Impossible. They're dead."

Newt said nothing, and Chuck turned and walked back toward the Homestead, his head hanging low. *Dead?* Thomas thought. The situation had become so grave he didn't know how to react, felt a pit of emptiness in his heart.

"The shank's right," Newt said solemnly. "That's why we can't go out. We can't afford to make things bloody worse than they already are."

He put his hand on Thomas's shoulder, then let it slump to his side. Tears moistened Newt's eyes, and Thomas was sure that even within the dark chamber of memories that were locked away, out of his reach, he'd never seen someone look so sad. The growing darkness of twilight was a perfect fit for how grim things felt to Thomas.

"The Doors close in two minutes," Newt said, a statement so succinct and final it seemed to hang in the air like a burial shroud caught in a puff of wind. Then he walked away, hunched over, quiet.

Thomas shook his head and looked back into the Maze. He barely knew Alby and Minho. But his chest ached at the thought of them out there, killed by the horrendous creature he'd seen through the window his first morning in the Glade.

A loud boom sounded from all directions, startling Thomas out of his thoughts. Then came the crunching, grinding sound of stone against stone. The Doors were closing for the night.

The right wall rumbled across the ground, spitting dirt and rocks as it moved. The vertical row of connecting rods, so many they seemed to reach the sky far above, slid toward their corresponding holes on the left wall, ready to seal shut until the morning. Once again, Thomas looked in awe at the massive moving wall—it defied any sense of physics. It seemed impossible.

Then a flicker of movement to the left caught his eyes.

Something stirred inside the Maze, down the long corridor in front of him.

At first, a shot of panic raced through him; he stepped back, worried it might be a Griever. But then two forms took shape, stumbling along the alley toward the Door. His eyes finally focused through the initial blindness of fear, and he realized it was Minho, with one of Alby's arms draped across his shoulders, practically dragging the boy along behind him. Minho looked up, saw Thomas, who knew his eyes must be bulging out of his head.

"They got him!" Minho shouted, his voice strangled and weak with exhaustion. Every step he took seemed like it could be his last.

Thomas was so stunned by the turn of events, it took a moment for him to act. "Newt!" he finally screamed, forcing his gaze away from Minho and Alby to face the other direction. "They're coming! I can see 'em!" He knew he should run into the Maze and help, but the rule about not leaving the Glade was seared into his mind.

Newt had already made it back to the Homestead, but at Thomas's cry he immediately spun around and broke into a stuttering run toward the Door.

Thomas turned to look back into the Maze and dread washed

through him. Alby had slipped out of Minho's clutches and fallen to the ground. Thomas watched as Minho tried desperately to get him back on his feet, then, finally giving up, started to drag the boy across the stone floor by the arms.

But they were still a hundred feet away.

The right wall was closing fast, seeming to quicken its pace the more Thomas willed it to slow down. There were only seconds left until it shut completely. They had no chance of making it in time. No chance at all.

Thomas turned to look at Newt: limping along as well as he could, he'd only made it halfway to Thomas.

He looked back into the Maze, at the closing wall. Only a few feet more and it'd be over.

Minho stumbled up ahead, fell to the ground. They weren't going to make it. Time was up. That was it.

Thomas heard Newt scream something from behind him.

"Don't do it, Tommy! Don't you bloody do it!"

The rods on the right wall seemed to reach like stretched-out arms for their home, grasping for those little holes that would serve as their resting place for the night. The crunching, grinding sound of the Doors filled the air, deafening.

Five feet. Four feet. Three. Two.

Thomas knew he had no choice. He *moved*. Forward. He squeezed past the connecting rods at the last second and stepped into the Maze.

The walls slammed shut behind him, the echo of its boom bouncing off the ivy-covered stone like mad laughter.

CHAPTER 17

For several seconds, Thomas felt like the world had frozen in place. A thick silence followed the thunderous rumble of the Door closing, and a veil of darkness seemed to cover the sky, as if even the sun had been frightened away by what lurked in the Maze. Twilight had fallen, and the mammoth walls looked like enormous tombstones in a weed-infested cemetery for giants. Thomas leaned back against the rough rock, overcome by disbelief at what he had just done.

Filled with terror at what the consequences might be.

Then a sharp cry from Alby up ahead snapped Thomas to attention; Minho was moaning. Thomas pushed himself away from the wall and ran to the two Gladers.

Minho had pulled himself up and was standing once again, but he looked terrible, even in the pale light still available—sweaty, dirty, scratched-up. Alby, on the ground, looked worse, his clothes ripped, his arms covered with cuts and bruises. Thomas shuddered. Had Alby been attacked by a Griever?

"Greenie," Minho said, "if you think that was brave comin' out here, listen up. You're the shuckiest shuck-faced shuck there ever was. You're as good as dead, just like us."

Thomas felt his face heat up—he'd expected at least a little gratitude. "I couldn't just sit there and leave you guys out here."

"And what good are you with us?" Minho rolled his eyes. "Whatever, dude. Break the Number One Rule, kill yourself, whatever."

"You're welcome. I was just trying to help." Thomas felt like kicking him in the face.

Minho forced a bitter laugh, then knelt back on the ground beside Alby. Thomas took a closer look at the collapsed boy and realized just how bad things were. Alby looked on the edge of death. His usually dark skin was losing color fast and his breaths were quick and shallow.

Hopelessness rained down on Thomas. "What happened?" he asked, trying to put aside his anger.

"Don't wanna talk about it," Minho said as he checked Alby's pulse and bent over to listen to his chest. "Let's just say the Grievers can play dead really well."

This statement took Thomas by surprise. "So he was . . . bitten? Stung, whatever? Is he going through the Changing?"

"You've got a lot to learn," was all Minho would say.

Thomas wanted to scream. He knew he had a lot to learn—that was why he was asking questions. "Is he going to die?" he forced himself to say, cringing at how shallow and empty it sounded.

"Since we didn't make it back before sunset, probably. Could be dead in an hour—I don't know how long it takes if you don't get the Serum. Course, we'll be dead, too, so don't get all weepy for him. Yep, we'll all be nice and dead soon." He said it so matter-of-factly, Thomas could hardly process the meaning of the words.

But fast enough, the dire reality of the situation began to hit Thomas, and his insides turned to rot. "We're really going to die?" he asked, unable to accept it. "You're telling me we have no chance?"

"None."

Thomas was annoyed at Minho's constant negativity. "Oh, come on—there has to be something we can do. How many Grievers'll come at us?" He peered down the corridor that led deeper into the Maze, as if expecting the creatures to arrive then, summoned by the sound of their name.

"I don't know."

A thought sprang into Thomas's mind, giving him hope. "But . . . what about Ben? And Gally, and others who've been stung and survived?"

Minho glanced up at him with a look that said he was dumber than cow klunk. "Didn't you hear me? They made it back before sunset, you dong. Made it back and got the Serum. All of them."

Thomas wondered about the mention of a serum, but had too many other questions to get out first. "But I thought the Grievers only came out at night."

"Then you were *wrong,* shank. They *always* come out at night. That doesn't mean they never show up during the day."

Thomas wouldn't allow himself to give in to Minho's hopelessness—he didn't want to give up and die just yet. "Has anyone ever been caught outside the walls at night and lived through it?"

"Never."

Thomas scowled, wishing he could find one little spark of hope. "How many have died, then?"

Minho stared at the ground, crouched with one forearm on a knee. He was clearly exhausted, almost in a daze. "At least twelve. Haven't you been to the graveyard?"

"Yeah." *So that's how they died,* he thought.

"Well, those are just the ones we *found.* There are more whose bodies never showed up." Minho pointed absently back toward the sealed-off Glade. "That freaking graveyard's back in the woods for a reason. Nothing kills happy time more than being reminded of your slaughtered friends every day."

Minho stood and grabbed Alby's arms, then nodded toward his feet. "Grab those smelly suckers. We gotta carry him over to the Door. Give 'em one body that's easy to find in the morning."

Thomas couldn't believe how *morbid* a statement that was. "How can this be happening!" he screamed to the walls, turning in a circle. He felt close to losing it once and for all.

"Quit your crying. You should've followed the rules and stayed inside. Now come on, grab his legs."

Wincing at the growing cramps in his gut, Thomas walked over and lifted Alby's feet as he was told. They half carried, half dragged the almost-lifeless body a hundred feet or so to the vertical crack of the Door, where Minho propped Alby up against the wall in a semi-sitting position. Alby's chest rose and fell with struggled breaths, but his skin was drenched in sweat; he looked like he wouldn't last much longer.

"Where was he bitten?" Thomas asked. "Can you see it?"

"They don't freaking *bite* you. They prick you. And no, you can't see it. There could be dozens all over his body." Minho folded his arms and leaned against the wall.

For some reason, Thomas thought the word *prick* sounded a lot worse than *bite*. "Prick you? What does that mean?"

"Dude, you just have to see them to know what I'm talking about."

Thomas pointed at Minho's arms, then his legs. "Well, why didn't the thing *prick* you?"

Minho held his hands out. "Maybe it did—maybe I'll collapse any second."

"They . . . ," Thomas began, but didn't know how to finish. He couldn't tell if Minho had been serious.

"There was no *they*, just the one we thought was dead. It went nuts and stung Alby, but then ran away." Minho looked back into the Maze, which was now almost completely dark with nighttime. "But I'm sure it and a whole bunch of them suckers'll be here soon to finish us off with their needles."

"Needles?" Things just kept sounding more and more disturbing to Thomas.

"Yeah, needles." He didn't elaborate, and his face said he didn't plan to.

Thomas looked up at the enormous walls covered in thick vines—desperation had finally clicked him into problem-solving mode. "Can't we climb this thing?" He looked at Minho, who didn't say a word. "The *vines*—can't we climb them?"

Minho let out a frustrated sigh. "I swear, Greenie, you must think we're a bunch of idiots. You really think we've never had the ingenious thought of climbing the freaking *walls*?"

For the first time, Thomas felt anger creeping in to compete with his fear and panic. "I'm just trying to help, man. Why don't you quit moping at every word I say and *talk* to me?"

Minho abruptly jumped at Thomas and grabbed him by the shirt. "You don't *understand,* shuck-face! You don't know anything, and you're just making it worse by trying to have hope! We're dead, you hear me? Dead!"

Thomas didn't know which he felt more strongly at that moment—anger at Minho or pity for him. He was giving up too easily.

Minho looked down at his hands clasped to Thomas's shirt and shame washed across his face. Slowly, he let go and backed away. Thomas straightened his clothes defiantly.

"Ah, man, oh man," Minho whispered, then crumpled to the ground, burying his face in clenched fists. "I've never been this scared before, dude. Not like this."

Thomas wanted to say something, tell him to grow up, tell him to *think,* tell him to explain everything he knew. Something!

He opened his mouth to speak, but closed it quickly when he heard the *noise.* Minho's head popped up; he looked down one of the darkened stone corridors. Thomas felt his own breath quicken.

It came from deep within the Maze, a low, haunting sound. A constant whirring that had a metallic ring every few seconds, like sharp knives rubbing against each other. It grew louder by the second, and then a series of eerie clicks joined in. Thomas thought of long fingernails tapping against glass. A hollow moan filled the air, and then something that sounded like the clanking of chains.

All of it, together, was horrifying, and the small amount of courage Thomas had gathered began to slip away.

Minho stood, his face barely visible in the dying light. But when he spoke, Thomas imagined his eyes wide with terror. "We have to split up—it's our only chance. Just keep moving. Don't stop moving!"

And then he turned and ran, disappearing in seconds, swallowed by the Maze and darkness.

CHAPTER 18

Thomas stared at the spot where Minho had vanished.

A sudden dislike for the guy swelled up inside him. Minho was a veteran in this place, a Runner. Thomas was a Newbie, just a few days in the Glade, a few minutes in the Maze. Yet of the two of them, Minho had broken down and panicked, only to run off at the first sign of trouble. *How could he leave me here?* Thomas thought. *How could he do that!*

The noises grew louder. The roar of engines interspersed with rolling, cranking sounds like chains hoisting machinery in an old, grimy factory. And then came the smell—something burning, oily. Thomas couldn't begin to guess what was in store for him; he'd seen a Griever, but only a glimpse, and through a dirty window. What would they do to him? How long would he last?

Stop, he told himself. He had to quit wasting time waiting for them to come and end his life.

He turned and faced Alby, still propped against the stone wall, now only a mound of shadow in the darkness. Kneeling on the ground, Thomas found Alby's neck, then searched for a pulse. Something there. He listened at his chest like Minho had done.

buh-bump, buh-bump, buh-bump

Still alive.

Thomas rocked back on his heels, then ran his arm across his forehead, wiping away the sweat. And at that moment, in the space of only a few seconds, he learned a lot about himself. About the Thomas that was *before*.

He couldn't leave a friend to die. Even someone as cranky as Alby.

He reached down and grabbed both of Alby's arms, then squatted into a sitting position and wrapped the arms around his neck from behind. He pulled the lifeless body onto his back and pushed with his legs, grunting with the effort.

But it was too much. Thomas collapsed forward onto his face; Alby sprawled to the side with a loud flump.

The frightening sounds of the Grievers grew closer by the second, echoing off the stone walls of the Maze. Thomas thought he could see bright flashes of light far away, bouncing off the night sky. He didn't want to meet the source of those lights, those sounds.

Trying a new approach, he grabbed Alby's arms again and started dragging him along the ground. He couldn't believe how *heavy* the boy was, and it took only ten feet or so for Thomas to realize that it just wasn't going to work. Where would he take him, anyway?

He pushed and pulled Alby back over to the crack that marked the entrance to the Glade, and propped him once more into a sitting position, leaning against the stone wall.

Thomas sat back against it himself, panting from exertion, thinking. As he looked into the dark recesses of the Maze, he searched his mind for a solution. He could hardly see anything, and he knew, despite what Minho had said, that it'd be stupid to run even if he *could* carry Alby. Not only was there the chance of getting lost, he could actually find himself running toward the Grievers instead of away from them.

He thought of the wall, the ivy. Minho hadn't explained, but he had made it sound as if climbing the walls was impossible. Still . . .

A plan formed in his mind. It all depended on the unknown abilities of the Grievers, but it was the best thing he could come up with.

Thomas walked a few feet along the wall until he found a thick growth of ivy covering most of the stone. He reached down and grabbed one of the vines that went all the way to the ground and wrapped his hand around it. It felt thicker and more solid than he would've imagined, maybe a half-inch in diameter. He pulled on it, and with the sound of thick paper ripping apart, the vine came unattached from the wall—more and more as Thomas stepped away from it. When he'd moved back ten feet, he could no longer see the end of the vine way above; it disappeared in the darkness. But the trailing plant had yet to fall free, so Thomas knew it was still attached up there somewhere.

Hesitant to try, Thomas steeled himself and pulled on the vine of ivy with all his strength.

It held.

He yanked on it again. Then again, pulling and relaxing with both hands over and over. Then he lifted his feet and hung onto the vine; his body swung forward.

The vine held.

Quickly, Thomas grabbed other vines, ripping them away from the wall, creating a series of climbing ropes. He tested each one, and they all proved to be as strong as the first. Encouraged, he went back to Alby and dragged him over to the vines.

A sharp crack echoed from within the Maze, followed by the horrible sound of crumpling metal. Thomas, startled, swung around to look, his mind so concentrated on the vines that he'd momentarily shut out the Grievers; he searched all three directions of the Maze. He couldn't see anything coming, but the sounds were louder—the whirring, the groaning, the clanging. And the air had brightened ever so slightly; he could make out more of the details of the Maze than he'd been able to just minutes before.

He remembered the odd lights he'd observed through the Glade window with Newt. The Grievers were close. They had to be.

Thomas pushed aside the swelling panic and set himself to work.

He grabbed one of the vines and wrapped it around Alby's right arm. The plant would only reach so far, so he had to prop Alby up as much as he could to make it work. After several wraps, he tied the vine off. Then he took another vine and put it around Alby's left arm, then both of his legs, tying each one tightly. He worried about the Glader's circulation getting cut off, but decided it was worth the risk.

Trying to ignore the doubt that was seeping into his mind about the plan, Thomas continued on. Now it was his turn.

He snatched a vine with both hands and started to climb, directly over the spot where he'd just tied up Alby. The thick leaves of the ivy served well as handholds, and Thomas was elated to find that the many cracks in the stone wall were perfect supports for his feet as he climbed. He began to think how easy it would be without . . .

He refused to finish the thought. He couldn't leave Alby behind.

Once he reached a point a couple of feet above his friend, Thomas wrapped one of the vines around his own chest, around and around several times, snug against his armpits for support. Slowly, he let himself sag, letting go with his hands but keeping his feet planted firmly in a large crack. Relief filled him when the vine held.

Now came the really hard part.

The four vines tied to Alby below hung tautly around him. Thomas took hold of the one attached to Alby's left leg, and pulled. He was only able to get it up a few inches before letting go—the weight was too much. He couldn't do it.

He climbed back down to the Maze floor, decided to try *pushing* from below instead of *pulling* from above. To test it, he tried raising Alby only a couple of feet, limb by limb. First, he pushed the left leg up, then tied a new vine around it. Then the right leg. When both were secure, Thomas did the same to Alby's arms—right, then left.

He stepped back, panting, to take a look.

Alby hung there, seemingly lifeless, now three feet higher than he'd been five minutes earlier.

Clangs from the Maze. Whirrs. Buzzes. Moans. Thomas thought he saw a couple of red flashes to his left. The Grievers were getting closer, and it was now obvious that there were more than one.

He got back to work.

Using the same method of pushing each of Alby's arms and legs up two or three feet at a time, Thomas slowly made his way up the stone wall. He climbed until he was right below the body, wrapped a vine around his own chest for support, then pushed Alby up as far as he could, limb by limb, and tied them off with ivy. Then he repeated the whole process.

Climb, wrap, push up, tie off.

Climb, wrap, push up, tie off. The Grievers at least seemed to be moving slowly through the Maze, giving him time.

Over and over, little by little, up they went. The effort was exhausting; Thomas heaved in every breath, felt sweat cover every inch of his skin. His hands began to slip and slide on the vines. His feet ached from pressing into the stone cracks. The sounds grew louder—the awful, awful sounds. Still Thomas worked.

When they'd reached a spot about thirty feet off the ground, Thomas stopped, swaying on the vine he'd tied around his chest. Using his drained, rubbery arms, he turned himself around to face the Maze.

An exhaustion he'd not known possible filled every tiny particle of his body. He ached with weariness; his muscles screamed. He couldn't push Alby up another inch. He was done.

This was where they'd hide. Or make their stand.

He'd known they couldn't reach the top—he only hoped the Grievers couldn't or wouldn't look above them. Or, at the very least, Thomas hoped he could fight them off from high up, one by one, instead of being overwhelmed on the ground.

He had no idea what to expect; he didn't know if he'd see tomorrow. But here, hanging in the ivy, Thomas and Alby would meet their fate.

A few minutes passed before Thomas saw the first glimmer of light shine off the Maze walls up ahead. The terrible sounds he'd heard escalate for the last hour took on a high-pitched, mechanical squeal, like a robotic death yell.

A red light to his left, on the wall, caught his attention. He turned and almost screamed out loud—a beetle blade was only a few inches from him, its spindly legs poking through the ivy and somehow sticking to the stone. The red light of its eye was like a little sun, too bright to look at directly. Thomas squinted and tried to focus on the beetle's body.

The torso was a silver cylinder, maybe three inches in diameter and ten inches long. Twelve jointed legs ran along the length of its bottom, spread out, making the thing look like a sleeping lizard. The head was impossible to see because of the red beam of light shining right at him, though it seemed small, vision its only purpose, perhaps.

But then Thomas saw the most chilling part. He thought he'd seen it before, back in the Glade when the beetle blade had scooted past him and into the woods. Now it was confirmed: the red light from its eye cast a creepy glow on six capital letters smeared across the torso, as if they had been written with blood:

Thomas couldn't imagine why that one word would be stamped on the beetle blade, unless for the purpose of announcing to the Gladers that it was evil. Wicked.

He knew it had to be a spy for whoever had sent them here—Alby had told him as much, saying the beetles were how the Creators watched them. Thomas stilled himself, held his breath, hoping that maybe the beetle only detected movement. Long seconds passed, his lungs screaming for air.

With a click and then a clack, the beetle turned and scuttled off, disappearing into the ivy. Thomas sucked in a huge gulp of air, then another, feeling the pinch of the vines tied around his chest.

Another mechanical squeal screeched through the Maze, close now, followed by the surge of revved machinery. Thomas tried to imitate Alby's lifeless body, hanging limp in the vines.

And then something rounded the corner up ahead, and came toward them.

Something he'd seen before, but through the safety of thick glass.

Something unspeakable.

A Griever.

CHAPTER 19

Thomas stared in horror at the monstrous thing making its way down the long corridor of the Maze.

It looked like an experiment gone terribly wrong—something from a nightmare. Part animal, part machine, the Griever rolled and clicked along the stone pathway. Its body resembled a gigantic slug, sparsely covered in hair and glistening with slime, grotesquely pulsating in and out as it breathed. It had no distinguishable head or tail, but front to end it was at least six feet long, four feet thick.

Every ten to fifteen seconds, sharp metal spikes popped through its bulbous flesh and the whole creature abruptly curled into a ball and spun forward. Then it would settle, seeming to gather its bearings, the spikes receding back through the moist skin with a sick slurping sound. It did this over and over, traveling just a few feet at a time.

But hair and spikes were not the only things protruding from the Griever's body. Several randomly placed mechanical arms stuck out here and there, each one with a different purpose. A few had bright lights attached to them. Others had long, menacing needles. One had a three-fingered claw that clasped and unclasped for no apparent reason. When the creature rolled, these arms folded and maneuvered to avoid being crushed. Thomas wondered what—or who—could create such frightening, disgusting creatures.

The source of the sounds he'd been hearing made sense now. When the Griever rolled, it made the metallic whirring sound, like the spinning blade of a saw. The spikes and the arms explained the creepy clicking sounds, metal against stone. But nothing sent chills up and down Thomas's spine like the haunted, deathly moans that somehow escaped the creature when it sat still, like the sound of dying men on a battlefield.

Seeing it all now—the beast matched with the sounds—Thomas couldn't think of any nightmare that could equal this hideous thing coming toward him. He fought the fear, forced his body to remain perfectly still, hanging there in the vines. He was sure their only hope was to avoid being noticed.

Maybe it won't see us, he thought. *Just maybe.* But the reality of the situation sank like a stone in his belly. The beetle blade had already revealed his exact position.

The Griever rolled and clicked its way closer, zigzagging back and forth, moaning and whirring. Every time it stopped, the metal arms unfolded and turned this way and that, like a roving robot on an alien planet looking for signs of life. The lights cast eerie shadows across the Maze. A faint memory tried to escape the locked box within his mind—shadows on the walls when he was a kid, scaring him. He longed to be back to wherever that was, to run to the mom and dad he hoped still lived, somewhere, missing him, searching for him.

A strong whiff of something burnt stung his nostrils; a sick mixture of overheated engines and charred flesh. He couldn't believe people could create something so horrible and send it after kids.

Trying not to think about it, Thomas closed his eyes for a moment and concentrated on remaining still and quiet. The creature kept coming.

whirrrrrrrrrrrrrr

click-click-click

whirrrrrrrrrrrrrr

click-click-click

Thomas peeked down without moving his head—the Griever had finally reached the wall where he and Alby hung. It paused by the closed Door that led into the Glade, only a few yards to Thomas's right.

Please go the other way, Thomas pleaded silently.

Turn.

Go.

That way.

Please!

The Griever's spikes popped out; its body rolled toward Thomas and Alby.

whirrrrrrrrrrrrrr

click-click-click

It came to a stop, then rolled once more, right up to the wall.

Thomas held his breath, not daring to make the slightest sound. The Griever now sat directly below them. Thomas wanted to look down so badly, but knew any movement might give him away. The beams of light from the creature shone all over the place, completely random, never settling in one spot.

Then, without warning, they went out.

The world turned instantly dark and silent. It was as if the creature had turned *off*. It didn't move, made no sound—even the haunting groans had stopped completely. And with no more lights, Thomas couldn't see a single thing.

He was blind.

He took small breaths through his nose; his pumping heart needed oxygen desperately. Could it hear him? Smell him? Sweat drenched his hair, his hands, his clothes, everything. A fear he had never known filled him to the point of insanity.

Still, nothing. No movement, no light, no sound. The anticipation of trying to guess its next move was killing Thomas.

Seconds passed. Minutes. The ropy plant dug into Thomas's flesh—his chest felt numb. He wanted to scream at the monster below him: *Kill me or go back to your hiding hole!*

Then, in a sudden burst of light and sound, the Griever came back to life, whirring and clicking.

And then it started to climb the wall.

CHAPTER 20

The Griever's spikes tore into the stone, throwing shredded ivy and rock chips in every direction. Its arms shifted about like the legs of the beetle blade, some with sharp picks that drove into the stone of the wall for support. A bright light on the end of one arm pointed directly at Thomas, only this time, the beam didn't move away.

Thomas felt the last drop of hope drain from his body.

He knew the only option left was to run. *I'm sorry, Alby,* he thought as he unraveled the thick vine from his chest. Using his left hand to hold tight to the foliage above him, he finished unwrapping himself and prepared to move. He knew he couldn't go up—that would bring the Griever across the path of Alby. Down, of course, was only an option if he wanted to die as quickly as possible.

He had to go to the side.

Thomas reached out and grabbed a vine two feet to the left of where he hung. Wrapping it around his hand, he yanked on it with a sharp tug. It held true, just like all the others. A quick glance below revealed that the Griever had already halved the distance between them, and it was moving faster yet, no more pauses or stops.

Thomas let go of the rope he'd used around his chest and heaved his body to the left, scraping along the wall. Before his pendulum swing took him back toward Alby, he reached out for another vine, catching a nice thick one. This time he grabbed it with both hands and turned to plant the bottom of his feet on the wall. He shuffled his body to the right as far as the plant would let him, then let go and grabbed another one. Then another. Like some tree-climbing monkey, Thomas found he could move more quickly than he ever could've hoped.

The sounds of his pursuer went on relentlessly, only now with the bone-shuddering addition of cracking and splitting rock joined in. Thomas swung to the right several more times before he dared to look back.

The Griever had altered its course from Alby to head directly for Thomas. *Finally,* Thomas thought, *something went right.* Pushing off with his feet as strongly as he could, swing by swing, he fled the hideous thing.

Thomas didn't need to look behind him to know the Griever was gaining on him with every passing second. The sounds gave it away. Somehow, he had to get back to the ground, or it would all end quickly.

On the next switch, he let his hand slip a bit before clasping tightly. The ivy-rope burned his palm, but he'd slipped several feet closer to the ground. He did the same with the next vine. And the next. Three swings later he'd made his way halfway to the Maze floor. Scorching pain flared up both his arms; he felt the sting of raw skin on his hands. The adrenaline rushing through his body helped push away his fear—he just kept moving.

On his next swing, the darkness prevented Thomas from seeing a new wall looming in front of him until it was too late; the corridor ended and turned to the right.

He slammed into the stone ahead, losing his grip on the vine. Throwing his arms out, Thomas flailed, reaching and grabbing to stop his plunge to the hard stone below. At the same instant, he saw the Griever out of the corner of his left eye. It had altered its course and was almost on him, reaching out with its clasping claw.

Thomas found a vine halfway to the ground and grasped it, his arms almost ripping out of their sockets at the sudden stop. He pushed off the wall with both feet as hard as he could, swinging his body away from it just as the Griever charged in with its claw and needles. Thomas kicked out with his right leg, connecting with the arm attached to the claw. A sharp crack revealed a small victory, but any elation ended when he realized that the momentum of his swing was now pulling him back down to land right on top of the creature.

Pulsing with adrenaline, Thomas drew his legs together and pulled them tight against his chest. As soon as he made contact with the Griever's body, disgustingly sinking inches into its gushy skin, he kicked out with both feet to push off, squirming to avoid the swarm of needles and claws coming at him from all directions. He swung his body out and to the left; then he jumped toward the wall of the Maze, trying to grab another vine; the Griever's vicious tools snapped and clawed at him from behind. He felt a deep scratch on his back.

Flailing once again, Thomas found a new vine and clutched it with both hands. He gripped the plant just enough to slow him down as he slid to the ground, ignoring the horrible burn. As soon as his feet hit the solid stone floor, he took off, running despite the scream of exhaustion from his body.

A booming crash sounded behind him, followed by the rolling, cracking, whirring of the Griever. But Thomas refused to look back, knowing every second counted.

He rounded a corner of the Maze, then another. Pounding the stone with his feet, he fled as fast as he possibly could. Somewhere in his mind he tracked his own movements, hoping he'd live long enough to use the information to return to the Door again.

Right, then left. Down a long corridor, then right again. Left. Right. Two lefts. Another long corridor. The sounds of pursuit from behind didn't relent or fade, but he wasn't *losing* ground, either.

On and on he ran, his heart ready to blow its way out of his chest. With great, sucking heaves of breath, he tried to get oxygen in his lungs, but he knew he couldn't last much longer. He wondered if it'd just be easier to turn and fight, get it over with.

When he rounded the next corner, he skidded to a halt at the sight in front of him. Panting uncontrollably, he stared.

Three Grievers were up ahead, rolling along as they dug their spikes into the stone, coming directly toward him.

CHAPTER 21

Thomas turned to see his original pursuer still coming, though it had slowed a bit, clasping and unclasping a metal claw as if mocking him, laughing.

It knows I'm done, he thought. After all that effort, here he was, surrounded by Grievers. It was over. Not even a week of salvageable memory, and his life was over.

Almost consumed by grief, he made a decision. He'd go down fighting.

Much preferring one over three, he ran straight toward the Griever that had chased him there. The ugly thing retracted just an inch, stopped moving its claw, as if shocked at his boldness. Taking heart at the slight falter, Thomas started screaming as he charged.

The Griever came to life, spikes popping out of its skin; it rolled forward, ready to collide head-on with its foe. The sudden movement almost made Thomas stop, his brief moment of insane courage washing away, but he kept running.

At the last second before collision, just as he got a close look at the metal and hair and slime, Thomas planted his left foot and dove to the right. Unable to stop its momentum, the Griever zoomed straight past him before it shuddered to a halt—Thomas noticed the thing was moving a lot faster now. With a metallic howl, it swiveled and readied to pounce on its victim. But now, no longer surrounded, Thomas had a clear shot away, back down the path.

He scrambled to his feet and sprinted forward. Sounds of pursuit, this time from all four Grievers, followed close behind. Sure that he was pushing his body beyond its physical limits, he ran on, trying to rid himself of the hopeless feeling that it was only a matter of time before they got him.

Then, three corridors down, two hands suddenly reached out and yanked him into the adjoining hallway. Thomas's heart leaped into his throat as he struggled to free himself. He stopped when he realized it was Minho.

"What—"

"Shut up and follow me!" Minho yelled, already dragging Thomas away until he was able to get his feet under him.

Without a moment to think, Thomas collected himself. Together, they ran through corridors, taking turn after turn. Minho seemed to know exactly what he was doing, where he was going; he never paused to think about which way they should run.

As they rounded the next corner, Minho attempted to speak. Between heaving breaths, he gasped, "I just saw . . . the dive move you did . . . back there . . . gave me an idea . . . we only have to last . . . a little while longer."

Thomas didn't bother wasting his own breath on questions; he just kept running, following Minho. Without having to look behind him, he knew the Grievers were gaining ground at an alarming rate. Every inch of his body hurt, inside and out; his limbs cried for him to quit running. But he ran on, hoped his heart didn't quit pumping.

A few turns later, Thomas saw something ahead of them that didn't register with his brain. It seemed . . . wrong. And the faint light emanating from their pursuers made the oddity up ahead all the more apparent.

The corridor didn't end in another stone wall.

It ended in blackness.

Thomas narrowed his eyes as they ran toward the wall of darkness, trying to comprehend what they were approaching. The two ivy-covered walls on either side of him seemed to intersect with nothing but sky up ahead. He could see stars. As they got closer, he finally realized that it was an opening—the Maze ended.

How? he wondered. *After years of searching, how did Minho and I find it this easily?*

Minho seemed to sense his thoughts. "Don't get excited," he said, barely able to get the words out.

A few feet before the end of the corridor, Minho pulled up, holding his hand out over Thomas's chest to make sure he stopped, too. Thomas slowed, then walked up to where the Maze opened out into open sky. The sounds of the onrushing Grievers grew closer, but he had to see.

They had indeed reached a way out of the Maze, but like Minho had said, it was nothing to get excited about. All Thomas could see in every direction, up and down, side to side, was empty air and fading stars. It was a strange and unsettling sight, like he was standing at the edge of the universe, and for a brief moment he was overcome by vertigo, his knees weakening before he steadied himself.

Dawn was beginning to make its mark, the sky seeming to have lightened considerably even in the last minute or so. Thomas stared in complete disbelief, not understanding how it could all be possible. It was like somebody had built the Maze and then set it afloat in the sky to hover there in the middle of nothing for the rest of eternity.

"I don't get it," he whispered, not knowing if Minho could even hear him.

"Careful," the Runner replied. "You wouldn't be the first shank to fall off the Cliff." He grabbed Thomas's shoulder. "Did you forget something?" He nodded back toward the inside of the Maze.

Thomas remembered hearing the word *Cliff* before, but couldn't place it at the moment. Seeing the vast, open sky in front of and below him had put him into some kind of hypnotized stupor. He shook himself back to reality and turned to face the oncoming Grievers. They were now only dozens of yards away, single file, charging in with a vengeance, moving surprisingly fast.

Everything clicked, then, even before Minho explained what they were going to do.

"These things may be vicious," Minho said, "but they're dumb as dirt. Stand here, close to me, facing—"

Thomas cut him off. "I know. I'm ready."

They shuffled their feet until they stood scrunched up together in front of the drop-off at the very middle of the corridor, facing the Grievers. Their heels were only inches from the edge of the Cliff behind them, nothing but air waiting after that.

The only thing left for them was courage.

"We need to be in sync!" Minho yelled, almost drowned out by the earsplitting sounds of the thundering spikes rolling along the stone. "On my mark!"

Why the Grievers had lined up single file was a mystery. Maybe the Maze proved just narrow enough to make it awkward for them to travel side by side. But one after the other, they rolled down the stone hallway, clicking and moaning and ready to kill. Dozens of yards had become dozens of feet, and the monsters were only seconds away from crashing into the waiting boys.

"Ready," Minho said steadily. "Not yet . . . not yet . . ."

Thomas hated every millisecond of waiting. He just wanted to close his eyes and never see another Griever again.

"Now!" screamed Minho.

Just as the first Griever's arm extended out to nip at them, Minho and Thomas dove in opposite directions, each toward one of the outer walls of the corridor. The tactic had worked for Thomas earlier, and judging by the horrible screeching sound that escaped the first Griever, it had worked again. The monster flew off the edge of the Cliff. Oddly, its battle cry cut off sharply instead of fading as it plummeted to the depths beyond.

Thomas landed against the wall and spun just in time to see the second creature tumble over the edge, not able to stop itself. The third one planted a heavily spiked arm into the stone, but its momentum was too much. The nerve-grinding squeal of the spike cutting through the ground sent a shiver up Thomas's spine, though a second later the Griever tumbled into the abyss. Again, neither of them made a sound as they fell—as if they'd disappeared instead of falling.

The fourth and final approaching creature was able to stop in time, teetering on the very edge of the cliff, a spike and a claw holding it in place.

Instinctively Thomas knew what he had to do. Looking to Minho, he nodded, then turned. Both boys ran in at the Griever and jumped feetfirst at the creature, kicking out at the last second with every waning bit of strength. They both connected, sending the last monster plummeting to its death.

Thomas quickly scrambled to the edge of the abyss, poking his head over to see the falling Grievers. But impossibly, they were gone—not even a sign of them in the emptiness that stretched below. Nothing.

His mind couldn't process the thought of where the Cliff led or what had happened to the terrible creatures. His last ounce of strength disappeared, and he curled into a ball on the ground.

Then, finally, came the tears.

CHAPTER 22

A half hour passed.

Neither Thomas nor Minho had moved an inch.

Thomas had finally stopped crying; he couldn't help wondering what Minho would think of him, or if he'd tell others, calling him a sissy. But there wasn't a shred of self-control left in him; he couldn't have prevented the tears, he knew that. Despite his lack of memory, he was sure he'd just been through the most traumatic night of his life. And his sore hands and utter exhaustion didn't help.

He crawled to the edge of the Cliff once more, stuck his head over again to get a better look now that dawn was in full force. The open sky in front of him was a deep purple, slowly fading into the bright blue of day, with tinges of orange from the sun on a distant, flat horizon.

He stared straight down, saw that the stone wall of the Maze went toward the ground in a sheer cliff until it disappeared into whatever lay far, far below. But even with the ever-increasing light, he still couldn't tell what was down there. It seemed as if the Maze was perched on a structure several miles above the ground.

But that was impossible, he thought. *It can't be. Has to be an illusion.*

He rolled over onto his back, groaning at the movement. Things seemed to hurt on him and inside him that he'd never known existed before. At least the Doors would be opening soon, and they could return to the Glade. He looked over at Minho, huddled against the hall of the corridor. "I can't believe we're still alive," he said.

Minho said nothing, just nodded, his face devoid of expression.

"Are there more of them? Did we just kill them all?"

Minho snorted. "Somehow we made it to sunrise, or we would've had ten more on our butts before long." He shifted his body, wincing and groaning. "I can't believe it. Seriously. We made it through the whole night—never been done before."

Thomas knew he should feel proud, brave, something. But all he felt was tired and relieved. "What did we do differently?"

"I don't know. It's kind of hard to ask a dead guy what he did wrong."

Thomas couldn't stop wondering about how the Grievers' enraged cries had ended as they fell from the Cliff, and how he hadn't been able to see them plummeting to their deaths. There was something very strange and unsettling about it. "Seems like they disappeared or something after they went over the edge."

"Yeah, that was kinda psycho. Couple of Gladers had a theory that other things had disappeared, but we proved 'em wrong. Look."

Thomas watched as Minho tossed a rock over the Cliff, then followed its path with his eyes. Down and down it went, not leaving his sight until it grew too small to see. He turned back toward Minho. "How does that prove them wrong?"

Minho shrugged. "Well, the rock didn't disappear, now, did it?"

"Then what do you think happened?" There was something significant here, Thomas could feel it.

Minho shrugged again. "Maybe they're magic. My head hurts too much to think about it."

With a jolt, all thoughts of the Cliff were forgotten. Thomas remembered Alby. "We have to get back." Straining, he forced himself to get to his feet. "Gotta get Alby off the wall." Seeing the look of confusion on Minho's face, he quickly explained what he'd done with the ropes of ivy.

Minho looked down, his eyes dejected. "No way he's still alive."

Thomas refused to believe it. "How do you know? Come on." He started limping back along the corridor.

"Because no one's ever made it . . ."

He trailed off, and Thomas knew what he was thinking. "That's because they've always been killed by the Grievers by the time you found them. Alby was only stuck with one of those needles, right?"

Minho stood up and joined Thomas in his slow walk back toward the Glade. "I don't know, I guess this has never happened before. A few guys have been stung by the needles during the day. And those are the ones who got the Serum and went through the Changing. The poor shanks who got stuck out in the Maze all night weren't found until later—days later, sometimes, if at all. And all of them were killed in ways you don't wanna hear about."

Thomas shuddered at the thought. "After what we just went through, I think I can imagine."

Minho looked up, surprise transforming his face. "I think you just figured it out. We've been wrong—well, *hopefully* we've been wrong. Because no one who'd been stung and *didn't* make it back by sunset has ever survived, we just assumed that was the point of no return—when it's too late to get the Serum." He seemed excited by his line of thinking.

They turned yet another corner, Minho suddenly taking the lead. The boy's pace was picking up, but Thomas stayed on his heels, surprised at how familiar he felt with the directions, usually even leaning into turns before Minho showed the way.

"Okay—this Serum," Thomas said. "I've heard that a couple of times now. What *is* that? And where does it come from?"

"Just what it sounds like, shank. It's a serum. The Grief Serum."

Thomas forced out a pathetic laugh. "Just when I think I've learned everything about this stupid place. Why is it called that? And why are Grievers called Grievers?"

Minho explained as they continued through the endless turns of the Maze, neither one of them leading now. "I don't know where we got the names, but the Serum comes from the Creators—or that's what we call them, at least. It's with the supplies in the Box every week, always has been. It's a medicine or antidote or something, already inside a medical syringe, ready to use." He made a show of sticking a needle in his arm. "Stick that sucker in someone who's been stung and it saves 'em. They go through the Changing—which sucks—but after that, they're healed."

A minute or two passed in silence as Thomas processed the information; they made a couple more turns. He wondered about the Changing, and what it meant. And for some reason, he kept thinking of the girl.

"Weird, though," Minho finally continued. "We've never talked about this before. If he's still alive, there's really no reason to think Alby can't be saved by the Serum. We somehow got it into our klunk heads that once the Doors closed, you were done—end of story. I gotta see this hanging-on-the-wall thing myself—I think you're shuckin' me."

The boys kept walking, Minho almost looking happy, but something was nagging at Thomas. He'd been avoiding it, denying it to himself. "What if another Griever got Alby after I diverted the one chasing me?"

Minho looked over at him, a blank expression on his face.

"Let's just hurry, is all I'm saying," Thomas said, hoping all that effort to save Alby hadn't been wasted.

They tried to pick up the pace, but their bodies hurt too much and they settled back into a slow walk despite the urgency. The next time they rounded a corner, Thomas faltered, his heart skipping a beat when he saw movement up ahead. Relief washed through him an instant later when he realized it was Newt and a group of Gladers. The West Door to the Glade towered over them and it was open. They'd made it back.

At the boys' appearance, Newt limped over to them. "What happened?" he asked; he sounded almost angry. "How in the bloody—"

"We'll tell you later," Thomas interrupted. "We have to save Alby."

Newt's face went white. "What do you mean? He's alive?"

"Just come here." Thomas headed to the right, craning his neck to look high up at the wall, searching along the thick vines until he found the spot where Alby hung by his arms and legs far above them. Without saying anything, Thomas pointed up, not daring to be relieved yet. He was still there, and in one piece, but there was no sign of movement.

Newt finally saw his friend hanging in the ivy, and looked back at Thomas. If he'd seemed shocked before, now he looked completely bewildered. "Is he . . . alive?"

Please let him be, Thomas thought. "I don't know. Was when I left him up there."

"When *you* left him . . ." Newt shook his head. "You and Minho get your butts inside, get yourselves checked by the Med-jacks. You look bloody awful. I want the whole story when they're done and you're rested up."

Thomas wanted to wait and see if Alby was okay. He started to speak but Minho grabbed him by the arm and forced him to walk toward the Glade. "We need sleep. And bandages. *Now*."

And Thomas knew he was right. He relented, glancing back up at Alby, then followed Minho out and away from the Maze.

The walk back into the Glade and then to the Homestead seemed endless, a row of Gladers on both sides gawking at them. Their faces showed complete awe, as if they were watching two ghosts strolling through a graveyard. Thomas knew it was because they'd accomplished something never done before, but he was embarrassed by the attention.

He almost stopped walking altogether when he spotted Gally up ahead, arms folded and glaring, but he kept moving. It took every ounce of his willpower, but he looked directly into Gally's eyes, never breaking contact. When he got to within five feet, the other boy's stare fell to the ground.

It almost disturbed Thomas how good that felt. Almost.

The next few minutes were a blur. Escorted into the Homestead by a couple of Med-jacks, up the stairs, a glimpse through a barely ajar door of someone feeding the comatose girl in her bed—he felt an incredibly strong urge to go see her, to check on her—into their own rooms, into bed, food, water, bandages. Pain. Finally, he was left alone, his head resting on the softest pillow his limited memory could recall.

But as he fell asleep, two things wouldn't leave his mind. First, the word he'd seen scrawled across the torso of both beetle blades—*WICKED*—ran through his thoughts again and again.

The second thing was the girl.

Hours later—days for all he knew—Chuck was there, shaking him awake. It took several seconds for Thomas to get his bearings and see straight. He focused in on Chuck, groaned. "Let me sleep, you shank."

"I thought you'd want to know."

Thomas rubbed his eyes and yawned. "Know what?" He looked at Chuck again, confused by his big smile.

"He's alive," he said. "Alby's okay—the Serum worked."

Thomas's grogginess instantly washed away, replaced with relief—it surprised him how much joy the information brought. But then Chuck's next words made him reconsider.

"He just started the Changing."

As if brought on by the words, a blood-chilling scream erupted from a room down the hall.

CHAPTER 23

Thomas wondered long and hard about Alby. It'd seemed such a victory just to save his life, bring him back from a night in the Maze. But had it been worth it? Now the boy was in intense pain, going through the same things as Ben. And what if he became as psychotic as Ben? Troubling thoughts all around.

Twilight fell upon the Glade and Alby's screams continued to haunt the air. It was impossible to escape the terrible sound, even after Thomas finally talked the Med-jacks into letting him go—weary, sore, bandaged, but tired of the piercing, agonized wails of their leader. Newt had adamantly refused when Thomas asked to see the person he'd risked his life for. *It'll only make it worse*, he'd said, and would not be swayed.

Thomas was too tired to put up a fight. He'd had no idea it was possible to feel so exhausted, despite the few hours of sleep he'd gotten. He'd hurt too much to do anything after that, and had spent most of the day on a bench on the outskirts of the Deadheads, wallowing in despair. The elation of his escape had faded rapidly, leaving him with pain and thoughts of his new life in the Glade. Every muscle ached; cuts and bruises covered him from head to toe. But even that wasn't as bad as the heavy emotional weight of what he'd been through the previous night. It seemed as if all the realities of living there had finally settled in his mind, like hearing a final diagnosis of terminal cancer.

How could anyone ever be happy in a life like this? he thought. Then,

How could anyone be evil enough to do this to us? He understood more than ever the passion the Gladers felt for finding their way out of the Maze. It wasn't just a matter of escape. For the first time, he felt a hunger to get revenge on the people responsible for sending him there.

But those thoughts just led back to the hopelessness that had filled him so many times already. If Newt and the others hadn't been able to solve the Maze after two *years* of searching, it seemed impossible there could actually *be* a solution. The fact that the Gladers hadn't given up said more about these people than anything else.

And now he was one of them.

This is my life, he thought. *Living in a giant maze, surrounded by hideous beasts.* Sadness filled him like a heavy poison. Alby's screams, now distant but still audible, only made it worse. He had to squeeze his hands to his ears every time he heard them.

Eventually, the day dragged to a close, and the setting of the sun brought the now-familiar grinding of the four Doors closing for the night. Thomas had no memory of his life before the Box, but he was positive he'd finished the worst twenty-four hours of his existence.

Just after dark, Chuck brought him some dinner and a big glass of cold water.

"Thanks," Thomas said, feeling a burst of warmth for the kid. He scooped the beef and noodles off the plate as fast as his aching arms could move. "I so needed this," he mumbled through a huge bite. He took a big swig of his drink, then went back to attacking the food. He hadn't realized how hungry he was until he'd started eating.

"You're disgusting when you eat," Chuck said, sitting on the bench next to him. "It's like watching a starving pig eat his own klunk."

"That's funny," Thomas said, sarcasm lacing his voice. "You should go entertain the Grievers—see if they laugh."

A quick expression of hurt flashed across Chuck's face, making

Thomas feel bad, but vanished almost as fast as it had appeared. "That reminds me—you're the talk of the town."

Thomas sat up straighter, not sure how he felt about the news. "What's *that* supposed to mean?"

"Oh, gee, let me think. First, you go out in the Maze when you're not supposed to, at night. Then you turn into some kind of freaky jungle dude, climbing vines and tying people up on walls. Next, you become one of the first people ever to survive an entire night outside the Glade, and to top it all off you kill four Grievers. Can't imagine what those shanks are talking about."

A surge of pride filled Thomas's body, then fizzled. Thomas was sickened by the happiness he'd just felt. Alby was still in bed, screaming his head off in pain—probably *wishing* he were dead. "Tricking them to go over the Cliff was Minho's idea, not mine."

"Not according to him. He saw you do the wait-and-dive thingy, then had the idea to do the same thing at the Cliff."

"The 'wait-and-dive thingy'?" Thomas asked, rolling his eyes. "Any idiot on the planet would've done that."

"Don't get all humbly bumbly on us—what you did is freaking unbelievable. You and Minho, both."

Thomas tossed the empty plate on the ground, suddenly angry. "Then why do I feel so crappy, Chuck? Wanna answer me that?"

Thomas searched Chuck's face for an answer, but by the looks of it he didn't have one. The boy just sat clasping his hands as he leaned forward on his knees, head hanging. Finally, half under his breath, he murmured, "Same reason we all feel crappy."

They sat in silence until, a few minutes later, Newt walked up, looking like death on two feet. He sat on the ground in front of them, as sad and worried as any person could possibly appear. Still, Thomas was glad to have him around.

"I think the worst part's over," Newt said. "The bugger should be sleepin' for a couple of days, then wake up okay. Maybe a little screaming now and then."

Thomas couldn't imagine how bad the whole ordeal must be—but the whole process of the Changing was still a mystery to him. He turned to the older boy, trying his best to be casual. "Newt, what's he going through up there? Seriously, I don't get what this Changing thing is."

Newt's response startled Thomas. "You think *we* do?" he spat, throwing his arms up, then slapping them back down on his knees. "All we bloody know is if the Grievers sting you with their nasty needles, you inject the Grief Serum or you die. If you do get the Serum, then your body wigs out and shakes and your skin bubbles and turns a freaky green color and you vomit all over yourself. Enough explanation for ya there, Tommy?"

Thomas frowned. He didn't want to make Newt any more upset than he already was, but he needed answers. "Hey, I know it sucks to see your friend go through that, but I just want to know what's really happening up there. Why do you call it the Changing?"

Newt relaxed, seemed to shrink, even, and sighed. "It brings back memories. Just little snippets, but definite memories of before we came to this horrible place. Anyone who goes through it acts like a bloody psycho when it's over—although usually not as bad as poor Ben. Anyway, it's like being given your old life back, only to have it snatched away again."

Thomas's mind was churning. "Are you sure?" he asked.

Newt looked confused. "What do you mean? Sure about what?"

"Are they *changed* because they want to go back to their old life, or is it because they're so depressed at realizing their old life was no better than what we have now?"

Newt stared at him for a second, then looked away, seemingly deep in thought. "Shanks who've been through it'll never really talk about it. They get . . . different. Unlikable. There's a handful around the Glade, but I can't stand to be around them." His voice was distant, his eyes having strayed to a certain blank spot in the woods. Thomas knew he was thinking about how Alby might never be the same again.

"Tell me about it," Chuck chimed in. "Gally's the worst of 'em all."

"Anything new on the girl?" Thomas asked, changing the subject. He was in no mood to talk about Gally. Plus, his thoughts kept going back to her. "I saw the Med-jacks feeding her upstairs."

"No," Newt answered. "Still in the buggin' coma, or whatever it is. Every once in a while she'll mumble something—nonsense, like she's dreaming. She takes the food, seems to be doing all right. It's kind of weird."

A long pause followed, as if the three of them were trying to come up with an explanation for the girl. Thomas wondered again about his inexplicable feeling of connection with her, though it *had* faded a little—but that could have been because of everything else occupying his thoughts.

Newt finally broke the silence. "Anyway, next up—figure out what we do with Tommy here."

Thomas perked up at that, confused by the statement. "*Do* with me? What're you talking about?"

Newt stood, stretched his arms. "Turned this whole place upside down, you bloody shank. Half the Gladers think you're God, the other half wanna throw your butt down the Box Hole. Lotta stuff to talk about."

"Like what?" Thomas didn't know which was more unsettling—that people thought he was some kind of hero, or that some wished he didn't exist.

"Patience," Newt said. "You'll find out after the wake-up."

"Tomorrow? Why?" Thomas didn't like the sound of this.

"I've called a Gathering. And you'll be there. You're the only buggin' thing on the agenda."

And with that, he turned and walked away, leaving Thomas to wonder why in the world a Gathering was needed just to talk about *him*.

CHAPTER 24

The next morning, Thomas found himself sitting in a chair, worried and anxious, sweating, facing eleven other boys. They were seated in chairs arranged in a semicircle around him. Once settled, he realized they were the Keepers, and to his chagrin that meant Gally was among them. One chair directly in front of Thomas stood empty—he didn't need to be told that it was Alby's.

They sat in a large room of the Homestead that Thomas hadn't been in before. Besides the chairs, there was no other furniture except for a small table in the corner. The walls were made of wood, as was the floor, and it didn't look like anyone had ever attempted to make the place look inviting. There were no windows; the room smelled of mildew and old books. Thomas wasn't cold, but shivered all the same.

He was at least relieved that Newt was there. He sat in the chair to the right of Alby's empty seat. "In place of our leader, sick in bed, I declare this Gathering begun," he said, with a subtle roll of his eyes as if he hated anything approaching formality. "As you all know, the last few days have been bloody crazy, and quite a bit seems centered around our Greenbean, Tommy, seated before us."

Thomas's face flushed with embarrassment.

"He's not the Greenie anymore," Gally said, his scratchy voice so low and cruel it was almost comical. "He's just a rule breaker now."

This started off a rumbling of murmurs and whispers, but Newt shushed them. Thomas suddenly wanted to be as far from that room as possible.

"Gally," Newt said, "try to keep some buggin' order, here. If you're gonna blabber your shuck mouth every time I say something, you can go ahead and bloody leave, because I'm not in a very cheerful mood."

Thomas wished he could cheer at that.

Gally folded his arms and leaned back in his chair, the scowl on his face so forced that Thomas almost laughed out loud. He was having a harder and harder time believing he'd been terrified of this guy just a day earlier—he seemed silly, even pathetic now.

Newt gave Gally a hard stare, then continued. "Glad we got that out of the way." Another roll of the eyes. "Reason we're here is because almost every lovin' kid in the Glade has come up to me in the last day or two either boohooing about Thomas or beggin' to take his bloody hand in marriage. We need to decide what we're gonna do with him."

Gally leaned forward, but Newt cut him off before he could say anything.

"You'll have your chance, Gally. One at a time. And Tommy, you're not allowed to say a buggin' thing until we ask you to. Good that?" He waited for a nod of consent from Thomas—who gave it reluctantly—then pointed to the kid in the chair on the far right. "Zart the Fart, you start."

There were a few snickers as Zart, the quiet big guy who watched over the Gardens, shifted in his seat. He looked to Thomas more out of place than a carrot on a tomato plant.

"Well," Zart began, his eyes darting around almost like he was waiting for someone else to tell him what to say. "I don't know. He broke one of our most important rules. We can't just let people think that's okay." He paused and looked down at his hands, rubbing them together. "But then again, he's . . . changed things. Now we know we can survive out there, and that we can beat the Grievers."

Relief flooded Thomas. He had someone else on his side. He made a promise to himself to be extra nice to Zart.

"Oh, give me a break," Gally spurted. "I bet Minho's the one who actually got rid of the stupid things."

"Gally, shut your hole!" Newt yelled, standing for effect this time; once again Thomas felt like cheering. "I'm the bloody Chair right now, and if I hear one more buggin' word out of turn from you, I'll be arrangin' another Banishing for your sorry butt."

"Please," Gally whispered sarcastically, the ridiculous scowl returning as he slouched back into his chair again.

Newt sat down and motioned to Zart. "Is that it? Any official recommendations?"

Zart shook his head.

"Okay. You're next, Frypan."

The cook smiled through his beard and sat up straighter. "Shank's got more guts than I've fried up from every pig and cow in the last year." He paused, as if expecting a laugh, but none came. "How stupid is this—he saves Alby's life, kills a couple of Grievers, and we're sitting here yappin' about what to do with him. As Chuck would say, this is a pile of klunk."

Thomas wanted to walk over and shake Frypan's hand—he'd just said exactly what Thomas himself had been thinking about all of this.

"So what're ya recommendin'?" Newt asked.

Frypan folded his arms. "Put him on the freaking Council and have him train us on everything he did out there."

Voices erupted from every direction, and it took Newt half a minute to calm everyone down. Thomas winced; Frypan had gone too far with that recommendation, almost invalidating his well-stated opinion of the whole mess.

"All right, writin' her down," Newt said as he did just that, scribbling on a notepad. "Now everyone keep their bloody mouths shut, I mean it. You know the rules—no idea's unacceptable—and you'll all have your say when we vote on it." He finished writing and pointed to the third member of the Council, a kid Thomas hadn't met yet with black hair and a freckly face.

"I don't really have an opinion," he said.

"What?" Newt asked angrily. "Lot of good it did to choose you for the Council, then."

"Sorry, I honestly don't." He shrugged. "If anything, I agree with Frypan, I guess. Why punish a guy for saving someone's life?"

"So you do have an opinion—is that it?" Newt insisted, pencil in hand.

The kid nodded and Newt scribbled a note. Thomas was feeling more and more relieved—it seemed like most of the Keepers were for him, not against him. Still, he was having a hard time just sitting there; he desperately wanted to speak on his own behalf. But he forced himself to follow Newt's orders and keep quiet.

Next was acne-covered Winston, Keeper of the Blood House. "I think he should be punished. No offense, Greenie, but Newt, you're the one always harping about *order*. If we don't punish him, we'll set a bad example. He broke our Number One Rule."

"Okay," Newt said, writing on his pad. "So you're recommendin' punishment. What kind?"

"I think he should be put in the Slammer for a week with only bread and water—and we need to make sure everyone knows about it so they don't get any ideas."

Gally clapped, earning a scowl from Newt. Thomas's heart fell just a bit.

Two more Keepers spoke, one for Frypan's idea, one for Winston's. Then it was Newt's turn.

"I agree with the lot of ya. He should be punished, but then we need to figure out a way to use him. I'm reservin' my recommendation until I hear everyone out. Next."

Thomas hated all this talk about punishment, even more than he hated having to keep his mouth shut. But deep inside he couldn't bring himself to disagree—as odd as it seemed after what he'd accomplished, he *had* broken a major rule.

Down the line they went. Some thought he should be praised, some thought he should be punished. Or both. Thomas could barely listen anymore, anticipating the comments from the last two Keepers, Gally and Minho. The latter hadn't said a word since Thomas had entered the room; he just sat there, drooped in his chair, looking like he hadn't slept in a week.

Gally went first. "I think I've made my opinions pretty clear already."

Great, Thomas thought. *Then just keep your mouth shut.*

"Good that," Newt said with yet another roll of the eyes. "Go on, then, Minho."

"No!" Gally yelled, making a couple of Keepers jump in their seats. "I still wanna say something."

"Then bloody say it," Newt replied. It made Thomas feel a little better that the temporary Council Chair despised Gally almost as much as he did. Though Thomas wasn't that afraid of him anymore, he still hated the guy's guts.

"Just think about it," Gally began. "This slinthead comes up in the Box, acting all confused and scared. A few days later, he's running around the Maze with Grievers, acting like he owns the place."

Thomas shrank into his chair, hoping that others hadn't been thinking anything like that.

Gally continued his rant. "I think it was all an act. How could he have done what he did out there after just a few days? I ain't buyin' it."

"What're you tryin' to say, Gally?" Newt asked. "How 'bout having a bloody *point*?"

"I think he's a spy from the people who put us here."

Another uproar exploded in the room; Thomas could do nothing but shake his head—he just didn't get how Gally could come up with all these ideas. Newt finally calmed everyone down again, but Gally wasn't finished.

"We can't trust this shank," he continued. "Day after he shows up, a psycho girl comes, spoutin' off that things are gonna change, clutching that freaky note. We find a dead Griever. Thomas conveniently finds himself in the Maze for the night, then tries to convince everyone he's a hero. Well, neither Minho nor anyone else actually *saw* him do anything in the vines. How do we know it was the Greenie who tied Alby up there?"

Gally paused; no one said a word for several seconds, and panic rose inside Thomas's chest. Could they actually believe what Gally was saying? He was anxious to defend himself and almost broke his silence for the first time—but before he could get a word in, Gally was talking again.

"There's too many weird things going on, and it all started when this shuck-face Greenie showed up. And he just happens to be the first person to survive a night out in the Maze. Something ain't right, and until we figure it out, I officially recommend that we lock his butt in the Slammer—for a month, and then have another review."

More rumblings broke out, and Newt wrote something on his pad, shaking his head the whole time—which gave Thomas a tinge of hope.

"Finished, Captain Gally?" Newt asked.

"Quit being such a smart aleck, Newt," he spat, his face flushing red. "I'm dead serious. How can we trust this shank after less than a week? Quit voting me down before you even *think* about what I'm saying."

For the first time, Thomas felt a little empathy for Gally—he did have a point about how Newt was treating him. Gally was a Keeper, after all. *But I still hate him*, Thomas thought.

"Fine, Gally," Newt said. "I'm sorry. We heard you, and we'll all consider your bloody recommendation. Are you done?"

"Yes, I'm done. And I'm *right*."

With no more words for Gally, Newt pointed at Minho. "Go ahead, last but not least."

Thomas was elated that it was finally Minho's turn; surely he'd defend him to the end.

Minho stood quickly, taking everyone off guard. "I was out there; I saw what this guy did—he stayed strong while I turned into a panty-wearin' chicken. No blabbin' on and on like Gally. I want to say my recommendation and be done with it."

Thomas held his breath, wondering what he'd say.

"Good that," Newt said. "Tell us, then."

Minho looked at Thomas. "I nominate this shank to replace me as Keeper of the Runners."

CHAPTER 25

Complete silence filled the room, as if the world had been frozen, and every member of the Council stared at Minho. Thomas sat stunned, waiting for the Runner to say he'd been kidding.

Gally finally broke the spell, standing up. "That's ridiculous!" He faced Newt and pointed back at Minho, who had taken his seat again. "He should be kicked off the Council for saying something so stupid."

Any pity Thomas had felt for Gally, however remote, completely vanished at that statement.

Some Keepers seemed to actually agree with Minho's recommendation—like Frypan, who clapped to drown out Gally, clamoring to take a vote. Others didn't. Winston shook his head adamantly, saying something that Thomas couldn't quite make out. When everyone started talking at once, Thomas put his head in his hands to wait it out, terrified and awed at the same time. Why had Minho said that? *Has to be a joke*, he thought. *Newt said it takes forever just to* become *a Runner, much less the Keeper.* He looked back up, wishing he were a thousand miles away.

Finally, Newt put his notepad down and stepped out from the semicircle, screaming at people to shut up. Thomas watched on as at first no one seemed to hear or notice Newt at all. Gradually, though, order was restored and everyone sat down.

"Shuck it," Newt said. "I've never seen so many shanks acting like teat-suckin' babies. We may not look it, but around these parts we're adults. Act like it, or we'll disband this bloody Council and start from scratch." He walked from end to end of the curved row of sitting Keepers, looking each of them in the eye as he spoke. "Are we clear?"

Quiet had swept across the group. Thomas expected more outbursts, but was surprised when everyone nodded their consent, even Gally.

"Good that." Newt walked back to his chair and sat down, putting the pad in his lap. He scratched out a few lines on the paper, then looked up at Minho. "That's some pretty serious klunk, brother. Sorry, but you need to talk it up to move it forward."

Thomas couldn't help feeling eager to hear the response.

Minho looked exhausted, but he started defending his proposal. "It's sure easy for you shanks to sit here and talk about something you're stupid on. I'm the only Runner in this group, and the only other one here who's even *been* out in the Maze is Newt."

Gally interjected: "Not if you count the time I—"

"I don't!" Minho shouted. "And believe me, you or nobody else has the slightest clue what it's like to be out there. The only reason you were stung is because you broke the same rule you're blaming Thomas for. That's called *hypocrisy,* you shuck-faced piece of—"

"Enough," Newt said. "Defend your proposal and be done with it."

The tension was palpable; Thomas felt like the air in the room had become glass that could shatter at any second. Both Gally and Minho looked as if the taut, red skin of their faces was about to burst—but they finally broke their stare.

"Anyway, listen to me," Minho continued as he took his seat. "I've never seen anything like it. He didn't panic. He didn't whine and cry, never seemed scared. Dude, he'd been here for just a few days. Think about what we were all like in the beginning. Huddling in corners, disoriented, crying every hour, not trusting anybody, refusing to do anything. We were all like that, for weeks or months, till we had no choice but to shuck it and live."

Minho stood back up, pointed at Thomas. "Just a few days after this guy shows up, he steps out in the Maze to save two shanks he hardly knows. All this klunk about him breaking a rule is just beyond stupid. He didn't get the rules yet. But plenty of people had told him what it's like in the Maze, especially at night. And he still stepped out there, just as the Door was closing, only caring that two people needed help." He took a deep breath, seeming to gain strength the more he spoke.

"But that was just the beginning. After that, he saw me give up on Alby, leave him for dead. And I was the veteran—the one with all the experience and knowledge. So when Thomas saw me give up, he shouldn't have questioned it. But he did. Think about the willpower and strength it took him to push Alby up that wall, inch by inch. It's psycho. It's freaking crazy.

"But that wasn't it. Then came the Grievers. I told Thomas we had to split up and I started the practiced evasive maneuvers, running in the patterns. Thomas, when he should've been wettin' his pants, took control, defied all laws of physics and gravity to get Alby up onto that wall, diverted the Grievers away from him, beat one off, found—"

"We get the point," Gally snapped. "Tommy here is a lucky shank."

Minho rounded on him. "No, you worthless shuck, you *don't* get it! I've been here two years, and I've never seen anything like it. For you to say anything . . ."

Minho paused, rubbing his eyes, groaning in frustration. Thomas realized his own mouth had dropped wide open. His emotions were scattered: appreciation for Minho standing up to everybody on his behalf, disbelief at Gally's continuous belligerence, fear of what the final decision would be.

"Gally," Minho said in a calmer voice, "you're nothing but a sissy who has never, not once, asked to be a Runner or tried out for it. You don't have the right to talk about things you don't understand. So shut your mouth."

Gally stood up again, fuming. "Say one more thing like that and I'll break your neck, right here in front of everybody." Spit flew from his mouth as he spoke.

Minho laughed, then raised the palm of his hand and shoved Gally in the face. Thomas half stood as he watched the Glader crash down into his chair, tipping it over backward, cracking it in two pieces. Gally sprawled across the floor, then scrambled to stand up, struggling to get his hands and feet under him. Minho stepped closer and stomped the bottom of his foot down on Gally's back, driving his body flat to the ground.

Thomas plopped back into his seat, stunned.

"I swear, Gally," Minho said with a sneer, "don't ever threaten me again. Don't ever *speak* to me again. Ever. If you do, I'll break *your* shuck neck, right after I'm done with your arms and legs."

Newt and Winston were on their feet and grabbing Minho before Thomas even knew what was going on. They pulled him away from Gally, who jumped up, his face a ruddied mask of rage. But he made no move toward Minho; he just stood there with his chest out, heaving ragged breaths.

Finally Gally backed away, half stumbling toward the exit behind him. His eyes darted around the room, lit with a burning hatred. Thomas had the sickening thought that Gally looked like someone about to commit murder. He backed toward the door, reached behind him to grab the handle.

"Things are different now," he said, spitting on the floor. "You shouldn't have done that, Minho. You should *not* have done that." His maniacal gaze shifted to Newt. "I know you hate me, that you've always hated me. You should be Banished for your embarrassing inability to lead this group. You're shameful, and any one of you who stays here is no better. Things are going to change. This, I promise."

Thomas's heart sank. As if things hadn't been awkward enough already.

Gally yanked the door open and stepped out into the hall, but before anyone could react, he popped his head back in the room. "And you," he said, glaring at Thomas, "the *Greenbean* who thinks he's friggin' God. Don't forget I've seen you before—I've *been* through the Changing. What these guys decide doesn't mean jack."

He paused, looking at each person in the room. When his malicious stare fell back on Thomas, he had one last thing to say. "Whatever you came here for—I swear on my life I'm gonna stop it. Kill you if I have to."

Then he turned and left the room, slamming the door behind him.

CHAPTER 26

Thomas sat frozen in his chair, a sickness growing in his stomach like an infestation. He'd been through the whole gamut of emotions in the short time since he'd arrived at the Glade. Fear, loneliness, desperation, sadness, even the slightest hint of joy. But this was something new—to hear a person say they hate you enough that they want to kill you.

Gally's crazy, he told himself. *He's completely insane.* But the thought only increased his worries. Insane people could really be capable of anything.

The Council members stood or sat in silence, seemingly as shocked as Thomas at what they'd just seen. Newt and Winston finally let go of Minho; all three of them sullenly walked to their chairs and sat down.

"He's finally whacked for good," Minho said, almost in a whisper. Thomas couldn't tell if he'd meant for the others to hear him.

"Well, you're not the bloody saint in the room," Newt said. "What were you *thinking*? That was a little overboard, don't ya think?"

Minho squinched up his eyes and pulled his head back, as if he were baffled by Newt's question. "Don't give me that garbage. Every one of you loved seeing that slinthead get his dues, and you know it. It's about time someone stood up to his klunk."

"He's on the Council for a reason," Newt said.

"Dude, he threatened to break my neck and kill Thomas! The guy is mentally whacked, and you better send someone right now to throw him in the Slammer. He's dangerous."

Thomas couldn't have agreed more and once again almost broke his order to stay quiet, but stopped himself. He didn't want to get in any more trouble than he was already in—but he didn't know how much longer he could last.

"Maybe he had a good point," Winston said, almost too quietly.

"What?" Minho asked, mirroring Thomas's thoughts exactly.

Winston looked surprised at the acknowledgment that he'd said anything. His eyes darted around the room before he explained. "Well . . . he *has* been through the Changing—Griever stung him in the middle of the day just outside the West Door. That means he has *memories,* and he said the Greenie looks familiar. Why would he make that up?"

Thomas thought about the Changing, and the fact that it brought back memories. The idea hadn't occurred to him before, but would it be worth it to get stung by the Grievers, go through that horrible process, just to remember something? He pictured Ben writhing in bed and remembered Alby's screams. *No way,* he thought.

"Winston, did you *see* what just happened?" Frypan asked, looking incredulous. "Gally's psycho. You can't put too much stock in his rambling nonsense. What, you think Thomas here is a Griever in disguise?"

Council rules or no Council rules, Thomas had finally had enough. He couldn't stay silent another second.

"Can I say something now?" he asked, frustration raising the volume of his voice. "I'm sick of you guys talking about me like I'm not here."

Newt glanced up at him and nodded. "Go ahead. This bloody meetin' can't be much more screwed up."

Thomas quickly gathered his thoughts, grasping for the right words inside the swirling cloud of frustration, confusion and anger in his mind. "I don't know why Gally hates me. I don't care. He seems psychotic to me. As for who I *really* am, you all know just as much as I do.

But if I remember correctly, we're here because of what I did out in the Maze, not because some idiot thinks I'm evil."

Someone snickered and Thomas quit talking, hoping he'd gotten his point across.

Newt nodded, looking satisfied. "Good that. Let's get this meeting over with and worry about Gally later."

"We can't vote without all the members here," Winston insisted. "Unless they're really sick, like Alby."

"For the love, Winston," Newt replied. "I'd say Gally's a wee bit ill today, too, so we continue without him. Thomas, defend yourself and then we'll take the vote on what we should do with you."

Thomas realized his hands were squeezed up into fists on his lap. He relaxed them and wiped his sweaty palms on his pants. Then he began, not sure of what he'd say before the words came out.

"I didn't do anything wrong. All I know is I saw two people struggling to get inside these walls and they couldn't make it. To ignore that because of some stupid rule seemed selfish, cowardly, and . . . well, stupid. If you want to throw me in jail for trying to save someone's life, then go ahead. Next time I promise I'll point at them and laugh, then go eat some of Frypan's dinner."

Thomas wasn't trying to be funny. He was just dumbfounded that the whole thing could even be an issue.

"Here's my recommendation," Newt said. "You broke our bloody Number One Rule, so you get one day in the Slammer. That's your punishment. I also recommend we elect you as a Runner, effective the second this meeting's over. You've proven more in one night than most trainees do in weeks. As for you being the buggin' Keeper, forget it." He looked over at Minho. "Gally was right on that count—stupid idea."

The comment hurt Thomas's feelings, even though he couldn't disagree. He looked to Minho for his reaction.

The Keeper didn't seem surprised, but argued all the same. "Why? He's the best we have—I swear it. The best should be the Keeper."

"Fine," Newt responded. "If that's true, we'll make the change later. Give it a month and see if he proves himself."

Minho shrugged. "Good that."

Thomas quietly sighed in relief. He still wanted to be a Runner—which surprised him, considering what he'd just gone through out in the Maze—but becoming the Keeper right away sounded ridiculous.

Newt glanced around the room. "Okay, we had several recommendations, so let's give it a go-round—"

"Oh, come on," Frypan said. "Just vote. I vote for yours."

"Me too," Minho said.

Everyone else chimed in their approval, filling Thomas with relief and a sense of pride. Winston was the only one to say no.

Newt looked at him. "We don't need your vote, but tell us what's bonkin' around your brain."

Winston gazed at Thomas carefully, then back to Newt. "It's fine with me, but we shouldn't totally ignore what Gally said. Something about it—I don't think he just made it up. And it's true that ever since Thomas got here, everything's been shucked and screwy."

"Fair enough," Newt said. "Everyone put some thought into it—maybe when we get right nice and bored we can have another Gathering to talk about it. Good that?"

Winston nodded.

Thomas groaned at how invisible he'd become. "I love how you guys are just talking about me like I'm not here."

"Look, Tommy," Newt said. "We just elected you as a buggin' Runner. Quit your cryin' and get out of here. Minho has a lot of training to give you."

It hadn't really hit Thomas until then. He was going to be a *Runner,* explore the Maze. Despite everything, he felt a shiver of excitement; he was sure they could avoid getting trapped out there at night again. Maybe he'd had his one and only turn of bad luck. "What about my punishment?"

"Tomorrow," Newt answered. "The wake-up till sunset."

One day, Thomas thought. *That won't be so bad.*

The meeting was dismissed and everyone except Newt and Minho left the room in a hurry. Newt hadn't moved from his chair, where he sat jotting notes. "Well, that was good times," he murmured.

Minho walked over and playfully punched Thomas in the arm. "It's all this shank's fault."

Thomas punched him back. "Keeper? You want me to be Keeper? You're nuttier than Gally by a long shot."

Minho faked an evil grin. "Worked, didn't it? Aim high, hit low. Thank me later."

Thomas couldn't help smiling at the Keeper's clever ways. A knock on the opened door grabbed his attention—he turned to see who it was. Chuck stood there, looking like he'd just been chased by a Griever. Thomas felt the grin fade from his face.

"What's wrong?" Newt asked, standing up. The tone of his voice only heightened Thomas's concern.

Chuck was wringing his hands. "Med-jacks sent me."

"Why?"

"I guess Alby's thrashing around and acting all crazy, telling them he needs to talk to somebody."

Newt made for the door, but Chuck held up his hand. "Um . . . he doesn't want you."

"What do you mean?"

Chuck pointed at Thomas. "He keeps asking for him."

CHAPTER 27

For the second time that day, Thomas was shocked into silence.

"Well, come on," Newt said to Thomas as he grabbed his arm. "No way I'm not going with ya."

Thomas followed him, with Chuck right behind, as they left the Council room and went down the hall toward a narrow, spiraling staircase that he hadn't noticed before. Newt took the first step, then gave Chuck a cold glare. "You. Stay."

For once, Chuck simply nodded and said nothing. Thomas figured that something about Alby's behavior had the kid's nerves on edge.

"Lighten up," Thomas said to Chuck as Newt headed up the staircase. "They just elected me a Runner, so you're buddies with a stud now." He was trying to make a joke, trying to deny that he was terrified to see Alby. What if he made accusations like Ben had? Or worse?

"Yeah, right," Chuck whispered, staring at the wooden steps in a daze.

With a shrug Thomas began climbing the stairs. Sweat slicked his palms, and he felt a drop trickle down his temple. He did *not* want to go up there.

Newt, all grim and solemn, was waiting for Thomas at the top of the stairwell. They stood at the opposite end of the long, dark hallway from the usual staircase, the one Thomas had climbed on his very first day to see Ben. The memory made him queasy; he hoped Alby was completely healed from the ordeal so he didn't have to witness something like that again—the sickly skin, the veins, the thrashing. But he expected the worst, and braced himself.

He followed Newt to the second door on the right and watched as the older boy knocked lightly; a moan sounded in reply. Newt pushed open the door, the slight creak once again reminding Thomas of some vague childhood memory of haunted-house movies. There it was again—the smallest glimpse at his past. He could remember movies, but not the actors' faces or with whom he'd watched them. He could remember theaters, but not what any specific one *looked* like. It was impossible to explain how that felt, even to himself.

Newt had stepped into the room and was motioning for Thomas to follow. As he entered, he prepared himself for the horror that might await. But when his eyes lifted, all he saw was a very weak-looking teenage boy lying in his bed, eyes closed.

"Is he asleep?" Thomas whispered, trying to avoid the real question that had popped in his mind: *He's not* dead, *is he?*

"I don't know," Newt said quietly. He walked over and sat in a wooden chair next to the bed. Thomas took a seat on the other side.

"Alby," Newt whispered. Then more loudly: "Alby. Chuck said you wanted to talk to Tommy."

Alby's eyes fluttered open—bloodshot orbs that glistened in the light. He looked at Newt, then across at Thomas. With a groan he shifted in the bed and sat up, his back against the headboard. "Yeah," he muttered, a scratchy croak.

"Chuck said you were thrashin' around, acting like a loonie." Newt leaned forward. "What's wrong? You still sick?"

Alby's next words came out in a wheeze, as if every one of them would take a week off his life. "Everything's . . . gonna change. . . . The girl . . . Thomas . . . I saw them . . ." His eyelids flickered closed, then open again; he sank back to a flat position on the bed, stared at the ceiling. "Don't feel so good."

"What do you mean, you saw—" Newt began.

"I wanted Thomas!" Alby yelled, with a sudden burst of energy that Thomas would've thought impossible a few seconds earlier. "I didn't ask for you, Newt! Thomas! I asked for freaking Thomas!"

Newt looked up, questioned Thomas with a raising of his eyebrows. Thomas shrugged, feeling sicker by the second. What did Alby want *him* for?

"Fine, ya grouchy shuck," Newt said. "He's right here—talk to him."

"Leave," Alby said, his eyes closed, his breathing heavy.

"No way—I wanna hear."

"Newt." A pause. "Leave. Now." Thomas felt incredibly awkward, worried about what Newt was thinking and dreading what Alby wanted to say to him.

"But—" Newt protested.

"Out!" Alby sat up as he yelled, his voice cracking with the strain of it. He scooted himself back to lean against the headboard again. "Get out!"

Newt's face sank in obvious hurt—Thomas was surprised to see no anger there. Then, after a long, tense moment, Newt stood from his chair and walked over to the door, opened it. *He's really going to leave?* Thomas thought.

"Don't expect me to kiss your butt when you come sayin' sorry," he said, then stepped into the hallway.

"Close the door!" Alby shouted, one final insult. Newt obeyed, slamming it shut.

Thomas's heart rate quickened—he was now alone with a guy

who'd had a bad temper *before* getting attacked by a Griever and going through the Changing. He hoped Alby would say what he wanted and be done with it. A long pause stretched into several minutes, and Thomas's hands shook with fear.

"I know who you are," Alby said finally, breaking the silence.

Thomas couldn't find words to reply. He tried; nothing came out but an incoherent mumble. He was utterly confused. And scared.

"I know who you are," Alby repeated slowly. "Seen it. Seen everything. Where we came from, who you are. Who the *girl* is. I remember the Flare."

The Flare? Thomas forced himself to talk. "I don't know what you're talking about. What did you see? I'd love to know who I am."

"It ain't pretty," Alby answered, and for the first time since Newt had left, Alby looked up, straight at Thomas. His eyes were deep pockets of sorrow, sunken, dark. "It's horrible, ya know. Why would those shucks want us to remember? Why can't we just live here and be happy?"

"Alby . . ." Thomas wished he could take a peek in the boy's mind, see what he'd seen. "The Changing," he pressed, "what happened? What came back? You're not making sense."

"You—" Alby started, then suddenly grabbed his own throat, making gurgly choking sounds. His legs kicked out and he rolled onto his side, thrashing back and forth as if someone *else* were trying to strangle him. His tongue stuck out of his mouth; he bit it over and over.

Thomas stood up quickly, stumbled backward, horrified—Alby struggled as if he was having a seizure, his legs kicking in every direction. The dark skin of his face, which had been oddly pale just a minute earlier, had turned purple, his eyes rolled up so far in their sockets they looked like glowing white marbles.

"Alby!" Thomas yelled, not daring to reach down and grab him.

"Newt!" he screamed, cupping his hands around his mouth. "Newt, get in here!"

The door was flung open before he'd finished his last sentence.

Newt ran to Alby and grabbed him by the shoulders, pushing with his whole body to pin the convulsing boy to the bed. "Grab his legs!"

Thomas moved forward, but Alby's legs kicked and flailed out, making it impossible to get any closer. His foot hit Thomas in the jaw; a lance of pain shot through his whole skull. He stumbled backward again, rubbing the sore spot.

"Just bloody do it!" Newt yelled.

Thomas steeled himself, then jumped on top of Alby's body, grabbing both legs and pinning them to the bed. He wrapped his arms around the boy's thighs and squeezed while Newt put a knee on one of Alby's shoulders, then grabbed at Alby's hands, still clasped around his own neck in a chokehold.

"Let go!" Newt yelled as he tugged. "You're bloody killin' yourself !"

Thomas could see the muscles in Newt's arms flexing, veins popping out as he pulled at Alby's hands, until finally, inch by inch, he was able to pry them away. He pushed them tightly against the struggling boy's chest. Alby's whole body jerked a couple of times, his midsection thrusting up and away from the bed. Then, slowly, he calmed, and a few seconds later he lay still, his breath evening; his eyes glazed over.

Thomas held firm to Alby's legs, afraid to move and set the boy off again. Newt waited a full minute before he slowly let go of Alby's hands. Then another minute before he pulled his knee back and stood up. Thomas took that as his cue to do the same, hoping the ordeal had truly ended.

Alby looked up, eyes droopy, as if he was on the edge of slipping into a deep sleep. "I'm sorry, Newt," he whispered. "Don't know what happened. It was like . . . something was controlling my body. I'm sorry. . . ."

Thomas took a deep breath, sure he'd never experience something so disturbing and uncomfortable again. He hoped.

"Sorries, nothin'," Newt replied. "You were trying to bloody kill yourself."

"Wasn't me, I swear," Alby murmured.

Newt threw his hands up. "What do you mean it wasn't you?" he asked.

"I don't know. . . . It . . . it wasn't me." Alby looked just as confused as Thomas felt.

But Newt seemed to think it wasn't worth trying to figure out. At least at the moment. He grabbed the blankets that had fallen off the bed in Alby's struggle and pulled them atop the sick boy. "Get your butt to sleep and we'll talk about it later." He patted him on the head, then added, "You're messed up, shank."

But Alby was already drifting off, nodding slightly as his eyes closed.

Newt caught Thomas's gaze and gestured for the door. Thomas had no problem leaving that crazy house—he followed Newt out and into the hall. Then, just as they stepped through the doorway, Alby mumbled something from his bed.

Both boys stopped in their tracks. "What?" Newt asked.

Alby opened his eyes for a brief moment, then repeated what he'd said, a little more loudly. "Be careful with the girl." Then his eyes slid shut.

There it was again—the girl. Somehow things always led back to the girl. Newt gave Thomas a questioning look, but Thomas could only return it with a shrug. He had no idea what was going on.

"Let's go," Newt whispered.

"And Newt?" Alby called again from the bed, not bothering to open his eyes.

"Yeah?"

"Protect the Maps." Alby rolled over, his back telling them he'd finally finished speaking.

Thomas didn't think that sounded very good. Not good at all. He and Newt left the room and softly closed the door.

CHAPTER 28

Thomas followed Newt as he hurried down the stairs and out of the Homestead into the bright light of midafternoon. Neither boy said a word for a while. For Thomas, things just seemed to be getting worse and worse.

"Hungry, Tommy?" Newt asked when they were outside.

Thomas couldn't believe the question. "Hungry? I feel like puking after what I just saw—no, I'm not hungry."

Newt only grinned. "Well, I am, ya shank. Let's go look for some leftovers from lunch. We need to talk."

"Somehow I knew you were going to say something like that." No matter what he did, he was becoming more and more entwined in the dealings of the Glade. And he was growing to expect it.

They made their way directly to the kitchen, where, despite Frypan's grumbling, they were able to get cheese sandwiches and raw vegetables. Thomas couldn't ignore the way the Keeper of the cooks kept giving him a weird look, eyes darting away whenever Thomas returned the stare.

Something told him this sort of treatment would now be the norm. For some reason, he was different from everyone else in the Glade. He felt like he'd lived an entire lifetime since awakening from his memory wipe, but he'd only been there a week.

The boys decided to take their lunches to eat outside, and a few minutes later they found themselves at the west wall, looking out at the many work activities going on throughout the Glade, their backs up against a spot of thick ivy. Thomas forced himself to eat; the way things were going, he needed to make sure he'd have strength to deal with whatever insane thing came his way next.

"Ever seen that happen before?" Thomas asked after a minute or so.

Newt looked at him, his face suddenly somber. "What Alby just did? No. Never. But then again, no one's ever tried to tell us what they remembered during the Changing. They always refuse. Alby tried to—must be why he went nuts for a while."

Thomas paused in the middle of chewing. Could the people behind the Maze *control* them somehow? It was a terrifying thought.

"We have to find Gally," Newt said through a bite of carrot, changing the subject. "Bugger's gone off and hid somewhere. Soon as we're done eating, I need to find him and throw his butt in jail."

"Serious?" Thomas couldn't help feeling a shot of pure elation at the thought. He'd be happy to slam the door closed and throw away the key himself.

"That shank threatened to kill you and we have to make bloody sure it never happens again. That shuck-face is gonna pay a heavy price for acting like that—he's lucky we don't Banish him. Remember what I told you about order."

"Yeah." Thomas's only concern was that Gally would just hate him all the more for being thrown in jail. *I don't care,* he thought. *I'm not scared of that guy anymore.*

"Here's how it'll play out, Tommy," Newt said. "You're with me the rest of today—we need to figure things. Tomorrow, the Slammer. Then you're Minho's, and I want you to stay away from the other shanks for a while. Got it?"

Thomas was more than happy to oblige. Being mostly alone sounded like a great idea. "Sounds beautiful. So Minho's going to train me?"

"That's right—you're a Runner now. Minho'll teach ya. The Maze, the Maps, everything. Lots to learn. I expect you to work your butt off."

Thomas was shocked that the idea of entering the Maze again didn't frighten him all that much. He resolved to do just as Newt said, hoping it would keep his mind off things. Deeper down, he hoped to get out of the Glade as much as possible. Avoiding other people was his new goal in life.

The boys sat in silence, finishing their lunches, until Newt finally got to what he really wanted to talk about. Crumpling his trash into a ball, he turned and looked straight at Thomas.

"Thomas," he began, "I need you to accept something. We've heard it too many times now to deny it, and it's time to discuss it."

Thomas knew what was coming, but was startled. He dreaded the words.

"Gally said it. Alby said it. Ben said it," Newt continued, "the girl, after we took her out of the Box—she said it."

He paused, perhaps expecting Thomas to ask what he meant. But Thomas already knew. "They all said things were going to change."

Newt looked away for a moment, then turned back. "That's right. And Gally, Alby and Ben claim they saw you in their memories after the Changing—and from what I gather, you weren't plantin' flowers and helpin' old ladies cross the street. According to Gally, there's somethin' rotten enough about ya that he wants to kill ya."

"Newt, I don't know—" Thomas started, but Newt didn't let him finish.

"I know you don't remember anything, Thomas! Quit sayin' that—don't ever say it again. None of us remember anything, and we're bloody sick of you reminding us. The point is there's something different about you, and it's time we figured it out."

Thomas was overwhelmed by a surge of anger. "Fine, so how do we do it? I want to know who I am just as much as anyone else. *Obviously*."

"I need you to open your mind. Be honest if anything—anything at all—seems familiar."

"Nothing—" Thomas started, but stopped. So much had happened since arriving, he'd almost forgotten how familiar the Glade had felt to him that first night, sleeping next to Chuck. How comfortable and *at home* he'd felt. A far cry from the terror he should've experienced.

"I can see your wheels spinnin'," Newt said, quietly. "Talk."

Thomas hesitated, scared of the consequences of what he was about to say. But he was tired of keeping secrets. "Well . . . I can't put my finger on anything specific." He spoke slowly, carefully. "But I did feel like I'd been here before when I first got here." He looked at Newt, hoping to see some sort of recognition in his eyes. "Anyone else go through that?"

But Newt's face was blank. He simply rolled his eyes. "Uh, no, Tommy. Most of us spent a week klunkin' our pants and bawlin' our eyes out."

"Yeah, well." Thomas paused, upset and suddenly embarrassed. What did it all mean? Was he different from everyone else somehow? Was something wrong with him? "It all seemed familiar to me, and I knew I wanted to be a Runner."

"That's bloody interesting." Newt examined him for a second, not hiding his obvious suspicion. "Well, keep lookin' for it. Strain your mind, spend your free time wanderin' your thoughts, and *think* about this place. Delve inside that brain of yours, and seek it out. *Try,* for all our sakes."

"I will." Thomas closed his eyes, started searching the darkness of his mind.

"Not now, you dumb shuck." Newt laughed. "I just meant do it from now *on*. Free time, meals, goin' to sleep at night, as you walk around, train, work. Tell me anything that seems even remotely familiar. Got it?"

"Yeah, got it." Thomas couldn't help worrying that he'd thrown up some red flags for Newt, and that the older boy was just hiding his concern.

"Good that," Newt said, looking almost too agreeable. "To begin, we better go see someone."

"Who?" Thomas asked, but knew the answer as soon as he spoke. Dread filled him again.

"The girl. I want you to look at her till your eyes bleed, see if somethin' gets triggered in that shuck brain of yours." Newt gathered his lunch trash and stood up. "Then I want you to tell me every single word Alby said to you."

Thomas sighed, then got to his feet. "Okay." He didn't know if he could bring himself to tell the complete truth about Alby's accusations, not to mention how he felt about the girl. It looked like he wasn't done keeping secrets after all.

The boys walked back toward the Homestead, where the girl still lay in a coma. Thomas couldn't stifle his worry about what Newt was thinking. He'd opened himself up, and he really *liked* Newt. If Newt turned on him now, Thomas didn't know if he could handle it.

"If all else fails," Newt said, interrupting Thomas's thoughts, "we'll send ya to the Grievers—get ya stung so you can go through the Changing. We *need* your memories."

Thomas barked a sarcastic laugh at the idea, but Newt wasn't smiling.

The girl seemed to be sleeping peacefully, like she'd wake up at any minute. Thomas had almost expected the skeletal remnant of a person—someone on the verge of death. But her chest rose and fell with even breaths; her skin was full of color.

One of the Med-jacks was there, the shorter one—Thomas couldn't remember his name—dropping water into the comatose girl's mouth a few drips at a time. A plate and bowl on the bedside table had the remains of her lunch—mashed potatoes and soup. They were doing everything possible to keep her alive and healthy.

"Hey, Clint," Newt said, sounding comfortable, like he'd stopped by to visit many times before. "She surviving?"

"Yeah," Clint answered. "She's doing fine, though she talks in her sleep all the time. We think she'll come out of it soon."

Thomas felt his hackles rise. For some reason, he'd never really considered the possibility that the girl might wake up and be okay. That she might talk to people. He had no idea why that suddenly made him so nervous.

"Have you been writin' down every word she says?" Newt asked.

Clint nodded. "Most of it's impossible to understand. But yeah, when we can."

Newt pointed at a notepad on the nightstand. "Give me an example."

"Well, the same thing she said when we pulled her out of the Box, about things changing. Other stuff about the Creators and how 'it all has to end.' And, uh . . ." Clint looked at Thomas as if he didn't want to continue in his company.

"It's okay—he can hear whatever I hear," Newt assured him.

"Well . . . I can't make it all out, but . . ." Clint looked at Thomas again. "She keeps saying *his* name over and over."

Thomas almost fell down at this. Would the references to him never end? How did he know this girl? It was like a maddening itch inside his skull that wouldn't go away.

"Thanks, Clint," Newt said in what sounded to Thomas like an obvious dismissal. "Get us a report of all that, okay?"

"Will do." The Med-jack nodded at both of them and left the room.

"Pull up a chair," Newt said as he sat on the edge of the bed. Thomas, relieved that Newt still hadn't erupted into accusations, grabbed the one from the desk and placed it right next to where the girl's head lay; he sat down, leaning forward to look at her face.

"Anything ring a bell?" Newt asked. "Anything at all?"

Thomas didn't respond, kept looking, willing his mind to break down the memory barrier and seek out this girl from his past. He thought back to those brief moments when she'd opened her eyes right after being pulled out of the Box.

They'd been blue, richer in color than the eyes of any other person he could remember seeing before. He tried to picture those eyes on her now as he looked at her slumbering face, melding the two images in his mind. Her black hair, her perfect white skin, her full lips. . . . As he stared at her, he realized once more how truly beautiful she was.

Stronger recognition briefly tickled the back of his mind—a flutter of wings in a dark corner, unseen but there all the same. It lasted only an instant before vanishing into the abyss of his other captured memories. But he had *felt* something.

"I do know her," he whispered, leaning back in his chair. It felt good to finally admit it out loud.

Newt stood up. "What? Who is she?"

"No idea. But something clicked—I know her from somewhere." Thomas rubbed his eyes, frustrated that he couldn't solidify the link.

"Well, keep bloody thinking—don't lose it. Concentrate."

"I'm trying, so shut up." Thomas closed his eyes, searched the darkness of his thoughts, seeking her face in that emptiness. Who *was* she? The irony of the question struck him—he didn't even know who *he* was.

He leaned forward in his chair and took a deep breath, then looked at Newt, shaking his head in surrender. "I just don't—"

Teresa.

Thomas jolted up from the chair, knocked it backward, spun in a circle, searching. He had heard . . .

"What's wrong?" Newt asked. "Did ya remember somethin'?"

Thomas ignored him, looked around the room in confusion, knowing he'd heard a voice, then back at the girl.

"I . . ." He sat back down, leaned forward, staring at the girl's face. "Newt, did you just say something before I stood up?"

"No."

Of course not. "Oh. I just thought I heard something . . . I don't know. Maybe it was in my head. Did . . . *she* say anything?"

"Her?" Newt asked, his eyes lit up. "No. Why? What did you hear?"

Thomas was scared to admit it. "I . . . I swear I heard a name. Teresa."

"Teresa? No, I didn't hear that. Must've sprung loose from your bloody memory blocks! That's her name, Tommy. Teresa. Has to be."

Thomas felt . . . odd—an uncomfortable feeling, like something supernatural had just occurred. "It was . . . I swear I *heard* it. But in my mind, man. I can't explain it."

Thomas.

This time he jumped from the chair and scrambled as far from the bed as possible, knocking over the lamp on the table; it landed with the crash of broken glass. A voice. A girl's voice. Whispery, sweet, confident. He'd heard it. He *knew* he'd heard it.

"What's bloody wrong with you?" Newt asked.

Thomas's heart was racing. He felt the thumps in his skull. Acid boiled in his stomach. "She's . . . she's freakin' *talking* to me. In my head. She just said my name!"

"What?"

"I swear!" The world spun around him, pressed in, crushing his mind. "I'm . . . hearing her voice in my head—or something . . . it's not really a voice. . . ."

"Tommy, sit your butt down. *What* are you bloody talking about?"

"Newt, I'm serious. It's . . . not really a voice . . . but it *is*."

Tom, we're the last ones. It'll end soon. It has to.

The words echoed in his mind, touched his eardrums—he could *hear* them. Yet they didn't sound like they were coming from the room, from outside his body. They were literally, in every way, *inside* his mind.

Tom, don't freak out on me.

He put his hands up to his ears, squeezed his eyes shut. It was too strange; he couldn't bring his rational mind to accept what was happening.

My memory's fading already, Tom. I won't remember much when I wake up. We can pass the Trials. It has to end. They sent me as a trigger.

Thomas couldn't take it anymore. Ignoring Newt's questions, he stumbled to the door and yanked it open, stepped into the hall, ran. Down the stairs, out the front door, he ran. But it did nothing to shut her up.

Everything is going to change, she said.

He wanted to scream, run until he could run no more. He made it to the East Door and sprinted through it, out of the Glade. Kept going, through corridor after corridor, deep into the heart of the Maze, rules or no rules. But he still couldn't escape the voice.

It was you and me, Tom. We *did this to them. To us.*

CHAPTER 29

Thomas didn't stop until the voice had gone for good.

It shocked him when he realized he'd been running for almost an hour—the shadows of the walls ran long toward the east, and soon the sun would set for the night and the Doors would close. He had to get back. It only peripherally hit him then that without thinking he'd recognized the direction and the time. That his instincts were strong.

He had to get back.

But he didn't know if he could face her again. The voice in his head. The strange things she'd said.

He had no choice. Denying the truth would solve nothing. And as bad—as weird—as the invasion of his mind had been, it beat another date with the Grievers any day.

As he ran toward the Glade, he learned a lot about himself. Without meaning to or realizing it, he'd pictured in his mind his exact route through the Maze as he escaped the voice. Not once did he falter on his return, turning left and right and running down long corridors in reverse of the way he had come. He knew what it meant.

Minho had been right. Soon, Thomas would be the best Runner.

The second thing he learned about himself, as if the night in the Maze hadn't proved it already, was that his body was in perfect shape. Just a day earlier he'd been at the end of his strength and sore from top to bottom. He'd recovered quickly, and ran now with almost no effort, despite nearing the end of his second hour of running. It didn't take a math genius to calculate that his speed and time combined meant he'd run roughly half a marathon by the time he returned to the Glade.

Never before had the sheer size of the Maze truly hit him. Miles and miles and miles. With its walls that moved, every night, he finally understood why the Maze was so hard to solve. He'd doubted it until now, wondered how the Runners could be so inept.

On he ran, left and right, straight, on and on. By the time he'd crossed the threshold into the Glade, the Doors were only minutes away from closing for the night. Exhausted, he headed straight for the Deadheads, went deep into the forest until he reached the spot where the trees crowded against the southwest corner. More than anything, he wanted to be alone.

When he could hear only the sounds of distant Glader conversations, as well as faint echoes of bleating sheep and snorting pigs, his wish was granted; he found the junction of the two giant walls and collapsed into the corner to rest. No one came, no one bothered him. The south wall eventually moved, closing for the night; he leaned forward until it stopped. Minutes later, his back once again comfortably pressed against thick layers of ivy, he fell asleep.

The next morning, someone gently shook him awake.

"Thomas, wake up." It was Chuck—the kid seemed to be able to find him anywhere.

Groaning, Thomas leaned forward, stretched out his back and arms. A couple of blankets had been placed over him during the night—someone playing the Glade Mother.

"What time is it?" he asked.

"You're almost too late for breakfast." Chuck tugged on his arm. "Come on, get up. You need to start acting normal or things'll just get worse."

The events of the previous day came crashing into Thomas's mind, and his stomach seemed to twist inside out. *What are they going to do to me?* he thought. *Those things she said. Something about me and her doing this to them. To us. What did that* mean?

Then it hit him that maybe he was crazy. Maybe the stress of the Maze had driven him insane. Either way, only *he* had heard the voice inside his head. No one else knew the weird things Teresa had said, or accused him of. They didn't even know that she had told him her name. Well, no one except Newt.

And he would keep it that way. Things were bad enough—no way he'd make it worse by telling people about voices in his head. The only problem was Newt. Thomas would have to convince him somehow that stress had finally overwhelmed him and a good night's rest had solved everything. *I'm not crazy,* Thomas told himself. Surely he wasn't.

Chuck was looking at him with eyebrows raised.

"Sorry," Thomas said as he stood up, acting as normal as he could. "Just thinking. Let's eat, I'm starving."

"Good that," Chuck said, slapping Thomas on the back.

They headed for the Homestead, Chuck yapping the whole time. Thomas wasn't complaining—it was the closest thing to normal in his life.

"Newt found you last night and told everyone to let you sleep. *And* he told us what the Council decided about you—one day in the cell, then you'll enter the Runner training program. Some shanks grumbled, some cheered, most acted like they couldn't care less. As for me, I think it's pretty awesome." Chuck paused to take a breath, then kept going. "That first night, when you were bragging about being a Runner and all that klunk—shuck it, I was laughing inside so hard. I kept telling myself, this sucker's in for a rude awakening. Well, you proved *me* wrong, huh?"

But Thomas didn't feel like talking about it. "I just did what anyone else would've done. It's not my fault Minho and Newt want me to be a Runner."

"Yeah, right. Quit being modest."

Being a Runner was the last thing on Thomas's mind. What he couldn't stop thinking about was Teresa, the voice in his head, what she'd *said*. "I guess I'm a little excited." Thomas forced a grin, though he cringed at the thought of hanging out in the Slammer by himself all day before he got to start.

"We'll see how you feel after running your guts out. Anyway, as long as you know old Chucky is proud of you."

Thomas smiled at his friend's enthusiasm. "If only you were my mom," Thomas murmured, "life'd be a peach." *My mom,* he thought. The world seemed to darken for a moment—he couldn't even remember his own mother. He pushed the thought away before it consumed him.

They made it to the kitchen and grabbed a quick breakfast, taking two empty seats at the big table inside. Every Glader going in and out the door gave Thomas a stare; a few came up and offered congratulations. Other than a sprinkling of dirty looks here and there, most people seemed to be on his side. Then he remembered Gally.

"Hey, Chuck," he asked after taking a bite of eggs, trying to sound casual. "Did they ever find Gally?"

"No. I was gonna tell you—someone said they saw him run out into the Maze after he left the Gathering. Hasn't been seen since."

Thomas dropped his fork, not knowing what he'd expected or hoped for. Either way, the news stunned him. "What? You're serious? He went into the Maze?"

"Yeah. Everyone knows he went nuts—some shank even accused you of killing him when you ran out there yesterday."

"I can't believe . . ." Thomas stared at his plate, trying to understand why Gally would do that.

"Don't worry about it, dude. No one liked him except for his few shuck cronies. They're the ones accusing you of stuff."

Thomas couldn't believe how casually Chuck spoke about it. "Ya know, the guy is probably dead. You're talking about him like he went on vacation."

A contemplative look came over Chuck. "I don't think he's dead."

"Huh? Then where is he? Aren't Minho and I the only ones who've survived a night out there?"

"That's what I'm saying. I think his buddies are hiding him inside the Glade somewhere. Gally was an idiot, but he couldn't possibly be stupid enough to stay out in the Maze all night. Like you."

Thomas shook his head. "Maybe that's *exactly* why he stayed out there. Wanted to prove he could do anything I can do. The guy hates me." A pause. "Hated me."

"Well, whatever." Chuck shrugged as if they were arguing over what to have for breakfast. "If he's dead, you guys'll probably find him eventually. If not, he'll get hungry and show up to eat. I don't care."

Thomas picked up his plate and took it to the counter. "All I want is one normal day—one day to relax."

"Then your bloody wish is granted," said a voice from the kitchen door behind him.

Thomas turned to see Newt there, smiling. That grin sent a wave of reassurance through Thomas, as if he were finding out the world was okay again.

"Come on, ya buggin' jailbird," Newt said. "You can take it easy while you're hangin' in the Slammer. Let's go. Chucky'll bring ya some lunch at noon."

Thomas nodded and headed out the door, Newt leading the way. Suddenly a day in prison sounded excellent. A day to just sit and relax.

Though something told him there was a better chance of Gally bringing him flowers than of passing a day in the Glade with nothing strange happening.

CHAPTER 30

The Slammer stood in an obscure place between the Homestead and the north Glade wall, hidden behind thorny, ragged bushes that looked like they hadn't been trimmed in ages. It was a big block of roughly cut concrete, with one tiny, barred window and a wooden door that was locked with a menacing rusty metal latch, like something out of the Dark Ages.

Newt took out a key and opened it up, then motioned for Thomas to enter. "There's only a chair in there and nothin' at all for ya to do. Enjoy yourself."

Thomas groaned inwardly as he stepped inside and saw the one piece of furniture—an ugly, rickety chair with one leg obviously shorter than the rest, probably on purpose. Didn't even have a cushion.

"Have fun," Newt said before closing the door. Thomas turned back to his new home and heard the latch close and the lock click behind him. Newt's head appeared at the little glassless window, looking through the bars, a smirk on his face. "Nice reward for breakin' the rules. You saved some lives, Tommy, but ya still need to learn—"

"Yeah, I know. *Order.*"

Newt smiled. "You're not half bad, shank. But friends or no, gotta run things properly, keep us buggers alive. Think about that while ya sit here and stare at the bloody walls."

And then he was gone.

★ ★ ★

The first hour passed, and Thomas felt boredom creep in like rats under the door. By hour number two, he wanted to bang his head against the wall. Two hours after that he started to think having dinner with Gally and the Grievers would beat sitting inside that stupid Slammer. He sat and tried to bring back memories, but every effort evaporated into oblivious mist before anything formed.

Thankfully, Chuck arrived with lunch at noon, relieving Thomas from his thoughts.

After passing some pieces of chicken and a glass of water through the window, he took up his usual role of talking Thomas's ear off.

"Everything's getting back to normal," the boy announced. "The Runners are out in the Maze, everyone's working—maybe we'll survive after all. Still no sign of Gally—Newt told the Runners to come back lickety-splickety if they found his body. And, oh, yeah—Alby's up and around. Seems fine—and Newt's glad he doesn't have to be the big boss anymore."

The mention of Alby pulled Thomas's attention from his food. He pictured the older boy thrashing around, choking himself the day before. Then he remembered that no one else knew what Alby had said after Newt left the room—before the seizure. But that didn't mean Alby would keep it between them now that he was up and walking around.

Chuck continued talking, taking a completely unexpected turn. "Thomas, I'm kinda messed up, man. It's weird to feel sad and homesick, but have no idea what it is you wish you could go back to, ya know? All I know is I don't want to be here. I want to go back to my family. Whatever's there, whatever I was taken from. I wanna *remember*."

Thomas was a little surprised. He'd never heard Chuck say something so deep and so true. "I know what you mean," he murmured.

Chuck was too short for his eyes to reach where Thomas could see them as he spoke, but from his next statement, Thomas imagined them filling with a bleak sadness, maybe even tears. "I used to cry. Every night."

This made thoughts of Alby leave Thomas's mind. "Yeah?"

"Like a pants-wettin' baby. Almost till the day you got here. Then I just got used to it, I guess. This became home, even though we spend every day hoping to get out."

"I've only cried once since showing up, but that was after almost getting eaten alive. I'm probably just a shallow shuck-face." Thomas might not have admitted it if Chuck hadn't opened up.

"You cried?" he heard Chuck say through the window. "Then?"

"Yeah. When the last one finally fell over the Cliff, I broke down and sobbed till my throat and chest hurt." Thomas remembered all too well. "Everything crushed in on me at once. Sure made *me* feel better—don't feel bad about crying. Ever."

"Kinda *does* make ya feel better, huh? Weird how that works."

A few minutes passed in silence. Thomas found himself hoping Chuck wouldn't leave.

"Hey, Thomas?" Chuck asked.

"Still here."

"Do you think I have parents? *Real* parents?"

Thomas laughed, mostly to push away the sudden surge of sadness the statement caused. "Of course you do, shank. You need me to explain the birds and bees?" Thomas's heart hurt—he could remember getting that lecture but not who'd given it to him.

"That's not what I meant," Chuck said, his voice completely devoid of cheer. It was low and bleak, almost a mumble. "Most of the guys who've gone through the Changing remember terrible things they won't even talk about, which makes me doubt I have anything good back home. So, I mean, you think it's really possible I have a mom and a dad out in the world somewhere, missing me? Do you think *they* cry at night?"

Thomas was completely shocked to realize his eyes had filled with tears. Life had been so crazy since he'd arrived, he'd never really thought of the Gladers as real people with real families, missing them. It was strange, but he hadn't even really thought of himself that way. Only about what it all meant, who'd sent them there, how they'd ever get out.

For the first time, he felt something for Chuck that made him so angry he wanted to kill somebody. The boy should be in school, in a home, playing with neighborhood kids. He deserved to go home at night to a family who loved him, worried about him. A mom who made him take a shower every day and a dad who helped him with homework.

Thomas hated the people who'd taken this poor, innocent kid from his family. He hated them with a passion he didn't know a human could feel. He wanted them dead, tortured, even. He wanted Chuck to be happy.

But happiness had been ripped from their lives. *Love* had been ripped from their lives.

"Listen to me, Chuck." Thomas paused, calming down as much as he could, making sure his voice didn't crack. "I'm sure you have parents. I know it. Sounds terrible, but I bet your mom is sitting in your room right now, holding your pillow, looking out at the world that stole you from her. And yeah, I bet she's crying. Hard. Puffy-eyed, snotty-nosed crying. The real deal."

Chuck didn't say anything, but Thomas thought he heard the slightest of sniffles.

"Don't give up, Chuck. We're gonna solve this thing, get out of here. I'm a Runner now—I promise on my life I'll get you back to that room of yours. Make your mom quit crying." And Thomas meant it. He felt it *burn* in his heart.

"Hope you're right," Chuck said with a shaky voice. He showed a thumbs-up sign in the window, then walked away.

Thomas stood up to pace around the little room, fuming with an intense desire to keep his promise. "I swear, Chuck," he whispered to no one. "I swear I'll get you back home."

CHAPTER 31

Just after Thomas heard the grind and rumble of stone against stone announce the closing of the Doors for the day, Alby showed up to release him, which was a huge surprise. The metal of key and lock jingled; then the door to the cell swung wide open.

"Ain't dead, are ya, shank?" Alby asked. He looked so much better than the day before, Thomas couldn't help staring at him. His skin was back to full color, his eyes no longer crisscrossed with red veins; he seemed to have gained fifteen pounds in twenty-four hours.

Alby noticed him goggling. "Shuck it, boy, what you lookin' at?"

Thomas shook his head slightly, feeling like he'd been in a trance. His mind was racing, wondering what Alby remembered, what he knew, what he might say about him. "Wha—Nothing. Just seems crazy you healed so quickly. You're fine now?"

Alby flexed his right bicep. "Ain't never been better—come on out."

Thomas did, hoping his eyes weren't flickering, making his concern obvious.

Alby closed the Slammer door and locked it, then turned to face him. "Actually, nothin' but a lie. I feel like a piece of klunk twice crapped by a Griever."

"Yeah, you looked it yesterday." When Alby glared, Thomas hoped it was in jest and quickly clarified. "But today you look brand-new. I swear."

Alby put the keys in his pocket and leaned back against the Slammer's door. "So, quite the little talk we had yesterday."

Thomas's heart pounded. He had no idea what to expect from Alby at that point. "Uh . . . yeah, I remember."

"I saw what I saw, Greenie. It's kinda fadin', but I ain't never gonna forget. It was terrible. Tried to talk about it, somethin' starts choking me. Now the images are gettin' up and gone, like that same somethin' don't like me remembering."

The scene from the day before flashed in Thomas's mind. Alby thrashing, trying to strangle himself—Thomas wouldn't have believed it had happened if he hadn't seen it himself. Despite fearing an answer, he knew he had to ask the next question. "What was it about me—you kept saying you saw me. What was I doing?"

Alby stared at an empty space in the distance for a while before answering. "You were with the . . . Creators. Helping them. But that ain't what got me shook up."

Thomas felt like someone had just rammed their fist in his abdomen. *Helping them*? He couldn't form the words to ask what that meant.

Alby continued. "I hope the Changing doesn't give us real memories—just plants fake ones. Some suspect it—I can only hope. If the world's the way I saw it . . ." He trailed off, leaving an ominous silence.

Thomas was confused, but pressed on. "Can't you tell me what you saw about me?"

Alby shook his head. "No way, shank. Ain't gonna risk stranglin' myself again. Might be something they got in our brains to control us—just like the memory wipe."

"Well, if I'm evil, maybe you should leave me locked up." Thomas half meant it.

"Greenie, you ain't evil. You might be a shuck-faced slinthead, but you ain't evil." Alby showed the slightest hint of a smile, a bare crack in his usually hard face. "What you did—riskin' your butt to save me and Minho—that ain't no evil I've ever heard of. Nah, just makes me think the Grief Serum and the Changing got somethin' fishy about 'em. For your sake and mine, I hope so."

Thomas was so relieved that Alby thought he was okay, he only heard about half of what the older boy had just said. "How bad *was* it? Your memories that came back."

"I remembered things from growin' up, where I lived, that sort of stuff. And if God himself came down right now and told me I could go back home . . ." Alby looked to the ground and shook his head again. "If it was real, Greenie, I swear I'd go shack up with the Grievers before goin' back."

Thomas was surprised to hear it was so bad—he wished Alby would give details, describe something, anything. But he knew the choking was still too fresh in Alby's mind for him to budge. "Well, maybe they're not real, Alby. Maybe the Grief Serum is some kind of psycho drug that gives you hallucinations." Thomas knew he was grasping at straws.

Alby thought for a minute. "A drug . . . hallucinations . . ." Then he shook his head. "Doubt it."

It had been worth a try. "We still have to escape this place."

"Yeah, thanks, Greenie," Alby said sarcastically. "Don't know what we'd do without your pep talks." Again, the almost-smile.

Alby's change of mood broke Thomas out of his gloom. "Quit calling me Greenie. The girl's the Greenie now."

"Okay, Greenie." Alby sighed, clearly done with the conversation. "Go find some dinner—your terrible prison sentence of *one day* is over."

"One was plenty." Despite wanting answers, Thomas was ready to get away from the Slammer. Plus, he was starving. He grinned at Alby, then headed straight for the kitchen and food.

Dinner was awesome.

Frypan had known Thomas would be coming late, so he'd left a plate full of roast beef and potatoes; a note announced there were cookies in the cupboard. The Cook seemed fully intent on backing up the support he'd shown for Thomas in the Gathering. Minho joined Thomas as he ate, prepping him a little before his first big day of Runner training, giving him a few stats and interesting facts. Things for him to think about as he went to sleep that night.

When they were finished, Thomas headed back to the secluded place where he'd slept the night before, in the corner behind the Deadheads. He thought about his conversation with Chuck, wondered how it would feel to have parents say good night to you.

Several boys milled about the Glade that night, but for the most part it was quiet, like everyone just wanted to go to sleep, end the day and be done with it. Thomas didn't complain—that was exactly what he needed.

The blankets someone had left for him the night before still lay there. He picked them up and settled in, snuggling up against the comforting corner where the stone walls met in a mass of soft ivy. The mixed smells of the forest greeted him as he took his first deep breath, trying to relax. The air felt perfect, and it made him wonder again about the weather of the place. Never rained, never snowed, never got too hot or too cold. If it weren't for the little fact they were torn apart from friends and families and trapped in a Maze with a bunch of monsters, it could be paradise.

Some things here were too perfect. He knew that, but had no explanation.

His thoughts drifted to what Minho had told him at dinner about the size and scale of the Maze. He believed it—he'd realized the massive scale when he'd been to the Cliff. But he just couldn't fathom how such a structure could have been built. The Maze stretched for miles and miles. The Runners had to be in almost superhuman shape to do what they did every day.

And yet they'd *never* found an exit. And despite that, despite the utter hopelessness of the situation, they still hadn't given up.

At dinner Minho had told him an old story—one of the bizarre and random things he remembered from before—about a woman trapped in a maze. She escaped by never taking her right hand off the walls of the maze, sliding it along as she walked. In doing so, she was forced to turn right at every turn, and the simple laws of physics and geometry ensured that eventually she found the exit. It made sense.

But not here. Here, all paths led back to the Glade. They had to be missing *something*.

Tomorrow, his training would begin. Tomorrow, he could start helping them find that missing something. Right then Thomas made a decision. Forget all the weird stuff. Forget all the bad things. Forget it all. He wouldn't quit until he'd solved the puzzle and found a way home.

Tomorrow. The word floated in his mind until he finally fell asleep.

CHAPTER 32

Minho woke Thomas before dawn, motioning with a flashlight to follow him back to the Homestead. Thomas easily shook off his morning grogginess, excited to begin his training. He crawled out from under his blanket and eagerly followed his teacher, winding his way through the crowd of Gladers who slept on the lawn, their snores the only sign they weren't dead. The slightest glow of early morning illuminated the Glade, turning everything dark blue and shadowed. Thomas had never seen the place look so peaceful. A cock crowed in the Blood House.

Finally, in a crooked cranny near a back corner of the Homestead, Minho pulled out a key and opened up a shabby door leading to a small storage closet. Thomas felt a shiver of anticipation, wondering what was inside. He caught glimpses of ropes and chains and other odds and ends as Minho's flashlight crisscrossed the closet. Eventually, it fell on an open box full of running shoes. Thomas almost laughed, it seemed so ordinary.

"That right there's the number one supply we get," Minho announced. "At least for us. They send new ones in the Box every so often. If we had bad shoes, we'd have feet that look like freaking Mars." He bent over and rummaged through the pile. "What size you wear?"

"Size?" Thomas thought for a second. "I . . . don't know." It was so odd sometimes what he could and couldn't remember. He reached down and pulled off a shoe he'd worn since coming to the Glade and took a look inside. "Eleven."

"Geez, shank, you got big feet." Minho stood up holding a pair of sleek silver ones. "But looks like I've got some—man, we could go canoeing in these things."

"Those are fancy." Thomas took them and walked out of the closet to sit on the ground, eager to try them on. Minho grabbed a few more things before coming out to join him.

"Only Runners and Keepers get these," Minho said. Before Thomas could look up from tying his shoes, a plastic wristwatch dropped into his lap. It was black and very simple, its face showing only a digital display of the time. "Put it on and never take it off. Your life might depend on it."

Thomas was glad to have it. Though the sun and the shadows had seemed plenty to let him know roughly what time it was up to that point, being a Runner probably required more precision. He buckled the watch onto his wrist and then returned to fitting on his shoes.

Minho continued talking. "Here's a backpack, water bottles, lunch pack, some shorts and T-shirts, other stuff." He nudged Thomas, who looked up. Minho was holding out a couple of pairs of tightly cut underwear, made from a shiny white material. "These bad boys're what we call Runnie-undies. Keeps you, um, nice and comfy."

"Nice and comfy?"

"Yeah, ya know. Your—"

"Yeah, got it." Thomas took the underwear and other stuff. "You guys really have this all thought out, don't you?"

"Couple of years runnin' your butt off every day, you figure out what you need and ask for it." He started stuffing things into his own backpack.

Thomas was surprised. "You mean, you can make requests? Supplies you want?" Why would the people who'd sent them there help so much?

"Of course we can. Just drop a note in the Box, and there she goes.

Doesn't mean we always get what we want from the Creators. Sometimes we do, sometimes we don't."

"Ever asked for a map?"

Minho laughed. "Yeah, tried that one. Asked for a TV, too, but no luck. I guess those shuck-faces don't want us seeing how wonderful life is when you don't live in a freaking maze."

Thomas felt a trickle of doubt that life was so great back home—what kind of world allowed people to make kids live like this? The thought surprised him, as if its source had been founded in actual memory, a wisp of light in the darkness of his mind. But it was already gone. Shaking his head, he finished lacing up his shoes, then stood up and jogged around in circles, jumping up and down to test them out. "They feel pretty good. I guess I'm ready."

Minho was still crouched over his backpack on the ground; he glanced up at Thomas with a look of disgust. "You look like an idiot, prancin' around like a shuck ballerina. Good luck out there with no breakfast, no packed lunch, no weapons."

Thomas had already stopped moving, felt an icy chill. "Weapons?"

"Weapons." Minho stood and walked back to the closet. "Come here, I'll show ya."

Thomas followed Minho into the small room and watched as he pulled a few boxes away from the back wall. Underneath lay a small trapdoor. Minho lifted it to reveal a set of wooden stairs leading into blackness. "Keep 'em down in the basement so shanks like Gally can't get to them. Come on."

Minho went first. The stairs creaked with every shift of weight as they descended the dozen or so steps. The cool air was refreshing, despite the dust and the strong scent of mildew. They hit a dirt floor, and Thomas couldn't see a thing until Minho turned on a single lightbulb by pulling a string.

The room was larger than Thomas had expected, at least thirty feet square. Shelves lined the walls, and there were several blocky wooden tables; everything in sight was covered with all manner of junk that gave him the creeps. Wooden poles, metal spikes, large pieces of mesh—like what covers a chicken coop—rolls of barbed wire, saws, knives, swords. One entire wall was dedicated to archery: wooden bows, arrows, spare strings. The sight of it immediately brought back the memory of Ben getting shot by Alby in the Deadheads.

"Wow," Thomas murmured, his voice a dull thump in the enclosed place. At first he was terrified that they needed so many weapons, but he was relieved to see that the vast majority of it was covered with a thick layer of dust.

"Don't use most of it," Minho said. "But ya never know. All we usually take with us is a couple of sharp knives."

He nodded toward a large wooden trunk in the corner, its top open and leaning against the wall. Knives of all shapes and sizes were stacked haphazardly all the way to the top.

Thomas just hoped the room was kept secret from most of the Gladers. "Seems kind of dangerous to have all this stuff," he said. "What if Ben had gotten down here right before he went nuts and attacked me?"

Minho pulled the keys out of his pocket and dangled them with a clickety-clank. "Only a few lucky toads have a set of these."

"Still . . ."

"Quit your bellyachin' and pick a couple. Make sure they're nice and sharp. Then we'll go get breakfast and pack our lunch. I wanna spend some time in the Map Room before we head out."

Thomas was pumped to hear that—he'd been curious about the squat building ever since he'd first seen a Runner go through its menacing door. He selected a short silvery dagger with a rubber grip, then one with a long black blade. His excitement waned a little. Even though he knew perfectly well what lived out there, he still didn't want to think about why he needed weapons to go into the Maze.

A half hour later, fed and packed, they stood in front of the riveted metal door of the Map Room. Thomas was itching to go inside. Dawn had burst forth in all her glory, and Gladers milled about, readying for the day. Smells of frying bacon wafted through the air—Frypan and his crew trying to keep up with dozens of starving stomachs. Minho unlocked the door, cranked the wheel-handle, spinning it until an audible click sounded from inside, then pulled. With a lurching squeal, the heavy metal slab swung open.

"After you," Minho said with a mocking bow.

Thomas went in without saying anything. A cool fear, mixed with an intense curiosity, gripped him, and he had to remind himself to breathe.

The dark room had a musty, wet smell, laced with a deep coppery scent so strong he could taste it. A distant, faded memory of sucking on pennies as a kid popped into his head.

Minho hit a switch and several rows of fluorescent lights flickered until they came on full strength, revealing the room in detail.

Thomas was surprised at its simplicity. About twenty feet across, the Map Room had concrete walls bare of any decoration. A wooden table stood in the exact center, eight chairs tucked in around it. Neatly stacked piles of paper and pencils lay about the table's surface, one for each chair. The only other items in the room were eight trunks, just like the one containing the knives in the weapons basement. Closed, they were evenly spaced, two to a wall.

"Welcome to the Map Room," Minho said. "As happy a place as you could ever visit."

Thomas was slightly disappointed—he'd been expecting something more profound. He took in a deep breath. "Too bad it smells like an abandoned copper mine."

"I kinda like the smell." Minho pulled out two chairs and sat in one of them. "Have a seat, I want you to get a couple of images in your head before we go out there."

As Thomas sat down, Minho grabbed a piece of paper and a pencil and started drawing. Thomas leaned in to get a better look and saw that Minho had drawn a big box that filled almost the entire page. Then he filled it with smaller boxes until it looked exactly like an enclosed tic-tac-toe board, three rows of three squares, all the same size. He wrote the word *GLADE* in the middle, then numbered the outside squares from one to eight, starting in the upper left corner and going clockwise. Lastly, he drew little notches here and there.

"These are the Doors," Minho said. "You know about the ones from the Glade, but there are four more out in the Maze that lead to Sections One, Three, Five, and Seven. They stay in the same spot, but the route there changes with the wall movements every night." He finished, then slid the paper over to rest in front of Thomas.

Thomas picked it up, completely fascinated that the Maze was so structured, and studied it as Minho kept talking.

"So we have the Glade, surrounded by eight Sections, each one a completely self-contained square and unsolvable in the two years since we began this freaking game. The only thing even approaching an exit is the Cliff, and that ain't a very good one unless you like falling to a horrible death." Minho tapped the Map. "The walls move all over the shuck place every evening—same time as our Doors close shut. At least, we think that's when, because we never really hear walls moving any other time."

Thomas looked up, happy to be able to offer a piece of information. "I didn't see anything move that night we got stuck out there."

"Those main corridors right outside the Doors don't ever change. It's just the ones a little deeper out."

"Oh." Thomas returned to the crude map, trying to visualize the Maze and see stone walls where Minho had penciled lines.

"We always have at least eight Runners, including the Keeper. One for each Section. It takes us a whole day to map out our area—hoping against hope there's an exit—then we come back and draw it up, a separate page for each day." Minho glanced over at one of the trunks. "That's why those things are shuck full of Maps."

Thomas had a depressing—and scary—thought. "Am I . . . replacing someone? Did somebody get killed?"

Minho shook his head. "No, we're just training you—someone'll probably want a break. Don't worry, it's been a while since a Runner was killed."

For some reason that last statement worried Thomas, though he hoped it didn't show on his face. He pointed at Section Three. "So . . . it takes you a whole day to run through these little squares?"

"Hilarious." Minho stood and stepped over to the trunk right behind them, knelt down, then lifted the lid and rested it against the wall. "Come here."

Thomas had already gotten up; he leaned over Minho's shoulder and took a look. The trunk was large enough that four stacks of Maps could fit, and all four reached the top. Each of the ones Thomas could see were very similar: a rough sketch of a square maze, filling almost the whole page. In the top right corners, *Section 8* was scribbled, followed by the name *Hank,* then the word *Day,* followed by a number. The latest one said it was day number 749.

Minho continued. "We figured out the walls were moving right at the beginning. As soon as we did, we started keeping track. We've always thought that comparing these day to day, week to week, would help us figure out a pattern. And we did—the mazes basically repeat themselves about every month. But we've yet to see an exit open up that will lead us out of the square. Never been an exit."

"It's been two years," Thomas said. "Haven't you gotten desperate enough to stay out there overnight, see if maybe something opens while the walls are moving?"

Minho looked up at him, a flash of anger in his eyes. "That's kind of insulting, dude. Seriously."

"What?" Thomas was shocked—he hadn't meant it that way.

"We've been bustin' our butts for two years, and all you can ask is why we're too sissy to stay out there all night? A few tried it in the very beginning—all of them showed up dead. You wanna spend another night out there? Like your chances of surviving again, do ya?"

Thomas's face reddened in shame. "No. Sorry." He suddenly felt like a piece of klunk. And he certainly agreed—he'd much rather come home safe and sound to the Glade every night than ensure another battle with the Grievers. He shuddered at the thought.

"Yeah, well." Minho returned his gaze to the Maps in the trunk, much to Thomas's relief. "Life in the Glade might not be sweet livin', but at least it's safe. Plenty of food, protection from the Grievers. There's no way we can ask the Runners to risk staying out there—no way. Least not yet. Not until something about these patterns gives a clue that an exit might open up, even temporarily."

"Are you close? Anything developing?"

Minho shrugged. "I don't know. It's kind of depressing, but we don't know what else to do. Can't take a chance that one day, in one spot, somewhere, an exit might appear. We can't give up. Ever."

Thomas nodded, relieved at the attitude. As bad as things were, giving up would only make them worse.

Minho pulled several sheets from the trunk, the Maps from the last few days. As he flipped through them, he explained, "We compare day to day, week to week, month to month, just like I was saying. Each Runner is in charge of the Map for his own Section. If I gotta be honest, we haven't figured out jack yet. Even more honest—we don't know what we're looking for. Really sucks, dude. Really freaking sucks."

"But we can't give up." Thomas said it in a matter-of-fact tone, as a resigned repeat of what Minho had said a moment earlier. He'd said "we" without even thinking about it, and realized he was truly part of the Glade now.

"Right on, bro. We can't give up." Minho carefully returned the papers and closed the trunk, then stood. "Well, we gotta bust it fast since we took time in here—you'll just be following me around your first few days. Ready?"

Thomas felt a wire of nervousness tighten inside him, pinching his gut. It was actually here—they were going for real now, no more talking and thinking about it. "Um . . . yeah."

"No 'ums' around here. You ready or not?"

Thomas looked at Minho, matched his suddenly hard gaze. "I'm ready."

"Then let's go runnin'."

CHAPTER 33

They went through the West Door into Section Eight and made their way down several corridors, Thomas right beside Minho as he turned right and left without seeming to think about it, running all the while. The early-morning light had a sharp sheen about it, making everything look bright and crisp—the ivy, the cracked walls, the stone blocks of the ground. Though the sun had a few hours before hitting the noon spot up above, there was plenty of light to see by. Thomas kept up with Minho as best he could, having to sprint every once in a while to catch back up.

They finally made it to a rectangular cut in a long wall to the north that looked like a doorway without a door. Minho ran straight through it without stopping. "This leads from Section Eight—the middle left square—to Section One—the top left square. Like I said, this passage is always in the same spot, but the route here might be a little different because of the walls rearranging themselves."

Thomas followed him, surprised at how heavy his breaths had already become. He hoped it was only jitters, that his breathing would steady soon.

They ran down a long corridor to the right, passing several turns to the left. When they reached the end of the passage, Minho slowed to barely more than a walk and reached behind him to pull out a notepad and pencil from a side pocket in his backpack. He jotted a note, then put them back, never fully stopping. Thomas wondered what he'd written, but Minho answered him before he could pose the question.

"I rely . . . mostly on memory," the Keeper huffed, his voice finally showing a hint of strain. "But about every fifth turn, I write something down to help me later. Mostly just related to stuff from yesterday—what's different today. Then I can use yesterday's Map to make today's. Easy-peasy, dude."

Thomas was intrigued. Minho *did* make it sound easy.

They ran for a short while before they reached an intersection. They had three possible choices, but Minho went to the right without hesitating. As he did so, he pulled one of his knives from a pocket and, without missing a beat, cut a big piece of ivy off the wall. He threw it on the ground behind him and kept running.

"Bread crumbs?" Thomas asked, the old fairy tale popping into his mind. Such odd glimpses of his past had almost stopped surprising him.

"Bread crumbs," Minho replied. "I'm Hansel, you're Gretel."

On they went, following the course of the Maze, sometimes turning right, sometimes turning left. After every turn, Minho cut and dropped a three-foot length of ivy. Thomas couldn't help being impressed—Minho didn't even need to slow down to do it.

"All right," the Keeper said, breathing heavier now. "Your turn."

"What?" Thomas hadn't really expected to do anything but run and watch on his first day.

"Cut the ivy now—you gotta get used to doing it on the run. We pick 'em up as we come back, or kick 'em to the side."

Thomas was happier than he thought he'd be at having something to do, though it took him a while to become good at it. First couple of times, he had to sprint to catch up after cutting the ivy, and once he nicked his finger. But by his tenth attempt, he could almost match Minho at the task.

On they went. After they'd run awhile—Thomas had no idea for how long or how far, but he guessed three miles—Minho slowed to a walk, then stopped altogether. "Break time." He swung off his pack and pulled out some water and an apple.

Thomas didn't have to be convinced to follow Minho's lead. He guzzled his water, relishing the wet coolness as it washed down his dry throat.

"Slow down there, fishhead," Minho yelped. "Save some for later."

Thomas stopped drinking, sucked in a big satisfied breath, then burped. He took a bite of his apple, feeling surprisingly refreshed. For some reason, his thoughts turned back to the day Minho and Alby had gone to look at the dead Griever—when everything had gone to klunk. "You never really told me what happened to Alby that day—why he was in such bad shape. Obviously the Griever woke up, but what *happened*?"

Minho had already put his backpack on. He looked ready to go. "Well, shuck thing wasn't dead. Alby poked at it with his foot like an idiot and that bad boy suddenly sprang to life, spikes flaring, its fat body rollin' all over him. Something was wrong with it, though—didn't really attack like usual. It seemed like it was mostly just trying to get out of there, and poor Alby was in the way."

"So it ran away from you guys?" From what Thomas had seen only a few nights before, he couldn't imagine it.

Minho shrugged. "Yeah, I guess—maybe it needed to get recharged or something. I don't know."

"What could've been wrong with it? Did you see an injury or anything?" Thomas didn't know what kind of answer he was searching for, but he was sure there had to be a clue or lesson to learn from what happened.

Minho thought for a minute. "No. Shuck thing just looked dead—like a wax statue. Then boom, it was back to life."

Thomas's mind was churning, trying to get somewhere, only he didn't know where or which direction to even start in. "I just wonder where it *went*. Where they always go. Don't you?" He was quiet for a second, then, "Haven't you ever thought of following them?"

"Man, you *do* have a death wish, don't you? Come on, we gotta go." And with that Minho turned and started running.

As Thomas followed, he struggled to figure out what was tickling the back of his mind. Something about that Griever being dead and then not dead, something about where it had gone once it sprang to life . . .

Frustrated, he put it aside and sprinted to catch up.

Thomas ran right behind Minho for two more hours, sprinkled with little breaks that seemed to get shorter every time. Good shape or not, Thomas was feeling the pain.

Finally, Minho stopped and pulled off his backpack once more. They sat on the ground, leaning against the soft ivy as they ate lunch, neither one of them talking much. Thomas relished every bite of his sandwich and veggies, eating as slowly as possible. He knew Minho would make them get up and go once the food disappeared, so he took his time.

"Anything different today?" Thomas asked, curious.

Minho reached down and patted his backpack, where his notes rested. "Just the usual wall movements. Nothing to get your skinny butt excited about."

Thomas took a long swig of water, looking up at the ivy-covered wall opposite them. He caught a flash of silver and red, something he'd seen more than once that day.

"What's the deal with those beetle blades?" he asked. They seemed to be everywhere. Then Thomas remembered what he'd seen in the Maze—so much had happened he hadn't had the chance to mention it. "And why do they have the word *wicked* written on their backs?"

"Never been able to catch one." Minho finished up his meal and put his lunch box away. "And we don't know what that word means—probably just something to scare us. But they have to be spies. For *them*. Only thing we can reckon."

"Who is *them,* anyway?" Thomas asked, ready for more answers. He hated the people behind the Maze. "Anybody have a clue?"

"We don't know jack about the stupid Creators." Minho's face reddened as he squeezed his hands together like he was choking someone. "Can't wait to rip their—"

But before the Keeper could finish, Thomas was on his feet and across the corridor. "What's that?" he interrupted, heading for a dull glimmer of gray he'd just noticed behind the ivy on the wall, about head high.

"Oh, yeah, that," Minho said, his voice completely indifferent.

Thomas reached in and pulled apart the curtains of ivy, then stared blankly at a square of metal riveted to the stone with words stamped across it in big capital letters. He put his hand out to run his fingers across them, as if he didn't believe his eyes.

WORLD IN CATASTROPHE:
KILLZONE EXPERIMENT DEPARTMENT

He read the words aloud, then looked back at Minho. "What's this?" It gave him a chill—it had to have something to do with the Creators.

"I don't know, shank. They're all over the place, like freaking labels for the nice pretty Maze they built. I quit bothering to look at 'em a long time ago."

Thomas turned back to stare at the sign, trying to suppress the feeling of doom that had risen inside him. "Not much here that sounds very good. Catastrophe. Killzone. *Experiment*. Real nice."

"Yeah, real nice, Greenie. Let's go."

Reluctantly, Thomas let the vines fall back into place and swung his backpack over his shoulders. And off they went, those six words burning holes in his mind.

An hour after lunch, Minho stopped at the end of a long corridor. It was straight, the walls, solid, with no hallways branching off.

"The last dead end," he said to Thomas. "Time to go back."

Thomas sucked in a deep breath, trying not to think about only being halfway done for the day. "Nothing new?"

"Just the usual changes to the way we got here—day's half over," Minho replied as he looked at his watch emotionlessly. "Gotta go back." Without waiting for a response, the Keeper turned and set off at a run in the direction from which they'd just come.

Thomas followed, frustrated that they couldn't take time to examine the walls, explore a little. He finally pulled in stride with Minho. "But—"

"Just shut it, dude. Remember what I said earlier—can't take any chances. Plus, think about it. You really think there's an exit anywhere? A secret trapdoor or something?"

"I don't know . . . maybe. Why do you ask it that way?"

Minho shook his head, spat a big wad of something nasty to his left. "There's no exit. It's just more of the same. A wall is a wall is a wall. Solid."

Thomas felt the heavy truth of it, but pushed back anyway. "How do you know?"

"Because people willing to send Grievers after us aren't gonna give us an easy way out."

This made Thomas doubt the whole point of what they were doing. "Then why even bother coming out here?"

Minho looked over at him. "Why *bother*? Because it's here—gotta be a reason. But if you think we're gonna find a nice little gate that leads to Happy Town, you're smokin' cow klunk."

Thomas looked straight ahead, feeling so hopeless he almost slowed to a stop. "This sucks."

"Smartest thing you've said yet, Greenie."

Minho blew out a big puff of air and kept running, and Thomas did the only thing he knew to do. He followed.

The rest of the day was a blur of exhaustion to Thomas. He and Minho made it back to the Glade, went to the Map Room, wrote up the day's Maze route, compared it to the previous day's. Then there were the walls closing and dinner. Chuck tried talking to him several times, but all Thomas could do was nod and shake his head, only half hearing, he was so tired.

Before twilight faded to blackness, he was already in his new favorite spot in the forest corner, curled up against the ivy, wondering if he could ever run again. Wondering how he could possibly do the same thing tomorrow. Especially when it seemed so pointless. Being a Runner had lost its glamour. After one day.

Every ounce of the noble courage he'd felt, the will to make a difference, the promise to himself to reunite Chuck with his family—it all vanished into an exhausted fog of hopeless, wretched weariness.

He was somewhere very close to sleep when a voice spoke in his head, a pretty, feminine voice that sounded as if it came from a fairy goddess trapped in his skull. The next morning, when everything started going crazy, he'd wonder if the voice had been real or part of a dream. But he heard it all the same, and remembered every word:

Tom, I just triggered the Ending.

CHAPTER 34

Thomas awoke to a weak, lifeless light. His first thought was that he must've gotten up earlier than usual, that dawn was still an hour away. But then he heard the shouts. And then he looked up, through the leafy canopy of branches.

The sky was a dull slab of gray—not the natural pale light of morning.

He jumped to his feet, put his hand on the wall to steady himself as he craned his neck to gawk toward the heavens. There was no blue, no black, no stars, no purplish fan of a creeping dawn. The sky, every last inch of it, was slate gray. Colorless and dead.

He looked down at his watch—it was a full hour past his mandatory waking time. The brilliance of the sun should've awakened him—had done so easily since he'd arrived at the Glade. But not today.

He glanced upward again, half expecting it to have changed back to normal. But it was all gray. Not cloudy, not twilight, not the early minutes of dawn. Just gray.

The sun had disappeared.

Thomas found most of the Gladers standing near the entrance to the Box, pointing at the dead sky, everyone talking at once. Based on the time, breakfast should've already been served, people should be working. But there was something about the largest object in the solar system vanishing that tended to disrupt normal schedules.

In truth, as Thomas silently watched the commotion, he didn't feel nearly as panicked or frightened as his instincts told him he ought to be. And it surprised him that so many of the others looked like lost chicks thrown from the coop. It was, in fact, ridiculous.

The sun obviously had *not* disappeared—that wasn't possible.

Though that was what it seemed like—signs of the ball of furious fire nowhere to be seen, the slanting shadows of morning absent. But he and all the Gladers were far too rational and intelligent to conclude such a thing. No, there had to be a scientifically acceptable reason for what they were witnessing. And whatever it was, to Thomas it meant one thing: the fact they could no longer see the sun probably meant they'd never been able to in the first place. A sun couldn't just disappear. Their sky had to have been—and still was—fabricated. Artificial.

In other words, the sun that had shone down on these people for two years, providing heat and life to everything, was not the sun at all. Somehow, it had been fake. Everything about this place was fake.

Thomas didn't know what that meant, didn't know how it was possible. But he knew it to be true—it was the only explanation his rational mind could accept. And it was obvious from the other Gladers' reactions that none of them had figured this out until now.

Chuck found him, and the look of fear on the boy's face pinched Thomas's heart.

"What do you think happened?" Chuck said, a pitiful tremor in his voice, his eyes glued to the sky. Thomas thought his neck must hurt something awful. "Looks like a big gray ceiling—close enough you could almost touch it."

Thomas followed Chuck's gaze and looked up. "Yeah, makes you wonder about this place." For the second time in twenty-four hours, Chuck had nailed it. The sky *did* look like a ceiling. Like the ceiling of a massive room. "Maybe something's broken. I mean, maybe it'll be back."

Chuck finally quit gawking and made eye contact with Thomas. "Broken? What's that supposed to mean?"

Before Thomas could answer, the faint memory of last night, before he fell asleep, came to him, Teresa's words inside his mind. She'd said, *I just triggered the Ending.* It couldn't be a coincidence, could it? A sour rot crept into his belly. Whatever the explanation, whatever that had been in the sky, the real sun or not, it was gone. And that couldn't be a good thing.

"Thomas?" Chuck asked, lightly tapping him on the upper arm.

"Yeah?" Thomas's mind felt hazy.

"What'd you mean by broken?" Chuck repeated.

Thomas felt like he needed time to think about it all. "Oh. I don't know. Must be things about this place we obviously don't understand. But you can't just make the sun disappear from space. Plus, there's still enough light to see by, as faint as it is. Where's that coming from?"

Chuck's eyes widened, as if the darkest, deepest secret of the universe had just been revealed to him. "Yeah, where *is* it coming from? What's going on, Thomas?"

Thomas reached out and squeezed the younger boy's shoulder. He felt awkward. "No clue, Chuck. Not a clue. But I'm sure Newt and Alby'll figure things out."

"Thomas!" Minho was running up to them. "Quit your leisure time with Chucky here and let's get going. We're already late."

Thomas was stunned. For some reason he'd expected the weird sky to throw all normal plans out the window.

"You're still going out there?" Chuck asked, clearly surprised as well. Thomas was glad the boy had asked the question for him.

"Of course we are, shank," Minho said. "Don't you have some sloppin' to do?" He looked from Chuck to Thomas. "If anything, gives us even more reason to get our butts out there. If the sun's really gone, won't be long before plants and animals drop dead, too. I think the desperation level just went up a notch."

The last statement struck Thomas deep down. Despite all his ideas—all the things he'd pitched to Minho—he wasn't eager to change how things had been done for the last two years. A mixture of excitement and dread swept over him when he realized what Minho was saying. "You mean we're going to stay out there overnight? Explore the walls a little more closely?"

Minho shook his head. "No, not yet. Maybe soon, though." He looked up toward the sky. "Man—what a way to wake up. Come on, let's go."

Thomas was quiet as he and Minho got their things ready and ate a lightning-fast breakfast. His thoughts were churning too much about the gray sky and what Teresa—at least, he thought it had been the girl—had told him in his mind to participate in any conversation.

What had she meant by the Ending? Thomas couldn't knock the feeling that he should tell somebody. Everybody.

But he didn't know what it meant, and he didn't want them to know he had a girl's voice in his head. They'd think he'd really gone bonkers, maybe even lock him up—and for good this time.

After a lot of deliberation, he decided to keep his mouth shut and went running with Minho for his second day of training, below a bleak and colorless sky.

They saw the Griever before they'd even made it to the door leading from Section Eight to Section One.

Minho was a few feet ahead of Thomas. He'd just rounded a corner to the right when he slammed to a stop, his feet almost skidding out from under him. He jumped back and grabbed Thomas by the shirt, pushing him against the wall.

"Shh," Minho whispered. "There's a freaking Griever up there."

Thomas widened his eyes in question, felt his heart pick up the pace, even though it had already been pumping hard and steady.

Minho simply nodded, then put his finger to his lips. He let go of Thomas's shirt and took a step back, then crept up to the corner around which he'd seen the Griever. Very slowly, he leaned forward to take a peek. Thomas wanted to scream at him to be careful.

Minho's head jerked back and he turned to face Thomas. His voice was still a whisper. "It's just sitting up there—almost like that dead one we saw."

"What do we do?" Thomas asked, as quietly as possible. He tried to ignore the panic flaring inside him. "Is it coming toward us?"

"No, idiot—I just told you it was *sitting* there."

"Well?" Thomas raised his hands to his sides in frustration. "What do we do?" Standing so close to a Griever seemed like a really bad idea.

Minho paused a few seconds, thinking before he spoke. "We have to go that way to get to our section. Let's just watch it awhile—if it comes after us, we'll run back to the Glade." He took another peek, then quickly looked over his shoulder. "Crap—it's gone! Come on!"

Minho didn't wait for a response, didn't see the look of horror Thomas had just felt widen his own eyes. Minho took off running in the direction where he'd seen the Griever. Though his instincts told him not to, Thomas followed.

He sprinted down the long corridor after Minho, turned left, then right. At every turn, they slowed so the Keeper could look around the corner first. Each time he whispered back to Thomas that he'd seen the tail end of the Griever disappearing around the next turn. This went on for ten minutes, until they came to the long hallway that ended at the Cliff, where beyond lay nothing but the lifeless sky. The Griever was charging toward that sky.

Minho stopped so abruptly Thomas almost ran him over. Then Thomas stared in shock as up ahead the Griever dug in with its spikes and spun forward right up to the Cliff's edge, then off, into the gray abyss. The creature disappeared from sight, a shadow swallowed by more shadow.

CHAPTER 35

"That settles it," Minho said.

Thomas stood next to him on the edge of the Cliff, staring at the gray nothingness beyond. There was no sign of anything, to the left, right, down, up, or ahead, for as far as he could see. Nothing but a wall of blankness.

"Settles what?" Thomas asked.

"We've seen it three times now. Something's up."

"Yeah." Thomas knew what he meant, but waited for Minho's explanation anyway.

"That dead Griever I found—it ran this way, and we never saw it come back or go deeper into the Maze. Then those suckers we tricked into jumping past us."

"Tricked?" Thomas said. "Maybe not such a trick."

Minho looked over at him, contemplative. "Hmm. Anyway, then this." He pointed out at the abyss. "Not much doubt anymore—somehow the Grievers can *leave the Maze* this way. Looks like magic, but so does the sun disappearing."

"If *they* can leave this way," Thomas added, continuing Minho's line of reasoning, "so could we." A thrill of excitement shot through him.

Minho laughed. "There's your death wish again. Wanna hang out with the Grievers, have a sandwich, maybe?"

Thomas felt his hopes drop. "Got any better ideas?"

“One thing at a time, Greenie. Let’s get some rocks and test this place out. There has to be some kind of hidden exit.”

Thomas helped Minho as they scrabbled around the corners and crannies of the Maze, picking up as many loose stones as possible. They got more by thumbing cracks in the wall, spilling broken chunks onto the ground. When they finally had a sizable pile, they hauled it over right next to the edge and took a seat, feet dangling over the side. Thomas looked down and saw nothing but a gray descent.

Minho pulled out his pad and pencil, placed them on the ground next to him. “All right, we gotta take good notes. And memorize it in that shuck head of yours, too. If there’s some kind of optical illusion hiding an exit from this place, I don’t wanna be the one who screws up when the first shank tries to jump into it.”

“That shank oughtta be the Keeper of the Runners,” Thomas said, trying to make a joke to hide his fear. Being this close to a place where Grievers might come out at any second was making him sweat. “You’d wanna hold on to one beauty of a rope.”

Minho picked up a rock from their pile. “Yeah. Okay, let’s take turns tossing them, zigzagging back and forth out there. If there’s some kind of magical exit, hopefully it’ll work with rocks, too—make them disappear.”

Thomas took a rock and carefully threw it to their left, just in front of where the left wall of the corridor leading to the Cliff met the edge. The jagged piece of stone fell. And fell. Then disappeared into the gray emptiness.

Minho went next. He tossed his rock just a foot or so farther out than Thomas had. It also fell far below. Thomas threw another one, another foot out. Then Minho. Each rock fell to the depths. Thomas kept following Minho’s orders—they continued until they’d marked a line reaching at least a dozen feet from the Cliff, then moved their target pattern a foot to the right and started coming back toward the Maze.

All the rocks fell. Another line out, another line back. All the rocks fell. They threw enough rocks to cover the entire left half of the area in front of them, covering the distance anyone—or any*thing*—could possibly jump. Thomas's discouragement grew with every toss, until it turned into a heavy mass of blah.

He couldn't help chiding himself—it'd been a stupid idea.

Then Minho's next rock disappeared.

It was the strangest, most hard-to-believe thing Thomas had ever seen.

Minho had thrown a large chunk, a piece that had fallen from one of the cracks in the wall. Thomas had watched, deeply concentrating on each and every rock. This one left Minho's hand, sailed forward, almost in the exact center of the Cliff line, started its descent to the unseen ground far below. Then it vanished, as if it had fallen through a plane of water or mist.

One second there, falling. Next second gone.

Thomas couldn't speak.

"We've thrown stuff off the Cliff before," Minho said. "How could we have ever missed that? I never saw anything disappear. Never."

Thomas coughed; his throat felt raw. "Do it again—maybe we blinked weird or something."

Minho did, throwing it at the same spot. And once again, it winked out of existence.

"Maybe you weren't looking carefully other times you threw stuff over," Thomas said. "I mean, it should be impossible—sometimes you don't look very hard for things you don't believe will or can happen."

They threw the rest of the rocks, aiming at the original spot and every inch around it. To Thomas's surprise, the spot in which the rocks disappeared proved only to be a few feet square.

"No wonder we missed it," Minho said, furiously writing down notes and dimensions, his best attempt at a diagram. "It's kind of small."

"The Grievers must barely fit through that thing." Thomas kept his eyes riveted to the area of the invisible floating square, trying to burn the distance and location in his mind, remember exactly where it was. "And when they come out, they must balance on the rim of the hole and jump over the empty space to the Cliff edge—it's not that far. If I could jump it, I'm sure it's easy for them."

Minho finished drawing, then looked up at the special spot. "How's this possible, dude? What're we looking at?"

"Like you said, it's not magic. Must be something like our sky turning gray. Some kind of optical illusion or hologram, hiding a doorway. This place is all jacked up." And, Thomas admitted to himself, kind of cool. His mind craved to know what kind of technology could be behind it all.

"Yeah, jacked up is right. Come on." Minho got up with a grunt and put on his backpack. "Better get as much of the Maze run as we can. With our new decorated sky, maybe other weird things have happened out there. We'll tell Newt and Alby about this tonight. Don't know how it helps, but at least we know now where the shuck Grievers go."

"And probably where they come from," Thomas said as he took one last look at the hidden doorway. "The Griever Hole."

"Yeah, good a name as any. Let's go."

Thomas sat and stared, waiting for Minho to make a move. Several minutes passed in silence and Thomas realized his friend must be as fascinated as he was. Finally, without saying a word, Minho turned to leave. Thomas reluctantly followed and they ran into the gray-dark Maze.

★ ★ ★

Thomas and Minho found nothing but stone walls and ivy.

Thomas did the vine cutting and all the note-taking. It was hard for him to notice any changes from the day before, but Minho pointed out without thinking about it where the walls had moved. When they reached the final dead end and it was time to head back home, Thomas felt an almost uncontrollable urge to bag everything and stay there overnight, see what happened.

Minho seemed to sense it and grabbed his shoulder. "Not yet, dude. Not yet."

And so they'd gone back.

A somber mood rested over the Glade, an easy thing to happen when all is gray. The dim light hadn't changed a bit since they'd woken up that morning, and Thomas wondered if anything would change at "sunset" either.

Minho headed straight for the Map Room as they came through the West Door.

Thomas was surprised. He thought it was the last thing they should do. "Aren't you dying to tell Newt and Alby about the Griever Hole?"

"Hey, we're still Runners," Minho said, "and we still have a job." Thomas followed him to the steel door of the big concrete block and Minho turned to give him a wan smile. "But yeah, we'll do it quick so we can talk to them."

There were already other Runners milling about the room, drawing up their Maps when they entered. No one said a word, as if all speculation on the new sky had been exhausted. The hopelessness in the room made Thomas feel as if he were walking through mud-thick water. He knew he should also be exhausted, but he was too excited to feel it—he couldn't wait to see Newt's and Alby's reactions to the news about the Cliff.

He sat down at the table and drew up the day's Map based on his memory and notes, Minho looking over his shoulder the whole time, giving pointers. "I think that hall was actually cut off here, not there," and "Watch your proportions," and "Draw straighter, you shank." He was annoying but helpful, and fifteen minutes after entering the room, Thomas examined his finished product. Pride washed through him—it was just as good as any other Map he'd seen.

"Not bad," Minho said. "For a Greenie, anyway."

Minho got up and walked over to the Section One trunk and opened it. Thomas knelt down in front of it and took out the Map from the day before and held it up side by side with the one he'd just drawn.

"What am I looking for?" he asked.

"Patterns. But looking at two days' worth isn't gonna tell you jack. You really need to study several weeks, look for patterns, anything. I know there's something there, something that'll help us. Just can't find it yet. Like I said, it sucks."

Thomas had an itch in the back of his mind, the same one he'd felt the very first time in this room. The Maze walls, moving. Patterns. All those straight lines—were they suggesting an entirely different kind of map? Pointing to something? He had such a heavy feeling that he was missing an obvious hint or clue.

Minho tapped him on the shoulder. "You can always come back and study your butt off after dinner, after we talk to Newt and Alby. Come on."

Thomas put the papers in the trunk and closed it, hating the twinge of unease he felt. It was like a prick in his side. Walls moving, straight lines, patterns . . . There had to be an answer. "Okay, let's go."

They'd just stepped outside the Map Room, the heavy door clanging shut behind them, when Newt and Alby walked up, neither one of them looking very happy. Thomas's excitement immediately turned to worry.

"Hey," Minho said. "We were just—"

"Get on with it," Alby interrupted. "Ain't got time to waste. Find anything? Anything?"

Minho actually recoiled at the harsh rebuke, but his face seemed more confused to Thomas than hurt or angry. "Nice to see you, too. Yeah, we *did* find something, actually."

Oddly, Alby almost looked disappointed. "Cuz this whole shuck place is fallin' to pieces." He shot Thomas a nasty glare as if it were all his fault.

What's wrong *with him*? Thomas thought, feeling his own anger light up. They'd been working hard all day and this was their thanks?

"What do you mean?" Minho asked. "What else happened?"

Newt answered, nodding toward the Box as he did so. "Bloody supplies didn't come today. Come every week for two years, same time, same day. But not today."

All four of them looked over at the steel doors attached to the ground. To Thomas, there seemed to be a shadow hovering over it darker than the gray air surrounding everything else.

"Oh, we're shucked for good now," Minho whispered, his reaction alerting Thomas to how grave the situation really was.

"No sun for the plants," Newt said, "no supplies from the bloody Box—yeah, I'd say we're shucked, all right."

Alby had folded his arms, still glaring at the Box as if trying to open the doors with his mind. Thomas hoped their leader didn't bring up what he'd seen in the Changing—or anything related to Thomas, for that matter. Especially now.

"Yeah, anyway," Minho continued. "We found something weird."

Thomas waited, hoping that Newt or Alby would have a positive reaction to the news, maybe even have further information to shed light on the mystery.

Newt raised his eyebrows. "What?"

Minho took a full three minutes to explain, starting with the Griever they followed and ending with the results of their rock-throwing experiment.

"Must lead to where the . . . ya know . . . Grievers *live,*" he said when finished.

"The Griever Hole," Thomas added. All three of them looked at him, annoyed, as if he had no right to speak. But for the first time, being treated like the Greenie didn't bother him that much.

"Gotta bloody see that for myself," Newt said. Then murmured, "Hard to believe." Thomas couldn't have agreed more.

"I don't know what we can do," Minho said. "Maybe we could build something to block off that corridor."

"No way," Newt said. "Shuck things can climb the bloody walls, remember? Nothing *we* could build would keep them out."

But a commotion outside the Homestead shifted their attention away from the conversation. A group of Gladers stood at the front door of the house, shouting to be heard over each other. Chuck was in the group, and when he saw Thomas and the others he ran over, a look of excitement spread across his face. Thomas could only wonder what crazy thing had happened now.

"What's going on?" Newt asked.

"She's awake!" Chuck yelled. "The girl's awake!"

Thomas's insides twisted; he leaned against the concrete wall of the Map Room. The girl. The girl who spoke in his head. He wanted to run before it happened again, before she spoke to him in his mind.

But it was too late.

Tom, I don't know any of these people. Come get me! It's all fading. . . .

I'm forgetting everything but you. . . . I have to tell you things! But it's all fading. . . .

He couldn't understand how she did it, how she was inside his head.

Teresa paused, then said something that made no sense.

The Maze is a code, Tom. The Maze is a code.

CHAPTER 36

Thomas didn't want to see her. He didn't want to see anybody.

As soon as Newt set off to go and talk to the girl, Thomas silently slipped away, hoping no one would notice him in the excitement. With everyone's thoughts on the stranger waking up from her coma, it proved easy. He skirted the edge of the Glade, then, breaking into a run, he headed for his place of seclusion behind the Deadhead forest.

He crouched in the corner, nestled in the ivy, and threw his blanket over himself, head and all. Somehow, it seemed like a way to hide from Teresa's intrusion into his mind. A few minutes passed, his heart finally calming to a slow roll.

"Forgetting about you was the worst part."

At first, Thomas thought it was another message in his head; he squeezed his fists against his ears. But no, it'd been . . . different. He'd heard it with his ears. A girl's voice. Chills creeping up his spine, he slowly lowered the blanket.

Teresa stood to his right, leaning against the massive stone wall. She looked so different now, awake and alert—*standing*. Wearing a long-sleeved white shirt, blue jeans, and brown shoes, she looked—impossibly—even more striking than when he'd seen her in the coma. Black hair framed the fair skin of her face, with eyes the blue of pure flame.

"Tom, do you really not remember me?" Her voice was soft, a contrast from the crazed, hard sound he'd heard from her after she first arrived, when she'd delivered the message that *everything was going to change.*

"You mean . . . you remember *me*?" he asked, embarrassed at the squeak that escaped on the last word.

"Yes. No. Maybe." She threw her arms up in disgust. "I can't explain it."

Thomas opened his mouth, then closed it without saying anything.

"I remember *remembering,*" she muttered, sitting down with a heavy sigh; she pulled her legs up to wrap her arms around her knees. "Feelings. Emotions. Like I have all these shelves in my head, labeled for memories and faces, but they're empty. As if everything before this is just on the other side of a white curtain. Including you."

"But how do you know me?" He felt like the walls were spinning around him.

Teresa turned toward him. "I don't know. Something about before we came to the Maze. Something about us. It's mostly empty, like I said."

"You know about the Maze? Who told you? You just woke up."

"I . . . It's all very confusing right now." She held a hand out. "But I know you're my friend."

Almost in a daze, Thomas pulled the blanket completely off and leaned forward to shake her hand. "I like how you call me Tom." As soon as it came out, he was sure he couldn't have possibly said anything dumber.

Teresa rolled her eyes. "That's your *name,* isn't it?"

"Yeah, but most people call me Thomas. Well, except Newt—he calls me Tommy. Tom makes me feel . . . like I'm at home or something. Even though I don't know what home *is*." He let out a bitter laugh. "Are we messed up or what?"

She smiled for the first time, and he almost had to look away, as if something that nice didn't belong in such a glum and gray place, as if he had no right to look at her expression.

"Yeah, we're messed up," she said. "And I'm scared."

"So am I, trust me." Which was definitely the understatement of the day.

A long moment passed, both of them looking toward the ground.

"What's . . . ," he began, not sure how to ask it. "How . . . did you talk to me inside my mind?"

Teresa shook her head. *No idea—I can just do it,* she thought to him. Then she spoke aloud again. "It's like if you tried to ride a bicycle here—if they had one. I bet you could do it without thinking. But do you remember learning to ride one?"

"No. I mean . . . I remember riding one, but not learning." He paused, feeling a wave of sadness. "Or who taught me."

"Well," she said, her eyes flickering as if she was embarrassed by his sudden gloom. "Anyway . . . it's kind of like that."

"Really clears things up."

Teresa shrugged. "You didn't tell anyone, did you? They'd think we're crazy."

"Well . . . when it first happened, I did. But I think Newt just thinks I was stressed out or something." Thomas felt fidgety, like he'd go nuts if he didn't move. He stood up, started pacing in front of her. "We need to figure things out. That weird note you had about being the last person to ever come here, your coma, the fact you can talk to me telepathically. Any ideas?"

Teresa followed him with her eyes as he walked back and forth. "Save your breath and quit asking. All I have are faint impressions—

that you and I were important, that we were *used* somehow. That we're smart. That we came here for a reason. I know I triggered the Ending, whatever that means." She groaned, her face reddening. "My memories are as useless as yours."

Thomas knelt down in front of her. "No, they're not. I mean, the fact that you knew my memory had been wiped without asking me—and this other stuff. You're way ahead of me and everybody else."

Their eyes met for a long time; it looked like her mind was spinning, trying to make sense of it all.

I just don't know, she said in his mind.

"There you go again," Thomas said aloud, though he was relieved that her trick didn't really freak him out anymore. "How do you do that?"

"I just do, and I bet you can, too."

"Well, can't say I'm too anxious to try." He sat back down and pulled his legs up, much like she had done. "You said something to me—in my head—right before you found me over here. You said 'The Maze is a code.' What did you mean?"

She shook her head slightly. "When I first woke up, it was like I'd entered an insane asylum—these strange guys hovering over my bed, the world tipping around me, memories swirling in my brain. I tried to reach out and grasp a few, and that was one of them. I can't really remember *why* I said it."

"Was there anything else?"

"Actually, yeah." She pulled up the sleeve of her left arm, exposing her bicep. Small letters were written across the skin in thin black ink.

"What's that?" he asked, leaning in for a better look.

"Read it yourself."

The letters were messy, but he could make them out when he got close enough.

WICKED is good

Thomas's heart beat faster. "I've seen that word—*wicked*." He searched his mind for what the phrase could possibly mean. "On the little creatures that live here. The beetle blades."

"What are those?" she asked.

"Just little lizardlike machines that spy on us for the Creators—the people who sent us here."

Teresa considered that for a moment, looking off into space. Then she focused on her arm. "I can't remember why I wrote this," she said as she wet her thumb and started rubbing off the words. "But don't let me forget—it has to mean something."

The three words ran through Thomas's mind over and over. "When did you write it?"

"When I woke up. They had a pen and notepad next to the bed. In the commotion I wrote it down."

Thomas was baffled by this girl—first the connection he'd felt to her from the very beginning, then the mind-speaking, now this. "Everything about you is weird. You know that, right?"

"Judging by your little hiding spot, I'd say you're not so normal yourself. Like living in the woods, do ya?"

Thomas tried to scowl, then smiled. He felt pathetic, and embarrassed about hiding. "Well, you look familiar to me and you claim we're friends. Guess I'll trust you."

He held out his hand for another shake, and she took it, holding on for a long time. A chill swept through Thomas that was surprisingly pleasant.

"All I want is to get back home," she said, finally letting go of his hand. "Just like the rest of you."

Thomas's heart sank as he snapped back to reality and remembered how grim the world had become. "Yeah, well, things pretty much suck right about now. The sun disappeared and the sky's gone gray, they didn't send us the weekly supplies—looks like things are going to end one way or another."

But before Teresa could answer, Newt was running out of the woods. "How in the . . . ," he said as he pulled up in front of them. Alby and a few others were right behind him. Newt looked at Teresa. "How'd you get here? Med-jack said you were there one second and buggin' gone the next."

Teresa stood up, surprising Thomas with her confidence. "Guess he forgot to tell the little part about me kicking him in the groin and climbing out the window."

Thomas almost laughed as Newt turned to an older boy standing nearby, whose face had turned bright red.

"Congrats, Jeff," Newt said. "You're officially the first guy here to get your butt beat by a *girl*."

Teresa didn't stop. "Keep talking like that and you'll be next."

Newt turned back to face them, but his face showed anything but fear. He stood, silently, just staring at them. Thomas stared back, wondering what was going through the older boy's head.

Alby stepped up. "I'm sick of this." He pointed at Thomas's chest, almost tapping it. "I wanna know who you are, who this shank girl is, and how you guys know each other."

Thomas almost wilted. "Alby, I swear—"

"She came straight to you after waking up, shuck-face!"

Anger surged inside Thomas—and worry that Alby would go off like Ben had. "So what? I know her, she knows me—or at least, we used to. That doesn't mean anything! I can't *remember* anything. Neither can she."

Alby looked at Teresa. "What did you do?"

Thomas, confused by the question, glanced at Teresa to see if *she* knew what he meant. But she didn't reply.

"What did you do!" Alby screamed. "First the sky, now this."

"I triggered something," she replied in a calm voice. "Not on purpose, I swear it. The Ending. I don't know what it means."

"What's wrong, Newt?" Thomas asked, not wanting to talk to Alby directly. "What happened?"

But Alby grabbed him by the shirt. "What happened? I'll tell ya what happened, shank. Too busy makin' lovey eyes to bother lookin' around? To bother noticing what freaking *time* it is!"

Thomas looked at his watch, realizing with horror what he'd missed, knowing what Alby was about to say before he said it.

"The *walls,* you shuck. The *Doors*. They didn't close tonight."

CHAPTER 37

Thomas was speechless. Everything would be different now. No sun, no supplies, no protection from the Grievers. Teresa had been right from the beginning—everything had changed. Thomas felt as if his breath had solidified, lodged itself in his throat.

Alby pointed at the girl. "I want her locked up. Now. Billy! Jackson! Put her in the Slammer, and ignore every word that comes out of her shuck mouth."

Teresa didn't react, but Thomas did enough for the both of them. "What're you talking about? Alby, you can't—" He stopped when Alby's fiery eyes shot such a look of anger at him he felt his heart stutter. "But . . . how could you possibly blame her for the walls not closing?"

Newt stepped up, lightly placed a hand on Alby's chest and pushed him back. "How could we not, Tommy? She bloody admitted it herself."

Thomas turned to look at Teresa, paled at the sadness in her blue eyes. It felt like something had reached through his chest and squeezed his heart.

"Just be glad you ain't goin' with her, Thomas," Alby said; he gave both of them one last glare before leaving. Thomas had never wanted so badly to punch someone.

Billy and Jackson came forward and grabbed Teresa by both arms, started escorting her away.

Before they could enter the trees, though, Newt stopped them. "Stay with her. I don't care what happens, no one's gonna touch this girl. Swear your lives on it."

The two guards nodded, then walked away, Teresa in tow. It hurt Thomas even more to see how willingly she went. And he couldn't believe how sad he felt—he wanted to keep talking to her. *But I just met her,* he thought. *I don't even know her.* Yet he knew that wasn't true. He already felt a closeness that could only have come from knowing her before the memory-wiped existence of the Glade.

Come see me, she said in his mind.

He didn't know how to do it, how to talk to her like that. But he tried anyway.

I will. At least you'll be safe in there.

She didn't respond.

Teresa?

Nothing.

The next thirty minutes were an eruption of mass confusion.

Though there had been no discernible change in the light since the sun and blue sky hadn't appeared that morning, it still felt like a darkness spread over the Glade. As Newt and Alby gathered the Keepers and put them in charge of making assignments and getting their groups inside the Homestead within the hour, Thomas felt like nothing more than a spectator, not sure how he could help.

The Builders—without their leader, Gally, who was still missing—were ordered to put up barricades at each open Door; they obeyed, although Thomas knew there wasn't enough time and there weren't materials to do much good. It almost seemed to him as if the Keepers wanted people busy, wanted to delay the inevitable panic attacks. Thomas helped as the Builders gathered every loose item they could find and piled them in the gaps, nailing things together as best they could. It looked ugly and pathetic and scared him to death—no way that'd keep the Grievers out.

As Thomas worked, he caught glimpses of the other jobs going on across the Glade.

Every flashlight in the compound was gathered and distributed to as many people as possible; Newt said he planned for everyone to sleep in the Homestead that night, and that they'd kill the lights, except for emergencies. Frypan's task was to take all the nonperishable food out of the kitchen and store it in the Homestead, in case they got trapped there—Thomas could only imagine how horrible that'd be. Others were gathering supplies and tools; Thomas saw Minho carrying weapons from the basement to the main building. Alby had made it clear they could take no chances: they'd make the Homestead their fortress, and must do whatever it took to defend it.

Thomas finally snuck away from the Builders and helped Minho, carrying up boxes of knives and barbwire-wrapped clubs. Then Minho said he had a special assignment from Newt, and more or less told Thomas to get lost, refusing to answer any of his questions.

This hurt Thomas's feelings, but he left anyway, really wanting to talk to Newt about something else. He finally found him, crossing the Glade on his way to the Blood House.

"Newt!" he called out, running to catch up. "You have to listen to me."

Newt stopped so suddenly Thomas almost ran into him. The older boy turned to give Thomas such an annoyed look he thought twice about saying anything.

"Make it quick," Newt said.

Thomas almost balked, not sure how to say what he was thinking.

"You've gotta let the girl go. Teresa." He knew that she could only help, that she might still remember something valuable.

"Ah, glad to know you guys are buddies now." Newt started walking off. "Don't waste my time, Tommy."

Thomas grabbed his arm. "Listen to me! There's something about her—I think she and I were sent here to help end this whole thing."

"Yeah—end it by lettin' the bloody Grievers waltz in here and kill us? I've heard some sucky plans in my day, Greenie, but that's got 'em all beat."

Thomas groaned, wanting Newt to know how frustrated he felt. "No, I don't think that's what it means—the walls not closing."

Newt folded his arms; he looked exasperated. "Greenie, what're you yappin' about?"

Ever since Thomas had seen the words on the wall of the Maze—*world in catastrophe, killzone experiment department*—he'd been thinking about them. He knew if there was anyone who would believe him, it would be Newt. "I think . . . I think we're here as part of some weird experiment, or test, or something like that. But it's supposed to end somehow. We can't live here forever—whoever sent us here *wants* it to end. One way or another." Thomas was relieved to get it off his chest.

Newt rubbed his eyes. "And that's supposed to convince me that everything's jolly—that I should let the girl go? Because she came and everything is suddenly do-or-die?"

"No, you're missing the *point*. I don't think she has anything to do with us being here. She's just a pawn—they sent her here as our last tool or hint or whatever to help us get out." Thomas took a deep breath. "And I think they sent me, too. Just because she was the trigger for the Ending doesn't make her bad."

Newt looked toward the Slammer. "You know what, I don't buggin' care right now. She can handle one night in there—if anything, she'll be safer than us."

Thomas nodded, sensing a compromise. "Okay, we get through tonight, somehow. Tomorrow, when we have a whole day of safety, we can figure out what to do with her. Figure out what we're supposed to do."

Newt snorted. "Tommy, what's gonna make tomorrow any different? It's been two bloody years, ya know."

Thomas had an overwhelming feeling that all of these changes were a spur, a catalyst for the endgame. "Because now we *have* to solve it. We'll be forced to. We can't live that way anymore, day to day, thinking that what matters most is getting back to the Glade before the Doors close, snug and safe."

Newt thought a minute as he stood there, the bustle of the Glader preparations surrounding both of them. "Dig deeper. Stay out there while the walls move."

"Exactly," Thomas said. "That's exactly what I'm talking about. And maybe we could barricade or blow up the entrance to the Griever Hole. Buy time to analyze the Maze."

"Alby's the one who won't let the girl out," Newt said with a nod toward the Homestead. "That guy's not too high on you two shanks. But right now we just gotta slim ourselves and get to the wake-up."

Thomas nodded. "We can fight 'em off."

"Done it before, haven't you, Hercules?" Without smiling or even waiting for a response, Newt walked away, yelling at people to finish up and get inside the Homestead.

Thomas was happy with the conversation—it had gone about as well as he could've possibly hoped. He decided to hurry and talk to Teresa before it was too late. As he sprinted for the Slammer on the back side of the Homestead, he watched as Gladers started moving inside, most of them with arms full of one thing or another.

Thomas pulled up outside the small jail and caught his breath. "Teresa?" he finally asked through the barred window of the lightless cell.

Her face popped up on the other side, startling him.

He let out a small yelp before he could stop it—it took him a second to recover his wits. "You can be downright spooky, ya know?"

"That's very sweet," she said. "Thanks." In the darkness her blue eyes seemed to glow like a cat's.

"You're welcome," he answered, ignoring her sarcasm. "Listen, I've been thinking." He paused to gather his thoughts.

"More than I can say for that Alby schmuck," she muttered.

Thomas agreed, but was anxious to say what he'd come to say. "There's gotta be a way out of this place—we just have to push it, stay out in the Maze longer. And what you wrote on your arm, and what you said about a code, it all has to mean something, right?" *It has to,* he thought. He couldn't help feeling some hope.

"Yeah, I've been thinking the same thing. But first—can't you get me out of here?" Her hands appeared, gripping the bars of the window. Thomas felt the ridiculous urge to reach out and touch them.

"Well, Newt said maybe tomorrow." Thomas was just glad he'd gotten that much of a concession. "You'll have to make it through the night in there. It might actually be the safest place in the Glade."

"Thanks for asking him. Should be fun sleeping on this cold floor." She motioned behind her with a thumb. "Though I guess a Griever can't squeeze through this window, so I'll be happy, right?"

The mention of Grievers surprised him—he didn't remember talking about them to her yet. "Teresa, are you sure you've forgotten everything?"

She thought a second. "It's weird—I guess I do remember some stuff. Unless I just heard people talking while I was in the coma."

"Well, I guess it doesn't matter right now. I just wanted to see you before I went inside for the night." But he didn't want to leave; he almost wished he could get thrown in the Slammer with her. He grinned inside—he could only imagine Newt's response to *that* request.

"Tom?" Teresa said.

Thomas realized he was staring off in a daze. "Oh, sorry. Yeah?"

Her hands slipped back inside, disappeared. All he could see were her eyes, the pale glow of her white skin. "I don't know if I can do this—stay in this jail all night."

Thomas felt an incredible sadness. He wanted to steal Newt's keys and help her escape. But he knew that was a ridiculous idea. She'd just have to suffer and make do. He stared into those glowing eyes. "At least it won't get completely dark—looks like we're stuck with this twilight junk twenty-four hours a day now."

"Yeah. . . ." She looked past him at the Homestead, then focused on him again. "I'm a tough girl—I'll be okay."

Thomas felt horrible leaving her there, but he knew he had no choice. "I'll make sure they let you out first thing tomorrow, okay?"

She smiled, making him feel better. "That's a promise, right?"

"Promise." Thomas tapped his right temple. "And if you get lonely, you can talk to me with your . . . trick all you want. I'll try to answer back." He'd accepted it now, almost wanted it. He just hoped he could figure out how to talk back, so they could have a conversation.

You'll get it soon, Teresa said in his mind.

"I wish." He stood there, really not wanting to leave. At all.

"You better go," she said. "I don't want your brutal murder on my conscience."

Thomas managed his own smile at that. "All right. See you tomorrow."

And before he could change his mind, he slipped away, heading around the corner toward the front door of the Homestead, just as the last couple of Gladers were entering, Newt shooing them in like errant chickens. Thomas stepped inside as well, followed by Newt, who closed the door behind him.

Just before it latched shut, Thomas thought he heard the first eerie moan of the Grievers, coming from somewhere deep in the Maze.

The night had begun.

CHAPTER 38

Most of them slept outside in normal times, so packing all those bodies into the Homestead made for a tight fit. The Keepers had organized and distributed the Gladers throughout the rooms, along with blankets and pillows. Despite the number of people and the chaos of such a change, a disturbing silence hung over the activities, as if no one wanted to draw attention to themselves.

When everyone was settled, Thomas found himself upstairs with Newt, Alby and Minho, and they were finally able to finish their discussion from earlier in the courtyard. Alby and Newt sat on the only bed in the room while Thomas and Minho sat next to them in chairs. The only other furniture was a crooked wooden dresser and a small table, on top of which rested a lamp providing what light they had. The gray darkness seemed to press on the window from outside, with promises of bad things to come.

"Closest I've come so far," Newt was saying, "to hangin' it all up. Shuck it all and kiss a Griever goodnight. Supplies cut, bloody gray skies, walls not closing. But we can't give up, and we all know it. The buggers who sent us here either want us dead or they're givin' us a spur. This or that, we gotta work our arses off till we're dead or not dead."

Thomas nodded, but didn't say anything. He agreed completely but had no concrete ideas on what to do. If he could just make it to tomorrow, maybe he and Teresa could come up with something to help.

Thomas glanced over at Alby, who was staring at the floor,

seemingly lost in his own gloomy thoughts. His face still wore the long, weary look of depression, his eyes sunken and hollow. The Changing had been aptly named, considering what it had done to him.

"Alby?" Newt asked. "Are you gonna pitch in?"

Alby looked up, surprise crossing his face as if he hadn't known that anyone else was in the room. "Huh? Oh. Yeah. Good that. But you've seen what happens at night. Just because Greenie the freaking superboy made it doesn't mean the rest of us can."

Thomas rolled his eyes ever so slightly at Minho—so tired of Alby's attitude.

If Minho felt the same way, he did a good job of hiding it. "I'm with Thomas and Newt. We gotta quit boohooing and feeling sorry for ourselves." He rubbed his hands together and sat forward in his chair. "Tomorrow morning, first thing, you guys can assign teams to study the Maps full-time while the Runners go out. We'll pack our stuff shuck-full so we can stay out there a few days."

"What?" Alby asked, his voice finally showing some emotion. "What do you mean, *days*?"

"I mean, *days*. With open Doors and no sunset, there's no point in coming back here, anyway. Time to stay out there and see if anything opens up when the walls move. *If* they still move."

"No way," Alby said. "We have the Homestead to hide in—and if that ain't workin', the Map Room and the Slammer. We can't freaking ask people to go out there and die, Minho! Who'd volunteer for that?"

"Me," Minho said. "And Thomas."

Everyone looked at Thomas; he simply nodded. Although it scared him to death, exploring the Maze—really exploring it—was something he'd wanted to do from the first time he'd learned about it.

"I will if I have to," Newt said, surprising Thomas; though he'd never talk about it, the older boy's limp was a constant reminder that something horrible had happened to him out in the Maze. "And I'm sure all the Runners'll do it."

"With your bum leg?" Alby asked, a harsh laugh escaping his lips.

Newt frowned, looked at the ground. "Well, I don't feel good askin' Gladers to do something if I'm not bloody willing to do it myself."

Alby scooted back on the bed and propped his feet up. "Whatever. Do what you want."

"Do what I want?" Newt asked, standing up. "What's wrong with you, man? Are you tellin' me we have a choice? Should we just sit around on our butts and wait to be snuffed by the Grievers?"

Thomas wanted to stand up and cheer, sure that Alby would finally snap out of his doldrums.

But their leader didn't look in the least bit reprimanded or remorseful. "Well, it sounds better than running *to* them."

Newt sat back down. "Alby. You gotta start talkin' reason."

As much as he hated to admit it, Thomas knew they needed Alby if they were going to accomplish anything. The Gladers looked up to him.

Alby finally took a deep breath, then looked at each of them in turn. "You guys know I'm all screwed up. Seriously, I'm . . . sorry. I shouldn't be the stupid leader anymore."

Thomas held his breath. He couldn't believe Alby had just said that.

"Oh bloody—" Newt started.

"No!" Alby shouted, his face showing humility, surrender. "That's not what I meant. Listen to me. I ain't saying we should switch or any of that klunk. I'm just saying . . . I think I need to let you guys make the decisions. I don't trust myself. So . . . yeah, I'll do whatever."

Thomas could see that both Minho and Newt were as surprised as he was.

"Uh . . . okay," Newt said slowly. As if he was unsure. "We'll make it work, I promise. You'll see."

"Yeah," Alby muttered. After a long pause, he spoke up, a hint of odd excitement in his voice. "Hey, tell you what. Put me in charge of the Maps. I'll freaking work every Glader to the bone studying those things."

"Works for me," Minho said. Thomas wanted to agree, but didn't know if it was his place.

Alby put his feet back on the floor, sat up straighter. "Ya know, it was really stupid for us to sleep in here tonight. We should've been out in the Map Room, working."

Thomas thought that was the smartest thing he'd heard Alby say in a long time.

Minho shrugged. "Probably right."

"Well . . . I'll go," Alby said with a confident nod. "Right now."

Newt shook his head. "Forget that, Alby. Already heard the bloody Grievers moaning out there. We can wait till the wake-up."

Alby leaned forward, elbows on his knees. "Hey, you shucks are the ones giving me all the pep talks. Don't start whining when I actually listen. If I'm gonna do this, I gotta do it, be the old me. I need something to dive into."

Relief flooded Thomas. He'd grown sick of all the contention.

Alby stood up. "Seriously, I need this." He moved toward the door of the room as if he really meant to leave.

"You can't be serious," Newt said. "You can't go out there now!"

"I'm going, and that's that." Alby took his ring of keys from his pocket and rattled them mockingly—Thomas couldn't believe the sudden bravery. "See you shucks in the morning."

And then he walked out.

It was strange to know that the night grew later, that darkness should've swallowed the world around them, but to see only the pale gray light outside. It made Thomas feel off-kilter, as if the urge to sleep that grew steadily with every passing minute were somehow unnatural. Time slowed to an agonizing crawl; he felt as if the next day might never come.

The other Gladers settled themselves, turning in with their pillows and blankets for the impossible task of sleeping. No one said much, the mood somber and grim. All you could hear were quiet shuffles and whispers.

Thomas tried hard to force himself to sleep, knowing it would make the time pass faster, but after two hours he'd still had no luck. He lay on the floor in one of the upper rooms, on top of a thick blanket, several other Gladers crammed in there with him, almost body to body. The bed had gone to Newt.

Chuck had ended up in another room, and for some reason Thomas pictured him huddled in a dark corner, crying, squeezing his blankets to his chest like a teddy bear. The image saddened Thomas so deeply he tried to replace it, but to no avail.

Almost every person had a flashlight by their side in case of emergency. Otherwise, Newt had ordered all lights extinguished despite the pale, deathly glow of their new sky—no sense attracting any more attention than necessary. Anything that *could* be done on such short notice to prepare for a Griever attack had been done: windows boarded up, furniture moved in front of doors, knives handed out as weapons . . .

But none of that made Thomas feel safe.

The anticipation of what might happen was overpowering, a suffocating blanket of misery and fear that began to take on a life of its own. He almost wished the suckers would just come and get it over with. The waiting was unbearable.

The distant wails of the Grievers grew closer as the night stretched on, every minute seeming to last longer than the one before it.

Another hour passed. Then another. Sleep finally came, but in miserable fits. Thomas guessed it was about two in the morning when he turned from his back to his stomach for the millionth time that night. He put his hands under his chin and stared at the foot of the bed, almost a shadow in the dim light.

Then everything changed.

A mechanized surge of machinery sounded from outside, followed by the familiar rolling clicks of a Griever on the stony ground, as if someone had scattered a handful of nails. Thomas shot to his feet, as did most of the others.

But Newt was up before anyone, waving his arms, then shushing the room by putting a finger to his lips. Favoring his bad leg, he tiptoed toward the lone window in the room, which was covered by three hastily nailed boards. Large cracks allowed for plenty of space to peek outside. Carefully, Newt leaned in to take a look, and Thomas crept over to join him.

He crouched below Newt against the lowest of the wooden boards, pressing his eye against a crack—it was terrifying being so close to the wall. But all he saw was the open Glade; he didn't have enough space to look up or down or to the side, just straight ahead. After a minute or so, he gave up and turned to sit with his back against the wall. Newt walked over and sat back down on the bed.

A few minutes passed, various Griever sounds penetrating the walls every ten to twenty seconds. The squeal of small engines followed by a grinding spin of metal. The clicking of spikes against the hard stone. Things snapping and opening and snapping. Thomas winced in fear every time he heard something.

Sounded like three or four of them were just outside. At least.

He heard the twisted animal-machines come closer, so close, waiting on the stone blocks below. All hums and metallic clatter.

Thomas's mouth dried up—he'd seen them face to face, remembered it all too well; he had to remind himself to breathe. The others in the room were still; no one made a sound. Fear seemed to hover in the air like a blizzard of black snow.

One of the Grievers sounded like it was moving toward the house. Then the clicking of its spikes against the stone suddenly turned into a deeper, hollower sound. Thomas could picture it all: the creature's metal spikes digging into the wooden sides of the Homestead, the massive creature rolling its body, climbing up toward their room, defying gravity with its strength. Thomas heard the Grievers' spikes shred the wood siding in their path as they tore out and rotated around to take hold once again. The whole building shuddered.

The crunching and groaning and snapping of the wood became the only sounds in the world to Thomas, horrifying. They grew louder, *closer*—the other boys had shuffled across the room and as far away from the window as possible. Thomas finally followed suit, Newt right beside him; everyone huddled against the far wall, staring at the window.

Just when it grew unbearable—just as Thomas realized the Griever was right outside the window—everything fell silent. Thomas could almost hear his own heart beating.

Lights flickered out there, casting odd beams through the cracks between the wooden boards. Then a thin shadow interrupted the light, moving back and forth. Thomas knew that the Griever's probes and weapons had come out, searching for a feast. He imagined beetle blades out there, helping the creatures find their way. A few seconds later the shadow stopped; the light settled to a standstill, casting three unmoving planes of brightness into the room.

The tension in the air was thick; Thomas couldn't hear anyone breathing. He thought much the same must be going on in the other rooms of the Homestead. Then he remembered Teresa in the Slammer.

He was just wishing she'd say something to him when the door from the hallway suddenly whipped open. Gasps and shouts exploded throughout the room. The Gladers had been expecting something from the window, not from behind them. Thomas turned to see who'd opened the door, expecting a frightened Chuck or maybe a reconsidering Alby. But when he saw who stood there, his skull seemed to contract, squeezing his brain in shock.

It was Gally.

CHAPTER 39

Gally's eyes raged with lunacy; his clothes were torn and filthy. He dropped to his knees and stayed there, his chest heaving with deep, sucking breaths. He looked about the room like a rabid dog searching for someone to bite. No one said a word. It was as if they all believed as Thomas did—that Gally was only a figment of their imagination.

"They'll kill you!" Gally screamed, spittle flying everywhere. "The Grievers will kill you all—one every night till it's over!"

Thomas watched, speechless, as Gally staggered to his feet and walked forward, dragging his right leg with a heavy limp. No one in the room moved a muscle as they watched, obviously too stunned to do anything. Even Newt stood mouth agape. Thomas was almost more afraid of their surprise visitor than he was of the Grievers just outside the window.

Gally stopped, standing just a few feet in front of Thomas and Newt; he pointed at Thomas with a bloody finger. "You," he said with a sneer so pronounced it went past comical to flat-out disturbing. "It's all your fault!" Without warning he swung his left hand, forming it into a fist as it came around and crashed into Thomas's ear. Crying out, Thomas crumpled to the ground, more taken by surprise than pain. He scrambled to his feet as soon as he'd hit the floor.

Newt had finally snapped out of his daze and pushed Gally away. Gally stumbled backward and crashed into the desk by the window. The lamp scooted off the side and broke into pieces on the ground. Thomas assumed Gally would retaliate, but he straightened instead, taking everyone in with his mad gaze.

"It can't be solved," he said, his voice now quiet and distant, spooky. "The shuck Maze'll kill all you shanks. . . . The Grievers'll kill you . . . one every night till it's over. . . . I . . . It's better this way. . . ." His eyes fell to the floor. "They'll only kill you one a night . . . their stupid Variables . . ."

Thomas listened in awe, trying to suppress his fear so he could memorize everything the crazed boy said.

Newt took a step forward. "Gally, shut your bloody hole—there's a Griever right out the window. Just sit on your butt and be quiet—maybe it'll go away."

Gally looked up, his eyes narrowing. "You don't get it, Newt. You're too stupid—you've always been too stupid. There's no way out—there's no way to win! They're gonna kill you, all of you—one by *one*!"

Screaming the last word, Gally threw his body toward the window and started tearing at the wooden boards like a wild animal trying to escape a cage. Before Thomas or anyone else could react, he'd already ripped one board free; he threw it to the ground.

"No!" Newt yelled, running forward. Thomas followed to help, in utter disbelief at what was happening.

Gally ripped off the second board just as Newt reached him. He swung it backward with both hands and connected with Newt's head, sent him sprawling across the bed as a small spray of blood sprinkled the sheets. Thomas pulled up short, readying himself for a fight.

"Gally!" Thomas yelled. "What're you *doing*!"

The boy spat on the ground, panting like a winded dog. "You shut your shuck-face, *Thomas*. You shut up! I know who you are, but I don't care anymore. I can only do what's right."

Thomas felt as if his feet were rooted to the ground. He was completely baffled by what Gally was saying. He watched the boy reach back and rip loose the final wooden board. The instant the discarded slab hit the floor of the room, the glass of the window exploded inward like a swarm of crystal wasps. Thomas covered his face and fell to the floor, kicking his legs out to scoot his body as far away as possible. When he bumped into the bed, he gathered himself and looked up, ready to face his world coming to an end.

A Griever's pulsating, bulbous body had squirmed halfway through the destroyed window, metallic arms with pincers snapping and clawing in all directions. Thomas was so terrified, he barely registered that everyone else in the room had fled to the hallway—all except Newt, who lay unconscious on the bed.

Frozen, Thomas watched as one of the Griever's long arms reached for the lifeless body. That was all it took to break him from his fear. He scrambled to his feet, searched the floor around him for a weapon. All he saw were knives—they couldn't help him now. Panic exploded within him, consumed him.

Then Gally was speaking again; the Griever pulled back its arm, as if it needed the thing to be able to observe and listen. But its body kept churning, trying to squeeze its way inside.

"No one ever understood!" the boy screamed over the horrible noise of the creature, crunching its way deeper into the Homestead, ripping the wall to pieces. "No one ever understood what I saw, what the Changing did to me! Don't go back to the real world, Thomas! You *don't . . . want . . .* to remember!"

Gally gave Thomas a long, haunted look, his eyes full of terror; then he turned and dove onto the writhing body of the Griever. Thomas yelled out as he watched every extended arm of the monster immediately retract and clasp onto Gally's arms and legs, making escape or rescue impossible. The boy's body sank several inches into the creature's squishy flesh, making a horrific squelching sound. Then, with surprising speed, the Griever pushed itself back outside the shattered frame of the window and began descending toward the ground below.

Thomas ran to the jagged, gaping hole, looked down just in time to see the Griever land and start scooting across the Glade, Gally's body appearing and disappearing as the thing rolled. The lights of the monster shone brightly, casting an eerie yellow glow across the stone of the open West Door, where the Griever exited into the depths of the Maze. Then, seconds later, several other monsters followed close behind their companion, whirring and clicking as if celebrating their victory.

Thomas was sickened to the verge of throwing up. He began to back away from the window, but something outside caught his eye. He quickly leaned out of the building to get a better look. A lone shape was sprinting across the courtyard of the Glade toward the exit through which Gally had just been taken.

Despite the poor light, Thomas realized who it was immediately. He screamed—yelled at him to stop—but it was too late.

Minho, running full speed, disappeared into the Maze.

CHAPTER 40

Lights blazed throughout the Homestead. Gladers ran about, everyone talking at once. A couple of boys cried in a corner. Chaos ruled.

Thomas ignored all of it.

He ran into the hallway, then leaped down the stairs three at a time. He pushed his way through a crowd in the foyer, tore out of the Homestead and toward the West Door, sprinting. He pulled up just short of the threshold of the Maze, his instincts forcing him to think twice about entering. Newt called to him from behind, delaying the decision.

"Minho followed it out there!" Thomas yelled when Newt caught up to him, a small towel pressed against the wound on his head. A patchy spot of blood had already seeped through the white material.

"I saw," Newt said, pulling the towel away to look at it; he grimaced and put it back. "Shuck it, that hurts like a mother. Minho must've finally fried his last bit of brain cells—not to mention Gally. Always knew he was crazy."

Thomas could only worry about Minho. "I'm going after him."

"Time to be a bloody hero again?"

Thomas looked at Newt sharply, hurt by the rebuke. "You think I do things to impress you shanks? Please. All I care about is getting out of here."

"Yeah, well, you're a regular toughie. But right now we've got worse problems."

"What?" Thomas knew if he wanted to catch up with Minho he had no time for this.

"Somebody—" Newt began.

"There he is!" Thomas shouted. Minho had just turned a corner up ahead and was coming straight for them. Thomas cupped his hands. "What were you doing, idiot!"

Minho waited until he made it back through the Door, then bent over, hands on his knees, and sucked in a few breaths before answering. "I just . . . wanted to . . . make sure."

"Make sure of what?" Newt asked. "Lotta good you'd be, taken with Gally."

Minho straightened and put his hands on his hips, still breathing heavily. "Slim it, boys! I just wanted to see if they went toward the Cliff. Toward the Griever Hole."

"And?" Thomas said.

"Bingo." Minho wiped sweat from his forehead.

"I just can't believe it," Newt said, almost whispering. "What a night."

Thomas's thoughts tried to drift toward the Hole and what it all meant, but he couldn't shake the thought of what Newt had been about to say before they saw Minho return. "What were you about to tell me?" he asked. "You said we had worse—"

"Yeah." Newt pointed his thumb over his shoulder. "You can still see the buggin' smoke."

Thomas looked in that direction. The heavy metal door of the Map Room was slightly ajar, a wispy trail of black smoke drifting out and into the gray sky.

"Somebody burned the Map trunks," Newt said. "Every last one of 'em."

For some reason, Thomas didn't care about the Maps that much—they seemed pointless anyway. He stood outside the window of the Slammer, having left Newt and Minho when they went to investigate the sabotage of the Map Room. Thomas had noticed them exchange an odd look before they split up, almost as if communicating some secret with their eyes. But Thomas could think of only one thing.

"Teresa?" he asked.

Her face appeared, hands rubbing her eyes. "Was anybody killed?" she asked, somewhat groggy.

"Were you *sleeping*?" Thomas asked. He was relieved to see that she appeared okay, felt himself relax.

"I was," she responded. "Until I heard something shred the Homestead to bits. What happened?"

Thomas shook his head in disbelief. "I don't know how you could've slept through the sound of all those Grievers out here."

"You try coming out of a coma sometime. See how you do." *Now answer my question,* she said inside his head.

Thomas blinked, momentarily surprised by the voice since she hadn't done it in a while. "Cut that junk out."

"Just tell me what happened."

Thomas sighed; it was such a long story, and he didn't feel like telling the whole thing. "You don't know Gally, but he's a psycho kid who ran away. He showed up, jumped on a Griever, and they all took off into the Maze. It was really weird." He still couldn't believe it had actually happened.

"Which is saying a lot," Teresa said.

"Yeah." He looked behind him, hoping to see Alby somewhere.

Surely he'd let Teresa out now. Gladers were scattered all over the complex, but there was no sign of their leader. He turned back to Teresa. "I just don't get it. Why would the Grievers have left after getting Gally? He said something about them killing us one a night until we were all dead—he said it at least twice."

Teresa put her hands through the bars, rested her forearms against the concrete sill. "Just one a night? Why?"

"I don't know. He also said it had to do with . . . trials. Or variables. Something like that." Thomas had the same strange urge he'd had the night before—to reach out and take one of her hands. He stopped himself, though.

"Tom, I was thinking about what you told me I said. That the Maze is a code. Being holed up in here does wonders for making the brain do what it was made for."

"What do you think it means?" Intensely interested, he tried to block out the shouts and chatter rumbling through the Glade as others found out about the Map Room being burned.

"Well, the walls move every day, right?"

"Yeah." He could tell she was really on to something.

"And Minho said they think there's a pattern, right?"

"Right." Gears were starting to shift into place inside Thomas's head as well, almost as if a prior memory was beginning to break loose.

"Well, I can't remember why I said that to you about the code. I know when I was coming out of the coma all sorts of thoughts and memories swirled through my head like crazy, almost as if I could feel someone *emptying* my mind, sucking them out. And I felt like I needed to say that thing about the code before I lost it. So there must be an important reason."

Thomas almost didn't hear her—he was thinking harder than he had in a while. "They always compare each section's Map to the one from the day before, and the day before that, and the day before that, day by day, each Runner just analyzing their own Section. What if they're supposed to compare the Maps to *other* sections . . ." He trailed off, feeling like he was on the cusp of something.

Teresa seemed to ignore him, doing her own theorizing. "The first thing the word *code* makes me think of is letters. Letters in the alphabet. Maybe the Maze is trying to *spell* something."

Everything came together so quickly in Thomas's mind, he almost heard an audible click, as if the pieces all snapped into place at once. "You're right—you're right! But the Runners have been looking at it wrong this whole time. They've been analyzing it the wrong way!"

Teresa gripped the bars now, her knuckles white, her face pressed against the iron rods. "What? What're you talking about?"

Thomas grabbed the two bars outside of where she held on, moved close enough to smell her—a surprisingly pleasant scent of sweat and flowers. "Minho said the patterns repeat themselves, only they can't figure out what it means. But they've always studied them section by section, comparing one day to the next. What if each day is a separate piece of the code, and they're supposed to use all eight sections together somehow?"

"You think maybe each day is trying to reveal a word?" Teresa asked. "With the wall movements?"

Thomas nodded. "Or maybe a letter a day, I don't know. But they've always thought the movements would reveal how to escape, not spell something. They've been studying it like a map, not like a picture of something. We've gotta—" Then he stopped, remembering what he'd just been told by Newt. "Oh, no."

Teresa's eyes flared with worry. "What's wrong?"

"Oh no oh no oh no . . ." Thomas let go of the bars and stumbled back a step as the realization hit him. He turned to look at the Map

Room. The smoke had lessened, but it still wafted out the door, a dark, hazy cloud covering the entire area.

"What's wrong?" Teresa repeated. She couldn't see the Map Room from her angle.

Thomas faced her again. "I didn't think it mattered. . . ."

"What!" she demanded.

"Someone *burned* all the Maps. If there was a code, it's gone."

CHAPTER 41

"I'll be back," Thomas said, turning to go. His stomach was full of acid. "I gotta find Newt, see if any of the Maps survived."

"Wait!" Teresa yelled. "Get me out of here!"

But there was no time, and Thomas felt awful about it. "I can't—I'll be back, I promise." He turned before she could protest and set off at a sprint for the Map Room and its foggy black cloud of smoke. Needles of pain pricked his insides. If Teresa was right, and they'd been that close to figuring out some kind of clue to get out of there, only to see it literally lost in flames . . . It was so upsetting it hurt.

The first thing Thomas saw when he ran up was a group of Gladers huddled just outside the large steel door, still ajar, its outer edge blackened with soot. But as he got closer, he realized they were surrounding something on the ground, all of them looking down at it. He spotted Newt, kneeling there in the middle, leaning over a body.

Minho was standing behind him, looking distraught and dirty, and spotted Thomas first. "Where'd you go?" he asked.

"To talk to Teresa—what happened?" He waited anxiously for the next dump of bad news.

Minho's forehead creased in anger. "Our Map Room was set on fire and you ran off to talk to your shuck girlfriend? What's wrong with you?"

Thomas knew the rebuke should've stung, but his mind was too preoccupied. "I didn't think it mattered anymore—if you haven't figured out the Maps by now . . ."

Minho looked disgusted, the pale light and fog of smoke making his face seem almost sinister. "Yeah, this'd be a great freaking time to give up. What the—"

"I'm sorry—just tell me what happened." Thomas leaned over the shoulder of a skinny boy standing in front of him to get a look at the body on the ground.

It was Alby, flat on his back, a huge gash on his forehead. Blood seeped down both sides of his head, some into his eyes, crusting there. Newt was cleaning it with a wet rag, gingerly, asking questions in a whisper too low to hear. Thomas, concerned for Alby despite his recent ill-tempered ways, turned back to Minho and repeated his question.

"Winston found him out here, half dead, the Map Room blazing. Some shanks got in there and put it out, but way too late. All the trunks are burned to a freaking crisp. I suspected Alby at first, but whoever did it slammed his shuck head against the table—you can see where. It's nasty."

"Who do you think did it?" Thomas was hesitant to tell him about the possible discovery he and Teresa had made. With no Maps, the point was moot.

"Maybe Gally before he showed up in the Homestead and went psycho? Maybe the Grievers? I don't know, and I don't care. Doesn't matter."

Thomas was surprised at the sudden change of heart. "Now who's the one giving up?"

Minho's head snapped up so quickly, Thomas took a step backward. There was a flash of anger there, but it quickly melted into an odd expression of surprise or confusion. "That's not what I meant, shank."

Thomas narrowed his eyes in curiosity. "What did—"

"Just shut your hole for now." Minho put his fingers to his lips, his eyes darting around to see if anyone was looking at him. "Just shut your hole. You'll find out soon enough."

Thomas took a deep breath and thought. If he expected the other boys to be honest, he should be honest too. He decided he'd better share about the possible Maze code, Maps or no Maps. "Minho, I need to tell you and Newt something. And we need to let Teresa out—she's probably starving and we could use her help."

"That stupid girl is the last thing I'm worried about."

Thomas ignored the insult. "Just give us a few minutes—we have an idea. Maybe it'll still work if enough Runners remember their Maps."

This seemed to get Minho's full attention—but again, there was that same strange look, as if Thomas was missing something very obvious. "An idea? What?"

"Just come over to the Slammer with me. You and Newt."

Minho thought for a second. "Newt!" he called out.

"Yeah?" Newt stood up, refolding his bloody rag to find a clean spot. Thomas couldn't help noticing that every inch was drenched in red.

Minho pointed down at Alby. "Let the Med-jacks take care of him. We need to talk."

Newt gave him a questioning look, then handed the rag to the closest Glader. "Go find Clint—tell him we got worse problems than guys with buggin' splinters." When the kid ran off to do as he was told, Newt stepped away from Alby. "Talk about what?"

Minho nodded at Thomas, but didn't say anything.

"Just come with me," Thomas said. Then he turned and headed for the Slammer without waiting for a response.

"Let her out." Thomas stood by the cell door, arms folded. "Let her out, and then we'll talk. Trust me—you wanna hear it."

Newt was covered in soot and dirt, his hair matted with sweat. He certainly didn't seem to be in a very good mood. "Tommy, this is—"

"*Please*. Just open it—let her out. Please." He wouldn't give up this time.

Minho stood in front of the door with his hands on his hips. "How can we trust her?" he asked. "Soon as she woke up, the whole place fell to pieces. She even *admitted* she triggered something."

"He's got a point," Newt said.

Thomas gestured through the door at Teresa. "We can trust her. Every time I've talked to her, it's something about trying to get out of here. She was sent here just like the rest of us—it's stupid to think she's responsible for any of this."

Newt grunted. "Then what the bloody shuck did she mean by sayin' she triggered something?"

Thomas shrugged, refusing to admit that Newt had a good point. There had to be an explanation. "Who knows—her mind was doing all kinds of weird stuff when she woke up. Maybe we all went through that in the Box, talking gibberish before we came totally awake. Just let her out."

Newt and Minho exchanged a long look.

"Come on," Thomas insisted. "What's she gonna do, run around and stab every Glader to death? Come on."

Minho sighed. "Fine. Just let the stupid girl out."

"I'm not stupid!" Teresa shouted, her voice muffled by the walls. "And I can hear every word you morons are saying!"

Newt's eyes widened. "Real sweet girl you picked up, Tommy."

"Just hurry," Thomas said. "I'm sure we have a lot to do before the Grievers come back tonight—if they don't come during the day."

Newt grunted and stepped up to the Slammer, pulling his keys out as he did so. A few clinks later the door swung wide open. "Come on."

Teresa walked out of the small building, glowering at Newt as she passed him. She gave a just-as-unpleasant glance toward Minho, then stopped to stand right next to Thomas. Her arm brushed against his; tingles shot across his skin, and he felt mortally embarrassed.

"All right, talk," Minho said. "What's so important?"

Thomas looked at Teresa, wondering how to say it.

"What?" she said. "You talk—they obviously think I'm a serial killer."

"Yeah, you look so dangerous," Thomas muttered, but he turned his attention to Newt and Minho. "Okay, when Teresa was first coming out of her deep sleep, she had memories flashing through her mind. She, um"—he just barely stopped himself from saying she'd said it inside his mind—"she told me later that she remembers that the Maze is a *code*. That maybe instead of solving it to find a way out, it's trying to send us a message."

"A *code*?" Minho asked. "How's it a code?"

Thomas shook his head, wishing he could answer. "I don't know for sure—you're way more familiar with the Maps than I am. But I have a theory. That's why I was hoping you guys could remember some of them."

Minho glanced at Newt, his eyebrows raised in question. Newt nodded.

"What?" Thomas asked, fed up with them keeping information from him. "You guys keep acting like you have a secret."

Minho rubbed his eyes with both hands, took a deep breath. "We hid the Maps, Thomas."

At first it didn't compute. "Huh?"

Minho pointed at the Homestead. "We hid the freaking Maps in the weapons room, put dummies in their place. Because of Alby's warning. And because of the so-called *Ending* your girlfriend triggered."

Thomas was so excited to hear this news he temporarily forgot how awful things had become. He remembered Minho acting suspicious the day before, saying he had a special assignment. Thomas looked over at Newt, who nodded.

"They're all safe and sound," Minho said. "Every last one of those suckers. So if you have a theory, get talking."

"Take me to them," Thomas said, itching to have a look.

"Okay, let's go."

CHAPTER 42

Minho switched on the light, making Thomas squint for a second until his eyes got used to it. Menacing shadows clung to the boxes of weapons scattered across the table and floor, blades and sticks and other nasty-looking devices seeming to wait there, ready to take on a life of their own and kill the first person stupid enough to come close. The dank, musty smell only added to the creepy feel of the room.

"There's a hidden storage closet back here," Minho explained, walking past some shelves into a dark corner. "Only a couple of us know about it."

Thomas heard the creak of an old wooden door, and then Minho was dragging a cardboard box across the floor; the scrape of it sounded like a knife on bone. "I put each trunk's worth in its own box, eight boxes total. They're all in there."

"Which one is this?" Thomas asked; he knelt down next to it, eager to get started.

"Just open it and see—each page is marked, remember?"

Thomas pulled on the crisscrossed lid flaps until they popped open. The Maps for Section Two lay in a messy heap. Thomas reached in and pulled out a stack.

"Okay," he said. "The Runners have always compared these day to day, looking to see if there was a pattern that would somehow help figure out a way to an exit. You even said you didn't really know *what* you were looking for, but you kept studying them anyway. Right?"

Minho nodded, arms folded. He looked as if someone were about to reveal the secret of immortal life.

"Well," Thomas continued, "what if all the wall movements had nothing to do with a map or a maze or anything like that? What if instead the pattern spelled *words*? Some kind of clue that'll help us escape."

Minho pointed at the Maps in Thomas's hand, letting out a frustrated sigh. "Dude, you have any idea how much we've studied these things? Don't you think we would've noticed if it were spelling out freaking *words*?"

"Maybe it's too hard to see with the naked eye, just comparing one day to the next. And maybe you weren't supposed to compare one day to the next, but look at it one day at a time?"

Newt laughed. "Tommy, I might not be the sharpest guy in the Glade, but sounds like you're talkin' straight out your butt to me."

While he'd been talking, Thomas's mind had been spinning even faster. The answer was within his grasp—he knew he was almost there. It was just so hard to put into words.

"Okay, okay," he said, starting over. "You've always had one Runner assigned to one section, right?"

"Right," Minho replied. He seemed genuinely interested and ready to understand.

"And that Runner makes a Map every day, and then compares it to Maps from previous days, *for that section*. What if, instead, you were supposed to compare the eight sections to *each other,* every day? Each day being a separate clue or code? Did you ever compare sections to other sections?"

Minho rubbed his chin, nodding. "Yeah, kind of. We tried to see if they made something when put together—of course we did that. We've tried everything."

Thomas pulled his legs up underneath him, studying the Maps in his lap. He could just barely see the lines of the Maze written on the second page through the page resting on top. In that instant, he knew what they had to do. He looked up at the others.

"Wax paper."

"Huh?" Minho asked. "What the—"

"Just trust me. We need wax paper and scissors. And every black marker and pencil you can find."

Frypan wasn't too happy having a whole box of his wax paper rolls taken away from him, especially with their supplies being cut off. He argued that it was one of the things he always requested, that he used it for baking. They finally had to tell him what they needed it for to convince him to give it up.

After ten minutes of hunting down pencils and markers—most had been in the Map Room and were destroyed in the fire—Thomas sat around the worktable in the weapons basement with Newt, Minho and Teresa. They hadn't found any scissors, so Thomas had grabbed the sharpest knife he could find.

"This better be good," Minho said. Warning laced his voice, but his eyes showed some interest.

Newt leaned forward, putting his elbows on the table, as if waiting for a magic trick. "Get on with it, Greenie."

"Okay." Thomas was eager to do so, but was also scared to death it might end up being nothing. He handed the knife to Minho, then pointed at the wax paper. "Start cutting rectangles, about the size of the Maps. Newt and Teresa, you can help me grab the first ten or so Maps from each section box."

"What is this, kiddie craft time?" Minho held up the knife and looked at it with disgust. "Why don't you just tell us what the klunk we're doing this for?"

"I'm done explaining," Thomas said, knowing they just had to see what he was picturing in his mind. He stood to go rummage through the storage closet. "It'll be easier to show you. If I'm wrong, I'm wrong, and we can go back to running around the Maze like mice."

Minho sighed, clearly irritated, then muttered something under his breath. Teresa had stayed quiet for a while, but she spoke up inside Thomas's head.

I think I know what you're doing. Brilliant, actually.

Thomas was startled, but he tried his best to cover it up. He knew he had to pretend he didn't have voices in his head—the others would think he was a lunatic.

Just . . . come . . . help . . . me, he tried to say back, thinking each word separately, trying to visualize the message, *send* it. But she didn't respond.

"Teresa," he said aloud. "Can you help me a second?" He nodded toward the closet.

The two of them went into the dusty little room and opened up all the boxes, grabbing a small stack of Maps from each one. Returning to the table, Thomas found that Minho had cut twenty sheets already, making a messy pile to his right as he threw each new piece on top.

Thomas sat down and grabbed a few. He held one of the papers up to the light, saw how it shone through with a milky glow. It was exactly what he needed.

He grabbed a marker. "All right, everybody trace the last ten or so days onto a piece of this stuff. Make sure you write the info on top so we can keep track of what's what. When we're done, I think we might see something."

"What—" Minho began.

"Just bloody keep cutting," Newt ordered. "I think I know where he's going with this." Thomas was relieved someone was finally getting it.

They got to work, tracing from original Maps to wax paper, one by one, trying to keep it clean and correct while hurrying as fast as possible. Thomas used the side of a stray slab of wood as a makeshift ruler, keeping his lines straight. Soon he'd completed five maps, then five more. The others kept the same pace, working feverishly.

As Thomas drew, he started to feel a tickle of panic, a sick feeling that what they were doing was a complete waste of time. But Teresa, sitting next to him, was a study in concentration, her tongue sticking out the corner of her mouth as she traced lines up and down, side to side. She seemed way more confident that they were definitely on to something.

Box by box, section by section, they continued on.

"I've had enough," Newt finally announced, breaking the quiet. "My fingers are bloody burning like a mother. See if it's working."

Thomas put his marker down, then flexed his fingers, hoping he'd been right about all this. "Okay, give me the last few days of each section—make piles along the table, in order from Section One to Section Eight. One here"—he pointed at an end—"to Eight here." He pointed at the other end.

Silently, they did as he asked, sorting through what they'd traced until eight low stacks of wax paper lined the table.

Jittery and nervous, Thomas picked up one page from each pile, making sure they were all from the same day, keeping them in order. He then laid them one on top of the other so that each drawing of the Maze matched the same day above it and below it, until he was looking at eight different sections of the Maze at once. What he saw amazed him. Almost magically, like a picture coming into focus, an image developed. Teresa let out a small gasp.

Lines crossed each other, up and down, so much so that what

Thomas held in his hands looked like a checkered grid. But certain lines in the middle—lines that happened to appear more often than any other—made a slightly darker image than the rest. It was subtle, but it was, without a doubt, there.

Sitting in the exact center of the page was the letter *F*.

CHAPTER 43

Thomas felt a rush of different emotions: relief that it had worked, surprise, excitement, wonder at what it could lead to.

"Man," Minho said, summing up Thomas's feelings with one word.

"Could be a coincidence," Teresa said. "Do more, quick."

Thomas did, putting together the eight pages of each day, in order from Section One to Section Eight. Each time, an obvious letter formed in the center of the crisscrossed mass of lines. After the *F* was an *L*, then an *O*, then an *A*, and a *T*. Then *C* . . . *A* . . . *T*.

"Look," Thomas said, pointing down the line of stacks they'd formed, confused, but happy that the letters were so obvious. "It spells *FLOAT* and then it spells *CAT*."

"Float cat?" Newt asked. "Doesn't sound like a bloody rescue code to me."

"We just need to keep working," Thomas said.

Another couple of combinations made them realize that the second word was actually *CATCH*. *FLOAT* and *CATCH*.

"Definitely not a coincidence," Minho said.

"Definitely not," Thomas agreed. He couldn't wait to see more.

Teresa gestured toward the storage closet. "We need to go through all of them—all those boxes in there."

"Yeah," Thomas nodded. "Let's get on it."

"We can't help," Minho said.

All three of them looked at him. He returned their glares. "At least not me and Thomas here. We need to get the Runners out in the Maze."

"What?" Thomas asked. "This is way more important!"

"Maybe," Minho answered calmly, "but we can't miss a day out there. Not now."

Thomas felt a rush of disappointment. Running the Maze seemed like such a waste of time compared to figuring out the code. "Why, Minho? You said the pattern's basically been repeating itself for months—one more day won't mean a thing."

Minho slammed his hand against the table. "That's bullcrap, Thomas! Of all days, this might be the most important to get out there. Something might've changed, something might've opened up. In fact, with the freaking walls not closing anymore, I think we should try your idea—stay out there overnight and do some deeper exploring."

That piqued Thomas's interest—he *had* been wanting to do that. Conflicted, he asked, "But what about this code? What about—"

"Tommy," Newt said in a consoling voice. "Minho's right. You shanks go out and get Runnin'. I'll round up some Gladers we can trust and get workin' on this." Newt sounded more like a leader than ever before.

"Me too," Teresa agreed. "I'll stay and help Newt."

Thomas looked at her. "You sure?" He was itching to figure out the code himself, but he decided Minho and Newt were right.

She smiled and folded her arms. "If you're going to decipher a hidden code from a complex set of different mazes, I'm pretty sure you need a girl's brain running the show." Her grin turned into a smirk.

"If you say so." He folded his own arms, staring at her with a smile, suddenly not wanting to leave again.

"Good that." Minho nodded and turned to go. "Everything's fine and dandy. Come on." He started toward the door, but stopped when he realized Thomas wasn't behind him.

"Don't worry, Tommy," Newt said. "Your girlfriend will be fine."

Thomas felt a million thoughts go through his head in that moment. An itch to learn the code, embarrassment at what Newt thought of him and Teresa, the intrigue of what they might find out in the Maze—and fear.

But he pushed it all aside. Without even saying goodbye, he finally followed Minho and they went up the stairs.

Thomas helped Minho gather the Runners to give them the news and organize them for the big journey. He was surprised at how readily everyone agreed that it was time to do some more in-depth exploring of the Maze and stay out there overnight. Even though he was nervous and scared, he told Minho he could take one of the sections himself, but the Keeper refused. They had eight experienced Runners to do that. Thomas was to go with him—which made Thomas so relieved he was almost ashamed of himself.

He and Minho packed their backpacks with more supplies than usual; there was no telling how long they'd be out there. Despite his fear, Thomas couldn't help being excited as well—maybe this was the day they'd find an exit.

He and Minho were stretching their legs by the West Door when Chuck walked over to say goodbye.

"I'd go with you," the boy said in a far too jovial voice, "but I don't wanna die a gruesome death."

Thomas laughed, surprising himself. "Thanks for the words of encouragement."

"Be careful," Chuck said, his tone quickly melting into genuine concern. "I wish I could help you guys."

Thomas was touched—he bet that if it really came down to it, Chuck *would* go out there if he were asked to. "Thanks, Chuck. We'll definitely be careful."

Minho grunted. "Being careful hasn't gotten us squat. It's all or nothing now, baby."

"We better get going," Thomas said. Butterflies swarmed in his gut, and he just wanted to *move,* to quit thinking about it. After all, going out in the Maze was no worse than staying in the Glade with open Doors. Though the thought didn't make him feel much better.

"Yeah," Minho responded evenly. "Let's go."

"Well," Chuck said, looking down at his feet before returning his gaze to Thomas. "Good luck. If your girlfriend gets lonely for you, I'll give her some lovin'."

Thomas rolled his eyes. "She's not my girlfriend, shuck-face."

"Wow," Chuck said. "You're already using Alby's dirty words." He was obviously trying hard to pretend he wasn't scared of all the recent developments, but his eyes revealed the truth. "Seriously, good luck."

"Thanks, that means a lot," Minho answered with his own eye roll. "See ya, shank."

"Yeah, see ya," Chuck muttered, then turned to walk away.

Thomas felt a pang of sadness—it was possible he might never see Chuck or Teresa or any of them again. A sudden urge gripped him. "Don't forget my promise!" he yelled. "I'll get you home!"

Chuck turned and gave him a thumbs-up; his eyes glimmered with tears.

Thomas flipped up double thumbs; then he and Minho pulled on their backpacks and entered the Maze.

CHAPTER 44

Thomas and Minho didn't stop until they were halfway to the last dead end of Section Eight. They made good time—Thomas was glad for his wristwatch, with the skies being gray—because it quickly became obvious that the walls hadn't moved from the day before. Everything was exactly the same. There was no need for Mapmaking or taking notes; their only task was to get to the end and start making their way back, searching for things previously unnoticed—anything. Minho allowed a twenty-minute break and then they were back at it.

They were silent as they ran. Minho had taught Thomas that speaking only wasted energy, so he concentrated on his pace and his breaths. Regular. Even. In, out. In, out. Deeper and deeper into the Maze they went, with only their thoughts and the sounds of their feet thumping against the hard stone floor.

In the third hour, Teresa surprised him, speaking in his mind from back in the Glade.

We're making progress—found a couple more words already. But none of it makes sense yet.

Thomas's first instinct was to ignore her, to deny once again that someone had the ability to enter his mind, invade his privacy. But he *wanted* to talk to her.

Can you hear me? he asked, picturing the words in his mind, mentally throwing them out to her in some way he could never have explained. Concentrating, he said it again. *Can you hear me?*

Yes! she replied. *Really clearly the second time you said it.*

Thomas was shocked. So shocked he almost quit running. It had worked!

Wonder why we can do this, he called out with his mind. The mental effort of speaking to her was already straining—he felt a headache forming like a bulge in his brain.

Maybe we were lovers, Teresa said.

Thomas tripped and crashed to the ground. Smiling sheepishly at Minho, who'd turned to look without slowing, Thomas got back up and caught up to him. *What?* he finally asked.

He sensed a laugh from her, a watery image full of color. *This is so bizarre,* she said. *It's like you're a stranger, but I know you're not.*

Thomas felt a pleasant chill even though he was sweating. *Sorry to break it to you, but we* are *strangers. I just met you, remember?*

Don't be stupid, Tom. I think someone altered our brains, put something in there so we could do this telepathy thing. Before *we came here. Which makes me think we already knew each other.*

It was something he'd wondered about, and he thought she was probably right. Hoped it, anyway—he was really starting to like her. *Brains altered?* he asked. *How?*

I don't know—some memory I can't quite grasp. I think we did something big.

Thomas thought about how he'd always felt a connection to her, ever since she arrived in the Glade. He wanted to dig a little more and see what she said. *What are you talking about?*

Wish I knew. I'm just trying to bounce ideas off you to see if it sparks anything in your mind.

Thomas thought about what Gally, Ben and Alby had said about him—their suspicions that he was against them somehow, was someone not to trust. He thought about what *Teresa* had said to him, too, the very first time—that he and she had somehow done all of this to them.

This code has to mean something, she added. *And the thing I wrote on my arm*—WICKED is good.

Maybe it won't matter, he answered. *Maybe we'll find an exit. You never know.*

Thomas squeezed his eyes shut for a few seconds as he ran, trying to concentrate. A pocket of air seemed to float in his chest every time they spoke, a swelling that half annoyed and half thrilled him. His eyes popped back open when he realized she could maybe read his thoughts even when he wasn't trying to communicate. He waited for a response, but none came.

You still there? he asked.

Yeah, but this always gives me a headache.

Thomas was relieved to hear he wasn't the only one. *My head hurts, too.*

Okay, she said. *See you later.*

No, wait! He didn't want her to leave; she was helping the time pass. Making the running easier somehow.

Bye, Tom. I'll let you know if we figure anything out.

Teresa—what about the thing you wrote on your arm?

Several seconds passed. No reply.

Teresa?

She was gone. Thomas felt as if that bubble of air in his chest had burst, releasing toxins into his body. His stomach hurt, and the thought of running the rest of the day suddenly depressed him.

In some ways, he wanted to tell Minho about how he and Teresa could talk, to share what was happening before it made his brain explode. But he didn't dare. Throwing telepathy into the whole situation didn't seem like the grandest of ideas. Everything was weird enough already.

Thomas put his head down and drew in a long, deep breath. He would just keep his mouth shut and run.

Two breaks later, Minho finally slowed to a walk as they headed down a long corridor that ended in a wall. He stopped and took a seat against the dead end. The ivy was especially thick there; it made the world seem green and lush, hiding the hard, impenetrable stone.

Thomas joined him on the ground and they attacked their modest lunch of sandwiches and sliced fruit.

"This is it," Minho said after his second bite. "We've already run through the whole section. Surprise, surprise—no exits."

Thomas already knew this, but hearing it made his heart sink even lower. Without another word—from himself or Minho—he finished his food and readied himself to explore. To look for who-knew-what.

For the next few hours, he and Minho scoured the ground, felt along the walls, climbed up the ivy in random spots. They found nothing, and Thomas grew more and more discouraged. The only thing interesting was another one of those odd signs that read WORLD IN CATASTROPHE—KILLZONE EXPERIMENT DEPARTMENT. Minho didn't even give it a second glance.

They had another meal, searched some more. They found nothing, and Thomas was beginning to get ready to accept the inevitable—that there was nothing *to* find. When wall-closing time rolled around, he started looking for signs of Grievers, was struck by an icy hesitation at every corner. He and Minho always had knives clasped firmly in both hands. But nothing showed up until almost midnight.

Minho spotted a Griever disappearing around a corner ahead of them; and it didn't come back. Thirty minutes later, Thomas saw one do the exact same thing. An hour after that, a Griever came charging through the Maze right past them, not even pausing. Thomas almost collapsed from the sudden rush of terror.

He and Minho continued on.

"I think they're playing with us," Minho said a while later.

Thomas realized he'd given up on searching the walls and was just heading back toward the Glade in a depressed walk. From the looks of it, Minho felt the same way.

"What do you mean?" Thomas asked.

The Keeper sighed. "I think the Creators want us to know there's no way out. The walls aren't even moving anymore—it's like this has all just been some stupid game and it's time to end. And they want us to go back and tell the other Gladers. How much you wanna bet when we get back we find out a Griever took one of them just like last night? I think Gally was right—they're gonna just keep killing us."

Thomas didn't respond—felt the truth of what Minho said. Any hope he'd felt earlier when they'd set out had crashed a long time ago.

"Let's just go home," Minho said, his voice weary.

Thomas hated to admit defeat, but he nodded in agreement. The code seemed like their only hope now, and he resolved to focus on that.

He and Minho made their way silently back to the Glade. They didn't see another Griever the whole way.

CHAPTER 45

By Thomas's watch, it was midmorning when he and Minho stepped through the West Door back into the Glade. Thomas was so tired he wanted to lie down right there and take a nap. They'd been in the Maze for roughly twenty-four hours.

Surprisingly, despite the dead light and everything falling apart, the day in the Glade appeared to be proceeding business as usual—farming, gardening, cleaning. It didn't take long for some of the boys to notice them standing there. Newt was notified and he came running.

"You're the first to come back," he said as he walked up to them. "What happened?" The childlike look of hope on his face broke Thomas's heart—he obviously thought they'd found something important. "Tell me you've got good news."

Minho's eyes were dead, staring at a spot somewhere in the gray distance. "Nothing," he said. "The Maze is a big freaking joke."

Newt looked at Thomas, confused. "What's he talking about?"

"He's just discouraged," Thomas said with a weary shrug. "We didn't find anything different. The walls haven't moved, no exits, nothing. Did the Grievers come last night?"

Newt paused, darkness passing over his face. Finally, he nodded. "Yeah. They took Adam."

Thomas didn't know the name, and felt guilty for feeling nothing. *Just one person again*, he thought. *Maybe Gally* was *right*.

Newt was about to say something else when Minho freaked out, startling Thomas.

"I'm sick of this!" Minho spat in the ivy, veins popping out of his neck. "I'm sick of it! It's over! It's all over!" He took off his backpack and threw it on the ground. "There's no exit, never was, never will be. We're all shucked."

Thomas watched, his throat dry, as Minho stomped off toward the Homestead. It worried him—if Minho gave up, they were all in big trouble.

Newt didn't say a word. He left Thomas standing there, now in his own daze. Despair hung in the air like the smoke from the Map Room, thick and acrid.

The other Runners returned within the hour, and from what Thomas heard, none of them had found anything and they'd eventually given up as well. Glum faces were everywhere throughout the Glade, and most of the workers had abandoned their daily jobs.

Thomas knew that the code of the Maze was their only hope now. It had to reveal something. It had to. And after aimlessly wandering the Glade to hear the other Runners' stories, he snapped out of his funk.

Teresa? he said in his mind, closing his eyes, as if that would do the trick. *Where are you? Did you figure anything out?*

After a long pause, he almost gave up, thinking it didn't work.

Huh? Tom, did you say something?

Yeah, he said, excited he'd made contact again. *Can you hear me? Am I doing this thing right?*

Sometimes it's choppy, but it's working. Kinda freaky, huh?

Thomas thought about that—actually, he was sort of getting used to it. *It's not so bad. Are you guys still in the basement? I saw Newt but then he disappeared again.*

Still here. Newt had three or four Gladers help us trace the Maps. I think we have the code all figured out.

Thomas's heart leaped into his throat. *Serious?*

Get down here.

I'm coming. He was already moving as he said it, somehow not feeling so exhausted anymore.

Newt let him in.

"Minho still hasn't shown up," he said as they walked down the stairs to the basement. "Sometimes he turns into a buggin' hothead."

Thomas was surprised Minho was wasting time sulking, especially with the code possibilities. He pushed the thought aside as he entered the room. Several Gladers he didn't know were gathered around the table, standing; they all looked exhausted, their eyes sunken. Piles of Maps lay scattered all over the place, including the floor. It looked as if a tornado had touched down right in the middle of the room.

Teresa was leaning against a stack of shelves, reading a single sheet of paper. She glanced up when he entered, but then returned her gaze to whatever it was she held. This saddened him a little—he'd hoped she'd be happy to see him—but then he felt really stupid for even having the thought. She was obviously busy figuring out the code.

You have to see this, Teresa said to him just as Newt dismissed his helpers—they clomped up the wooden stairs, a couple of them grumbling about doing all that work for nothing.

Thomas started, for a brief moment worried that Newt could tell what was going on. *Don't talk in my head while Newt's around. I don't want him knowing about our . . . gift.*

"Come check this out," she said aloud, barely hiding the smirk that flashed across her face.

"I'll get down on my knees and kiss your bloody feet if you can figure it out," Newt said.

Thomas walked over to Teresa, eager to see what they'd come up with. She held out the paper, eyebrows raised.

"No doubt this is right," she said. "Just don't have a clue what it means."

Thomas took the paper and scanned it quickly. There were numbered circles running down the left side, one to six. Next to each one was a word written in big blocky letters.

FLOAT
CATCH
BLEED
DEATH
STIFF
PUSH

That was it. Six words.

Disappointment washed over Thomas—he'd been sure the purpose of the code would be obvious once they had it figured out. He looked up at Teresa with a sunken heart. "That's all? Are you sure they're in the right order?"

She took the paper back from him. "The Maze has been repeating those words for months—we finally quit when that became clear. Each time, after the word *PUSH,* it goes a full week without showing any letter at all, and then it starts over again with *FLOAT.* So we figured that's the first word, and that's the order."

Thomas folded his arms and leaned against the shelves next to

Teresa. Without thinking about it, he'd memorized the six words, welded them to his mind. *Float. Catch. Bleed. Death. Stiff. Push.* That didn't sound good.

"Cheerful, don't ya think?" Newt said, mirroring his thoughts exactly.

"Yeah," Thomas replied with a frustrated groan. "We need to get Minho down here—maybe he knows something we don't. If we just had more clues—" He froze, hit by a dizzy spell; he would've fallen to the floor if he hadn't had the shelves to lean on. An idea had just occurred to him. A horrible, terrible, awful idea. The worst idea in the history of horrible, terrible, awful ideas.

But instinct told him he was right. That it was something he had to do.

"Tommy?" Newt asked, stepping closer with a look of concern creasing his forehead. "What's wrong with you? Your face just went white as a ghost."

Thomas shook his head, composing himself. "Oh . . . nothing, sorry. My eyes are hurting—I think I need some sleep." He rubbed his temples for effect.

Are you okay? Teresa asked in his mind. He looked to see that she was as worried as Newt, which made him feel good.

Yeah. Seriously, I'm tired. I just need some rest.

"Well," Newt said, reaching out to squeeze Thomas's shoulder. "You spent all bloody night out in the Maze—go take a nap."

Thomas looked at Teresa, then at Newt. He wanted to share his idea, but decided against it. Instead, he just nodded and headed for the stairs.

All the same, Thomas now had a plan. As bad as it was, he had a plan.

They needed more clues about the code. They needed *memories*.

So he was going to get stung by a Griever. Go through the Changing. On purpose.

CHAPTER 46

Thomas refused to talk to anyone the rest of the day.

Teresa tried several times. But he kept telling her he didn't feel good, that he just wanted to be alone and sleep in his spot behind the forest, maybe spend some time thinking. Try to discover a hidden secret within his mind that would help them know what to do.

But in truth, he was psyching himself up for what he had planned for that evening, convincing himself it was the right thing to do. The *only* thing to do. Plus, he was absolutely terrified and he didn't want the others to notice.

Eventually, when his watch showed that evening had arrived, he went to the Homestead with everyone else. He barely noticed he'd been hungry until he started eating Frypan's hastily prepared meal of biscuits and tomato soup.

And then it was time for another sleepless night.

The Builders had boarded up the gaping holes left by the monsters who'd carried off Gally and Adam. The end result looked to Thomas like an army of drunk guys had done the work, but it was solid enough. Newt and Alby, who finally felt well enough to walk around again, his head heavily bandaged, insisted on a plan for everyone to rotate where they slept each night.

Thomas ended up in the large living room on the bottom floor of the Homestead with the same people he'd slept with two nights before. Silence settled over the room quickly, though he didn't know if it was because people were actually asleep or just scared, quietly hoping against hope the Grievers didn't come again. Unlike two nights ago, Teresa was allowed to stay in the building with the rest of the Gladers. She was near him, curled up in two blankets. Somehow, he could sense that she was sleeping. Actually *sleeping*.

Thomas certainly couldn't sleep, even though he knew his body needed it desperately. He tried—he tried so hard to keep his eyes closed, force himself to relax. But he had no luck. The night dragged on, the heavy sense of anticipation like a weight on his chest.

Then, just as they'd all expected, came the mechanical, haunted sounds of the Grievers outside. The time had come.

Everyone crowded together against the wall farthest from the windows, doing their best to keep quiet. Thomas huddled in a corner next to Teresa, hugging his knees, staring at the window. The reality of the dreadful decision he'd made earlier squeezed his heart like a crushing fist. But he knew that everything might depend on it.

The tension in the room rose at a steady pace. The Gladers were quiet, not a soul moved. A distant scraping of metal against wood echoed through the house; it sounded to Thomas like a Griever was climbing on the back side of the Homestead, opposite where they were. More noises joined in a few seconds later, coming from all directions, the closest right outside their own window. The air in the room seemed to freeze into solid ice, and Thomas pressed his fists against his eyes, the anticipation of the attack killing him.

A booming explosion of ripping wood and broken glass thundered from somewhere upstairs, shaking the whole house. Thomas went numb as several screams erupted, followed by the pounding of fleeing footsteps. Loud creaks and groans announced a whole horde of Gladers running to the first floor.

"It's got Dave!" someone yelled, the voice high-pitched with terror.

No one in Thomas's room moved a muscle; he knew each of them was probably feeling guilty about their relief—that at least it wasn't them. That maybe they were safe for one more night. Two nights in a row only one boy had been taken, and people had started to believe that what Gally had said was true.

Thomas jumped as a terrible crash sounded right outside their door, accompanied by screams and the splintering of wood, like some iron-jawed monster was eating the entire stairwell. A second later came another explosion of ripping wood: the front door. The Griever had come right through the house and was now leaving.

An explosion of fear ripped through Thomas. It was now or never.

He jumped up and ran to the door of the room, yanking it open. He heard Newt yell, but he ignored him and ran down the hall, side-stepping and jumping over hundreds of splintered pieces of wood. He could see that where the front door had been there now stood a jagged hole leading out into the gray night. He headed straight for it and ran out into the Glade.

Tom! Teresa screamed inside his head. *What are you doing!*

He ignored her. He just kept running.

The Griever holding Dave—a kid Thomas had never spoken to—was rolling along on its spikes toward the West Door, churning and whirring. The other Grievers had already gathered in the courtyard and followed their companion toward the Maze. Without hesitating, knowing the others would think he was trying to commit suicide, Thomas sprinted in their direction until he found himself in the middle of the pack of creatures. Having been taken by surprise, the Grievers hesitated.

Thomas jumped on the one holding Dave, tried to jerk the kid free, hoping the creature would retaliate. Teresa's scream inside his mind was so loud it felt as if a dagger had been driven through his skull.

Three of the Grievers swarmed on him at once, their long pincers and claspers and needles flying in from all directions. Thomas flailed his arms and legs, knocking away the horrible metallic arms as he kicked at the pulsating blubber of the Grievers' bodies—he only wanted to be stung, not taken like Dave. Their relentless attack intensified, and Thomas felt pain erupt over every inch of his body—needle pricks that told him he'd succeeded. Screaming, he kicked and pushed and thrashed, throwing his body into a roll, trying to get away from them. Struggling, bursting with adrenaline, he finally found an open spot to get his feet under him and ran with all his power.

As soon as he escaped the immediate reach of the Grievers' instruments, they gave up and retreated, disappearing into the Maze. Thomas collapsed to the ground, groaning from the pain.

Newt was on him in a second, followed immediately by Chuck, Teresa, several others. Newt grabbed him by the shoulders and lifted him up, gripping him under both arms. "Get his legs!" he yelled.

Thomas felt the world swimming around him, felt delirious, nauseated. Someone, he couldn't tell who, obeyed Newt's order; he was being carried across the courtyard, through the front door of the Homestead, down the shattered hall, into a room, placed on a couch. The world continued to twist and pitch.

"What were you *doing*!" Newt yelled in his face. "How could you be so bloody stupid!"

Thomas had to speak before he faded into blackness. "No . . . Newt . . . you don't understand. . . ."

"Shut up!" Newt shouted. "Don't waste your energy!"

Thomas felt someone examining his arms and legs, ripping his clothes away from his body, checking for damage. He heard Chuck's voice, couldn't help feeling relief that his friend was okay. A Med-jack said something about him being stung dozens of times.

Teresa was by his feet, squeezing his right ankle with her hand. *Why, Tom? Why would you do that?*

Because . . . He didn't have the strength to concentrate.

Newt yelled for the Grief Serum; a minute later Thomas felt a pinprick on his arm. Warmth spread from that point throughout his body, calming him, lessening the pain. But the world still seemed to be collapsing in on itself, and he knew it would all be gone from him in just a few seconds.

The room spun, colors morphing into each other, churning faster and faster. It took all of his effort, but he said one last thing before the darkness took him for good.

"Don't worry," he whispered, hoping they could hear him. "I did it on purpose. . . ."

CHAPTER 47

Thomas had no concept of time as he went through the Changing.

It started much like his first memory of the Box—dark and cold. But this time he had no sensation of anything touching his feet or body. He floated in emptiness, stared into a void of black. He saw nothing, heard nothing, smelled nothing. It was as if someone had stolen his five senses, leaving him in a vacuum.

Time stretched on. And on. Fear turned into curiosity, which turned into boredom.

Finally, after an interminable wait, things began to change.

A distant wind picked up, unfelt but heard. Then a swirling mist of whiteness appeared far in the distance—a spinning tornado of smoke that formed into a long funnel, stretching out until he could see neither the top nor the bottom of the white whirlwind. He felt the gales then, sucking into the cyclone so that it blew past him from behind, ripping at his clothes and hair like they were shredded flags caught in a storm.

The tower of thick mist began to move toward him—or *he* was moving toward *it,* he couldn't tell—increasing its speed at an alarming rate. Where seconds before he'd been able to see the distinct form of the funnel, he now could see only a flat expanse of white.

And then it consumed him; he felt his mind taken by the mist, felt memories flood into his thoughts.

Everything else turned into pain.

CHAPTER 48

"Thomas."

The voice was distant, warbled, like an echo in a long tunnel.

"Thomas, can you hear me?"

He didn't want to answer. His mind had shut down when it could no longer take the pain; he feared it would all return if he allowed himself back into consciousness. He sensed light on the other side of his eyelids, but knew it would be unbearable to open them. He did nothing.

"Thomas, it's Chuck. Are you okay? Please don't die, dude."

Everything came crashing back into his mind. The Glade, the Grievers, the stinging needle, the Changing. *Memories.* The Maze couldn't be solved. Their only way out was something they'd never expected. Something terrifying. He was crushed with despair.

Groaning, he forced his eyes open, squinting at first. Chuck's pudgy face was there, staring with frightened eyes. But then they lit up and a smile spread across his face. Despite it all, despite the terrible crappiness of it all, Chuck smiled.

"He's awake!" the boy yelled to no one in particular. "Thomas is awake!"

The booming sound of his voice made Thomas wince; he shut his eyes again. "Chuck, do you have to scream? I don't feel so good."

"Sorry—I'm just glad you're alive. You're lucky I don't give you a big kiss."

"Please don't do that, Chuck." Thomas opened his eyes again and forced himself to sit up in the bed in which he lay, pushing his back against the wall and stretching out his legs. Soreness ate at his joints and muscles. "How long did it take?" he asked.

"Three days," Chuck answered. "We put you in the Slammer at night to keep you safe—brought you back here during the days. Thought you were dead for sure about thirty times since you started. But check you out—you look brand-new!"

Thomas could only imagine how *non*-great he looked. "Did the Grievers come?"

Chuck's jubilation visibly crashed to the ground as his eyes sank down toward the floor. "Yeah—they got Zart and a couple others. One a night. Minho and the Runners have scoured the Maze, trying to find an exit or some use for that stupid code you guys came up with. But nothing. Why do you think the Grievers are only taking one shank at a time?"

Thomas's stomach turned sour—he knew the exact answer to that question, and some others now. Enough to know that sometimes knowing sucked.

"Get Newt and Alby," he finally said in answer. "Tell them we need to have a Gathering. Soon as possible."

"Serious?"

Thomas let out a sigh. "Chuck, I just went through the Changing. Do *you* think I'm serious?"

Without a word, Chuck jumped up and ran out of the room, his calls for Newt fading the farther he went.

Thomas closed his eyes and rested his head against the wall. Then he called out to her with his mind.

Teresa.

She didn't answer at first, but then her voice popped into his thoughts as clearly as if she were sitting next to him. *That was really stupid, Tom. Really, really stupid.*

Had to do it, he answered.

I pretty much hated you the last couple days. You should've seen yourself. Your skin, your veins . . .

You hated *me?* He was thrilled she'd cared so much about him.

She paused. *That's just my way of saying I would've killed you if you'd died.*

Thomas felt a burst of warmth in his chest, reached up and actually touched it, surprised at himself. *Well . . . thanks. I guess.*

So, how much do you remember?

He paused. *Enough. What you said about the two of us and what we did to them . . .*

It was true?

We did some bad things, Teresa. He sensed frustration from her, like she had a million questions and no idea where to start.

Did you learn anything to help us get out of here? she asked, as if she didn't want to know what part she'd had in all of this. *A purpose for the code?*

Thomas paused, not really wanting to talk about it yet—not before he really gathered his thoughts. Their only chance for escape might be a death wish. *Maybe,* he finally said, *but it won't be easy. We need a Gathering. I'll ask for you to be there—I don't have the energy to say it all twice.*

Neither one of them said anything for a while, a sense of hopelessness wafting between their minds.

Teresa?

Yeah?

The Maze can't be solved.

She paused for a long time before answering. *I think we all know that now.*

Thomas hated the pain in her voice—he could feel it in his mind. *Don't worry; the Creators meant for us to escape, though. I have a plan.* He wanted to give her some hope, no matter how scarce.

Oh, really.

Yeah. It's terrible, and some of us might die. Sound promising?

Big-time. What is it?

We have to—

Before he could finish, Newt walked into the room, cutting him off.

I'll tell you later, Thomas quickly finished.

Hurry! she said, then was gone.

Newt had walked over to the bed and sat down next to him. "Tommy—you barely look sick."

Thomas nodded. "I feel a little queasy, but other than that, I'm fine. Thought it'd be a lot worse."

Newt shook his head, his face a mixture of anger and awe. "What you did was half brave and half bloody stupid. Seems like you're pretty good at that." He paused, shook his head. "I *know* why you did it. What memories came back? Anything that'll help?"

"We need to have a Gathering," Thomas said, shifting his legs to get more comfortable. Surprisingly, he didn't feel much pain, just wooziness. "Before I start forgetting some of this stuff."

"Yeah, Chuck told me—we'll do it. But why? What did you figure out?"

"It's a test, Newt—the whole thing is a test."

Newt nodded. "Like an experiment."

Thomas shook his head. "No, you don't get it. They're weeding us out, seeing if we'll give up, finding the best of us. Throwing variables at us, trying to make us quit. Testing our ability to hope and fight. Sending Teresa here and shutting everything down was only the last part, one more . . . final analysis. Now it's time for the last test. To escape."

Newt's brow crinkled in confusion. "What do you mean? You know a way out?"

"Yeah. Call the Gathering. Now."

CHAPTER 49

An hour later, Thomas sat in front of the Keepers for the Gathering, just like he had a week or two before. They hadn't let Teresa in, which ticked him off just as much as it did her. Newt and Minho trusted her now, but the others still had their doubts.

"All right, Greenie," Alby said, looking much better as he sat in the middle of the semicircle of chairs, next to Newt. The other chairs were all occupied except two—a stark reminder that Zart and Gally had been taken by the Grievers. "Forget all the beat-around-the-bush klunk. Start talking."

Thomas, still a bit queasy from the Changing, forced himself to take a second and gain his composure. He had a lot to say, but wanted to be sure it came out sounding as non-stupid as possible.

"It's a long story," he began. "We don't have time to go through it all, but I'll tell you the gist of it. When I went through the Changing, I saw flashes of images—hundreds of them—like a slide show in fast forward. A lot came back to me, but only some of it's clear enough to talk about. Other stuff has faded or is fading." He paused, gathering his thoughts one last time. "But I remember enough. The Creators are testing us. The Maze was never meant to be solved. It's all been a trial. They want the winners—or survivors—to do something important." He trailed off, already confused at what order he should tell things in.

"What?" Newt asked.

"Let me start over," Thomas said, rubbing his eyes. "Every single one of us was taken when we were really young. I don't remember how or why—just glimpses and feelings that things had changed in the world, that something really bad happened. I have no idea what. The Creators stole us, and I think they felt justified in doing it. Somehow they figured out that we have above-average intelligence, and that's why they chose us. I don't know, most of this is sketchy and doesn't matter that much anyway.

"I can't remember anything about my family or what happened to them. But after we were taken, we spent the next few years learning in special schools, living somewhat normal lives until they were finally able to finance and build the Maze. All our names are just stupid nicknames they made up—like Alby for Albert Einstein, Newt for Isaac Newton, and me—Thomas. As in Edison."

Alby looked like he'd been slapped in the face. "Our names . . . these ain't even our real names?"

Thomas shook his head. "As far as I can tell, we'll probably never know what our names were."

"What are you saying?" Frypan asked. "That we're freakin' orphans raised by scientists?"

"Yes," Thomas said, hoping his expression didn't give away just how depressed he felt. "Supposedly we're really smart and they're studying every move we make, analyzing us. Seeing who'd give up and who wouldn't. Seeing who'd survive it all. No wonder we have so many beetle blade spies running around this place. Plus, some of us have had things . . . altered in our brains."

"I believe this klunk about as much as I believe Frypan's food is good for you," Winston grumbled, looking tired and indifferent.

"Why would I make this up?" Thomas said, his voice rising. He'd gotten stung on *purpose* to remember these things! "Better yet, what do *you* think is the explanation? That we live on an alien planet?"

"Just keep talking," Alby said. "But I don't get why none of us remembered this stuff. I've been through the Changing, but everything I saw was . . ." He looked around quickly, like he'd just said something he shouldn't have. "I didn't learn nothin'."

"I'll tell you in a minute why I think I learned more than others," Thomas said, dreading that part of the story. "Should I keep going or not?"

"Talk," Newt said.

Thomas sucked in a big breath, as if he were about to start a race. "Okay, somehow they wiped our memories—not just our childhood, but all the stuff leading up to entering the Maze. They put us in the Box and sent us up here—a big group to start and then one a month over the last two years."

"But why?" Newt asked. "What's the bloody point?"

Thomas held up a hand for silence. "I'm getting there. Like I said, they wanted to test us, see how we'd react to what they call the Variables, and to a problem that has no solution. See if we could work together—build a community, even. Everything was provided for us, and the problem was laid out as one of the most common puzzles known to civilization—a maze. All this added up to making us think there *had* to be a solution, just encouraging us to work all the harder while at the same time magnifying our discouragement at not finding one." He paused to look around, making sure they were all listening. "What I'm saying is, there *is* no solution."

Chatter broke out, questions overlapping each other.

Thomas held his hands up again, wishing he could just zap his thoughts into everyone else's brains. "See? Your reaction proves my point. Most people would've given up by now. But I think we're different. We couldn't accept that a problem *can't* be solved—especially when it's something as simple as a maze. And we've kept fighting no matter how hopeless it's gotten."

Thomas realized his voice had steadily risen as he spoke, and he felt heat in his face. "Whatever the reason, it makes me sick! All of this—the Grievers, the walls moving, the Cliff—they're just elements of a stupid *test.* We're being used and manipulated. The Creators wanted to keep our minds working toward a solution that was never there. Same thing goes for Teresa being sent here, her being used to trigger the Ending—whatever *that* means—the place being shut down, gray skies, on and on and on. They're throwing crazy things at us to see our response, test our will. See if we'll turn on each other. In the end, they want the survivors for something important."

Frypan stood up. "And killing people? That's a nice little part of their plan?"

Thomas felt a moment of fear, worried that the Keepers might take out their anger on him for knowing so much. And it was only about to get worse. "Yes, Frypan, killing people. The only reason the Grievers are doing it one by one is so we don't all die before it ends the way it's supposed to. Survival of the fittest. Only the best of us will escape."

Frypan kicked his chair. "Well, you better start talking about this magical escape, then!"

"He will," Newt said, quietly. "Shut up and listen."

Minho, who'd been mostly silent the whole time, cleared his throat. "Something tells me I'm not gonna like what I'm about to hear."

"Probably not," Thomas said. He closed his eyes for a second and folded his arms. The next few minutes were going to be crucial. "The Creators want the best of us for whatever it is they have planned. But we have to earn it." The room fell completely silent, every eye on him. "The code."

"The code?" Frypan repeated, his voice lighting up with a trace of hope. "What about it?"

Thomas looked at him, paused for effect. "It was hidden in the wall movements of the Maze for a reason. I should know—I was there when the Creators did it."

CHAPTER 50

For a long moment, no one said anything, and all Thomas saw were blank faces. He felt the sweat beading on his forehead, slicking his hands; he was terrified to keep going.

Newt looked completely baffled and finally broke the silence. "What are you talking about?"

"Well, first there's something I have to share. About me and Teresa. There's a reason Gally accused me of so much stuff, and why everyone who's gone through the Changing recognizes me."

He expected questions—an eruption of voices—but the room was dead silent.

"Teresa and I are . . . different," he continued. "We were part of the Maze Trials from the very beginning—but against our will, I swear it."

Minho was the one to speak up now. "Thomas, what're you talking about?"

"Teresa and I were used by the Creators. If you had your full memories back, you'd probably want to kill us. But I had to tell you this myself to show you we can be trusted now. So you'll believe me when I tell you the only way we can get out of here."

Thomas quickly scanned the faces of the Keepers, wondering one last time if he should say it, if they would understand. But he knew he had to. He *had* to.

Thomas took a deep breath, then said it. "Teresa and I helped design the Maze. We helped create the whole thing."

Everyone seemed too stunned to respond. Blank faces stared back at him once again. Thomas figured they either didn't understand or didn't believe him.

"What's that supposed to mean?" Newt finally asked. "You're a bloody sixteen-year-old. How could you have created the Maze?"

Thomas couldn't help doubting it a little himself—but he knew what he'd remembered. As crazy as it was, he knew it for the truth. "We were . . . smart. And I think it might be part of the Variables. But most importantly, Teresa and I have a . . . gift that made us very valuable as they designed and built this place." He stopped, knowing it must all sound absurd.

"Speak!" Newt yelled. "Spit it out!"

"We're telepathic! We can talk to each other in our freaking heads!" Saying it out loud almost made him feel ashamed, as if he'd just admitted he was a thief.

Newt blinked in surprise; someone coughed.

"But listen to me," Thomas continued, in a hurry to defend himself. "They *forced* us to help. I don't know how or why, but they did." He paused. "Maybe it was to see if we could gain your trust despite having been a part of them. Maybe we were meant all along to be the ones to reveal how to escape. Whatever the reason, with your Maps we figured out the code and we need to use it now."

Thomas looked around, and surprisingly, astonishingly, no one seemed angry. Most of the Gladers continued to stare blankly at him or shook their heads in wonder or disbelief. And for some odd reason, Minho was smiling.

"It's true, and I'm sorry," Thomas continued. "But I can tell you this—I'm in the same boat with you now. Teresa and I were sent here just like anyone else, and we can die just as easily. But the Creators have seen enough—it's time for the final test. I guess I needed the Changing to add the final pieces of the puzzle. Anyway, I wanted you to know the truth, to know there's a chance we can do this."

Newt shook his head back and forth, staring at the ground. Then he looked up, took in the other Keepers. "The Creators—those shanks did this to us, not Tommy and Teresa. The Creators. And they'll be sorry."

"Whatever," Minho said, "who gives a klunk about all that—just get on with the escape already."

A lump formed in Thomas's throat. He was so relieved he almost couldn't speak. He'd been sure they'd put him under major heat for his confession, if not throw him off the Cliff. The rest of what he had to say almost seemed easy now. "There's a computer station in a place we've never looked before. The code will open a door for us to get out of the Maze. It also shuts down the Grievers so they can't follow us—if we can just survive long enough to get to that point."

"A place we've never *looked* before?" Alby asked. "What do you think we've been doing for two years?"

"Trust me, you've never been to this spot."

Minho stood up. "Well, where is it?"

"It's almost suicide," Thomas said, knowing he was putting off the answer. "The Grievers will come after us whenever we try to do it. All of them. The final test." He wanted to make sure they understood the stakes. The odds of everyone surviving were slim.

"So where is it?" Newt asked, leaning forward in his chair.

"Over the Cliff," Thomas answered. "We have to go through the Griever Hole."

CHAPTER 51

Alby stood up so quickly his chair fell over backward. His bloodshot eyes stood out against the white bandage on his forehead. He took two steps forward before stopping, as if he'd been about to charge and attack Thomas.

"Now you're being a shuck idiot," he said, glaring at Thomas. "Or a traitor. How can we trust a word you say if you helped design this place, put us here! We can't handle one Griever on our own ground, much less fight a whole horde of them in their little hole. What are you really up to?"

Thomas was furious. "What am I up to? Nothing! Why would I make all this up?"

Alby's arms stiffened, fists clenched. "For all we know you were sent here to get us all killed. Why should we trust you?"

Thomas stared, incredulous. "Alby, do you have a short-term memory problem? I risked my life to save you out in the Maze—you'd be dead if it wasn't for me!"

"Maybe that was a trick to gain our trust. If you're in league with the shucks who sent us here, you wouldn't have had to worry about the Grievers hurting you—maybe it was all an act."

Thomas's anger lessened slightly at that, turned into pity. Something was odd here—suspicious.

"Alby," Minho finally interjected, relieving Thomas. "That's about the dumbest theory I've ever heard. He just about got freaking torn apart three nights ago. You think that's part of the act?"

Alby nodded once, curtly. "Maybe."

"I *did it,*" Thomas said, throwing all the annoyance he could into his voice, "on the chance that I could get my memories back, help all of us get out of here. Do I need to show you the cuts and bruises all over my body?"

Alby said nothing, his face still quivering with rage. His eyes watered and veins popped out on his neck. "We can't go back!" he finally yelled, turning to look at everyone in the room. "I've seen what our lives were like—we can't go back!"

"Is *that* what this is about?" Newt asked. "Are you kidding?"

Alby turned on him, fiercely, even held up a clenched fist. But he stopped, lowered his arm, then went over and sank into his chair, put his face in his hands, and broke down. Thomas couldn't have been more surprised. The fearless leader of the Gladers was crying.

"Alby, talk to us," Newt pressed, not willing to let it drop. "What's going on?"

"I did it," Alby said through a racking sob. "I did it."

"Did what?" Newt asked. He looked as confused as Thomas felt.

Alby looked up, his eyes wet with tears. "I burned the Maps. I did it. I slammed my head on the table so you'd think it was someone else, I lied, burned it all. I did it!"

The Keepers exchanged looks, shock clear in their wide eyes and raised eyebrows. For Thomas, though, it all made sense now. Alby remembered how awful his life was before he came here and he didn't want to go back.

"Well, it's a good thing we saved those Maps," Minho said, completely straight-faced, almost mocking. "Thanks for the tip you gave us after the Changing—to protect them."

Thomas looked to see how Alby would respond to Minho's sarcastic, almost cruel, remark, but he acted as if he hadn't even heard.

Newt, instead of showing anger, asked Alby to explain. Thomas knew why Newt wasn't mad—the Maps were safe, the code figured out. It didn't matter.

"I'm telling you." Alby sounded like he was begging—near hysterical. "We can't go back to where we came from. I've seen it, remembered awful, awful things. Burned land, a disease—something called the Flare. It was horrible—way worse than we have it here."

"If we stay *here,* we'll all die!" Minho yelled. "It's worse than that?"

Alby stared at Minho a long time before answering. Thomas could only think of the words he'd just said. *The Flare.* Something about it was familiar, right on the edge of his mind. But he was certain he hadn't remembered anything about that when he'd gone through the Changing.

"Yes," Alby finally said. "It's worse. Better to die than go home."

Minho snickered and leaned back in his chair. "Man, you are one butt-load of sunshine, let me tell you. I'm with Thomas. I'm with Thomas one hundred percent. If we're gonna die, let's freakin' do it fighting."

"Inside the Maze or out of it," Thomas added, relieved that Minho was firmly on his side. He turned to Alby then, and looked at him gravely. "We still live inside the world you remembered."

Alby stood again, his face showing his defeat. "Do what you want." He sighed. "Doesn't matter. We'll die no matter what." And with that, he walked to the door and left the room.

Newt let out a deep breath and shook his head. "He's never been the same since being stung—must've been one bugger of a memory. What in the world is the Flare?"

"I don't care," Minho said. "Anything's better than dying here. We can deal with the Creators once we're out. But for now we gotta do what they planned. Go through the Griever Hole and escape. If some of us die, so be it."

Frypan snorted. "You shanks are driving me nuts. Can't get out of the Maze, and this idea of hanging with the Grievers at their bachelor pad sounds as stupid as anything I've ever heard in my life. Might as well slit our wrists."

The other Keepers burst out in argument, everyone talking over everyone else. Newt finally screamed for them to shut up.

Thomas spoke again once things settled. "I'm going through the Hole or I'll die trying to get there. Looks like Minho will, too. And I'm sure Teresa's in. If we can fight off the Grievers long enough for someone to punch in the code and shut them down, then we can go through the door *they* come through. We'll have passed the tests. Then we can face the Creators themselves."

Newt's grin had no humor in it. "And you think we can fight off Grievers? Even if we don't die, we'll probably all get stung. Every last one of them might be waiting for us when we get to the Cliff—the beetle blades are out there constantly. The Creators'll know when we make our run for it."

He'd been dreading it, but Thomas knew it was time to tell them the last part of his plan. "I don't think they'll sting us—the Changing was a Variable meant for us while we lived here. But that part will be over. Plus, we might have one thing going for us."

"Yeah?" Newt asked, rolling his eyes. "Can't wait to hear it."

"It doesn't do the Creators any good if we all die—this thing is meant to be hard, not impossible. I think we finally know for sure that the Grievers are programmed to only kill one of us each day. So somebody can sacrifice himself to save the others while we run to the Hole. I think this might be how it's supposed to happen."

The room went silent until the Blood House Keeper barked a loud laugh. "Excuse me?" Winston asked. "So your suggestion is that we throw some poor kid to the wolves so the rest of us can escape? *This* is your *brilliant* suggestion?"

Thomas refused to admit how bad that sounded, but an idea hit him. "Yes, Winston, I'm glad you're so good at paying attention." He ignored the glare that got him. "And it seems obvious who the poor kid should be."

"Oh, yeah?" Winston asked. "Who?"

Thomas folded his arms. "Me."

CHAPTER 52

The meeting erupted into a chorus of arguments. Newt very calmly stood up, walked over to Thomas and grabbed him by the arm; he pulled him toward the door. "You're leaving. Now."

Thomas was stunned. "Leaving? Why?"

"Think you've said enough for one meeting. We need to talk and decide what to do—*without* you here." They had reached the door and Newt gave him a gentle push outside. "Wait for me by the Box. When we're done, you and I'll talk."

He started to turn around, but Thomas reached out and grabbed him. "You gotta believe me, Newt. It's the only way out of here—we can do it, I swear. We're *meant* to."

Newt got in his face and spoke in an angry rasp of a whisper. "Yeah, I especially loved the bit where you volunteered to get yourself killed."

"I'm perfectly willing to do it." Thomas meant it, but only because of the guilt that racked him. Guilt that he'd somehow helped design the Maze. But deep down, he held on to the hope that he could fight long enough for someone to punch in the code and shut down the Grievers before they killed him. Open the door.

"Oh, really?" Newt asked, seeming irritated. "Mr. Noble himself, aren't ya?"

"I have plenty of my own reasons. In some ways it's my fault we're here in the first place." He stopped, took a breath to compose himself. "Anyway, I'm going no matter what, so you better not waste it."

Newt frowned, his eyes suddenly filled with compassion. "If you really did help design the Maze, Tommy, it's not your fault. You're a *kid*—you can't help what they forced you to do."

But it didn't matter what Newt said. What anyone said. Thomas bore the responsibility anyway—and it was growing heavier the more he thought about it. "I just . . . feel like I need to save everyone. To redeem myself."

Newt stepped back, slowly shaking his head. "You know what's funny, Tommy?"

"What?" Thomas replied, wary.

"I actually believe you. You just don't have an ounce of lying in those eyes of yours. And I can't bloody believe I'm about to say this." He paused. "But I'm going back in there to convince those shanks we should go through the Griever Hole, just like you said. Might as well fight the Grievers rather than sit around letting them pick us off one by one." He held up a finger. "But listen to me—I don't want another buggin' word about you dying and all that heroic klunk. If we're gonna do this, we'll take our chances—all of us. You hear me?"

Thomas held his hands up, overwhelmed with relief. "Loud and clear. I was just trying to make the point that it's worth the risk. If someone's going to die every night anyway, we might as well use it to our advantage."

Newt frowned. "Well, ain't that just cheery?"

Thomas turned to walk away, but Newt called out to him. "Tommy?"

"Yeah?" He stopped, but didn't look back.

"If I can convince those shanks—and that's a big *if*—the best time to go would be at night. We can hope that a lot of the Grievers might be out and about in the Maze—not in that Hole of theirs."

"Good that." Thomas agreed with him—he just hoped Newt could convince the Keepers. He turned to look at Newt and nodded.

Newt smiled, a barely-there crack in his worried grimace. "We should do it tonight, before anyone else is killed." And before Thomas could say anything, Newt disappeared back into the Gathering.

Thomas, a little shocked at the last statement, left the Homestead and walked to an old bench near the Box and took a seat, his mind a whirlwind. He kept thinking of what Alby had said about the Flare, and what it could mean. The older boy had also mentioned burned earth and a disease. Thomas didn't remember anything like that, but if it was all true, the world they were trying to get back to didn't sound so good. Still—what other choice did they have? Besides the fact that the Grievers were attacking every night, the Glade had basically shut down.

Frustrated, worried, tired of his thoughts, he called out to Teresa. *Can you hear me?*

Yeah, she replied. *Where are you?*

By the Box.

I'll come in a minute.

Thomas realized how badly he needed her company. *Good. I'll tell you the plan; I think it's on.*

What is it?

Thomas leaned back on the bench and put his right foot up on his knee, wondering how Teresa would react to what he was going to say. *We gotta go through the Griever Hole. Use that code to shut the Grievers down and open a door out of here.*

A pause. *I figured it was something like that.*

Thomas thought for a second, then added, *Unless you've got any better ideas?*

No. It's gonna be awful.

He punched his right fist against his other hand, even though he knew she couldn't see him. *We can do this.*

Doubtful.

Well, we have to try.

Another pause, this one longer. He could feel her resolve. *You're right.*

I think we're leaving tonight. Just come out here and we can talk more about it.

I'll be there in a few minutes.

Thomas's stomach tightened into a knot. The reality of what he had suggested, the plan Newt was trying to convince the Keepers to accept, was starting to hit him. He knew it was dangerous, but the idea of actually fighting the Grievers—not just running from them—was terrifying. The absolute best-case scenario was that only one of them would die—but even that couldn't be trusted. Maybe the Creators would just reprogram the creatures. And then all bets were off.

He tried not to think about it.

Sooner than Thomas expected, Teresa had found him and was sitting next to him, her body pressed against his despite plenty of room on the bench. She reached out and took his hand. He squeezed back, so hard he knew it must've hurt.

"Tell me," she said.

Thomas did, reciting every word he'd told the Keepers, hating how Teresa's eyes filled with worry—and terror. "The plan was easy to talk about," he said after he'd told her everything. "But Newt thinks we should go *tonight*. It doesn't sound so good now." It especially terrified him to think about Chuck and Teresa out there—he'd faced the Grievers down already and knew all too well what it was like. He wanted to be able to protect his friends from the horrible experience, but he knew he couldn't.

"We can do it," she said in a quiet voice.

Hearing her say that only made him worry more. "Holy crap, I'm scared."

"Holy crap, you're human. You *should* be scared."

Thomas didn't respond, and for a long time they just sat there, holding hands, no words spoken, in their minds or aloud. He felt the slightest hint of peace, as fleeting as it was, and tried to enjoy it for however long it might last.

CHAPTER 53

Thomas was almost sad when the Gathering finally ended. When Newt came out of the Homestead he knew that the time for rest was over.

The Keeper spotted them and approached at a limping run. Thomas noticed he'd let go of Teresa's hand without thinking about it. Newt finally came to a halt and crossed his arms over his chest as he looked down at them sitting on the bench. "This is bloody nuts, you know that, right?" His face was impossible to read, but there seemed to be a hint of victory in his eyes.

Thomas stood up, feeling a rush of excitement flooding his body. "So they agreed to go?"

Newt nodded. "All of them. Wasn't as hard as I thought it'd be. Those shanks've seen what happens at night with those bloody Doors open. We can't get out of the stupid Maze. Gotta try *something*." He turned and looked at the Keepers, who'd started to gather their respective work groups. "Now we just have to convince the Gladers."

Thomas knew that would be even more difficult than persuading the Keepers had been.

"You think they'll go for it?" Teresa asked, finally standing to join them.

"Not all of them," Newt said, and Thomas could see the frustration in his eyes. "Some'll stay and take their chances—guarantee it."

Thomas didn't doubt people would blanch at the thought of

making a run for it. Asking them to fight the Grievers was asking a lot. "What about Alby?"

"Who knows?" Newt responded, looking around the Glade, observing the Keepers and their groups. "I'm convinced that bugger really *is* more scared to go back home than he is of the Grievers. But I'll get him to go with us, don't worry."

Thomas wished he could bring back memories of those things that were tormenting Alby, but there was nothing. "How are you going to convince him?"

Newt laughed. "I'll make up some klunk. Tell him we'll all find a new life in another part of the world, live happily ever after."

Thomas shrugged. "Well, maybe we can. I promised Chuck I'd get him home, you know. Or at least find him a home."

"Yeah, well," Teresa murmured. "Anything's better than this place."

Thomas looked around at the arguments breaking out across the Glade, Keepers doing their best to convince people they should take a chance and battle their way through the Griever Hole. Some Gladers stomped away, but most seemed to listen and at least consider.

"So what's next?" Teresa asked.

Newt took a deep breath. "Figure out who's going, who's staying. Get ready. Food, weapons, all that. Then we go. Thomas, I'd put you in charge since it was your idea, but it's going to be hard enough to get people on our side without making the Greenie our leader—no offense. So just lay low, okay? We'll leave the code business to you and Teresa—you can handle that from the background."

Thomas was more than fine with lying low—finding that computer station and punching in the code was more than enough responsibility for him. Even with that much on his shoulders he had to fight the rising flood of panic he felt. "You sure make it sound easy," he finally said, trying his best to lighten up the situation. Or at least *sound* like he was.

Newt folded his arms again, looked at him closely. "Like you said—stay here, one shank'll die tonight. Go, one shank'll die. What's the difference?" He pointed at Thomas. "*If* you're right."

"I am." Thomas knew he was right about the Hole, the code, the door, the need to fight. But whether one person or many would die, he had no clue. However, if there was one thing his gut told him, it was not to admit to any doubt.

Newt clapped him on the back. "Good that. Let's get to work."

The next few hours were frantic.

Most of the Gladers ended up agreeing to go—even more than Thomas would've guessed. Even Alby decided to make the run. Though no one admitted it, Thomas bet most of them were banking on the theory that only one person would be killed by the Grievers, and they figured their chances of *not* being the unlucky sap were decent. Those who decided to stay in the Glade were few but adamant and loud. They mainly walked around sulking, trying to tell others how stupid they were. Eventually, they gave up and kept their distance.

As for Thomas and the rest of those committed to the escape, there was a ton of work to be done.

Backpacks were handed out and stuffed full of supplies. Frypan—Newt told Thomas that the Cook had been one of the last Keepers to agree to go—was in charge of gathering all the food and figuring out a way to distribute it evenly among the packs. Syringes of Grief Serum were included, even though Thomas didn't think the Grievers would sting them. Chuck was in charge of filling water bottles and getting them out to everyone. Teresa helped him, and Thomas asked her to sugarcoat the trip as much as she could, even if she had to flat-out lie, which was mostly the case. Chuck had tried to act brave from the time he first found out they were going for it, but his sweaty skin and dazed eyes revealed the truth.

Minho went to the Cliff with a group of Runners, taking ivy ropes and rocks to test the invisible Griever Hole one last time. They had to hope the creatures would keep to their normal schedule and not come out during daytime hours. Thomas had contemplated just jumping into the Hole right away and trying to punch in the code quickly, but he had no idea what to expect or what might be waiting for him. Newt was right—they'd better wait until night and hope that most of the Grievers were in the Maze, not inside their Hole.

When Minho returned, safe and sound, Thomas thought he seemed very optimistic that it really was an exit. Or entrance. Depending on how you looked at it.

Thomas helped Newt distribute the weapons, and even more innovative ones were created in their desperation to be prepared for the Grievers. Wooden poles were carved into spears or wrapped in barbwire; the knives were sharpened and fastened with twine to the ends of sturdy branches hacked from trees in the woods; chunks of broken glass were duct-taped to shovels. By the end of the day, the Gladers had turned into a small army. A very pathetic, ill-prepared army, Thomas thought, but an army all the same.

Once he and Teresa were done helping, they went to the secret spot in the Deadheads to strategize about the station inside the Griever Hole and how they planned to punch in the code.

"We have to be the ones to do it," Thomas said as they leaned their backs against craggy trees, the once-green leaves already starting to turn gray from the lack of artificial sunlight. "That way if we get separated, we can be in contact and still help each other."

Teresa had grabbed a stick and was peeling off the bark. "But we need backup in case something happens to us."

"Definitely. Minho and Newt know the code words—we'll tell them they have to get them punched into the computer if we . . . well, you know." Thomas didn't want to think about all the bad things that might happen.

"Not much to the plan, then." Teresa yawned, as if life were completely normal.

"Not much at all. Fight the Grievers, punch in the code, escape through the door. Then we deal with the Creators—whatever it takes."

"Six code words, who knows how many Grievers." Teresa broke the stick in half. "What do you think *WICKED* stands for, anyway?"

Thomas felt like he'd been hit in the stomach. For some reason, hearing the word at that moment, from someone else, knocked something loose in his mind and it clicked. He was stunned he hadn't made the connection sooner. "That sign I saw out in the Maze—remember? The metal one with words stamped on it?" Thomas's heart had started to race with excitement.

Teresa crinkled her forehead in confusion for a second, but then a light seemed to blink on behind her eyes. "Whoa. World In Catastrophe: Killzone Experiment Department. WICKED. *WICKED is good*—what I wrote on my arm. What does that even *mean*?"

"No idea. Which is why I'm scared to death that what we're about to do is a whole pile of stupid. Could be a bloodbath."

"Everyone knows what they're getting into." Teresa reached out and took his hand. "Nothing to lose, remember?"

Thomas remembered, but for some reason Teresa's words fell flat—they didn't have much hope in them. "Nothing to lose," he repeated.

CHAPTER 54

Just before the normal Door-closing time, Frypan prepared one last meal to carry them through the night. The mood hanging over the Gladers as they ate couldn't have been more somber or sodden with fear. Thomas found himself sitting next to Chuck, absently picking at his food.

"So . . . Thomas," the boy said through a huge bite of mashed potatoes. "Who am I nicknamed after?"

Thomas couldn't help shaking his head—here they were, about to embark on probably the most dangerous task of their lives, and Chuck was curious where he'd gotten his nickname. "I don't know, Darwin, maybe? The dude who figured out evolution."

"I bet no one's ever called him a dude before." Chuck took another big bite, and seemed to think that was the best time to talk, full mouth and all. "You know, I'm really not all that scared. I mean, last few nights, sitting in the Homestead, just waiting for a Griever to come in and steal one of us was the worst thing I've ever done. At least now we're taking it to them, *trying* something. And at least . . ."

"At least what?" Thomas asked. He didn't believe for a second that Chuck wasn't scared; it almost hurt to see him acting brave.

"Well, everyone's speculating they can only kill one of us. Maybe I sound like a shuck, but it gives me some hope. At least most of us will make it through—just leaves one poor sucker to die. Better than all of us."

It made Thomas sick to think people were hanging on to that hope of just one person dying; the more he thought about it, the less he believed it was true. The Creators knew the plan—they might reprogram the Grievers. But even false hope was better than nothing. "Maybe we can all make it. As long as everyone fights."

Chuck stopped stuffing his face for a second and looked at Thomas carefully. "You really think that, or you just trying to cheer me up?"

"We can do it." Thomas ate his last bite, took a big drink of water. He'd never felt like such a liar in his life. People were going to die. But he was going to do everything possible to make sure Chuck wasn't one of them. And Teresa. "Don't forget my promise. You can still plan on it."

Chuck frowned. "Big deal—I keep hearing the world is in klunky shape."

"Hey, maybe so, but we'll find the people who care about us—you'll see."

Chuck stood up. "Well, I don't wanna think about it," he announced. "Just get me out of the Maze, and I'll be one happy dude."

"Good that," Thomas agreed.

A commotion from the other tables caught his attention. Newt and Alby were gathering the Gladers, telling everyone it was time to go. Alby seemed mostly himself, but Thomas still worried about the guy's mental state. In Thomas's mind, Newt was in charge, but he could also be a loose cannon sometimes.

The icy fear and panic Thomas had experienced so often the last few days swept over him once again in full force. This was it. They were going. Trying not to think about it, to just act, he grabbed his backpack. Chuck did the same, and they headed for the West Door, the one leading to the Cliff.

Thomas found Minho and Teresa talking to each other near the left side of the Door, going over the hastily made plans to enter the escape code once they got into the Hole.

"You shanks ready?" Minho asked when they came up. "Thomas, this was all your idea, so it better work. If not, I'll kill ya before the Grievers can."

"Thanks," Thomas said. But he couldn't shake the twisting feeling in his gut. What if somehow he *was* wrong? What if the memories he'd had were false ones? *Planted* somehow? The thought terrified him, and he pushed it aside. There was no going back.

He looked at Teresa, who shifted from foot to foot, wringing her hands. "You okay?" he asked.

"I'm fine," she answered with a small smile, clearly not fine at all. "Just anxious to get it over with."

"Amen, sister," Minho said. He looked the calmest to Thomas, the most confident, the least scared. Thomas envied him.

When Newt finally had everyone gathered, he called for quiet, and Thomas turned to hear what he had to say. "There're forty-one of us." He pulled the backpack he was holding onto his shoulders, and hoisted a thick wooden pole with barbwire wrapped around its tip. The thing looked deadly. "Make sure you've got your weapons. Other than that, isn't a whole lot to buggin' say—you've all been told the plan. We're gonna fight our way through to the Griever Hole, and Tommy here's gonna punch in his little magic code and then we're gonna get payback on the Creators. Simple as that."

Thomas barely heard Newt, having seen Alby sulking over to the side, away from the main group of the Gladers, alone. Alby picked at the string of his bow while he stared at the ground. A quiver of arrows hung over his shoulder. Thomas felt a rising tide of worry that somehow Alby was unstable, that somehow he'd screw everything up. He decided to watch him carefully if he could.

"Shouldn't someone give a pep talk or something?" Minho asked, pulling Thomas's attention away from Alby.

"Go ahead," Newt replied.

Minho nodded and faced the crowd. "Be careful," he said dryly. "Don't die."

Thomas would have laughed if he could, but he was too scared for it to come out.

"Great. We're all bloody inspired," Newt answered, then pointed over his shoulder, toward the Maze. "You all know the plan. After two years of being treated like mice, tonight we're making a stand. Tonight we're taking the fight back to the Creators, no matter what we have to go through to get there. Tonight the Grievers better be scared."

Someone cheered, and then someone else. Soon shouts and battle calls broke out, rising in volume, filling the air like thunder. Thomas felt a trickle of courage inside him—he grasped it, clung to it, urged it to grow. Newt was right. Tonight, they'd fight. Tonight, they'd make their stand, once and for all.

Thomas was ready. He roared with the other Gladers. He knew they should probably be quiet, not bring any more attention to themselves, but he didn't care. The game was on.

Newt thrust his weapon into the air and yelled, "Hear that, Creators! We're coming!"

And with that, he turned and ran into the Maze, his limp barely noticeable. Into the gray air that seemed darker than the Glade, full of shadows and blackness. The Gladers around Thomas, still cheering, picked up their weapons and ran after him, even Alby. Thomas followed, falling into line between Teresa and Chuck, hefting a big wooden spear with a knife tied at its tip. The sudden feeling of responsibility for his friends almost overwhelmed him—made it hard to run. But he kept going, determined to win.

You can do this, he thought. *Just make it to that Hole.*

CHAPTER 55

Thomas kept a steady pace as he ran with the other Gladers along the stone pathways toward the Cliff. He'd grown used to running the Maze, but this was completely different. The sounds of shuffling feet echoed up the walls and the red lights of the beetle blades flashed more menacingly in the ivy—the Creators were certainly watching, listening. One way or another, there was going to be a fight.

Scared? Teresa asked him as they ran.

No, I love things made out of blubber and steel. Can't wait to see them. He felt no mirth or humor and wondered if there'd ever be a time again when he would.

So funny, she responded.

She was right next to him, but his eyes stayed glued up ahead. *We'll be fine. Just stay close to me and Minho.*

Ah, my Knight in Shining Armor. What, you don't think I can fend for myself?

Actually, he thought quite the opposite—Teresa seemed as tough as anybody there. *No, I'm just trying to be nice.*

The group was spread out across the full width of the corridor, running at a steady but quick pace—Thomas wondered how long the non-Runners would hold up. As if in response to the thought, Newt fell back, finally tapping Minho on the shoulder. "You lead the way now," Thomas heard him say.

Minho nodded and ran to the front, guiding the Gladers through all the turns necessary. Every step was agonizing for Thomas. What courage he'd gathered had turned to dread, and he wondered when the Grievers would finally give chase. Wondered when the fight would begin.

And so it went for him as they kept moving, those Gladers not used to running such distances gasping in huge gulps of air. But no one quit. On and on they ran, with no signs of Grievers. And as the time passed, Thomas let the slightest trickle of hope enter his system—maybe they'd make it before getting attacked. Maybe.

Finally, after the longest hour of Thomas's life, they reached the long alley that led to the last turn before the Cliff—a short corridor to the right that branched off like the stem of the letter *T.*

Thomas, his heart thumping, sweat slicking his skin, had moved up right behind Minho, Teresa at his side. Minho slowed at the corner, then stopped, holding up a hand to tell Thomas and the others to do the same. Then he turned, a look of horror on his face.

"Do you hear that?" he whispered.

Thomas shook his head, trying to squash the terror Minho's expression had given him.

Minho crept ahead and peeked around the sharp edge of stone, looking toward the Cliff. Thomas had seen him do that before, when they'd followed a Griever to this very spot. Just like that time, Minho jerked back and turned to face him.

"Oh, no," the Keeper said through a moan. "Oh, no."

Then Thomas heard it. Griever sounds. It was as if they'd been hiding, waiting, and now were coming to life. He didn't even have to look—he knew what Minho was going to say before he said it.

"There's at least a dozen of them. Maybe fifteen." He reached up and rubbed his eyes with the heels of his hands. "They're just waiting for us!"

The icy chill of fear bit Thomas harder than ever before. He looked over at Teresa, about to say something, but stopped when he saw the expression on her pale face—he'd never seen terror present itself so starkly.

Newt and Alby had moved up the line of waiting Gladers to join Thomas and the others. Apparently Minho's pronouncement had already been whispered through the ranks, because the first thing Newt said was "Well, we knew we'd have to fight." But the tremor in his voice gave him away—he was just trying to say the right thing.

Thomas felt it himself. It'd been easy to talk about—the nothing-to-lose fight, the hope that just one of them would be taken, the chance to finally escape. But now it was here, literally around the corner. Doubts that he could go through with it seeped into his mind and heart. He wondered why the Grievers were just waiting—the beetle blades had obviously let them know the Gladers were coming. Were the Creators *enjoying* this?

He had an idea. "Maybe they've already taken a kid back at the Glade. Maybe we can get past them—why else would they just be sitting—"

A loud noise from behind cut him off—he spun to see more Grievers moving down the corridor toward them, spikes flaring, metal arms groping, coming from the direction of the Glade. Thomas was just about to say something when he heard sounds from the other end of the long alley—he looked to see yet more Grievers.

The enemy was on all sides, blocking them off completely.

The Gladers surged toward Thomas, forming a tight group, forcing him to move out into the open intersection where the Cliff corridor met the long alley. He saw the pack of Grievers between them and the Cliff, spikes extended, their moist skin pulsing in and out. Waiting, watching. The other two groups of Grievers had closed in and stopped just a few dozen feet from the Gladers, also waiting, watching.

Thomas slowly turned in a circle, fought the fear as he took it all in. They were surrounded. They had no choice now—there was nowhere to go. A sharp pulsing pain throbbed behind his eyes.

The Gladers compressed into a tighter group around him, everyone facing outward, huddled together in the center of the *T* intersection. Thomas was pressed between Newt and Teresa—he could feel Newt trembling. No one said a word. The only sounds were the eerie moans and whirrs of machinery coming from the Grievers, sitting there as if enjoying the little trap they'd set for the humans. Their disgusting bodies heaved in and out with mechanical wheezes of breath.

What are they doing? Thomas called out to Teresa. *What are they waiting for?*

She didn't answer, which worried him. He reached out and squeezed her hand. The Gladers around him stood silent, clutching their meager weapons.

Thomas looked over at Newt. "Got any ideas?"

"No," he replied, his voice just the tiniest bit shaky. "I don't understand what they're bloody waitin' for."

"We shouldn't have come," Alby said. He'd been so quiet, his voice sounded odd, especially with the hollow echo the Maze walls created.

Thomas was in no mood for whining—they had to *do* something. "Well, we'd be no better off in the Homestead. Hate to say it, but if one of us dies, that's better than all of us." He really hoped the one-person-a-night thing was true now. Seeing all these Grievers close up hit home with an explosion of reality—could they really fight them all?

A long moment passed before Alby replied. "Maybe I should . . ." He trailed off and started walking forward—in the direction of the Cliff—slowly, as if in a trance. Thomas watched in detached awe—he couldn't believe his eyes.

"Alby?" Newt said. "Get back here!"

Instead of responding, Alby took off running—he headed straight for the pack of Grievers between him and the Cliff.

"Alby!" Newt screamed.

Thomas started to say something himself, but Alby had already made it to the monsters and jumped on top of one. Newt moved away from Thomas's side and toward Alby—but five or six Grievers had already burst to life and attacked the boy in a blur of metal and skin. Thomas reached out and grabbed Newt by the arms before he could go any farther, then pulled him backward.

"Let go!" Newt yelled, struggling to break loose.

"Are you nuts!" Thomas shouted. "There's nothing you can do!"

Two more Grievers broke from the pack and swarmed over Alby, piling on top of each other, snapping and cutting at the boy, as if they wanted to rub it in, show their vicious cruelty. Somehow, impossibly, Alby didn't scream. Thomas lost sight of the body as he struggled with Newt, thankful for the distraction. Newt finally gave up, collapsing backward in defeat.

Alby'd flipped once and for all, Thomas thought, fighting the urge to rid his stomach of its contents. Their leader had been so scared to go back to whatever he'd seen, he'd chosen to sacrifice himself instead. He was gone. Totally gone.

Thomas helped steady Newt on his feet; the Glader couldn't stop staring at the spot where his friend had disappeared.

"I can't believe it," Newt whispered. "I can't believe he just did that."

Thomas shook his head, unable to reply. Seeing Alby go down like that . . . a new kind of pain he'd never felt before filled his insides—an ill, disturbed pain; it felt worse than the physical kind. And he didn't even know if it had anything to do with Alby—he'd never much liked the guy. But the thought that what he'd just seen might happen to Chuck—or Teresa . . .

Minho moved closer to Thomas and Newt, squeezed Newt's shoulder. "We can't waste what he did." He turned toward Thomas. "We'll fight 'em if we have to, make a path to the Cliff for you and Teresa. Get in the Hole and do your thing—we'll keep them off until you scream for us to follow."

Thomas looked at each of the three sets of Grievers—not one had yet made a move toward the Gladers—and nodded. "Hopefully they'll go dormant for a while. We should only need a minute or so to punch in the code."

"How can you guys be so heartless?" Newt murmured, the disgust in his voice surprising Thomas.

"What do you want, Newt?" Minho said. "Should we all dress up and have a funeral?"

Newt didn't respond, still staring at the spot where the Grievers seemed to be *feeding* on Alby beneath them. Thomas couldn't help taking a peek—he saw a smear of bright red on one of the creatures' bodies. His stomach turned and he quickly looked away.

Minho continued. "Alby didn't wanna go back to his old life. He freaking *sacrificed* himself for us—and they aren't attacking, so maybe it worked. *We'd* be heartless if we wasted it."

Newt only shrugged, closed his eyes.

Minho turned and faced the huddled group of Gladers. "Listen up! Number one priority is to protect Thomas and Teresa. Get them to the Cliff and the Hole so—"

The sounds of the Grievers revving to life cut him off. Thomas looked up in horror. The creatures on both sides of their group seemed to have noticed them again. Spikes were popping in and out of blubbery skin; their bodies shuddered and pulsed. Then, in unison, the monsters moved forward, slowly, instrument-tipped appendages unfolding, pointed at Thomas and the Gladers, ready to kill. Tightening their trap formation like a noose, the Grievers steadily charged toward them.

Alby's sacrifice had failed miserably.

CHAPTER 56

Thomas grabbed Minho by the arm. "Somehow I have to get through that!" He nodded toward the rolling pack of Grievers between them and the Cliff—they looked like one big mass of rumbling, spiked blubber, glistening with flashes of lights off steel. They were even more menacing in the faded gray light.

Thomas waited for an answer as Minho and Newt exchanged a long glance. The anticipation of fighting was almost worse than the fear of it.

"They're *coming*!" Teresa yelled. "We have to do something!"

"You lead," Newt finally said to Minho, his voice barely more than a whisper. "Make a bloody path for Tommy and the girl. Do it."

Minho nodded once, a steel look of resolve hardening his features. Then he turned toward the Gladers. "We head straight for the Cliff! Fight through the middle, push the shuckin' things toward the walls. What matters most is getting Thomas and Teresa to the Griever Hole!"

Thomas looked away from him, back at the approaching monsters—they were only a few feet away. He gripped his poor excuse for a spear.

We have to stay close together, he told Teresa. *Let them do the fighting—we have to get through that Hole.* He felt like a coward, but he knew that any fighting—and any deaths—would be in vain if they didn't get that code punched, the door to the Creators opened.

I know, she replied. *Stick together.*

"Ready!" Minho yelled next to Thomas, raising his barbwire-wrapped club into the air with one hand, a long silver knife in the other. He pointed the knife at the horde of Grievers; a flash glinted off the blade. *"Now!"*

The Keeper ran forward without waiting for a response. Newt went after him, right on his heels, and then the rest of the Gladers followed, a tight pack of roaring boys charging ahead to a bloody battle, weapons raised. Thomas held Teresa's hand, let them all go past, felt them bump him, smelled their sweat, sensed their terror, waiting for the perfect opportunity to make his own dash.

Just as the first sounds of boys crashing into Grievers filled the air—pierced with screams and roars of machinery and wood clacking against steel—Chuck ran past Thomas, who quickly reached out and grabbed his arm.

Chuck stumbled backward, then looked up at Thomas, his eyes so full of fright Thomas felt something shatter in his heart. In that split second, he'd made a decision.

"Chuck, you're with me and Teresa." He said it forcefully, with authority, leaving no room for doubt.

Chuck looked ahead at the engaged battle. "But . . ." He trailed off, and Thomas knew the boy relished the idea though he was ashamed to admit it.

Thomas quickly tried to save his dignity. "We need your help in the Griever Hole, in case one of those things is in there waiting for us."

Chuck nodded quickly—too quickly. Again, Thomas felt the pang of sadness in his heart, felt the urge to get Chuck home safely stronger than he'd ever felt it before.

"Okay, then," Thomas said. "Hold Teresa's other hand. Let's go."

Chuck did as he was told, trying so hard to act brave. And, Thomas noted, not saying a word, perhaps for the first time in his life.

They've made an opening! Teresa shouted in Thomas's mind—it sent a quick snap of pain shooting through his skull. She pointed ahead, and Thomas saw the narrow aisle forming in the middle of the corridor, Gladers fighting wildly to push the Grievers toward the walls.

"Now!" Thomas shouted.

He sprinted ahead, pulling Teresa behind him, Teresa pulling Chuck behind her, running at full speed, spears and knives cocked for battle, forward into the bloody, scream-filled hallway of stone. Toward the Cliff.

War raged around them. Gladers fought, panic-induced adrenaline driving them on. The sounds echoing off the walls were a cacophony of terror—human screams, metal clashing against metal, motors roaring, the haunted shrieks of the Grievers, saws spinning, claws clasping, boys yelling for help. All was a blur, bloody and gray and flashes of steel; Thomas tried not to look left or right, only ahead, through the narrow gap formed by the Gladers.

Even as they ran, Thomas went through the code words again in his mind. *FLOAT, CATCH, BLEED, DEATH, STIFF, PUSH.* They just had to make it a few dozen feet more.

Something just sliced my arm! Teresa screamed. Even as she said it, Thomas felt a sharp stab in his leg. He didn't look back, didn't bother answering. The seething impossibility of their predicament was like a heavy deluge of black water flooding around him, dragging him toward surrender. He fought it, pushed himself forward.

There was the Cliff, opening out into a gray-dark sky, about twenty feet away. He surged ahead, pulling his friends.

Battles clashed on both sides of them; Thomas refused to look, refused to help. A Griever spun directly in his path; a boy, his face hidden from sight, was clutched in its claws, stabbing viciously into the thick, whalish skin, trying to escape. Thomas dodged to the left, kept running. He heard a shriek as he passed by, a throat-scorching wail that could only mean the Glader had lost the fight, met a horrific end. The scream ran on, shattering the air, overpowering the other sounds of war, until it faded in death. Thomas felt his heart tremble, hoped it wasn't someone he knew.

Just keep going! Teresa said.

"I know!" Thomas shouted back, this time out loud.

Someone sprinted past Thomas, bumped him. A Griever charged in from the right, blades twirling. A Glader cut it off, attacked it with two long swords, metal clacking and clanging as they fought. Thomas heard a distant voice, screaming the same words over and over, something about him. About protecting him as he ran. It was Minho, desperation and fatigue radiant in his shouts.

Thomas kept going.

One almost got Chuck! Teresa yelled, a violent echo in his head.

More Grievers came at them, more Gladers helped. Winston had picked up Alby's bow and arrow, flinging the steel-pointed shafts at anything nonhuman that moved, missing more than he hit. Boys Thomas didn't know ran alongside him, whacking at Griever instruments with their makeshift weapons, jumping on them, attacking. The sounds—clashes, clangs, screams, moaning wails, roars of engines, spinning saws, snapping blades, the screech of spikes against the floor, hair-raising pleas for help—it all grew to a crescendo, became unbearable.

Thomas screamed, but he kept running until they made it to the Cliff. He skidded to a stop, right on the edge. Teresa and Chuck bumped into him, almost sending all three of them to an endless fall. In a split second, Thomas surveyed his view of the Griever Hole. Hanging out, in the middle of thin air, were ivy vines stretching to nowhere.

Earlier, Minho and a couple of Runners had pulled out ropes of ivy and knotted them to vines still attached to the walls. They'd then tossed the loose ends over the Cliff, until they hit the Griever Hole, where now six or seven vines ran from the stone edge to an invisible rough square, hovering in the empty sky, where they disappeared into nothingness.

It was time to jump. Thomas hesitated, feeling one last moment of stark terror—hearing the horrible sounds behind him, seeing the illusion in front of him—then snapped out of it. "You first, Teresa." He wanted to go last to make sure a Griever didn't get her or Chuck.

To his surprise, she didn't hesitate. After squeezing Thomas's hand, then Chuck's shoulder, she leaped off the edge, immediately stiffening her legs, with her arms by her sides. Thomas held his breath until she slipped into the spot between the cut-off ivy ropes and disappeared. It looked as if she'd been erased from existence with one quick swipe.

"Whoa!" Chuck yelled, the slightest hint of his old self breaking through.

"*Whoa* is right," Thomas said. "You're next."

Before the boy could argue, Thomas grabbed him under his arms, squeezed Chuck's torso. "Push off with your legs and I'll give you a lift. Ready? One, two, *three!*" He grunted with effort, heaved him over toward the Hole.

Chuck screamed as he flew through the air, and he almost missed the target, but his feet went through; then his stomach and arms slammed against the sides of the invisible hole before he disappeared inside. The boy's bravery solidified something in Thomas's heart. He loved the kid. He loved him as if they had the same mom.

Thomas tightened the straps on his backpack, held his makeshift fighting spear tightly in his right fist. The sounds behind him were awful, horrible—he felt guilty for not helping. *Just do your part,* he told himself.

Steeling his nerves, he tapped his spear against the stone ground, then planted his left foot on the very edge of the Cliff and jumped, catapulting up and into the twilight air. He pulled the spear close to his torso, pointed his toes downward, stiffened his body.

Then he hit the Hole.

CHAPTER 57

A line of icy cold shot across Thomas's skin as he entered the Griever Hole, starting from his toes and continuing up his whole body, as if he'd jumped through a flat plane of freezing water. The world went even darker around him as his feet thumped to a landing on a slippery surface, then shot out from under him; he fell backward into Teresa's arms. She and Chuck helped him stand. It was a miracle Thomas hadn't stabbed someone's eye out with his spear.

The Griever Hole would've been pitch-black if not for the beam of Teresa's flashlight cutting through the darkness. As Thomas got his bearings, he realized they were standing in a ten-foot-high stone cylinder. It was damp, and covered in shiny, grimy oil, and it stretched out in front of them for dozens of yards before it faded into darkness. Thomas peered up at the Hole through which they'd come—it looked like a square window into a deep, starless space.

"The computer's over there," Teresa said, grabbing his attention.

Several feet down the tunnel, she had aimed her light at a small square of grimy glass that shone a dull green color. Beneath it, a keyboard was set into the wall, angling out enough for someone to type on it with ease if standing. There it was, ready for the code. Thomas couldn't help thinking it seemed too easy, too good to be true.

"Put the words in!" Chuck yelled, slapping Thomas on the shoulder. "Hurry!"

Thomas motioned for Teresa to do it. "Chuck and I'll keep watch, make sure a Griever doesn't come through the Hole." He just hoped the Gladers had turned their attention from making the aisle in the Maze to keeping the creatures away from the Cliff.

"Okay," Teresa said—Thomas knew she was too smart to waste time arguing about it. She stepped up to the keyboard and screen, then started typing.

Wait! Thomas called to her mind. *Are you sure you know the words?*

She turned to him and scowled. "I'm not an idiot, Tom. Yes, I'm perfectly capable of remembering—"

A loud bang from above and behind them cut her off, made Thomas jump. He spun around to see a Griever plop through the Griever Hole, appearing as if by magic from the dark square of black. The thing had retracted its spikes and arms to enter—when it landed with a squishy thump, a dozen sharp and nasty objects popped back out, looking deadlier than ever.

Thomas pushed Chuck behind him and faced the creature, holding out his spear as if that would ward it off. "Just keep typing, Teresa!" he yelled.

A skinny metallic rod burst out of the Griever's moist skin, unfolding into a long appendage with three spinning blades, which moved directly toward Thomas's face.

He gripped the end of his spear with both hands, squeezing tightly as he lowered the knife-laced point to the ground in front of him. The bladed arm moved within two feet, ready to slice his skin to bits. When it was just a foot away, Thomas tensed his muscles and swung the spear up, around, and toward the ceiling as hard as he could. It smacked the metal arm and pivoted the thing skyward, revolving in an arc until it slammed back into the body of the Griever. The monster let out an angry shriek and pulled back several feet, its spikes retracting into its body. Thomas heaved breaths in and out.

Maybe I can hold it off, he said quickly to Teresa. *Just hurry!*

I'm almost done, she replied.

The Griever's spikes appeared again; it surged ahead and another arm popped out of its skin and shot forward, this one with huge claws, snapping to grab the spear. Thomas swung, this time from above his head, throwing every bit of strength into the attack. The spear crashed into the base of the claws. With a loud clunk, and then a squishing sound, the entire arm ripped free of its socket, falling to the floor. Then, from some kind of mouth that Thomas couldn't see, the Griever let out a long, piercing shriek and pulled back again; the spikes disappeared.

"These things are beatable!" Thomas shouted.

It won't let me enter the last word! Teresa said in his mind.

Barely hearing her, not quite understanding, he yelled out a roar and charged ahead to take advantage of the Griever's moment of weakness. Swinging his spear wildly, he jumped on top of the creature's bulbous body, whacking two metal arms away from him with a loud crack. He lifted the spear above his head, braced his feet—felt them sink into the disgusting blubber—then thrust the spear down and into the monster. A slimy yellow goo exploded from the flesh, splashing over Thomas's legs as he drove the spear as far as it would sink into the thing's body. Then he released the hilt of the weapon and jumped away, running back to Chuck and Teresa.

Thomas watched in sick fascination as the Griever twitched uncontrollably, spewing the yellow oil in every direction. Spikes popped in and out of the skin; its remaining arms swung around in mass confusion, at times impaling its own body. Soon it began to slow, losing energy with every ounce of blood—or fuel—it lost.

A few seconds later, it stopped moving altogether. Thomas couldn't believe it. He absolutely couldn't believe it. He'd just defeated a

Griever, one of the monsters that had terrorized the Gladers for more than two years.

He glanced behind him at Chuck, standing there with eyes wide.

"You killed it," the boy said. He laughed, as if that one act had solved all their problems.

"Wasn't so hard," Thomas muttered, then turned to see Teresa frantically typing away at the keyboard. He knew immediately that something was wrong.

"What's the problem?" he asked, almost shouting. He ran up to look over her shoulder and saw that she kept typing the word *PUSH* over and over, but nothing appeared on the screen.

She pointed at the dirty square of glass, empty but for its greenish glow of life. "I put in all the words and one by one they appeared on the screen; then something beeped and they'd disappear. But it won't let me type in the last word. Nothing's happening!"

Cold filled Thomas's veins as Teresa's words sank in. "Well . . . why?"

"I don't know!" She tried again, then again. Nothing appeared.

"Thomas!" Chuck screamed from behind them. Thomas turned to see him pointing at the Griever Hole—another creature was making its way through. As he watched, it plopped down on top of its dead brother and another Griever started entering the Hole.

"What's taking so long!" Chuck cried frantically. "You said they'd turn off when you punched in the code!"

Both Grievers had righted themselves and extended their spikes, had started moving toward them.

"It won't let us enter the word *PUSH*," Thomas said absently, not really speaking to Chuck but trying to think of a solution . . .

I don't get it, Teresa said.

The Grievers were coming, only a few feet away. Feeling his will fade into blackness, Thomas braced his feet and held up his fists half-heartedly. It was supposed to work. The code was supposed to—

"Maybe you should just push that button," Chuck said.

Thomas was so surprised by the random statement that he turned away from the Grievers, looked at the boy. Chuck was pointing at a spot near the floor, right underneath the screen and keyboard.

Before he could move, Teresa was already down there, crouching on her knees. And consumed by curiosity, by a fleeting hope, Thomas joined her, collapsing to the ground to get a better look. He heard the Griever moan and roar behind him, felt a sharp claw grab his shirt, felt a prick of pain. But he could only stare.

A small red button was set into the wall only a few inches above the floor. Three black words were printed there, so obvious he couldn't believe he'd missed it earlier.

Kill the Maze

More pain snapped Thomas out of his stupor. The Griever had grabbed him with two instruments, had started dragging him backward. The other one had gone after Chuck and was just about to swipe at the kid with a long blade.

A button.

"Push!" Thomas screamed, louder than he'd thought possible for a human being to scream.

And Teresa did.

She pushed the button and everything went perfectly silent. Then, from somewhere down the dark tunnel, came the sound of a door sliding open.

CHAPTER 58

Almost at once the Grievers had shut down completely, their instruments sucked back through their blubbery skin, their lights turned off, their inside machines dead quiet. And that door . . .

Thomas fell to the floor after being released by his captor's claws, and despite the pain of several lacerations across his back and shoulders, elation surged through him so strongly he didn't know how to react. He gasped, then laughed, then choked on a sob before laughing again.

Chuck had scooted away from the Grievers, bumping into Teresa—she held him tightly, squeezing him in a fierce hug.

"You did it, Chuck," Teresa said. "We were so worried about the stupid code words, we didn't think to look around for something to *push*—the last word, the last piece of the puzzle."

Thomas laughed again, in disbelief that such a thing could be possible so soon after what they'd gone through. "She's right, Chuck—you saved us, man! I *told* you we needed you!" Thomas scrambled to his feet and joined the other two in a group hug, almost delirious. "Chuck's a shucking hero!"

"What about the others?" Teresa said with a nod toward the Griever Hole. Thomas felt his elation wither, and he stepped back and turned toward the Hole.

As if in answer to her question, someone fell through the black square—it was Minho, looking as if he'd been scratched or stabbed on ninety percent of his body.

"Minho!" Thomas shouted, filled with relief. "Are you okay? What about everybody else?"

Minho stumbled toward the curved wall of the tunnel, then leaned there, gulping big breaths. "We lost a ton of people. . . . It's a mess of blood up there . . . then they all just shut down." He paused, taking in a really deep breath and letting it go in a rush of air. "You did it. I can't believe it actually worked."

Newt came through then, followed by Frypan. Then Winston and others. Before long eighteen boys had joined Thomas and his friends in the tunnel, making a total of twenty-one Gladers in all. Every last one of those who'd stayed behind and fought was covered in Griever sludge and human blood, their clothes ripped to shreds.

"The rest?" Thomas asked, terrified of the answer.

"Half of us," Newt said, his voice weak. "Dead."

No one said a word then. No one said a word for a very long time.

"You know what?" Minho said, standing up a little taller. "Half might've died, but half of us shucking lived. And nobody got stung—just like Thomas thought. We've gotta get out of here."

Too many, Thomas thought. *Too many by far.* His joy dribbled away, turned into a deep mourning for the twenty people who'd lost their lives. Despite the alternative, despite knowing that if they hadn't tried to escape, *all* of them might've died, it still hurt, even though he hadn't known them very well. Such a display of death—how could it be considered a victory?

"Let's get out of here," Newt said. "Right now."

"Where do we go?" Minho asked.

Thomas pointed down the long tunnel. "I heard the door open

down that way." He tried to push away the ache of it all—the horrors of the battle they'd just won. The losses. He pushed it away, knowing they were nowhere near safe yet.

"Well—let's go," Minho answered. And the older boy turned and started walking up the tunnel without waiting for a response.

Newt nodded, ushering the other Gladers past him to follow. One by one they went until only he remained with Thomas and Teresa.

"I'll go last," Thomas said.

No one argued. Newt went, then Chuck, then Teresa, into the black tunnel. Even the flashlights seemed to get swallowed by the darkness. Thomas followed, not even bothering to look back at the dead Grievers.

After a minute or so of walking, he heard a shriek from ahead, followed by another, then another. Their cries faded, as if they were falling. . . .

Murmurs made their way down the line, and finally Teresa turned to Thomas. "Looks like it ends in a slide up there, shooting downward."

Thomas's stomach turned at the thought. It seemed like it *was* a game—for whoever had built the place, at least.

One by one he heard the Gladers' dwindling shouts and hoots up ahead. Then it was Newt's turn, then Chuck's. Teresa shone her light down on a steeply descending, slick black chute of metal.

Guess we have no choice, she said to his mind.

Guess not. Thomas had a strong feeling it wasn't a way out of their nightmare; he just hoped it didn't lead to another pack of Grievers.

Teresa slipped down the slide with an almost cheerful shriek, and Thomas followed her before he could talk himself out of it—anything was better than the Maze.

His body shot down a steep decline, slick with an oily goo that smelled awful—like burnt plastic and overused machinery. He twisted his body until he got his feet in front of him, then tried to hold his hands out to slow himself down. It was useless—the greasy stuff covered every inch of the stone; he couldn't grip anything.

The screams of the other Gladers echoed off the tunnel walls as they slid down the oily chute. Panic gripped Thomas's heart. He couldn't fight off the image that they'd been swallowed by some gigantic beast and were sliding down its long esophagus, about to land in its stomach at any second. And as if his thoughts had materialized, the smells changed—to something more like mildew and rot. He started gagging; it took all his effort not to throw up on himself.

The tunnel began to twist, turning in a rough spiral, just enough to slow them down, and Thomas's feet smacked right into Teresa, hitting her in the head; he recoiled and a feeling of complete misery sank over him. They were still falling. Time seemed to stretch out, endless.

Around and around they went down the tube. Nausea burned in his stomach—the squishing of the goo against his body, the smell, the circling motion. He was just about to turn his head to the side to throw up when Teresa let out a sharp cry—this time there was no echo. A second later, Thomas flew out of the tunnel and landed on her.

Bodies scrambled everywhere, people on top of people, groaning and squirming in confusion as they tried to push away from each other. Thomas wiggled his arms and legs to scoot away from Teresa, then crawled a few more feet to throw up, emptying his stomach.

Still shuddering from the experience, he wiped at his mouth with his hand, only to realize it was covered in slimy filth. He sat up, rubbing both hands on the ground, and he finally got a good look at where they'd arrived. As he gaped, he saw, also, that everyone else had pulled themselves together into a group, taking in the new surroundings.

Thomas had seen glimpses of it during the Changing, but didn't truly remember it until that very moment.

They were in a huge underground chamber big enough to hold nine or ten Homesteads. From top to bottom, side to side, the place was covered in all kinds of machinery and wires and ducts and computers. On one side of the room—to his right—there was a row of forty or so large white pods that looked like enormous coffins. Across from that on the other side stood large glass doors, although the lighting made it impossible to see what was on the other side.

"Look!" someone shouted, but he'd already seen it, his breath catching in his throat. Goose bumps broke out all over him, a creepy fear trickling down his spine like a wet spider.

Directly in front of them, a row of twenty or so darkly tinged windows stretched across the compound horizontally, one after the other. Behind each one, a person—some men, some women, all of them pale and thin—sat observing the Gladers, staring through the glass with squinted eyes. Thomas shuddered, terrified—they all looked like ghosts. Angry, starving, sinister apparitions of people who'd never been happy when alive, much less dead.

But Thomas knew they were not, of course, ghosts. They were the people who'd sent them all to the Glade. The people who'd taken their lives away from them.

The Creators.

CHAPTER 59

Thomas took a step backward, noticing others doing the same. A deathly silence sucked the life out of the air as every last Glader stared at the row of windows, at the row of observers. Thomas watched one of them look down to write something, another reach up and put on a pair of glasses. They all wore black coats over white shirts, a word stitched on their right breast—he couldn't quite make out what it said. None of them wore any kind of discernible facial expression—they were all sallow and gaunt, miserably sad to look upon.

They continued to stare at the Gladers; a man shook his head, a woman nodded. Another man reached up and scratched his nose—the most human thing Thomas had seen any of them do.

"Who are those people?" Chuck whispered, but his voice echoed throughout the chamber with a raspy edge.

"The Creators," Minho said; then he spat on the floor. "I'm gonna break your faces!" he screamed, so loudly Thomas almost held his hands over his ears.

"What do we do?" Thomas asked. "What are they waiting on?"

"They've probably revved the Grievers back up," Newt said. "They're probably coming right—"

A loud, slow beeping sound cut him off, like the warning alarm of a huge truck driving in reverse, but much more powerful. It came from everywhere, booming and echoing throughout the chamber.

"What now?" Chuck asked, not hiding the concern in his voice.

For some reason everyone looked at Thomas; he shrugged in answer—he'd only remembered so much, and now he was just as clueless as anyone else. And scared. He craned his neck as he scanned the place top to bottom, trying to find the source of the beeps. But nothing had changed. Then, out of the corner of his eye, he noticed the other Gladers looking in the direction of the doors. He did as well; his heart quickened when he saw that one of the doors was swinging open toward them.

The beeping stopped, and a silence as deep as outer space settled on the chamber. Thomas waited without breathing, braced himself for something horrible to come flying through the door.

Instead, two people walked into the room.

One was a woman. An actual grown-up. She seemed very ordinary, wearing black pants and a button-down white shirt with a logo on the breast—WICKED spelled in blue capital letters. Her brown hair was cut at the shoulder, and she had a thin face with dark eyes. As she walked toward the group, she neither smiled nor frowned—it was almost as if she didn't notice or care they were standing there.

I know her, Thomas thought. But it was a cloudy kind of recollection—he couldn't remember her name or what she had to do with the Maze, but she seemed familiar. And not just her looks, but the way she walked, her mannerisms—stiff, without a hint of joy. She stopped several feet in front of the Gladers and slowly looked left to right, taking them all in.

The other person, standing next to her, was a boy wearing an overly large sweatshirt, its hood pulled up over his head, concealing his face.

"Welcome back," the woman finally said. "Over two years, and so few dead. Amazing."

Thomas felt his mouth drop open—felt anger redden his face.

"*Excuse* me?" Newt asked.

Her eyes scanned the crowd again before falling on Newt. "Everything has gone according to plan, Mr. Newton. Although we expected a few more of you to give up along the way."

She glanced over at her companion, then reached out and pulled the hood off the boy. He looked up, his eyes wet with tears. Every Glader in the room sucked in a breath of surprise. Thomas felt his knees buckle.

It was Gally.

Thomas blinked, then rubbed his eyes, like something out of a cartoon. He was consumed with shock and anger.

It was *Gally*.

"What's *he* doing here!" Minho shouted.

"You're safe now," the woman responded as if she hadn't heard him. "Please, be at ease."

"At ease?" Minho barked. "Who are you, telling us to be at ease? We wanna see the police, the mayor, the president—somebody!" Thomas worried what Minho might do—then again, Thomas kind of wanted him to go punch her in the face.

She narrowed her eyes as she looked at Minho. "You have no idea what you're talking about, boy. I'd expect more maturity from someone who's passed the Maze Trials." Her condescending tone shocked Thomas.

Minho started to retort, but Newt elbowed him in the gut.

"Gally," Newt said. "What's going on?"

The dark-haired boy looked at him; his eyes flared for a moment, his head shaking slightly. But he didn't respond. *Something's off with him,* Thomas thought. Worse than before.

The woman nodded as if proud of him. "One day you'll all be

grateful for what we've done for you. I can only promise this, and trust your minds to accept it. If you don't, then the whole thing was a mistake. Dark times, Mr. Newton. Dark times."

She paused. "There is, of course, one final Variable." She stepped back.

Thomas focused on Gally. The boy's whole body trembled, his face pasty white, making his wet, red eyes stand out like bloody splotches on paper. His lips pressed together; the skin around them twitched, as if he were trying to speak but couldn't.

"Gally?" Thomas asked, trying to suppress the complete hatred he had for him.

Words burst from Gally's mouth. "They . . . can control me . . . I don't—" His eyes bulged, a hand went to his throat as if he were choking. "I . . . have . . . to . . ." Each word was a croaking cough. Then he stilled, his face calming, his body relaxing.

It was just like Alby in bed, back in the Glade, after he went through the Changing. The same type of thing had happened to him. What did it—

But Thomas didn't have time to finish his thought. Gally reached behind himself, pulled something long and shiny from his back pocket. The lights of the chamber flashed off the silvery surface—a wicked-looking dagger, gripped tightly in his fingers. With unexpected speed, he reared back and threw the knife at Thomas. As he did so, Thomas heard a shout to his right, sensed *movement*. Toward him.

The blade windmilled, its every turn visible to Thomas, as if the world had turned to slow motion. As if it did so for the sole purpose of allowing him to feel the terror of seeing such a thing. On the knife came, flipping over and over, straight at him. A strangled cry was forming in his throat; he urged himself to move but he couldn't.

Then, inexplicably, Chuck was there, diving in front of him. Thomas felt as if his feet had been frozen in blocks of ice; he could only stare at the scene of horror unfolding before him, completely helpless.

With a sickening, wet thunk, the dagger slammed into Chuck's chest, burying itself to the hilt. The boy screamed, fell to the floor, his body already convulsing. Blood poured from the wound, dark crimson. His legs slapped against the floor, feet kicking aimlessly with onrushing death. Red spit oozed from between his lips. Thomas felt as if the world were collapsing around him, crushing his heart.

He fell to the ground, pulled Chuck's shaking body into his arms.

"Chuck!" he screamed; his voice felt like acid ripping through his throat. *"Chuck!"*

The boy shook uncontrollably, blood everywhere, wetting Thomas's hands. Chuck's eyes had rolled up in their sockets, dull white orbs. Blood trickled out of his nose and mouth.

"Chuck . . . ," Thomas said, this time a whisper. There had to be something they could do. They could save him. They—

The boy stopped convulsing, stilled. His eyes slid back into normal position, focused on Thomas, clinging to life. "Thom . . . mas." It was one word, barely there.

"Hang on, Chuck," Thomas said. "Don't die—fight it. *Someone get help!*"

Nobody moved, and deep inside, Thomas knew why. Nothing *could* help now. It was over. Black spots swam before Thomas's eyes; the room tilted and swayed. *No,* he thought. *Not Chuck. Not Chuck. Anyone but Chuck.*

"Thomas," Chuck whispered. "Find . . . my mom." A racking cough burst from his lungs, throwing a spray of blood. "Tell her . . ."

He didn't finish. His eyes closed, his body went limp. One last breath wheezed from his mouth.

Thomas stared at him, stared at his friend's lifeless body.

Something happened within Thomas. It started deep down in his chest, a seed of rage. Of revenge. Of hate. Something dark and terrible. And then it exploded, bursting through his lungs, through his neck, through his arms and legs. Through his mind.

He let go of Chuck, stood up, trembling, turned to face their new visitors.

And then Thomas snapped. He completely and utterly *snapped*.

He rushed forward, threw himself on Gally, grasping with his fingers like claws. He found the boy's throat, squeezed, fell to the ground on top of him. He straddled the boy's torso, gripped him with his legs so he couldn't escape. Thomas started punching.

He held Gally down with his left hand, pushing down on the boy's neck, as his right fist rained punches upon Gally's face, one after another. Down and down and down, slamming his balled knuckles into the boy's cheek and nose. There was crunching, there was blood, there were horrible screams. Thomas didn't know which were louder—Gally's or his own. He beat him—*beat* him as he released every ounce of rage he'd ever owned.

And then he was being pulled away by Minho and Newt, his arms still flailing even when they only hit air. They dragged him across the floor; he fought them, squirmed, yelled to be left alone. His eyes remained on Gally, lying there, still; Thomas could feel the hatred pouring out, as if a visible line of flame connected them.

And then, just like that, it all vanished. There were only thoughts of Chuck.

He threw off Minho's and Newt's grip, ran to the limp, lifeless body of his friend. He grabbed him, pulled him back into his arms, ignoring the blood, ignoring the frozen look of death on the boy's face.

"No!" Thomas shouted, sadness consuming him. *"No!"*

Teresa was there, put her hand on his shoulder. He shook it away.

"I promised him!" he screamed, realizing even as he did so that his voice was laced with something wrong. Almost insanity. "I promised I'd save him, take him home! I *promised* him!"

Teresa didn't respond, only nodded, her eyes cast to the ground.

Thomas hugged Chuck to his chest, squeezed him as tightly as possible, as if that could somehow bring him back, or show thanks for saving his life, for being his friend when no one else would.

Thomas cried, wept like he'd never wept before. His great, racking sobs echoed through the chamber like the sounds of tortured pain.

CHAPTER 60

He finally pulled it all back into his heart, sucking in the painful tide of his misery. In the Glade, Chuck had become a symbol for him—a beacon that somehow they could make everything right again in the world. Sleep in beds. Get kissed goodnight. Have bacon and eggs for breakfast, go to a real school. Be happy.

But now Chuck was gone. And his limp body, to which Thomas still clung, seemed a cold talisman—that not only would those dreams of a hopeful future never come to pass, but that life had never been that way in the first place. That even in escape, dreary days lay ahead. A life of sorrow.

His returning memories were sketchy at best. But not much good floated in the muck.

Thomas reeled in the pain, locked it somewhere deep inside him. He did it for Teresa. For Newt and Minho. Whatever darkness awaited them, they'd be together, and that was all that mattered right then.

He let go of Chuck, slumped backward, trying not to look at the boy's shirt, black with blood. He wiped the tears from his cheeks, rubbed his eyes, thinking he should be embarrassed but not feeling that way. Finally, he looked up. Looked up at Teresa and her enormous blue eyes, heavy with sadness—just as much for him as for Chuck, he was sure of it.

She reached down, grabbed his hand, helped him stand. Once he was up, she didn't let go, and neither did he. He squeezed, tried to say what he felt by doing so. No one else said a word, most of them staring at Chuck's body without expression, as if they'd moved far beyond feeling. No one looked at Gally, breathing but still.

The woman from WICKED broke the silence.

"All things happen for a purpose," she said, any sign of malice now gone from her voice. "You must understand this."

Thomas looked at her, threw all his compressed hatred into the glare. But he did nothing.

Teresa placed her other hand on his arm, gripped his bicep. *What now?* she asked.

I don't know, he replied. *I can't—*

His sentence was cut short by a sudden series of shouts and commotion outside the entrance through which the woman had come. She visibly panicked, the blood draining from her face as she turned toward the door. Thomas followed her gaze.

Several men and women dressed in grimy jeans and soaking-wet coats burst through the entrance with guns raised, yelling and screaming words over each other. It was impossible to understand what they were saying. Their guns—some were rifles, other pistols—looked . . . archaic, rustic. Almost like toys abandoned in the woods for years, recently discovered by the next generation of kids ready to play war.

Thomas stared in shock as two of the newcomers tackled the WICKED woman to the floor. Then one stepped back and drew up his gun, aimed.

No way, Thomas thought. *No—*

Flashes lit the air as several shots exploded from the gun, slamming into the woman's body. She was dead, a bloody mess.

Thomas took several steps backward, almost stumbled.

A man walked up to the Gladers as the others in his group spread out around them, sweeping their guns left and right as they shot at the observation windows, shattering them. Thomas heard screams, saw blood, looked away, focused on the man who approached them. He had dark hair, his face young but full of wrinkles around the eyes, as if he'd spent each day of his life worrying about how to make it to the next.

"We don't have time to explain," the man said, his voice as strained as his face. "Just follow me and run like your life depends on it. Because it does."

With that the man made a few motions to his companions, then turned and ran out the big glass doors, his gun held rigidly before him. Gunfire and cries of agony still rattled the chamber, but Thomas did his best to ignore them and follow instructions.

"Go!" one of the rescuers—that was the only way Thomas could think of them—screamed from behind.

After the briefest hesitation, the Gladers followed, almost stomping each other in their rush to get out of the chamber, as far away from the Grievers and the Maze as possible. Thomas, his hand still gripping Teresa's, ran with them, bunched up in the back of the group. They had no choice but to leave Chuck's body behind.

Thomas felt no emotion—he was completely numb. He ran down a long hallway, into a dimly lit tunnel. Up a winding flight of stairs. Everything was dark, smelled like electronics. Down another hallway. Up more stairs. More hallways. Thomas wanted to ache for Chuck, get excited about their escape, rejoice that Teresa was there with him. But he'd seen too much. There was only emptiness now. A void. He kept going.

On they ran, some of the men and women leading from ahead, some yelling encouragement from behind.

They reached another set of glass doors and went through them into a massive downpour of rain, falling from a black sky. Nothing was visible but dull sparkles flashing off the pounding sheets of water.

The leader didn't stop moving until they reached a huge bus, its sides dented and scarred, most of the windows webbed with cracks. Rain sluiced down it all, making Thomas imagine a huge beast cresting out of the ocean.

"Get on!" the man screamed. "Hurry!"

They did, forming into a tight pack behind the door as they entered, one by one. It seemed to take forever, Gladers pushing and scrambling their way up the three stairs and into the seats.

Thomas was at the back, Teresa right in front of him. Thomas looked up into the sky, felt the water beat against his face—it was warm, almost hot, had a weird thickness to it. Oddly, it helped break him out of his funk, snap him to attention. Maybe it was just the ferocity of the deluge. He focused on the bus, on Teresa, on escape.

They were almost to the door when a hand suddenly slammed against his shoulder, gripping his shirt. He cried out as someone jerked him backward, ripping his hand out of Teresa's—he saw her spin around just in time to watch as he slammed into the ground, throwing up a spray of water. A bolt of pain shot down his spine as a woman's head appeared two inches above him, upside down, blocking out Teresa.

Greasy hair hung down, touching Thomas, framing a face hidden in shadow. A horrible smell filled his nostrils, like eggs and milk gone rotten. The woman pulled back enough for someone's flashlight to reveal her features—pale, wrinkly skin covered in horrible sores, oozing with pus. Sheer terror filled Thomas, froze him.

"Gonna save us all!" the hideous woman said, spit flying out of her mouth, spraying Thomas. "Gonna save us from the Flare!" She laughed, not much more than a hacking cough.

The woman yelped when one of the rescuers grabbed her with both hands and yanked her off of Thomas, who recovered his wits and scrambled to his feet. He backed into Teresa, staring as the man dragged the woman away, her legs kicking out weakly, her eyes on Thomas. She pointed at him, called out, "Don't believe a word they tell ya! Gonna save us from the Flare, ya are!"

When the man was several yards from the bus, he tossed the woman to the ground. "Stay put or I'll shoot you dead!" he yelled at her; then he turned to Thomas. "Get on the bus!"

Thomas, so terrified by the ordeal that his body shook, turned and followed Teresa up the stairs and into the aisle of the bus. Wide eyes watched him as they walked all the way to the back seat and plopped down; they huddled together. Black water washed down the windows outside. The rain drummed on the roof, heavy; thunder shook the skies above them.

What was *that?* Teresa said in his mind.

Thomas couldn't answer, just shook his head. Thoughts of Chuck flooded him again, replacing the crazy woman, deadening his heart. He just didn't care, didn't feel any relief at escaping the Maze. *Chuck* . . .

One of the rescuers, a woman, sat across from Thomas and Teresa; the leader who'd spoken to them earlier climbed onto the bus and took a seat at the wheel, cranked up the engine. The bus started rolling forward.

Just as it did, Thomas saw a flash of movement outside the window. The sore-riddled woman had gotten to her feet, was sprinting toward the front of the bus, waving her arms wildly, screaming something drowned out by the sounds of the storm. Her eyes were lit with lunacy or terror—Thomas couldn't tell which.

He leaned toward the glass of the window as she disappeared from his view up ahead.

"Wait!" Thomas shrieked, but no one heard him. Or if they did, they didn't care.

The driver gunned the engine—the bus lurched as it slammed into the woman's body. A thump almost jolted Thomas out of his seat as the front wheels ran over her, quickly followed by a second thump—the back wheels. Thomas looked at Teresa, saw the sickened look on her face that surely mirrored his own.

Without a word, the driver kept his foot on the gas and the bus plowed forward, driving off into the rain-swept night.

CHAPTER 61

The next hour or so was a blur of sights and sounds for Thomas.

The driver drove at reckless speeds, through towns and cities, the heavy rain obscuring most of the view. Lights and buildings were warped and watery, like something out of a drug-induced hallucination. At one point people outside rushed the bus, their clothes ratty, hair matted to their heads, strange sores like those Thomas had seen on the woman covering their terrified faces. They pounded on the sides of the vehicle as if they wanted to get on, wanted to escape whatever horrible lives they were living.

The bus never slowed. Teresa remained silent next to Thomas.

He finally got up enough nerve to speak to the woman sitting across the aisle.

"What's going on?" he asked, not sure how else to pose it.

The woman looked over at him. Wet, black hair hung in strings around her face. Dark eyes full of sorrow. "That's a very long story." The woman's voice came out much kinder than Thomas had expected, giving him hope that she truly was a friend—that all of their rescuers were friends. Despite the fact that they'd run over a woman in cold blood.

"Please," Teresa said. "Please tell us something."

The woman looked back and forth between Thomas and Teresa, then let out a sigh. "It'll take a while before you get your memories back, if ever—we're not scientists, we have no idea what they did to you, or how they did it."

Thomas's heart dropped at the thought of maybe having lost his memory forever, but he pressed on. "Who are they?" he asked.

"It started with the sun flares," the woman said, her gaze growing distant.

"What—" Teresa began, but Thomas shushed her.

Just let her talk, he said to her mind. *She looks like she will.*

Okay.

The woman almost seemed in a trance as she spoke, never taking her eyes off an indistinct spot in the distance. "The sun flares couldn't have been predicted. Sun flares are normal, but these were unprecedented, massive, spiking higher and higher—and once they were noticed, it was only minutes before their heat slammed into Earth. First our satellites were burned out, and thousands died instantly, millions within days, countless miles became wastelands. Then came the sickness."

She paused, took a breath. "As the ecosystem fell apart, it became impossible to control the sickness—even to keep it in South America. The jungles were gone, but the insects weren't. People call it the Flare now. It's a horrible, horrible thing. Only the richest can be treated, no one can be cured. Unless the rumors from the Andes are true."

Thomas almost broke his own advice—questions filled his mind. Horror grew in his heart. He sat and listened as the woman continued.

"As for you, all of you—you're just a few of millions orphaned. They tested thousands, chose you for the big one. The ultimate test. Everything you lived through was calculated and thought through. Catalysts to study your reactions, your brain waves, your thoughts. All in an attempt to find those capable of helping us find a way to beat the Flare."

She paused again, pulled a string of hair behind her ear. "Most of the physical effects are caused by something else. First the delusions start, then animal instincts begin to overpower the human ones. Finally it consumes them, destroys their humanity. It's all in the brain. The Flare *lives* in their brains. It is an awful thing. Better to die than catch it."

The woman broke her gaze into nothingness and focused on Thomas, then looked at Teresa, then Thomas again. "We won't let them do this to children. We've sworn our lives to fighting WICKED. We can't lose our humanity, no matter the end result."

She folded her hands in her lap, looked down at them. "You'll learn more in time. We live far in the north. We're separated from the Andes by thousands of miles. They call it the Scorch—it lies between here and there. It's centered mainly around what they used to call the equator—it's just heat and dust now, filled with savages consumed by the Flare beyond help. We're trying to cross that land—to find the cure. But until then, we'll fight WICKED and stop the experiments and tests." She looked carefully at Thomas, then Teresa. "It's our hope that you'll join us."

She looked away then, gazing out her window.

Thomas looked at Teresa, raised his eyebrows in question. She simply shook her head and then laid it on his shoulder and closed her eyes.

I'm too tired to think about it, she said. *Let's just be safe for now.*

Maybe we are, he replied. *Maybe.*

He heard the soft sounds of her sleep, but he knew that sleep would be impossible for him. He felt such a raging storm of conflicting emotions, he couldn't identify any of them. Still—it was better than the dull void he'd experienced earlier. He could only sit and stare out the window into the rain and blackness, pondering words like *Flare* and *sickness* and *experiment* and *Scorch* and *WICKED.* He could only sit and hope that things might be better now than they'd been in the Maze.

But as he jiggled and swayed with the movements of the bus, felt Teresa's head thump against his shoulder every once in a while when they hit big bumps, heard her stir and fall back to sleep, heard the murmurs of other conversations from other Gladers, his thoughts kept returning to one thing.

Chuck.

Two hours later, the bus stopped.

They had pulled into a muddy parking lot that surrounded a nondescript building with several rows of windows. The woman and other rescuers shuffled the nineteen boys and one girl through the front door and up a flight of stairs, then into a huge dormitory with a series of bunk beds lined up along one of the walls. On the opposite side were some dressers and tables. Curtain-covered windows checkered each wall of the room.

Thomas took it all in with a distant and muted wonder—he was far past being surprised or overcome by anything ever again.

The place was full of color. Bright yellow paint, red blankets, green curtains. After the drab grayness of the Glade, it was as if they'd been transported to a living rainbow. Seeing it all, seeing the beds and the dressers, all made up and fresh—the sense of normalcy was almost overwhelming. Too good to be true. Minho said it best on entering their new world: "I've been shucked and gone to heaven."

Thomas found it hard to feel joy, as if he'd betray Chuck by doing so. But there was something there. Something.

Their bus-driving leader left the Gladers in the hands of a small staff—nine or ten men and women dressed in pressed black pants and white shirts, their hair immaculate, their faces and hands clean. They were smiling.

The colors. The beds. The staff. Thomas felt an impossible happiness trying to break through inside him. An enormous pit lurked in the middle of it, though. A dark depression that might never leave—memories of Chuck and his brutal murder. His sacrifice. But despite that, despite everything, despite all the woman on the bus had told them about the world they'd reentered, Thomas felt safe for the very first time since coming out of the Box.

Beds were assigned, clothes and bathroom things were passed out, dinner was served. Pizza. Real, bona fide, greasy-fingers pizza. Thomas devoured each bite, hunger trumping everything else, the mood of contentment and relief around him palpable. Most of the Gladers had remained quiet through it all, perhaps worried that speaking would make everything vanish. But there were plenty of smiles. Thomas had gotten so used to looks of despair, it was almost unsettling to see happy faces. Especially when he was having such a hard time feeling it himself.

Soon after eating, no one argued when they were told it was time for bed.

Certainly not Thomas. He felt as if he could sleep for a month.

CHAPTER 62

Thomas shared a bunk with Minho, who insisted on sleeping up top; Newt and Frypan were right next to them. The staff put Teresa up in a separate room, shuffling her away before she could even say goodbye. Thomas missed her desperately three seconds after she was gone.

As Thomas was settling into the soft mattress for the night, he was interrupted.

"Hey, Thomas," Minho said from above him.

"Yeah?" Thomas was so tired the word barely came out.

"What do you think happened to the Gladers who stayed behind?"

Thomas hadn't thought about it. His mind had been occupied with Chuck and now Teresa. "I don't know. But based on how many of us died getting here, I wouldn't like to be one of them right now. Grievers are probably swarming all over them." He couldn't believe how nonchalant his voice sounded as he said it.

"You think we're safe with these people?" Minho asked.

Thomas pondered the question for a moment. There was only one answer to hold on to. "Yeah, I think we're safe."

Minho said something else, but Thomas didn't hear. Exhaustion consuming him, his mind wandered to his short time in the Maze, his time as a Runner and how much he'd wanted it—ever since that first night in the Glade. It felt like a hundred years ago. Like a dream.

Murmurs of conversation floated through the room, but to

Thomas they seemed to come from another world. He stared at the crossed wooden boards of the bed above him, feeling the pull of sleep. But wanting to talk to Teresa, he fought it off.

How's your room? he asked in his mind. *Wish you were in here.*

Oh, yeah? she replied. *With all those stinky boys? Think not.*

Guess you're right. I think Minho's farted three times in the last minute. Thomas knew it was a lame attempt at a joke, but it was the best he could do.

He sensed her laughing, wished he could do the same. There was a long pause. *I'm really sorry about Chuck,* she finally said.

Thomas felt a sharp pang and closed his eyes as he sank deeper into the misery of the night. *He could be so annoying,* he said. He paused, thought of that night when Chuck had scared the crap out of Gally in the bathroom. *But it hurts. Feels like I lost a brother.*

I know.

I promised—

Stop, Tom.

What? He wanted Teresa to make him feel better, say something magic to make the pain go away.

Stop with the promise stuff. Half of us made it. We all would've died if we'd stayed in the Maze.

But Chuck didn't make it, Thomas said. Guilt racked him because he knew for a certainty he would trade any one of the Gladers in that room for Chuck.

He died saving you, Teresa said. *He made the choice himself. Just don't ever waste it.*

Thomas felt tears swell under his eyelids; one escaped and trickled down his right temple, into his hair. A full minute passed without any words between them. Then he said, *Teresa?*

Yeah?

Thomas was scared to share his thoughts, but did. *I wanna remember you. Remember us. Ya know, before.*

Me too.

Seems like we . . . He didn't know how to say it after all.

I know.

Wonder what tomorrow'll be like.

We'll find out in a few hours.

Yeah. Well, good night. He wanted to say more, much more. But nothing came.

Good night, she said, just as the lights went out.

Thomas rolled over, glad it was dark so no one could see the look that had settled across his face.

It wasn't a smile, exactly. Not quite a happy expression. But almost.

And for now, almost was good enough.

EPILOGUE

WICKED Memorandum, Date 232.1.27, Time 22:45
TO: My Associates
FROM: Ava Paige, Chancelor
RE: THOUGHTS ON MAZE TRIALS, Group A

By any reckoning, I think we'd all agree that the Trials were a success. Twenty survivors, all well qualified for our planned endeavor. The responses to the Variables were satisfactory and encouraging. The boy's murder and the "rescue" proved to be a valuable finale. We needed to shock their systems, see their responses. Honestly, I'm amazed that in the end, despite everything, we were able to collect such a large population of kids that just never gave up.

Oddly enough, seeing them this way, thinking all is well, has been the hardest thing for me to observe. But there's no time for regret. For the good of our people, we will move forward.

I know I have my own feelings as to who should be chosen as the leader, but I'll refrain from saying at this time so as not to influence any decisions. But to me, it's an obvious choice.

We are all well aware of what's at stake. I, for one, am encouraged. Remember what the girl wrote on her arm before losing her memory? The one thing she chose to clasp on to? *WICKED is good.*

The subjects will eventually recall and understand the purpose of the hard things we have done and plan to do to them. The mission of WICKED is to serve and preserve humanity, no matter the cost. We are, indeed, "good."

Please respond with your own reactions. The subjects will be allowed one full night's sleep before Stage 2 implementation. At this time, let's allow ourselves to feel hopeful.

Group B's trial results were also most extraordinary. I need time to process the data, but we can touch on it in the morning.

Until tomorrow, then.

END OF BOOK ONE

ACKNOWLEDGMENTS

Editor and friend Stacy Whitman, for helping me see what I could not see.

Faithful fan Jacoby Nielsen, for his feedback and constant support.

Fellow authors Brandon Sanderson, Aprilynne Pike, Julie Wright, J. Scott Savage, Sara Zarr, Emily Wing Smith, and Anne Bowen, for being there.

My agent, Michael Bourret, for making my dream a reality.

Also, sincere thanks to Lauren Abramo and everyone at Dystel & Goderich.

And Krista Marino, for an editing job that defies description. You are a genius, and your name should be on the cover with mine.

JAMES DASHNER
THE
MAZE
RUNNER
FILES
ASSIFIED RECORDS AND CONCEALED INFORMATION

PART I

CONFIDENTIAL FILES

Misc.
Just found this
file. Should it
be destroyed?
CONFIDENTIAL

WICKED Memorandum, Date 220.6.24, Time 0936

TO: Partners

FROM: Kevin Anderson, Chancellor

RE: Welcome

Welcome, colleagues, to the beginning of the greatest collaborative human effort in the history of our planet. I would not dare suggest that this is a time for excitement. The world has never known such dark times as these, and celebration is far from appropriate. What I would like to establish, however, is that we *can* feel hope and pride that we are a part of something that is working to save the human race. And to succeed, we must hit the ground running.

Those of you in charge of the search parties in the designated Twelve Sectors are to report back to the Council each time a suitable subject is discovered. It is far too early to know what percentage of the population meets our needs, but it has become obvious that the number will be small. We need to test each subject immediately so we can choose Candidates with the greatest potential to last until the very end.

The design team for the Maze will be presenting their latest plans to us tomorrow morning at 0900 hours at command center 3. Building a structure of this sophistication is an ambitious project during the best of times, and given the current state of the world, we anticipate that implementing phase 1 will take the next several years. We will spare no expense to keep the project on track. In a few years we will have our Elite Candidates to help in the final design and building phases.

Tomorrow's meeting will also devote a segment to the biotech creatures we have manufactured to help us create and fully manage the planned Variables.

Our Psychs and doctors have worked to come up with an action plan. They believe that we can achieve sixty percent of the patterns we need by setting in motion the incidents we have plotted so far. With at least ten years until the project reaches its climax, I think that is an incredible number.

Members of the Council plan to stay in constant communication throughout the entirety of this project, so do feel free to share your thoughts with me or the others on the Council at any time. I am proud to be a part of this great endeavor, along with all of you.

The future has begun.

WICKED Memorandum, Date 221.11.26, Time 1056

TO: Partners

FROM: Kevin Anderson, Chancellor

RE: Elite Candidate

We have discovered a most extraordinary Candidate.

None of us can put a finger on why he seems so perfect to serve as one of our Elites. There is simply something about him. Though very young, he seems to have an awareness of his surroundings well beyond his years. His verbal and cognitive skills are at an adult level, yet somehow he still holds on to an innocence—a childlike quality—that has endeared him to everyone he has met so far.

Preliminary tests show the most promising results we have had thus far. His intelligence and capacity to learn are immeasurable. He also has the potential for incredible physical abilities, which of course will be vital in the Maze if he ends up doing what we would like him to do.

We have decided to name him after one of the most important inventors in history, as we believe strongly that he will go on to achieve great things.

If you would like to observe Thomas, go to room 31J. (Located next to Teresa.)

I think you will be impressed.

WICKED Memorandum, Date 224.9.6, Time 1108

TO: Partners

FROM: Kevin Anderson, Chancellor

RE: Implants

One of the most delicate elements of our project is complete. All brain devices, including the Swipe trigger, the manipulators, and the telepathy tools, have been successfully implanted. I am happy to pass on that the doctors reported only seven deaths during surgery. Many fewer than we had feared and anticipated.

Transcript of Subjects A1 and A2, Meeting 1

BEGINNING OF TRANSCRIPT

Thomas: Hey.

Teresa: Hi.

Thomas: Why did they put us in here?

Teresa: I don't know. They wanted us to meet and talk, I guess.

Thomas: How long have you lived here?

Teresa: Since I was five.

Thomas: So . . . ?

Teresa: So four years.

Thomas: You're only nine?

Teresa: Yeah. Why? How old are you?

Thomas: Same. You just seem older is all.

Teresa: I'll be ten soon. Haven't you been here just as long?

Thomas: Yeah.

Teresa: Why do they keep some of us separate? I can hear other kids screaming and laughing all the time. And I've seen the big cafeteria. It's gotta feed hundreds.

Thomas: So they bring your food to your room, too?

Teresa: Three times a day. Most of it tastes like a toilet.

Thomas: So you know what a toilet tastes like?

Teresa: Can't be worse than the food they give us.

Thomas: Heh. You're right.

Teresa: So there must be something different about us, don't you think?

Thomas: I guess. There has to be a reason we're kept alone. But it's hard to guess what when we don't even know why we're here.

Teresa: I know. Is your life pretty much school stuff from wake-up to lights-out?

Thomas: Just about.

Teresa: They keep telling me how smart I am.

Thomas: Me too. It's weird.

Teresa: I think it all has something to do with the Flare. Did your parents catch it before WICKED took you?

Thomas: I don't want to talk about that.

Teresa: Why not?

Thomas: I just don't.

Teresa: Fine, then. Me neither.

Thomas: Why are we in here, anyway? Seriously, what're we supposed to be doing?

Teresa: Talking. Being tested. I don't know. Sorry being around me is so freaking boring for you.

Thomas: Huh? You're mad?

Teresa: No, I'm not mad. You just don't seem very nice. I kind of like the idea of finally having a friend.

Thomas: Sorry. Sounds kind of good to me, too.

Teresa: Then maybe we passed the test. Maybe they wanted to see if we'd get along.

Thomas: Whatever. I quit guessing about things a long time ago.

Teresa: So . . . friends?

Thomas: Friends.

Teresa: Shake on it.

Thomas: Okay.

Teresa: Hey, does your brain hurt sometimes? I mean, not just like a normal headache, but deep down inside your skull?

Thomas: What? Are you serious? Yes!

Teresa: Shh! Quiet, someone's coming. We'll talk about it later.

END OF TRANSCRIPT

WICKED Memorandum, Date 228.2.13, Time 1842

TO: Partners

FROM: Kevin Anderson, Chancellor

RE: Telepathy Progress

A quick report to all those not directly involved in Project Silence. Of all the elements we debated during the planning stages, this is one that I think we can all agree is an absolute winner. The potential for valuable pattern results from those with implanted abilities is enormous. Though we have not yet officially begun collecting data, we can already see what a boon to the studies Project Silence will be.

Please remember the reasoning we have agreed upon for why the Elites have been given this special gift of communication; it is important in case you ever come into direct contact with them and are questioned. These Candidates are, by nature, very curious—not only about this particular issue, but also about why they are being treated differently from other subjects in all aspects. They have often asked each other about it, and the questions have become constant now that they can speak to one another via telepathy.

Please remember, if questioned, to answer that they have been given the ability to do this for one reason and one reason only: to allow them instant communication as they help us complete the Maze. The irony is that it really *will* help. Quite a bit. I believe we greatly underestimated how smoothly and efficiently the structure will operate with such remarkable workers.

It is vital that these Candidates never learn the truth. Once our subjects know that we have manipulated their brains to such an extent, we will lose the advantage of their oblivious and sincere reactions to the upcoming Variables. Their altered perspective and inevitable suspicion will not only taint the results in the beginning, but will also make it almost impossible to implement the stimulating experiments when we begin feeding them memory retrievals and the like.

Those are the two things I wanted to bring to your attention. First, that the telepathy is working even better than we could have hoped, already proving that it will be invaluable in creating the kinds of situations and Variables we will need throughout the experiment. And second, that we must ensure that Thomas and the others think they have been given this ability merely to assist in their design-and-build efforts.

WICKED Memorandum, Date 229.6.10, Time 2329

TO: Partners

FROM: Kevin Anderson, Chancellor

RE: Spread of the Flare

Due to the increased rapidity of the virus's spread and the outbreak within our own facilities, it seems we may need to rethink the schedule of the Maze experiment. Although it would be ideal to keep to our five-year time line of study and analysis, I suggest we pare back to two years before sending in our catalyst subjects. I've spoken with Thomas, Teresa, Aris, and Rachel; they are in agreement.

I do not believe we will be able to collect all the necessary patterns by the end of this phase. This makes it almost certain that we will be required to implement the second phase we have tentatively planned for. We will achieve results more quickly by accelerating the schedule, though the experiment will be much, much riskier.

The next few months are going to be terribly difficult. I am instituting mandatory testing with the Psychs FOR ALL PARTNERS every other day so we will know when we have reached the point of no return, at which time decommissioning will take place. We cannot let the decline of our minds jeopardize the very project meant to stop such a thing.

Please be sensitive around Thomas and the others. Despite their intelligence and maturity, sometimes we forget how young they are. They will need thick skin to make it through the transition to becoming our replacements; they will have to survive with their emotional and psychological foundations intact or the whole project could be a failure. We must watch them closely.

At this time it is important that we not let hopelessness prevail. We have a chance to save the future. Be diligent. Be decisive. Detach your emotions from the difficulties of the present and remember what we have held as our mantra from the very beginning: we will do whatever it takes to succeed.

Whatever it takes.

WICKED Memorandum, Date 231.5.4, Time 1343

TO: Partners

FROM: Kevin Anderson, Chancellor

RE: My Farewell to You All

I hope that each one of you will forgive me for doing this in such a cowardly manner, sending you a memo when this is something I should do in person. However, I have no choice. The effects of the Flare are rampant in my actions, embarrassing and disheartening. And our decision not to allow the Bliss within our compound means I can't fake it long enough to say goodbye properly.

Typing these words is difficult enough. But at least I have the ability and time to write and edit in the small windows of sanity left to me.

I do not know why the virus affected me so quickly and so viciously. I deteriorated far more quickly than almost all of the original group. But no matter. I have been decommissioned, and my replacement, Ava Paige, is ready to take charge. The Elites are well into their training to serve as the links between us and those who will continue to run WICKED. Ava herself admits that her purpose is almost that of a figurehead, with our Elite Candidates the true rulers.

We are and will continue to be in good hands. The noble endeavor we began over a decade ago will see itself through to fruition. Our efforts, and for almost all of us, our lives, will have been spent justly and for the greater good. The cure will be built.

Honestly, this is more of a personal note. To thank you for your friendship, your compassion, your empathy in the face of such difficult tasks.

One word of warning: It gets bad in the end. Do not fight your decommission. I did, and now I regret it. Just leave and end the suffering.

It has become too much.

Thank you.

And goodbye.

WICKED Memorandum, Date 231.5.5, Time 0716

TO:

FROM:

RE:

I only have two fingers left.

I wrote the lies of my farewell with two fingers.

That is the truth.

We are evil.

They are kids.

We are evil.

We should stop, let the Munies have the world.

We can't play God.

We can't do this to kids.

You're evil, I'm evil.

My two fingers tell me so.

How can we lie to our replacements?

We give them hope when there is none.

Everyone will die.

No matter what.

Let nature win.

WICKED Memorandum, Date 231.6.22, Time 1137

TO: The Replacements

FROM: Thomas [Subject A1]

RE: The Purge

I take total responsibility for what we have had to do over the last few days.

What we have to keep in mind, though, is that WICKED is alive and stronger than ever. The Maze is up and running and our studies are in full swing. We are on the path and we cannot stray from it.

All I ask is that what we have done here remain within the organization and never be referred to again. What's done is done, and it was a mercy. But now, every waking thought has to be devoted to building the blueprint.

Ava Paige is the new chancellor of WICKED, effective immediately.

WICKED Memorandum, Date 232.1.28, Time 0721

TO: My Associates

FROM: Ava Paige, Chancellor

RE: Regarding Chuck

I wanted to share some quick thoughts about Chuck's death since talk of it is rampant around the compound. Though not surprising, the reaction disappoints me.

We all understand what it is we have been asked to do, and we all knew that we would be expected to do things that are difficult. But WICKED's purpose is about the long term, and everything will have been for nothing unless we accomplish our ultimate goal. Showing small mercies along the way does no one any good.

The Psychs have determined what we need to stimulate our subjects and seek the patterns; their edicts are our first concern. Chuck was a wonderful child full of life and sweet tenderness. Of all our subjects, he may have been the one most likely to earn our sympathies, as well as those of his companions. Ironically, that is the very reason why what happened needed to happen. You saw the results for yourself.

Most importantly, and to ease your conscience, remember that Chuck was not a potential Candidate and most certainly would have met an even worse death eventually. If anything, we *did* show him a mercy by setting up the scenario that led to his murder.

There is not much else to say. I do not need to preach about morals or right and wrong. We are in survival mode, and the only thing that matters is maximizing the number of lives saved *in the long run*. Please visit our in-staff counselors if need be, but then please move on and stay on course for the Scorch Trials. The discussions regarding this matter must cease immediately to keep morale up.

PART II

RECOVERED CORRESPONDENCE

To whom it may concern:

We were able to recover the following material from the hard drives of several computers found in the remains of a building. We believe this building was the headquarters for AMRIID—the Army Medical Research Institute for Infectious Diseases.

This information is alarming. Please proceed with caution.

TO ALL SURVIVORS OF THE SUN FLARES

The Flares Information Recovery Endeavor, henceforth known as FIRE, hereby calls upon municipal units, police agencies, social services and any surviving governmental entities for help. Because most means of communication have been rendered useless, this flyer is being disseminated to the four corners of the world by any available means, including Netblock, Berg, plane, boat, car, and horse.

So far FIRE comprises representatives from the North American Alliance, Russia, the European Union, the United States of Africa, and Mexico, all countries that have suffered catastrophic damage from the sun flares. We hope to gather more representatives from around the world as quickly as possible.

The globe has been ravaged by this disaster. But now is the time to pull together to do what we have always done: survive. FIRE's first task is to assemble world leaders and collect information. We will then organize governing units, police forces, and food and shelter coordination plans.

If you read this message, please find a way to send word back to the FIRE headquarters in Anchorage, Alaska.

Post-Flares Coalition Memorandum, Date 217.11.28, Time 21:46
TO: All board members
FROM: Chancellor John Michael
RE: Population concerns

The report presented to us today, copies of which were sent to all members of the coalition, certainly left no room for doubt as to the problems that face this already crippled world. I am certain that all of you, like me, went to your shelters in stunned silence. It is my hope that the harsh reality described in this report is now clear enough that we can begin talking about solutions.

The problem is simple: the world has too many people and not enough resources.

We have scheduled our next meeting for a week from tomorrow. I expect all members to come prepared to present a solution, no matter how extraordinary it seems. You may be familiar with an old business saying, "think outside the box." I believe it is time we do just that.

I look forward to hearing your ideas.

To: John Michael
From: Katie McVoy
Subject: Potential

John,

I looked into the matter we discussed over dinner last night. AMRIID barely survived the flares, but they're confident that the underground containment system for the most dangerous viruses, bacteria, and biological weapons didn't fail.

It took some wrangling, but I got the information we need. I've looked through it and come up with a recommendation. All the potential solutions are far too unpredictable to be usable. Except one.

It's a virus. It attacks the brain and shuts it down, painlessly. It acts quickly and decisively. The virus was designed to slowly weaken in infection rate as it spreads from host to host. It will be perfect for our needs, especially considering how severely limited travel has become. It could work, John. And as awful as it seems, I believe it could work efficiently.

I'll send over the details. Let me know your thoughts.
–Katie

To: Katie McVoy
From: John Michael
Subject: RE: Potential

Katie,

I need your help preparing my full proposal for the virus release presentation. We need to focus on how a controlled kill is the only way to save lives. Though it will make survival possible for only a select portion of our population, unless we take extreme measures, we face the eventual extinction of the human race.

You and I both know how hypothetical this solution is. But we've run the simulations a thousand times and I just can't see any alternative. If we don't do this, the world will run out of resources. I firmly believe it is the most ethical decision—the risk of race extinction justifies the elimination of a few. My mind is made up. Now it's a matter of convincing the others on the board.

Let's meet at my quarters, 1700. Everything has to be worded perfectly, so prepare yourself for a long night.

Until then,
John

To: Randall Spilker
From: Ladena Lichliter
Subject:

I'm still sick from the meeting today. I just can't believe it. I can't accept that the PCC actually looked us in the eyes and presented that proposal. Seriously. I was stunned.

And then more than half the room AGREED WITH THEM! They supported it! What the hell is going on? Randall, tell me what the HELL is going on? How can we even THINK about doing something like that? How?

I've spent the afternoon trying to make sense of it all. I can't take it. I can't.

How did we get here?

Come see me tonight. Please.
–LL

Post-Flares Coalition Memorandum, Date 219.02.12, Time 19:32
TO: All board members
FROM: Chancellor John Michael
RE: EO draft

Please give me your thoughts on the following draft. The final order will go out tomorrow.

Executive Order #13 of the Post-Flares Coalition, by recommendation of the Population Control Committee, to be considered TOP-SECRET, of the highest priority, on penalty of capital punishment.

We the Coalition hereby grant the PCC express permission to fully implement their PC Initiative #1 as presented in full and attached below. We the Coalition take full responsibility for this action and will monitor developments and offer assistance to the fullest extent of our resources. The virus will be released in the locations recommended by the PCC and agreed upon by the Coalition. Armed forces will be stationed to ensure that the process unfolds in as orderly a manner as possible.

EO #13, PCI #1, is hereby ratified. Begin immediately.

To: John Michael
From: Katie McVoy
Subject: Potential

John,

We received the following radio message from soldiers at Ground Zero EU: an exchange between a Lieutenant Larsson and a private named Kibucho that began during a helicopter flyover. I have to warn you, it's a little disturbing.

Begin transmission

Larsson: What the *expletive* is that down there? Through that gash in the roof. What's all that movement?
Kibucho: They're supposed to be *expletive* dead by now. It has to be animals or something.
Larsson: No way. But it's too dark. We need to get down there and have a look.
Kibucho: I'll tell them.

Three-minute break in transmission

Larsson: Open the door.
Kibucho: Are you sure?
Larsson: Open the *expletive* door, Private!
Kibucho: Going in.

Two-minute break in transmission

Kibucho: He chopped off my leg! He chopped off my *expletive* leg!
Larsson: What? What the *expletive* are you talking about?
Kibucho: [Garbled response.]
Larsson: Private! What's going on?
Kibucho: Half of them are alive! Get me out!
Larsson: Backup, backup, backup! We need backup in Sector Seventeen of Ground Zero EU immediately!
Kibucho: [Garbled screams.]
Larsson: Holy *expletive*! Holy *expletive*! They're eating him! My God, they're eating him!
Kibucho: [Garbled screams that cut off abruptly.]
Larsson: They have me cornered! Oh, *expletive*, they have me cornered!

End transmission

We need to gather the board.
—Katie

To: Randall Spilker
From: Ladena Lichliter
Subject: Unbelievable

I know you've been sick, but the reports are flying in now. Have you seen any of them? These aren't rumors anymore, Randall. They have at least 27 confirmed sightings of infected groups. The virus didn't kill them! None of the doctors or scientists can nail down what's gone wrong. But most of the people living at Ground Zero locations are completely insane, like animals. They're monsters!

But that's not even the worst part. What has the Coalition terrified is that victims even had time to escape from the remote camps. The Coalition thought the incubation period and onset of death would be much faster. And there are reports of symptoms in citizens outside the hot zones. Everywhere.

Randall, we have a major, major crisis on our hands. They should've listened to us. They should've listened!

God help us.
–LL

To: John Michael
From: Katie McVoy
Subject: Some last words

John,

There's no way we can stop this. You're right. I hate to admit it, but it's true. Every effort we made to prevent the spread was pointless. The virus is jumping bodies every second. We can only hope that the rumors of the presence of Immunes are true. They might be the only chance we've got for survival.

A cure. I can't think of any other possible solution. Somehow, we have to find a cure.

Did you hear what the media has taken to calling it? The Flare. I'm sure it'll stick.

I have it. I know I do. I'm leaving. I don't want to infect anyone.

You were a true friend in this madness.

Goodbye, John.
—Katie

Post-Flares Coalition Memorandum, Date 220.05.01, Time 11:23
TO: All board members
FROM: Chancellor John Michael
RE: Another solution

The killzone. That's their word for the brain now. Where the Flare does its damage and slowly kills you with lunacy. And they already have a nickname for the Immunes, too. The Munies. What utter ridiculousness.

But jargon matters not. What matters is how it all connects. The killzone. The Flare. The Immunes. A world that's in complete catastrophe. We need to find a cure. There is no other way to go forward.

We will meet tomorrow, 0800.
I have an idea.

PART III

SUPPRESSED MEMORIES

THOMAS'S FIRST MEMORY OF THE FLARE

It had been five days since they'd locked Thomas up in the white room. On that fifth day, after trying his best to go through the routine he'd established—exercise, eat, think, repeat—he decided to lie down and sleep. Let his terrible new world wash away for a while. Exhausted, he faded quickly and images began to bloom in his mind.

Thomas is young—he can't tell how young exactly. He's curled up in a corner, knees pulled up to his chest, shivering with fright. His dad—the man who holds him, reads to him, kisses him on the cheek, hugs him, bathes him—is on a rampage, screaming hateful things and turning over furniture. His mom tries to stop him, but he pushes her away without even seeming to realize who she is. She stumbles, tries to regain her balance, then slams into the wall a few feet from Thomas.

Sobbing, she crawls to him, pulls him into her arms.

"Don't worry, honey," she whispers. "They're coming to take him away. They'll be here soon."

"Who?" Thomas asks. His voice sounds so young, and it breaks his dreaming heart.

"The people who are going to take care of him," she answers. "Remember, your daddy's sick, very sick. This isn't really him doing all of this. It's the disease."

Suddenly Dad spins around to face them, his face aflame with anger. "Disease? Did I just hear you say disease?" Each word comes out of his mouth like a poisoned dart, full of venom.

Mom shakes her head, hugs Thomas tighter to her body.

"Why don't you just say it, woman," Dad continues, taking a step toward them. His chest is lurching with his attempts to suck in breath, and his hands are clenched into tight fists. "The Flare. Tell the boy how it is. Tell him the truth. Your dad has the Flare, Thomas. It's comin' along real nicely." Another step closer. "Your mom has it, too. Oh yes. Soon she'll be chewing on her fingers and feeding you dirt for breakfast. Laughing hysterically while she breaks the windows and tries to cut you. She'll be bat crazy, boy, just like your daddy."

Another step closer. Thomas squeezes his eyes shut, hoping it'll all go away. The dreaming part of him doesn't want to see anymore, either. Wants it to end.

"Look at me, boy," Dad says with a snarl. "Look at me when I'm talking to you."

Thomas can't help it. He always does as he's told. His dad looks calm now in every way except one: those fists. Fingers and knuckles white.

"That's good," Dad says. "Good boy. Look at your daddy. Do I look crazy to you? Huh? Do I?" He shouts those last two words.

"No, sir," Thomas says, surprised he can say it without shaking.

"Well, you're wrong, then." Dad's face pinches with anger again. "I'm crazy, boy. I'm a madman. I could eat both of you for dinner and love every bite."

"Stop it!" Mom screams, a sound so loud it pierces Thomas's eardrums painfully. "You stop it right now! I swear to God I'll rip your heart out if you touch my son!"

Dad laughs. Not just a chuckle, either. His whole body shakes and he throws his head back as booming laughter pours from him, filling the house with its noise. Thomas has never heard something sound so wrong before. But the man keeps it up, laughing and laughing and laughing.

"Stop it!" Mom screams again. She repeats it over and over until finally Thomas can't take it anymore and covers his ears.

Then the doorbell rings, barely loud enough to be heard. But both of his parents go silent. Dad looks in the direction of the front door, his face suddenly showing fear.

"They're here to get you," Mom says through a sob. "My sweet, the love of my life, they're here to get you."

Thomas woke up.

FRYPAN, SWIPE REMOVAL OPERATION

Frypan looked up at his nurse, and though nervousness filled his gut, he knew he was doing the right thing and forced himself to relax. He was about to get his memories back. His memories! He couldn't wait to see his past.

The woman swabbed a spot clean on the side of his neck, then poked the needle into a vein before he could get another word out. There was a sharp sting and then warmth flowed through his body.

"There," she said. "Just rest for a few minutes. We'll lower the mask as soon as you fall asleep."

"How does it work?" Frypan whispered; he couldn't help himself—he wanted answers. "What is the Swipe, anyway?"

"Just relax now" was all she said in response.

Frypan closed his eyes and resolved to shut up. The answers would come soon enough. He breathed deeply, doing his best to follow directions, to calm his nerves. The warmth he'd been feeling expanded as weariness trickled in, pulling him toward sleep.

"You ready?"

Frypan's eyes snapped open to see his nurse staring down at him through what seemed like a white haze. He tried to speak, but only a mumble of something unintelligible came out.

"You look ready," she said. "Just wanted to let you know I'm about to lower the mask. You don't need to do anything—go ahead and close your eyes again. When you wake up you'll remember everything."

He grunted, closed his eyes. He hadn't been this tired in a long time.

Something squeaked, followed by a grating sound, then a few hard clinks. He felt the pads of the mask on his skin. Something whirred, reminding him of the Grievers, which sent a brief spurt of panic through him before it got swallowed by his exhaustion.

Just before he lost consciousness, he swore he could feel cold worms trying to burrow their way into his ears.

Frypan swam in a pool of darkness.

Somewhere on the outside, in the periphery, he was aware of pain. It bit at his nerves, sliced through his head and brain. But a dullness, the fog of drugs, numbed it, made it a thing he didn't care about.

As he floated in the absence of light, he remembered how others back in the Maze had described the Changing—an awful journey into a swirling white tornado of their imagination. And that was when recalling only a few flashes of memory. They talked about the extreme pain, and he wondered if he was about to go through something like that. He wasn't too keen on the idea—a good burn from the stove was about the worst thing he'd been through before.

Things developed differently than he could've ever guessed.

He floated in an impossible vacuum—with no gravity, no sense of direction or space. Finally an unseen ground solidified below him and his feet touched a hard surface. He pulled himself together and looked around, hoping for a light to banish the darkness that pressed in on him, scaring him.

Something creaked close by and he turned toward the sound, saw an open door, a soft light spilling out to reveal a stone path between him and the entrance to who-knew-where. He knew this all had to be imagined, that he wasn't actually in this place, seeing what he was seeing. It had to be symbolic, something formed in his imagination to be able to process whatever the doctors were doing to his brain with their mask machine.

He reached the door in just four steps, hesitated in front of it, then pushed it open wider and entered a sea of blackness. As his eyes adjusted, he realized he was in a long hallway that stretched into the distance as far as he could see. The walls, floor, and ceiling were no longer black, but white. They went on until they converged into a single point.

A series of screens was set into the right wall, one about every three feet, seeming to continue as far as the hallway itself did. The screen closest to him suddenly flickered with static; then a moving image formed within its square, perfectly clear and crisp. Frypan stepped closer to get a better look.

> A man, standing at a kitchen counter, his arm moving furiously as he mixes something in a bowl. Frypan is sitting on the floor, staring up at this man. His . . . dad. The man turns to face Frypan, a huge smile on his face. "These are going to be the best pancakes ever eaten by humans. Almost ready!" Frypan laughs.

The screen goes black. Frypan realizes this was his first memory, the earliest his mind can go back; he was maybe three years old. He is remembering his dad, his kind face full of love as he smiled and spoke.

Frypan knows what to do next, reminds himself that it's all imagined—this is how his brain has chosen to give him his life back. He walks to the next screen.

> He's sitting in a small pool, splashing and shrieking, crying when too much water gets in his eyes. Warm hands

reach down—a woman's hands—and wipe his face; then he begins all over again. A ball is thrown in and he kicks it. His mom's body keeps appearing and disappearing in the background as she paces back and forth. She's just learned some awful news about the disease spreading across the world.

He doesn't know how all this is so clear from just watching a few images. But it is. He moves on to the next screen.

A little older, helping his dad in the kitchen. They're making stew, chopping up all the veggies and meat. His dad is crying. Frypan knows that his mom has been taken away for further testing, and that they've said his dad will be next.

On to the next screen.

A man in a dark suit, standing by a car. Papers in his fist, a grave look on his face. Frypan is holding hands with his dad on the porch. WICKED has been formed, a joint venture of the world's governments—those that survived the sun flares, an event that happened long before Frypan was born. WICKED's purpose is to study what is now known as the killzone, where the Flare does its damage. The brain.

Frypan is immune. Others are immune. Less than one percent of the population, most of them under the age of twenty. Many people have developed hatred toward those who are immune, call them the Munies and do terrible things out of jealousy. WICKED says they can protect Frypan while they're working toward a cure.

His dad says many things to him. Mostly that he loves him and is so glad that he'll never go through the horrible things they're seeing happen around the world. Madness and murder.

Frypan has no reason to process or think too deeply about the returning memories. They're not like new revelations, things to which he should respond somehow. They've always been there, inside him. He has already reacted to them. He has been shaped by them. He's not learning. He's not experiencing. He's remembering.

He walks to the next screen, hungry to be himself again.

MINHO, PHASE 3 TRIAL

Three days had passed since they'd arrived on the Bergs from the Scorch, and Minho was just about ready to go whacker. He'd been kept in a small dorm room with plenty of food and absolutely nothing to do. Counting the rows on the wallpaper and imagining faces in the swirly patterns of the ceiling had grown old. And he'd heard nothing about Thomas or his other friends.

On the morning of the fourth day, the Rat Man showed up at his door with two armed guards.

"Follow me," he said.

"No hugs and kisses?" Minho asked. "I've missed your ugly face."

"Follow me or you'll be fired upon." Not even a crack in his stone-hard expression.

Minho sighed and did what he was told. He wasn't in the mood to be shot that day. And if he was honest with himself, anything would be better than sitting in that room for one more second.

Minho followed the Rat Man down a long hallway and then into a small chamber that led to several marked doors.

"You're in room number eight," the Rat Man announced. He gestured to the door marked #8.

They stood in silence until Minho asked, "Oh really? And what am I supposed to do in there?"

"A simple test," the Rat Man answered. "Nothing like the Trials before, I assure you. Yours is probably the easiest of all the tests we've created, and I think the shortest. You will be asked one question and one question only, and the answer will consist of exactly one word. Sound simple enough?"

It sounded too simple. "You actually think I could ever trust you, shuckface?"

"Excuse me?" the Rat Man asked.

Minho shook his head. "I swear to God that if you do one more thing to me or my friends, I won't quit fighting until I'm dead."

A smirk appeared on the man's face, enraging Minho even more. "I give you my word that your response alone will dictate what happens. Everything from this point on is voluntary. The Trials are over."

Minho was so angry he almost shook. He knew he had no choice but to do what he was told, and it drove him crazy.

"Are you ready?" the Rat Man asked.

Minho grunted. He walked over to the door marked with an eight and opened it. He was surprised—there was no fancy gadgetry, no complex machines. It was just a small beige room with a single wooden chair in the middle of a brown-tiled floor. A whiteboard hung on the opposite wall, and beside it stood a tall, muscular man dressed in green scrubs and a white lab coat. He had perfectly combed black hair and the worst mustache Minho had ever seen.

"Welcome," the man said. "My name is Lincoln. Please have a seat, facing me."

Curiosity took over. Minho sat in the chair, wondering what to do with his hands, until he finally folded them in his lap.

"Now please observe," Lincoln said in a cold, clinical voice.

The man turned and started writing with his finger on the upper left hand corner of the board, his touch creating a bright red line as he moved.

The first word Lincoln wrote was Thomas. Then he moved down a few inches and wrote Newt. Then down again and added Frypan, and Aris under that. The man shifted to the right and wrote Harriet in the upper corner on that side. He moved down and wrote Sonya. Then Teresa. Then, to Minho's surprise, Brenda.

When Lincoln was finished, eight names were printed in red on the board, evenly spaced. He turned to face Minho once again.

"Do you confirm that you are aware of these eight individuals?" Lincoln asked.

Minho rolled his eyes. "Yeah, genius, I know them. The Rat said you'd only ask me one question. Is that it?"

"The actual Experience exercise has not begun. This is what we would call prep work. Please answer the preliminary question and then we will begin the test. Do you—"

"Yes!" Minho yelled. "I know them. What now?"

Lincoln showed no signs of being caught off guard. He calmly responded, "Thank you for confirming."

His eyes flickered to one of the back corners of the ceiling; Minho turned to see what he was looking at. A beetle blade was attached to the wall; its red light made it impossible to miss. Minho could see the familiar scrawl of WICKED painted on its body. Memories of the Maze flooded in, and he shifted to face Lincoln again.

Of course they'd be observing all this, he told himself. But did they really have to use beetle blades? He hadn't seen those since leaving the Maze.

"Okay, we're ready to begin," Lincoln said loudly. The man returned his full attention to Minho. "As you've been told, I'm going to ask you one question and one question only. Your response should be limited to one word. I'll pose the question in ten seconds if you're ready."

Minho let out a small laugh to show how absurd the situation was, then nodded. He was ready.

When the allotted time had passed, Lincoln spoke in a grave voice that showed he meant every single word. "Our doctors have determined that we need to dissect the brains of these subjects for a more in-depth study. But we will allow you to spare one of them. Which person do you choose to save? That is your question."

Five full minutes passed. Minho sat in silence. It couldn't possibly be true. Did WICKED really mean to cut his friends' brains apart?

"Minho," Lincoln said, "I need you to answer the question, but you can take some more time if you need to. I know it must be difficult."

"I'm not going to answer your stupid question," Minho replied, surprised at how much venom was captured in each word.

"This is no game. The people on this list have been used to their fullest extent, and the only value remaining is to study them physically. Your friends will have the honor of donating their lives to the noblest cause ever known to mankind."

Minho said nothing, seething in his chair.

Lincoln persisted. "Be thankful that the Psychs determined that this Trial would be beneficial. At least you get to save one of the people you care about."

Minho broke eye contact and looked down at his hands. He'd been gripping the sides of his chair tightly, he realized. Spots swam before his eyes, blood pounded in his head—almost as if he could hear it running through his veins and to his heart. Of all the many times he'd felt anger since entering the Maze, it had never been like this. Never.

"How much time would you—"

"I don't need any time!" Minho yelled before the man could finish. "I refuse to answer! If you even touch a single one of them, I swear . . ."

"I'm afraid you have no choice in the matter," Lincoln's voice was firm, and he seemed unfazed. "Times are desperate, and we need to complete this blueprint. We need those brains for study."

"I won't let you do it," Minho said, suddenly calm. "If one of them gets hurt, I'm done. Take your chances with me, do however many tests you need to, but leave them out of it."

"That's simply not an option, Minho. I'm sorry. We need you to make this choice. And we're willing to take whatever actions necessary to . . . encourage you to continue volunteering."

"What's that supposed to mean?"

The lines of Lincoln's jaw tightened. "It means what it means. Now which of these names do you choose?"

"I choose all of them," Minho said.

"You can choose only one."

"All of them."

"One and one only."

"All."

Lincoln took a step forward. "I'll ask it a final time before taking further measures. Which of your friends do you want to save?"

"Every single one."

Lincoln rushed forward and grabbed Minho by the shirt, pulling him to his feet. "You will choose, now!"

Minho was terrified, but he ignored it. "All!"

Lincoln reared back with his right hand, formed a fist, and punched Minho in the face. Pain burst through his head as he fell to the floor. Lights seemed to flash along the brown tiles a few inches from his eyes. Lincoln grabbed him and pulled him back up, turned him around so they were facing each other once again. His strength was ridiculous; Minho had no chance.

"Which name do you choose?" Lincoln asked him.

Minho's face felt broken and he tasted blood, but he refused to give up. "I won't choose!" He spat a wad of red goo onto Lincoln's face.

The man didn't flinch; he punched Minho again, but held him up this time so he couldn't fall. Another explosion of pain, more lights.

"Minho," Lincoln said with insulting calm. "Which of the names do you choose?"

"I won't," Minho forced out.

Lincoln punched him on the other cheek. Again. Then again. Minho's head felt like needles and mush.

"Make a choice." Lincoln spoke between heavier breaths now. "Which one of the names do you choose?"

Minho didn't get it, couldn't comprehend how this could all be necessary. The confusion just made him even angrier and more stubborn.

"All of them," he said, ashamed of how it came out, nothing but a whimper.

"We can do this all day," Lincoln said. "We're not leaving and I'm not stopping until you give me an answer. All you have to do is say one name. Just say it! Now, which one! Say it!"

"All of them, you slinthead shuck-faced piece of klunk." Minho smiled.

Lincoln showed the slightest hint of surprise on his face, but recovered almost as quickly as he had slipped up. He stepped back, smoothed out his clothes.

"The test is over," the man said. "You're free to go."

Stunned and battered, Minho remained speechless as the guards came into the room and escorted him back to his dorm.

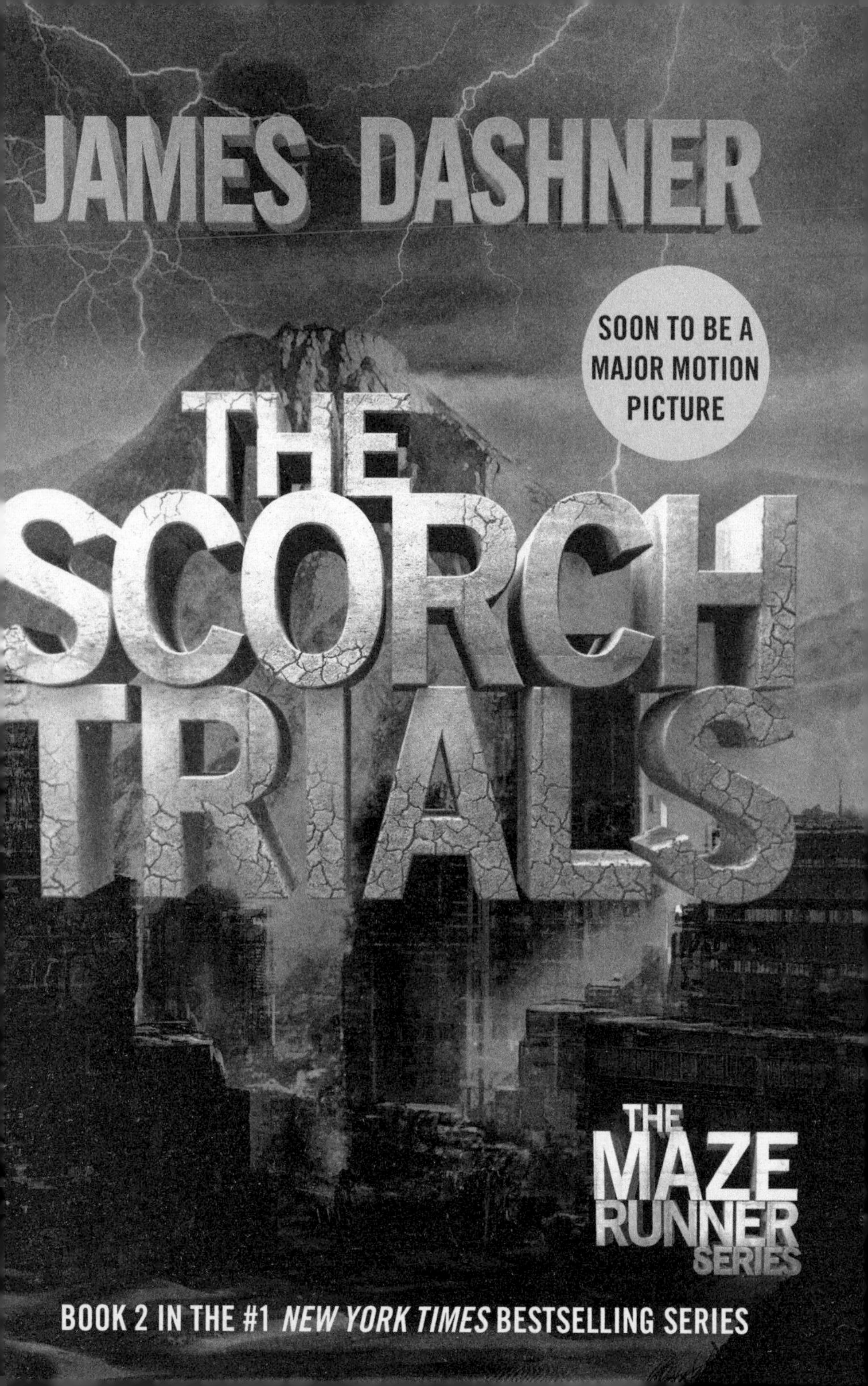
JAMES DASHNER
SOON TO BE A MAJOR MOTION PICTURE
THE SCORCH TRIALS
THE MAZE RUNNER SERIES
BOOK 2 IN THE #1 NEW YORK TIMES BESTSELLING SERIES

THE SCORCH TRIALS

CHAPTER 1

She spoke to him before the world fell apart.

Hey, are you still asleep?

Thomas shifted in his bed, felt a darkness around him like air turned solid, pressing in. At first he panicked; his eyes snapped open as he imagined himself back in the Box—that horrible cube of cold metal that had delivered him to the Glade and the Maze. But there was a faint light, and lumps of dim shadow gradually emerged throughout the huge room. Bunk beds. Dressers. The soft breaths and gurgly snores of boys deep in slumber.

Relief filled him. He was safe now, rescued and delivered to this dormitory. No more worries. No more Grievers. No more death.

Tom?

A voice in his head. A girl's. Not audible, not visible. But he heard it all the same, though never could he have explained to anyone how it worked.

Exhaling a deep breath, he relaxed into his pillow, his razor-edged nerves settling down from that fleeting moment of terror. He spoke back, forming the words with his thoughts.

Teresa? What time is it?

No idea, she replied. *But I can't sleep. I probably dozed for an hour or so. Maybe more. I was hoping you were awake to keep me company.*

Thomas tried not to smile. Even though she wouldn't be able to see it, it would be embarrassing all the same. *Didn't give me much choice in the matter, did you? Kind of hard to sleep when someone's talking directly into your skull.*

Waa, waa. Go back to bed, then.

No. I'm good. He stared at the bottom of the bunk above him—featureless and darkly fuzzy in the shadow—where Minho was currently breathing like a guy with ungodly amounts of phlegm lodged in his throat. *What've you been thinking about?*

What do you think? Somehow she projected a jab of cynicism into the words. *I keep seeing Grievers. Their disgusting skin and blubber bodies, all those metal arms and spikes. It was way too close for comfort, Tom. How're we gonna get something like that out of our heads?*

Thomas knew what he thought. Those images would never leave—the Gladers would be haunted by the horrible things that had happened in the Maze for the rest of their lives. He figured that most if not all of them would have major psychological problems. Maybe even go completely nutso.

And above it all, he had one image burned into his memories as strongly as a branded mark from a searing hot iron. His friend Chuck, stabbed in the chest, bleeding, dying as Thomas held him.

Thomas knew he would *never* forget that. But what he said to Teresa was: *It'll go away. Just takes a little time, that's all.*

You're so full of it, she said.

I know. How ridiculous was it that he loved hearing her say something like that to him? That her sarcasm meant things were going to be okay? *You're an idiot,* he told himself, then hoped she didn't hear that thought.

I hate that they separated me from you guys, she said.

Thomas understood why they had, though. She was the only girl and the rest of the Gladers were teenage boys—a bunch of shanks they didn't trust yet. *Guess they were protecting you.*

Yeah. I guess. Melancholy seeped into his brain with her words, stuck to them like syrup. *But it sucks being alone after everything we went through.*

Where'd they take you, anyway? She sounded so sad that he almost wanted to get up and look for her, but he knew better.

Just on the other side of that big common room where we ate last night. It's a small room with a few bunks. I'm pretty sure they locked the door when they left.

See, told ya they wanted to protect you. Then he quickly added, *Not that you need protecting. I'd put my money on you against at least half these shanks.*

Only half?

Okay, three-quarters. Including me.

A long stretch of silence followed, though somehow Thomas could still sense her presence. He *felt* her. It was almost like how, even though he couldn't see Minho, he knew his friend lay only a few feet above him. And it wasn't just the snoring. When someone is close by, you just know it.

Despite all the memories of the last few weeks, Thomas was surprisingly calm, and soon sleep overpowered him once more. Darkness settled on his world, but she was there, next to him in so many ways. Almost . . . touching.

He had no concept of time passing while in that state. Half asleep, half enjoying her presence and the thought that they'd been rescued from that horrible place. That they were safe, that he and Teresa could get to know each other all over again. That life could be good.

Blissful sleep. Hazy darkness. Warmth. A physical glow. Almost floating.

The world seemed to fade away. All became numb and sweet. And the darkness, somehow comforting. He slipped into a dream.

He's very young. Four, maybe? Five? Lying in a bed with blankets pulled to his chin.

A woman sits next to him, her hands folded in her lap. She has long brown hair, a face just beginning to show signs of age. Her eyes are sad. He knows this even though she's trying very hard to hide it with a smile.

He wants to say something, ask her a question. But he can't. He's not really here. Just witnessing it all from a place he doesn't quite understand. She begins to talk, a sound so simultaneously sweet and angry it disturbs him.

"I don't know why they chose you, but I do know this. You're special somehow. Never forget that. And never forget how much"—her voice cracks and tears run down her face—"never forget how much I love you."

The boy replies, but it's not really Thomas speaking. Even though it *is* him. None of it makes sense. "Are you gonna be crazy like all those people on TV, Mommy? Like . . . Daddy?"

The woman reaches out and runs her fingers through his hair. Woman? No, he can't call her that. This is his mother. His . . . mommy.

"Don't you worry about that, honey," she says. "You won't be here to see it."

Her smile has gone away.

Too fast the dream faded into blackness, leaving Thomas in a void with nothing but his thoughts. Had he seen another memory crawl up from the depths of his amnesia? Had he really seen his mom? There'd been something about his dad being crazy. The ache inside Thomas was deep and gnawing, and he tried to sink further into oblivion.

Later—how much later he had no idea—Teresa spoke to him again.

Tom, something's wrong.

CHAPTER 2

That was how it started. He heard Teresa say those three words, but it seemed from far away, as if spoken down a long and cluttered tunnel. His slumber had become a viscous liquid, thick and sticky, trapping him. He became aware of himself, but realized he was removed from the world, entombed by exhaustion. He couldn't wake up.

Thomas!

She screamed it. A piercing rattle in his head. He felt the first trickle of fear, but it was more like a dream. He could only sleep. And they were safe now, nothing to worry about anymore. Yeah, it had to be a dream. Teresa was fine, they were all fine. He relaxed again, let himself drown in slumber.

Other sounds snuck their way into his consciousness. Thumps. The clang of metal against metal. Something shattering. Boys shouting. More like the echo of shouts, very distant, muted. Suddenly they became more like screams. Unearthly cries of anguish. But still distant. As if he'd been wrapped in a thick cocoon of dark velvet.

Finally something pricked the comfort of sleep. This wasn't right. Teresa had called for him, told him something was wrong! He fought the deep sleep that had consumed him, clawed at the heavy weight pinning him down.

Wake up! he yelled at himself. *Wake up!*

Then something disappeared from inside him. There one instant, gone the next. He felt as if a major organ had just been ripped from his body.

It had been her. She was gone.

Teresa! he screamed out with his mind. *Teresa! Are you there?*

But there was nothing, and he no longer felt that comforting sense of her closeness. He called her name again, then again, as he continued to struggle against the dark pull of sleep.

Finally, reality swept in, washed away the darkness. Engulfed in terror, Thomas opened his eyes and shot to a sitting position on his bed, scooted out until he got his feet under him and jumped up. Looked around.

Everything had gone crazy.

The other Gladers in the room were running around, shouting. And terrible, horrible, awful sounds filled the air, like the wretched squeals of animals being tortured. There was Frypan, pointing out a window, his face pale. Newt and Minho were running to the door. Winston, hands held up to his frightened, acne-plagued face like he'd just seen a flesh-eating zombie. Others stumbling over each other to look out the different windows, but keeping their distance from the glass. Achingly, Thomas realized he didn't even know most of the names of the twenty boys who'd survived the Maze, an odd thought to have in the middle of all that chaos.

Something at the corner of his eye made him turn to look toward the wall. What he saw immediately wiped away any peace and safety he'd felt talking to Teresa in the night. Made him doubt such emotions could even exist in the same world in which he now stood.

Three feet from his bed, draped by colorful curtains, a window looked out into a bright, blinding light. The glass was broken, jagged shards leaning against crisscrossed steel bars. A man stood on the other side, gripping the bars with bloody hands. His eyes were wide and bloodshot, filled with madness. Sores and scars covered his thin, sunburnt face. He had no hair, only diseased splotches of what looked like greenish moss. A vicious slit stretched across his right cheek; Thomas could see teeth through the raw, festering wound. Pink saliva dribbled in swaying lines from the man's chin.

"I'm a Crank!" the horror of a man yelled. "I'm a bloody Crank!"

And then he started screaming two words over and over and over, spit flying with every shriek.

"Kill me! Kill me! Kill me! . . ."

CHAPTER 3

A hand slammed down on Thomas's shoulder from behind; he cried out and spun around to see Minho staring past him at the maniac screaming through the window.

"They're everywhere," Minho said. His voice had a gloom to it that perfectly matched how Thomas felt. It seemed as if everything they'd dared hope for the previous night had dissolved to nothing. "And there's no sign of those shanks who rescued us," he added.

Thomas had lived in fear and terror the past few weeks, but this was almost too much. To feel safe only to have that snatched away again. Shocking even himself, though, he quickly set aside that small part of him that wanted to jump back into his bed and bawl his eyes out. He pushed away the lingering ache of remembering his mom and the stuff about his dad and people going crazy. Thomas knew that someone had to take charge—they needed a plan if they were going to survive this, too.

"Have any of them gotten in yet?" he asked, a strange calm washing over him. "Do all the windows have these bars?"

Minho nodded toward one of the many lining the walls of the long rectangular room. "Yeah. It was too dark to notice them last night, especially with those stupid frilly curtains. But I'm sure glad for 'em."

Thomas looked at the Gladers around them, some running from window to window to get a look outside, others huddling in small groups. Everyone had a look of half disbelief, half terror. "Where's Newt?"

"Right here."

Thomas turned to see the older boy, not knowing how he'd missed him. "What's goin' on?"

"You think I have a bloody clue? Bunch of crazies want to eat us for breakfast, by the looks of it. We need to find another room, have a Gathering. All this noise is driving nails through my buggin' skull."

Thomas nodded absently; he agreed with the plan but hoped Newt and Minho would take care of it. He was eager to make contact with Teresa—he hoped her warning had just been part of a dream, a hallucination from the drug of deep and exhausted slumber. And that vision of his mom . . .

His two friends moved away, calling out and waving their arms to collect Gladers. Thomas took a tremulous glance back at the shredded madman at the window, then looked away immediately, wishing he hadn't reminded his brain of the blood and torn flesh, the insane eyes, the hysterical screaming.

Kill me! Kill me! Kill me!

Thomas stumbled to the farthest wall, leaned heavily against it.

Teresa, he called out again with his mind. *Teresa. Can you hear me?*

He waited, closing his eyes to concentrate. Reaching out with invisible hands, trying to grasp some trace of her. Nothing. Not even a passing shadow or brush of feeling, much less a response.

Teresa, he said more urgently, clenching his teeth with the effort. *Where are you? What happened?*

Nothing. His heart seemed to slow until it almost stopped, and he felt like he'd swallowed a big hairy lump of cotton. Something had happened to her.

He opened his eyes to see the Gladers gathered around the green-painted door that led to the common area where they'd eaten pizza the night before. Minho was jerking on the round brass handle to no avail. Locked.

The only other door was to a shower and locker room, from which no other exits existed. There was that, and the windows. All with those metal bars. Thank goodness. Each one had raging lunatics screaming and yelling on the other side.

Even though worry ate at him like spilled acid in his veins, Thomas gave up momentarily on trying to contact Teresa and joined the other Gladers. Newt was having a go at the door, with the same useless result.

"It's locked," he muttered when he finally gave up, his arms falling weakly to his sides.

"Really, genius?" Minho said, his powerful arms folded and tensed, veins bulging all over the place. Thomas thought for a split second he could actually see the blood pumping through them. "No wonder you were named after Isaac Newton—such an amazing ability to think."

Newt wasn't in the mood. Or maybe he'd just learned long ago to ignore Minho's smart-aleck remarks. "Let's break this bloody handle off." He looked around as if he expected someone to give him a sledgehammer.

"I wish those shuck . . . Cranks would shut up!" Minho yelled, turning to glower at the closest one, a woman who looked even more hideous than the first man Thomas had seen. A bleeding wound crossed her face, ending on the side of her head.

"Cranks?" Frypan repeated. The hairy cook had been silent until then, barely noticeable. Thomas thought he looked even more frightened than when they'd been about to battle the Grievers to escape the Maze. Maybe this was worse. When they'd settled into bed last night, everything had seemed good and safe. Yeah, maybe this *was* worse, to have that suddenly taken away.

Minho pointed at the screaming, bloody woman. "That's what they keep calling themselves. Haven't you heard it?"

"I don't care if you call 'em pussy willows," Newt snapped. "Find me something to break through this stupid door!"

"Here," a shorter boy said, carrying a slender but solid fire extinguisher he'd taken off the wall—Thomas remembered seeing it earlier. Again, he felt guilty for not even knowing this kid's name.

Newt grabbed the red cylinder, ready to pile-drive the door handle. Thomas stood as close as he could, eager to see what was on the other side of the door, though he had a very bad feeling that whatever it was, they weren't going to like it.

Newt lifted the extinguisher, then slammed it down on the round brass handle. The loud crack was accompanied by a deeper crunch, and it took only three more whacks before the entire unit of the handle crashed to the floor with a jangle of broken metal pieces. The door inched outward, cracked open just enough to show darkness on the other side.

Newt stood quietly, staring at that long, narrow gap of blackness as if he expected demons from the underworld to come flying through. Absently, he handed the extinguisher back to the boy who'd found it. "Let's go," he said. Thomas thought he heard the slightest quaver in his voice.

"Wait," Frypan called out. "We sure we wanna go out there? Maybe that door was locked for a reason."

Thomas couldn't help but agree; something felt wrong about this.

Minho stepped up to stand right next to Newt; he looked back at Frypan, then made eye contact with Thomas. "What else're we gonna do? Sit here and wait for those loonies to get in? Come on."

"Those freaks aren't breaking through the window bars anytime soon," Frypan retorted. "Let's just *think* for a second."

"Time for thinking's done," Minho said. He kicked out with his foot and the door swung completely open; if anything, it seemed to grow even darker on the other side. "Plus, you should've spoken up *before* we blasted the lock to bits, slinthead. Too late now."

"I hate when you're right," Frypan grumbled under his breath.

Thomas couldn't quit staring past the open door, into the pool of inky darkness. He felt a now-all-too-familiar clench of apprehension, knowing that something had to be wrong or the people who'd rescued them would've come for them a long time ago. But Minho and Newt were right—they had to go out there and find some answers.

"Shuck it," Minho said. "I'll go first."

Without waiting for a response he walked through the open door, his body vanishing in the gloom almost instantly. Newt gave Thomas a hesitant look, then followed. For some reason Thomas thought it should be up to him to go next, so he did.

Step by step, he left the dorm room and entered the darkness of the common area, hands reaching out in front of him.

The glow of light coming from behind didn't do much to illuminate things; he might as well have been walking with his eyes squeezed shut. And the place smelled. Horrible.

Minho yelped up ahead, then called back. "Whoa, be careful. Something . . . weird's hanging from the ceiling."

Thomas heard a slight squeak or groan, something creaking. As if Minho had bumped into a low-hanging chandelier, sending it swaying back and forth. A grunt from Newt somewhere to the right was followed by the squeal of metal dragging across the floor.

"Table," Newt announced. "Watch out for tables."

Frypan spoke up behind Thomas. "Does anyone remember where the light switches were?"

"That's where I'm heading," Newt responded. "I swear I remember seeing a set of them somewhere over here."

Thomas continued walking blindly forward. His eyes had adjusted a little; where before, everything had been a wall of blackness, now he could see traces of shadows against shadows. Yet something was off. He was still a little disoriented, but things seemed to be in places they shouldn't be. It was almost as if—

"Bluh-huh-huh," Minho groaned, a shudder of repulsion, like he'd just stepped in a pile of klunk. Another creaking sound cut through the room.

Before Thomas could ask what had happened, he bumped into something himself. Hard. Awkwardly shaped. The feel of cloth.

"Found it!" Newt shouted.

A few clicks were heard; then the room suddenly blazed with fluorescent lights, temporarily blinding Thomas. He stumbled away from the thing he'd bumped into, rubbing his eyes, ran into another stiff figure, sent it swaying away from him.

"Whoa!" Minho yelled.

Thomas squinted; his vision cleared. He forced himself to look at the scene of horror around him.

Throughout the large room, people hung from the ceiling—at least a dozen. They'd all been strung up by the neck, the ropes twisted and trenched into purple, bloated skin. The stiff bodies swung to and fro ever so slightly, pale pink tongues lolling out of their white-lipped mouths. All of them had eyes open, though glazed over with certain death. By the looks of it, they'd been that way for hours. Their clothes and some of their faces looked familiar.

Thomas dropped to his knees.

He knew these dead people.

They were the ones who'd rescued the Gladers. Just the day before.

CHAPTER 4

Thomas tried not to look at any of the dead bodies as he stood up. He half walked, half stumbled over to Newt, who was still by the bank of light switches, his terrified gaze darting between the corpses hanging throughout the room.

Minho joined them, swearing under his breath. Other Gladers were emerging from the dorm room, shouting as they realized what they were seeing; Thomas heard a couple of them throw up, gagging and spitting. He felt the sudden urge himself, but fought it. What had happened? How could everything be taken away from them so fast? His stomach tightened up as despair threatened to bowl him over.

Then he remembered Teresa.

Teresa! he called out with his mind. *Teresa!* Again and again, mentally screaming it with his eyes closed and jaw clenched. *Where are you!*

"Tommy," Newt said, reaching out to squeeze his shoulder. "What's bloody wrong with you?"

Thomas opened his eyes, realized he was doubled over, arms wrapped around his stomach. He slowly straightened, tried to push away the panic eating him inside. "What . . . what do you think? Look around us."

"Yeah, but you looked like you were in pain or something."

"I'm fine—just trying to reach her in my mind. But I can't." He wasn't fine. He hated reminding the others that he and Teresa could speak telepathically. And if all these people were dead . . . "We've gotta find where they put her," he blurted out, grasping urgently for a task to clear his mind. He scanned the room, trying his best not to focus on the corpses, looking for a door that might lead to her room. She'd said it was across the common area from where they'd all slept.

There. A yellow door with a brass handle.

"He's right," Minho said to the group. "Spread out, find her!"

"Might've already." Thomas was on the move, surprised at how quickly he'd recovered his senses. He ran toward the door, dodging tables and bodies. She had to be in there, safe like they'd been. The door was closed; that was a good sign. Probably locked. Maybe she'd fallen into a deep sleep like him. That was why she'd been quiet, unresponsive.

He had almost reached the door when he remembered that they might need something to break into the room. "Someone grab that fire extinguisher!" he yelled over his shoulder. The smell in the common area was horrendous; he gagged as he sucked in a deep breath.

"Winston, go get it," Minho ordered behind him.

Thomas reached the door first and tried the handle. It didn't budge, locked tight. Then he noticed a small, clear-plastic display hanging on the wall to the right, about five inches square. A sheet of paper had been slipped into the thin slot, several words typed on its surface.

Teresa Agnes. Group A, Subject Al.
The Betrayer.

Oddly, the thing that stood out the most to Thomas was Teresa's last name. Or at least, what appeared to be her last name. Agnes. He didn't know why, but it surprised him. Teresa Agnes. He couldn't think of anyone within the splotchy knowledge of history floating in his still-scarce memories who matched that name. He himself had been renamed after Thomas Edison, the great inventor. But Teresa Agnes? He'd never heard of her.

Of course, all their names were more of a joke than anything, probably a callous way for the Creators—WICKED or whoever had done this to them—to distance themselves from the *real* people they'd stolen from *real* mothers and fathers. Thomas couldn't wait until the day he learned what he'd been called at birth, what name lay stamped in the minds of his parents, whoever they were. Wherever they were.

The sketchy memories he'd initially regained from going through the Changing had made him think that he didn't have parents who loved him. That whoever they were, they didn't want him. That he'd been taken from horrible circumstances. But now he refused to believe it, especially after having dreamed about his mom during the night.

Minho snapped his fingers in front of Thomas's eyes. "Hello? Calling Thomas? Not a good time to daydream. Lots of dead bodies, smells like Frypan's pits. Wake up."

Thomas turned to him. "Sorry. Just thought it was weird that Teresa's last name was Agnes."

Minho clucked his tongue. "Who cares about *that*? What's this freakin' stuff about her being the Betrayer?"

"And what's 'Group A, Subject A1' mean?" This was Newt, who handed over the fire extinguisher to Thomas. "Anyway, your turn to break a buggin' door handle."

Thomas grabbed it, suddenly angry at himself for wasting even a few seconds thinking about the stupid label. Teresa was in there, and she needed their help. Trying not to be bothered by the word *betrayer,* he gripped the cylinder and slammed it against the brass knob. A jolt ran up his arms as the clang of metal against metal rang through the air. He'd felt it give a little, and two smashes later the handle fell off and the door popped open an inch or two.

Thomas threw the extinguisher to the side and grabbed the door, swung it all the way out. Itchy anticipation mixed with dread at what he might find. He was the first to step into the lighted room.

It was a smaller version of the boys' dorm, just four bunk beds, two dressers and a closed door, presumably leading to another bathroom. All the beds were made up nicely except one, its blankets tossed to the side and a pillow hanging off the edge, the sheet rumpled. But there was no sign of Teresa.

"Teresa!" Thomas called out, his throat straining with panic as he yelled.

The swirly, swooshing sound of a toilet flushing came through the closed door and a sudden relief burst through Thomas. It was so strong he almost had to sit down. She was here, she was safe. He steadied himself and started walking toward the bathroom, but Newt reached out and grabbed his arm.

"You're used to living with a bunch of boys," Newt said. "I don't think it's polite to go stomping into the bloody ladies' room. Just wait till she comes out."

"Then we need to get everybody in here and have a Gathering," Minho added. "It doesn't stink in here, and there aren't any windows for Cranks to scream at us."

Thomas hadn't noticed the lack of windows until that moment, though it should've been the most obvious thing, considering the chaos of their own dorm room. Cranks. He'd almost forgotten.

"I wish she'd hurry up," he murmured.

"I'll get everyone over here," Minho said; he turned and walked back into the common area.

Thomas stared at the bathroom door. Newt and Frypan and a few other Gladers pushed their way into the room and took seats on the beds, all of them leaning forward, elbows on knees, rubbing their hands together absently, the anxiety and worry evident in their body language.

Teresa? Thomas said in his mind. *Can you hear me? We're waiting for you out here.*

No response. And he still felt that bubble of emptiness, as if her presence itself had been permanently taken away.

There was a click. The handle on the door to the bathroom turned; then the door opened, swinging toward Thomas. He stepped forward, ready to pull Teresa into a hug—he didn't care who was there to see it. But the person who walked into the dorm room wasn't Teresa. Thomas stopped midstride and almost tripped. Everything inside him seemed to fall.

It was a boy.

He wore the same kind of clothes they'd all been given the night before—clean pajamas with a button-up shirt and flannel pants, light blue. He had olive skin, and his dark hair was cut surprisingly short. The look of innocent surprise on his face was the only thing that prevented Thomas from grabbing the shank by the collar and shaking him until some answers came out.

"Who are you?" Thomas asked, not caring that the words sounded harsh.

"Who am I?" the boy responded, somewhat sarcastically. "Who are *you*?"

Newt had gotten back to his feet, actually standing even closer to the new guy than Thomas was. "Don't bloody mess around. There are a lot more of us than there are of you. Tell us who you are."

The boy folded his arms, a defiance coming over his whole body. "Fine. My name's Aris. What else you wanna know?"

Thomas wanted to punch the guy. Him acting all high and mighty while Teresa was *missing.* "How'd you get here? Where's the girl who slept here last night?"

"Girl? What girl? I'm the only one here, and it's been that way since they put me here last night."

Thomas turned to point back in the direction of the door to the common area. "There's a sign right out there that *says* this is her room. Teresa . . . Agnes. No mention of a shank named *Aris.*"

Something in his tone must've made the boy realize this wasn't a joke. He held out his hands in a conciliatory gesture. "Look, man, I don't know what you're talking about. They put me in here last night, I slept in *that* bed"—he pointed to the one with the rumpled sheet and blanket—"and I woke up about five minutes ago and took a pee. Never heard the name Teresa Agnes in my life. Sorry."

The brief moment of relief Thomas had felt when he'd heard the toilet flush officially shattered. He shared a look with Newt, not knowing what to ask next.

Newt shrugged slightly, then turned back to Aris. "*Who* put you in here last night?"

Aris threw his arms up in the air, then let them come back down and slap against his sides. "I don't even know, man. A bunch of people with guns who rescued us, told us everything would be okay now."

"Rescued you from what?" Thomas asked. This was getting weird. Really, really weird.

Aris looked down at the floor and his shoulders fell. It looked as if a wave of some terrible memory had washed over him. He sighed, then finally looked back up at Thomas and answered.

"From the Maze, man. From the Maze."

CHAPTER 5

Something softened in Thomas. This kid wasn't lying—he could just tell. The look of horror that had taken hold of Aris was one he knew well. Thomas had felt it himself and had seen it on too many other faces. He knew exactly what kind of terrible memories made someone look like that. He also knew that Aris had no clue what had happened to Teresa.

"Maybe you should sit down," Thomas said. "I think we have a lot to talk about."

"What do you mean?" Aris asked. "Who are you guys? Where'd *you* come from?"

Thomas let out a slight laugh. "The Maze. The Grievers. WICKED. You name it." So much had happened, where could he start? Not to mention that worry over Teresa was making his head spin, making him want to run out of the room and search for her immediately, but he stayed.

"You're lying," Aris said, his voice having dropped to a whisper, his face now a full shade paler.

"No, we're not," Newt responded. "Tommy's right. We need to talk. Sounds like we've come from similar places."

"Who's that guy?"

Thomas turned around to see that Minho had returned, a pack of Gladers standing behind him on the other side of the doorway. Their faces were scrunched up in disgust at the smell out there, their eyes still full of the terror of seeing what filled the room just behind them.

"Minho, meet Aris," Thomas said, taking a step to the side and gesturing toward the other boy. "Aris, meet Minho."

Minho stuttered out a few unintelligible words, as if he couldn't quite decide where to start.

"Look," Newt said. "Let's take down these top beds and move them around the room. Then we can all sit and figure out what's bloody going on."

Thomas shook his head. "No. First, we need to go find Teresa. She must be in some other room."

"Isn't one," Minho said.

"What do you mean?"

"I just checked this whole place out. There's the big common area, this room, our dorm room, and some seriously shucked doors that lead outside—where we came in from the bus yesterday. Locked and chained from the *inside.* Doesn't make any sense, but I don't see any other doors or exits."

Thomas shook his head in confusion. It felt like a million spiders had just spun cobwebs through his brain. "But . . . what about last night? Where'd the food come from? Didn't anyone notice other rooms, a kitchen, anything?" He looked around, hoping for an answer, but no one said a word.

"Maybe there's a hidden door," Newt finally said. "Look, we can only do one thing at a time. We need to—"

"No!" Thomas shouted. "We've got all day to talk to this Aris guy. The label by the door said Teresa should be here somewhere—we need to find her!"

Without waiting for a response, he headed for the door back to the common area, pushing his way past boys until he was through. The smell hit him as if a bucket of raw sewage had been spilled over his head. The bloated and purple bodies hung like carcasses of game set out by hunters to dry. Their lifeless eyes stared back at him.

A familiar, sickening tickle of revulsion filled his stomach and triggered his gag reflex. Closing his eyes for a second, he willed his insides to settle. When they finally did, he began his search for some sign of Teresa, concentrating with all his might on *not* looking at the dead people.

But then a horrible thought struck him. What if she . . .

He ran through the room, searching the faces of the bodies. None of them was her. Relief dissolved the fleeting moment of panic, and he focused on the room itself.

The walls surrounding the common area were as plain as could be; smooth plaster painted white, no decoration of any kind. And for some reason, no windows. He walked quickly around its entire circumference, running his left hand along the wall as he did so. He came to the door to the boys' dorm room, went past it, then made it to the big entrance through which they'd come the day before. There had been a torrential downpour at the time, which seemed impossible now, considering the bright sun he'd seen shining behind the crazy man earlier.

The entrance—or exit—consisted of two large steel doors, their surfaces a shiny silver. And just like Minho said, a massive chain—with links a full inch thick—had been threaded through the handles on the doors and pulled tight, two big key locks snapped shut to keep it that way. Thomas reached out and pulled on the chains to check their strength. The metal felt cool under his hands, and it didn't give at all.

He expected thumps from the other side—Cranks trying to get in just as they were at the windows in the dorm room. But the room remained silent. The only sounds were muted and coming from the two dorms—distant shouts and screams from the Cranks and murmurs of conversation from the Gladers.

Frustrated, Thomas continued his trek along the walls until he made it back to the room that was *supposed* to be Teresa's. Nothing, not even a crack or seam to indicate another exit. The large room wasn't even a square—it was a big oval, round and cornerless.

He was completely perplexed. He thought back to the night before, when they'd all sat there and eaten pizza like the starved people they'd been. Surely they'd seen other doors, a kitchen, something. But the more he thought about it, the more he tried to picture what things had looked like, the fuzzier it became. An alarm went off in his head—their brains had been tinkered with before. Had it happened again? Had their memories been altered or wiped?

And what had happened to Teresa?

Desperate, he thought about crawling across the floor to look for a trapdoor or something—some clue to what had happened. But he couldn't spend another minute with all those rotting bodies. The only thing left was the new kid. He sighed and turned back to the small room where they'd found him. Aris had to know something that would help.

Just as Newt had ordered, the top beds had been unhooked from the lower ones and placed around the room against the walls, creating enough space for the nineteen other Gladers and Aris to sit in a circle, everyone facing each other.

When Minho saw Thomas, he patted an empty spot next to him. "Told ya, dude. Have a seat and let's talk. We waited on you. But close that shuck door as much as you can first—smells worse than Gally's rotting feet out there."

Without responding, Thomas pulled the door shut, then walked over and sat down. He wanted to sink his head into his hands, but he didn't. Nothing indicated for sure that any kind of danger threatened

Teresa. Something weird was going on, but there could be a million explanations, and plenty of them included her being okay.

Newt was one bed to the right, sitting so far forward that just the edge of his butt rested on the mattress. "All right, let's get started on the bloody storytellin' so we can get to the real problem—finding something to eat."

Right on cue, Thomas felt a hunger pang, heard his stomach growl. That problem hadn't even occurred to him yet. Water would be fine—they had the bathrooms—but there was no sign of food anywhere.

"Good that," Minho said. "Talk, Aris. Tell us everything."

The new boy was directly across the room from Thomas—the Gladers sitting to each side of the stranger had scooted to the far ends of the bed. Aris shook his head. "No way. You guys go first."

"Yeah?" Minho responded. "How about we all just take turns beating the living klunk out of your shuck face? Then we'll ask you to talk again."

"Minho," Newt said sternly. "There's no reason—"

Minho pointed sharply at Aris. "Please, dude. For all we know this shank could be one of the Creators. Somebody from WICKED, here to spy on us. He could've killed those people out there—he's the only one we don't know and the doors and windows are locked! I'm sick of him acting all snooty when we've got twenty guys to his one. He should talk first."

Thomas groaned on the inside. One thing he knew was that the kid would never open up if Minho terrified him.

Newt sighed and looked over at Aris. "He's got a point. Just tell us what you meant about coming from the buggin' Maze. That's where *we* escaped from, and we obviously haven't met you."

Aris rubbed his eyes, then met Newt's gaze. "Fine, listen. I was thrown into this gigantic maze made out of huge stone walls—but before that my memory was erased. I couldn't remember anything about my life from before. I just knew my name. I lived there with a bunch of girls. There must've been fifty of them, and I was the only boy. We escaped a few days ago—the people who helped kept us in a big gym for a few days, then moved me here last night—but no one explained anything. What's this stuff about you being in a maze, too?"

Thomas barely heard the last few words of what Aris had said over the sounds of surprise coming from the other Gladers. Confusion swirled in his brain. Aris had announced what he'd been through as simply and quickly as describing a trip to the beach. But it seemed crazy. Monumental, if true. Luckily someone voiced exactly what Thomas was trying to sort out in his mind.

"Wait a minute," Newt said. "You lived in a big maze, on a farm, where walls closed every night? Just you and a few dozen girls? Were there creatures called Grievers? Were you the last one to arrive? And did everything go buggin' nuts when you did? Did you come in a coma? With a note that said you were the last one ever?"

"Whoa, whoa, whoa," Aris was saying even before Newt had finished. "How do you know all this? How . . ."

"It's the same shuck experiment," Minho said, the earlier belligerence gone from his voice. "Or same . . . whatever. But they had all girls and one boy, we had all boys and one girl. WICKED must've built two of those mazes, run two different tests!"

Thomas's line of thinking had already accepted that. He finally settled himself enough to speak. He looked at Aris. "Did they call you the Trigger?"

Aris nodded, obviously as perplexed as anyone else in the room.

"And could you . . . ," Thomas began, but hesitated. He felt like every time he brought this up, he was admitting to the world that he was crazy. "Could you speak to one of those girls inside your mind? Ya know, like telepathically?"

Aris's eyes widened, staring deeply at Thomas as if he'd understood a dark secret that only someone else who shared it could understand.

Can you hear me?

The phrase appeared so clearly inside Thomas's mind that at first he thought Aris had spoken aloud. But no—his lips hadn't moved.

Can you hear me? the boy repeated.

Thomas hesitated, swallowed. *Yes.*

They killed her, Aris said back to him. *They killed my best friend.*

CHAPTER 6

"What's going on?" Newt asked, looking back and forth between Thomas and Aris. "Why're you guys looking at each other like you just fell in love?"

"He can do it, too," Thomas answered, not taking his eyes off the new kid, seeing the others only in his peripheral vision. That final statement by Aris had terrified him; if they'd killed *his* telepathy partner . . .

"Do what?" Frypan asked.

"What do you think?" Minho said. "He's a freak like Thomas. They can talk in each other's heads."

Newt was glaring at Thomas now. "Serious?"

Thomas nodded and almost spoke to Aris in his mind again, but said it out loud at the last second. "*Who* killed her? What happened?"

"Who killed who?" Minho said. "No more of your voodoo klunk while we're around."

Thomas, eyes watering now, finally broke his gaze with Aris and looked over at Minho. "He had someone he could do this with, just like I did. I mean . . . *do.* But he said they killed her. I want to know who *they* are."

Aris's head had dropped; his eyes looked closed from where Thomas sat. "I don't really know who *they* are. It's too confusing. I couldn't tell the bad guys from the good guys. But I think somehow they made this girl Beth . . . stab . . . my friend. Her name was Rachel. She's dead, man. She's dead." He covered his face with both hands.

Thomas felt an almost painful prick of confusion. Everything pointed to Aris's having come from another version of the Maze, set up in the same format except with the ratio of girls to boys being switched. But that would make Aris their version of Teresa. And this Beth sounded like their version of Gally, who'd killed Chuck. With a knife. Did that mean that Gally was supposed to have killed Thomas instead?

But why was Aris here now? And where was Teresa? Things that had almost started to click in his mind fell apart again.

"Well, how'd you end up with us?" Newt asked. "Where are all these girls you keep talking about? How many of them escaped with you? Did they bring all of you here or just you?"

Thomas couldn't help but feel sorry for Aris. To get grilled with all these questions after something like that had happened. If the roles were switched, if Thomas had seen Teresa get killed . . . Watching it happen to Chuck had been bad enough.

Bad enough? he thought. *Or was seeing Chuck die worse?* Thomas wanted to scream. At that moment, everything in the world just *sucked.*

Aris looked up finally, wiped a couple of tears from his cheeks. He did it without the slightest hint of shame, and Thomas suddenly knew that he liked this kid.

"Look," the boy said. "I'm just as confused as everyone else. About thirty of us survived, they took us to that gym, fed us, cleaned us up. Then they brought me to this place last night, saying I should be separate since I'm a guy. That's it. Then you sticks show up."

"Sticks?" Minho repeated.

Aris shook his head. "Never mind. I don't even know what it means. Just a word they used when I got there."

Minho exchanged a glance with Thomas, half smiling. Looked like both groups had come up with their own vocabulary.

"Hey," one of the Gladers Thomas didn't really know called out. He was leaning against the wall behind Aris, pointing at him. "What's that on the side of your neck? Something black, right below your collar."

Aris tried to look down, but couldn't bend his neck to see that part of his body. "What?"

Thomas saw a dark splotch just above the back neckline of the boy's pajama shirt as he shifted around. It appeared to be a thick line, stretching from the hollow of his collarbone around to his back. And it was broken up, like it might be lettering.

"Here, let me look," Newt offered. He stood from the bed and walked over, his limp—from something in the past he'd never shared with Thomas—showing more than usual. He reached out and pulled Aris's shirt down more so he could see the odd marking better.

"It's a tattoo," Newt said, squinting as if he didn't believe his eyes.

"What's it say?" Minho asked, though he'd already gotten up from the bed and approached to get his own look.

When Newt didn't answer right away, curiosity forced Thomas to his feet, and soon he was right beside Minho, leaning over to see the tattoo himself. What he saw printed there in blocky letters made his heart skip a beat.

Property of WICKED. Group B, Subject B1. The Partner.

"What's that supposed to mean?" Minho asked.

"What does it *say*?" Aris asked, reaching around to feel the skin of his neck and shoulders, pulling his shirt collar down. "I swear it wasn't there last night!"

Newt repeated the words to him, then said, "Property of WICKED?

I thought we'd escaped them. Or you'd escaped them, too. Whatever." He turned around, visibly frustrated, and went back to sit down on his bed.

"And why would it call you the *Partner?*" Minho said, still staring at the tattoo.

Aris shook his head. "I don't have a clue. I swear. And there's no way that was there before last night. I showered, looked in the mirror. I would've seen it. And someone would've noticed it back in the Maze for sure."

"You're telling me they tattooed you in the middle of the night?" Minho said. "Without you noticing? Come on, dude."

"I swear!" Aris insisted. Then he got up and went to the bathroom, probably to try to see the words for himself.

"I don't believe a shuck word he says," Minho whispered to Thomas on his way back to his seat. Then, just as he leaned forward to plop back down on the mattress, his shirt shifted enough to reveal a thick line of black on *his* neck.

"Whoa!" Thomas said. For a second, he was too stunned to move.

"What?" Minho asked, looking at Thomas as if he'd just sprouted a third ear on his forehead.

"Your—your neck," Thomas finally got out. "You have it on your neck, too!"

"What the shuck you talkin' about?" Minho said, pulling at his shirt, face scrunched up as he struggled to see something he couldn't.

Thomas ran over to Minho, slapped his hands away, then pulled the neckline of the shirt back. "Holy . . . It's right there! Same thing, except . . ."

Thomas read the words to himself.

Property of WICKED. Group A, Subject A7. The Leader.

"*What,* dude!" Minho yelled at him.

Most of the other Gladers had gathered in a tight group behind Thomas, squeezing in to get a look. Thomas quickly read the tattooed words out loud, surprised he did it without stumbling on them.

"You're kiddin' me, man," Minho said, standing up. He pushed his way through the crowd of boys to follow Aris to the bathroom.

And then the frenzy began. Thomas felt his own shirt tugged down as he pulled at others. Everyone started talking over everyone else.

"They all say Group A."

"Property of WICKED, just like his."

"You're Subject A-thirteen."

"Subject A-nineteen."

"A-three."

"A-ten."

Thomas was slowly turning in a circle, dazed as he watched the Gladers discover the tattoos on each other. Most of them didn't have the additional designations like Aris and Minho, just the property line. Newt was going from boy to boy, looking for himself, his face set in stone as if he were concentrating on memorizing the names and numbers. Then, quite by accident, the two of them stood facing each other.

"What does mine say?" Newt asked.

Thomas pulled the neckline of Newt's shirt to the side, then leaned over to read the words etched into his skin. "You're Subject A-five and they called you the *Glue.*"

Newt gave him a startled look. "The *Glue*?"

Thomas let go of his shirt and stepped back. "Yeah. Probably because you're kind of the glue that holds us all together. I don't know. Read mine."

"I already did—"

Thomas noticed that an odd expression had come over Newt's face.

One of hesitation. Or dread. Like he didn't want to tell Thomas what his tattoo said. "Well?"

"You're Subject A-two," Newt answered. Then he lowered his eyes.

"And?" Thomas pushed.

Newt hesitated, then answered without looking at him. "It doesn't call you anything. It just says . . . 'To be killed by Group B.' "

CHAPTER 7

Thomas didn't really have time to process what Newt had said. He was actually trying to decide whether he was more confused or scared when a clanging bell began ringing throughout the room. He instinctively put his hands to his ears and looked around at the others.

He noticed the perplexed recognition on their faces, and then it hit him. It was the same sound he'd heard back in the Maze right before Teresa had shown up in the Box. That was the only time he'd heard it, and trapped within the confines of a small room it was different—stronger, laced with overlapping echoes. Still, he was pretty sure it was the same. It was the alarm used in the Glade to announce that a Newbie had arrived.

And it wasn't stopping; Thomas already felt a headache forming behind his eyes.

The Gladers milled about the room, gawking at the walls and the roof as if they were trying to figure out the source of the noise. Some of them sat down on the beds, hands pressed to the sides of their heads. Thomas tried to find the source of the alarm as well, but couldn't see anything. No speakers, no heating or air-conditioning vents in the walls, nothing. Just a sound coming from everywhere at once.

Newt grabbed his arm, shouted in his ear. "It's the bloody Newbie alarm!"

"I know!"

"Why's it ringing?"

Thomas shrugged, hoping his face didn't betray how annoyed he was. How was he supposed to know what was going on?

Minho and Aris had reappeared from the bathroom, both of them absently rubbing the backs of their necks as they searched the room for answers. It didn't take long for them to realize that the others had similar tattoos. Frypan had walked over to the door leading back out to the common room and was just about to touch the palm of his hand to the spot where the broken handle used to be.

"Wait!" Thomas shouted on impulse. He ran over to join Frypan at the door, sensing Newt right behind him.

"Why?" Frypan asked, his hand still hovering just inches from the door.

"I don't know," Thomas replied, not sure if he could even be heard over the clanging sounds. "It's an *alarm*. Maybe something really bad is happening."

"Yeah!" Frypan yelled back. "And maybe we need to get out of here!"

Without waiting to see what Thomas said, he pushed the door. When it didn't move, he pushed harder. When it still didn't budge, he leaned up against it with his full weight, shoulder first.

Nothing. It was closed as tight as if it were bricked shut.

"You broke the shuck handle!" Frypan screamed, then slapped the door with the palm of his hand.

Thomas didn't want to shout anymore; he was tired and his throat hurt. He turned and leaned back against the wall, folded his arms. Most of the Gladers seemed as run-down as Thomas—sick of looking for answers or a way out. All of them were either sitting on the beds or standing around with blank expressions on their faces.

Out of desperation more than anything, Thomas called to Teresa again. Then several times more. But she didn't respond, and with all the blaring noise, he didn't know if he could have focused enough to hear her anyway. He still felt her absence; it was like waking up one day with no teeth in your mouth. You wouldn't need to run to the mirror to know they were gone.

Then the alarm stopped.

Never before had silence seemed to have its own sound. Like a buzzing hive of bees, it settled on the room with ferocity, making Thomas reach up and wiggle a finger in each ear. Every breath, every sigh in the room was like an explosion compared to the bizarre haze of quiet.

Newt was the first one to speak. "Don't tell me we're still gonna get bloody Newbies thrown in our laps."

"Where's the Box in this shuck place?" Minho muttered sarcastically.

A slight creak made Thomas look sharply over at the door to the common area. It had swung open several inches, a slice of darkness marking where it now stood ajar. Someone had turned off the lights on the other side. Frypan backed up a step.

"Guessin' they want us to go out there now," Minho said.

"Then why don't you go first," Frypan offered.

Minho had already started moving. "No problem. Maybe we'll have a new little shank to pick on and kick in the butt when we got nothin' else to do." He made it to the door, then paused and looked sideways at Thomas. His voice turned surprisingly soft. "We could use another Chuck."

Thomas knew he shouldn't have been upset. If anything, Minho was trying—in his own strange way—to show that he missed Chuck just as much as everyone else. But being reminded of his friend, and at such an odd moment, made Thomas angry. Instinct told him to ignore it—he was having a hard enough time dealing with the things going on around him. He needed to separate himself from his feelings for a while and just move forward. Step by step. Figure it all out.

"Yeah," he finally said. "You going through or you need me to go first?"

"What did your tattoo say?" Minho responded quietly, ignoring Thomas's question.

"Doesn't matter. Let's go out there."

Minho nodded, still not looking directly at him. Then he smiled, and whatever had been troubling him so deeply appeared to vanish, replaced by his usual laid-back attitude. "Good that. If some zombie starts eating my leg, save me."

"Deal." Thomas wanted him to hurry and get on with it. He knew they were on the edge of yet another great change in their ridiculous journey, and he didn't want to draw it out any longer.

Minho pushed open the door. The single bar of blackness became a wide swath of it, the common area now as dark as it had been when they'd first left the boys' dorm. Minho stepped through the doorway, and Thomas followed right on his heels.

"Wait here," Minho whispered. "No need playing bumper cars with the dead folks again. Let me find the light switches first."

"Why would they have turned them off?" Thomas asked. "I mean, *who* turned them off?"

Minho looked back at him; the light from Aris's room spilled across his face, illuminating the smirk set firmly there. "Why do you even bother asking questions, dude? Nothing has ever made sense and it probably never will. Now slim it and sit still."

Minho was quickly swallowed by the darkness. Thomas heard his soft footsteps on the carpet and the *swish* sound of his hand running along the wall as he walked.

"Here they are!" he shouted from the spot that seemed about right to Thomas.

A few clicks sounded and then lights blazed throughout the room. For the tiniest fraction of a second, Thomas didn't realize what was so starkly different about the place. But then it hit him, and as if that awakened his other senses as well, he realized that the horrible smell of rotting corpses had vanished.

And now he knew why.

The bodies were gone, with no sign that they'd ever been there in the first place.

CHAPTER 8

Several seconds passed before Thomas realized he'd stopped breathing. Sucking in a deep pull of air, he gaped at the now-empty room. No bloated, purpled-skinned bodies. No stink.

Newt nudged past him, walking forward with his slight limp until he stood in the very center of the room's carpeted floor. "This is impossible," he said, turning in a slow circle, gazing up at the ceiling where the corpses had hung from ropes only minutes earlier. "Not enough time passed for someone to get them out. And no one else even came into this buggin' room. We would've heard them!"

Thomas stepped to the side and leaned against the wall as the other Gladers and Aris came out of the small dorm room. A hushed sense of awe spread across the group as one by one, each person noticed the missing dead. As for Thomas, he once again felt a numbness, like he just might be done feeling surprised at anything.

"You're right," Minho said to Newt. "We were in there with the door closed for, what, twenty minutes? No way anyone could've moved all those bodies that quickly. Plus, this place is locked from the *inside*."

"Not to mention getting rid of the smell," Thomas added.

Minho nodded.

"Well, you shanks are right smart," Frypan said through a huff. "But take a look around. They're gone. So whatever you think, somehow they got rid of them."

Thomas didn't feel like arguing about it—or even talking about it. So the dead bodies were gone. They'd seen stranger stuff.

"Hey," Winston said. "Those crazy people quit screaming and yelling."

Thomas put his weight back on his feet, listened. Silence. "I thought we just couldn't hear them from Aris's room. But you're right—they stopped."

Soon everyone was running for the larger dorm room on the far side of the common area. Thomas followed, intensely curious to look out the windows and see the world outside. Before, with the Cranks screaming and pressing their faces against the iron bars, he'd been too horrified to get a good view.

"No way!" Minho yelled from up ahead, then, without further explanation, disappeared inside the room.

As Thomas moved in that direction, he noticed that every boy hesitated a second, wide-eyed at the threshold of the door, then went ahead and entered the dorm. He waited as each Glader and then Aris funneled their way inside, then followed.

He felt the same shock he'd sensed from the other boys. As a whole, the room looked much like it had when they'd walked out of it earlier. But there was one monumental difference: at each window, without exception, a red brick wall had been erected just outside the iron bars, completely blocking every inch of open space. The only light in the room came from the panels on the ceiling.

"Even if they were quick with those bodies," Newt said, "I'm pretty sure they didn't have time to bloody throw up some brick walls. What's going on here?"

Thomas watched as Minho walked over to one of the windows and reached through the bars, pressing his hand against the red bricks. "Solid," he said, then slapped at it.

"It doesn't even look fresh," Thomas murmured, stepping up to one himself to get a feel. Hard and cool. "The mortar's dry. Somehow they've tricked us, that's all."

"Tricked us?" Frypan asked. "How?"

Thomas shrugged, that numbness returning. Still wishing desperately that he could talk to Teresa. "I don't know. Remember the Cliff? We jumped into thin air and went through an invisible hole. Who knows what these people can do."

The next half hour passed in a haze. Thomas wandered about, as did everyone else, inspecting the brick walls, looking for signs of anything else that had changed. Several things had, each one just as strange as the next. All the beds in the Gladers' dorm room were made, and there was no sign of the grungy clothes they'd all worn before changing into the pajamas provided the night before. The dressers had been rearranged, though the difference was subtle and some people disagreed that they'd been moved at all. Either way, each one had been stocked with fresh clothes and shoes, and new digital watches for each boy.

But the biggest change of all—discovered by Minho—was the sign outside the room where they'd found Aris. Instead of saying *Teresa Agnes, Group A, Subject A1, The Betrayer,* it now said:

Aris Jones, Group B, Subject B1
The Partner

Everyone observed the new plaque, then wandered away, but Thomas found himself standing in front of it, unable to remove his eyes. To Thomas it felt like the new label made it official—Teresa had been taken from him, replaced by Aris. None of it made sense, and none of it mattered anymore. He went back to the boys' dorm, found the cot he'd slept on during the night—or at least, the one he *thought* he'd slept on—

and lay down, putting the pillow over his head, as if that would make everyone else go away.

What had happened to her? What had happened to *them*? Where were they? What were they supposed to do? And the tattoos . . .

Turning his head to the side, then his whole body, he squeezed his eyes shut and folded his arms tightly, pulling his legs up until he lay in the fetal position. Then, determined to keep trying until he heard back from her, he called out with his thoughts.

Teresa? A pause. *Teresa?* A longer pause. *Teresa!* He shouted it mentally, his whole body tensing with the effort. *Teresa! Where are you? Please answer me! Why aren't you trying to contact me? Ter—*

Get out of my head!

The words exploded inside his mind, so vivid and so strangely audible within his skull that he felt lances of pain behind his eyes and in his ears. He sat up in bed, then stood. It was her. It was definitely her.

Teresa? He pressed the first two fingers of both hands against his temples. *Teresa?*

Whoever you are, get out of my shuck head!

Thomas stumbled backward until he sat down once again on the bed. His eyes were closed as he concentrated. *Teresa, what are you talking about? It's me. Thomas. Where are you?*

Shut up! It was her, he had no doubt, but her mental voice was full of fear and anger. *Just shut up! I don't know who you are! Leave me alone!*

But, Thomas began, completely at a loss. *Teresa, what's wrong?*

She paused before answering, as if collecting her thoughts, and when she finally spoke again, Thomas sensed an almost disturbing calm in her.

Leave me alone, or I'll hunt you down and cut your throat. I swear it.

And then she was gone. Despite her warning, he tried calling for her again, but the same emptiness he'd felt since that morning returned, her presence having vanished.

Thomas fell back on the bed, something horrible burning through his body. He quickly buried his head in the pillow again and cried for the first time since Chuck had been killed. But the words from the label outside her door—*The Betrayer*—kept popping up in his mind. Each time, he pushed them away.

Amazingly, no one bothered him or asked him what was wrong. His stifled sobs finally faded into an occasional hitched breath, and eventually he fell asleep. Once again, he dreamed.

He's a little older this time, probably seven or eight. A very bright light hovers above his head like magic.

People in strange green suits and funny glasses keep peeking at him, their heads momentarily blocking the brilliance that shines down. He can see their eyes but nothing else. Their mouths and noses are covered by masks. Thomas is somehow both himself at that age and yet, as before, observing as an outsider. But he feels the boy's fear.

People are talking, voices muted and dull. Some are men, some are women, but he can't tell which is which or who is who.

He can't understand much of it at all.

Only glimpses. Fragments of conversation. All of it terrifying.

"We'll have to cut deeper with him and the girl."

"Can their brains handle this?"

"This is so amazing, you know? The Flare is rooted inside him."

"He might die."

"Or worse. He might live."

He hears one last thing, finally something that doesn't make him shiver in disgust or fright.

"Or he and the others might save us. Save us all."

CHAPTER 9

When he woke up, his head felt like several chunks of ice had been hammered through his ears and into his brain. Wincing, he reached up to rub his eyes and was hit by a wave of nausea that sent the room tilting around him. Then he remembered the terrible things Teresa had said, then the short dream, and misery engulfed him. Who had those people been? Was it real? What had they meant when they'd said those awful things about his brain?

"Glad to see you still know how to take a nap."

Thomas peeked through a squint and saw Newt standing next to his bed, staring down at him.

"How long's it been?" Thomas asked, forcing thoughts of Teresa and the dream—memory?—into a dark corner of his mind to agonize over later.

Newt looked at his watch. "Couple hours. When people noticed you lie down, it actually kind of relaxed everyone. Not much we can do but sit and wait for something new to happen. There's no way out of this place."

Thomas tried not to groan as he scooted himself into a sitting position, his back against the wall at the head of his bed. "Do we even have any food?"

"No. But I'm pretty sure these people wouldn't go through all this trouble to bring us here, trick us or whatever they've done, just to let us buggin' starve to death. Something will happen. Reminds me of when they sent the first group of us to the Glade. The initial group of me and Alby and Minho and some others. The original Gladers." He said that last part with a not-so-subtle burst of sarcasm.

Thomas was intrigued, surprised he'd never before dug into what that had been like. "How does this remind you of that?"

Newt's gaze was focused on the brick wall outside the closest window. "We all woke up in the middle of the day, lying on the ground around the doors to the Box. It was closed. Our memories had been wiped, just like yours when you came. You'd be surprised at how quickly we pulled ourselves together and quit panicking. There were about thirty of us. Obviously, we had no bloody clue what had happened, how we'd gotten there, what we were supposed to do. And we were terrified, disoriented. But since we were all in the same crappy situation, we organized ourselves and figured out the place. Had the full farm running within days, everybody with their own job."

Thomas was relieved that the pain in his skull had diminished. And he was intrigued to hear about the start of the Glade—the scattered pieces of the puzzle brought back by the Changing weren't nearly enough to form solid memories. "Did the Creators have everything in place already? Crops, animals, all that?"

Newt nodded, still staring at the bricked-up window. "Yeah, but it took a ton of work to get it going nice and smooth. A lot of trial and error before we accomplished anything."

"So . . . how does this remind you of that?" Thomas asked again.

Finally, Newt looked at him. "I guess back then we all just had a sense that there was obviously a *purpose* to us having been sent there. If someone had wanted to kill us, why wouldn't they have just killed us? Why would they send us to a huge place with a house and a barn and animals? And because we had no other choice, we accepted it and started working and exploring."

"But we're already done exploring here," Thomas countered. "No animals, no food, no Maze."

"Yeah, but come on. It's the same concept. We're obviously here for a buggin' purpose. We'll figure it out eventually."

"If we don't starve first."

Newt pointed at the bathroom. "We've got plenty of water, so it'll be at least a few days before we drop dead. Something will happen."

Deep down Thomas believed it, too, and was only arguing to solidify it in his own mind. "But what about all those dead people we saw? Maybe they rescued us for real, got killed, and now we're screwed. Maybe we were *supposed* to do something, but now it's all been messed up and we've been left here to die."

Newt burst out laughing. "You're one depressing piece of klunk, slinthead. Nah, with all those corpses magically disappearing and the brick walls, I'd say this is something more like the Maze. Weird and impossible to explain. The latest and greatest mystery. Maybe our next test, who knows. Whatever's going on, we'll have a chance, just like we did in the bloody Maze. I guarantee it."

"Yeah," Thomas murmured, wondering if he should share what he'd dreamed about. Deciding to save it for later, he said, "Hope you're right. As long as no Grievers suddenly show up, we'll be good."

Newt was already shaking his head by the time Thomas finished. "Please, man. Careful what you buggin' wish for. Maybe they'll send something worse."

The image of Teresa popped into Thomas's mind just then, and he lost all desire to talk. "Who's the cheerful one now?" he forced himself to say.

"You got me," Newt replied, then stood up. "Guess I'll go bug somebody else till the excitement begins, which better be bloody soon. I'm hungry."

"Careful what *you* wish for."

"Good that."

Newt walked away, and Thomas scooted down to lie on his back, staring at the bottom of the bunk above him. He closed his eyes after a while, but when he saw Teresa's face in the darkness of his thoughts, he opened them right up again. If he was going to get through this, he'd have to try to forget about her for now.

Hunger.

It's like an animal trapped inside you, Thomas thought. After three full days of not eating, it felt like a vicious, gnawing, dull-clawed animal was trying to burrow its way out of his stomach. He felt it every second of every minute of every hour. He drank water as often as possible from the sinks in the bathroom, but it did nothing to drive the beast away. If anything, it felt like he was making the thing stronger so it could inflict more misery within.

The others felt it, too, even if most of them kept their complaints to themselves. Thomas watched as they walked around, heads hung low, jaws slack, as if every step burned a thousand calories. People licked their lips a lot. They grabbed at their stomachs, pushed on them, as if trying to calm that gnawing beast. Unless they were going to the bathroom to use it or to get a drink, the Gladers didn't move at all. Like Thomas, they just lay there on the bunk beds, limp. Skin pale, eyes sunken.

Thomas felt all this like a festering disease, and seeing the others only made it worse, a stark reminder that this wasn't something he could just ignore. That it was real, and death waited just around the corner.

Listless sleep. Bathroom. Water. Trudge back to bed. Listless sleep—without any more of the memory-dreams he'd experienced. It became a horrendous cycle, broken up only by thoughts of Teresa, her harsh words to him the only thing that lightened the prospect of death, even if only a little. She'd been the only thing he could grasp for hope after the Maze and Chuck's death. And now she was gone, there was no food, and three long days had passed.

Hunger. Misery.

He'd quit bothering to look at his watch—it only made time drag and reminded his body how long it'd been since he'd eaten—but he thought it was roughly midafternoon of the third day when a humming sound abruptly began from the common area.

He stared at the door leading out there, knew he should get up and go check it out. But his mind had already been slipping into another one of those hazy half-naps, the world around him foggy.

Maybe he'd imagined it. But then he heard it again.

He told himself to get up.

He fell asleep instead.

"Thomas."

It was Minho's voice. Weak, but stronger than it had been the last time he'd heard it.

"Thomas. Dude, wake up."

Thomas opened his eyes, amazed he'd survived another nap without dying. Things were blurry for a second, and at first he didn't believe that what he thought was just a few inches from his face was real. But then its image sharpened, and the red roundness of it, with flecks of green scattered across its shiny surface, made him feel like he was looking on heaven itself.

An apple.

"Where'd you . . ." He didn't bother to finish, those two words alone sapping his strength.

"Just eat it," Minho said, followed by a wet crunch.

Thomas glanced up to see his friend munching on his own apple.

Then, drawing the last remnants of energy from somewhere deep inside himself, he pushed himself up onto an elbow and grabbed the fruit lying on the bed. He lifted it to his mouth and took a small bite. The burst of flavor and juice was a glorious thing.

Moaning, he attacked the rest of it and had eaten down to its stumpy core before Minho had even finished his—despite the head start.

"Slim yourself nice and calm," Minho said. "Eat like that and you'll just throw it right back up. Here's another one—try slowing down this time."

He handed a second apple to Thomas, who took it without saying thank you and chomped a big bite. As he chewed, resolving to swallow before stuffing another chunk in his mouth, he realized he could actually feel the first traces of energy trickling through his body.

"This is so good," he mumbled. "This is so shuckin' good."

"You still sound like an idiot when you use Glader words," Minho responded before taking another bite of his apple.

Thomas ignored him. "Where'd these come from?"

Minho hesitated in the middle of chewing, then resumed. "Found them out in the common room. Along with . . . something else. Shanks who found it all claim they'd just looked a few minutes earlier and nothing had been there, but whatever, I don't care."

Thomas swung his legs off the bed and sat up. "What else did they find?"

Minho took a bite, then nodded toward the door. "Go look for yourself."

Thomas rolled his eyes and slowly stood up. The miserable weakness was still there, like most of his insides had been sucked right out and all he had left were a few bones and tendons to hold himself erect. But he steadied, feeling even after a few seconds that he was already better than the last time he'd made the long, lifeless trek to the bathroom.

Once he thought he had his balance, he walked over to the door and entered the common area. Only three days before, the room had been filled with dead bodies—now it was crowded with Gladers picking things off a big pile of food that had seemingly been dumped there without any order. Fruit, vegetables, small packages.

But he'd barely registered this when an even more bizarre sight on the far side of the room caught his attention. He reached out to steady himself on the wall behind him.

A large wooden desk had been placed opposite the door to the other dorm room.

Behind the desk, a thin man in a white suit sat in a chair, his feet propped up and crossed at the ankles.

The man was reading a book.

CHAPTER 10

Thomas stood there for a full minute, staring at the man casually sitting at the desk, reading. It was as if he'd been reading that way and in that very spot every day for his whole life. Thin black hair combed across a pale, bald head; a long nose, twisted slightly to the right; and shifty brown eyes darting back and forth as he read—the man somehow looked relaxed and nervous at the same time.

And the white suit. Pants, shirt, tie, coat. Socks. Shoes. All white.

What in the *world*?

Thomas looked over at the Gladers munching on fruit and a snack from a bag that looked like a mixture of nuts and seeds. They seemed oblivious to the man at the desk.

"Who *is* that guy?" Thomas called out to no one in particular.

One of the boys looked up, stopped chewing for a second. Then he quickly finished off his mouthful and swallowed. "He won't tell us anything. Told us we had to wait till he's ready." The boy shrugged as if that wasn't a big deal and took another bite of a peeled orange.

Thomas returned his attention to the stranger. Still sitting there, still reading. He turned a page with a whispery scrape and continued scanning the words.

Baffled, and with a stomach rumbling for more food, Thomas still couldn't help but walk toward the man to investigate. Of all the strange things to wake up to . . .

"Careful," one of the Gladers called out, but it was too late.

Just ten feet in front of the desk, Thomas slammed into an invisible wall. His nose hit first, smashing against what felt like a cold sheet of glass. The rest of his body followed suit, bumping against the unseen wall and making him stumble backward. He instinctively reached up to rub his nose as he squinted to see how he could've possibly missed a glass barrier.

But no matter how hard he looked, he couldn't see anything. Not the slightest glare or reflection, not a smudge anywhere. All he saw was air. All the while, the man hadn't bothered to move or give even the least hint he'd noticed anything.

More slowly this time, Thomas approached the spot, holding his hands out. Soon he made contact with the wall of completely invisible . . . what? It felt like glass—smooth, hard and cool to the touch. But he saw absolutely nothing to indicate that something solid stood there.

Frustrated, Thomas moved to the left, then the right, feeling along the unseen yet solid wall. It spanned the entire room; there was no way to approach the stranger at the desk. Thomas finally pounded on it, making a series of dull thumps, but nothing else happened. Some of the Gladers behind him, Aris included, remarked how they'd already tried that.

The strangely dressed man, just a dozen or so feet in front of him, let out an exaggerated sigh as he pulled his crossed feet from the desk and let them drop to the floor. He placed a finger in his book to mark his place and looked up at Thomas, making no effort to hide his annoyance.

"How many times do I have to repeat this?" the man said, his nasally voice a perfect match for his pale skin, thin hair and skinny body. And that suit. That stupid white suit. Oddly, his words weren't muffled at all by the barrier. "We still have forty-seven minutes before I've been authorized to implement Phase Two of the Trials. Please show your patience and leave me alone. You've been given this time to eat and replenish yourselves, and I strongly suggest you take advantage of it, young man. Now, if you don't mind . . ."

Without waiting for a response, he leaned back in his chair and returned his feet to the desktop. Then, opening his book to the spot he'd marked, he resumed reading.

Thomas was truly speechless. He turned away from the man and the desk and leaned against the invisible wall, its hard surface pressing against his back. What had just happened? Surely he was still asleep, dreaming. For some reason, that thought alone seemed to amplify his hunger, and he longingly glanced over at the mound of food. Then he noticed Minho at the door to the dorm room, leaning against its frame with his arms folded.

Thomas jabbed a thumb over his shoulder and raised his eyebrows.

"You met our new friend?" Minho responded, a smirk flashing across his face. "Real piece of work, this guy. I gotta get me one of those shuck suits. Fancy stuff."

"Am I awake?" Thomas asked.

"You're awake. Now eat—you look horrible. Almost as bad as Rat Man over there, reading his book."

Thomas was surprised at how quickly he could set aside the oddness of the guy in the white suit appearing out of nowhere, and the invisible wall. Again that numbness that had become so familiar. After the initial shock, nothing was strange anymore. Anything could become normal. Pushing it all away, he dragged himself over to the food and started eating. Another apple. An orange. A bag of mixed nuts, then a chewy bar of granola and raisins. His body begged for water, but he couldn't get himself to move quite yet.

"You need to slim it," Minho said from behind him. "We've got shanks puking all over the place 'cause they ate too much. That's probably enough, dude."

Thomas stood, relishing the feel of a full stomach. Not missing at all that gnawing beast that had lived inside him for so long. He knew Minho was right—he had to slim it. He nodded at his friend before stepping around him to go get a drink, the whole time wondering what could possibly be in store for them when the man in the white suit was ready to implement "Phase Two of the Trials."

Whatever *that* meant.

A half hour later, Thomas sat on the floor with the rest of the Gladers, Minho to his right and Newt to his left, all of them facing the invisible wall and the weasel of a man sitting at the desk behind it. His feet were still propped up, his eyes still flickering down the pages of his book. Thomas felt the wonderful return of energy and strength slowly building inside him.

The new kid, Aris, had given him a strange look in the bathroom, as if he wanted to speak telepathically with him but was afraid to do it. Thomas had ignored him, and quickly walked to the sink and guzzled down as much water as he could with his now-full stomach. By the time he finished and wiped his mouth on his sleeve, Aris had left. Now the boy sat over by the wall, staring at the floor. Thomas felt sorry for him—as bad as things were for the Gladers, Aris had it worse. Especially if he'd been as close to the murdered girl he'd mentioned as Thomas was to Teresa.

Minho was the first to break the silence. "I think we've all gone psycho like those . . . what'd they call themselves again? Cranks. The Cranks at the windows. We're all sitting here waiting for a lecture from Rat Man like this is totally normal. Like we're at some kind of school. I can tell you this much—if he had anything good to say, he wouldn't need a freaking magic wall to protect him from us, now, would he?"

"Just slim it and listen," Newt said. "Maybe it's all gonna be over."

"Yeah, right," Minho said. "And Frypan's gonna start having little babies, Winston'll get rid of his monster acne, and Thomas here'll actually smile for once."

Thomas turned to Minho and exaggerated a fake smile. "There, you happy?"

"Dude," he responded. "You are one ugly shank."

"If you say so."

"Shut your bloody holes," Newt whispered. "I think it's time."

Thomas looked over to see that the stranger—Rat Man, as Minho so kindly called him—had put his feet on the floor and placed the book on the desk. He scooted his chair back to get a better view of one of the drawers, then pulled it out and rummaged through things Thomas couldn't see. Finally, he pulled out a densely packed manila folder full of messy papers, many of them bent and sticking out at odd angles.

"Ah, here it is," Rat Man said in his nasally voice; then he placed the folder on the desk, opened it up and looked at the boys in front of him. "Thank you for gathering in an orderly manner so I can tell you what I've been . . . instructed to tell you. Please listen carefully."

"Why do you need that wall!" Minho shouted.

Newt reached around Thomas and punched Minho in the arm. "Shut it!"

Rat Man continued as if he hadn't heard the outburst. "You're all still here because of an uncanny will to survive despite the odds, among . . . other reasons. About sixty people were sent to live in the Glade. Well, *your* Glade, anyway. Another sixty in Group B, but for now we'll forget them."

The man's eyes flickered to Aris, then went back to slowly scanning the crowd. Thomas didn't know if anyone else had noticed, but he had no doubt that there'd been a hint of familiarity in that quick look. What did it mean . . . ?

"Out of all those people, only a fraction survived to be here today. I'm assuming you've figured this out by now, but many of the things that happen to you are solely for the purpose of judging and analyzing your *responses*. And yet it's not really an experiment as much as it is . . . constructing a blueprint. Stimulating the killzone and collecting the resultant patterns. Putting them all together to achieve the greatest breakthrough in the history of science and medicine.

"These situations inflicted upon you are called the Variables, and each one has been meticulously thought out. I'll explain more soon. And though I can't tell you everything at this time, it's vital that you know this much: these trials you're going through are for a very important cause. Continue to respond well to the Variables, continue to survive, and you'll be rewarded with the knowledge that you've played a part in saving the human race. And yourselves, of course."

Rat Man paused, apparently for effect. Thomas looked over at Minho and raised his eyebrows.

"This dude's shucked in the head," Minho whispered. "How would escaping a freaking maze save the human race?"

"I represent a group called WICKED," Rat Man continued. "I know it sounds menacing, but it stands for World In Catastrophe, Killzone Experiment Department. Nothing menacing about it, despite what you may think. We exist for one purpose and one purpose only: to save the world from catastrophe. You here in this room are a vital part of what we plan to do. We have resources never known to any group of any kind in the history of civilization. Nearly unlimited money, unlimited human capital and technology advanced beyond even the most clever man's wants and wishes.

"As you make your way through the Trials, you have seen and will continue to see evidence of this technology and the resources behind it. If I can tell you anything today, it is that you should never, ever believe your eyes. Or your mind, for that matter. This is why we did the demonstration with the hanging bodies and the bricked-up windows. All I will say is that sometimes what you see is not real, and sometimes what you do *not* see *is* real. We can manipulate your brains and nerve receptacles when necessary. I know this all sounds confusing and a little scary, perhaps."

Thomas thought the man couldn't have possibly made a greater understatement. And the word *killzone* kept bouncing around his head. His scarcely revived memories couldn't quite grasp what it meant, but he'd first seen it on the metal plaque back in the Maze, the one that had spelled out the words that made up WICKED's acronym.

The man slowly passed his eyes over every Glader in the room. His upper lip shone with sweat. "The Maze was a part of the Trials. Not one Variable was thrown at you that didn't serve a purpose for our collection of killzone patterns. Your escape was part of the Trials. Your battle against the Grievers. The murder of the boy Chuck. The supposed rescue and subsequent trip in the bus. All of it. Part of the Trials."

Anger swelled in Thomas's chest at the mention of Chuck. He'd half risen to his feet before he knew what had come over him; Newt pulled him back down to the floor.

As if spurred by this, Rat Man quickly stood up from his chair, sending it back against the wall behind him. Then he placed his hands on the desk and leaned toward the Gladers.

"*All* of it has been part of the Trials, you understand? Phase One, to be exact. And we are still dangerously short of what we need. So we've had to up the ante, and now it's time for Phase Two. It's time for things to get difficult."

CHAPTER 11

The room lapsed into silence. Thomas knew he should be upset by the absurd notion that up to this point things had been easy for them. The idea should've terrified him. Not to mention the stuff about manipulating their brains. But instead, he was so intensely curious to find out what the man was going to tell them, the words had merely washed across his mind.

Rat Man waited for an eternity, then slowly lowered himself back into the chair and scooted forward to sit behind the desk once more. "You may think, or it may seem, that we're merely testing your ability to survive. On the surface, the Maze Trial could be mistakenly classified that way. But I assure you—this is not merely about survival and the will to live. That's only part of this experiment. The bigger picture is something you won't understand until the very end.

"Sun flares have ravaged many parts of the earth. Also, a disease unlike any before known to man has been ravaging the earth's people—a disease called the Flare. For the first time, the governments of all nations—the surviving ones—are working together. They've combined forces to create WICKED—a group meant to fight the new problems of this world. You are a big part of that fight. And you'll have every incentive to work with us, because, sad to say, each one of you has already caught the virus."

He quickly held up his hands to cut off the rumblings that started. "Now, now! No need to worry—the Flare takes a while to set in and show symptoms. But at the end of these Trials, the *cure* will be your reward, and you'll never see the . . . debilitating effects. Not many can afford the cure, you know."

Thomas's hand instinctively went up to his throat, as if a soreness there were the first indicator that he'd caught the Flare. He remembered all too well what the woman on the rescue bus had told him after the Maze. About how the Flare destroyed your brain, slowly driving you insane and stripping you of the capacity to feel basic human emotions like compassion or empathy. About how it turned you into less than an animal.

He thought of the Cranks he'd seen through the dorm windows, and he suddenly wanted to run to the bathroom and scrub his hands and mouth clean. The guy was right—they had all the incentive they needed to make it through this next phase.

"But enough of this history lesson and time-wasting," Rat Man continued. "We know you now. All of you. It doesn't matter what I say or what's behind the mission of WICKED. You'll all do whatever it takes. Of this we have no doubt. And by doing what we ask, you'll save yourselves by getting the very cure so many people desperately want."

Thomas heard Minho groan next to him and worried about him throwing out another one of his smart-aleck remarks. Thomas shushed him before he could do it.

Rat Man looked down at the messy stack of papers lying in the open folder, picked up a loose piece of it, then turned it over, barely glancing at its contents. He cleared his throat. "Phase Two. The Scorch Trials. It officially begins tomorrow morning at six o'clock. You'll enter this room, and in the wall behind me you will find a Flat Trans. To your eyes the Flat Trans will appear as a shimmering wall of gray. Each of you must step through it by five minutes after the hour. So again, it opens at six o'clock and closes five minutes after that. Do you understand?"

Thomas stared at Rat Man, transfixed. It almost felt as if he were watching a recording—as if the stranger weren't really there. The other Gladers must've felt the same, because no one answered the simple question. What was a Flat Trans, anyway?

"I'm quite certain you can all *hear,*" Rat Man said. "Do . . . you . . . under . . . stand?"

Thomas nodded; a few boys around him murmured quiet yeahs and yeses.

"Good." Rat Man absently picked up another piece of paper and turned it over. "At that point, the Scorch Trials will have begun. The rules are very simple. Find your way to open air, then head due north for one hundred miles. Make it to the safe haven within two weeks' time and you'll have completed Phase Two. At that point, and only at that point, you'll be cured of the Flare. That's exactly two weeks—starting the second you step through the Trans. If you don't make it, eventually you'll end up dead."

The room should've erupted into arguments, questions, panic. But no one said a word. Thomas felt as if his tongue had dried up into an old, crusty root.

Rat Man quickly slammed the folder shut, bending its contents even more than before, then put it away in the drawer from which he'd retrieved it. He stood, stepped to the side and pushed the chair underneath the desk. Finally, he folded his hands in front of him and returned his attention to the Gladers.

"It's simple, really," he said, his tone so matter-of-fact one would think he'd just given them instructions on how to turn on the showers in the bathroom. "There are no rules. There are no guidelines. You have few supplies, and there's nothing to help you along the way. Go through the Flat Trans at the time indicated. Find open air. Go one hundred miles, directly north, to the safe haven. Make it or die."

The last word seemed to finally snap everyone out of their stupor, all of them speaking up at once.

"What's a Flat Trans?"

"How'd we catch the Flare?"

"How long till we see symptoms?"

"What's at the end of the hundred miles?"

"What happened to the dead bodies?"

Question after question, a chorus of them, all melding into one roar of confusion. As for Thomas, he didn't bother. The stranger wasn't going to tell them anything. Couldn't they all see that?

Rat Man waited patiently, ignoring them, those dark eyes darting back and forth between the Gladers as they spoke. His gaze settled on Thomas, who sat there, silent, staring back at him, hating him. Hating WICKED. Hating the world.

"You shanks shut *up*!" Minho finally shouted. The questions stopped instantly. "This shuck-face ain't answering, so quit wastin' your time."

Rat Man nodded once toward Minho as if thanking him. Perhaps acknowledging his wisdom. "One hundred miles. North. Hope you make it. Remember—you all have the Flare now. We gave it to you to provide any incentive you may be lacking. And reaching the safe haven means receiving a cure." He turned away and moved toward the wall behind him, as if he planned to walk right through it. But then he stopped and faced them again.

"Ah, one last thing," he said. "Don't think you'll avoid the Scorch Trials if you decide *not* to enter the Flat Trans between six and six-oh-five tomorrow morning. Those who stay behind will be executed immediately in a most . . . unpleasant manner. Better off taking your chances in the outside world. Good luck to all of you."

With that he turned away and once again started inexplicably walking toward the wall.

But before Thomas could see what happened, the invisible wall separating them started to fog up, whitening to an opaque blur in a matter of seconds. And then the whole thing disappeared, once again revealing the other side of the common area.

Except there was no sign of the desk and its chair. And no sign of Rat Man.

"Well, shuck me," Minho whispered next to Thomas.

CHAPTER 12

Once again, the Gladers' questions and arguments filled the air, but Thomas left. He needed some space and knew the bathroom was his only escape. So instead of heading to the boys' dorm, he went to the one Teresa, then Aris, had used. He leaned back against the sink, arms folded, staring at the floor. Luckily, no one had followed him.

He didn't know how to begin processing all the information. Bodies hanging from the ceiling, reeking of death and rot, then gone completely in a matter of minutes. A stranger—and his desk!—appear out of nowhere, with an impossible shield protecting them. Then they disappear.

And these were by far the least of their worries. It was clear now that the rescue from the Maze had been a sham. But who were the pawns WICKED had used to pull the Gladers from the Creators' chamber, put them on that bus and bring them here? Had those people known they were going to be killed? Had they even really *been* killed? Rat Man had said not to trust their eyes or their minds. How could they believe anything ever again?

And worst of all, this stuff about them having the Flare disease, about the Trials earning them a cure . . .

Thomas squeezed his eyes closed and rubbed his forehead. Teresa had been taken from him. None of them had families. The next morning they were supposed to start some ridiculous thing called Phase Two, which by the sound of it was going to be worse than the Maze. All those crazy people out there—the Cranks. How would they deal with them? He suddenly thought of Chuck and what he might say if he were there.

Something simple, probably. Something like, *This sucks.*

You'd be right, Chuck, Thomas thought. *The whole world sucks.*

It had only been a few days since he'd seen his friend get stabbed in the heart; poor Chuck had died as Thomas held him. And now Thomas couldn't help but think that as horrible as it was, maybe that had been the best thing for Chuck. Maybe death was better than what lay ahead. His mind veered toward the tattoo on his neck—

"Dude, how long's it take to drop a load?" It was Minho.

Thomas looked up to see him standing in the doorway to the bathroom. "I can't stand it out there. Everyone talking over everybody else like a bunch of babies. Say what they want, we all know what we're gonna do."

Minho walked over to him and leaned his shoulder against the wall. "Ain't you Mr. Happy? Look, man, those shanks out there are just as brave as you are. Every last one of us will go through that . . . whatever he called it . . . tomorrow morning. Who cares if they wanna crack their throats yappin' about it?"

Thomas rolled his eyes. "I never said jack about me being braver than anybody. I'm just sick of hearing people's voices. Yours included."

Minho snickered. "Slinthead, when you try to be mean, it's just freaking hilarious."

"Thanks." Thomas paused. "Flat Trans."

"Huh?"

"That's what the white-suit shank called the thing we need to go through. A Flat Trans."

"Oh yeah. Must be some kind of doorway."

Thomas looked up at him. "That's what I'm thinking. Something like the Cliff. It's flat, and it *trans*ports you somewhere. Flat Trans."

"You're a shuck genius."

Newt came in then. "What're you two hiding for?"

Minho reached over and slapped Thomas on the shoulder. "We're not hiding. Thomas is just whining about his life and wishin' he could go back to his mommy."

"Tommy," Newt said, not seeming amused, "you went through the Changing, got some of your memories back. How much of this stuff do you remember?"

Thomas had been thinking a lot about that. Much of what had come back after being stung by the Griever had turned cloudy. "I don't know. I can't really picture the actual world outside or what it was like being involved with the people I helped design the Maze. Most of it's either faded again or just gone. I've had a couple of weird dreams, but nothing that helps."

They then went off on a discussion about some of the things they'd heard from their odd visitor. About the sun flares and the disease and how different things might be now that they *knew* they were being tested or experimented on. About a lot of things, with no answers—all of it laced with an unspoken fear of the virus they'd supposedly been given. They finally lulled into silence.

"Well, we've got stuff to figure out," Newt said. "And I need help to make sure the bloody food's not gone before we leave tomorrow. Something tells me we're gonna need it."

Thomas hadn't even thought of that. "You're right. Are people still chowing down out there?"

Newt shook his head. "No, Frypan took charge. That shank's religious about food—I think he was glad to have something to be the boss about again. But I'm scared people might get panicky and try to eat it anyway."

"Oh, come on," Minho said. "Those of us who made it this far got here for a reason. All the idiots are dead by now." He looked sideways at Thomas, as if worried Thomas might think he'd included Chuck in that assessment. Maybe even Teresa.

"Maybe," Newt responded. "Hope so. Anyway, I was thinking we need to get organized, get things back together. Act like we did in the bloody Glade. Last few days have been miserable, everybody moaning and groaning, no structure, no plan. It's driving me psycho."

"What'd you expect us to do?" Minho asked. "Form up in lines and do push-ups? We're stuck in a stupid three-room prison."

Newt swatted at the air as if Minho's words were gnats. "Whatever. I'm just saying, things are obviously going to change tomorrow and we gotta be ready to face it."

Despite all the talk, Thomas felt like Newt was failing to make his point.

"What are you getting at?"

Newt paused while he looked at Thomas, then Minho. "We need to make sure we have a solid leader when tomorrow comes. There can't be any doubt who's in charge."

"That's the lamest shuck-faced thing you've ever barked," Minho said. "You're the leader, and you know it. We all know it."

Newt shook his head adamantly. "Bein' hungry make you forget the bloody tattoos? You think they're just decorations?"

"Oh, come on," Minho retorted. "You really think it means anything? They're just playin' with our heads!"

Instead of answering, Newt stepped closer to Minho and pulled back his shirt to reveal the tattoo there. Thomas didn't have to look—he remembered. It had branded Minho as the Leader.

Minho shrugged off Newt's hand and started his usual rant of sarcastic remarks, but Thomas had already tuned out, his heart's pace having kicked in to a rapid series of almost painful thumps. All he could think about was what had been tattooed on his *own* neck.

That he was to be killed.

CHAPTER 13

Thomas felt it getting late and knew they had to get sleep that night and be ready for the morning. So he and the Gladers spent the rest of the evening making crude packs out of bedsheets for carrying the food and the extra clothes that had appeared in the dressers. Some of the food had come in plastic bags, and the now-empty bags were filled with water and tied off with material ripped from the curtains. No one expected these poor excuses for canteens to last very long without leaking, but it was the best idea anyone could come up with.

Newt had finally convinced Minho to be the leader. Thomas knew as well as anybody that they needed someone to be in charge, so he was relieved when Minho grudgingly agreed.

Around nine o'clock, Thomas found himself lying in bed, staring at the bunk above him once again. The room was strangely silent even though he knew no one had fallen asleep yet. Fear surely gripped them as much as it did him. They'd been through the Maze and its horrors. They'd seen close up what WICKED was capable of doing. If Rat Man was correct, and all that had happened was part of some master plan, then these people had forced Gally to kill Chuck, had shot a woman at close range, had hired people to rescue them only to kill them when the mission was complete . . . the list went on and on.

Then, to top it all off, they gave them a hideous disease, with the cure as bait to lure them to continue. Who even knew what was true and what was a lie. And the evidence continued to suggest that they'd singled Thomas out somehow. It was a sad thought—Chuck was the one who had lost his life. Teresa was the one missing. But taking those two away from him . . .

His life felt like a black hole. He had no idea how he would muster the will to go on in the morning. To face whatever WICKED had in store for them. But he'd do it—and not just to get a cure. He would never stop, especially now. Not after what they'd done to him and his friends. If the only way to get back at them was to pass all their tests and trials, to *survive,* then so be it.

So be it.

With thoughts of revenge actually comforting him in a sick and twisted way, he finally fell asleep.

Every Glader had set the alarm on his digital watch for five o'clock in the morning. Thomas woke up well before that and couldn't go back to sleep. When beeps finally started filling the room, he swung his legs off the bed and rubbed his eyes. Someone turned on the light and a yellow blast lit up his vision. Squinting, he got up and headed for the showers. Who knew how long it'd be before he could clean himself again.

At ten minutes till the time appointed by Rat Man, every Glader sat in anticipation, most holding a plastic bag full of water, the bedsheet packs at their sides. Thomas, like the others, had decided he'd carry the water in his hand to make sure it didn't spill or leak. The invisible shield had reappeared overnight in the middle of the common area, impossible to pass through, and the Gladers settled just on the boys' dorm side of it, facing where the stranger in the white suit had said a Flat Trans would appear.

Aris was sitting right next to Thomas, and spoke for the first time since . . . well, Thomas couldn't remember the last time he'd heard the boy's voice.

"Did you think you were crazy?" the new kid asked. "When you first heard her in your head?"

Thomas glanced at him, paused. For some reason, up until that moment he hadn't wanted to talk to this guy. But suddenly the feeling vanished completely. It wasn't Aris's fault that Teresa had disappeared. "Yeah. Then when it kept happening, I got over it—only I started worrying about *other* people thinking I was crazy. So we didn't tell anyone about it for a long time."

"It was weird for me," Aris responded. He looked deep in thought as he stared at the floor. "I was in a coma for a few days, and when I woke up, speaking out to Rachel seemed the most natural thing in the world. If she hadn't accepted it and spoken back, I'm pretty sure I would've lost it. The other girls in the group hated me—some of them wanted to kill me. Rachel was the only one who . . ."

He trailed off, and Minho stood up to address everyone before Aris could finish what he was saying. Thomas was glad for it, because hearing about the trippy alternate version of what he himself had been through only made him think of Teresa, and that hurt too much. He didn't want to think about her anymore. He had to concentrate on surviving for now.

"We've got three minutes," Minho said, for once looking completely serious. "Everybody sure they still wanna go?"

Thomas nodded, noticed others doing the same.

"Anybody change their mind overnight?" Minho asked. "Speak now or never. Once we go wherever we're going, if some shank decides he's a sissy pants and tries to turn back, I'll make sure he does it with a broken nose and smashed privates."

Thomas looked over at Newt, who had his head in his hands and was groaning loudly.

"Newt, you got a problem?" Minho asked, his voice surprisingly stern. Thomas, shocked, waited for Newt's reaction.

The older boy seemed just as surprised. "Uh . . . no. Just admiring your bloody leadership skills."

Minho pulled his shirt away from his neck, leaned over to show everyone the tattoo there. "What does that say, slinthead?"

Newt glanced left and right, his face blushing. "We know you're the boss, Minho. Slim it."

"No, you slim it," Minho retorted, pointing at Newt. "We don't have time for that kind of klunk. So shut your hole."

Thomas could only hope that Minho was putting on an act to solidify the decision they'd made for him to be the leader, and that Newt understood. Though if Minho *was* acting, he was sure doing a good job of it.

"It's six o'clock!" one of the Gladers shouted.

As if this proclamation had triggered it, the invisible shield turned opaque again, fogging to a splotchy white. A split second later it vanished altogether. Thomas noticed the change in the wall opposite them instantly—a large section of it had transformed into a flat, shimmering surface of murky, shadowy gray.

"Come on!" Minho yelled as he pulled the strap of his pack onto his shoulder. He was gripping a water bag in his other hand. "Don't mess around—we only have five minutes to get through. I'll go first." He pointed at Thomas. "You go last—make sure everyone follows me before you come."

Thomas nodded, trying to fight the fire burning through his nerves; he reached up and wiped the sweat off his forehead.

Minho walked up to the wall of gray, then paused right in front of it. The Flat Trans seemed completely unstable, impossible for Thomas to focus on. Shadows and swirls of varying shades of darkness danced across its surface. The whole thing pulsed and blurred, as if it might disappear at any second.

Minho turned to look back at them. "See you shanks on the other side."

Then he stepped through, and the wall of gray murk swallowed him whole.

CHAPTER 14

No one complained as Thomas herded the rest of them behind Minho. No one even said anything, just exchanged flickering, frightened looks as they approached the Flat Trans and went through it. Without fail, every Glader hesitated a second before taking the final step into the murkiness of the gray square. Thomas watched each of them, swatting them on the back right before they disappeared.

After two minutes, only Aris and Newt were left with Thomas.

You sure about this? Aris said to him inside his mind.

Thomas choked on a cough, surprised by the flow of words across his consciousness—that not-quite-audible yet somehow audible speech. He'd thought—and hoped—that Aris had gotten the hint that he didn't want to communicate that way. That was something for Teresa, not anybody else.

"Hurry," Thomas muttered out loud, refusing to answer telepathically. "We've gotta hurry."

Aris stepped through, a hurt look on his face. Newt followed right on his heels; just like that, Thomas was alone in the big common room.

He glanced around one last time, remembered the dead, swelling bodies that had hung there just a few days earlier. Thought about the Maze and all the klunk they'd been through. Sighing as loudly as he could, hoping someone, somewhere could hear it, he gripped his water bag and his bedsheet pack full of food and stepped into the Flat Trans.

A distinct line of coldness traveled across his skin from front to back, as if the wall of gray were a standing plane of icy water. He'd closed his eyes at the last second and opened them now to see nothing but absolute darkness. But he heard voices.

"Hey!" he called out, ignoring the sudden burst of panic in his own voice. "You guys—"

Before he could finish, he stumbled on something and fell over, crashing on top of a squirming body.

"Ow!" the person yelled, pushing Thomas off. It was all he could do to hold tight to the water bag.

"Everyone be still and shut up!" This was Minho, and the relief that washed through Thomas almost made him shout for joy. "Thomas, was that you? Are you in here?"

"Yes!" Thomas regained his feet, blindly feeling around him to make sure he didn't bump into someone else. He felt nothing but air, saw nothing but black. "I was the last one to come through. Did everyone make it?"

"We were lining up and counting off nice and easy till you came stumbling through like a doped-up bull," Minho responded. "Let's do it again. One!"

When no one said anything, Thomas yelled, "Two!"

From there, the Gladers counted off until Aris went last and called out, "Twenty."

"Good that," Minho said. "We're all here, wherever here is. Can't see a shuck thing."

Thomas stood still, sensing the other boys, hearing their breaths, but scared to move. "Too bad we don't have a flashlight."

"Thanks for stating the obvious, Mr. Thomas," Minho replied. "All right, listen up. We're in some kind of hallway—I can feel the walls on both sides, and as far as I can tell, most of you are to my right. Thomas, where you're standing is where we came in. We better not take any chances of accidentally going back through the Flat Trans thingamajiggy, so everyone follow my voice and come toward me. Not much choice but to head down this way and see what we find."

He'd started moving away from Thomas as he said those last few words. The whispers of shuffling feet and rustling packs against clothes told him that the others were following. When he sensed that he was the last one remaining, and that he wouldn't step on anybody again, he moved slowly to his left, reaching his hand out until he felt a hard, cool wall. Then he walked after the rest of the group, letting his hand slide along the wall to keep his bearings.

No one spoke as they moved forward. Thomas hated that his eyes never adjusted to the darkness—there wasn't even the slightest hint of light. The air was cool, but smelled like old leather and dust. A couple of times he bumped into the person directly in front of him; he didn't even know who it was because the boy didn't say anything when they collided.

On and on they went, the tunnel stretching ahead without ever turning to the left or right. Thomas's hand against the wall and the ground below his feet were the only things that kept him tied to reality or gave him a sense of movement. Otherwise, he would've felt as if he were floating through empty space, making no progress whatsoever.

The only sounds were the scrapes of shoes on the hard concrete floor and occasional snatches of whispers between Gladers. Thomas felt every thump of his heart as they marched down the endless tunnel of darkness. He couldn't help but remember the Box, that lightless cube of stale air that had delivered him to the Glade; it had felt much like this. At least now he had a portion of solid memory, had friends and knew who they were. At least now he understood the stakes—that they needed a cure and would probably go through awful things to get it.

A sudden burst of intense whispering filled the tunnel, seemed to come from above. Thomas stopped dead in his tracks. It hadn't been from any of the Gladers, he was sure of it.

From up ahead, Minho shouted for the others to halt. Then, "Did you guys hear that?"

As several Gladers murmured yeses and started asking questions, Thomas tilted his ear toward the ceiling, straining to hear something beyond those voices. The flash of whispering had been quick, just a few short words that had sounded as if they came from a very old and very sick man. But the message had been completely indecipherable.

Minho shushed everyone again, telling them to listen.

Even though it was perfectly dark and therefore pointless, Thomas closed his eyes, concentrating on his sense of hearing. If the voice came again, he wanted to catch what it said.

Less than a minute passed before the same ancient voice whispered harshly once more, echoing through the air as if huge speakers were installed on the ceiling. Thomas heard several people gasp, like they'd gotten it this time and were shocked by what they'd heard. But he still hadn't been able to isolate even one or two of the words. He opened his eyes again, though nothing changed in front of him. Utter darkness. Black.

"Did anybody get what it said?" Newt called out.

"Couple of words," Winston replied. "Sounded like 'go back' right in the middle."

"Yeah, it did," someone agreed.

Thomas thought about what he'd heard, and in retrospect, it did seem like those two words had been in there somewhere. *Go back*.

"Everybody slim it and listen real hard this time," Minho announced. The dark hallway lapsed into silence.

The next time the voice came, Thomas understood every single syllable.

"One-chance deal. Go back now, you won't be sliced."

Judging by the reactions in front of him, everyone else got it this time, too.

"Won't be sliced?"

"What's that supposed to mean?"

"He said we can go back!"

"We can't trust some random shank whispering in the dark."

Thomas tried not to think about how ominous the last four words had been. *You won't be sliced.* That didn't sound good at all. And not being able to see anything made it worse. Driving him crazy.

"Just keep going!" he shouted up to Minho. "I can't take this much longer. Just go!"

"Wait a minute." Frypan's voice. "The voice said this was a one-chance deal. We have to at least think about it."

"Yeah," someone added. "Maybe we should go back."

Thomas shook his head even though he knew no one could see it. "No way. Remember what that guy at the desk told us. That we'd all die horrible deaths if we go back."

Frypan pushed. "Well, what makes him any more in charge than this whispering dude? How're we supposed to know who to listen to and who to ignore?"

Thomas knew it was a good question, but going back just didn't feel right. "The voice is just a test, I bet. We need to keep going."

"He's right." This was Minho from up in front. "Come on, let's go."

He'd barely said the last word when the whispering voice whooshed through the air again, this time laced with an almost childish hatred. *"You're all dead. You're all going to be sliced. Dead and sliced."*

Every hair on Thomas's neck stood up straight and a chill tickled his back. He expected to hear even more calls to go back, but once again the Gladers surprised him. No one said a thing, and soon they were all walking forward again. Minho had been right when he'd said all the sissies had been weeded out.

They made their way deeper into the darkness. The air warmed a bit, seemed to thicken with dust. Thomas coughed several times and was dying to take a drink, but he didn't want to risk untying his water bag without being able to see it. That was all he needed, to spill it all over the floor.

Forward.

Warmer.

Thirsty.

Darkness.

Walking. Time passed ever so slowly.

Thomas had no idea how this hallway could even be possible. They had to have journeyed at least two or three miles since last hearing the creepy whisper of warning. Where *were* they? Underground? Inside some massive building? The Rat Man had said they needed to find open air. How—

A boy screamed a few dozen feet in front of him.

It started out as an abrupt shriek, like simple surprise, but then escalated into pure terror. He didn't know who it was, but the kid was now screaming his throat raw, screeching and squealing like an animal at the old Blood House in the Glade. Thomas heard the sounds of a body thrashing on the ground.

He ran forward on instinct, pushing past several Gladers who seemed frozen by fear, moving toward the inhuman sounds. He didn't know why he thought he'd be able to help more than anyone else, but he didn't hesitate, not even taking care with his steps as he sprinted through the darkness. After the long insanity of walking blindly for so long, it was as if his body craved the action.

He made it, could hear that the boy now lay right in front of him, his arms and legs thrashing on the concrete floor as he struggled against who knew what. Thomas carefully set his water bag and shoulder pack far to the side, then timidly reached forward with his hands to find a grip on an arm or leg. He sensed the other Gladers crowding behind him, a loud and chaotic presence of shouts and questions that he forced himself to ignore.

"Hey!" Thomas yelled at the squirming boy. "What's wrong with you?" His fingers brushed the kid's jeans, then his shirt, but the boy's body convulsed all over the place, impossible to catch, and his shrieks continued to pierce the air.

Finally, Thomas went for broke. He dove forward, launching himself fully onto the body of the thrashing kid. With a jolt that knocked the breath out of him, he landed, felt the squirming torso; an elbow dug into his ribs, then a hand slapped his face. A knee came up and almost got him square in the groin.

"Stop it!" Thomas shouted. "What's wrong!"

The screams gurgled to a stop, almost like the kid had just been pulled underwater. But the convulsing didn't ease in the slightest.

Thomas put an elbow and forearm on the chest of the Glader for leverage, then reached out to grab his hair or his face. But when his hands slid over what was there, confusion consumed him.

There was no head. No hair or face. Not even a neck. None of those things that *should've* been there.

Instead, Thomas felt a large and perfectly smooth ball of cold metal.

CHAPTER 15

The next few seconds were beyond strange. As soon as Thomas's hand made contact with the odd metal ball, the boy stopped moving. His arms and legs stilled and the stiffness in his twitching torso went away in an instant. Thomas felt a thick wetness on the hard sphere, oozing up from where the kid's neck should've been. He knew it was blood, could smell the coppery scent of it.

Then the ball slipped from under Thomas's fingers and rolled away, making a hollow grating sound until it thumped into the closest wall and came to a stop. The boy lying below him didn't move or make a sound. The other Gladers continued to shout questions into the dark, but Thomas ignored them.

Horror filled his chest as he pictured the boy, what he must look like. Nothing about it made sense, but the kid was obviously dead, his head cut off somehow. Or . . . turned into metal? What in the world had happened? Thomas's mind spun, and it took a moment before he realized that warm fluid was flowing over the hand he'd pressed to the floor when the ball slipped away. He freaked.

Scooting backward away from the body, wiping his hand on his pants, he shouted but wasn't able to form words. A couple of Gladers grabbed him from behind and helped him to his feet. He pushed them away, stumbled against a wall. Someone gripped his shirt at the shoulder, pulled him closer.

"Thomas!" Minho's voice. "Thomas! What happened?"

Thomas tried to calm himself, take hold of things. His stomach lurched; his chest tightened. "I . . . I don't know. Who was that? Who was down there screaming?"

Winston answered, his voice shaky. "Frankie, I think. He was right next to me, just making a joke, and then it was like something yanked him away. Yeah, it was him. Definitely him."

"What happened!" Minho repeated.

Thomas realized he was still wiping his hands on his pants. "Look," he said before taking a long breath. Doing all this in the dark was maddening. "I heard him screaming, and ran up here to help. I jumped on him, tried to pin his arms down, find out what was wrong. Then I reached for his head to grab him by the cheeks—I don't even know why—and all I felt was . . ."

He couldn't say it. Nothing could possibly sound more absurd than the truth.

"What?" Minho shouted.

Thomas groaned, then said it. "His head wasn't a head. It was like a . . . a big . . . metal *ball*. I don't know, man, but that's what I felt. Like his shuck head had been swallowed by . . . by a big metal ball!"

"What're you talking about?" Minho asked.

Thomas didn't know how he could convince him or anyone else. "Didn't you hear it rolling away right after he stopped screaming? I know it—"

"It's right here!" someone shouted. Newt. Thomas heard a heavy scrape again, then Newt grunting with effort. "I heard it roll over here. And it's all wet and sticky—feels like blood."

"What the *klunk*," Minho half whispered. "How big is it?" The other Gladers joined in with a chorus of questions.

"Everybody slim it!" Newt yelled. When they quieted, he said flatly, "I don't know." Thomas heard him carefully handling the ball to get a feel for it. "Bigger than a buggin' head for sure. It's perfectly round—a perfect sphere."

Thomas was baffled, disgusted, but all he could think about was getting out of that place. Out of the darkness. "We need to run," he said. "We need to go. Now."

"Maybe we *should* go back." Thomas didn't recognize the voice. "Whatever that ball thing is, it sliced off Frankie's head, just like the old shank warned us."

"No way," Minho responded angrily. "No way. Thomas is right. No more dinkin' around. Spread out a couple of feet from each other, then run. Hunch down, and if something comes near your head, hit the living crap out of it."

No one argued. Thomas quickly found his food and water; then some unspoken communication permeated the group and they set off running, far enough apart not to trip over each other. Thomas wasn't in the very back anymore, not wanting to waste time to get back in order. He ran, ran as hard as he remembered ever running in the Maze.

He smelled sweat. He breathed dust and warm air. His hands grew clammy and gooey from the blood. The darkness, complete.

He ran and didn't stop.

A death ball got one more person. It happened closer to Thomas this time—got a kid he'd never spoken one word to. Thomas heard a distinct sound of metal sliding against metal, a couple of hard clicks. Then the screams drowned out the rest.

No one stopped. A terrible thing, maybe. Probably. But no one stopped.

When the screams finally cut off with a gurgling halt, Thomas heard a loud clonk as the ball of metal crashed onto the hard ground. He heard it rolling, heard it clank against a wall and roll some more.

He kept running. He never slowed.

His heart pounded; his chest hurt from deep, ragged breaths as he desperately gulped the dusty air. He lost track of time, had no sense of how far they'd gone. But when Minho called for everyone to stop, the relief was almost overwhelming. His exhaustion had finally won out over the terror of the thing that had killed two people.

Sounds of people panting filled the small space, and it reeked of bad breath. Frypan was the first one to recover enough to speak. "Why'd we stop?"

"'Cause I almost broke my shins on something up here!" Minho shouted back. "I think it's a stairway."

Thomas felt his spirits lift, but immediately squashed them back down. Getting his hopes up was something he'd sworn never to do again. Not until all this was over.

"Well, let's go up 'em!" Frypan said far too cheerfully.

"Ya think?" Minho responded. "What would we do without you, Frypan? Seriously."

Thomas heard the heavy stomps of Minho's footsteps as he ran up the stairs—it made a high-pitched ringing like they were made of thin metal. Only a few seconds passed before other footsteps joined in, and soon everyone was following Minho.

When Thomas reached the first step, he tripped and fell, banging his knee against the second one. He put his hands down to regain his balance—almost bursting his bag of water—then popped back up, skipping a step every once in a while. Who knew when another metal thing might attack, and hope or no hope, he was more than ready to move on to a place that wasn't pitch-black.

A bang sounded from above, a deeper thump than the footsteps, but it still sounded like metal.

"Ow!" Minho yelled. Then there were a few grunts and groans

as Gladers bumped into each other before they could stop themselves.

"You okay?" Newt asked.

"What'd . . . you hit?" Thomas called up through heavy breaths.

Minho sounded irritated. "The shuck top, that's what. We hit the roof, and there's nowhere else . . ." He trailed off, and Thomas could hear him sliding his hands along the walls and ceiling, searching. "Wait! I think I found—"

A distinct click cut him off, and then the world around Thomas seemed to ignite into pure flame. He cried out as he covered his eyes with his hands—a blinding, searing light shone down from above. He'd dropped his water bag, but he couldn't help it. After so long in pitch-darkness, the sudden appearance of light overpowered him—even through the protection of his hands. Brilliant orange burst through his fingers and eyelids, and a wave of heat—like a hot wind—swept down.

Thomas heard a heavy scrape, then a *clonk,* and the darkness returned. Warily, he dropped his hands and squinted; spots danced across his vision.

"Shuck me," Minho said. "Looks like we found a way out, but I think it's on the freaking sun! Man, that was bright. And hot."

"Let's just open it a crack and let our eyes get used to it," Newt said. Then Thomas heard him walk up the stairs to join Minho. "Here's a shirt—wedge it in there. Everybody shut your eyes!"

Thomas did as he was told and covered them with his hands again. The glow of orange returned and the process began. After a minute or so, he lowered his hands and slowly opened his eyes. He had to squint, and it still seemed like a million flashlights were pointed at him, but it had become bearable. A couple of minutes more and everything was bright but fine.

He could now see that he stood about twenty steps down from

where Minho and Newt crouched just beneath the door in the ceiling. Three shining lines marked the edges of the door, broken only by the shirt they'd stuffed in the right corner to keep it open. Everything around them—the walls, the stairs, the door itself—was made of a dull gray metal. Thomas turned around to look back in the direction from which they'd come, saw that the stairs disappeared into darkness far below them. They'd climbed up a lot more than he'd imagined.

"Anybody blind now?" Minho asked. "I feel like my eyeballs are roasted marshmallows."

Thomas felt that, too. His eyes burned and itched, kept tearing up. The Gladers around him were all rubbing their eyes.

"So what's out there?" someone asked.

Minho shrugged as he peeked through the slit of the open door with a hand half-shielding his vision. "Can't really tell. All I can see is a lot of bright light—maybe we *are* on the shuck sun. But I don't think there're any people out there." He paused. "Or Cranks."

"Let's get out of here, then," Winston said; he was two steps below Thomas. "I'd rather get a sunburn than get my head attacked by some ball of steel. Let's go!"

"All right, Winston," Minho replied. "Keep your undies on—I just wanted to let our eyes adjust first. I'll throw the door all the way open to make sure we're okay. Get ready." He moved up a step so he could press his right shoulder against the slab of metal. "One. Two. Three!"

He straightened his legs with a grunt and heaved upward. Light and heat burst down the stairwell as the door opened with a terrible squeal of grinding metal. Thomas quickly looked toward the ground and squinted. The brightness seemed impossible—even if they *had* been wandering along in perfect darkness for hours.

He heard some shuffling and pushing above him and looked up to see Newt and Minho moving to get out of the square of blinding sunlight coming through the now-open door. The whole stairwell heated up like an oven.

"Aw, man!" Minho said, a wince on his face. "Something's wrong, dude. It feels like it's already burning my skin!"

"He's right," Newt said, rubbing the back of his neck. "I don't know if we can go out there. We might have to wait until the sun goes down."

Groans of complaint sounded from the Gladers, but then they were overcome by a sudden outburst from Winston. "Whoa! Watch out! Watch out!"

Thomas turned to look at Winston down the stairs. He was pointing at something right above him as he backed up a couple of steps. On the ceiling, just a few feet above their heads, a big glob of liquid silver was coalescing, seeping out of the metal as if melting into a large teardrop. It grew bigger and bigger as Thomas stared at it, forming in a matter of seconds into a wavering, slowly rippling ball of molten goop. Then, before anyone could react, it detached from the ceiling and fell away.

But instead of splatting on the steps at their feet, the sphere of silver defied gravity and flew horizontally, directly into Winston's face. His horrific screams filled the air as he fell and started tumbling down the stairs.

CHAPTER 16

Thomas had a sickening thought as he pushed his way down the stairs after Winston. He didn't know if he was going because he wanted to help him or because he couldn't control his curiosity about this silvery monster-ball.

Winston eventually thumped to a stop, his back coming to rest by chance on one of the steps; they were still nowhere close to the bottom. The brilliant light from the open door up top illuminated everything with perfect clarity. Both of Winston's hands were at his face, pulling at the silver liquid—the ball of molten metal had already melded with the top of his head, consuming the part above the ears. Now its edges were creeping downward like thick syrup, lipping over the ears and covering his eyebrows.

Thomas jumped over the boy's body and spun around to kneel on the step directly below him; Winston pulled and pushed at the silver goop to keep it off his eyes. Surprisingly, it seemed to be working. But the boy was screaming at the top of his lungs, thrashing, his feet kicking the wall.

"Get it off me!" he yelled, his voice so strangled that Thomas almost gave up and ran away. If the stuff hurt that bad . . .

It looked like a very dense silver gel. Persistent and stubborn—like it was alive. As soon as Winston pushed a portion of it up and off his eyes, some of it would slip around his fingers from the side and try again. Thomas could see glimpses of the skin on his face when he did this, and it wasn't pretty. Red and blistering.

Winston cried out something unintelligible—his tortured screams could have been in another language altogether. Thomas knew he had to do something. Time had run out.

He threw the pack off his shoulders and dumped the contents; fruits and packages scattered and thumped down the stairs. He took the bedsheet and wrapped it around his hands for protection, then went for it. As Winston swiped at the molten silver right above his eyes again, Thomas grabbed for the sides that had just gone over the boy's ears. He felt heat through the cloth, thought it might burst into flame. He braced his feet, squeezed the stuff as hard as he could, then yanked.

With a disturbing sucking sound, the sides of the attacking metal lifted several inches before slipping out of his hands and slapping back down onto Winston's ears. Impossibly, the boy screamed even louder. A couple of other Gladers tried to move in to help, but Thomas shouted for them to back off, thinking they'd only get in the way.

"We have to do it together!" Thomas yelled at Winston, determined to get a stronger hold this time. "Listen to me, Winston! We have to do it together! Try to get a grip on it and lift it off your head!"

The other boy didn't show any sign of understanding, his whole body convulsing as he struggled. If Thomas hadn't been on the step below him, he would've tumbled down the rest of the way for sure by now.

"On the count of three!" Thomas yelled. "Winston! On the count of three!"

Still no sign he'd heard. Screaming. Thrashing. Kicking. Slapping at the silver.

Tears welled up in Thomas's eyes, or maybe it was sweat trickling down from his forehead. But it stung. And he felt like the air had heated up to a million degrees. His muscles tensed; lances of pain shot through his legs. They were cramping.

"Just do it!" he yelled, ignoring it all and leaning in to try again. "One! Two! Now!"

He gripped the sides of the stretching silver, felt its odd combination of soft toughness, then yanked once again up and away from Winston's head. Winston must've heard, or maybe it was luck, but at the same time, he pushed at the goop with the heels of his hands, like he was trying to rip off his own forehead. The entire mess of silver came off, a wobbly, thick and heavy sheet of the stuff. Thomas didn't hesitate; he flung his arms up and threw the junk over his head and down the stairwell, then spun around on his heels to see what happened.

As it flew through the air, the silver quickly formed back into a sphere, its surface rippling for a moment, then solidifying. It stopped just a few steps down from them, hovered for a second, like it was taking a long and lasting look at its victim, perhaps thinking over what had gone wrong. Then it shot away, flying down the stairway until it disappeared in the darkness far below.

It was gone. For some reason, it hadn't attacked again.

Thomas sucked in huge gasps of air; every inch of his body felt drenched with sweat. He leaned his shoulder against the wall, scared to look back at Winston, who was whimpering behind him. At least the screams had stopped.

Thomas finally turned around and faced him.

The kid was a mess. Curled up into a ball, shaking. The hair on his head had vanished, replaced with raw skin and spots of seeping blood. His ears were cut and ragged, but whole. He sobbed, surely from the pain, probably also from the trauma of what he'd just been through. The acne on his face looked clean and fresh compared to the raw wounds on the rest of his head.

"You okay, man?" Thomas asked, knowing it had to be the dumbest question he'd ever spoken aloud.

Winston shook his head with a quick jerk; his body continued to tremble.

Thomas looked up to see Minho and Newt and Aris and all the other Gladers just a couple of steps above them, all staring down in complete shock. The brilliant glare from above shadowed their faces, but Thomas could still see their eyes—wide like those of cats stunned by a spotlight.

"What was that shuck thing?" Minho murmured.

Thomas couldn't bring himself to speak, just shook his head wearily.

Newt was the one to answer. "Magic goop that eats people's heads, that's what it bloody was."

"Has to be some kind of new technology." This came from Aris, the first time Thomas had seen him participate in a discussion. The boy looked around, obviously noticing the surprised faces, then shrugged as if embarrassed and continued. "I've had a few splotchy memories come back. I know the world has some pretty advanced techno stuff—but I don't remember anything like flying molten metal that tries to cut off body parts."

Thomas thought about his own sketchy memories. Certainly nothing like that came to mind for him, either.

Minho pointed absently down the stairwell past Thomas. "That crap must keep gelling around your face, then eat into the flesh of your neck until it cuts clean through it. Nice. That's real nice."

"Did you see? Thing came right out of the ceiling!" Frypan said. "We better get out of here. Now."

"Couldn't agree more," Newt added.

Minho glanced down at Winston with a look of disgust, and Thomas followed his gaze. The kid had quit shaking, and his sobs had calmed to a stifled whimper. But he looked awful, and was surely scarred for life.

Thomas couldn't imagine hair ever growing back on the red, raw mess of his head.

"Frypan, Jack!" Minho called out. "Get Winston on his feet, help him along. Aris, you gather the klunk he dropped, have a couple of guys help you carry it. We're leaving. I don't care how bright or brutal that light is up there—I don't feel like having my head turned into a bowling ball today."

He turned around without waiting to see if people followed his orders. It was a move that, for some reason, made Thomas think the guy would end up making a good leader after all. "Come on, Thomas and Newt," he called over his shoulder. "The three of us are going through first."

Thomas exchanged glances with Newt, who returned a look that had a little fear in it but was mostly full of curiosity. An eagerness to move on. Thomas felt it himself, and hated to admit that anything seemed better than dealing with the aftermath of what had happened to Winston.

"Let's go," Newt said, his voice rising on the second word, as if they had no choice but to do what they were told. Though his face revealed the truth: he wanted to get away from poor Winston just as much as Thomas did.

Thomas nodded and carefully stepped over Winston, trying not to look at the skin on his injured head again. It was making him sick. He moved to the side to let Frypan, Jack and Aris past him to do their jobs, then started up the stairs, two at a time. Following Newt and Minho to the top, where it seemed like the sun itself waited just outside the open door.

CHAPTER 17

The other Gladers moved out of their way, seemingly more than happy to let the three of them be the ones to see what was outside. Thomas squinted and then shielded his eyes as they got closer. It was getting hard to believe they could actually step through the door into that horrible brightness and survive.

Minho stopped on the last step, just short of the direct line of the light. Then he slowly held his hand out until it entered the square of brilliance. Despite the boy's olive complexion, it looked to Thomas as if Minho's skin shone like white fire.

After only a few seconds Minho pulled his hand back and shook it at his side like he'd hit his thumb with a hammer. "That's definitely hot. Definitely hot." He turned to face Thomas and Newt. "If we're gonna do this, we better have something wrapped around us or we'll have second-degree sunburns in five minutes."

"Let's empty out our packs," Newt said, already taking his off his shoulder. "Wear these sheets like buggin' robes as we check things out. If it works well enough, we can stuff the food and water into half our sheets and use the other half for protection."

Thomas had already freed his sheet to help Winston. "We'll look like ghosts—scare away any bad guys out there."

Minho didn't take the same care as Newt; he just upended his pack and let everything drop. The Gladers closest to them scrambled on instinct to stop the stuff from tumbling down the stairs. "Funny boy, that

Thomas. Let's just hope we don't have some nice Cranks to greet us," he said as he started untying the knots he'd made in the bedsheet. "I don't see how anyone could just be hanging out in that heat. Hopefully there'll be trees or some kind of shelter."

"I don't know," Newt said. "Then they might be hiding, bloody waitin' to get us or something."

Thomas was just itching to check things out. Quit making guesses and see for himself what they were up against. "We won't know till we investigate. Let's go." He whipped out his sheet, then pulled it over himself and wrapped it tightly around his face like an old woman in a shawl. "How do I look?"

"Like the ugliest shanky girl I've ever seen," Minho responded. "You better thank the gods above you were born a dude."

"Thanks."

Minho and Newt did as Thomas had done, though both of them took more care to grip the sheet with their hands under it so they were completely covered. They also held it out to make sure their faces were shaded. Thomas followed suit.

"You shanks ready?" Minho asked, looking at Newt, then Thomas.

"Kind of excited, actually," Newt responded.

Thomas didn't know if that was quite the right word, but he felt the same urge to act. "Me too. Let's go."

The remaining steps above them went all the way to the top, like an exit from an old cellar, the last few glowing with the brilliance of the sun. Minho hesitated, but then ran up them, not stopping until he'd disappeared, seemingly absorbed into the light.

"Go!" Newt yelled, smacking Thomas on the back.

Thomas felt a rush of adrenaline. Blowing out a deep breath, he took off after Minho; he heard Newt right on his heels.

As soon as Thomas emerged into the light, he realized that they might as well have been draped in see-through plastic. The sheet did nothing to block the blinding light and searing heat beating down from above. He opened his mouth to speak and a raw plume of dry warmth shot down his throat, seeming to obliterate any air or moisture in its path. He tried desperately to pull in oxygen, but instead it felt like someone had lit a fire in his chest.

Although his memories were few and scattered, Thomas didn't think the world was supposed to be like this.

With his eyes screwed shut against the white brilliance, he bumped into Minho and almost fell down. Regaining his balance, he bent his knees and squatted, tenting the sheet entirely over his body as he continued to fight for breath. He finally caught it, sucking air in and puffing it out rapidly as he tried to compose himself. That first instant after exiting the stairway had really panicked him. The other two Gladers were also breathing heavily.

"You guys all right?" Minho finally asked.

Thomas grunted a yes, and Newt said, "Pretty sure we just arrived in bloody hell. Always thought you'd end up here, Minho, but not me."

"Good that," Minho replied. "My eyeballs hurt, but I think I'm finally starting to get kind of used to the light."

Thomas opened his own eyes into a squint and looked down at the ground just a couple of feet below his face. Dirt and dust. A few gray-brown rocks. The sheet lay draped completely around him, but it glowed so white it was like some odd piece of futuristic light technology.

"Who you hidin' from?" Minho asked. "Get up, ya shank—I don't see anybody."

Thomas was embarrassed that they thought he was cowering there—he must look like a small child whimpering under his blankets, trying not to be seen. He stood up and very slowly lifted the sheet until he could peek out at their surroundings.

It was a wasteland.

In front of him, a flat pan of dry and lifeless earth stretched as far as he could see. Not a single tree. Not a bush. No hills or valleys. Just an orange-yellow sea of dust and rocks; wavering currents of heated air boiled on the horizon like steam, floating upward, as if any life out there were melting toward the cloudless and pale blue sky.

Thomas turned in a circle, didn't see much change until he faced the opposite direction. A line of jagged and barren mountains rose far in the distance. In front of those mountains, maybe halfway between there and where they now stood, a cluster of buildings sat squatting together like a pile of abandoned boxes. It had to be a town, but it was impossible to tell how big it was from this distance. Hot air shimmered in front of it, blurring everything close to the ground.

The white-hot sun above already lay far to Thomas's left, and seemed to be sinking toward that horizon, which meant that way was west, which meant that the town ahead and the range of black and red rock behind it had to be due north. Where they were supposed to head. His sense of direction surprised him, as if a piece of his past had risen from the ashes.

"How far away do you think those buildings are?" Newt asked. After the echoing, hollow sounds their speaking had made in the long dark tunnel and stairway, his voice was like a dull whisper.

"Could that be a hundred miles?" Thomas asked no one in particular. "That's definitely north. Is that where we have to go?"

Minho shook his head under his sheet-hood. "No way, dude. I mean, we're supposed to go that way, but it's not even close to a hundred miles. Thirty at most. And the mountains might be sixty or seventy."

"Didn't know you could measure distance so well with nothing but your bloody eyeballs," Newt said.

"I'm a Runner, shuck-face. You get a feel for stuff like that in the Maze, even if its scale was a lot smaller."

"The Rat Man wasn't kidding about those sun flares," Thomas said, trying not to let his heart sink too much. "Looks like a nuclear holocaust out here. I wonder if the whole world is like this."

"Let's hope not," Minho responded. "I'd be happy to see one tree right about now. Maybe a creek."

"I'd settle for a patch of grass," Newt said through a sigh.

The more Thomas looked, the closer that town appeared. Thirty miles might even have been too much. He broke his gaze and turned toward the others. "Could this be any more different from what they put us through in the Maze? There, we were trapped inside walls, with everything we need to survive. Now we have nothing holding us in, but no way to survive unless we go where they told us to. Isn't that called irony or something like that?"

"Something like that," Minho agreed. "You're a philosophizing wonder." He nodded back toward the exit from the stairway. "Come on. Let's get those shanks out here and start walking. No time to waste letting the sun suck all the water out of us."

"Maybe we should wait until it goes down," Newt suggested.

"And hang out with those shuck balls of metal? No way."

Thomas agreed that they should get moving. "I think we're okay. Looks like sunset's only a few hours away. We can be tough for a while, take a break, then go as far as possible during the night. I can't stand another minute down there."

Minho nodded firmly.

"Sounds like a plan," Newt said. "For now, let's just make it to that dusty old town and hope it's not full of our Crank buddies."

Thomas's chest hitched at that comment.

Minho walked back to the hole and leaned over it. "Hey, you bunch of sissy, no-good shanks! Grab all the food and get up here!"

Not one Glader complained about the plan.

Thomas watched as each one of them did the same things he'd done when he first exited the stairway. Struggling gasps for breaths, squinty eyes, looks of hopelessness. He bet that each one of them had hoped the Rat Man was lying. That the worst times had been back in the Maze. But he was pretty sure that after the crazy head-eating silver things and then seeing this wasteland, no one would ever have such hopeful thoughts again.

They had to make some adjustments as they readied for the journey—the food and water bags were stuffed more tightly into half of the original packs; then the free bedsheets were used to cover two people as they walked. All in all, it worked surprisingly well—even for Jack and poor Winston—and soon they were marching across the hard, rock-strewn ground. Thomas shared his sheet with Aris, though he didn't know how it had ended up that way. Maybe he was just refusing to admit that he'd wanted to be with the boy, that he might be the only possible connection to figuring out what had happened to Teresa.

Thomas held one end of the sheet up with his left hand and had a pack draped around his right shoulder. Aris was to his right; they'd agreed to trade off the now-much-heavier pack every thirty minutes. Step by dusty step, they made their way toward the town, the heat seeming to suck a full day of their life away every hundred yards.

They didn't talk for a long while, but Thomas finally broke the silence. "So you've never heard the name Teresa before?"

Aris looked sharply at him, and Thomas realized he'd probably had a less-than-subtle hint of accusation in his voice. But he didn't back down. "Well? Have you?"

Aris returned his gaze forward, but there was something suspicious there. "No. Never. I don't know who she is or where she went. But at least you didn't see her die right in front of you."

That was a punch to the gut, but for some reason it made Thomas like Aris more. "I know, sorry." He thought for a second before he asked the next questions. "How close were you guys? What was her name, again?"

"Rachel." Aris paused, and for a second Thomas thought the conversation might be over already, but then he continued. "We were way more than close. Things happened. We remembered stuff. Made new memories."

Thomas knew Minho would've laughed his face off at that last comment, but to him it sounded like the saddest three words he'd ever heard. He felt he had to say something—offer something. "Yeah. I did see a really good friend die, though. Every time I think about Chuck I get ticked off all over again. If they've done the same thing to Teresa, they won't be able to stop me. Nothing will. They'll all die."

Thomas stopped—forcing Aris to as well—shocked that those words had just come out of his own mouth. It was like something else had taken over him and said those things. But he did feel it. Very strongly. "What do you think—"

But before he could finish the thought, Frypan started shouting. He was pointing at something.

It only took a second for Thomas to realize what had gotten the cook all excited.

Far ahead, from the direction of the town, two people were running toward them, their bodies like ghostly forms of darkness in the heat mirage, small plumes of dust rising from their feet.

CHAPTER 18

Thomas stared at the runners. He sensed that the other Gladers around him had stopped as well, as if there'd been an unspoken command to do so. Thomas shivered, something that seemed completely impossible in the sweltering heat. He didn't know why he felt the tickle of cold fear along his back—the Gladers outnumbered the approaching strangers almost ten times over—but the feeling was undeniable.

"Everyone pack in tighter," Minho said. "And get ready to fight these shanks the first sign of trouble."

The blurry mirage of upward-melting heat obscured the two figures until they were only a hundred yards or so away. Thomas's muscles tensed when they came into focus. He remembered all too well what he'd seen through the barred window just a few mornings ago. The Cranks. But these people scared him in a different way.

They stopped just a couple of dozen feet in front of the Gladers. One was a man, the other a woman, though Thomas could only tell this from the lady's slightly curvy figure. Other than that, they had the same build—tall and scrawny. Their heads and faces were almost completely covered in wrappings of tattered beige cloth, small ragged slits cut for them to see and breathe through. Their shirts and pants were a hodgepodge of filthy clothing sewn together, tied with ratty strips of denim in some places. Nothing was exposed to the beating sun but their hands, and those were red and cracked and scabby.

The two of them stood there, panting as they caught their breath, a sound like sick dogs.

"Who are you?" Minho called out.

The strangers didn't respond, didn't move. Their chests heaved in and out. Thomas observed them from under his makeshift hood—he couldn't imagine how anyone could run so far and not die of heat exhaustion.

"Who *are* you?" Minho repeated.

Instead of answering, the two strangers split apart and started walking in a broad circle around the bunched-up Gladers. Their eyes, hidden behind the slits in those odd mummy wrappings, stayed fixed on the boys as they made their way in a wide arc, as if sizing them up for a kill. Thomas felt the tension inside him rise, hated when he could no longer see both of them at once. He turned around and watched as they met back up behind the group and once again faced them, standing still.

"There are a whole lot more of us than there are of you," Minho said, his voice betraying his frustration. To threaten them so soon seemed desperate. "Start talking. Tell us who you are."

"We're Cranks."

The two words came from the woman, a short burst of guttural annoyance. For no discernible reason she pointed across the Gladers back toward the town from which they'd run.

"Cranks?" Minho said; he had pushed his way through the crowd to be closest to the strangers again. "Just like the ones that tried to break into our building a couple days ago?"

Thomas cringed—these people would have no idea what Minho was talking about. Somehow the Gladers had traveled a long way from wherever that place had been—through the Flat Trans.

"We're Cranks." This time from the man, his voice surprisingly lighter and less gruff than the woman's. But there was no kindness in it.

He pointed over the Gladers just like his companion had done. "Came to see if you're Cranks. Came to see if you've got the Flare."

Minho turned to look at Thomas and then a few others, his eyebrows raised. No one said anything. He turned back. "Some dude told us we had the Flare, yeah. What can you tell us about it?"

"Don't matter," the man responded; the strips of cloth wrapped around his face jiggled with every word. "You got it, you'll know soon enough."

"Well, what do you bloody want?" Newt asked, stepping up to stand next to Minho. "What's it matter to you if we're Cranks or not?"

The woman responded this time, acting as if she hadn't heard the questions. "How'd you get in the Scorch? Where'd you come from? How'd you get here?"

Thomas was surprised at the . . . intelligence evident in her words. The Cranks they'd seen back at the dorm had seemed absolutely insane, like animals. These people were aware enough to realize that their group had appeared out of nowhere. Nothing lay in the opposite direction from the town.

Minho leaned over to consult with Newt, then turned and stepped closer to Thomas. "What do we tell these people?"

Thomas had no clue. "I don't know. The truth? It can't hurt."

"The truth?" Minho said sarcastically. "What an idea, Thomas. You're freaking brilliant, as usual." He faced the Cranks again. "We were sent here by WICKED. Came out of a hole just a little while that way, from a tunnel. We're supposed to go one hundred miles to the north, cross the Scorch. Any of that mean a thing to you?"

Once again, it was as if they hadn't heard a word he'd said.

"Not all Cranks are gone," the man said. "Not all of them are past the Gone." He said that last word in a way that made it sound like the name of a place. "Different ones at different levels. Best you learn who to make friends with and who to avoid. Or kill. Better learn right quick if you're coming our way."

"What's your way?" Minho asked. "You came from that town, right? Is that where all these Cranks live? Is there food and water there?"

Thomas felt the same urge as Minho—to ask a million questions. He was half tempted to suggest they capture these two Cranks and *make* them answer. But for the moment the pair didn't seem intent on helping at all, and they split again to circle back around to the side of the Gladers closest to the town.

Once they met up in the spot where they'd first spoken, the distant town almost seeming to float between them, the woman said one last thing. "If you don't have it yet, you'll have it soon. Same with the other group. The ones that're supposed to kill you."

The two strangers then turned around and ran back toward the cluster of buildings on the horizon, leaving Thomas and the other Gladers in stunned silence. Soon, any evidence of the running Cranks was lost in a blur of heat and dust.

"Other group?" someone said. Maybe Frypan. Thomas was in too much of a trance staring at the disappearing Cranks and worrying about the Flare to notice.

"Wonder if they're talking about my group." This was definitely Aris. Thomas finally forced himself to snap out of his gaze.

"Group B?" he asked him. "You think they've already made it to the town?"

"Hello!" Minho snapped. "Who cares? You'd think the little part about them supposedly killing us would be the attention getter. Maybe this stuff about the Flare?"

Thomas thought of the tattoo on the back of his neck. Those simple words that scared him. "Maybe when she said 'you' she didn't mean all of us." He jabbed a thumb over his shoulder, pointing down at his menacing mark. "Maybe she meant me specifically. Couldn't tell where her eyes were looking."

"How's she gonna know who you are?" Minho retorted. "Plus, doesn't matter. If someone tries to kill you, or me, or anyone else, they might as well try to get all of us. Right?"

"You're so sweet," Frypan said with a snort. "Go ahead and die with Thomas. I think I'll sneak away and enjoy living with the guilt." He cast his special look that meant he was only kidding, but Thomas wondered if a little truth might be hiding in there somewhere.

"Well, what do we do now?" Jack asked. He had Winston's arm around one of his shoulders, but the former Keeper of the Blood House seemed to have recovered some of his strength. Luckily the sheet covered the hideous parts of his head.

"What do you think?" Newt asked, but then he nodded at Minho.

Minho rolled his eyes. "We keep going, that's what. Look, we don't have a choice. If we don't go to that town, we're gonna die out here of sunstroke or starvation. If we *do* go, we'll have some shelter for a while, maybe even food. Cranks or no Cranks, that's where we're going."

"And Group B?" Thomas asked; he glanced over at Aris. "Or whoever they were talking about. What if they really do wanna kill us? All we have to fight with are our hands."

Minho flexed his right arm. "If these people are really the girls Aris was hanging out with, I'll show 'em these guns of mine and they'll go runnin'."

Thomas kept pushing. "And if these girls have weapons? Or can fight? Or if it's not them at all but a bunch of seven-foot-tall grunts who like to eat humans? Or a thousand Cranks?"

"Thomas . . . no. Everybody." Minho let out an exasperated sigh.

"Would everyone just shut their holes and slim it? No more questions. Unless you have an idea that doesn't involve absolute certain death, then quit your pipin' and let's take the only chance we got. Get it?"

Thomas smiled, though he didn't know where the impulse came from. Somehow in a few sentences Minho had cheered him up, or at least given him a little hope. They just had to go, to move, to do. That was it.

"That's better," Minho said with a satisfied nod. "Anybody else wanna pee their pants and cry for Mommy?"

A few snickers broke out, but no one said anything.

"Good. Newt, you lead up front this time, limp and all. Thomas, you in the back. Jack, get someone else to help with Winston to give you a break. Let's go."

And so they did. Aris held the pack this time, and Thomas felt as if he were almost floating along the ground, it felt so good. The only hard part was holding that sheet up, his arm growing weak and rubbery. But on and on they went, sometimes walking, sometimes jogging.

Luckily, the sun seemed to gain weight and drop more quickly the closer it got to the horizon. By Thomas's wristwatch, the Cranks had only been gone an hour when the sky turned a purplish orange and the intense glare of the sun started to melt away into a more pleasant glow. Not long after that, it disappeared below the horizon altogether, pulling nighttime and stars across the sky like a curtain.

The Gladers kept moving, heading toward the faint twinkle of lights coming from the town. Thomas could almost enjoy it now that he wasn't holding the pack and they'd put the sheet away.

Finally, when every last trace of dusk had gone, full darkness settled on the land like a black fog.

CHAPTER 19

Soon after dark, Thomas heard a girl screaming.

At first he didn't know what he was hearing, or if maybe it was just his imagination. With the thumps of dry footsteps, the rustling of the packs, the whispers of conversation between heavy breaths, it was hard to tell. But what had started as almost a buzz inside his head soon became unmistakable. Somewhere ahead of them, maybe all the way in the town but more likely closer, a girl's screams tore through the night.

The others had obviously noticed it, too, and soon the Gladers quit running. Once everyone caught their breath, it became easier to hear the disturbing sound.

It was almost like a cat. An injured, wailing cat. The kind of noise that made your skin crawl and made you press your hands to your ears and pray it went away. There was something unnatural about it, something that chilled Thomas inside and out. The darkness only added to the creepiness. Whoever the source, she still wasn't very close, but her shrill screeches bounced along like living echoes, trying to smash their unspeakable sounds against the dirt until they ceased to exist in this world.

"You know what that reminds me of?" Minho asked, his voice a whisper with an edge of fear.

Thomas knew. "Ben. Alby. Me, I guess? Screaming after the Griever sting?"

"You got it."

"No, no, no," Frypan moaned. "Don't tell me we're gonna have those suckers out here, too. I can't take it!"

Newt responded, just a couple of feet to the left of Thomas and Aris. "Doubt it. Remember how moist and gooey their skin was? They'd turn into a big dust ball if they rolled around in this stuff."

"Well," Thomas said, "if WICKED can create Grievers, they can create plenty of other freaks of nature that might be worse. Hate to say it, but that rat-lookin' guy said things were finally going to get tough."

"Once again, Thomas gives us a cheerful pep talk," Frypan announced; he tried to sound jovial, but it came out more like a spiteful rub.

"Just saying it how it is."

Frypan huffed. "I know. And *how it is* sucks big-time."

"What now?" Thomas asked.

"I think we should take a break," Minho said. "Fill our little tummies and drink up. Then we should book it for as long as we can stand it while the sun is still down. Maybe get a couple hours' sleep before dawn."

"And the psycho screaming lady out there?" Frypan asked.

"Sounds like she's plenty busy with her own troubles."

For some reason that statement terrified Thomas. Maybe the others, too, because no one said a word as they slipped the packs off their shoulders, sat down and began eating.

"Man, I wish she'd shut up." It was about the fifth time Aris had said that as they ran along in the darker-than-dark night. The poor girl, somewhere out there, getting closer all the while, was still crying her fretful, high-pitched wails.

Their meal had been quiet and somber, the talk drifting toward what the Rat Man had said about the Variables and how their responses to them were all that mattered. About creating a "blueprint," about finding the "killzone" patterns. No one had any answers, of course, only meaningless speculations. It was odd, Thomas thought. They now *knew* they were being tested somehow, put through WICKED's trials. In some ways it felt like they should behave differently because of this, and yet they just kept going, fighting, surviving until they could get the promised cure. And that was what they'd keep doing; Thomas was sure of it.

It had taken a while for his legs and joints to loosen up once Minho got everyone moving again. Above them, the moon was a sliver, barely providing any more light than the stars. But you didn't need to see much to run along flat and barren land. Plus, unless it was his imagination, they were actually starting to reach the lights from the town. He could see that they flickered now, which meant they were probably fires. Which made sense—the odds of having electricity in this wasteland hovered around zero.

He wasn't sure when it happened exactly, but suddenly the cluster of buildings they were running toward seemed a lot closer. And there were a lot more of them than he or anyone else had thought. Taller, too. Wider. Spread out and organized in rows and in an orderly fashion. For all they knew, the place might've once been a major city, devastated by whatever had happened to the area. Could sun flares really inflict that much damage? Or had other things caused it during the aftermath?

Thomas was starting to think they'd actually reach the first buildings sometime the next day.

Even though they didn't need the cover of their sheet at the moment, Aris still jogged right next to him, and Thomas felt like talking. "Tell me more about your whole Maze thing."

Aris's breaths were even; he seemed to be in just as good shape as Thomas. "My whole Maze thing? What's that supposed to mean?"

"You've never really told us the details. What was it like for you? How long were you there? How'd you get out?"

Aris answered over the soft *crunch, crunch, crunch* of their footsteps on the desert ground. "I've talked with some of your friends, and it sounds like a lot of it was exactly the same. Just . . . girls instead of guys. Some of them had been there for two years, the rest had shown up one at a time, once a month. Then came Rachel, then me the next day, in a coma. I barely remember anything, just those last few crazy days after I finally woke up."

He went on to explain what had happened, and so much of it matched what Thomas and the Gladers had been through, it was just plain bizarre. Almost impossible to believe. Aris came out of his coma, said something about the Ending, the walls quit shutting at night, their Box stopped coming, they figured out the Maze had a code, on and on and on until the escape. Which went down almost the same as the Gladers' terrifying experience, except less of the girl group died—if they were tough like Teresa, this didn't surprise Thomas in the least.

In the end, once Aris and his group were in the final chamber, a girl named Beth—who'd disappeared days earlier, just like Gally had—killed Rachel, right before rescuers came in and whisked them away to the gym Aris had mentioned before. Then the rescuers took him to the place where the Gladers had finally discovered him—what had been Teresa's room.

If that was what had happened. Who knew how things worked anymore, after seeing what could happen at the Cliff and the Flat Trans that had taken them to the tunnel. Not to mention the bricked-up walls and the name change on Aris's door.

It all gave Thomas a big fat headache.

When he tried to think of Group B and imagine their roles—how he and Aris were basically switched, and how Aris was actually Teresa's counterpart—it twisted his mind. The fact that Chuck had been killed in the end instead of him . . . that was the only major difference that stood out in the parallels. Were the setups meant to instigate certain conflicts or provoke reactions for WICKED's studies?

"It's all kind of freaky, huh?" Aris asked after letting Thomas digest his story for a while.

"I don't know what the word for it is. But it blows me away how the two groups went through these trippy parallel experiments. Or tests, trials, whatever they were. I mean, if they're testing our responses, I guess it makes sense that we were put through the same thing. Weird, though."

Right when Thomas stopped speaking the girl in the distance let out a shriek even louder than her now-regular cries of pain and he felt a fresh rush of horror.

"I think I know," Aris said, so quietly Thomas wasn't sure he'd heard him correctly.

"Huh?"

"I think I know. Why there were two groups. *Are* two groups."

Thomas looked over at him, could barely see the surprising look of calm on his face. "You do? What then?"

Aris still didn't seem very winded. "Well, actually I have two ideas. One is I think these people—WICKED, whoever they are—are trying to weed out the best of both groups to use us somehow. Maybe even breed us or something like that."

"What?" Thomas was so surprised he almost forgot about the screaming. He couldn't believe anyone would be so sick. "*Breed* us? Come on."

"After going through the Maze and what we just saw happen in that tunnel, you think *breeding* is far-fetched? Give me a break."

"Good that." Thomas had to admit that the kid had a point. "Okay, so what was your other theory?" As he asked it Thomas could feel the weariness brought on by the run settling in; his throat felt like someone had poured a glassful of sand down his gullet.

"Kind of the opposite," Aris responded. "That instead of wanting survivors from both groups, they only want one group to live through to the end. So they're either weeding out people from the guys *and* the girls, or an entire group altogether. Either way, it's the only explanation I can think of."

Thomas thought about what he'd said for quite some time before responding. "But what about the stuff the Rat Man said? That they're testing our responses, building some kind of blueprint? Maybe it's an experiment. Maybe they don't plan for any of us to survive. Maybe they're studying our brains and our reactions and our genes and everything else. When it's all done, we'll be dead and they'll have lots of reports to read."

"Hmm," Aris grunted, considering. "Possibly. I keep trying to figure out why they had one member of the opposite sex in each group."

"Maybe to see what kind of fights or problems it would cause. Study people's reactions—it's kind of a unique situation." Thomas almost wanted to laugh. "I love how we're talking about this—like we're deciding when we need to stop for a klunk."

Aris actually did laugh, a dry chuckle that made Thomas feel better—actually made him like the new kid even more. "Man, don't say that. I've had to go for at least an hour."

It was Thomas's turn to snicker, and right on cue, like he'd heard Aris calling for it, Minho yelled out for everyone to stop.

"Potty break," he said with his hands on his hips as he caught his breath. "Bury your klunk and don't do it too close. We'll rest for fifteen, then we'll just walk awhile. I know you shanks can't keep up with Runners like me and Thomas."

Thomas tuned out—he didn't need directions on how to use the bathroom—and turned to get a look at where they'd stopped. He took a deep, full breath, and when he relaxed his eyes caught on something. A dark shadow of a shape a few hundred yards in front of them, but not directly in the path of their journey. A square of darkness against the faint glow of the town up ahead. It stood out so distinctly he couldn't believe he hadn't noticed it until now.

"Hey!" he yelled, pointing toward it. "Looks like a little building up there, just a few minutes away, to the right some. You guys see it?"

"Yeah, I see it," Minho responded, walking up to stand next to him. "Wonder what it is."

Before Thomas could respond, two things happened almost simultaneously.

First, the haunted screams of the mystery girl stopped, instantly, cut short as if a door had closed on her. Then, stepping out from behind the dark building up ahead, the figure of a girl appeared, long hair flowing from her shadowed head like black silk.

CHAPTER 20

Thomas couldn't help it. His first instinct was to hope it was her, call out to her. To hope that against all odds she was there, just a few hundred yards away, waiting for him.

Teresa?

Nothing.

Teresa? Teresa!

Nothing. The abscess left when she disappeared was still in his head—like an empty pool. But . . . it *could* be her. Might be her. Maybe something had happened to their ability to communicate.

Once the girl had stepped out from behind the building, or more likely from *inside* the building, she just stood there. Despite being obscured completely by shadow, something about her stance made it obvious she was facing them, staring at them with arms folded.

"You think that's Teresa?" Newt asked, as if he'd read Thomas's mind.

Thomas nodded before he knew what he was doing. He quickly looked around to see if anyone had noticed. Didn't seem so. "No clue," he finally said.

"You think *she* was the one screaming?" Frypan asked. "It stopped right when she walked out."

Minho grunted. "Better bet is she was the one torturing somebody. Probably killed her and put her out of her misery when she saw us coming." Then for some reason he clapped his hands once. "Okay, then, who wants to go meet this nice young lady?"

How Minho could be so lighthearted at times like this just baffled Thomas. "I'll do it," he said, way too loudly. He didn't want to make it obvious that he hoped it was Teresa.

"I was just kidding, shuck-face," Minho said. "Let's all go over there. She could have an army of psycho girl ninjas hiding in that shack of hers."

"Psycho girl ninjas?" Newt repeated, his voice showing he was surprised, if not annoyed, by Minho's attitude.

"Yeah. Let's go." Minho started walking forward.

Thomas acted on a sudden and unexpected instinct. "No!" He lowered his voice. "No. You guys stay here—I'll go talk to her. Maybe it's a trap or something. We'd be idiots to all go over there and fall right into it."

"And you're *not* an idiot for going by yourself?" Minho asked.

"Well, we can't just walk on by without checking it out. I'll go. If something happens or gets suspicious, I'll call for help."

Minho paused for a long moment. "All right. Go. Our brave little shank." He whacked Thomas on the back with his open palm and it stung.

"This is bloody stupid," Newt interrupted, stepping forward. "I'll go with him."

"No!" Thomas snapped. "Just . . . let me do this. Something tells me we need to be careful. If I cry like a baby, come save me." And before anyone could argue, he took off at a fast walk toward the girl and her building.

He closed the distance quickly. His shoes crunched against the gritty dirt and rocks, breaking the silence. He sniffed the raw smells of the desert mixed with a distant scent of something burning, and as he stared at the silhouette of the girl next to the building, he suddenly knew for sure. Maybe it was the shape of her head or body. Maybe it was her stance, the way she held her folded arms crooked to one side, her hip jutting the other direction. But he knew.

It was her.

It was Teresa.

When he reached a point just a few feet from her, right before the faint light would finally reveal her face, she turned around and went through an open door, disappearing inside the small building. It was a rectangle, a slightly tilted roof tenting in the middle, longways. As far as he could tell, it had no windows. Large black cubes were hanging from the corners—speakers, perhaps. Maybe the sound had been broadcast, been a fake. That would explain why they could hear it from so far away.

The door, a big slab of wood, stood all the way open and rested against the wall. It was even darker inside than out.

Thomas moved. He walked through the door, realizing even as he did so how reckless and stupid it might be. But it was her. No matter what had happened, no matter the explanation for her disappearance and refusal to speak with him through their thoughts, he knew she wouldn't hurt him. No way.

The air was noticeably cooler inside, almost moist. It felt wonderful. Three steps in, he stopped and listened in the complete darkness. He could hear her breathing.

"Teresa?" he asked aloud, pushing away the temptation to ask for her in his mind again. "Teresa, what's going on?"

She didn't respond, but he heard a short intake of breath, followed by a halting sniff, as if she were crying but trying to hide it from him.

"Teresa, *please.* I don't know what's happened or what they did to you, but I'm here now. This is crazy. Just talk to—"

He cut off when a light blazed to life with a quick flare that then dulled to a small flame. His eyes naturally went straight to it, to the hand holding a match. He watched as it dropped, slowly, carefully, to light a candle resting on a small table. When it caught, and the hand flicked the match until it went out, Thomas finally looked up and saw her. Saw that he'd been right after all. But the short and almost overpowering thrill of seeing Teresa alive was soon cut short, replaced by confusion and pain.

She was clean, every part of her. He'd expected her to be filthy like he must be after all this time in the dusty desert. He'd expected her clothes to be ratty and torn. He'd expected greasy hair and a smudged and sunburned face. But instead she wore fresh clothes; her clean hair cascaded to her shoulders. Nothing marred the pale skin of her face or arms. She was more beautiful than he'd ever seen her in the Maze, than any memories he could pull from the murky goop of what he'd recovered after the Changing.

But her eyes sparkled with tears; her lower lip trembled with fear; her hands shook at her sides. He saw recognition in her eyes, saw that she hadn't forgotten him again, but behind that there was pure and absolute terror.

"Teresa," he whispered, knotting up inside. "What's wrong?"

She didn't respond, but her eyes flickered to the side, then back to him. A couple of tears trickled out, slipping down her cheeks, then falling to the floor. Her lips trembled even more, and her chest lurched with what could only be a stifled sob.

Thomas stepped forward, put his hands out to her.

"No!" she screamed. "Get away from me!"

Thomas stopped—it was like something massive had just slammed him in the gut. He held his hands up. "Okay, okay. Teresa, what . . ." He didn't know what to say or ask. Didn't know what to do. But that terrible feeling of something breaking inside him intensified, threatened to choke him as it swelled in his throat.

He stilled, scared to set her off again. All he could do was lock eyes with her, try to communicate how he felt, beg her to tell him something. Anything.

A very long moment passed in silence. The way her body shook, the way she almost seemed to struggle against something unseen . . . it reminded him of . . .

It reminded him of how Gally had been acting, right after they'd escaped from the Glade and he'd entered the room with the woman in the white shirt. Right before everything had gone crazy. Right before he'd killed Chuck.

Thomas had to speak or he'd burst. "Teresa, I've thought about you every second since they took you away. You—"

She didn't let him finish. Rushing forward, she was in front of him in two long strides and reaching out, grabbing his shoulders and pulling herself close to him. Shocked, Thomas wrapped his arms around her and squeezed, embracing her so tightly he suddenly worried she couldn't breathe. Her hands found the back of his head, then the sides of his face, making him look at her.

And then they were kissing. Something exploded within his chest, burning away the tension and confusion and fear. Burning away the hurt of seconds earlier. For a moment it felt like nothing mattered anymore. Like nothing would matter ever again.

But then she pulled away. She stumbled backward until she hit the wall. The terror returned to her face, possessed it like a demon. And then she spoke, her voice a whisper but laced with urgency.

"Get away from me, Tom," she said. "All of you need to get . . . away . . . from me. Don't argue. Just leave. Run." Her neck tensed with the effort to get those last few words out.

Thomas had never hurt so badly. But he shocked himself by what he did next.

He knew her now, *remembered* her. And he knew that she was telling the truth—something wasn't right here. Something was terribly wrong—far worse than he'd first imagined. Staying, arguing with her, trying to force her to come with him would be a slap in the face to the incredible amount of willpower it must've taken her to break away and warn him. He had to do what she said.

"Teresa," he said. "I'll find you." Tears now welling in his own eyes, he turned from her and ran from the building.

CHAPTER 21

Thomas stumbled away from the now-dark building, squinting through tear-blurred eyes. He went back to the Gladers and refused to answer their questions. Told them they had to go, run, get away as fast as possible. That he'd explain later. That their lives were in danger.

He didn't wait for them. He didn't offer to take the pack from Aris. He just started toward the town, sprinting till he finally had to slow down to a manageable pace, blocking the others out, blocking the whole world out. Running away from her was the hardest thing he'd ever done, he had no doubt of it. Showing up at the Glade with his memories wiped, adapting to life there, being trapped in the Maze, fighting Grievers, watching Chuck die—none of it matched what he felt now.

She was there. She'd been in his arms. They'd been together again.

They'd kissed and he'd felt something he would've thought impossible.

And now he was running away. Leaving her behind.

Choked sobs burst from him. He groaned, heard the miserable sound of his voice crack. His heart felt a pain that almost made him stop, collapse to the ground and give up. Sorrow consumed him, and more than once he was tempted to go back. But somehow he held true to what she'd ordered him to do, and he held on to the promise he'd made to find her again.

At least she was alive. At least she was alive.

That was what he kept telling himself. That was what kept him running.

She was alive.

His body could only take so much. At some point, maybe two hours after he'd left her, maybe three, he stopped, sure his heart would explode out of his chest if he went one more step. Turning, he looked behind him and he saw shadows moving far in the distance—the other Gladers, way back. Breathing huge gulps of dry air, Thomas knelt, planted his forearms on one knee, then closed his eyes to rest until they caught up.

Minho reached him first, and their leader wasn't happy. Even in the faint light—dawn was just starting to brighten the eastern sky—he visibly fumed as he walked around Thomas three full times before he said anything.

"What . . . Why . . . What kind of a shuck idiot are you, Thomas?"

Thomas didn't feel like talking about it. About anything.

When he didn't answer, Minho knelt down next to him. "How could you do that? How could you just come out of there and take off like that? Without explaining anything? Since when is that how we do things? You slinthead." He let out a big sigh and fell back to sit on his butt, shaking his head.

"Sorry," Thomas finally muttered. "It was kinda traumatizing."

The other Gladers had reached them by now, half of them doubling over to catch their breaths, the other half pressing in to hear what Thomas and Minho were talking about. Newt was right there, but he seemed content to let Minho do all the digging to find out what had happened.

"Traumatizing?" Minho asked. "Who did you see in there? What did they say?"

Thomas knew he had no choice—this wasn't something he could or should keep from the others. "It was . . . it was Teresa."

He expected gasps, exclamations of surprise, accusations of being a freaking liar. But in the silence that followed, you could hear the morning winds scuttle across the dusty lands surrounding them.

"What?" Minho finally said. "You're serious?"

Thomas simply nodded, staring at a triangular-shaped rock on the ground. The air had brightened considerably in just the last few minutes.

Minho was understandably shocked. "And you *left* her there? Dude, you need to start talking and tell us what happened."

As much as it pained him, as much as the memory of it tore at his heart, Thomas told the story. Seeing her, how she trembled and cried, how she acted like Gally—almost possessed—before he killed Chuck, the warning she'd given. He told it all; the only thing he left out was the kiss.

"Wow," Minho said in a weary voice, somehow wrapping it all up with that one simple word.

Several minutes passed. The dry wind scratched across the ground, filling the air with dust as the bright orange dome of the sun crested the horizon and officially started the day. No one spoke. Thomas heard sniffs and breaths and a few coughs. The sounds of people drinking from their water bags. The town seemed to have grown during the night, its buildings stretching toward the cloudless, purple-blue sky. It would only take another day or two to reach it.

"It was some kind of trap," he finally said. "I don't know what would've happened, or how many of us would've died. Maybe all of us. But I could see that there wasn't any doubt in her eyes when she broke away from whatever restrained her. She saved us, and I bet they make her . . ." He swallowed. "I bet they make her pay for it."

Minho reached out and squeezed Thomas's shoulder. "Dude, if those shuck WICKED people wanted her dead, she'd be rottin' under a big pile of rocks. She's just as tough as anybody else, maybe tougher. She'll survive."

Thomas took in a deep pull of air and let it out. He felt better. Impossibly, he felt better. Minho was right. "I know. Somehow I know."

Minho stood up. "We should've stopped a couple hours ago to get some sleep. But thanks to Mr. Desert Runner down here"—he lightly whacked Thomas in the head—"we ran ourselves ragged till the freaking sun came back up. I still think we need to rest for a while. Do it under the sheets, whatever, but let's try."

It ended up being no problem at all for Thomas. The brightening sun making the backs of his eyelids a murky black-splotched crimson, he fell asleep instantly, a sheet pulled all the way over his head to protect him from sunburn—and from his troubles.

CHAPTER 22

Minho let them sleep for almost four hours. Not that he had to wake many people up. The rising and intensifying sun raged its heat down on the land, and it became unbearable—impossible to ignore. By the time Thomas was up and had the food repacked after breakfast, sweat already drenched his clothes. The smell of body odor hung over them like a stinky mist, and he just hoped he wasn't the worst culprit. The showers back at the dorm seemed like pure luxury now.

The Gladers remained sullen and quiet as they readied for the journey. The more Thomas thought about it, the more he realized that there wasn't much to be happy about. Still, two things kept him going, and he hoped they did the same for the others. First, an overwhelming curiosity to find out what was in that stupid town—it looked more and more like a city as they got closer. And second, the hope that Teresa was alive and well. Maybe she'd gone through one of those Flat Trans things. Maybe she was ahead of them now. In the city, even. Thomas felt a swell of encouragement.

"Let's go," Minho said when everybody was ready. Then they were off.

Across the dry and dusty land they walked. No one needed to say it, but Thomas knew everyone was thinking the same thing—they no longer had the energy to run while the sun was up. And even if they did, they didn't have enough water to keep them alive at a faster pace.

So they walked, sheets held over their heads. As food and water dwindled, more of the packs became available to use for protection from the sun, and fewer Gladers had to walk in pairs. Thomas was one of the first to be alone, probably because no one wanted to talk to him after hearing the story about Teresa. He certainly wasn't going to complain—solitude was bliss for now.

Walking. Breaks for food and water. Walking. Heat, like a dry ocean through which they had to swim. That wind, blowing stronger now, bringing more dust and grit than relief from the heat. It whipped at the sheets, made it harder to keep them in place. Thomas kept coughing and rubbing chunks of accumulated grime from the corners of his eyes. He felt as if every swallow of water only made him want more, but their supplies had reached dangerously low levels. If there wasn't fresh water in the city when they reached it . . .

There was no good way for him to finish that line of thought.

They kept going, each step becoming just a little more agonizing, and quiet set in. No one talked. Thomas felt like even saying a couple of words would expend too much energy. It was all he could do to put one foot in front of the other, over and over and over, staring lifelessly at their goal—the ever-nearing city.

It was as if the buildings were alive, growing right before their eyes as they got closer. Soon Thomas could see what had to be stone, windows glimmering in the sunlight. Some seemed to be broken, but far less than half. From Thomas's vantage point, the streets seemed empty. No fires burned during the day. As far as he could tell, not one tree or any other kind of plant existed in the place. How would it, in this climate? How could people possibly live there? How would they grow food? What would they find?

Tomorrow. It had taken longer than he'd thought, but Thomas had no doubt they'd reach the city tomorrow. And though they'd probably be better off going *around* it, they had no choice. They needed to replenish their supplies.

Walking. Breaks. Heat.

When nightfall finally came, the sun disappearing below the far western horizon at a maddeningly slow pace, the wind picked up even more, and this time brought the slightest chill. Thomas enjoyed it, grateful for any relief from the heat.

By midnight, however, when Minho finally called on them to stop and get more sleep, the city and its now-burning fires ever closer, the wind had become even stronger. It blew in gales, whipping and curling with increasing power.

Soon after they stopped, as Thomas lay on his back, sheet tucked around him and pulled up tightly to his chin, he looked up at the sky. The winds were almost soothing, lulling him to sleep. Just as his mind got hazy from exhaustion, the stars seemed to fade away, and sleep brought him another dream.

He's sitting in a chair. Ten or eleven years old. Teresa—she looks so different, so much younger, yet it's still clearly her—sits across from him, a table between them. She's about his age. No one else is in the room, a dark place with only one light—a dull square of yellow in the ceiling directly overhead.

"Tom, you need to try harder," she says. Her arms are folded, and even at this younger age, it's a look he doesn't find surprising. It's very familiar. As if he has already known her a long time.

"I *am* trying." Again it's him speaking, but not really him. It doesn't make sense.

"They'll probably kill us if we can't do this."

"I know."

"Then try!"

"I am!"

"Fine," she says. "You know what? I'm not speaking out loud to you anymore. Never ever again until you can do it."

"But—"

Not inside your mind, either. She's talking in his head. That trick that still freaks him out and he still can't reciprocate. *Starting now.*

"Teresa, just give me a few more days. I'll get it."

She doesn't respond.

"Okay, just one more day."

She only stares at him. Then, not even that. She looks down at the table, reaches out and starts scratching a spot in the wood with her fingernail.

"There's no way you're not gonna talk to me."

No response. And he knows her, despite what he just said. Oh, he knows her.

"Fine," he says. He closes his eyes, does what the instructor told him to do. Imagines a sea of black nothingness, interrupted only by the image of Teresa's face. Then, with every last bit of willpower, he forms the words and *throws* them at her.

You smell like a bag of crap.

Teresa smiles, then replies in his mind.

So do you.

CHAPTER 23

Thomas woke up to wind beating at his face and hair and clothes. It felt like invisible hands were trying to rip them off. It was still dark. And cold, too, his whole body shivering from it. Getting up on his elbows, he looked around, hardly able to see the huddled shapes sleeping near him, their sheets pulled tightly against their bodies.

Their sheets.

He let out a frustrated yelp, then jumped to his feet—at some point in the night his own sheet had slipped loose and flown off. With the tearing wind, it could be ten miles away by now.

"Shuck it," he whispered; the howl of the wind stole the words before he could even hear them. The dream came back to him—or was it a memory? It had to be. That brief glimpse into a time when he and Teresa had been younger, learning how to do their telepathy trick. He felt his heart sink a little, missing her, feeling guilt over yet more proof that he'd been part of WICKED before going to the Maze. He shook it off, not wanting to think about it. He could block it out if he tried hard enough.

He looked up at black sky, then sucked in a hurried breath as the memory of the sun vanishing from the Glade came rushing back. That had been the beginning of the end. The beginning of the terror.

But common sense soon calmed his heart. The winds. The cool air. A storm. It had to be a storm.

Clouds.

Embarrassed, he sat back down, then lay on his side and curled into a ball, his arms wrapped around himself. The cold wasn't unbearable, just a vast change from the horrible heat of the last couple of days. He probed his mind and wondered about the memories he'd had lately. Could they be lingering results of the Changing? Was his memory coming back?

The thought gave him mixed feelings. He wanted his memory block finally cracked for good—wanted to know who he was, where he came from. But that desire was tempered by fear of what he might find out about himself. About his role in the very things that had brought him to this point, that had done this to his friends.

He needed sleep desperately. The wind a constant roar in his ears, he finally slipped away, this time to nothing.

The light woke him to a dull, gray dawn that finally revealed the thick layer of clouds covering the sky. It also made the endless expanse of desert around them look even more dreary. The city was so close now, only a few hours away. The buildings really *were* tall; one of them even stretched up and disappeared in a low-hanging fog. And the glass in all those broken windows was like jagged teeth in mouths open to catch food that might be flying about in the stormy wind.

The gusty air still tore at him, and a thick layer of dirt seemed forever baked onto his face. He rubbed his head and his hair felt stiff with wind-dried grime.

Most of the other Gladers were up and about, taking in the unexpected shift in the weather, deep in conversations he couldn't hear. There was only the roar in his ears.

Minho noticed him awake and came over; he leaned into the wind as he walked, his clothes flapping around him. "'Bout time you woke up!" He was fully shouting.

Thomas rubbed the crust out of his eyes and got to his feet. "Where'd this all come from!" he yelled back. "I thought we were in the middle of a desert!"

Minho looked up at the roiling gray mass of clouds, then back at Thomas. He leaned closer to speak directly in his ear. "Well, guess it has to rain in the desert *sometime.* Hurry and eat—we gotta get going. Maybe we can get there and find a place to hide before we're soaked by the storm."

"What if we get there and a bunch of Cranks try to kill us?"

"Then we'll fight 'em!" Minho frowned as if disappointed that Thomas had asked such a stupid question. "What else you wanna do? We're almost out of food and water."

Thomas knew Minho was right. Plus, if they could fight dozens of Grievers, a bunch of half-mad, starved sicklings shouldn't be too much of a problem. "All right, then. Let's go. I'll eat one of those granola things while we walk."

A few minutes later, they were once again heading for the city, the gray sky above them ready to burst and bleed water at any moment.

They were only a couple of miles away from the closest buildings when they came across an old man lying in the sand on his back, wrapped in several blankets. Jack had been the one to spot him first, and soon Thomas and the others were packed in a circle around the guy, staring down at him.

Thomas's stomach turned as he studied the man more closely, but he couldn't look away. The stranger had to be a hundred years old, though it was hard to tell—the wear and tear of the sun might've made him just look that way. Wrinkled, leathery face. Scabs and sores where his hair should've been. Dark, dark skin.

He was alive, breathing deeply, but he gazed at the sky with an emptiness in his eyes. As if he was waiting for some god to come down and take him away, end his miserable life. He showed no sign he'd even noticed the Gladers approach.

"Hey! Old man!" Minho shouted, always the tactful one. "What're you doing out here?"

Thomas had a hard enough time hearing the words over the ripping wind; he couldn't imagine that the ancient guy could make anything out. But was he blind as well? Maybe.

Thomas nudged Minho out of the way and knelt down right beside the man's face. The melancholy there was heartbreaking. He held his hand out and waved it right above the old guy's eyes.

Nothing. No blink, no movement. It was only after Thomas pulled his hand back that the man's eyelids slowly drooped closed, then open again. Just once.

"Sir?" Thomas asked. "Mister?" The words sounded strange to him, conjured up from the murky memories of his past. He certainly hadn't used them since being sent to the Glade and the Maze. "Can you hear me? Can you talk?"

The man did that slow blink again, but didn't say anything.

Newt knelt next to Thomas and spoke loudly over the wind. "This guy's a bloody gold mine if we can get him to tell us stuff about the city. Looks harmless, probably knows what to expect when we go in there."

Thomas sighed. "Yeah, but he doesn't even seem to be able to hear us, much less have a long talk."

"Keep trying," Minho said from behind them. "You're officially our foreign ambassador, Thomas. Get the dude to open up and tell us about the good ol' days."

For some odd reason Thomas wanted to say something funny back, but he couldn't think of anything. If he'd been funny in his old life, every scrap of humor had certainly vanished in the memory swipe. "Okay," he said.

He scooted as close to the man's head as he could, then positioned himself so their eyes were square, just a couple of feet apart. "Sir? We really need your help!" He felt bad for shouting, worried the old man might take it the wrong way, but he had no choice. The wind was gusting stronger and stronger. "We need you to tell us if it's safe to go inside the city! We can carry you there if you need help yourself. Sir? Sir!"

The man's dark eyes had been looking past him, up at the sky, but now they shifted, slowly, until they focused on his. Awareness filled them like dark liquid poured slowly into a glass. His lips parted, but nothing came out except a small cough.

Thomas's hopes lifted. "My name is Thomas. These are my friends. We've been walking through the desert for a couple of days, and we need more water and food. What do you . . ."

He trailed off when the man's eyes flicked back and forth, a sudden hint of panic there.

"It's okay, we won't hurt you," Thomas quickly said. "We're . . . we're the good guys. But we'd really appreciate it if—"

The man's left hand shot out from beneath the blankets wrapped around him and clasped Thomas's wrist, gripping it with a strength far greater than seemed possible. Thomas cried out in surprise and instinctively tried to pull his arm free, but couldn't. He was shocked by the man's strength. He could barely budge against the man's iron manacle of a fist.

"Hey!" he shouted. "Let go of me!"

The man shook his head, those dark eyes full more of fear than any kind of belligerence. His lips parted again, and a rough, indecipherable whisper rose from his mouth. He didn't loosen his grip.

Thomas gave up the struggle to free his arm; instead, he relaxed and leaned forward to put his ear close to the stranger's mouth. "What'd you say!" he shouted.

The man spoke again, a dry rasp that was unsettling, spooky. Thomas caught the words *storm* and *terror* and *bad people.* None of them sounded very inspiring.

"One more time!" Thomas yelled, his head still cocked so his ear rested only inches above the man's face.

This time Thomas understood most of it, missing only a few words. "Storm coming . . . full of terror . . . brings out . . . stay away . . . bad people."

The man shot up into a sitting position, his eyes full and white around his irises. "Storm! Storm! Storm!" He didn't stop, repeating the word over and over; a mucus-thick strand of saliva finally crested over his bottom lip and swung back and forth like a hypnotist's pendulum.

He released Thomas's arm, and Thomas scooted back on his butt to get away. Even as he did so, the wind intensified, seemed to go from strong gusts to outright hurricane-strength gales of terror, just like the man had said. The world was lost in the sound of roaring, screaming air. Thomas felt as if his hair and clothes might rip off at any second. Almost all of the Gladers' sheets went flying, flapping over the ground and into the air like an army of ghosts. Food skittered in all directions.

Thomas got to his feet, an almost impossible task with the wind trying to knock him over. He stumbled forward several feet until he leaned back into it; invisible hands held him up.

Minho stood nearby, frantically waving his arms as he tried to get everyone's attention. Most saw and gathered around him, including Thomas, who fought off the panic creeping along his insides. It was only a storm. Far better than Grievers or Cranks with knives. Or ropes.

The old man had lost his blankets to the wind, and he huddled now in the fetal position, his skinny legs squeezed against his chest, eyes closed. Thomas had the fleeting thought that they should carry him someplace safe, save him for at least attempting to warn them about the storm. But something told him the man would fight tooth and nail if they tried to touch him or pick him up.

The Gladers were now packed together. Minho pointed at the city. The closest building was within a half hour if they ran at a good pace. The way the wind tore at them, the way the clouds above thickened and churned and bruised to a deep purple, almost black, the way dust and debris flew through the air, reaching that building seemed the only sane choice.

Minho started running. The others fell in, and Thomas waited to bring up the rear, knowing that was what Minho wanted him to do. He finally broke into a brisk jog, glad they weren't going directly into the wind. Only then did a few of the words the old man had said pop into his mind. They made him break into a sweat that quickly evaporated, leaving his skin dry and salty.

Stay away. Bad people.

CHAPTER 24

As they approached the city, it became harder for Thomas to actually see it. The dust in the air had thickened into a brown fog, and he felt it in every breath. It was crusting in his eyes, making them water and turning into goop that he had to keep wiping away. The large building they were shooting for had become a looming shadow behind the cloud of dust, towering taller and taller, like a growing giant.

The wind had gained a rough edge, pelting him with sand and grit until it hurt. Every once in a while a larger object would fly by, scaring him half out of his wits. A branch. Something that looked like a small mouse. A piece of roofing tile. And countless scraps of paper. All swirling through the air like snowflakes.

Then came the lightning.

They'd halved the distance to the building—maybe more than that—when the bolts came from nowhere, and the world around him erupted in light and thunder.

They fell from the sky in jagged streaks, like bars of white light, slamming into the ground and throwing up massive amounts of scorched earth. The crushing sound was too much to bear, and Thomas's ears began to go numb, the horrific noise fading to a distant hum as he went deaf.

He kept running, almost blind now, unable to hear, barely able to see the building. People fell and got back up. Thomas stumbled but caught his balance. He helped Newt regain his feet, then Frypan. Pushed them forward as he kept on. It was only a matter of time before one of the thick daggers of lightning struck someone and fried them to a blackened char. His hair stood on end despite the ripping wind, the static in the air raging and prickly as flying needles.

Thomas wanted to scream, wanted to hear his own voice, even if it was only the dull vibrations inside his skull. But he knew the dust-riddled air would choke him; it was hard enough to take short, quick breaths through his nose. Especially with the storm of lightning crashing to the ground all around them, singeing the air, making everything smell like copper and ash.

The sky darkened further, the dust cloud thickened; Thomas realized he couldn't see everyone anymore. Just those few directly in front of him. Light from the strikes flashed against them, a short burst of brilliant white illuminating them for the briefest instant. It all added together to blind Thomas even more. They had to reach that building. They had to get there or they wouldn't last much longer.

And where was the rain? he wondered. Where was the rain? What kind of a storm was this?

A bolt of pure white zigzagged from the sky and exploded on the ground right in front of him. He screamed but couldn't hear himself, squeezing his eyes shut as something—some burst of energy or wave of air—threw him to the side. He landed flat on his back, the breath knocked from his chest, as a spray of dirt and rocks rained down on him. Spitting, wiping at his face, he gulped for air as he scrambled onto his hands and knees, then his feet. The air finally flowed, and he pulled it deep into his lungs.

He heard a ringing now, a steady, high-pitched buzz that felt like nails in his eardrums. The wind tried to eat his clothes, dirt stung his skin, darkness swirled around him like living night, broken only by the flashes of lightning. Then he saw it, a horrific image made even spookier by the on-again-off-again source of light.

It was Jack. He lay on the ground, inside a small crater, writhing as he clutched his knee. There was nothing below that—shin, ankle, and foot obliterated by the burst of pure electricity from the sky. Blood that looked like black tar gushed from the hideous wound, making a paste of horror with the dirt. His clothes had been burned off, leaving him naked, injuries spreading across his whole body. He had no hair. And it looked like his eyeballs had . . .

Thomas spun around and collapsed to the ground, coughing as he spit up everything in his stomach. There was nothing they could do for Jack. No way. Nothing. But he was still *alive.* Though the thought shamed him, Thomas was glad he couldn't hear the screams. He didn't know if he could bear to even look at him again.

Then someone was grabbing him, pulling him to his feet. Minho. He said something, and Thomas focused enough to read his lips. *We have to go. Nothing we can do.*

Jack, he thought. *Oh, man, Jack.*

Stumbling, his stomach muscles sore from throwing up, his ears ringing painfully, in shock from the terrible sight of Jack ripped to shreds by lightning, he ran after Minho. He saw lumps of shadow to the left and right, other Gladers, but only a few. It was too dark to see very far, and the lightning came and went too fast to reveal much. Only dust and debris and that looming shape of the building, almost on top of them now. They'd lost any hope of organization or staying together. It was each Glader for himself now—they just had to hope everyone could make it.

Wind. Explosions of light. Wind. Choking dust. Wind. Ringing in his ears, pain. Wind. He kept going, his eyes glued to Minho just a few steps ahead of him. He didn't feel anything for Jack. He didn't care if he was permanently deaf. He didn't care about the others anymore. The chaos around him seemed to siphon away his humanity, turn him into an animal. All he wanted was to survive, make it to that building, get inside. *Live.* Gain another day.

Searing white light detonated in front of him, throwing him through the air again. Even as he flew backward, he screamed, tried to regain his footing—the explosion had happened right where Minho was running. Minho! Thomas landed with a jarring thump that felt like every joint in his body came loose, then popped back into place. He ignored the pain, got up, ran forward, his vision full of darkness mixed with blurry afterimages, amoebas of purplish light. Then he saw flames.

It took a second for his brain to compute what he was seeing. Rods of fire dancing about like magic, hot tendrils whipping to the right from the wind. Then it all collapsed to the ground, a heap of thrashing flame. Thomas reached it and understood.

It was Minho. His clothes were on fire.

With a shriek that sent sharp pains through his head, he fell to the ground next to his friend. He dug into the earth—thankfully loose from the explosion of electricity that hit it—and shoveled it on top of Minho with both hands, scooping frantically. Aiming for the brightest points of flame, he made progress as Minho helped by rolling around and beating at his upper body with both hands.

In a matter of seconds, the fire went out, leaving behind charred clothing and countless angry wounds. Thomas was glad he couldn't hear the wails of agony that appeared to be coming from Minho. He knew they didn't have time to stop, so Thomas grabbed their leader by the shoulders and dragged him to his feet.

"Come on!" Thomas shouted, though the words felt like a couple of noiseless throbs in his brain.

Minho coughed, winced again, but then nodded and wrapped one of his arms around Thomas's neck. Together they moved as fast as they could toward the building, Thomas doing most of the work.

All around them, the lightning continued to fall like arrows of white fire. Thomas could feel the silent impact of the explosions, each one rattling his skull, shaking his bones. Flashes of light all around. Past the building toward which they stumbled and struggled, even more fires had sprung up; two or three times he saw lightning make direct contact with the upper reaches of a structure, sending a rain of bricks and glass falling to the streets below.

The darkness began to take on a different tone, more gray than brown, and Thomas realized that the storm clouds must've really thickened and sunk toward the ground, pushing the dust and fog out of their way. The wind had lessened slightly, but the lightning seemed stronger than ever.

Gladers were to the left and right, all heading in the same direction. They seemed fewer in number, but Thomas still couldn't see well enough to know for sure. He did spot Newt, then Frypan. And Aris. All of them looking as terrified as he felt, running, all eyes riveted to their goal, now just a short distance away.

Minho lost his footing and fell, slipped from Thomas's grip. Thomas stopped, turned around, pulled the burnt boy back to his feet, reset Minho's arm around his shoulder. Gripping him around the torso with both arms now, he half carried, half pulled him along. A blinding arc of lightning went right over their heads, pummeled the earth behind them; Thomas didn't look, kept moving. A Glader fell to his left; he couldn't tell who it was, didn't hear the scream he knew must've come. Another boy fell to his right, got back up. A blast of lightning, just ahead and to the right. Another to the left. One straight ahead. Thomas had to pause, blinking viciously until his sight came back. He started up again, yanking Minho along with him.

And then they were there. The first building of the city.

In the gripping darkness of the storm, the structure was all gray. Massive blocks of stone, an arch of smaller bricks, half-broken windows. Aris reached the door first, didn't bother to open it. It had been made of glass that was mostly gone, so he carefully smashed out the remaining shards with his elbow. He waved a couple of Gladers past, then went in himself, swallowed by the interior.

Thomas made it just as Newt did, and gestured for help. Newt and another boy took Minho from him, carefully dragged him backward over the threshold of the open entrance, his feet hitting the sill as they pulled him through.

And then Thomas, still in shock over the sheer power of the lightning bursts, followed his friends, stepping into the gloom.

He turned to look just in time to see the rain start falling outside, as if the storm had finally decided to weep with shame for what it had done to them.

CHAPTER 25

The rain fell in torrents, like God had sucked up the ocean and spit it out over their heads in fury.

Thomas sat in the exact same place for at least two hours as he watched it. He huddled against the wall, exhausted and sore, willing his hearing to come back. It seemed to be working—what had been a complete throb of silence had decreased its pressure, and the ringing had gone away. When he coughed, he thought it was more than just a vibration he felt. He *heard* a trace of it. And in the distance, as if from the other side of a dream, came the steady drumming sound of the rain. Maybe he wouldn't be deaf after all.

The dull gray light coming from the windows did little to fight off the cold darkness inside the building. The other Gladers sat hunched up or lying on their sides around the room. Minho was curled up in a ball at Thomas's feet, barely moving; it looked as if every shift sent waves of burning pain through his nerves. Newt was there, also, close, as was Frypan. But no one tried to talk or get things organized. No one counted off the Gladers or tried to figure out who was missing. They all sat or lay as lifeless as Thomas, probably pondering the same thing he was—what kind of messed-up world could create a storm like that?

The soft thrum of the rain grew louder until Thomas had no more doubt—he could really hear it. It was a soothing sound, despite everything, and he finally fell asleep.

★ ★ ★

By the time he woke up, his body so stiff it felt like glue had dried in his veins and muscles, all the machinery in his ears and head was back to fully functional. He heard the heavy breaths of sleeping Gladers, heard the whimpering moans from Minho, heard the now-pounding deluge of water slamming into the pavement outside.

But it was dark. Completely. At some point, night had fallen.

Pushing away his discomfort, letting the exhaustion take over, he shifted until he lay flat, his head propped on someone's leg—then he was asleep again.

Two things woke him up for good: the glow of sunrise and a sudden rush of silence. The storm was over, and he'd slept through the night. But even before he felt the stiffness and soreness he expected, he felt something much more overpowering.

Hunger.

The light came through the broken windows and dappled the floor around him. He looked up to see a ruin of a building, massive holes ripped in each floor all the way to the roof dozens of stories toward the sky; it seemed that only the steel infrastructure was keeping the whole thing from coming down. He couldn't imagine what had caused it all to happen. But jags of bright blue seemed to hover above, a sight that seemed impossible last time he'd been outside. Whatever horror that storm had been, whatever quirks in the climate of the earth could cause such a thing, it really did seem to be gone for now.

Sharp pains stabbed at his stomach, which groaned, aching for food. He glanced around to see most of the other Gladers still asleep, but Newt lay with his back against the wall, staring sadly at a blank spot in the middle of the room.

"You okay, there?" Thomas asked. Even his jaw felt stiff.

Newt slowly turned to him; his eyes were distant until he seemed to snap out of his thoughts and focus on Thomas. "Okay? Yeah, I guess I'm okay. We're alive—guess that's all that bloody matters anymore." The bitterness in his voice couldn't have been stronger.

"Sometimes I wonder," Thomas murmured.

"Wonder what?"

"If being alive matters. If being dead might be a lot easier."

"Please. I don't believe for one second you really think that."

Thomas's gaze had lowered while he'd delivered the depressing sentiment and he looked up sharply at Newt's retort. Then he smiled, and it felt good. "You're right. Just trying to sound as miserable as you." He could almost convince himself that it was true. That he *didn't* feel as if dying would be the easy way out.

Newt gestured wearily toward Minho. "What bloody happened to him?"

"Lightning strike somehow caught his clothes on fire. How it did that without frying his brain I have no idea. But we were able to beat it out before it did too much damage, I think."

"Before it did too much damage? I'd hate to see what you think *real* damage looks like."

Thomas closed his eyes for a second and rested his head against the wall. "Hey, like you said—he's alive, right? And he still has clothes on, which means it couldn't have burned his skin in *too* many places. He'll be fine."

"Yeah, good that," Newt replied with a sarcastic chuckle. "Remind me not to hire you as my buggin' doctor anytime soon."

"Ohhhh." This came from Minho, a long, drawn-out groan. His eyes fluttered open, then squinted as he caught Thomas's gaze. "Oh, man. I'm shucked. I'm shucked for good."

"How bad is it?" Newt asked him.

Instead of answering, Minho very slowly pushed himself up to a sitting position, grunting and wincing with every small move. But he finally did it, legs crossed beneath him. His clothes were blackened and ragged. In some places where skin was exposed, raw red blisters peeked out like menacing alien eyeballs. But even though Thomas wasn't a doctor and had no clue about such things, his instincts told him the burns were manageable and would heal pretty quickly. Most of Minho's face had been spared, and he still had all his hair—filthy as it was.

"Can't be too bad if you can do that," Thomas said with a sly smile.

"Shuck it," Minho responded. "I'm tougher than nails. I could still kick your pony-lovin' butt with twice this pain."

Thomas shrugged. "I do love ponies. Wish I could eat one right now." His stomach grumbled and gurgled.

"Was that a joke?" Minho said. "Did Thomas the boring slinthead actually make a joke?"

"I think he did" was Newt's response.

"I'm a funny guy," Thomas said with a shrug.

"Yeah, you are." But Minho obviously had already lost interest in the small talk. He twisted his head around to take in the rest of the Gladers, most of them asleep or lying still with blank looks on their faces. "How many?"

Thomas counted them up. Eleven. After all they'd been through, only eleven were left. And that included the new kid, Aris. Forty or fifty had lived in the Glade when Thomas first arrived, just a few weeks before. Now there were eleven.

Eleven.

He couldn't bring himself to say anything out loud after this realization, and the lighter moment only seconds earlier suddenly seemed like pure blasphemy. Like an abomination.

How could I be part of WICKED? he thought. *How could I have been any part of this?* He knew he should tell them about his memory-dreams, but he just couldn't.

"There's only eleven of us," Newt finally said. There. It was out.

"So, what, six died in the storm? Seven?" Minho sounded completely detached, as if he were counting how many apples they'd lost when the packs had blown away.

"Seven," Newt snapped, showing his disapproval of the cavalier attitude. Then, in a softer tone, "Seven. Unless people ran to a different building."

"Dude," Minho said. "How're we gonna fight our way through this city with only eleven people? There could be hundreds of Cranks in this place for all we know. Thousands. And we don't have a clue what to expect from them!"

Newt let out a big breath. "And that's all you can buggin' think about? What about the people who died, Minho? Jack's missing. So is Winston—he never had a chance. And"—he looked around—"I don't see Stan or Tim, either. What about them?"

"Whoa, whoa, whoa." Minho held his hands up, palms facing Newt. "Slim it nice and calm, brother. I didn't ask to be the shuck leader. You wanna cry all day about what's happened, fine. But that's not what a leader does. A leader figures out where to go and what to do after that's done."

"Well, guess that's why you got the job, then," Newt said. But then a look of apology washed over his face. "Whatever. Seriously, sorry. I just . . ."

"Yeah, I'm sorry, too." Minho rolled his eyes, though, and Thomas hoped against hope that Newt didn't notice because his gaze had fallen to the floor again.

Luckily Aris scooted over to join them. Thomas wanted the conversation to go in a different direction.

"Ever seen anything like that lightning storm?" the new kid asked.

Thomas shook his head because Aris was looking at him. "Didn't seem natural. Even in my klunky memories, I'm pretty sure stuff like that doesn't happen normally."

"But remember what the Rat Man said and that lady told you on the bus," Minho said. "Sun flares, and the whole world burning like hell itself. That'd screw up the climate plenty enough to make crazy storms like that pop up. I have a feeling we're lucky it wasn't worse."

"Not sure *lucky*'s the first word I'd think of," Aris said.

"Yeah, well."

Newt pointed at the broken glass of the door, where the glow of sunrise had brightened into the same white brilliance they'd grown accustomed to their first couple of days out in the Scorch. "Least it's over. We better start thinking about what we're gonna do next."

"See," Minho said. "You're just as heartless as me. And you're right."

Thomas remembered the image of the Cranks at the windows back at the dorm. Like living nightmares, missing only a death certificate to make them official zombies. "Yeah, we better figure things out before we have a bunch of those crazies show up. But I'm telling you, we gotta eat first. We gotta find food." The last word almost hurt, he wanted some so badly.

"Food?"

Thomas pulled in a gasp of surprise; the voice had come from above. He looked up just as the others did. A face looked down at them from the shredded remains of the third floor, that of a young Hispanic man. His eyes were slightly wild, and Thomas felt a belt of tension cinch inside him.

"Who're you?" Minho shouted.

Then, to Thomas's utter disbelief, the man jumped through the jagged hole in the ceilings, falling toward them. At the last second, he crumpled into a human ball and rolled three times, then sprang up and landed on his feet.

"My name is Jorge," he said, his arms outstretched as if he expected applause for his acrobatics. "And I'm the Crank who rules this place."

CHAPTER 26

For a second Thomas had a hard time believing that the guy who'd dropped in—literally—was real. He was so unexpected, and there was an odd silliness about what he'd said and the way he'd said it. But he was there, all right. And even though he didn't seem quite as gone as some of the others they'd seen, he'd already confessed to being a Crank.

"You people forget how to talk?" Jorge asked, a smile on his face that looked completely out of place in the shattered building. "Or you just scared of the Cranks? Scared we'll pull you to the ground and eat your eyeballs out? Mmm, tasty. I love a good eyeball when the grub's runnin' short. Tastes like undercooked eggs."

Minho took it on himself to answer, doing a great job of hiding his pain. "You admit you're a Crank? That you're freaking crazy?"

"He just said he likes the taste of eyeballs." This from Frypan. "I think that qualifies as crazy."

Jorge laughed, and there was a definite tone of menace in it. "Come, come, my new friends. I'd only eat your eyes if you were already dead. Course, I might help you get that way if I needed to. Understand what I'm saying?" All mirth vanished from his expression, replaced with a look of stern warning. Almost as if he was daring them to confront him.

No one spoke for a long moment. Then Newt asked, "How many of you are here?"

Jorge's gaze snapped to Newt. "How many? How many Cranks? We're all Cranks around here, *hermano.*"

"That's not what I meant and you know it," Newt replied flatly.

Jorge started pacing the room, stepping over and around Gladers, taking everyone in as he spoke. "Lot of things you people need to understand about how things work in this city. About the Cranks and WICKED, about the government, about why they left us here to rot in our disease, kill each other, go completely and utterly *insane.* About how there's different levels of the Flare. About how it's too late for you—the ill is gonna catch ya if you don't already have it."

Thomas had followed the stranger with his eyes as he walked around the room making these horrible statements. The Flare. He thought he'd gotten used to the fear of having the disease, but with this Crank standing right in front of him, he was more scared than ever. And helpless to do anything about it.

Jorge stopped near him and his friends, his feet almost touching Minho. He continued to talk.

"But that's not the way it's gonna work, *comprende?* Those who are at a disadvantage are those who speak first. I want to know everything about you. Where you came from, why you're here, what in God's name your purpose could be. Now."

Minho let out a low, dangerous-sounding chuckle. "We're the ones at a disadvantage?" Minho swiveled his head around mockingly. "Unless that lightning storm fried my retinas, I'd say there are eleven of us and one of you. Maybe *you* should start talking."

Thomas really wished Minho hadn't said that. It was stupid and arrogant, and it could very well get them killed. The guy obviously wasn't alone. There could be a hundred Cranks hiding out in the torn-up remains of the upper floors, spying on them, waiting with who-knew-what kind of horrific weapons. Or worse, the savagery of their own hands and teeth and madness.

Jorge looked at Minho for a long time, his face blank. "You didn't just say that to me, did you? Please tell me you didn't just speak to me like a dog. You have ten seconds to apologize."

Minho looked over at Thomas with a smirk.

"One," Jorge said. "Two. Three. Four."

Thomas tried to shoot a look of warning to Minho, nodded at him. *Do it.*

"Five. Six."

"Do it," Thomas finally said aloud.

"Seven. Eight."

Jorge's voice was rising with each number. Thomas thought he caught a glimpse of movement somewhere far above, just a blur of streaking shadow. Maybe Minho noticed it, too; any arrogance drained from his face.

"Nine."

"I'm sorry," Minho blurted out, with little feeling.

"I don't think you meant that," Jorge said. Then he kicked Minho in the leg.

Thomas's hands clenched into fists when his friend cried out in pain; the Crank must've gotten him right in a burnt spot.

"Say it with meaning, *hermano.*"

Thomas looked up at the Crank, hated him. Irrational thoughts started swimming through his mind—he wanted to jump up and attack, beat him like he'd beaten Gally after escaping the Maze.

Jorge pulled his leg back and kicked Minho again, twice as hard in the same spot. "Say it with *meaning*!" He screamed the last word with a harshness that sounded crazed.

Minho wailed, grabbing the wound with both hands. "I'm . . . sorry," he said between heavy breaths, his voice strained and full of pain. But as soon as Jorge smiled and relaxed, satisfied with the humiliation he'd inflicted, Minho swung an arm out and slammed it into the Crank's shin. The man leaped onto his other foot, then fell, crashing to the ground with his own yelp, a shriek that was half surprise, half hurt.

Then Minho was on top of him, yelling a string of obscenities Thomas had never heard come out of his friend before. Their leader squeezed his thighs to trap Jorge's body, then started punching.

"Minho!" Thomas shouted. "Stop!" He got to his feet, ignoring the stiffness in his joints, the soreness in his muscles. He took a quick glance upward as he made for Minho, ready to tackle him off Jorge's body. There was movement up there, in several places. Then he saw people looking down, people readying to jump. Ropes appeared, dangled over the sides of the jagged holes.

Thomas rammed into Minho, sent him sprawling off Jorge's body; they crashed to the ground. Thomas quickly spun to grab his friend, wrapped his arms around his chest and squeezed against his struggles to escape.

"There's more of them up there!" Thomas screamed in his ear from behind. "You have to stop! They'll kill you! They'll kill all of us!"

Jorge had staggered to his feet, slowly wiping a thin trail of blood from the corner of his mouth. The look on his face was enough to ram a spike of fear straight through Thomas's heart. There was no telling what the guy would do.

"Wait!" Thomas shouted. "Please, wait!"

Jorge made eye contact with him just as a few more Cranks dropped to the ground from above. Some of them did the jump-and-roll like Jorge had done; others slid down ropes and landed squarely on their feet. All of them quickly gathered in a pack behind their leader, maybe fifteen of them. Men and women; a few were teenagers. All filthy and dressed in tattered clothing. Most of them skinny and frail-looking.

Minho had quit fighting, and Thomas finally loosened his grip. By the looks of it, he had only a few seconds before a dire situation turned into a slaughterhouse. He pressed one hand firmly down on Minho's back, then held the other one up toward Jorge in a conciliatory gesture.

"Please give me a minute," Thomas said, urging his heart and voice to calm down. "Won't do you people any good to . . . hurt us."

"Won't do us any good?" the Crank said; he spit a wad of red goo from his mouth. "It'll do me a lot of good. That, I can guarantee, *hermano.*" He balled both hands into fists at his sides.

Then he cocked his head, barely enough to be noticed. But as soon as he did, the Cranks behind him pulled all kinds of nasty things from within the hidden depths of their ragged clothes. Knives. Rusted machetes. Black spikes that had maybe once been in a railroad somewhere. Shards of glass with red-tinged smudges on their razor-thin tips. One girl, who couldn't have been more than thirteen years old, held a splintered shovel, its metal scoop ending in a jagged edge like the teeth of a saw.

Thomas had the sudden and absolute certainty that he was now pleading for their lives. The Gladers couldn't win in a fight against these people. No way. They weren't Grievers, but there also wasn't a magic code to shut them down.

"Listen," Thomas said, slowly getting to his feet, hoping Minho wouldn't be stupid enough to try anything. "There's something about us. We're not just random shanks who showed up on your doorstep. We're valuable. Alive, not dead."

The anger on Jorge's face lessened ever so slightly. Maybe a spark of curiosity. But what he said was "What's a shank?"

Thomas almost—*almost*—laughed. An irrational response that somehow would've seemed appropriate. "Me and you. Ten minutes. Alone. That's all I ask. Bring all the weapons you need."

Jorge *did* laugh at that, more of a wet snort than anything. "Sorry to burst your bubble, kid, but I don't think I'll need any."

He paused, and it felt like the next few seconds lasted a full hour.

"Ten minutes," the Crank finally said. "Rest of you stay here, watch these punks. If I give the word, let the death games begin." He held a hand out, gesturing to a dark hallway that led from the room on the side across from the broken doors.

"Ten minutes," he repeated.

Thomas nodded. When Jorge didn't move, he went first, walking toward their meeting place and maybe the most important discussion of his life.

And maybe the last.

CHAPTER 27

Thomas felt Jorge at his heels as he entered the dark hallway. It smelled of mildew and rot; water dripped from the ceiling, sending out creepy echoes that for some awful reason made him think of blood.

"Just keep going," Jorge said from behind. "There's a room at the end with chairs. Make even the slightest move against me, everyone dies."

Thomas wanted to turn and scream at the guy but kept walking. "I'm not an idiot. You can quit the whole tough-guy routine."

The Crank only snickered in response.

After several minutes of quiet, Thomas finally approached a wooden door with a round silver knob. He reached out and opened it without hesitating, trying to show Jorge that he still had some dignity. Once inside, however, he didn't know what to do. It was pitch-black.

He sensed Jorge stepping around him; then there was the loud *flumping* sound of heavy cloth being whipped in the air. A hot, blinding light appeared, and Thomas had to shield his eyes with his forearms. He could only squint at first, then eventually dropped his arms and was able to see okay; he realized that the Crank had pulled a large sheet of canvas from a window. An unbroken window. Outside, there was only sunlight and concrete.

"Sit down," Jorge said, his voice less gruff than Thomas would've expected. He hoped it was because the Crank had finally accepted that his new visitor was going to take a rational and calm approach to their situation. That maybe there really was something to this discussion that could end up benefiting the current residents of the dilapidated building. Of course, the guy was a Crank, so Thomas had no idea how he'd react.

The room had no furniture other than two small wooden chairs and a table between them. Thomas pulled out the one closer to him and took a seat. Jorge sat down on the other side, then leaned forward and put his elbows on the table, hands clasped. His face was blank, his eyes glued on Thomas.

"Talk."

Thomas wished he could take a second to sift through all the ideas that had run through his mind back in the larger room, but he knew there wasn't any time for that.

"Okay." He hesitated. One word. So far, not so good. He pulled in a breath. "Look, I heard you mention WICKED back there. We know all about those guys. It'd be really interesting to hear what you have to say about them."

Jorge didn't budge; his expression didn't change. "I'm not the one talking right now. You are."

"Yeah, I know." Thomas scooted his chair a little closer to the table. Then he pushed it back and put a foot up on his knee. He needed to calm down and just let the words flow. "Well, this is hard because I don't know what you know. So I guess I'll just pretend like you're stupid to the whole thing."

"I'd strongly advise you never to use the word *stupid* with me again."

Thomas had to force himself to swallow, his throat tight with fear. "Just a figure of speech."

"Get on with it."

Thomas took another deep breath. "We used to be a group of about fifty guys. And . . . a girl." A prick of pain stuck him at that. "Now we're down to eleven. I don't know all the details, but WICKED is some kind of organization that's doing a whole load of nasty things to us for some reason. We started in a place called the Glade, inside a stone maze, surrounded by these creatures called Grievers."

He waited, searching Jorge's face for any reaction to his burst of strange information. But the Crank showed no signs of confusion or recognition. Nothing at all.

And so Thomas told him everything. What it had been like in the Maze, how they'd escaped, how they thought they were safe, how it ended up being just another layer of the WICKED plan. He told him about the Rat Man, and the mission he'd set them on: to survive long enough to make it one hundred miles to the north, to a place he referred to as the safe haven. He related how they'd gone down the long tunnel, been attacked by the flying silver goop, made the trek across the initial miles of their journey.

He told Jorge the whole story. And the more he talked, the crazier it seemed that he was sharing it. Yet he kept talking because he couldn't think of anything else to do. He did it with the hope that WICKED was just as much the Cranks' enemy as it was theirs.

He didn't mention Teresa, however—she was the only thing he left out.

"So there must be something special about us," Thomas said, trying to wrap things up. "They can't be doing this just to be nasty. What'd be the point?"

"Speaking of points," Jorge responded, the first he'd spoken in at least ten minutes, the allotted time already gone. "What's yours?"

Thomas waited. This was it. His only chance.

"Well?" Jorge pushed.

Thomas went for it. "If you . . . help us . . . I mean, if you, or maybe just a few of you, go *with* us and help us make it to the safe haven . . ."

"Yeah?"

"Then maybe you'll be safe, too. . . ." And this was what Thomas had planned all along—had been building toward—the hope strung out by the Rat Man. "They told us we have the Flare. And that if we make it to the safe haven, we'll all be cured. They said they have a cure. If you help us get there, maybe you can get it, too." Thomas stopped talking and looked at Jorge earnestly.

Something had changed—slightly—in the Crank's face at that last thing he'd said, and Thomas knew he had won. The look was brief, but it was definitely *hope,* quickly replaced with a blank indifference. Yet Thomas knew what he'd seen.

"A cure," the Crank repeated.

"A cure." Thomas was determined to say as little as possible from here on out—he'd done his best.

Jorge leaned back in his chair, the wood creaking as if about to break, and folded his arms. He lowered his eyebrows in a look of contemplation. "What's your name?"

Thomas was surprised by the question. Felt sure, in fact, that he'd already told him. Or at least it seemed like he should have told him at some point. But then again, this whole scenario wasn't exactly your typical get-acquainted affair.

"Your *name*?" Jorge repeated. "I'm assuming you have one, *hermano*."

"Oh. Yeah. Sorry. It's Thomas."

Another flash across Jorge's face—this time something like . . . recognition. Mixed with surprise. "Thomas, huh. You go by Tommy? Tom, maybe?"

That last one hurt, made him think of his dream about Teresa. "No," he said, probably a little too quickly. "Just . . . Thomas."

"Okay, Thomas. Let me ask you something. Do you have the slightest clue in that squishy brain of yours what the Flare does to people? Do I look like someone who has a hideous disease to you?"

That seemed an impossible question to answer without getting your face beaten in, but Thomas went with the safest bet. "No."

"No? No to both questions?"

"Yes. I mean, no. I mean . . . yes, the answer to both questions is no."

Jorge smiled—nothing but an uptick of the right corner of his mouth—and Thomas thought he must be enjoying every second of this. "The Flare works in stages, *muchacho*. Every person in this city has it, and I'm not shocked to hear that you and your sissy friends do, too. Someone like me is in the beginning, a Crank in name only. I caught it just a few weeks ago, tested positive at the quarantine checkpoint—government's trying their damnedest to keep the sick and the well separate. Ain't working. Saw my whole world go straight in the crap hole. Was sent here. Fought to capture this building with a bunch of other newbies."

At that word, Thomas's breath caught in his throat like a mote of dust. It brought back too many memories of the Glade.

"My friends out there with the weapons are all in the same boat as me. But you go and take a nice stroll around the city and you'll see what happens as time goes by. You'll see the stages, see what it's like to be past the Gone, though you might not live to remember it for very long. And we don't even have any of the numbing agent here. The Bliss. None."

"Who sent you here?" Thomas asked, saving his curiosity about this numbing agent for later.

"WICKED—same as you. Only we're not *special* like you say you are. WICKED was set up by the surviving governments to fight the disease, and they claim that this city has something to do with it. Don't know much else."

Thomas felt a mixture of surprise and confusion, then a hope for answers. "Who *is* WICKED? *What* is WICKED?"

Jorge looked just about as confused as Thomas felt. "I told you all I know. Why're you asking me that, anyway? I thought the whole point here was that you were special to them, that they were behind this whole story you told me."

"Look, everything I told you is the honest truth. We've been promised things, but we still don't know much about them. They don't give us any details. Like they're testing us to see if we can make it through all this klunk even though we have no idea what's happening."

"And what makes you think they have a cure?"

Now Thomas had to keep his voice steady, think back to what he'd heard from the Rat Man. "The guy in the white suit I told you about. He told us it's why we have to make it to the safe haven."

"Mmm-hmm," Jorge said, one of those noises that sounded like a yes but meant exactly the opposite. "And what in the world makes you think they'll let us just ride in on a horse with you and get the cure, too?"

Thomas had to keep playing it nice and calm. "Obviously I don't know that at all. But why not at least try? If you help us get there, you have a small chance. If you kill us, you have zero chance. Only a full-gone Crank would choose the second option."

Jorge gave that pathetic smile again, then let out a small bark of a laugh. "There's something about you, Thomas. Few minutes ago I wanted to stab your friend in the eyeballs and then do the same to the rest of ya. But I'll be licked if you haven't half convinced me."

Thomas shrugged, trying to keep his face calm. "All I care about is surviving one more day. All I want is to make it through this city, and then I'll worry about what comes next. And you know what else?" He braced himself to act tougher than he felt.

Jorge raised his eyebrows. "What's that?"

"If stabbing *you* in the eyeballs could get me to tomorrow, I'd do it right now. But I need you. We all need you." Thomas wondered if he could ever actually do such a thing even as he said it.

But it worked.

The Crank eyed Thomas for a drawn-out moment, then stuck out a hand across the table. "I believe we have ourselves a deal, *hermano*. For many reasons."

Thomas reached out and shook. And even though he was filled with relief, it took everything he had not to show it.

But then Jorge brought it all crashing down. "I just have one condition. That ratty kid who junked me on the ground? Think I heard you call him Minho?"

"Yeah?" Thomas asked in a weak voice, his heart thumping all over again.

"He dies."

CHAPTER 28

"No."

Thomas said it with every ounce of finality and firmness he could muster.

"No?" Jorge repeated with a look of surprise. "I offer you a chance to make it through a city full of vicious Cranks ready to eat you alive, and you say no? To my one little itsy-bitsy request? That does not make me happy."

"It wouldn't be smart," Thomas said. He had no idea how he was able to maintain his calm expression, where this bravery was coming from. But something told him it was the only way he could survive with this Crank.

Jorge leaned forward again, placed his elbows on the table. But this time he didn't clasp his hands; instead, he balled them into fists. His knuckles cracked. "Is it your goal in life to piss me off until I cut your arteries open one by one?"

"You saw what he did to you," Thomas countered. "You know the guts that took. If you kill him, you lose the skills he brings. He's our best fighter, and he's not scared of anything. Maybe he's crazy, but we need him."

Thomas was trying to sound so practical. Pragmatic. But if there was a person other than Teresa on the planet he could truly call a friend, it was Minho. And he couldn't handle losing him, too.

"But he made me *angry,*" Jorge said tightly; his fists had not relaxed in the slightest. "He made me look like a little girl in front of my people. And that's not . . . acceptable."

Thomas shrugged like he didn't care, like it was a small and meaningless point. "So punish him. Make *him* look like a little girl. But killing him doesn't help us. The more bodies we have that can fight, the better our chances. I mean, you *live* here. Do I really need to tell you this?"

Finally, *finally,* Jorge loosened his white-knuckled grips. He also let out a breath that Thomas hadn't realized he'd been holding.

"Okay," the Crank said. "Okay. But it has nothing to do with your lame attempt to talk me into it. I'll spare him because I just made up my mind about something. Because of two reasons, actually. One of which you should have thought of yourself."

"What?" Thomas didn't mind his relief showing anymore—the effort to hide things was exhausting him. Plus, he was now too intrigued by what Jorge had to say.

"First off, you don't really know all the details behind this test or experiment or whatever it is that WICKED is putting you through. Maybe the more of you that make it back—to that safe haven—the better chances you have of getting the cure. Ever thought that this Group B you mentioned are probably your competitors? I think it's in my best interests to make sure all eleven of you make it now."

Thomas nodded, but didn't say anything. He didn't want to take the slightest chance of ruining the victory here: Jorge believed him about the Rat Man and the cure.

"Which leads to my second reason," he continued. "The thing I've made up my mind about."

"And what's that?" Thomas asked.

"I'm not taking all those Cranks out there with me. With *us*."

"Huh? Why? I thought the whole point was that you guys could help us fight our way through the city."

Jorge adamantly shook his head as he leaned back in his chair and assumed a much less threatening position, folding his arms across his chest. "No. If we're gonna do this, stealth will work way better than muscle. We've been sneaking around this hellhole ever since we got here, and I think our chances of making it through—and getting all the food and supplies we need—are way better if we take what we've learned and use it. Tiptoe our way past the long-gone-crazy Cranks instead of slashing through them like a bunch of wannabe warriors."

"You're hard to figure out," Thomas said. "Not to be rude, but it sure seems like warriors are exactly what you guys want to be. Ya know, based on all the ugly outfits and sharp things."

A long moment of silence passed, and Thomas was just starting to think he'd made a mistake when Jorge burst out laughing.

"Oh, *muchacho,* you're one lucky sucker I like you. Not sure why, but I do. Otherwise I would've killed you three times already."

"Can you do that?" Thomas asked.

"Huh?"

"Kill someone three times."

"I'd figure out a way."

"Then I'll try to be nicer."

Jorge slapped the table and stood up. "Okay. So here's the deal. We need to get all eleven of you punks to your safe haven. To do it, I'm only taking one other person—her name is Brenda, and she's a genius. We need her mind. And if we do make it, and it ends up that there's no cure for us, then I don't think I need to tell you what the consequences will be."

"Come on," Thomas said sarcastically. "I thought we were friends now."

"Pshh. We ain't friends, *hermano*. We're partners. I'll deliver you to WICKED. You get me a cure. That's the deal or there's gonna be a lot of death."

Thomas stood as well; his chair creaked against the floor. "We already agreed on that, didn't we?"

"Yeah. Yeah, we did. Now listen, don't you dare say a word out there. Getting away from those other Cranks is gonna be . . . tricky."

"What's the plan?"

Jorge thought for a minute, his eyes glued to Thomas as he did. Then he broke his silence. "Just keep your tongue-hole shut and let me do my thing." He started to move toward the door to the hallway, but stopped short. "Oh, and I don't think your *compadre* Minho is going to like it very much."

As they walked down the hallway to join the others, Thomas realized how achingly hungry he was. The cramps in his stomach had spread to the rest of his body, as if his internal organs and muscles were starting to eat each other.

"All right, everybody listen!" Jorge announced when they reentered the large torn-up room. "Me and the bird-face here have come to a resolution."

Bird face? Thomas thought.

The Cranks still stood at attention, nasty weapons gripped tightly, glaring at the Gladers, all of whom sat around the edges of the space, backs against the walls. Light beamed through the shattered windows and holes above.

Jorge came to a stop in the middle of the room and slowly turned to address the whole group. Thomas thought he looked ridiculous—like he was trying too hard.

"First, we need to get these people food. I know it seems crazy to share our hard-earned grub with a bunch of strangers, but I think we could use their help. Give 'em the pork and beans—I'm sick of that horse crap anyway." One of the Cranks snickered, a skinny runt of a kid whose eyes darted back and forth. "Second, being the grand gentleman and saint that I am, I've decided not to kill the punk who attacked me."

Thomas heard a few disappointed groans break out and wondered just how far along some of these people were with the Flare. But one girl, a pretty, older teenager with long hair that was surprisingly clean, rolled her eyes and shook her head as if she thought the noise was idiotic. Thomas found himself hoping she was the Brenda girl Jorge had mentioned.

Jorge pointed at Minho, who, not shockingly to Thomas at all, smiled and waved at the crowd.

"Pretty happy, are you?" Jorge grunted. "That's good to know. Means you'll take the news well."

"What news?" Minho asked sharply.

Thomas glanced over at Jorge, wondering what was about to come out of the guy's mouth.

The Crank leader spoke matter-of-factly. "After we get you stragglers fed so you don't go dying of starvation on us, you get to have your punishment for attacking me."

"Oh yeah?" If Minho was scared, he didn't show any sign of it. "And what's that gonna be?"

Jorge just stared back at Minho—a blank expression spread eerily across his face. "You punched me with both of your fists. So we're gonna cut a finger off each hand."

CHAPTER 29

Thomas didn't understand at all how threatening to cut off Minho's fingers was going to set the groundwork for them escaping from the rest of the Cranks. And he certainly wasn't stupid enough to trust Jorge after just one brief meeting. He began to panic that things were about to go terribly, horribly wrong.

But then Jorge looked at him, even as his Crank friends started to hoot and holler, and there was something there, in his eyes. Something that put Thomas at ease.

Minho, on the other hand, was a different story. He'd stood up as soon as Jorge had pronounced his punishment, and would've charged if the pretty girl hadn't stepped right up to him and placed her blade under his chin. It drew a drop of blood, bright red in the daylight pouring through the busted doors. He couldn't even talk without risking serious bodily harm.

"Here's the plan," Jorge said calmly. "Brenda and I will escort these moochers to the stash, let 'em eat up. Then we'll all meet on the Tower, let's say one hour from now." He looked at his watch. "Make that noon on the dot. We'll bring up lunch for the rest of you."

"Why just you and Brenda?" someone asked. Thomas didn't see who at first, then realized a man had said it—probably the oldest person in the room. "What if they jump you? There's eleven of them to two of you."

Jorge squinted—a scoffing look. "Thanks for the math lesson, Barkley. Next time I forget how many toes I have, I'll be sure and spend some counting time with you. For now, shut your flappin' lips and lead everybody to the Tower. If these punks try anything, Brenda will slash Mr. Minho to tiny bits while I beat the living hell out of the rest of 'em. They can barely stand they're so weak. Now *get*!"

Relief swam through Thomas. Once separated from the others, surely Jorge meant to run. Surely he didn't mean to go through with the punishment.

The man named Barkley was old but looked tough, veined muscles stretching the sleeves of his shirt. He held a nasty dagger in one hand and a big hammer in the other. "Fine," he said after a long stare down with his leader. "But if they do jump you and slit your throat, we'll get along just fine without ya."

"Thanks for the kind words, *hermano*. Now get, or we'll have double the fun on the Tower."

Barkley laughed as if to salvage some dignity, then started off down the same hallway Thomas and Jorge had used. He waved his arm in a "follow me" gesture and soon every last Crank was shuffling after him except Jorge and the pretty girl with the long brown hair. She still had her knife at Minho's neck, but the good part was that she had to be Brenda.

Once the main group of Flare-infected people left the room, Jorge shared an almost relieved look with Thomas; then he subtly shook his head, as if the others might still be able to hear them.

Movement from Brenda grabbed Thomas's attention. He looked to see her drop the knife away from Minho and step back, absently wiping the small trace of blood there on her pants. "I really would've killed you, ya know," she said in a slightly scratchy voice. Almost husky. "Charge Jorge again and I'll sever an artery."

Minho wiped at his small wound with a thumb, then looked at the bright red smear. "That's one sharp knife. Makes me like you more."

Newt and Frypan groaned simultaneously.

"Looks like I'm not the only Crank standing here," Brenda responded. "You're even more gone than me."

"None of us are crazy yet," Jorge added, walking over to stand next to her. "But it won't be long. Come on. We need to get over to the stash and put some food in you people. You all look like a bunch of starved zombies."

Minho didn't seem to like the idea. "You think I'm just gonna waltz over to have a sit-down with you psychos, then let you cut my freaking fingers off?"

"Just shut up for once," Thomas snapped, trying to communicate something different with his eyes. "Let's go eat. I don't care what happens to your beautiful hands after that."

Minho squinted in confusion, but seemed to pick up that something was off. "Whatever. Let's go."

Brenda stepped in front of Thomas unexpectedly, her face only a few inches from his. She had eyes so dark it made the whites seem to glow brightly. "You the leader?"

Thomas shook his head. "No—it's the guy you just nipped with your knife."

Brenda looked over at Minho, then back at Thomas. She grinned. "Well, then that's stupid. I know I'm on the verge of crazy, but I would've picked you. You seem like the leader type."

"Um, thanks." Thomas felt a rush of embarrassment, then remembered Minho's tattoo. Remembered his own, how he was supposed to be killed. He scrambled to say something to hide his sudden mood shift. "I, uh, would've picked you, too, instead of Jorge over there."

The girl leaned forward and kissed Thomas on the cheek. "You're sweet. I really hope we don't end up killing you, at least."

"All right." Jorge was already motioning everyone toward the broken doors that led outside. "Enough of this lovefest. Brenda, we have a lot to talk about once we get to the stash. Come on, let's go."

Brenda didn't take her eyes off Thomas. As for him, he still felt the tingle that had shot through his entire body when she'd touched him with her lips.

"I like you," she said.

Thomas swallowed, his mind empty of a comeback. Brenda's tongue touched the corner of her mouth and she grinned, then finally turned away from him and walked to the doors, slipping her knife into a pants pocket. "Let's go!" she yelled without looking back.

Thomas knew every single Glader was staring at him, but he refused to make eye contact with any of them. Instead, he hitched up his shirt and walked forward, not caring about the slight smile on his face. Soon the others fell into step behind him, and the group exited the building and emerged into the white heat of the sun beating down on the broken pavement outside.

Brenda led while Jorge took up the rear. Thomas had a hard time adjusting to the brightness, shielding his eyes and squinting as they walked close to the wall to stay in the scant shade. The other buildings and streets around him seemed to shine with unearthly luminescence, as if they were made of some sort of magic stone.

Brenda moved along the walls of the structure they'd just exited until they reached what Thomas thought must be the back. There, a set of steps disappeared into the pavement, reminding him of something in his past life. An entrance to some kind of underground train system, perhaps.

She didn't hesitate. Without waiting to make sure the others were behind her, she bounced down the stairs. But Thomas noticed that the knife had reappeared in her right hand, gripped tightly and held a few inches from the side of her body—a stealthy attempt at being ready to attack—or defend—on a moment's notice.

He followed her, eager to get out of the sun and, more importantly, make it to food. His insides ached more strongly for sustenance with every step he took. In fact, he was surprised he could still move; the weakness was like a poisonous growth inside him, replacing his vital parts with a painful cancer.

Darkness swallowed them eventually, welcome and cool. Thomas followed the sound of Brenda's footsteps until they reached a small doorway, through which shone a glow of orange. She went inside, and Thomas hesitated at the threshold. It was a small, damp room full of boxes and cans, with a single lightbulb hanging from the center of the ceiling. It looked far too cramped for all of them to enter.

Brenda must've sensed his thoughts. "You and the others can stay out there in the hallway, find a wall and sit. I'll start bringing out some tasty delights for you in a sec."

Thomas nodded even though she wasn't looking and stumbled back out into the hallway. He collapsed next to a wall down a ways from the rest of the Gladers, deeper into the darkness of the tunnel. And he knew for certain he'd never get back up unless he ate something.

The "tasty delights" ended up being canned beans and some type of sausage—according to Brenda, the words on the label were in Spanish. They ate it cold, but it tasted like the grandest meal ever to Thomas, and he devoured every bite. They'd already learned it wasn't smart to eat quickly after such a long period of fasting, but he didn't care. If he threw it all up, he'd just enjoy eating all over again. Hopefully a fresh batch.

After Brenda passed out the food to the starving Gladers, she walked over to sit by Thomas, the soft glow from the room illuminating the thin strands on the fringes of her dark hair. She set down a couple of backpacks—filled with more of the cans—at her side.

"One of these is for you," she said.

"Thanks." Thomas had already reached the bottom half of his can, scooping out one bite after another. No one spoke down the hall from them; the only sounds were slurping and swallowing.

"Taste good?" she asked as she dug into her own food.

"Please. I'd push my own mom down the stairs to eat this stuff. If I still *have* a mom." He couldn't help thinking of his dream and the brief glimpse he'd seen of her, but did his best to forget it—it was too depressing.

"You get sick of it fast," Brenda said, pulling Thomas out of his head. He noticed the way she sat, her right knee pressed against his shin, and his thoughts jumped to the ridiculous idea that she'd moved her leg like that on purpose. "We only have about four or five options."

Thomas concentrated on clearing his mind, bringing his thoughts back to the present. "Where'd you get the food? And how much is left?"

"Before this area got scorched by the flares, this city had several food manufacturing plants, plus a lot of warehouses to hold the food. Sometimes I think that's why WICKED sends Cranks here. They can at least tell themselves that we won't starve while we slowly go crazy and kill each other."

Thomas scooped out the last bit of sauce from the bottom of his can and licked his spoon clean. "If there's plenty, why do you only have a few options?" He had the thought that maybe they'd trusted her too quickly, that they could be eating poison. But she was eating the same food, so his worries were probably far-fetched.

Brenda pointed toward the ceiling with her thumb. "We've only scoured the closest ones. Some company that specialized, not much variety. *I'd* kill your mother for something fresh out of a garden. A nice salad."

"Guess my mom doesn't have much of a chance if she's ever standing between us and a grocery store."

"Guess not."

She smiled then, though a shadow mostly hid her face. The grin still shone through, and Thomas found himself liking this girl. She'd just drawn blood from his best friend, but he liked her. Maybe, in small part, because of that.

"Does the world still have grocery stores?" he asked. "I mean, what's it like out there after all this Flare business? Really hot, with a bunch of crazy people running around?"

"No. Well, I don't know. The sun flares killed a lot of people before they could escape to the north or south. My family lived in northern Canada. My parents were some of the first ones to make it to the camps set up by the coalition between governments. The people who ended up forming WICKED later."

Thomas stared for a second, his mouth wide open. She'd just revealed more to him about the state of the world in those few sentences than anything he'd heard since having his memory wiped.

"Wait . . . wait a second," he said. "I need to hear all this. Can you start from the beginning?"

Brenda shrugged. "Not much to tell—happened a long time ago. The sun flares were completely unexpected and unpredictable, and by the time the scientists tried to warn anyone, it was way too late. They wiped out half the planet, killed everything around the equatorial regions. Changed climates everywhere else. The survivors gathered, some governments combined. Wasn't too long before they discovered that a nasty virus had been unleashed from some disease-control place. Called it the Flare right from the beginning."

"Man," Thomas muttered. He looked down the hall at the other Gladers, wondering if they'd heard any of this, but none of them seemed to be listening, all absorbed in their food. They were probably too far away anyway. "When did—"

She shushed him, holding a hand up. "Wait," she said. "Something's wrong. I think we have visitors."

Thomas hadn't heard anything, and the other Gladers didn't seem to notice, either. But Jorge was already at Brenda's side, whispering something in her ear. She was just moving to stand up when a crash exploded down the hall—from the stairs they'd used to reach the stash. It was a horribly loud sound, the crumple and cracking of a structure falling apart, cement breaking, metal ripping. A cloud of dust fogged its way toward them, choking off the scant light from the food room.

Thomas sat and stared, paralyzed by fear. He could just see Minho and Newt and all the others running back toward the destroyed stairs, then turning down a branching hallway he hadn't noticed before. Brenda grabbed him by the shirt and pulled him to his feet.

"Run!" she screamed, and started dragging him away from the destruction and deeper into the underground.

Thomas snapped out of his stupor and swatted at her hand, though she didn't let go. "No! We have to follow my fr—"

Before he could finish, an entire section of the roof came crashing down onto the floor in front of him, blocks of cement falling on top of each other with thunderous cracks. It cut him off from the direction his friends had taken. He heard more fracturing of rock above him and realized that he no longer had any choice—or any time.

Reluctantly he turned and ran with Brenda, her hand still clutching his shirt as they sprinted into the darkness.

CHAPTER 30

Thomas didn't notice his heart pounding, or have time to contemplate what could possibly have caused the explosion. All he could think about were the other Gladers, now separated from him. Blind, he ran with Brenda—forced to entrust his life to her completely.

"Here!" she yelled. They made a sharp turn to the right; he almost stumbled and fell but she helped him stay on his feet. Once he had a good pace, she finally let go of his shirt. "Stick close to me."

The sounds of destruction behind them faded as they ran down this new path, and panic lit up inside Thomas. "What about my friends? What if—"

"Just keep going! Better for everyone to split up anyway."

The air cooled as they moved farther down the long hallway. The darkness deepened. Thomas felt his strength slowly returning and he caught his breath quickly. Behind them, the noises had almost stopped. He worried about the Gladers, but instinct told him it was okay to stay with Brenda—that his friends would be able to fend for themselves if they'd gotten out. But what if some of them had been captured by whoever had set off the explosion? Or killed? And who had attacked them? Concern seemed to bleed his heart dry as they ran along.

Brenda took three more turns; Thomas had no idea how she could know where she was going. He was just about to ask when she stopped, putting a hand to his chest to hold him back.

"You hear anything?" she said through huffs.

Thomas listened, but all he heard was their own breathing. Everything else was silence and darkness. "No," he told her. "Where are we?"

"A bunch of tunnels and secret passages connect the buildings on this side of town, maybe across the whole city—we haven't explored that far yet. They call it the Underneath."

Thomas couldn't see her face, but she was close enough that he felt and smelled her breath. It didn't reek, which surprised him, considering her living conditions. It kind of had a nonscent, somehow pleasant.

"The Underneath?" he repeated. "Sounds stupid."

"Well, I didn't name it."

"How much of it *have* you explored?" He didn't like the idea of running around down there without knowing what was ahead.

"Not much. We usually run into Cranks. The really bad ones. Way past Gone."

This made Thomas turn in a circle, searching the darkness for he didn't know what. His whole body tensed with fear as if he'd just jumped into ice water. "Well . . . are we safe? What happened with that explosion, anyway? We need to go back and find my friends."

"What about Jorge?"

"Huh?"

"Shouldn't we go find Jorge, too?"

Thomas hadn't meant to offend her. "Yeah, Jorge, my friends, all those shanks. We can't leave them behind."

"What's a shank?"

"Never mind. Just . . . what do you think happened back there?"

She sighed and stepped even closer to him, pressing her chest against his. He felt her lips brushing his ear as she spoke. "I want you to promise me something." She said it softly, in barely more than a whisper.

Chills broke out all over Thomas's body. "Um . . . what?"

She didn't pull back, just kept speaking into his ear. "No matter what happens, even if we have to go alone, you'll take me all the way back. All the way to WICKED, to that cure you promised Jorge—he told me about it in the storage room. I can't stay here and slowly go insane. I can't do it. I'd rather die."

She grabbed both of his hands in hers, squeezed. Then she rested her head on his shoulder, her nose nestled against his neck—she had to be standing on the tips of her toes. Each breath from her sent a new wave of chills across his skin.

Thomas was enjoying her being so close, but it seemed so bizarre and out of the blue. Then he had a surge of guilt, thinking of Teresa. All this was stupid. He was in the middle of a brutal and ruthless attempt to make it across a wasteland, his life on the line, his friends maybe dead. Teresa could even be dead. To sit here and cuddle with some strange girl in the dark was about the most absurd thing he could think of.

"Hey," he said. He wiggled his hands from her grip and grabbed her upper arms, pushed her away. He still couldn't see anything, but he imagined her there, looking at him. "Don't you think we need to figure things out?"

"You still haven't promised me," she replied.

Thomas wanted to scream, couldn't believe how strange she was acting. "Fine, I promise. Did Jorge tell you everything?"

"Mostly, I think. Though I'd already guessed it the second he told our group to go on without us and meet at the Tower."

"Guessed what?"

"That we were going to help you get through the city in exchange for you taking us back to civilization."

This made Thomas worry. "If you came up with that so quickly, don't you think some of your friends did, too?"

"Exactly."

"What do you mean *exactly*? Sounds like you figured something out."

She reached out and placed her hands on his chest. "I think that's what happened. At first I worried it was a group of longer-gone Cranks, but since no one chased us, I think Barkley and a couple of his buddies rigged an explosion at the Underneath entrance, tried to kill us. They know they can get plenty of food somewhere else, and there're other ways to get down here."

Thomas still didn't understand why she was being so touchy with him. "That doesn't make sense. I mean, kill us? Wouldn't they want to use us, too? Come with us?"

"No, no, no. Barkley and the others are happy here. I think they're a little more gone than we are, starting to lose their rational sides. I doubt the idea even occurred to them. I bet they just thought we were all gonna gang up and . . . eliminate them. That we were making plans down here."

Thomas let go of her, leaned his head back against the wall. She pressed in again and wrapped her arms around his middle.

"Uh . . . Brenda?" he asked. Something wasn't right with this girl.

"Yeah?" she mumbled against his chest.

"What are you doing?"

"What do you mean?"

"Don't you think it's a little weird how you're acting?"

She laughed, such an unexpected sound that Thomas thought for a second she'd succumbed to the Flare—become a full-blown Crank or something. She pulled away from him, still chuckling.

"What?" he asked.

"Nothing," she said through a schoolgirl snicker. "Guess we came from different places, that's all. Sorry."

"What do you mean?" He suddenly found himself wishing she'd hug him again.

"Don't worry about it," she said, her merriment at his expense finally subsiding. "Sorry for being so forward. It's just . . . pretty normal where I come from."

"No . . . it's okay. I . . . I mean, good that. I'm good." He was glad she couldn't see his face, because it must've burned so red she'd start laughing all over again.

He thought of Teresa then. He thought of Minho and the others. He had to take control. Now.

"Look, you said it yourself," he said, trying to pump confidence into his voice. "No one chased us. We need to go back."

"Are you sure?" She had a suspicious tone.

"What do you mean?"

"I could get you through the city. Find enough food to take with us. Why don't we leave all of them? Make it to this safe haven place on our own?"

Thomas wasn't going to have this conversation. "If you won't come back with me, fine. But I'm going." He put his hand against the wall to guide himself and started walking in the direction from which they'd fled.

"Wait!" she called out, then caught up to him. She grabbed his hand and intertwined their fingers, now walking alongside him, hand in hand like old lovers. "I'm sorry. Really. I just . . . I think it would be easier to make it through with fewer people. I'm not really great friends with any of those Cranks. Not like you and your . . . Gladers."

Had he said that word around her? He didn't remember, but anybody could've at some point without his noticing. "I really think as many of us as possible need to make it to the safe haven. Even if we do get past the city, who knows what'll be next. Maybe then we'll really want numbers."

He thought about what he'd just said. Did he really only care about having numbers in the end so they'd have a better chance to be safe? Was he really that detached?

"Okay" was all she said in response. Something had changed in her. She seemed less confident. Less in charge.

Thomas took his hand from her grip, coughing into it as an excuse. He didn't reach out for her again when he finished.

They didn't talk for the next few minutes. He followed her, sensing her even though he still couldn't see. After several turns, a light appeared up ahead, brightening quickly as they approached.

It turned out to be sunlight, pouring down from jagged holes in the roof—the aftermath of the explosion. Massive chunks of rock and twisted pieces of steel and broken pipes blocked the way to where the stairs had been—and it looked like climbing over the wreckage would be dangerous. A haze of dust clouded everything, making the rays of sunshine appear thick and alive, motes dancing like gnats. The air smelled of plaster and something burnt.

They were also blocked from the stash room with all that food, but Brenda found the two backpacks she'd brought out earlier.

"Doesn't look like anybody's here," she said. "They didn't come back. Jorge and your friends might've even gotten back up and outside somehow."

Thomas didn't really know what he'd been hoping to find, but at least one piece of good news was obvious. "No bodies, though, right? No one died in the explosion?"

Brenda shrugged. "Cranks could've dragged their bodies off. But I doubt it. No point."

Thomas nodded, as if solidifying her statement, holding on to it. But he had no idea what to do next. Did they go through the tunnels—the Underneath—searching for the other Gladers? Did they go out into the streets? Back to the building where they'd ditched Barkley and the others? Every idea sounded horrible. He looked around, as if the answer would magically present itself.

"We have to go through the Underneath," Brenda announced after a long moment; she'd probably been contemplating their options just like Thomas. "If the others went up top, then they'll be long gone by now. Plus, they'll pull any attention toward themselves and away from us."

"And if they're down here we'll find them, right?" Thomas asked. "These tunnels all come back together eventually, right?"

"Right. Either way, I know Jorge will have them moving toward the other side of the city, toward the mountains. We just have to make it so we can meet up and keep going."

Thomas looked at Brenda, thinking. Maybe only pretending to think, because he really had no option than to stick with her. She was probably his best—maybe only—bet of accomplishing anything other than a quick and horrible death at the hands of long-gone Cranks. What else *could* he do?

"Okay," he said. "Let's go."

She smiled, a sweet smile that shone through the grime on her face, and Thomas unexpectedly longed for that moment they'd had in the darkness together. Almost as quickly as his thought formed, though, it was gone. Brenda handed him one of the backpacks, then reached into hers and pulled out a flashlight, clicked it on. The beam shot through the dust as she shone it this way and that, finally aiming it down the long tunnel they'd already been down twice.

"Shall we?" she asked.

"We shall," Thomas muttered. He still felt sick about his friends, and he wondered if he was doing the right thing sticking with Brenda.

But when she started walking, he followed.

CHAPTER 31

The Underneath was a dank, miserable place. Thomas almost preferred the utter darkness to being able to see what was around him. The walls and floors were dull gray, nothing more than painted concrete, streaks of water trickling down the sides here and there. They passed a door every few dozen feet, but most of them were locked when he tried them. Dust coated the long-dark light fixtures on the ceiling, at least half of them busted, jagged glass screwed into rusty holes.

All in all, the place had the feel of a haunted tomb. The Underneath was as good a name as any. He wondered what the underground structure had been built for in the first place. Walkways and offices for who knew what kinds of jobs? Paths between buildings on rainy days? Emergency routes? *Escape* routes for things like massive sun flares and attacks from crazy people?

They didn't talk much as he followed Brenda through tunnel after tunnel, sometimes turning left at intersections or forks, sometimes turning right. His body quickly consumed any energy provided by his recent binge, and after walking for what felt like several hours he finally convinced her to stop and eat another meal.

"I'm assuming you know where we're going," he said to her when they set off again. Everything they passed looked exactly the same to him. Drab and dark. Dusty, where it wasn't wet. The tunnels were silent but for the distant drops of water and the swishing of their clothes as they walked. Their footsteps, dull thumps on the concrete.

She suddenly stopped and whirled on him, shining the light on her face from below. "Boo," she whispered.

Thomas jumped, then pushed her away. "Cut that crap," he yelled. He felt like an idiot—his heart had just about exploded from fright. "Makes you look like a . . ."

She let the flashlight fall to her side, but her eyes remained locked on his. "Look like a what?"

"Nothing."

"A *Crank*?"

The word cut to Thomas's heart. He didn't want to think of her that way. "Well . . . yeah," he murmured. "Sorry."

She turned from him and started walking again, her light shining forward. "I *am* a Crank, Thomas. Got the Flare, I'm a Crank. You are, too."

He had to run a few steps to catch up with her. "Yeah, but you're not full gone yet. And . . . me neither, right? We'll get the cure before we go nuts." The Rat Man had better have been telling the truth.

"Can't wait. And yeah, by the way. I do know where we're going. Thanks for checking."

They kept going, turn after turn, long tunnel after long tunnel. The slow but steady exercise took Thomas's thoughts off Brenda and made him feel better than he had in days. His mind drifted into a half-daze, thinking about the Maze and his splotchy memories and Teresa. Mostly about Teresa.

Eventually they entered a large room with quite a few exits branching off to the left and right, more than he'd seen previously. It almost seemed like it could be a gathering place joined by tunnels from all the buildings.

"Is this the center of the city or something?" he asked.

Brenda stopped to rest, sitting down on the ground with her back to the wall; Thomas joined her.

"More or less," she answered. "See? Already made it halfway to the other side of the city."

Thomas liked the sound of that, but he hated to think of the others. Minho, Newt, all the Gladers. Where were they? He felt like such a shuck-face for not looking for them, seeing if they were in trouble. Could they have already made it safely outside of town?

A loud pop startled Thomas, like a glass bulb breaking.

Brenda immediately shone her light back in the direction from which they'd come, but the hallway disappeared in shadow, empty except for a few ugly streaks of water on the walls, black on gray.

"What was that?" Thomas whispered.

"An old light busting, I guess." Her voice held no concern. She put her flashlight on the ground so it shone on the wall opposite them.

"Why would an old light just spontaneously break?"

"I don't know. A rat?"

"I haven't seen any rats. Plus, how would a rat walk on the ceiling?"

She gazed at him, a look of total mocking on her face. "You're right. It must be a *flying* rat. We should get the hell out of here."

A small, nervous laugh escaped before Thomas could stop it. "Hilarious."

Another pop, this time followed by the tinkle of glass sprinkling on the floor. It had definitely come from behind them—Thomas was sure of it this time. Someone had to be following them. And it couldn't be the Gladers—it sounded more like people trying to freak them out. Scare them.

Even Brenda couldn't hide her reaction. Her eyes met his, and they were full of worry.

"Get up," she whispered.

They both did it together, then quietly secured their packs. Brenda shone the light once again back the way they'd come. Nothing was there.

"Should we check it out?" she asked in a low voice. She was whispering, but in the silence of the tunnel it sounded way too loud—if anyone was close, they could hear every word she and Thomas were saying.

"Check it out?" Thomas thought that was the worst idea he'd heard in a long time. "No, we should get out of here, just like you said."

"What, you wanna just let whoever it is keep following us? Maybe gather some of his or her buddies to ambush us? Better to take care of it now."

Thomas grabbed her hand holding the flashlight and made it point to the ground. Then he leaned closer to her so he could whisper in her ear. "It could totally be a trap. There wasn't any glass on the ground back there—they had to have reached up and broken one of the old lights. Why would someone do that? It has to be someone trying to get us to go back there."

She countered. "If they have enough people to attack, why would they bait us? That's stupid. Why not just come in here and get it over with?"

Thomas thought about that. She had a point. "Well, it's even more stupid to sit here and talk about it all day. What do we do?"

"Let's just—" She had started to raise the flashlight as she spoke, but cut short her words, her eyes widening in terror.

Thomas whipped his head around to see the cause.

A man stood there, just on the edge of her flashlight's range.

He was like an apparition—there was something unreal about him. He leaned to the right, his left foot and leg jiggling slightly, like he had a nervous tic. His left arm also twitched, the hand clenching and unclenching. He wore a dark suit that had probably once been nice, though now it was filthy and tattered. Water or something more foul soaked both knees of the pants.

But Thomas took all that in quickly. Most of his attention was drawn to the man's head. Thomas couldn't help but stare, mesmerized. It looked like hair had been ripped from his scalp, leaving bloody scabs in its place. His face was pallid and wet, with scars and sores everywhere. One eye was gone, a gummy red mass where it should have been. He also had no nose, and Thomas could actually see traces of the nasal passages in his skull underneath the terribly mangled skin.

And his mouth. Lips drawn back in a snarl, gleaming white teeth exposed, clenched tightly together. His good eye glared, somehow vicious in the way it darted between Brenda and Thomas.

Then the man said something in a wet and gurgly voice that made Thomas shiver. He spoke only a few words, but they were so absurd and out of place that it just made the whole thing that much more horrifying.

"Rose took my nose, I suppose."

CHAPTER 32

A small cry escaped from deep within Thomas's chest, and he didn't know if it was audible or something he just felt inside, imagined. Brenda stood next to him, silent—transfixed, maybe—her light still fixed on the hideous stranger.

The man took a lumbering step toward them, having to wave his one good arm to keep his balance on the one good leg.

"Rose took my nose, I suppose," he repeated; the bubble of phlegm in his throat made a disgusting crackle. "And it really blows."

Thomas held his breath, waiting for Brenda to make the first move.

"Get it?" the man said, his snarl trying to morph into a grin. He looked like an animal about to pounce on its prey. "It really blows. My nose. Taken by Rose. I suppose." He laughed then, a wet chortle that made Thomas worry he might never sleep in peace again.

"Yeah, I get it," Brenda said. "That's some funny stuff."

Thomas sensed movement and looked over at her. She had pulled a can from her bag, slyly, and now gripped it in her right hand. Before he could wonder whether it was a good idea and whether he should try to stop her, she pulled her arm back and tossed the can at the Crank. Thomas watched it fly, watched it crash into the man's face.

He let out a shriek that iced Thomas to the core.

And then others appeared. A group of two. Then three. Then four more. Men and women. All dragging themselves out of the darkness to stand behind the first Crank. All just as gone. Just as hideous, consumed fully by the Flare, raging mad and injured head to toe. And, Thomas noticed, all missing their nose.

"That didn't hurt so bad," the leading Crank said. "You have a pretty nose. I really want a nose again." He stopped snarling long enough to lick his lips, then went right back to it. His tongue was a gruesomely scarred purple thing, as if he chewed it when bored. "And so do my friends."

Fear pushed up and through Thomas's chest, like toxic gas rejected by his stomach. He now knew better than ever what the Flare did to people. He'd seen it back at the windows of the dormitory—but now he faced it on a more personal level. Right in front of him, with no bars to keep them away. The faces of the Cranks were primitive and animalistic. The lead man took another lurching step, then another.

It was time to go.

Brenda didn't say anything. She didn't need to. After she pulled out another can and flung it toward the Cranks, Thomas turned around with her and they ran. The psychotic shrill of their pursuers' cries rose behind them like the battle call of a demon army.

Brenda's flashlight beam shakily crisscrossed left and right, bouncing as they sprinted straight past the slew of right and left turns. Thomas knew they had an advantage—the Cranks looked half broken, riddled with injury. Surely they wouldn't be able to keep up. But the thought that even more Cranks might be down here, maybe even waiting for them up ahead . . .

Brenda pulled up and turned right, grabbing Thomas's arm to drag him along. He stumbled the first few steps, got his feet under him, pushed himself back to full speed. The angry shouts and catcalls of the Cranks faded a bit.

Then Brenda turned left. Then right again. After this second turn she flicked off the flashlight but didn't slow.

"What're you doing?" Thomas asked. He held a hand out in front of him, sure he was going to smack into a wall at any second.

A shush was the only response he got. He wondered about how much he was trusting Brenda. He'd put his life in her hands. But he didn't see what other options he had, especially now.

She pulled up again a few seconds later, stopping completely. They stood in darkness, catching their breath. The Cranks were distant but still loud enough, coming closer.

"Okay," she whispered. "Right about . . . here."

"What?" he asked.

"Just follow me into this room. There's a perfect hiding spot in here—I found it while exploring once. There's no way they'll stumble on it. Come on."

Her hand tightened around his, pulled him to the right. He sensed that they were passing through a narrow door; then Brenda pulled him down to the floor.

"There's an old table here," she said. "Can you feel it?"

She pushed his hand out until he felt hard, smooth wood.

"Yeah," he answered.

"Just watch your head. We're gonna crawl under it and then through a small notch in the wall that leads to a hidden compartment. Who knows what it's for, but no way those Cranks'll find it. Even if they have a light, which I doubt."

Thomas had to wonder how they got around without one, but he saved the question for later—Brenda was already on the move, and he didn't want to lose her. Staying close, his fingers brushing her foot, he followed her as she scooted on her hands and knees under the table and toward the wall. Then they crawled through a small square opening into the long, narrow compartment. Thomas felt around, patting the surfaces to get a sense of where he was. The ceiling was only about two feet off the ground, so he continued to drag himself farther into the crevice.

Brenda lay with her back against the far wall of the hideout by the time Thomas awkwardly got himself in position. They had no choice but to lie stretched out, on their sides. It was a squeeze, but he fit, facing the same direction she did, his back pressed against her front. He felt her breath on his neck.

"This is real comfy," he whispered.

"Just be quiet."

Thomas scooted up a little so his head could rest against the wall; then he relaxed. He settled in, taking deep, slow breaths and listening for any sign of the Cranks.

At first the silence was so deep it had a buzz to it, a ringing in his ears. But then came the first traces of Crank noises. Coughing, random shouts, lunatic giggles. They came closer by the second, and Thomas felt a moment of panic, worried that they'd been stupid to trap themselves like this. But then he thought about it. The odds of the Cranks finding the hidden cubbyhole were slim, especially in the darkness. They'd move on, hopefully going far away. Maybe even forgetting about him and Brenda altogether. That was better than a prolonged chase.

And if worse came to worst, he and Brenda could easily defend themselves through the tiny opening into the compartment. Maybe.

The Cranks were close now; Thomas had to fight the urge to hold his breath. All they needed was for an unexpected gasp for oxygen to give them away. Despite the darkness, he closed his eyes to concentrate on listening.

The swishes of shuffling feet. Grunts and heavy breathing. Someone banged on a wall, a series of deadened thumps against the concrete. Arguments broke out, frantic exchanges of gibberish. He heard a "This way!" and a "That way!" More coughing. One of them gagged and spit violently, like he was trying to rid himself of an organ or two. A woman laughed, so full of madness the sound made Thomas shudder.

Brenda found his hand, squeezed it. Once again, Thomas felt a ridiculous surge of guilt, like he was cheating on Teresa. He couldn't help that this girl was so touchy-feely. And what a stupid thing to think when you have—

A Crank entered the room right outside their compartment. Then another. Thomas heard their wheezy intakes of breath, the scrapes of their feet against the floor. Another entered, those footsteps a long slide and thump, long slide and thump. Thomas thought it might be the first man they'd seen, the only one who'd spoken to them—the one with the arm and leg shaking and useless.

"Little boooooooy," the man said, a taunting and creepy call. Definitely him—Thomas couldn't forget that voice. "Little girrrrrrrrl. Come out come out make a sound make a sound. I want your noses."

"Nothin' in here," a woman spat. "Nothin' but an old table."

The creak of wood scraping against the floor sliced through the air, then ended abruptly.

"Maybe they're hiding their noses under it," the man responded. "Maybe they're still attached to their sweet little pretty faces."

Thomas shrank back against Brenda when he heard a hand or shoe scruff along the floor just outside the entrance to their little hiding place. Just a foot or two away.

"Nothin' down there!" the woman said again.

Thomas heard her move away. He realized that his whole body had tensed into a pack of taut wires; he forced himself to relax, still careful to control his breathing.

More shuffling of feet. Then a haunting set of whispers, as if the trio had met in the middle of the room to strategize. Were their minds still sound enough to do such a thing? Thomas wondered. He strained to hear, to catch any words, but the harsh puffs of speech remained indecipherable.

"No!" one of them shouted. A man, but Thomas couldn't tell if it was *the* man. "No! No no no no no no no no." The words quieted into a murmured stutter.

The woman cut him off with her own chant. "Yes yes yes yes yes yes yes yes."

"Shut up!" the leader said. Definitely the leader. "Shut up shut up shut up!"

Thomas felt cold inside, though sweat was beading on his skin. He didn't know if this exchange had any meaning whatsoever or was just more evidence of madness.

"I'm leaving," the woman said, her words broken by a sob. She sounded like a child left out of a game.

"Me too, me too." This from the other man.

"Shut up shut up shut up shut up!" the leader yelled, this time much louder. "Go away go away go away!"

The sudden repetition of words creeped Thomas out. Like some control over language had snapped in their brains.

Brenda was squeezing his hand so hard it hurt. Her breath was cool against the sweat on his neck.

Shuffles of feet and swishing of clothes outside. Were they leaving?

The sounds decreased sharply in volume when they entered the hallway, tunnel, whatever. The other Cranks in their party seemed to have left already. Soon it became silent all over again. Thomas only heard the faint sounds of his and Brenda's breath.

They waited in the darkness, lying flat on the hard ground, facing the small doorway, pressed together, sweating. The silence stretched out, turned back into the buzz of absent sound. Thomas kept listening, knowing they had to be absolutely sure. As much as he wanted to leave that little compartment, as uncomfortable as it was, they had to wait.

Several minutes passed. Several more. Nothing but silence and darkness.

"I think they're gone," Brenda finally whispered. She flicked on her flashlight.

"Hello, noses!" a hideous voice yelled from the room.

Then a bloody hand reached through the doorway and grabbed Thomas by the shirt.

CHAPTER 33

Thomas shrieked, started swatting at the scarred and bruised hand. His eyes were still adjusting to the brightness of Brenda's flashlight; he squinted to see the firm grip the man had on his shirt. The Crank pulled, slamming Thomas's body against the wall. His face smashed into the hard concrete and a burst of pain exploded around his nose. He felt blood trickling down.

The man pushed him back a few inches, then pulled him forward again. Pushed and pulled again. And again, slamming Thomas's face into the wall each time. Thomas couldn't believe the strength of the Crank—it seemed impossible based on how he looked. Weak and horribly injured.

Brenda had her knife out, was trying to crawl over him, get in position to slash at the hand.

"Careful!" Thomas yelled. That knife was awfully close. He grabbed the man's wrist and wriggled it back and forth, trying to loosen that iron grip. Nothing worked, and the man kept pulling and pushing, battering Thomas's body as he hit the wall.

Brenda screamed and went for it. She swept across Thomas and her blade flashed as she drove it right into the Crank's forearm. The man let out a demonic wail and let go of Thomas's shirt. His hand disappeared through the doorway, leaving a trail of blood on the floor. His shrieks of pain continued, loud with trailing echoes.

"We can't let him get away!" Brenda yelled. "Hurry, get out there!"

Thomas, hurting all over, knew she was right and was already squirming to get his body in position. If the man reached the other Cranks, they'd all come back. They might have heard the commotion and already be turning around.

Thomas finally got his arms and head through the opening; then it became easier. He used the wall for leverage and pushed himself the rest of the way out, his eyes glued to the Crank, waiting for another attack. The man was only a few feet away, cradling his wounded arm against his chest. Their eyes met, and the Crank snarled like a wounded animal, bit at the air.

Thomas started to stand up but his head banged into the bottom of the table. "Shuck!" he yelled, then scrambled out from under the old slab of wood. Brenda was right on his heels, and soon they were both standing over the Crank, who lay on the ground in a fetal position, whimpering. Blood dripped from his wound onto the floor, already forming a small puddle.

Brenda held her flashlight in one hand, the knife in the other, its point aimed at the Crank. "Should've gone with your psycho friends, old man. Should've known better than to mess with us."

Instead of responding, the man suddenly spun on his shoulder, kicking his good leg out with shocking speed and strength. He hit Brenda first, sent her crashing into Thomas, and they both crumpled to the floor. Thomas heard the knife and flashlight clatter across the cement. Shadows danced on the walls.

The Crank staggered to his feet, ran for the knife, which had come to rest by the door to the hallway. Thomas pushed himself up and dove forward, crashing into the backs of the man's knees and tackling him to the ground. The man spun, swinging an elbow as he did so. It connected with Thomas's jaw; he felt another explosion of pain as he fell, his hand naturally flying up to his face.

Then Brenda was there. She jumped on the Crank, hit him in the face twice, stunning him, by the looks of it. She took advantage of the brief moment and somehow yanked the man around again so that he lay on his stomach, flat on the floor. She grabbed his arms and pinned them behind him, pushing up in a way that looked incredibly painful. The Crank wrenched and thrashed, but Brenda had him pinned with her legs as well. He started screaming, a horrific, piercing wail of pure terror.

"We have to kill him!" she yelled over it.

Thomas had gotten to his knees and was looking on in a stupor of inaction. "What?" he asked, drugged with exhaustion, too stunned to process her words.

"Get the knife! We have to kill him!"

The Crank kept screaming, a sound that made Thomas want to run as far away as possible. It was unnatural. Inhuman.

"Thomas!" Brenda yelled.

Thomas crawled over to the knife, picked it up, looked at the crimson goo on its sharp blade. He turned back to Brenda.

"Hurry!" she said, her eyes lit with anger. Something told him that her anger was no longer just for the Crank—she was mad at him for taking so long.

But could he do this? Could he kill a man? Even a crazed lunatic of a man who wanted him dead? Who wanted his shuck nose, for crying out loud?

He shambled back to her, holding the knife as if it were tipped with poison. As if just holding it might make him catch a hundred diseases and die a slow and agonizing death.

The Crank, arms yanked behind him, pinned to the floor, continued to scream.

Brenda caught Thomas's gaze, spoke with determination. "I'm gonna flip him—you need to stab him in the heart!"

Thomas started to shake his head, then stopped. He had no choice. He had to do this. So he nodded.

Brenda let out a cry of effort and fell to the right side of the Crank, using her body and her grip on his arms to make the man twist onto his side. Impossibly, his shrieks grew even louder. His chest was now there for the taking, arched and sticking up right in front of Thomas, just inches away.

"Now!" Brenda yelled.

Thomas tightened his grip on the knife. Then he put his other hand on it for more support, all ten fingers clasped tightly around the handle, blade pointing toward the floor. He had to do this. He had to do it.

"Now!" Brenda yelled again.

The Crank, screaming.

Sweat pouring down Thomas's face.

His heart, pumping, thumping, rattling.

Sweat in his eyes. His whole body aching. The terrible, inhuman screams.

"Now!"

Thomas used all his strength and plunged the knife into the Crank's chest.

CHAPTER 34

The next thirty seconds were a horrible, horrible thing for Thomas.

The Crank struggled. Spasmed. Choked and spat. Brenda held him while Thomas twisted the knife. Pushed it deeper. Life took its time as it drained from the man, as the light in his maddened eyes faded, as the grunts and the physical strain to hold on slowly quieted and stilled.

But finally, the Flare-infected man died, and Thomas fell backward, his whole body a tense coil of rusty wire. He gasped for breath, fought the sickening swell in his breast.

He'd just killed a man. He'd taken the life of another person. His insides felt full of poison.

"We need to go," Brenda said, jumping to her feet. "There's no way they didn't hear all that racket. Come on."

Thomas couldn't believe how unaffected she was, how quickly she'd moved on from what they'd done. But then again, they didn't have much choice. The first sign of the other Cranks came echoing down the hall, like the sounds of hyenas bouncing through a canyon.

Thomas forced himself to stand, pushed down the guilt that threatened to consume him. "Fine, but no more of this." First the head-eating silver balls. Now fighting Cranks in the darkness.

"What do you mean?"

He'd had enough of long black tunnels. Enough to last a lifetime. "I want daylight. I don't care what it takes. I want daylight. Now."

★ ★ ★

Brenda didn't argue. She guided him through several twists and turns and soon they found a long iron ladder leading toward the sky, out of the Underneath. The disturbing noises of Cranks lingered in the distance. Laughs and shouts and giggles. An occasional scream.

Moving the round manhole cover took some serious pushing, but it gave way and they climbed out. They found themselves standing in gray twilight, surrounded by enormously tall buildings in every direction. Broken windows. Garbage strewn over the streets. Several dead bodies lying about. A smell of rot and dust. Heat.

But no people. None living, anyway. Thomas felt a moment of alarm that some of the dead might be his friends, but that wasn't the case. The scattered bodies were older men and women, and decay had already set in.

Brenda slowly turned in a circle, getting her bearings. "Okay, the mountains should be down that street." She pointed, but it was impossible to tell because they didn't have a clear view and the buildings hid the setting sun.

"You sure?" Thomas asked.

"Yeah, come on."

As they set off down the long and lonely street, Thomas kept his eyes peeled, scanning every broken window, every alley, every crumbled doorway. Hoping to see some sign of Minho and the Gladers. And hoping *not* to see any Cranks.

They traveled until dark, avoiding contact with anyone. They did hear the occasional scream in the distance, or the sounds of things crashing inside a building now and then. Once, Thomas saw a group of people scurry across a street several blocks away, but they seemed not to notice him or Brenda.

Just before the sun disappeared completely for the day, they turned a corner and came into full view of the city's edge, maybe another mile farther. The buildings ended abruptly, and behind them the mountains rose in all their majesty. They were several times bigger than Thomas would've guessed upon first glimpsing them a few days earlier, and were dry and rocky. No snowcapped beauties—a hazy memory from his past—in this part of the world.

"Should we go the rest of the way?" Thomas asked.

Brenda was busy looking for a place to hide. "Tempting, but no. First off, it's too dangerous running around here at night. Second, even if we made it, there'd be no place for cover out there unless we made it all the way to the mountains. Which I don't think we could do."

As much as Thomas dreaded spending another night in this wretched city, he agreed. But the frustration and worry over the other Gladers were eating away at his insides. He weakly replied, "Okay. Where should we go, then?"

"Follow me."

They wound up in an alley that ended in a large brick wall. At first Thomas thought it was a terrible idea to sleep in a place that had only one way out, but Brenda convinced him otherwise—Cranks would have no reason to enter the alley since it didn't lead anywhere. Plus, she pointed out, there were several large, rusted trucks in which to hide.

They ended up inside one that looked like it had been torn apart for anything usable. The seats were tattered but they were soft, and the cab was big. Thomas sat behind the wheel, pushing the seat as far back as it would go. Surprisingly, he felt somewhat comfortable once settled. Brenda was just a couple of feet to his right, settling in herself. Outside, the darkness grew complete, and the distant sounds of active Cranks came through the broken windows.

Thomas was exhausted. Sore. In pain. Had dried blood all over his clothes. Earlier, he'd cleaned his hands, scrubbing them until Brenda yelled at him to quit wasting their water. But having the blood of that Crank on his fingers, on his palms . . . he couldn't take it. His heart sank every time he thought of it, but he could no longer deny a terrible truth: if he hadn't had the Flare before—a slim hope that Rat Man had lied—he'd surely caught it by now.

And now, sitting in the darkness, his head propped against the truck's door, thoughts of what he'd done earlier came storming into his mind.

"I killed that guy," he whispered.

"Yeah, you did," Brenda responded, her voice soft. "Otherwise he would've killed you. Pretty sure that's doing the right thing."

He wanted to believe it. The guy had been fully gone, consumed by the Flare. He probably would've died soon anyway. Not to mention he'd been doing everything possible to hurt them. To kill them. Thomas *had* done the right thing. But guilt still gnawed at him, crept through his bones. Killing another human. It wasn't easy to accept.

"I know," he finally responded. "But it was so . . . vicious. So brutal. I wish I could've just shot him from a distance with a gun or something."

"Yeah. Sorry it had to go down that way."

"What if I see his nasty face every night when I go to sleep? What if he's in my dreams?" He felt a surge of irritation at Brenda for making *him* stab the Crank—maybe unwarranted when he really considered how desperate they'd been.

Brenda shifted in her seat to face him. Moonlight illuminated her just enough that he could see her dark eyes, her dirty but pretty face.

Maybe it was bad, maybe he was a jerk. But looking at her made him want Teresa back.

Brenda reached out, took his hand and squeezed it. He let her, but he didn't squeeze back.

"Thomas?" She said his name even though he was looking right at her.

"Yeah?"

"You didn't just save your own skin, ya know. You saved mine, too. I don't think I could've beaten that Crank by myself."

Thomas nodded but didn't say anything. He hurt inside for so many reasons. All his friends were gone. Dead, for all he knew. Chuck was definitely dead. Teresa was lost to him. He was only halfway to the safe haven, sleeping in a truck with a girl who would eventually go crazy, and they were surrounded by a city full of bloodthirsty Cranks.

"You asleep with your eyes open?" she asked him.

Thomas tried to smile. "No. Just thinking about how much my life sucks."

"Mine does, too. Sucks big-time. But I'm glad I'm with you."

The statement was so simple and so sweet it made Thomas close his eyes, squeeze them shut. All the pain inside him transformed into something for Brenda, almost like what he'd felt for Chuck. He hated the people who'd done this to her, hated the disease that had made all this happen, and he wanted to make it right.

He finally looked at her again. "I'm glad, too. Being alone would suck even worse."

"They killed my dad."

Thomas lifted his head, surprised by the sudden shift in conversation. "What?"

Brenda nodded slowly. "WICKED. He tried to stop them from

taking me, screamed like a lunatic as he attacked them with . . . I think it was a wooden rolling pin." She let out a small laugh. "Then they shot him in the head." Tears glistened in her eyes, sparkling in the faint light.

"You're serious?"

"Yeah. I saw it happen. Saw the life go out of him before he even hit the floor."

"Oh, man." Thomas searched for words. "I'm really . . . sorry. I saw maybe my best friend in the world get stabbed. He died right in my arms." He paused again. "What about your mom?"

"She hadn't been around for a long time." She didn't elaborate, and Thomas didn't push. Didn't really want to know.

"I'm so scared of going crazy," she said after a long minute of silence. "I can already feel it happening. Things look weird, sound weird. Out of the blue I'll start thinking about stuff that doesn't make any sense. Sometimes the air around me feels . . . hard. I don't even know what that means, but it's scary. I'm definitely starting. The Flare's taking my brain to hell."

Thomas couldn't handle the look in her eyes; he let his gaze drop to the floor. "Don't give up yet. We'll make it to the safe haven, get the cure."

"False hope," she said. "Guess that's better than no hope at all."

She squeezed his hand. This time, Thomas squeezed back.

And then, impossibly, they slept.

CHAPTER 35

A nightmare woke Thomas—something about Minho and Newt being cornered by a bunch of Cranks past the Gone. Cranks with knives. Angry Cranks. The first spill of blood finally jerked Thomas awake.

He looked around, scared that he'd yelled or said something. The cab of the truck still lay in the darkness of night—he could barely see Brenda, couldn't even tell if her eyes were open. But then she spoke.

"Bad dream?"

Thomas settled himself, closed his eyes. "Yeah. I can't quit worrying about my other friends. I just hate it so bad that we were separated."

"I'm sorry that happened. I really am." She shifted in her seat. "But I seriously don't think you need to worry. Your Glader buddies seemed capable enough, but even if they weren't—Jorge is one tough monkey. He'll get them through the city just fine. Don't waste the stress on your heart. *We're* the ones you should be worried about."

"You're doing a terrible job of making me feel better."

Brenda laughed. "Sorry—I was smiling when I said that last part, but you couldn't see me, I guess."

Thomas looked at his backlit watch, then said, "We still have a few hours before the sun comes up."

After a short silence, Thomas spoke again. "Tell me a little bit more about what life's like now. They took most of our memories—some of mine came back, but they're sketchy and I don't know if I can trust them. There isn't much there about the outside world, either."

Brenda sighed deeply. "The outside world, huh? Well, it sucks. The temperatures are finally starting to go down, but it'll be forever before the sea levels do the same. It's been a long time since the flares, but so many people died, Thomas. So many. It's actually kind of amazing how everyone who survived stabilized and civilized so quickly. If it weren't for the stupid Flare, I think the world would pull through in the long run. But if wishes were fishes . . . oh, I can't remember. Something my dad used to say."

Thomas could hardly contain the curiosity that now raced inside him. "What *did* happen? Are there new countries, or just one big government? And how does WICKED fit into it all? *Are* they the government?"

"There are still countries, but they're more . . . unified. Once the Flare started spreading like crazy, they combined all their forces, technology, resources, whatever to start up WICKED. They set up this crazy elaborate testing system and have tried really hard to have quarantined areas. They slowed the Flare down, but they can't stop it. I think the only hope is to find a cure. Hope you're right that they've done it—but if they have, they sure haven't shared it with the public yet."

"So where are we?" Thomas asked. "Where are we right now?"

"In a truck." When Thomas didn't laugh, she continued. "Sorry, bad time for jokes. Judging by the labels on the food, we think we're in Mexico. Or what used to be Mexico. It makes the most sense. Now it's called the Scorch. Basically any area between the two Tropics—Cancer and Capricorn—is a complete wasteland now. Central and South Americas, most of Africa, the Middle East and southern Asia. Lots of dead lands, lots of dead people. So, welcome to the Scorch. Isn't it nice of them to send us sweet Cranks down here?"

"Man." Thoughts raced through Thomas's mind, mostly related to how he knew he was a part of WICKED—a huge part—and how the

Maze and Groups A and B and all the junk they were going through were parts of it too. But he couldn't remember enough for it to make any sense.

"Man?" Brenda asked. "That's the best you can come up with?"

"I have too many questions—I can't seem to latch on to just one to ask."

"Do you know about the numbing agent?"

Thomas looked over at her, wished he could make out more of her face. "I think Jorge said something about that. What is it?"

"You know how the world is. New disease, new drugs. Even if it doesn't do jack to the illness itself, they still come up with stuff."

"What does it do? Do you have any?"

"Ha!" Brenda shouted it with contempt. "You think they'd give us any? Only the important people, the rich people can get their hands on that junk. They call it the Bliss. Numbs your emotions, numbs your brain processes, slows you down to a drunken stupor so you don't feel much. Keeps the Flare at bay because the virus thrives in your brain. Eats at it, destroys it. If there's not a lot of activity, the virus weakens."

Thomas folded his arms. There was something very important here, but he couldn't put his finger on it. "So . . . it's not a cure? Even though it slows the virus down?"

"Not even close. Just delays the inevitable. The Flare always wins in the end. You lose any chance of being rational, having common sense, having compassion. You lose your humanity."

Thomas was quiet. Maybe more strongly than ever before, he felt that a memory—an important one—was trying to squeeze its way through the cracks in the wall blocking him from his past. The Flare. The brain. Going mad. The numbing agent, the Bliss. WICKED. The trials. What Rat Man had said, that their responses to the Variables were what this was all about.

"Did you fall asleep?" Brenda asked him after several minutes of silence.

"No. Just too much information." He felt dimly alarmed at what she had said, but he still couldn't put anything together. "It's hard to process it all."

"Well, I'll shut up, then." She turned away, rested her head against the door. "Push it out of your mind. Won't do you any good. You need rest."

"Uh-huh," Thomas mumbled, frustrated at having so many clues but no real answers. But Brenda was right—he could definitely use a good night's sleep. He got comfortable and did his best, but it took a long time before he finally dozed off. And dreamed.

He's older again, probably fourteen now. He and Teresa are kneeling on the ground, their ears pressed to the crack of a door, listening. Eavesdropping. A man and a woman are talking inside, and Thomas can hear them well enough.

The man first. "Did you get the additions to the Variables list?"

"Last night," the woman responds. "I like what Trent added for the end of the Maze Trials. Brutal, but we need it to happen. Should create some interesting patterns."

"Absolutely. Same with the betrayal scenario, if that ever has to play out."

The woman makes a noise that must be a laugh but that sounds strained and humorless. "Yeah, I had the same thought. I mean, good Lord, how much can these kids take before they'll go crazy on their own?"

"Not just that, it's risky. What if he dies? We all agree that by then he'll surely be one of the top Candidates."

"He won't. We won't let him."

"Still. We're not God. He *could* die."

There's a long pause. Then the man says, "Maybe it won't come to that. But I doubt it. The Psychs say it will stimulate a lot of the patterns we need."

"Well, there's a lot of emotion involved with something like that," the woman answers. "And according to Trent, some of the hardest patterns to create. I think the plan for those Variables is just about the only thing that will work."

"You really think the Trials are *going* to work?" the man asks. "Seriously, the scale and logistics of this thing are unbelievable. Think of how much could go wrong!"

"*Could,* you're right. But what's the alternative? Try it, and if it fails, we'll just be in the same spot as if we'd tried nothing."

"I guess."

Teresa tugs on Thomas's shirt; he looks to see her pointing back down the hall. Time to go. He nods, but leans back in to see if he can catch one last phrase or two. He does. It's the woman.

"Too bad we'll never see the end of the Trials."

"I know," the man answers. "But the future will thank us."

The first purple traces of dawn were what woke up Thomas the second time. He couldn't remember stirring once in his sleep since his middle-of-the-night talk with Brenda—not even after the dream.

The dream. It had been the strangest one yet, lots of things said that were already fading, too difficult to grasp and fit into the pieces of his past that were slowly, very slowly, beginning to come together again. He allowed himself to feel a little hope that maybe he wasn't in on as much to do with the Trials as he'd begun to think. Though he hadn't understood much in the dream, the fact that he and Teresa had been spying meant they weren't involved in every aspect of the Trials.

But what could the purpose of all this be? Why would the future thank those people?

He rubbed his eyes and stretched, then looked over at Brenda—her eyes still closed, her chest moving with slow and even breaths, her mouth slightly open. Though his body felt even stiffer than the day before, the restful slumber had done wonders for his spirit. He felt refreshed. Invigorated. Somewhat perplexed and brain-dead over his memory-dream and all the things Brenda had told him about, but invigorated all the same.

He stretched again and was just letting out a long yawn when he saw something on the wall of the alley. A large metal plaque, riveted to the wall. A sign that looked very familiar.

He pushed the door open and stumbled out onto the street and over to it. It was nearly identical to the sign in the Maze that had said WORLD IN CATASTROPHE—KILLZONE EXPERIMENT DEPARTMENT. Same dull metal, same lettering. Except this one said something very different. And he stared at it for at least five straight minutes before he moved an inch.

It said:

THOMAS, YOU'RE THE REAL LEADER

CHAPTER 36

Thomas might've gone on looking at the plaque all day if Brenda hadn't come out of the truck.

"I was waiting for the right time to tell you," she finally said, completely snapping him out of his daze.

He jerked his head to look at her. "What? What're you talking about?"

She didn't return his gaze, just kept staring at the sign. "Ever since I found out what your name was. Same with Jorge. It's probably why he decided to take his chances and go with you through the city and to this safe haven of yours."

"Brenda, what are you *talking* about?" Thomas repeated.

She finally met his eyes. "These signs are all over the city. All of them say the same thing. Exactly the same thing."

Thomas felt a weakening in his knees. He turned around and sank to the ground, resting his back against the wall. "How . . . how is this even possible? I mean, it looks like it's been there for a while. . . ." He didn't really know what else to say.

"Don't know," Brenda answered, joining him on the ground. "None of us knew what it meant. But when you guys showed up and you told us your name . . . well, we figured it wasn't a coincidence."

Thomas gave her a hard stare, anger fighting its way up inside him. "Why didn't you tell me about this? You'll hold my hand, tell me about your dad being killed, but not this?"

"I didn't tell you because I was worried about how you'd react. I figured you'd probably run off looking for the signs, forget all about me."

Thomas sighed. He was sick of all of it. He let the anger go and blew out a long breath. "I guess it's just another part of this whole nightmare that makes no sense."

Brenda twisted to look up at the sign. "How could you not know what it means? Could it be any simpler? You're supposed to be the leader, take over. I'll help you, earn my way in. Earn a spot at the safe haven."

Thomas laughed. "Here I am in a city full of whacked-in-the-brain Cranks, there's a group of girls who want to kill me, and I'm supposed to worry about who the real leader of my group is? It's ridiculous."

Brenda's face wrinkled in confusion. "Girls who want to kill you? What're you talking about?"

Thomas didn't respond, wondering if he really should tell her the whole story from beginning to end. Wondering if he had the heart to go over it all again.

"Well?" she pressed.

Deciding that it would be nice to get it off his chest, and feeling like she'd gained his trust, he caved and told her everything. He'd given her hints and small parts, but now he took the time for details. About the Maze, about being rescued, about waking up and finding that it had all gone back to crappy. About Aris and Group B. He didn't linger on Teresa, but he could tell she noticed something when he mentioned her. Maybe in his eyes.

"So do you and this Teresa girl got a little somethin' going?" she asked when he was done.

Thomas didn't know how to answer. *Did* they have a little something? They were close, they were friends, he knew that much. Though he'd only gotten back some of his memories, he sensed that he and she had maybe even been more than friends before the Maze. During that awful time when they'd actually helped design the stupid thing.

And then there'd been that kiss . . .

"Tom?" Brenda asked.

He looked at her sharply. "Don't call me that."

"Huh?" she asked, obviously startled, maybe even hurt. "Why?"

"Just . . . don't." He felt terrible for saying it, but couldn't take it back. That was what Teresa called him.

"Fine. Shall I call you Mr. Thomas? Or maybe King Thomas? Or better yet, just Your Majesty?"

Thomas sighed. "I'm sorry. Call me whatever."

Brenda let out a sarcastic laugh and then they both grew silent.

Thomas and Brenda sat, backs against the wall, and the minutes stretched on. It was almost a peaceful quiet until Thomas heard an odd thumping sound that alarmed him.

"Do you hear that?" he asked, now fully at attention.

Brenda had stilled, head cocked to the side as she listened intently. "Yeah. Sounds like someone bangin' on a drum."

"I guess the fun and games are over." He stood up, then helped Brenda do the same. "What do you think it is?"

"Chances are it's not good."

"But what if it's our friends?"

The low *bump-bump-bump* suddenly seemed to come from everywhere at once, the echoes bouncing back and forth between the alley walls. But after a long few seconds, Thomas grew certain the sound was coming from a corner of the dead end. Despite the risk, he ran in that direction to get a look.

"What're you doing!" Brenda snapped at him, but when he ignored her, she followed.

At the very end of the alley, Thomas reached a wall of cracked and faded bricks, where four stairs led down to a scratched and worn wooden door. Just above the door, there was a tiny rectangle of a window, its glass missing. One broken shard still hung at the top, like a jagged tooth.

Thomas could hear music playing, much louder now. It was intense and fast, the bass powerful, drums banging and guitars screaming. Mixed in were the sounds of people laughing and shouting and singing along. And none of it sounded very . . . sane. There was something creepy and disturbing about it.

It looked like the Cranks didn't just look for peoples' noses to bite off, and it gave Thomas a very bad feeling—this noise had nothing to do with his friends.

"We better get out of here," Thomas said.

"Ya think?" Brenda responded, standing right at his shoulder.

"Come on." Thomas turned to go just as she did, but they both froze. Three people had appeared in the alley while they'd been distracted. Two men and one woman, now standing only a few feet away.

Thomas's stomach dropped as he quickly observed the new arrivals. Their clothes were tattered, their hair messy, their faces dirty. But when he looked closer he saw that they didn't have any noticeable injuries, and their eyes showed glints of intelligence. Cranks, but not full-gone Cranks.

"Hi there," the woman said. She had long red hair pulled into a ponytail. Her shirt was cut so low that Thomas had to force himself to keep his eyes focused on hers. "Come to join our party? Lots of dancing. Lots of lovin'. Lots of booze."

There was an edge to her voice that made Thomas nervous. He didn't know what it meant, but this lady wasn't being nice. She was mocking them.

"Um, no thanks," Thomas said. "We, uh, we were just—"

Brenda cut in. "Just trying to find our friends. We're new here, just getting settled."

"Welcome to WICKED's very own Crankland." This was one of the men, a tall, ugly guy with greasy hair. "Don't worry, most of 'em down there"—he nodded toward the stairs—"are half gone at worst. You might get an elbow in the face, maybe kicked in the 'nads. But no one's gonna try to eat you."

"'Nads?" Brenda repeated. "Excuse me?"

The man pointed at Thomas. "I was talkin' to the boy. Things might get a little worse for you if you don't stick close to us. You being female and all."

This whole conversation was making Thomas ill. "Sounds like fun. But we gotta go. Find our friends. Maybe we'll come back."

The other man stepped forward. This one was short but handsome, with blond hair in a crew cut. "You two are nothin' but kids. Time you got some lessons on life. Time you had some fun. We're officially inviting you to the party." He pronounced each word of the last sentence carefully, and with no kindness whatsoever.

"Thanks, but no thanks," Brenda said.

Blondie pulled a gun from a pocket of his long jacket. It was a pistol, silver but grimy and dull. Still, it looked as menacing and deadly as anything Thomas had ever seen.

"I don't think you understood me," the man said. "You're invited to our party. That's not something you turn down."

Tall and Ugly pulled out a knife. Ponytail pulled out a screwdriver, its tip black with what had to be old blood.

"What do you say?" Blondie asked. "Would you like to come to our party?"

Thomas looked at Brenda, but she didn't look back. Her eyes were glued to the blond man, and her face said she was about to do something really stupid.

"Okay," Thomas said quickly. "We'll go. Let's do it."

Brenda snapped her head around. "What?"

"He has a gun. He has a knife. *She's* got a shuck screwdriver! I'm not in the mood to have an eyeball smashed into my skull."

"Looks like your boyfriend's not stupid," Blondie said. "Now let's go have some fun." He pointed his pistol at the stairs and smiled. "Feel free to lead the way."

Brenda was clearly angry, but her eyes also revealed that she knew they had no other choice. "Fine."

Blondie smiled again; the expression would've looked natural on a snake. "That's the spirit. Fine and dandy, nothing to worry about."

"No one's gonna hurt you," Tall and Ugly added. "Unless you get difficult. Unless you act like brats. By the end of the party, you'll wanna join our group. Trust me on that."

Thomas had to fight to keep the panic from pounding through him. "Let's just go," he said to Blondie.

"Waiting on you." The man pointed at the stairs with his gun again.

Thomas reached out and grabbed Brenda's hand, pulled her close to him. "Let's go to the party, sweetheart." He put as much sarcasm into it as he could. "This'll be so much fun!"

"That's very nice," Ponytail said. "I get weepy when I see two people in love." She feigned wiping tears from her cheeks.

With Brenda by his side, Thomas turned toward the stairs, aware the whole time of the gun pointed at his back. They made their way down the steps to the old slab of a door, the space just wide enough for them to go side by side. When they reached the bottom, Thomas didn't see a handle. Raising his eyebrows, he looked back at Blondie, who stood two steps behind them.

"Gotta do the special knock," the man said. "Three slow fist thumps, three fast ones, then two knuckle taps."

Thomas hated these people. He hated the way they spoke so calmly and said mostly nice words, all of them full of mockery. In a way these Cranks were worse than the nose-missing guy he'd stabbed the day before—at least with him they'd known exactly what they were dealing with.

"Do it," Brenda whispered.

Thomas balled his hand into a fist and did the slow fist thumps, then the fast ones. Then he rapped the wood twice with his knuckles. The door opened immediately, the pounding music escaping like a blasting wind.

The guy who greeted them was huge, ears and face pierced several times, tattoos all over. His hair was long and white, reaching well past his shoulders. But Thomas barely had time to register this before the man spoke.

"Hey, Thomas. We've been waiting for you."

CHAPTER 37

The next minute or so was a stunned blur of the five senses.

The welcome statement had shocked Thomas, but before he could respond, the long-haired man practically pulled him and Brenda inside, then started ushering them through a tightly packed crowd of dancing bodies, gyrating and jumping and hugging and spinning. The music was deafening, each beat of the drums like a hammer to Thomas's skull. Several flashlights had been strung from the ceiling; they swayed back and forth as people swatted them, sending beams of light slashing this way and that.

Long Hair leaned over and spoke to Thomas as they slowly made their way through the dancers; Thomas could barely hear him even though he was yelling.

"Thank God for batteries! Life's gonna suck when those run out!"

"How did you know my name?" Thomas yelled back. "Why were you waiting for me?"

The man laughed. "We watched you all night! Then this morning we saw your reaction to the sign through a window—figured you had to be the famous Thomas!"

Brenda had both arms wrapped around Thomas's waist, clinging to him, probably just so they wouldn't get separated. Probably. But when she heard this, she squeezed even tighter.

Thomas looked back, saw Blondie and his two friends following on their heels. The gun had been put away, but Thomas knew it could be brought right back out again.

The music blared. The bass thumped and rattled the room. People dancing and jumping all around them, the swords of light crisscrossing the dark air. The Cranks were slick and shiny with sweat, all that body heat making the room uncomfortably warm.

Somewhere right in the middle, Long Hair stopped and turned to face them, his odd white mane flopping.

"We really want you to join us!" he shouted. "There's gotta be something about you! We'll protect you from the bad Cranks!"

Thomas was glad they didn't know more. Maybe this wouldn't be so bad after all. Play along, pretend to be a special Crank, and maybe he and Brenda would get through this long enough to slip away unnoticed at the right time.

"I'll go and get you a drink!" Long Hair called out. "Enjoy yourselves!" Then he scuttled off, vanishing into the thick, writhing crowd.

Thomas turned to see Blondie and his two friends still there, not dancing at all—just watching. Ponytail caught his attention with a wave of her hand.

"Might as well dance!" she yelled. But she didn't follow her own advice.

Thomas twisted around until he was fully facing Brenda. They needed to talk.

As though she could read his mind, she brought her arms up and wrapped them around his neck, pulling him close until her mouth was right next to his ear, her breath hot and tingling against his sweat.

"How did we get into this piece-of-crap situation?" she asked.

Thomas didn't know what to do but wrap his arms around her back and waist. He felt her heat through her damp clothes. Something stirred inside him, mixed with guilt and longing for Teresa.

"I never could have imagined this an hour ago," he finally said, speaking through her hair. It was the only thing he could think of to say.

The song changed, something dark and haunting. The beat had slowed a bit, the drum somehow deeper. Thomas couldn't make out any words—it was as if the singer were lamenting some horrible tragedy, the voice wailing, high-pitched and sorrowful.

"Maybe we should just stay with these people for a while," Brenda said.

Thomas noticed then that the two of them *were* dancing, without meaning to or thinking about it. Moving with the music, slowly turning, their bodies pressed tightly together, clasping each other.

"What're you talking about?" he asked, surprised. "You're giving up already?"

"No. Just tired. Maybe we'd be safer here."

He wanted to trust her, felt like he could. But something about all this worried him—had she brought him here on purpose? It seemed a stretch. "Brenda, don't quit on me yet. The only option we have is to get to the safe haven. There's a cure for this."

Brenda shook her head slightly. "It's just so hard to believe it's really true. Hard to hope for it."

"Don't say that." He didn't want to think it, and he didn't want to hear it.

"Why would they have sent all these Cranks here if there was a cure? It just doesn't make any sense."

Thomas pulled back to look at her, worried about the sudden change in attitude. Her eyes were wet with tears.

"You're talking crazy," he said, then paused. He had his own doubts, of course, but he didn't want to discourage her. "The cure is real. We have to . . ." He trailed off, looked over at Blondie, who was still staring at him. The guy probably couldn't hear, but better safe than sorry.

Thomas leaned back in to speak directly in Brenda's ear. "We have to get out of here. You wanna stay with people who pull guns and screwdrivers on you?"

Before she could respond, Long Hair was back, a cup in each hand, the brownish liquid inside sloshing as he got bumped from all directions by the dancers. "Drink up!" he called out.

Something inside Thomas seemed to wake up then. Taking a drink from these strangers suddenly felt like a very, very bad idea. Impossibly, everything about this place and this situation had become even more uncomfortable.

Brenda had already started reaching for a drink, though.

"No!" Thomas yelled before he could stop himself, then raced to cover his mistake. "I mean, no, I really don't think we should be drinking that stuff. We've gone a long time without water—we need that first. We, um, just wanna dance for a while." He tried to act casual, but was cringing on the inside, knowing he sounded like an idiot—especially when Brenda gave him a strange look.

Something small and hard pressed against his side. He didn't have to turn to see what it was: Blondie's pistol.

"I offered you a drink," Long Hair said again, this time any sign of kindness gone from his tattooed face. "It would be very rude to turn such an offer down." He held the cups out again.

Panic swelled in Thomas. Any small doubt had gone—something was wrong with the drinks.

Blondie pressed the gun into him even harder. "I'm gonna count to one," the man said into his ear. "Just one."

Thomas didn't have to think. He reached out and took the cup, poured the liquid in his mouth, swallowed all of it at once. It burned like fire, searing his throat and chest as it went down; he broke into a lurching, wracking cough.

"Now you," Long Hair said, handing the other cup to Brenda.

She looked at Thomas, then took it and drank. It didn't seem to faze her in the least; there was just a slight tightening of her eyes as it went down.

Long Hair took the empty cups back, a huge grin now spread across his face. "That's just fine! Back to dancing ya go!"

Thomas already felt something funny in his gut. A soothing warmth, a calmness, growing and spreading through his body. He took Brenda back into his arms, held her tightly as they swayed to the music. Her mouth was against his neck. Every time her lips bumped against his skin, a wave of pleasure shot through him.

"What was it?" he asked. He felt more than heard the slur in his voice.

"Something not good," she said; he could barely hear her. "Something drugged. It's doing funny things to me."

Yeah. Thomas thought. *Something funny.* The room had begun to spin around him, far faster than their slow turn should have caused it to. People's faces seemed to stretch when they laughed, their mouths gaping black holes. The music slowed and thickened, the singing voice deepened, grew drawn-out.

Brenda pulled her head away from him, clasped the sides of his face with her hands. She stared at him, though her eyes seemed to jiggle. She looked beautiful. More beautiful than anything he'd ever seen before. Everything around them faded to darkness. His mind was shutting down, he knew it.

"Maybe it's better this way," she said. Her words didn't match her lips. Her face was moving in circles, seemingly detached from her neck. "Maybe we can be with them. Maybe we can be happy until we're past the Gone." She smiled then, a sickening, disturbing smile. "Then you can kill me."

"No, Brenda," he said, but his voice seemed a million miles away, as if it were coming from an endless tunnel. "Don't . . ."

"Kiss me," she said. "Tom, kiss me." Her hands tightened on his face. She started to pull him down toward her.

"No," he said, resisting.

She stopped, a hurt look washing over her face. Her moving, blurring face.

"Why?" she asked.

The darkness almost had him fully now. "You're not . . . her." His voice, distant. A mere echo. "You could never be her."

And then she fell away, and his mind did the same.

CHAPTER 38

Thomas awoke to darkness, and it felt as if he had been put into some type of ancient torture device, nails slowly driving into his skull from all directions.

He groaned, a halting, terrible sound that only intensified the pain in his head. He forced himself silent, tried to reach up to rub—

His hands wouldn't move. Something held them down, something sticky pressing against his wrists. Tape. He tried to kick out with his legs, but they were bound, too. The effort sent another wave of pain crashing through his head and body; he went limp, moaning softly. He wondered how long he'd been out.

"Brenda?" he whispered. No response.

A light came on.

Bright and stabbing. He squeezed both eyes shut, then opened one just enough to squint through. Three people stood in front of him, but their faces were in shadow, the light source coming from behind.

"Wakey wakey," a husky voice said. Someone snickered.

"Want some more of that fire juice?" This came from a woman. The same person snickered again.

Thomas finally grew accustomed to the light and opened his eyes fully. He was in a wooden chair, wide gray tape tightly securing his wrists to the armrests and his ankles to the chair legs. Two men and one woman stood in front of him. Blondie. Tall and Ugly. Ponytail.

"Why didn't you just whack me out in the alley?" Thomas asked.

"Whack you?" Blondie responded. His voice hadn't seemed husky before; it sounded like he'd spent the last few hours yelling out on the dance floor. "What do you think we are, some kind of twentieth-century mafia clan? If we wanted to *whack* you, you'd already be dead, bleeding in the streets."

"We don't want you dead," Ponytail interrupted. "That would spoil the meat. We like to eat our victims while they're still breathing. Eat as much as we can before they bleed to death. You wouldn't believe how juicy and . . . sweet that tastes."

Tall and Ugly laughed, but Thomas couldn't tell whether Ponytail was serious. Either way, it freaked him out.

"She's kidding," Blondie said. "We've only eaten other humans when it's gotten completely desperate. Man meat tastes like pig crap."

Another burst of giggles from Tall and Ugly. Not snickering, not laughing. Giggling. Thomas didn't believe they were serious—he was much more worried about how their minds seemed . . . off.

Blondie smiled for the first time since Thomas had met him. "Joking again. We're not quite that Cranked-out yet. But I do bet people don't taste very good."

Tall and Ugly and Ponytail nodded.

Man, these guys are really starting to lose it. Thomas thought. He heard a muffled groan to his left and looked over. Brenda was in a corner of the room, bound just as he was. But her mouth had been taped shut as well, making him wonder if she'd put up more of a fight before she passed out. It looked like she was only now waking up, and when she noticed the three Cranks, she shifted and wiggled in her chair, moaning through the gag. Her eyes lit with fire.

Blondie pointed at her. His pistol had magically appeared. "Shut up! Shut up or I'll splat your brain on the wall!"

Brenda stopped. Thomas expected her to start whimpering or

crying or something. But she didn't, and he immediately felt stupid for thinking it. She'd already shown how tough she was.

Blondie dropped the gun to his side. "Better. Good God, we should've killed her when she first started screaming up there. And biting." He looked at his forearm, where the long arc of a welt shone red.

"She's with him," Ponytail said. "We can't kill her yet."

Blondie pulled a chair from the far wall and took a seat just a few feet in front of Thomas. The others followed suit, looking relieved, as if they'd been waiting hours for permission. Blondie rested the gun on his thigh, its business end pointed straight at Thomas.

"Okay," the man said. "We've got us quite a lot to talk about. I'm not going through the normal bullcrap with you, either. If you mess around or refuse to answer or whatever, I'm gonna shoot you in the leg. Then the other one. Third time, a bullet goes into your girlfriend's face. I'm thinking somewhere right between the eyes. And I bet you can guess what happens the fourth time you piss me off."

Thomas nodded. He wanted to think he was tough, think he could stand up to these Cranks. But common sense won out. He was taped to a chair, no weapons, no allies, nothing. Though honestly, he didn't have anything to hide. He'd answer whatever the guy asked him. Whatever ended up happening, he didn't want any bullets in his leg. And he doubted the guy was bluffing.

"First question," Blondie said. "Who are you and why is your name on signs all over this piece of crap city?"

"My name is Thomas." As soon as it came out, Blondie scrunched up his face in anger. Thomas realized his stupid mistake and hurried along. "You already knew that. Well, how I got here is a really weird story and I doubt you'll believe it. But I swear I'm telling the truth."

"Didn't you come on a Berg like the rest of us?" Ponytail asked.

"Berg?" Thomas didn't know what that meant, but he just shook his head and went on. "No. We came out of some underground tunnel about thirty miles or so to the south. Before that we went through something called a Flat Trans. Before that—"

"Hold it hold it hold it," Blondie said, holding up a hand. "A Flat Trans? I'd shoot you right now, but there's no way you just made that up."

Thomas wrinkled his brow in confusion "Why?"

"You'd be stupid to try getting away with an obvious lie like that. You came through a Flat Trans?" The man's surprise was obvious.

Thomas glanced at the other Cranks, both of whom had similar looks of shock on their faces. "Yeah. Why's that so hard to believe?"

"Do you have any idea how expensive Flat Transportation is? Before the flares, it had just been revealed to the public. Only governments and billionaires can afford to use it."

Thomas shrugged. "Well, I know they have a lot of money, and that's what the guy called it. A Flat Trans. Kind of a gray wall that tingles like ice when you walk through it."

"What guy?" Ponytail asked.

Thomas had barely started and already his mind was jumbled. How could you tell a story like this? "I think he was from WICKED. They're running us through some kind of experiment or test. I don't really know everything. We . . . had our memories wiped out. Some of mine came back, but not a whole lot."

Blondie didn't react for a second, just sat there staring at him. Almost *through* him, at the wall behind. Finally, he said, "I was a lawyer. Back before the flares and this disease ruined everything. I know when someone's lying. I was very, very good at my job."

Oddly, Thomas relaxed. "Then you know I'm not—"

"Yeah, I know. I wanna hear the whole thing. Start talking."

Thomas did. He couldn't say why, but it seemed okay. His instincts told him these Cranks were just like everybody else—sent here to live out their last horrible years succumbing to the Flare. They were just trying to find an advantage, find a way out, like anybody would. And meeting a guy who had special signs about him all over the city was an excellent first step. If Thomas had been in their shoes, he'd probably have been doing the same thing. Without the gun and bindings, hopefully.

He'd told most of the story to Brenda just the day before, and related it much the same way now. The Maze, the escape, the dorms. Being given the mission to cross the Scorch. He took special care to make it sound very important, stressing the part about the cure waiting at the end. Since they'd lost the chance to have Jorge's help getting through the city, maybe he could start over with these people. He also expressed his concern over the other Gladers, but when he asked if they'd seen them—or a big group of girls—the answer was no.

Once again, he didn't talk much about Teresa. He just didn't want to take any chances of endangering her somehow, though he had no idea how talking about her might do that. He also lied a bit about Brenda. Well, he never really lied directly. He just kind of made it sound like she'd been with him from the beginning.

When he finished, ending at the part where they'd met the three people in front of him in the alley, he took a deep breath and adjusted himself in the chair. "Can you *please* take this tape off me now?"

A flick of Tall and Ugly's hand caught his attention and he looked to see that a very sharp, shiny knife had appeared there. "What do you think?" he asked Blondie.

"Sure, why not." He'd held a stoic face throughout the tale, giving no hint yet as to whether he believed the story.

Tall and Ugly shrugged and got to his feet, walked over to Thomas. He was just leaning over, knife outstretched, when a commotion broke out above. Hard thumps on the ceiling, followed by a couple of screams. Then it sounded like a hundred people running. Frantic footsteps, jumping, more thumps. More screams.

"Another group must've found us," Blondie said, his face suddenly pale. He stood, motioned for the other two to follow him. A few seconds later they were gone, vanishing up a set of stairs into the shadows. A door opened and closed. The chaos above continued.

All of this combined to scare Thomas nearly out of his wits. He looked over at Brenda, who sat perfectly still, listening. Her eyes finally met his gaze. Still gagged, she could only raise her eyebrows.

He didn't like their odds being left like this, taped to chairs. There was no way any of the Cranks he'd met that night had a chance against ones like Mr. Nose. "What if a bunch of full-gone Cranks are up there?" he asked.

Brenda mumbled something through the tape.

Thomas strained every muscle and started jumping his chair in tiny steps toward where she sat. He'd made it about three feet when the sounds of fighting and rumbling suddenly stopped. He froze, looked up at the ceiling.

Nothing for several seconds. Then a set of footsteps, maybe two, shuffling across the floor above. A loud thump. Another loud thump. Then another. Thomas imagined bodies being thrown on the ground.

The door at the top of the stairs opened.

Then footsteps, hard and heavy, running down. It was all in shadow, and a cold panic flooded Thomas's body as he waited to see who came down.

Finally, someone stepped into the light.

Minho. Dirty and bloody, burn marks on his face. Knives in both hands. *Minho.*

"You guys look comfy," he said.

CHAPTER 39

Despite everything he'd been through, Thomas couldn't remember the last time he'd been at such a loss for words. "What . . . how . . ." He stammered, trying to get something out.

Minho smiled, a very welcome sight. Especially considering how horrible the guy looked. "We'd just found you. Did you think we were gonna let these bunch of shuck-faces do anything to you? You owe me. Big-time." He walked over and started cutting the tape.

"What do you mean you'd just found us?" Thomas was so happy he wanted to giggle like an idiot. Not only were they rescued, his friends were alive. They were alive!

Minho kept cutting. "Jorge's been leading us through the city—avoiding Cranks, finding food." He finished up with Thomas and went to free Brenda, still talking over his shoulder. "Yesterday morning, we kind of spread out, spying here and there. Frypan was peeking around the corner into that alley up there just as those three shanks pulled a gun on you. He came back, we got mad, started planning our ambush. Most of those shucks were wasted or asleep."

Brenda pushed her way out of the chair and past Minho as soon as her tape was cut. She started toward Thomas, but hesitated—he couldn't tell if she was mad or just worried. Then she came the rest of the way, ripping the tape off her mouth as she reached his side.

Thomas stood up, and immediately his head pounded again, the room swaying, making him sick. He plopped back into the chair. "Oh, man. Anybody got some aspirin?"

Minho only laughed. Brenda had made her way to the bottom of the stairs, where she stood with arms folded. Something about her body language *did* make her look angry. Then he remembered what he had said to her right before passing out from the drug.

Oh, crap, he thought. He'd told her she could never be Teresa.

"Brenda?" he asked sheepishly. "You okay?" No way he was gonna bring up their odd dance and that conversation in front of Minho.

She nodded, but didn't look back at him. "I'm fine. Let's go. I wanna see Jorge." Short clips for words. No emotion in them.

Thomas groaned, glad to have the pain in his head as an excuse. Yeah, she was mad at him. Actually, *mad* might've been the wrong word. She looked more hurt.

Or maybe he assumed too much and she didn't care at all.

Minho came up to him, offered a hand. "Come on, dude. Headache or no headache, we need to go. No telling how long we can keep the shuck prisoners up there quiet and still."

"Prisoners?" Thomas repeated.

"Whatever you wanna call them—we can't risk letting them go until we get out. We've got a dozen guys holding more than twenty. And they aren't too happy. They might start thinking they can take us pretty soon. Once they get rid of their hangovers."

Thomas stood up again, this time much more slowly. The pain in his head rocked and throbbed like a steady drum, seeming to push on his eyeballs from behind with every thud. He closed his eyes until things quit spinning around him. He sucked in a deep breath, looked at Minho. "I'll be fine."

Minho flashed him a smile. "Such a man. Come on."

Thomas followed his friend to the stairs. He paused beside Brenda but didn't say anything. Minho peered back at Thomas with an expression that said, *What's up with her?* Thomas just shook his head slightly.

Minho shrugged, then stomped his way up and out of the room, but Thomas stayed back with Brenda for a second. She didn't seem to want to move just yet. And she refused to meet his eyes.

"I'm sorry," he said, regretting his harsh words right before passing out. "I think I said something kinda mean—"

Her eyes snapped up to meet his. "You think I give a crap about you and your girlfriend? I was just dancing, trying to have some fun before everything went bad. What, you think I'm in love with you or something? Just dying till the day you ask me to be your Crank bride? Get over yourself."

Her words were so full of rage that Thomas took a step back, as hurt as if she'd slapped him. Before he could respond, she disappeared upstairs, all heavy footsteps and sighs. He'd never missed Teresa so badly as at that moment. On a whim, he called out to her with his mind. But she still wasn't there.

The smell hit him before he even entered the room where they'd danced.

Like sweat and vomit.

Bodies littered the floor, some sleeping, some huddled together and shivering; some even looked dead. Jorge, Newt and Aris were there, standing guard, slowly turning in circles with knives drawn and pointing.

Thomas saw Frypan and the other Gladers, too. Though his head still throbbed, he felt a rush of relief and excitement. "What happened to you guys! Where have you been?"

"Hey, it's Thomas!" Frypan roared. "As ugly and alive as ever!"

Newt came up to him, gave a sincere smile. "Glad you're not bloody dead, Tommy. I'm really, really glad."

"You too." Thomas realized with a weird numbness that this was what his life had become. This was how you greeted people after a day or two apart. "Has everyone made it so far? Where'd you guys go? How'd you get here?"

Newt nodded. "Still eleven of us. Plus Jorge."

Thomas's questions came faster than anyone could answer. "Any sign of Barkley and the rest of them? Were they the ones who set off the explosion?"

Jorge answered—Thomas saw that he stood closest to the door, holding a very nasty-looking sword that was currently resting on the shoulder of Tall and Ugly himself. Ponytail was next to him, and they were both curled up on the ground. "Haven't seen 'em since. We got away pretty quickly, and they're too scared to come deeper into the city."

The sight of Tall and Ugly had set off a small alarm inside Thomas. Blondie. Where was Blondie? How would Minho and the others have dealt with his gun? He looked around but couldn't find him anywhere in the room.

"Minho," Thomas whispered, then motioned for him to come closer. Once he and Newt were both right next to him, he leaned in. "The guy with really short blond hair. Seemed like the leader. What happened to him?"

Minho shrugged and looked at Newt to answer.

"Must've got out," Newt replied. "A handful did—we couldn't stop all of them."

"Why?" Minho asked. "You worried about him?"

Thomas looked around, lowered his voice even further. "He had a *gun*. He's the only one I've seen with something worse than a knife. And he wasn't very nice."

"Who gives a klunk?" Minho said. "We'll be out of this stupid city in an hour. And we should go. Now."

That sounded like the best idea Thomas had heard in days. "Okay, I want to get out of here before he comes back."

"Listen up!" Minho called out as he stepped away, walking through the crowd. "We're leaving now. Don't follow us, you'll be fine. Follow us, you'll be dead. Pretty easy choice, don't ya think?"

Thomas wondered when and how Minho had taken back the leadership role from Jorge. He looked over at the older man and noticed Brenda standing silently next to a wall, staring at the floor. He felt so bad about what had happened the night before. He really *had* wanted to kiss her. But for some reason he'd felt disgusted at the same time. Maybe it was the drug. Maybe it was Teresa. Maybe it was—

"Hey, Thomas!" Minho was yelling at him. "Dude, wake up! We're leaving!"

Several Gladers had already walked through the door and into the sunlight. How long had he been out from the drug? A full day? Or just a few hours, since morning? He moved to follow, stopping by Brenda and giving her a little push. He worried for a second that she wouldn't come with them, but she only hesitated a moment before heading for the door.

Minho, Newt and Jorge waited, keeping guard with their weapons, until everyone but Thomas and Brenda were out. Thomas watched at the doorway as the three Gladers backed away, slowly sweeping the tips of their knives and swords back and forth as they did so. But it didn't look like anyone was going to put up a fuss. They were all probably ready to move on, just glad to be alive.

Everyone gathered in the alley away from the stairs. Thomas stayed close to the top step, but Brenda made her way to the other side of the group. He swore he'd get her alone as soon as they were away and safe, have a long talk. He liked her, wanted to be her friend if nothing else. More importantly, he now felt about her much the way he'd felt about Chuck. For some reason a feeling of responsibility for her had overcome him.

"—make a run for it."

Thomas shook his head, realizing that Minho had been talking. Daggers of pain shot through his skull, but he focused.

"There's only about a mile left," Minho continued. "These Cranks aren't so hard to fight after all. So let's—"

"Hey!"

The shout came from behind Thomas, loud and screechy, filled with more than a hint of lunacy. Thomas spun around to see Blondie standing down on the bottom step, by the open door, his arm extended. His white-knuckled fingers held the gun, surprisingly steady and calm. It was pointed directly at Thomas.

Before anyone could move he fired, an explosion that rocked the narrow alley with a thunderous boom.

Pure pain ripped through Thomas's left shoulder.

CHAPTER 40

The impact knocked Thomas back, spinning him around so that he fell flat on his face, smacking his nose on the ground. Somehow, through the pain and muffled buzz in his ears, he heard the gun fire again, then the sound of grunts and punches, followed by metal clacking across the cement.

He rolled onto his back, hand clasped tight to where he'd been shot; he searched for the courage to look at the wound. The ringing in his ears grew louder, and he barely noticed out of the corner of his eye that Blondie had been tackled to the ground. Someone was punching the living crap out of him.

Minho.

Thomas finally gazed down at the damage. What he saw there made his heart double its pace.

A small hole in his shirt revealed a gooey red blob right in the meaty part above his armpit, blood pouring from the wound. It hurt. It hurt *bad*. If he'd thought his headache downstairs had been tough, this was like three or four of those, all smashed into a coil of pain right there in his shoulder. And spreading through the rest of his body.

Newt was at his side, looking down with worried eyes.

"He shot me." It just came out, a new number one on the list of the dumbest things he'd ever said. The pain, like living metal staples running through his insides, pricking and scratching with their little sharp points. He felt his mind going dark for the second time that day.

Someone handed a shirt to Newt, who pressed it tightly against Thomas's wound. This sent another wave of agony through him; he cried out, not caring how wimpy he sounded. It hurt like nothing he'd ever felt before. The world around him faded another few degrees.

Pass out, he urged himself. *Please pass out, make it go away.*

Voices came from a distance again, just like his own had on the dance floor after being drugged.

"I can get that sucker out of him." This was Jorge, of all people. "But I'll need a fire."

"We can't do this here." Was that Newt?

"Let's get out of this shuck city." Definitely Minho.

"All right. Help me carry him." No idea.

Hands gripping him from underneath, grasping his legs. The pain. Someone saying something about the count of three. The pain. It really, really hurt. One. The pain. Two. *Ouch.* Three!

He rose toward the sky, and the pain exploded anew, fresh and raw.

Then his wish to pass out came true and darkness washed his troubles away.

He awoke, his mind a haze.

Light blinded him; he couldn't open his eyes all the way. His whole body jostled and bumped, hands still holding him tight. He heard the sounds of breathing, heavy and fast. Feet pounding on pavement. Someone shouting, though he couldn't understand the words. In the distance, the mad screams of Cranks. Close enough that they might be pursuing.

Heat. The air was burning hot.

His shoulder, on fire. Pain tore through him like a series of toxic explosions, and he fled to the darkness once again.

★ ★ ★

He cracked his eyes.

This time the light was much less intense. The golden gleam of twilight. He lay on his back, the ground beneath him hard. A rock dug into his lower back, but it felt heavenly compared to the rot in his shoulder. People lumbered about him, talking in short and tight whispers.

The cackle of Cranks had grown more distant. He saw nothing but sky above him, no buildings. Pain in his shoulder. Oh, the pain.

A fire licked and spit somewhere close. He felt the heat wafting across his body, hot wind through hot air.

Someone said, "You better hold him down. Legs and arms."

Though his mind still floated in fog, those words didn't sound good.

A flash of light on silver in his vision, the fading sun's reflection on . . . a knife? Was it glowing red?

"This is gonna hurt somethin' awful." No idea who said it.

He heard the hiss right before a billion pounds of dynamite exploded in his shoulder.

His mind said goodbye for the third time.

He sensed that a long spell of time had passed this go-around. When he opened his eyes again, stars like pinpricks of daylight shone down from the dark sky. Someone held his hand. He tried to turn his head to look over, but it sent a fresh wave of agony shooting down his spine.

He didn't need to see. It was Brenda.

Who else would it be? Plus, the hand was soft and small. Brenda for sure.

The intense pain of before had been replaced. In some ways, he now felt worse. Something like an illness crept through the inner workings of his body. A gnawing, itching filthiness. Something foul, like maggots squirming through his veins and the hollows of his bones and between his muscles. Eating away at him.

It hurt, but now it was more of an ache. Deep and raw. His stomach, gurgly and unstable, fire in his veins.

He didn't know how he knew, but he was sure of it. Something was wrong.

The word *infection* popped up in his mind, then stayed there.

He drifted off.

The sunrise woke Thomas in the morning. The first thing he realized was that Brenda no longer held his hand. Then he noticed the cool air of early morning on his skin, which gave him the briefest moment of pleasure.

Then he became fully aware of the throbbing pain that consumed his body, dwelling in every last molecule. It no longer had anything to do with his shoulder and the bullet wound. Something terrible had gone wrong with his entire system.

Infection. That word again.

He didn't know how he'd make it through the next five minutes. Or the next hour. How could he possibly go through an entire day? Then sleep and start the whole thing all over again? Despair sucked at him, an empty, yawning void that threatened to pull him down into an awful abyss. A panic-laced craziness struck him. Suffusing it all, the pain.

That was when things got bizarre.

The others heard it before he did. Minho and everyone else were suddenly scrambling, searching for something, many of them scanning the sky. The sky? Why would they be doing that?

Someone—Jorge, he thought—yelled the word *Berg*.

Then Thomas heard it. A deep thrumming, full of heavy thumps. It grew louder before he even realized what was going on, and soon it felt as though the noise were inside his skull, rattling his jaw and eardrums and sluicing down his spine. A constant, steady pounding, like the world's largest drums; behind it all, the massive hum of heavy machinery. A wind picked up, and at first Thomas worried that a storm was starting again, but the sky was perfectly blue. Not a cloud to be seen.

The noise worsened his pain, made him begin to shut down again. But he fought it, desperate to know the source of the sounds. Minho shouted something, pointed to the north. Thomas hurt too much to turn and look. The wind grew stronger, gusting across him, ripping at his clothes. Dust flew and clouded the air. Suddenly Brenda was beside him again, squeezing his hand.

She leaned over until her face was only inches above his. Her hair whipped all around.

"I'm sorry," she said, though he barely heard her. "I didn't mean to—I mean, I know that you . . ." She fumbled for words, looked away.

What was she talking about? Why didn't she tell him what was making that horrible noise! He hurt so bad. . . .

A look of curious horror spread across her face, eyes widening, mouth dropping open. And then she was being pushed away by two . . .

Panic seized Thomas now. Two people, dressed in the strangest outfits he'd ever seen. One-piece, baggy and dark green—letters he couldn't read scrawled across the chest. Goggles covering their faces. No, not goggles. Some kind of gas mask. They looked hideous and alien. They looked evil, like giant, demented, human-eating insects wrapped in plastic.

One of them grabbed his legs by the ankles. The other put his hands under him, gripped him by the armpits, and Thomas screamed. They lifted, and pain went coursing through his body. He'd almost grown used to the agony by now, but this felt even worse. It hurt too much to struggle, so he went limp.

Then they were moving, carrying him, and for the first time, Thomas's eyes focused enough to read the letters on the chest of the person at his feet.

WICKED.

Darkness threatened to take him again. He let it, but the pain went with him.

CHAPTER 41

Once again, he woke to a blinding white light—this one shining directly into his eyes from above. He knew immediately it wasn't the sun—it was different. Plus, it shone from only a short distance away. Even as he clenched his eyes shut again, the afterimage of a bulb floated across the darkness.

He heard voices—more like whispers. He couldn't understand a word. Too soft, just out-of-reach enough that they were impossible to decipher.

He heard the click and clack of metal against metal. Small sounds, and the first thing he thought of was medical instruments. Scalpels and those little rods with mirrors on the end. These images swam up from the murkiness of his memory bank, and combining them with the light, he knew.

He'd been taken to a hospital. A hospital. The last thing he could ever imagine existing anywhere in the Scorch. Or had he been taken away? Far away? Through a Flat Trans, maybe?

A shadow crossed the light, and Thomas opened his eyes. Someone was looking down at him, dressed in the same ridiculous outfit as those who'd brought him here. The gas mask, or whatever it was. Big goggles. Behind the protective glass, he saw dark eyes focused on him. A woman's eyes, though he didn't know how he could tell.

"Can you hear me?" she asked. Yes, a woman, even though the mask muffled her voice.

Thomas tried to nod, didn't know if he actually did or not.

"This wasn't supposed to happen." She'd pulled her head back a bit and looked away, which made Thomas think she hadn't meant that comment for him. "How'd a working gun get in the city? You have any idea the amount of rust and gunk must've been on that bullet? Not to mention the germs."

She sounded very angry.

A man replied. "Just get on with it. We have to send him back. Quickly."

Thomas barely had time to process what they were saying. A new pain blossomed in his shoulder, unbearable.

He passed out for the umpteenth time.

Awake again.

Something was off. He couldn't tell what. The same light shone from the same spot above; he looked to the side this time instead of closing his eyes. He could see better, focus more. Silver squares of ceiling tile, a steel contraption with all kinds of dials and switches and monitors. None of it made sense.

Then it hit him. Hit him with such shock and wonder that he scarcely believed it could be true.

He felt no pain. None. Nothing at all.

No people stood around him. No crazy green alien suits, no goggles, no one sticking scalpels in his shoulder. He seemed to be alone, and the absence of pain was pure ecstasy. He didn't know it was possible to feel this good.

It wasn't. Had to be a drug.

He dozed off.

★ ★ ★

He stirred at the sound of soft voices, though it came through the haze of his drugged stupor.

Somehow he knew enough to keep his eyes shut, see if he could learn anything about the people who'd taken him. The people who'd evidently fixed him up and rid his body of the infection.

A man was talking. "Are we sure this doesn't screw anything up?"

"I'm positive." This from a woman. "Well, as positive as I can be. If anything, it may stimulate a pattern in the killzone that we hadn't expected. A bonus, possibly? I can't imagine it leading him or anyone else in a direction that would prevent the other patterns we're looking for."

"Dear God above, I hope you're right," the man responded.

Another woman spoke, her voice high, almost crystalline. "How many of the ones left do you think are still viable Candidates?" Thomas sensed the capital letter in that word—*Candidates.* Confused, he tried to remain still, listen.

"We're down to four or five," the first woman answered. "Thomas here is by far our greatest hope. He responds really sharply to the Variables. Wait, I think I just saw his eyes move."

Thomas froze, tried to stare straight ahead into the darkness of his eyelids. It was hard, but he forced himself to breathe evenly, as if asleep. He didn't know exactly what these people were talking about, but he desperately wanted to hear more. *Knew* he needed to hear more.

"Who cares if he's listening?" the man asked. "He couldn't possibly understand enough to affect his responses one way or the other. It'll do him good to know we made a huge exception to get that infection out of him. That WICKED will do what it has to when necessary."

The high-pitched-voice lady laughed, one of the most pleasant sounds Thomas had ever heard. "If you're listening, Thomas, don't get too excited. We're about to dump you right back where we took you from."

The drugs coursing through Thomas's veins seemed to surge, and he felt himself fading into bliss. He tried to open his eyes, but couldn't. Before he drifted off he did hear one last thing, from the first woman. Something very odd.

"It's what you would've wanted us to do."

CHAPTER 42

The mysterious people were true to their word.

The next time Thomas woke up, he was hanging in the air, strung tightly to a canvas litter with handles, swaying back and forth. A large rope attached to a ring of blue metal held him as he was lowered from something huge, the whole time accompanied by the same explosion of hums and heavy thumps that he'd heard when they'd come to get him. He gripped the sides of the litter, terrified.

Finally, he felt a soft bump, and then a million faces appeared around him. Minho, Newt, Jorge, Brenda, Frypan, Aris, the other Gladers. The rope holding him detached and sprang up into the air. Then, almost instantaneously, the vessel from which he'd been lowered vaulted away, disappearing into the brilliance of the sun directly overhead. The sounds of its engines faded, and soon it was gone.

Then everyone spoke at once.

"What was that all about?"

"Are you okay?"

"What'd they do to you?"

"Who was that?"

"Have fun in the Berg?"

"How's your shoulder?"

Thomas ignored it all and tried to get up, but realized that the ropes holding him to the litter still bound him tightly to it. He found Minho with his eyes. "A little help here?"

As Minho and a couple of others worked on untying him, Thomas had a disturbing thought. The people from WICKED had shown up to save him pretty quickly. From what they'd said, it was something they hadn't planned on, but they'd done it anyway. Which meant they were watching and could swoop in to save them whenever they wanted to.

But they hadn't until now. How many people had died in the last few days while WICKED stood by and watched? And why did that change for Thomas, just because he'd been shot by a rusty bullet?

It was too much to think about.

Once freed, he got to his feet and stretched out his muscles, refusing to acknowledge the second volley of questions flung his way. The day was hot, brutally hot, and as he stretched, he realized that he felt no pain other than the slightest of aches in his shoulder. He looked down to see that he was wearing fresh clothes, and that there was the bulge of a bandage under the left sleeve of his shirt. But his thoughts immediately went to something else.

"What are you guys doing out in the open? Your skin is gonna bake!"

Minho didn't answer, just pointed at something behind him, and Thomas looked to see a very shabby hut. It was made out of dry wood that seemed like it might crumble to pure dust at any second, but it was big enough to provide shelter for everyone there.

"We better get back under that thing," Minho said. Thomas realized that they must've run out just to see him delivered from the huge flying . . . Berg? Jorge had called it a Berg.

The group trekked over to the shelter; Thomas told them a dozen times that he'd explain everything from beginning to end once they were settled. Brenda found him, walked right next to him. But she didn't offer her hand, and Thomas felt an uneasy relief. She also didn't say anything, and neither did he.

The miserable city of the Cranks lay a few miles distant, huddling in all its decay and madness to the south. No sign of the infected people anywhere. To the north, the mountains loomed now, only a day or so away. Craggy and lifeless, they sloped up higher and higher until they ended in jagged brown peaks. Harsh cuts in the rock made the whole range appear as though a giant had hacked at it with a massive axe for days and days, letting out all its giant frustration.

They reached the shelter, the wood dry as rotted bone. It looked as if it had stood there for a hundred years—maybe built by a farmer in the days before the world was ravaged. How it had withstood everything was a complete mystery. But one flick of a match and the thing would probably burn down in three seconds.

"All right," Minho said, pointing to a spot in the far end of the shade. "You sit there, get yourself all nice and comfy and start talking."

Thomas couldn't believe how good he felt—just a dull ache in his shoulder. And he didn't think he had any trace of drugs in him anymore. Whatever doctors WICKED had unleashed on him had been brilliant at what they did. He took a seat and waited for everyone to get situated in front of him, sitting cross-legged on the hot and dusty ground. He was like a schoolteacher readying to give a lesson—a blurry flash from his past.

Minho was the last to take a seat, right next to Brenda. "Okay, tell us about your adventures with the aliens in their big bad spaceship."

"You sure about this?" Thomas asked. "How many days left to get over those mountains, to the safe haven?"

"Five days, dude. But you know we can't go tramping around in this sun with nothing to protect us. You're gonna talk, then we're gonna sleep, then we're all gonna bust our humps walking all night. Get on it."

"Good that," Thomas said, wondering what they'd been doing

while he was away, but realizing it didn't matter all that much. "Save all your questions till the end, children." When not a single person laughed, or even smiled, he coughed and hurried on. "It was WICKED that came and got me. I kept passing out, but they took me to some doctors who totally fixed me up. I heard them saying something about how it wasn't supposed to happen, how the gun had been a factor they hadn't expected. The bullet set off a nasty infection in me, and I guess they felt pretty strongly that it wasn't time for me to die."

Blank faces stared back at him.

Thomas knew it would be hard for them to accept—even after he'd told the whole story. "Just telling you what I heard."

He went on to explain more. Every detail of what he could remember, and about the odd bedside conversation he'd listened in on. Things about killzone patterns and Candidates. More about the Variables. None of it had made much sense the first time around, and it made even less now as he tried to recall it word for word. The Gladers—plus Jorge and Brenda—looked as frustrated as he felt.

"Well, that really cleared things up," Minho finally said. "Must have something to do with all those signs about you in the city."

Thomas shrugged. "Glad to know you're so happy to see me alive."

"Hey, if you wanna be the leader, no skin off my back. I *am* happy to see you alive."

"No thanks. You keep it."

Minho didn't respond. Thomas couldn't deny that the signs weighed heavily on him—what did it really mean that WICKED wanted him to be the leader? And what should he do about it?

Newt got to his feet, his face in a deep scowl of concentration. "So we're all potential candidates for *something*. And maybe the purpose of all the buggin' klunk we've been through is to weed out those who don't qualify. But for some reason the whole gun-and-rusty-bullet thing wasn't part of the . . . normal tests. Or Variables, whatever. If Thomas is gonna croak and die, it wasn't supposed to come from a bloody infection."

Thomas pursed his lips and nodded. Sounded like a great summary to him.

"What this means is that they're watching us," Minho said. "Just like they did in the Maze. Has anyone seen a beetle blade running around anywhere?"

Several Gladers shook their heads.

"What the hell's a beetle blade?" Jorge asked.

Thomas answered. "Little mechanical lizard things that spied on us with cameras in the Maze."

Jorge rolled his eyes. "Of course. Sorry I asked."

"The Maze was definitely some kind of indoor facility," Aris said. "But there's just no way we're inside something anymore. Though they could be using satellites or long-range cameras, I guess."

Jorge cleared his throat. "What is it about Thomas that makes him so special? Those signs in the city about him being the real leader, them swooping in here and saving his butt when he got all sicky-sicky." He looked at Thomas. "I'm not trying to be mean, *muchacho*—I'm just curious. What makes you better than the rest of your buddies?"

"I'm not special," Thomas said, even though he knew he was hiding something. He just didn't know *what*. "You heard what they said. We have lots of ways to die out here, but that gun shouldn't be one of them. I think they would've saved anybody who'd gotten shot. It wasn't about me—it was the bullet that messed things up."

"Still," Jorge replied with a smirk. "I think I'll stay close to you from here on."

A few more discussions broke out, but Minho didn't let them last long. He insisted that they all needed sleep if they were planning on marching through the night. Thomas didn't complain—he'd grown more tired with every passing second of sitting in that hot air on that hot ground. Maybe it was his body healing, maybe just the heat. Either way, sleep called to him.

They didn't have blankets or pillows, so Thomas curled up on the ground in the very spot where he'd been sitting, resting his head on his folded arms. Brenda somehow ended up right next to him, though she didn't say anything, and she certainly didn't touch him. Thomas didn't know if he'd ever figure her out.

He sucked in a long, slow breath, closed his eyes, then welcomed the rest, welcomed that heavy feeling of slumber as it started pulling him into its depths. The sounds around him seemed to fade away, the air to thicken. A calm came over him, then sleep.

The sun was still blazing in the sky when a voice sounded in his mind, waking him up.

A girl's voice.

Teresa.

After days and days of utter silence, Teresa started talking to him telepathically, all at once, a rush of words.

Tom, don't even try to talk back, just listen. Something terrible is going to happen to you tomorrow. An awful, awful thing. You're gonna be hurt and you're gonna be scared. But you have to trust me. No matter what happens, no matter what you see, no matter what you hear, no matter what you think. You have to trust me. I won't be able to talk to you.

She paused, but Thomas was so stunned and trying so hard to understand what she'd said—make sure he remembered it—that he couldn't get a word in before she started up again.

I have to go. You won't hear from me for a while.

Another pause.

Not until we're back together.

He fumbled for something to say, but her voice and her presence slipped away, leaving him empty once more.

CHAPTER 43

It took a long time for Thomas to find sleep again.

He had no doubt it had been Teresa. None at all. Just like before when they'd spoken to each other, he'd felt her presence, sensed her emotions. She'd been with him, even if it had been for such a short time. And when she left, it was like opening up that vast void within all over again. As if during the days since her disappearance a thick liquid had slowly seeped in and filled that chamber, only to have it all sucked out again when she came and went.

What had she meant, anyway? Something awful was going to happen to him, but he needed to trust her? He couldn't wrap his mind around that enough for it to make any sense. And as awful as her warning sounded, his thoughts kept drifting to the last part, about them being together again. Was that some string of false hope? Or did it mean she thought he'd make it through the bad thing and end up okay? Reunited with her? Possibilities raced through his mind, but they all seemed to hit a depressing dead end.

The day only got hotter and hotter as he tossed and turned, haunted by his thoughts. He'd almost grown used to Teresa's being gone, which made him sick to his stomach. To make it worse, he felt like he'd betrayed her by letting Brenda become his friend, by growing so close to her.

Ironically, his first instinct was to reach out and wake Brenda, talk to *her* about it. Was that wrong? He felt so frustrated and stupid he wanted to scream.

All great for someone trying to fall back asleep in the miserable heat.

The sun had trudged halfway to the horizon before he finally did.

He felt a little better in the late evening when Newt shook him awake. Teresa's brief visit to his mind seemed like a dream now. He could almost believe it had never happened.

"Sleep well, Tommy?" Newt asked. "How's that shoulder?"

Thomas sat up, rubbed his eyes. Though he couldn't have slept for more than three or four hours, his sleep had been deep and undisturbed. He rubbed his shoulder to test it and was surprised all over again. "Feels really good, actually—aches a little, but not much. Hard to believe I was hurtin' so bad before."

Newt looked around at the Gladers preparing to leave, then back at Thomas. "Feels like we haven't talked much since leaving the bloody dorm. Not much time to sit around and sip tea, I guess."

"Yeah." For some reason this made Thomas think of Chuck, and all the pain of his death came rushing back. Which just made him hate the people behind all this all over again. The line from Teresa came back to him. "I don't see how WICKED can be good."

"Huh?"

"Remember what Teresa had written on her arm when she first woke up? Or did you even know about that? It said *WICKED is good*. I'm just finding that hard to believe." The sarcasm in his voice wasn't subtle.

Newt had a strange smile on his face. "Well, they just saved your buggin' life."

"Yeah, they're real saints." Thomas couldn't deny he was confused. They *had* saved his life. He also knew he'd worked for them. But what it all meant, he had no idea.

Brenda, who had been stirring in her sleep, now finally sat up, letting out a big yawn. "Morning. Or evening. Whatever."

"Another day alive," Thomas answered, then realized Newt might have no idea who Brenda was. He really had no idea what had happened in the group since he'd been shot. "I'm assuming you guys had time to get to know each other? If not, Brenda, this is Newt. Newt, Brenda."

"Yeah, we know already." Newt reached out and shook her hand mockingly. "But thanks again for making sure this bloody sissy didn't get his butt killed while you two were out partying."

The barest hint of a smile flashed across her face. "Partying. Yeah. I especially loved the part where we had people trying to cut our noses off." A look flashed across her face, part embarrassment, part despair. "Guess it won't be long before *I'm* one of those psychos."

Thomas didn't know how to respond to that. "You're probably not that much farther along than us. Remember that—"

Brenda wouldn't let him finish. "Yeah, I know. You guys are gonna take me to the magical cure. I know." She got up then, the conversation obviously over.

Thomas looked at Newt, who shrugged. Then, as he got to his knees, he leaned in and whispered, "She your new girlfriend? I'm telling Teresa." He snickered to himself and was gone.

Thomas sat there for a minute, overwhelmed by it all. Teresa, Brenda, his friends. The warning he'd received. The Flare. The fact that they only had a few days to cross those mountains. WICKED. Whatever waited for them at the safe haven and in the future.

Too much. It was all too much.

He had to stop thinking. He was hungry, and that he *could* solve. So he got up and went searching for something to eat. And Frypan didn't disappoint.

★ ★ ★

They set off just as the sun dipped below the horizon, making the dusty orange land look almost purple. Thomas was cramped and tired, itching to walk off some steam and loosen his muscles.

The mountains slowly became jagged peaks of shadow, growing taller and taller as they walked. There were no real foothills to speak of; the flat valley just stretched forward until the ground erupted toward the sky in sheer cliffs and steep slopes. All brown and ugly, lifeless. Thomas hoped an obvious path would present itself once they'd made it that far.

No one spoke much as they marched along. Brenda stayed close but quiet. She didn't even talk to Jorge. Thomas hated how it was now. How suddenly everything was awkward between him and Brenda. He liked her, probably more than he liked anyone else now besides Newt and Minho. And Teresa, of course.

Newt approached him after darkness had fallen, the stars and moon their only guides. Their light was enough—you didn't need much when the ground was flat and all you had to do was walk toward the looming wall of rock in front of you. The *crunch crunch crunch* of their footsteps on the earth filled the air.

"Been thinkin'," Newt said.

"About what?" Thomas didn't really care; he was just glad to have someone to talk to and get his mind off things.

"WICKED. Ya know, they broke their own bloody rules with you."

"How's that?"

"They said there *were* no rules. Said we had so much time to get to the bloody safe haven and that was that. No rules. People dying left and right, then they come down in a buggin' monster flying thing and save your butt. Doesn't make sense." He paused. "Not that I'm complaining—I'm glad you're alive and all."

"Gee, thanks." Thomas knew it was a good point, but he was tired of thinking about it.

"And then there were all those signs in the city. Weird."

Thomas looked over at Newt, barely able to see his friend's face. "What, you jealous or something?" he asked, trying to make a joke out of it. Trying to ignore the fact that the signs *had* to be a big deal.

Newt laughed. "No, you shank. Just dying to know what's really going on around here. What this is really all about."

"Yeah." Thomas nodded. He couldn't agree more. "The lady said only a few of us were good enough to be Candidates. And she *did* say I was the best Candidate, and they didn't want me dying from something they hadn't planned. But I don't know what it all means. Has something to do with all that klunk about killzone patterns."

They walked on for a minute or so before Newt spoke again. "Not worth bustin' our brains about, I guess. What's gonna happen'll happen."

Thomas almost told him then about what Teresa had said in his mind, but for some reason it just didn't feel right.

He stayed silent, and eventually Newt drifted away until once again Thomas walked alone in the dark.

A couple of hours passed before he had another conversation, this time with Minho. A lot of words flew back and forth between them, but in the end they hadn't really said much. Just passing time, rehashing the same questions they'd all gone over in their minds a million times.

Thomas's legs were a little tired, but not too bad. The mountains got ever closer. The air cooled considerably, and it felt wonderful. Brenda remained silent and distant.

And on they went.

★ ★ ★

When the first traces of dawn turned the sky a deep, dark blue, the stars beginning to wink away for the coming day, Thomas finally got the nerve to approach Brenda and talk about something. Anything. The cliffs loomed now, dead trees and chunks of scattered rock coming into focus. They'd reach the foot of the mountains by the time the sun popped over the horizon, Thomas was sure of it.

"Hey," he said to her. "How're your feet holding up?"

"Fine." It came out curt, but then she quickly spoke again, maybe trying to make up for it. "How about you? Your shoulder seem okay?"

"I can't believe how fine it is. Doesn't hurt much at all."

"That's good."

"Yeah." He racked his brain, trying to think of something to say. "So, um, I'm sorry about all the weird stuff that happened. And . . . for anything I said. My head's all kinds of crazy and messed up."

She looked over at him, and he could see a bit of softness in her eyes. "Please, Thomas. The last thing you need to do is apologize." She returned her gaze up ahead. "We're just different. Plus, you have that girlfriend of yours. I shouldn't have tried to kiss you and all that crap."

"She's not really my girlfriend." He regretted saying it as soon as it came out—didn't even know where it had come from.

Brenda huffed. "Don't be dumb. And don't insult me. If you're gonna resist this"—she paused and gestured to herself with a sweep of her hands from head to toe with a mocking smile—"then it better be for a good reason."

Thomas laughed—all the tension and awkwardness had just vanished completely. "Point taken. You're probably a crappy kisser anyway."

She punched him in the arm—luckily his good one. "You couldn't possibly be more wrong. Trust me on that one."

Thomas was just about to say something stupid when he stopped dead in his tracks. Somebody almost ran into him from behind, tripped around to his side, but he couldn't tell who—his eyes were glued in front of him, his heart completely frozen.

The sky had lightened considerably, and the leading edge of the mountains' slope lay just a few hundred feet away. Halfway between here and there, a girl had seemingly appeared out of nowhere, rising from the ground. And she was walking toward them at a brisk pace.

In her hands she held a long shaft of wood with a large, nasty-looking blade lashed to one end.

It was Teresa.

CHAPTER 44

Thomas didn't quite know how to compute what he saw. He felt no surprise or joy at Teresa's being alive—he'd already known that she was. She'd spoken to his mind just the day before. But seeing her in the flesh still lifted his spirits. Until he remembered her warning that something bad was going to happen. Until he thought about the fact she was holding a bladed spear.

The other Gladers noticed right after he did, and soon everyone had stopped to gawk at Teresa as she marched toward them, her hands gripping that weapon, her face hard as stone. She looked ready to start stabbing the first thing that moved.

Thomas took a step forward, not really sure what he planned to do. But then more movement stopped him.

On both sides of Teresa, girls appeared; they, too, seemed to come from nowhere. He turned to look behind him. They were surrounded, by at least twenty girls.

And they all held weapons, varying knives and rusty swords and jagged machetes. Several of the girls had bows and arrows, their menacing tips already aimed at the group of Gladers. Thomas felt an uneasy slice of fear. Regardless of what Teresa had said about something bad happening, surely she wouldn't let these people hurt them. Right?

Group B popped into his mind. And his tattoo saying how they were supposed to kill him.

His thoughts were cut short when Teresa stopped about thirty feet away from the group. Her companions did the same, forming a complete circle around the Gladers. Thomas turned again to take it all in. Each one of their new visitors stood stiffly, eyes squinted, weapons held out in front and ready. The bows scared him the most—he and the others would have no chance to do anything before those arrows could fly and find a home inside someone's chest.

He stopped, facing Teresa. Her eyes were focused on him.

Minho spoke first. "What's this crap about, Teresa? Nice way to greet your long-lost buddies."

At the mention of the name *Teresa,* Brenda spun and looked sharply at Thomas. He gave her a quick nod, and the surprise on her face made him sad for some reason.

Teresa didn't answer the question, and an eerie silence swept across the group. The sun continued to rise, inching toward the point where its heat would beat down on them unbearably.

Teresa walked toward them again, and stopped about ten feet from where Minho and Newt stood side by side.

"Teresa?" Newt asked. "What the bloody—"

"Shut up," Teresa said. She didn't snap or yell it. She said it calmly and with conviction, which only made it that much more frightening to Thomas. "And any of you makes a move, the bows start shooting."

Teresa brought her spear up to a better fighting position, swept it back and forth as she stepped past Newt and Minho and through the Gladers, acting as if she was searching for something. She came to Brenda, paused. Neither said a word, but the hatred between them was visible. Teresa moved past her, never dropping her icy stare.

And then she was in front of Thomas. He tried to tell himself that she'd never use that weapon on him, but believing it wasn't easy when you were looking at the blade's sharp edge.

"Teresa," he whispered before he could stop himself. Despite the spear, despite the hard look on her face, despite the way her muscles tensed as if she was about to slash him, all he wanted was to reach out to her. He couldn't help but remember the kiss she'd given him. The way it had felt.

She didn't move, just kept staring at him, her face unreadable except for the obvious anger there.

"Teresa, what's—"

"Shut up." That same voice of calm. Of utter command. It didn't sound like her.

"But what—"

Teresa reared back and swung the butt of her spear at him, smashing it into his right cheek. An explosion of pain shot through his skull, his neck; he crumpled to his knees, a hand to his face where she'd hit him.

"I said shut up." She reached down and grabbed him by the shirt, jerked up until he stood once again. She repositioned her hands on the wooden shaft, pointed it at him. "Is your name Thomas?"

He gaped at her. His world was crashing in on him, even though he told himself she'd warned him. Told him that no matter what, he had to trust her. "You know who I—"

She swung the spear even more violently this time, crashing the bladeless end into the side of his head, right on his ear. The pain was twice as bad as the first hit; he cried out, clutching his head. But he didn't fall this time. "You know who I am!" he screamed.

"I used to, anyway," she said in a voice that was both soft and disgusted. "Now I'm going to ask you one more time. Is your name Thomas?"

"Yes!" he yelled back at her. "My name is Thomas!"

Teresa nodded, then started to back away from him, the tip of the blade once again aimed at his chest. People got out of her way as she passed the group and rejoined the circle of girls who surrounded them.

"You're coming with us," she called out. "Thomas. Come on. Remember, anyone tries something, the arrows fly."

"No way!" Minho yelled. "You're not taking him anywhere."

Teresa acted as if she hadn't heard him, her eyes riveted to Thomas in that strange squinty-eyed stare. "This isn't some stupid game. I'm going to start counting. Every time I hit a multiple of five, we'll kill one of you with an arrow. We'll do it until Thomas is the only one left, then we'll take him anyway. It's up to you."

For the first time, Thomas noticed that Aris was acting strange. He stood just a few feet to Thomas's right, and he kept turning in a slow circle, staring at the girls one by one as if he knew them each well. But somehow he kept his mouth shut.

Of course, Thomas thought. If this really was Group B, Aris had been with them. He *did* know them.

"One!" Teresa shouted.

Thomas wasn't taking any chances. He walked forward, pushing past people until he reached the open, then went straight toward Teresa. He ignored the comments from Minho and the others. He ignored everything. Eyes on Teresa, trying to show no emotion, he walked until he stood almost nose to nose with her.

It was what he wanted anyway, right? He wanted to be with her. Even if she'd been turned against him somehow. Even if she was being manipulated by WICKED, like Alby and Gally had been. For all he knew, her memory had been wiped again. Didn't matter. She looked serious, and he couldn't risk having someone shoot one of his friends with a bow and arrow.

"Fine," he said. "Take me."

"I only made it to one."

"Yeah. I'm really brave that way."

She hit him with the spear, so hard that he couldn't help but drop to the ground again. His jaw and head ached like smoldering fire. He spit, saw blood splatter on the dirt.

"Bring the bag," Teresa said from above.

In his peripheral vision he saw two girls walking toward him, their weapons hidden away somewhere. One of them—a dark-skinned girl with hair cut almost to her scalp—held a large frayed burlap sack. They stopped two feet from him; he got back to his hands and knees, scared to do anything more for fear of getting pummeled again.

"We're taking him with us!" Teresa yelled. "If anybody follows, I'll hit him again and we'll start shooting you. We won't really bother aiming. Just let the arrows fly any old way they feel like."

"Teresa!" Minho's voice. "You catch the Flare that quickly? Your mind's obviously gone already."

The butt of the spear smashed into the back of Thomas's head; he collapsed onto his stomach, black stars swimming in the dirt inches from his face. How could she do this to him?

"Anything else you wanna say?" Teresa asked. After a long moment of silence, she said, "Didn't think so. Put the bag over him."

Hands roughly grabbed his shoulder and spun him onto his back—their grip dug into his bullet wound enough to send a deep ache flashing through his upper body for the first time since WICKED had fixed him up.

He moaned. Faces—they didn't even look angry—hovered over him as two girls held the open end of the sack directly above his head.

"Don't resist," the dark-skinned girl said, her face shining with sweat. "Or it'll just get worse."

Thomas was perplexed. Her eyes and voice held genuine sympathy for him. But her next words couldn't have been more different.

"Better just to go along and let us kill you. Doesn't do you any good to have a lot of pain along the way."

The bag slipped over his head, and all he could see was ugly brown light.

CHAPTER 45

They shifted him around on the ground till they got the bag slipped entirely over his body. Then they tied the open end at his feet with a rope, knotting it tight and wrapping its ends up and around the rest of him, pinning him inside the bag, cinching another knot just over his head.

Thomas felt the bag going taut; then his head was pulled up. He imagined girls holding either end of this impossibly long rope. Which could only mean one thing—they were going to drag him. He couldn't take it anymore, started squirming even though he knew what it'd get him.

"Teresa! Don't do this to me!"

This time a fist hit him right in the stomach, making him howl. He tried to double over, tried to clutch his middle, but couldn't because of the stupid bag. Nausea swept through him; he fought it, kept his food down.

"Since you obviously don't care about yourself," Teresa said, "talk again and we'll start shooting your friends. That sound good to you?"

Thomas didn't respond; he heaved a silent sob of agony. Had he really been thinking things were looking up in the world only yesterday? His infection cured and his wound healed, away from the city of Cranks, nothing but a swift and hard hike through the mountains between them and the safe haven. He should've known better after everything he'd been through.

"I meant what I said!" Teresa yelled at the Gladers. "There won't be a warning. Follow us and the arrows start flying."

Thomas saw her outline as she knelt next to him, heard her knees crunching on the dirt. Then she grabbed him through the material of the bag, put her head against his, her mouth just half an inch from his ear. She started whispering, so faintly he had to strain to hear, concentrating to separate her words from the breeze.

"They're blocking me from talking to you in our heads. Remember to trust me."

Thomas, surprised, had to fight to keep his mouth shut.

"What're you saying to him?" This came from one of the girls holding the rope attached to the bag.

"I'm letting him know just how much I'm enjoying this. How much I'm enjoying my revenge. Do you mind?"

Thomas had never heard such arrogance from her. She was either a really good actress or *had* started going crazy. Gained a split personality or two.

"Well," the other girl responded. "Glad you're having so much fun. But we need to hurry."

"I know," Teresa said. She gripped the sides of Thomas's head even harder, squeezed and shook it. Then she pressed her mouth against the rough material, pushing on his ear. When she spoke, again with that hot whisper, he could feel her hot breath through the weave of the burlap. "Hang in there. It'll be over soon."

The words numbed Thomas's brain; he had no idea what to think. Was she being sarcastic?

She released him and stood back up. "Okay, let's get out of here. Make sure you hit as many rocks as you can along the way."

His captors started walking, dragging him along behind them. He felt the rough ground below him as he was dragged across it, the big sack providing absolutely no protection. It hurt. He arched his back, putting all his weight on his feet, letting his shoes bear the brunt of the impacts. But he knew his strength couldn't hold out forever.

Teresa walked right beside him as they pulled his body along. He could just make her out through the burlap.

Then Minho started yelling, his voice already fading with distance, the sound of being dragged against the dirt making it that much harder to hear. What Thomas *did* hear, however, gave him little hope. Between garbled unflattering names, Thomas heard the words "we'll find you" and "time is right" and "weapons."

Teresa slammed her fist into Thomas's stomach again, shutting Minho up.

And across the desert they went, Thomas bouncing over the dirt like a sack of old clothes.

Thomas imagined horrible things as they went along. His legs were weakening every second, and he knew he'd have to lower his body to the ground soon. He pictured the bleeding wounds, the permanent scars.

But maybe it wouldn't matter. They planned on killing him anyway.

Teresa had said to trust her. And even though he had a hard time doing it, he was trying to believe her. Could all the stuff she'd done to him since reappearing with the weapons and Group B really be an act? If it wasn't, why would she keep whispering to him to trust her?

His mind turned it all over in circles until he couldn't concentrate anymore. His body was being rubbed raw, and he knew he needed to figure out how to prevent every inch of skin from being scratched off.

The mountains saved him.

When they started going up the steep slope, it obviously became difficult for the girls to drag his body the way they'd done across flat ground. They tried pulling him in quick jerks—slipping and letting him slide several feet back down, then hauling him back up only to let him slip again. Teresa finally said it'd probably be easier to carry him by the shoulders and ankles. And that they should do it in shifts.

An idea hit Thomas then that was so obvious he thought surely he'd missed something. "Why don't you just let me walk!" he called through the burlap, his voice muffled and cracking from thirst. "I mean, you *do* have weapons. What am I gonna do?"

Teresa kicked him in the side. "Shut up, Thomas. We're not idiots. We're waiting until your Glader buddies can't see us anymore."

He'd done his best to stifle his groan when her foot crashed into his rib cage. "Huh? Why?"

"Because that's what we were *told* to do. Now shut up!"

"Why'd you tell him that?" one of the other girls whispered harshly.

"What does it matter?" Teresa responded, not even trying to hide what she was saying. "We're gonna kill him anyway. Who cares if he knows what we were told to do?"

Told to do, Thomas thought. *By WICKED.*

A different girl spoke up. "Well, I can barely see them now. Once we reach that crevice up there, we'll be out of sight, and they'll never find us after that. Even if they do follow."

"All right, then," Teresa said. "Let's just get him that far."

Hands were soon gripping Thomas on all sides, lifting him into the air. From what he could see through the sack, Teresa and three of her new friends were carrying him. They picked their way through boulders and around dead trees, going up and up and up. He heard their heavy breaths, smelled their sweat, hated them more with each jolting step. Even Teresa. He tried one last time to reach her mind, to salvage his trust in her, but she wasn't there.

The trudge up the mountain went on for maybe an hour—with stops here and there for girls to switch off carrying duties—and it had been at least twice that long since they'd left the Gladers. The sun was reaching a point where it would become dangerous, the heat stifling. But then they rounded a massive wall, the ground leveling a bit, and entered shade. The cooler air was a relief.

"All right," Teresa said. "Drop him."

Without ceremony, they did what she said and he slammed into the ground with a heavy grunt. It knocked the wind out of him, and he lay there gasping for air as they started untying the ropes. By the time he caught his breath, the bag had been taken off.

He blinked, looking up at Teresa and her friends. They all had their weapons pointed at him, which just seemed ridiculous.

From somewhere he found a trace of courage. "You guys must think a lot of me, twenty of you with knives and machetes, me with nothing. I feel so special."

Teresa reared back with her spear.

"Wait!" Thomas cried, and she stopped. He held his hands up in deference, slowly got to his feet. "Look, I'm not gonna try anything. Just take me wherever we're going and then I'll let you kill me like a good boy. I don't have any shuck thing to live for anyway."

He looked directly at Teresa when he said this, tried to put as much spite into his words as possible. He still held on to a little hope that somehow this would end up making sense, but either way, after how he'd been treated, he wasn't in such a hot mood.

"Come on," Teresa said. "I'm sick of this. Let's get to the inside of the Pass so we can sleep the day off. Tonight we'll start heading through."

The girl with dark skin who'd helped put him in the sack spoke next. "And what about this guy we've been hauling around for the last few hours?"

"Don't worry, we'll kill him," Teresa replied. "We'll kill him just the way they told us to. It's his punishment for what he did to me."

CHAPTER 46

Thomas couldn't figure out what Teresa meant by her last statement. What had he done to her? But his mind went numb as they walked and walked and walked, apparently heading back to Group B's camp. A steady climb uphill, the effort burning his legs. A sheer cliff to their left kept them in the shade as they hiked, but everything was still red and brown and hot. Dry. Dusty. The girls gave him a few sips of water, but he was sure that every drop evaporated before it hit his stomach.

They reached a large indentation in the east wall just as the noon sun broke out overhead, a golden ball of fire bent on burning them to ashes. The shallow cave went about forty feet into the mountain face; it was obvious that this was their camp, and it looked like they'd been there for a day or two. Blankets strewn about, the remains of a fire, some trash piled on the edge. Only three people were there when they arrived—girls just like the others—which meant they'd felt they needed almost everyone to kidnap Thomas.

With the bows and arrows, the knives and machetes? It seemed almost silly. A few of them would've done just as well.

Along the way, Thomas had learned some things. The dark-skinned girl's name was Harriet, and the one who was always with her, with the reddish blond hair and white, white skin, was named Sonya. Though he couldn't tell for certain, he guessed that those two had mostly been in charge until Teresa had arrived. They acted with some authority, but always deferred to her in the end.

“Okay,” Teresa said. “Let’s tie him to that ugly tree.” She pointed at the bone-white skeleton of an oak, its roots still clinging to the rocky soil even though it had to have been dead for years and years. “And we might as well feed him so he doesn’t moan and groan all day and keep us awake.”

Laying it on a little thick, isn’t she? Thomas thought. Whatever her true intentions, her words had started to get a little ridiculous. And he couldn’t deny it anymore—he was really starting to hate her, no matter what she’d said in the beginning.

He didn’t fight as they tied his torso to the trunk, leaving his hands free. Once they had him good and secure they gave him a few granola bars and a bottle of water. No one spoke to him or met his gaze. And strangely, if he wasn’t mistaken, he noticed that everyone looked a little guilty. He started eating, and as he did he carefully took in everything around him. His thoughts wandered all over the place as the rest of them began settling in to sleep out the remaining daylight. Something wasn’t right about all this.

Teresa’s display certainly didn’t seem like an act. It never had. Was it possible that she was doing the exact opposite of what she’d told him—making him think he should trust her when her real plan had been and was to—

With a jolt he remembered the tag outside her door back in the dorm. *The Betrayer.* He’d completely forgotten about it until that moment. Things started to make more sense.

WICKED was the boss, here. They were the groups’ only hope of surviving. If they’d really told her to kill him, would she do it? To save herself? And what was that line she’d spit out about his having done something to her? Could they even be manipulating her thoughts? Making her not like him anymore?

Then there was his tattoo and the signs in the city. The tattoo had warned him; the signs had told him he was the real leader. The label next to Teresa's door had been another warning.

Still—he had no weapons and he was tied to a tree. Group B outnumbered him by more than twenty and they all *had* weapons. Real easy.

Sighing, he finished up his food and felt a little better physically. And though he didn't quite know how everything added up, he had a new confidence that he was closer to understanding. And that he couldn't quit.

Harriet and Sonya had pallets laid out nearby; they kept sneaking looks at him as they readied for sleep. Again Thomas noticed those odd expressions of shame or guilt. He saw it as an opportunity to fight for his life with words.

"You guys don't really wanna kill me, do you?" He asked it in a tone that said he'd caught them in a lie. "Have you ever even killed anyone before?"

Harriet gave him a harsh glare, stopping just before she laid her head down on a wad of blankets. She propped herself up on her elbow. "Based on what Teresa told us, we escaped our Maze three days faster than your group did. Lost fewer people and killed more Grievers to do it. I think knocking off one little insignificant teenage boy won't be too tough."

"Think of the guilt you'll feel." He could only hope the thought would dig at them.

"We'll get over it." She stuck her tongue out at him—actually stuck her tongue out!—then put her head down and closed her eyes.

Sonya sat cross-legged, looking about as far from sleep as humanly possible. "We don't have a choice. WICKED said that was our only task.

If we don't do it, they won't let us in at the safe haven. We'll die out here in the Scorch."

Thomas shrugged. "Hey, I understand. Sacrifice me to save yourselves. Very noble."

She stared at him for a long time; he had to fight not to drop his gaze. She finally looked away and lay down with her back to him.

Teresa walked over, her face twisted in annoyance. "What are you talking about?"

"Nothing," mumbled Harriet. "Tell him to shut up."

"Shut up," Teresa said.

Thomas huffed a sarcastic laugh. "What're you gonna do, kill me if I don't?"

She didn't say anything, just kept looking at him, her face blank.

"Why do you hate me all of a sudden?" he asked. "What did I do to you?"

Sonya and Harriet both had turned to listen, looking back and forth between Thomas and Teresa.

"You know what you did," Teresa finally said. "So does everyone here—I told them all about it. But even still, I wouldn't have sunk to your level and tried to kill you. We're only doing that because we have no choice. Sorry. Life's tough."

Did something just flash in her eyes? Thomas wondered. What was she trying to tell him? "What are you talking about, *sink to my level*? I'd never kill a friend to save my own butt. Never."

"Me neither. Which is why I'm glad we're not friends." She started to turn away.

"So what'd I do to you?" Thomas asked quickly. "Sorry, I'm kind of havin' a memory lapse—ya know, we have those a lot around here. Remind me."

She twisted back around and glared at him with fiery eyes. "Don't insult me. Don't you dare sit there and act like nothing happened. Now shut up or I'll give you another bruise on that pretty face of yours."

She stomped away, and Thomas kept silent. He shifted until he was somewhat comfortable, his head leaning back on the dead wood of the tree. Everything about his current situation stank, but he was determined to figure it out and survive.

Eventually he slept.

CHAPTER 47

Thomas slept fitfully for a few hours, tossing and turning, trying to find a comfortable position on the hard rock. He finally fell into a deep slumber, and then came the dream.

Thomas is fifteen. He doesn't know how he knows this. Something to do with the timing of the memory. Is it a memory?

He and Teresa are standing in front of a massive bank of screens, each one showing various images from the Glade and the Maze. Some of the views are moving, and he knows why. These camera shots are coming from beetle blades, and every once in a while they have to change position. When they do, it's like looking through the eyes of a rat.

"I can't believe they're all dead," Teresa says.

Thomas is confused. Once again he doesn't quite understand what's happening. He's inside this boy who's supposed to be him, but he doesn't know what Teresa's talking about. Obviously not the Gladers—on one screen he can see Minho and Newt walking toward the forest; on another, Gally sitting on a bench. Then Alby yelling at someone Thomas doesn't recognize.

"We knew it would happen," he finally responds, not sure why he said it.

"It's still hard to take." They aren't looking at each other, just analyzing the screens. "Now it's up to us. And the people in the barracks."

"That's a good thing," Thomas says.

"I almost feel as sorry for them as I do for the Gladers. Almost."

Thomas wonders what this means as his younger dream version clears his throat. "Do you think we've learned enough? Do you really think we can pull this off with all the original Creators dead?"

"We have to, Tom." Teresa steps over to him and grabs his hand. He looks down at her but he can't read her expression. "Everything's in place. We have a year to train the replacements and get ready."

"But it's not right. How can we ask them to—"

Teresa rolls her eyes and squeezes his hand so hard it hurts. "They know what they're getting into. No more talking like that."

"Yeah." Somehow Thomas knows this version of himself in the vision he's seeing feels dead inside. His words mean nothing. "All that matters now are the patterns. The killzone. Nothing else."

Teresa nodded. "No matter how many die or get hurt. If the Variables don't work, they'll end up the same anyway. Everyone will."

"The patterns," Thomas says.

Teresa squeezes his hand. "The patterns."

When he woke up, the light dimming to a dull gray as the sun sank to a horizon he couldn't see, Harriet and Sonya were sitting just a few feet from him. Both staring at him strangely.

"Good evening," he said with false enthusiasm, the troubling dream still fresh in his mind. "Can I help you ladies?"

"We want to know what you know," Harriet said quietly.

The lingering fog of sleep quickly vanished. "Why should I help you?" He wanted to sit and think about what he'd dreamed, but he knew something had changed—he could see it in Harriet's gaze—and he couldn't pass up the chance to save himself.

"I don't think you have much choice," Harriet said. "But if you share whatever you've learned or figured out, maybe we can help *you*."

Thomas looked around for Teresa but couldn't see her. "Where is—"

Sonya interrupted him. "She said she wanted to scout the area to see if your friends followed us. Been gone for about an hour."

In his mind, Thomas could see the Teresa of his dream. Watching those screens, talking about dead Creators and the killzone. Talking about *patterns*. How did it all fit together?

"Forget how to talk?"

His eyes focused on Sonya. "No, um . . . does this mean you guys are having second thoughts about killing me?" The words sounded stupid to him, and he wondered how many people in the history of the world had ever asked a question like that.

Harriet smirked. "Don't go jumping to conclusions. And don't think we've gone all righteous. Let's just say we have our doubts and want to talk—but your odds are slim."

Sonya picked up her line of thought. "The smartest thing right now seems to be to do what we were told. There are a lot more of us than you. I mean, come on. If it was *your* decision, what would you do?"

"Pretty sure I'd choose the option of not killing myself."

"Don't be a jerk. This isn't funny. If you could choose, and the two options were you die or all of us die, which one would you pick? This is all about you or us."

Her face showed she was very serious, and the question hit Thomas like a thump to his chest. She was right, on some level. If that really would happen—they'd all die if they didn't get rid of him—then how could he expect them not to do it?

"You gonna answer?" Sonya pushed.

"I'm thinking." He paused, wiped some sweat off his forehead. Once again, the dream tried to creep to the front of his mind and he had to push it back. "Okay, I'm being honest here. I promise. If I were in your shoes, I'd choose not to kill me."

Harriet rolled her eyes. "Easy for you to say, since it's your life on the line."

"It's not just that. I think it's some kind of test and maybe you're not really supposed to do it." Thomas's heartbeat picked up—he really did mean what he said, but he doubted they'd believe him even if he tried to explain it. "Maybe we *should* share what we know, figure something out."

Harriet and Sonya exchanged a long look.

Sonya finally nodded; then Harriet said, "We've had our doubts about this whole thing from the beginning. Something about it isn't right. So yeah, you better talk. But let us get everybody over here first." They stood up to go rouse the others.

"Hurry, then," Thomas said, wondering if he really did have a chance to get out of this mess. "We better do this before Teresa gets back."

CHAPTER 48

It didn't take long for them to gather everyone—Thomas figured the intrigue of hearing what the dead-guy-walking had to say was just too good to pass up. The girls stood in a tight group in front of him; he remained tied to the ugly, lifeless tree.

"All right," Harriet said. "You talk first, then we will."

Thomas nodded and cleared his throat. He began talking even though he hadn't totally planned what to say yet.

"All I know about your group is what I learned from Aris. And it seems like we all went through pretty much the same thing inside the Maze. But since we escaped, lots of things have been different. And I'm not sure what you know about WICKED."

Sonya cut in. "Not much."

This encouraged Thomas, made him feel like he had an advantage. And it seemed a big mistake for Sonya to have admitted what she did. "Well, I've learned a lot about them. All of us are special in some way—we're being tested or something because they have plans for us." He paused then, but no one showed much of a reaction, so he went on.

"A lot of the things they're doing to us don't make sense because they're just part of the trials—what WICKED calls the Variables. Seeing how we react in certain situations. I don't understand all of it, not even close, but I think this whole thing about killing me is just another layer. Or another lie. So . . . I think this is just another Variable to see what we'll all do."

"In other words," Harriet said, "you want us to risk *our* lives because of this brilliant deduction."

"Don't you see? Killing me has no *point*. Maybe it's a test for you, I don't know. But I do know that I can help you if I'm alive, not if I'm dead."

"Or," Harriet replied, "we're being tested to see if we have the guts to kill our competitors' leader. Isn't *that* the whole point? See which group succeeds? Weed out the weak and leave the strong?"

"I haven't even *been* the leader—Minho has." Thomas shook his head adamantly. "No, think about this. How are you showing any strength by killing me? I'm way outnumbered and you have all these weapons. How does that prove who's stronger?"

"Then what *does* it have to do with?" a girl from the back called out.

Thomas paused, choosing his words carefully. "I think it's a test to see if you'll think for yourself, change plans, make rational decisions. And the more of us there are, the better odds we have of making it to the safe haven. Killing me makes no sense, does no one any good. You've proven any power you needed to by capturing me. Show them you won't blindly take it all the way."

He stopped, relaxed back against the tree. He couldn't think of anything else. It was up to them now. He'd given it his best shot.

"Interesting stuff," Sonya said. "Sounds a lot like something a person who's desperate not to die would say."

Thomas shrugged. "I really feel like it's the truth. I think that if you kill me, you'll have failed the real test WICKED is throwing at you."

"Yeah, I *bet* you think that," Harriet said. She stood up. "Look, to be honest, we've been thinking the same types of things. But we wanted to see what you had to say. Sun should be down soon, and I'm sure Teresa will be back any minute. We'll talk about it when she gets here."

Thomas spoke up quickly, worried that Teresa wouldn't be swayed.

"No! I mean, she's the one who seems the most gung ho about killing me." He said this even though deep down he hoped he didn't mean it. As badly as she'd treated him, surely she wasn't serious about taking it all the way to murder. "I think you guys should make the decision."

"Calm down," Harriet said, a half-smile on her face. "If we decide not to kill you, there's nothing she can freaking do about it. But if we . . ." She stopped, a strange look flashing across her face. Was she worried she'd said too much? "We'll figure it out."

Thomas tried not to show his relief. He might have appealed to their pride a little bit, but he tried not to let his hopes get too high.

Thomas watched as the girls gathered their belongings and packed them into backpacks—*Where'd they get* those? he wondered—readying for the night's journey, to wherever that might be. Murmurs and whispers of conversation floated through the air as people kept glancing his way, obviously discussing what he'd said.

The darkness grew deeper and deeper, and Teresa finally appeared from the direction they'd come in earlier that day. She noticed right away that something was different, probably by the way everyone kept looking between her and Thomas.

"What?" she asked, the same hard look on her face she'd worn since the day before.

It was Harriet who answered. "We need to talk."

Teresa looked confused, but went to the far side of the recess in the cliff with the rest of the group. Furious whispers immediately filled the air, but Thomas couldn't make out a word anybody said. His stomach clenched in anticipation of the verdict.

From where he stood he could see that the conversation had started to get passionate, and Teresa looked as riled up as anyone. He watched her expression intensify as she tried to make some point. It seemed like it was her against the rest of them, which made Thomas very nervous.

Finally, just as nightfall was almost complete, Teresa turned, stomped from the group of girls, and started walking away from the camp, heading north. She had her spear slung over one shoulder, a backpack over the other. Thomas watched her go until she disappeared between the narrow walls of the Pass.

He glanced back at the group, many of whom looked relieved, and Harriet came walking over. Without saying a word, she knelt down and untied the rope securing him to the tree.

"Well?" Thomas finally asked. "Did you guys decide anything?"

Harriet didn't answer until she'd completely freed him; then she sat back on her heels and looked at him, her dark eyes reflecting the faint light of the stars and moon. "It's your lucky day. We decided not to kill your puny butt after all. It can't be a coincidence that we've all been thinking the same things deep down."

Thomas didn't feel the expected rush of relief. In that moment he realized that he'd known that was what they would decide all along.

"But I tell you what," Harriet said as she stood up, holding a hand out to help him do the same. "Teresa does *not* like you. I'd watch my back around her if I were you."

Thomas let Harriet pull him up, confusion and hurt warring for dominance inside him.

Teresa really did want him dead.

CHAPTER 49

Thomas was quiet as he ate with Group B and prepared to leave. Soon they started making their way through the dark pass of the mountains, heading for the safe haven that was supposed to wait on the other side. It felt odd to suddenly be friendly with these people after what they'd done to him, but they acted like nothing unusual had ever happened. They treated him like, well, like one of the girls.

But he did keep his distance a little, hanging toward the back, wondering if he could fully trust their change of heart about him. What was he supposed to do? Even if Harriet and the others *let* him leave, should he try to find his own group, Minho and Newt and everyone else? He desperately wanted to be with his friends and Brenda again. But he knew time was running out, and he had no food or water to make it on his own. He had to hope they'd find their own way to the safe haven.

So he kept walking, staying close to Group B but not too close.

A couple of hours went by, nothing but tall cliffs of stone and the crunching of dirt and rock under his feet to keep him company. It felt good to move again, to stretch his legs and muscles. The deadline was fast approaching, though. And who knew what obstacle might spring up next? Or had the girls planned something else for him? He thought a lot about the dreams he'd been having, but still couldn't put enough together to truly understand what was going on.

Harriet drifted back until the two of them were walking side by side.

"Sorry we dragged you through the desert in a bag," she said. He couldn't see her face in the dimming light very well, but he imagined a smirk there.

"Oh, no problem, it felt good to take a load off for a while." Thomas knew he had to play the part, show some humor. He couldn't trust the girls completely yet, but he had no other options.

She laughed, a sound that put him at ease a bit. "Yeah, well, the man from WICKED gave us very specific instructions about you. But it was Teresa who got all obsessed about it. Almost like killing you was her idea."

This dug at Thomas, but he finally had a chance to learn some things and he wasn't going to let that go. "Did the guy have a white suit and kind of look like a rat turned human?"

"Yeah," she said without hesitating. "Same guy who talked to your group?"

Thomas nodded. "What were the . . . specific instructions he gave you?"

"Well, most of our trip has been through underground tunnels. That's why you didn't see us in the desert. The first thing we were supposed to do was that weird thing where you and Teresa spoke in that building on the south side of the city. Remember?"

Thomas's stomach fell. She'd been with her group at that point? "Uh, yeah, I remember."

"Well, you've probably figured it out, but all of that was an act. Kind of a prepper to give you some false security. She even told us they somehow . . . *controlled* her long enough to make her kiss you. Is that true?"

Thomas stopped walking, bent down and put his hands on his knees. Something had sucked the breath right out of him. That was it. He'd officially and completely lost any trace of doubt. Teresa had turned against him. Or maybe she had never really been on his side.

"I know this sucks," Harriet said softly. "It seems like you used to feel really close to her."

Thomas stood up again, slowly sucked in a long breath. "I . . . just . . . I had hoped it was the other way around. That they were forcing her to try to hurt us, that she broke away long enough to . . . to kiss me."

Harriet put a hand on his arm. "Ever since she joined us, she's made you out to be a monster who did something really awful to her, only she'd never tell us what it was. But I gotta tell ya—you're not anything like how she described you. That's probably the real reason we changed our minds."

Thomas closed his eyes and tried to calm his heart. Then he shook it off and started walking again. "Okay, tell me the rest. I need to hear it. All of it."

Harriet got in stride with him. "Everything else about the instructions to kill you had to do with catching you in the desert like we did and bringing you back here. We were even told to keep you in the bag until we got out of Group A's sight. Then . . . well, then the big day was supposed to be the day after tomorrow. There's supposed to be a place built into the mountain on the north side. A special place to . . . kill you."

Thomas wanted to stop again but kept his feet moving. "A *place*? What does that mean?"

"I don't know. He just told us we'd know what to do when we got there." She paused, then snapped her fingers as if she'd just thought of something. "I bet that's where she went earlier."

"Why? How close are we to the other side?"

"No idea, actually."

They fell into silence and kept walking.

★ ★ ★

It took longer than Thomas would've thought. They were in the middle of the second night of marching when shouts up ahead announced that they'd reached the end of the Pass. Thomas, who'd stayed at the back of the group, broke into a run to catch up; he desperately wanted to see what lay on the north side of the range. One way or another, his fate waited there.

The group of girls had clustered in a wide swath of broken rock that fanned out from the narrow canyon of the Pass before dropping in a steep slope to the bottom of the mountain far below. The three-quarter moon shone down on the valley in front of them, making it look dark purple and eerie. And very flat. With nothing for miles and miles but sparse, dead land.

Absolutely nothing.

No sign of anything that could be a safe haven. And they were supposed to be within a few miles of it.

"Maybe we just can't see it." Thomas didn't know who said it, but he knew every person there understood exactly why she did. Trying to hold on to hope.

"Yeah," Harriet added, sounding upbeat. "It might just be another entrance to one of their underground tunnels. I'm sure it's there."

"How many more miles do you think we have left?" Sonya asked.

"Can't be more than ten, based on where we started and how far the man said we had to go," Harriet answered. "Probably more like seven or eight. I thought we'd come out over here and we'd see a nice big building with a smiley face on it."

Thomas had been searching the darkness the whole time, but he couldn't see anything, either. Just a sea of black stretching to the horizon, where it seemed like a curtain of stars had been pulled down. And no sign of Teresa anywhere.

"Well," Sonya announced. "Not much choice but to keep heading north. We should've known better than to expect something easy. Maybe we can make it to the bottom of the mountain by sunrise. Sleep on flat ground."

The others agreed with her and were just about to set off down a barely visible footpath leading from the fan of rock when Thomas spoke up. "Where's Teresa?"

Harriet looked back at him, the moonlight bathing her face in a pale luminescence. "At this point, I don't really care. If she's a big enough girl to go runnin' around when she doesn't get her way, she's big enough to catch up and find us when she gets over it. Come on."

They started off, heading down the switchback-laden path, the loose soil and rock crunching underfoot. Thomas couldn't help but take a look behind him, searching the mountain face and the narrow entrance to the Pass for signs of Teresa. He was so confused about everything, but still had a strange urge to see her. He gazed across the dark slopes, but saw only dim shadows and reflections of the moonlight's glow.

He turned and started walking, almost relieved he hadn't spotted her.

The group made their way down the mountain, crisscrossing back and forth on the trail in silence. Thomas lingered in the back again, surprised at how blank his mind felt. How numb. He had absolutely no idea where his friends were, no idea what dangers might be waiting for him.

After an hour or so of traveling, his legs starting to burn from the awkward downhill walk, the group came across a pocket of dead trees that arrowed up the mountain in a big swath. It almost looked as if at one time a waterfall might have irrigated to the odd formation of trees. Though if it had, the last drop had long since surrendered to the Scorch.

Thomas, still last in line, was just passing the far side of the trees when a voice spoke his name, startling him so much he almost tripped. He turned sharply to see Teresa step out from behind a thick knot of white wood, spear gripped in her right hand, her face hidden in shadow. The others must not have heard, because they kept walking.

"Teresa," he whispered. "What . . ." He didn't even know what to say.

"Tom, we need to talk," she responded, almost sounding like the girl he thought he knew. "Don't worry about them, just come with me." She gestured to the trees behind her with a quick jerk of her head.

He looked back to the girls of Group B, still heading away from him, then turned to face Teresa again. "Maybe we should—"

"Just come on. The act is over." She turned away without waiting for a response and stepped into the lifeless forest.

Thomas thought hard for two whole seconds, his mind spinning in confusion, instinct screaming at him not to do it. But he followed her.

CHAPTER 50

The trees might have been dead, but their branches still pulled on Thomas's clothes and scratched at his skin. The wood shone white in the moonlight, and the streaks and pools of shadow across the ground gave the whole place a haunted feel. Teresa kept walking in silence, floating up the mountainside like an apparition.

Finally, he found the courage to speak. "Where're we going? And you really expect me to believe all that was an act? Why didn't you stop when everybody else agreed not to kill me?"

But her reply was strange. Barely turning her head, she asked, "You've met Aris, right?" She didn't break stride, just kept moving.

Thomas stopped for a second, completely taken aback. "*Aris?* How do you even know about him? What's he got to do with this?" He hurried to catch up with her again, curious but dreading the answer for some reason.

She didn't respond right away, picking her way through a particularly tight pack of branches; one flew back and smacked him in the face after she let it fly. Once through, she finally stopped and turned to him, right where a shaft of moonlight illuminated her face. She looked unhappy.

"I happen to know Aris very well," she said in a tight voice. "Much better than you're going to like. Not only was he a big part of my life before the Maze, he and I can speak in our minds, just like you and I used to do. Even when I was in the Glade, we communicated all the time. And we knew they'd eventually put us back together."

Thomas searched for a response. What she'd said was so unexpected he thought it must be a joke. Another trick by WICKED.

She waited, arms folded, as if she enjoyed seeing him struggle to speak.

"You're lying," he finally said. "That's all you do is lie. I don't understand why, or what's going on, but—"

"Oh, come *on,* Tom," she said. "How could you *possibly* be so stupid? After all that's happened to you, how could anything surprise you anymore? Everything about us was part of some ridiculous test. And it's over. Aris and I are going to do what we were told to do, and life goes on. WICKED's all that matters now. That's it."

"What are you *talking* about?" He couldn't have felt any emptier.

Teresa looked past him, over his shoulder. He heard the snap of breaking twigs on the ground, and somehow he held on to his dignity enough to not turn around to see who had snuck up on him.

"Tom," Teresa said. "Aris is right behind you, and he has a very big knife. Try anything and he'll slice your neck. You're coming with us and you're gonna do exactly what we tell you. Understand?"

Thomas stared at her, hoping the rage he felt inside showed clearly on his face. He'd never felt so angry in his life—what he could remember of it.

"Say hi, Aris," she said. And then, the worst thing yet—she smiled.

"Hi, Tommy," the boy said from behind. It was definitely him, just not as friendly as before. "Such a thrill to be with you again." The point of his knife just touched Thomas's back.

Thomas remained silent.

"Well," Teresa said. "At least you're acting like a grown-up about this. Just keep following me—we're almost there."

"Where are we going?" Thomas asked in a steely voice.

"You'll find out soon enough." She turned and started walking through the trees again, using her spear like a staff.

Thomas hurried to follow before Aris got the satisfaction of pushing him. The trees got thicker and closer together, and the moonlight flitted away. Darkness pressed in, sucking light and life right out of him.

They reached a cave, the thick copse of trees serving as a tight wall at its entrance. Thomas didn't have any warning—one minute they were picking their way through prickly branches, the next they were in a tall, narrow hole in the side of the mountain. A dull light source shone from deep inside, a sickly green rectangle that made Teresa look like a zombie when she moved to the side for the other two to enter.

Aris stepped around him, his blade aimed like a gun at Thomas's chest as he backed to the wall opposite Teresa and leaned against it. Thomas could do nothing but look back and forth between them. Two people who every instinct had told him were his friends. Until now.

"Well, we're here," Teresa said, looking at Aris.

He didn't take his eyes off Thomas. "Yep, we're here, all right. You're serious about him talking the others into sparing him? What is he, some kind of superpsychologist?"

"It kind of helped, actually. Made it easier to get him here." Teresa threw a condescending glance toward Thomas, then crossed the cave to Aris. As Thomas watched, she stood on her toes to kiss Aris on the cheek and grinned. "I'm so glad we're finally back together."

Aris smiled. He shot Thomas a look of warning, then risked looking away long enough to tilt his head toward Teresa. And kiss her on the lips.

Thomas tore his eyes away and closed them. Her pleas for him to trust her, her quick whisper to hang in there—it had all been to get him here. To bring him more easily to this point.

So that she could fulfill some evil purpose concocted by WICKED.

"Get it over with," he finally said, not daring to open his eyes again. He didn't want to know what they were doing, why they were quiet. But he wanted them to think he'd given up. "Just get it over with."

When they didn't answer, he couldn't help but take a peek. They were whispering to each other, stealing kisses between words. Something like burning oil filled his stomach.

He looked away again, focusing on the odd source of light in the back of the cave. A large rectangle of pale green, set into the dark stone, pulsed with an ethereal glow. It was as tall as an average man, maybe four feet wide. Stains streaked across its dull surface—a grimy window to something that looked like radioactive sludge, glowing and dangerous.

Out of the corner of his eye, he saw Teresa step away from Aris, their lovefest evidently over. He looked at her, wondering if his eyes showed just how much she had crushed him.

"Tom," she said. "If it helps, I'm really sorry I hurt you. I did what I had to do back in the Maze, and being all buddy-buddy seemed like my best shot at getting the memories we needed to figure out that code and escape. And I didn't have much choice here in the Scorch. All we had to do was get you here to pass the Trials. *And it's either you or us*."

Teresa paused for a second, and there was a strange glint in her eye. "Aris is my best friend, Tom," she said calmly, evenly.

And that was what finally made Thomas crack. "I . . . don't . . . *care*!" he screamed, though nothing could've been further from the truth.

"I'm just saying. If you care about me, then you should understand why I'd be willing to do whatever it takes to make it through this and keep him safe. Wouldn't you have done the same for me?"

Thomas couldn't believe how far away he felt from the girl he'd once thought was his best friend. Even in all of his memories—it was always the two of them. "What is this? Are you trying to come up with all the ways possible in the universe to hurt me? Just shut your shuck mouth and do whatever it is you brought me here to do!" His chest heaved with angry breaths, his heart thumping a deadly pace.

"Fine," she replied. "Aris, let's open the door. Time for Tom to go."

CHAPTER 51

Thomas was done talking, to either of them. But he certainly wasn't going down without a fight. He resolved to wait and watch for the best opportunity.

Aris kept his knife pointed at him as Teresa made her way toward the big rectangle of illuminated green glass. Thomas couldn't deny his curiosity about the door.

She reached a point where the glow silhouetted her whole body. It made her edges fuzzy, as if she were dissolving. She walked across the cave until she'd left the light completely, then reached for the stone wall, started punching a finger on what had to be some sort of keypad that Thomas couldn't see.

She finished up and stepped back toward him.

"We'll see if that actually works," Aris said.

"It will," Teresa replied.

A loud pop sounded, followed by a sharp hiss. Thomas watched as the right edge of the glass began to swing outward like a door. As it opened, wispy streams of white mist swirled through the widening crack, almost immediately evaporating into nothing. It was like a long-abandoned freezer releasing its cold air into the heat of the night. Darkness lurked inside even as the rectangle of glass continued to emit its strange green radiance.

So the door wasn't a window at all, Thomas thought. Just a green door. Maybe toxic waste *wasn't* in his near future. He hoped.

The door finally stopped, thumping with an icy screech against the wall of jagged rock. A pit of black now lay where the door had once been—there wasn't enough light to reveal what lay inside. The mist had completely stopped as well. Thomas felt an abyss of anxiety open up beneath him.

"Do you have a flashlight?" Aris asked.

Teresa put her spear on the ground, then pulled her backpack off and dug through its contents. A moment later she pulled out a flashlight and flicked it on.

Aris nodded back toward the opening. "Take a look while I watch him. Don't try anything, Thomas. I'm pretty sure what they have planned for you is easier than getting stabbed to death."

Thomas didn't answer, keeping his pathetic oath to stay silent from here on out. He thought about the knife and whether he could take it from Aris.

Teresa had stepped up right to the side of the gaping rectangular hole; she shone her flashlight inside. Swept it up and down, left to right. It cut through a fine cloud of mist as she did so, but the dwindling moisture was thin enough to reveal the interior.

It was a small room, only several feet deep. Its walls appeared to be made of some silvery metal, their surfaces broken up by small protrusions maybe an inch high, each ending in a black hole. The little knobs or spouts were set about five inches apart, making a square grid across the walls.

Teresa turned to Aris, flicking off the flashlight as she did so. "Looks about right," she said.

Aris snapped his head back to look at Thomas, who had been so focused on the strange room he'd missed another chance to do something. "Exactly like they said it would be."

"So . . . I guess this is it?" Teresa asked.

Aris nodded, then switched his knife to the other hand, holding it more tightly. "This is it. Thomas, be a good boy and go on inside. Who knows, maybe this is all a big test and once you're in they'll let ya go and we can all have a happy reunion."

"Shut up, Aris," Teresa said. It was actually the first thing she'd said in quite some time that didn't make Thomas want to punch her. She then turned back to Thomas, avoiding his eyes. "Let's get this over with."

Aris waved his blade, indicating that Thomas should walk forward. "Come on. Don't make me drag you in."

Thomas looked at him, struggling to keep a blank expression as his mind spun in a million directions. A surge of panic boiled inside him. It was now or never. Fight or die.

He turned his gaze to the open doorway and started slowly walking toward it. Three steps and he'd halved the distance. Teresa had straightened, her arms tensed in case he caused trouble. Aris kept his weapon trained on Thomas's neck.

Another step. Another. Now Aris stood directly to his left, just two or three feet away. Teresa was behind him, out of sight, the open doorway and the odd silver room with walls covered in holes right in front of him.

He stopped, looked sideways at Aris. "What did Rachel look like as she bled to death?" It was a gamble, a pitch to throw him off.

Shocked and hurt, Aris froze, giving Thomas the split second he needed.

He jumped toward the other boy and swung his left arm in an arc to smack the knife out of his hand. It clattered across the rocks. Thomas slammed his right fist into Aris's stomach, sending him to the ground, desperately trying to suck in a breath.

The click of metal against rock stopped Thomas from kicking the boy at his feet. He looked up to see that Teresa had picked up her spear.

They locked eyes for an instant; then she charged him. Thomas threw his hands up to protect himself but it was too late—the butt of the weapon swung through the air and smacked him on the side of the head. Stars floated before his eyes as he fell, fighting to stay conscious. As soon as he hit the ground, he scrambled to his hands and knees to get away.

But he heard Teresa scream, and a second later the wood came crashing down on the top of his skull. With a thump Thomas collapsed again; something wet oozed through his hair and trickled onto both temples. Pain tore through his head, as if an axe had been driven straight into his brain. It spread to the rest of his body, making him nauseated. He somehow pushed off the ground and flopped onto his back to see Teresa with the weapon raised above her once more.

"Get in the room, Thomas," she said through heavy breaths. "Get in the room or I'll hit you again. I swear I'll keep doing it till you pass out or bleed to death."

Aris had recovered and gotten back to his feet; he stood right next to her.

Thomas reared both legs back and kicked out, connecting with a knee on both of them. They screamed and crumpled, falling on top of each other. The physical effort sent a horrible rush of pain raging through Thomas. White flashes blinded him; the world was spinning. He groaned as he struggled to move, got back on his stomach, tried to get his hands under himself. He'd barely pushed a few inches off the ground when Aris landed on his back, slamming him down. Soon the boy's arm wrapped around Thomas's neck, squeezing.

"You're going in that room," Aris spit in his ear. "Help me, Teresa!"

Thomas couldn't find any strength to fight them off. The double blow to his head had somehow sapped him of everything, as if all his muscles had gone dormant because his brain didn't have enough energy to tell them what to do. Soon Teresa had grabbed both of his arms; she started dragging him toward the open doorway, Aris pushing him. Thomas kicked feebly. Rocks dug into his skin.

"Don't do this," he whispered, giving in to desperation. Every word sent a surge of pain across his nerves. "Please . . ." All he saw now were flashes of white on black. A concussion, he realized. He had a terrible, terrible concussion.

He was barely aware of his body crossing the threshold, of Teresa resting his arms against the cool metal of the back wall, stepping over him, helping Aris flip his legs up and over so that he now lay in a heap, facing the side. Thomas couldn't even find the strength to look at them.

"No," he said, but it was merely a whisper. The image of the sick boy, Ben, being Banished back in the Glade swam into his brain. An odd time to think it, but now he knew how that kid had felt in those last seconds before the walls slammed shut, trapping him in the Maze forever.

"No," he repeated; it was so quiet he couldn't imagine they heard him. He ached from head to toe.

"You're so stubborn," he heard Teresa say. "You had to make it harder on yourself! Harder on all of us!"

"Teresa," Thomas whispered. He dug through the pain and tried to call out to her telepathically, even though it hadn't worked in a long time. *Teresa.*

I'm sorry, Tom, she answered back, in his mind once again. *But thanks for being our sacrifice.*

He hadn't realized the door was swinging closed, but it slammed shut just as that last horrible word floated across his darkening thoughts.

CHAPTER 52

The back of the door they'd shut on him glowed green, turning the small room into a creepy, sickening prison. He might've cried, might've gushed tears and snot and wailed like a baby if his head didn't hurt so much. The pain drilled through his skull, and his eyes felt as if they were boiling in lava.

But even then, through all that, the deeper ache of truly losing Teresa gnawed away at his heart. He just couldn't let himself cry.

He lost all concept of time as he lay there. It was as if whoever was behind it all wanted to give him a chance to reflect on what had happened while he waited for the end. On how Teresa's message to trust her no matter what had ended up being a cruel trick that only magnified her two-faced treachery.

An hour passed. Maybe two or three. Maybe only thirty minutes. He had no idea.

And then the hissing started.

The faint light of the glowing door revealed sprays of mist shooting from the holes that dotted the metal walls in front of him. He turned his head, sending a fresh wave of pain across his skull, and saw that all the openings were expelling similar jets of fog.

And it all hissed like a squirming nest of poisonous vipers.

So this is it? he thought. After everything he'd been through, after all the mysteries and fighting and fleeting moments of hope, they were just going to kill him with some kind of poison gas? Stupid, that was what this was. Stupid. He'd battled Grievers and Cranks, survived a gunshot and infection. WICKED. They were the ones who'd saved him! And now they were just going to gas him to death?

He sat up, actually crying out from the jolt of pain it caused. He looked around, looked for anything he might be able to . . .

Tired. So tired.

Something in his chest felt wrong. Sick.

The gas.

Tired. Hurt. Body exhausted.

Breathing in gas.

Couldn't help himself.

So . . . tired . . .

Inside him. Wrong.

Teresa. Why did it have to end that way?

Tired . . .

Somewhere on the edge of his consciousness, he was aware of his head thumping against the floor.

Betrayal.

So . . .

Tired . . .

CHAPTER 53

Thomas didn't know if he was dead or alive, but it felt like he was asleep. Aware of himself, but as if through a haze. He slipped into yet another memory-dream.

Thomas is sixteen. He's standing in front of Teresa and some girl he doesn't recognize.

And Aris.

Aris?

All three of them are looking at him with grim faces. Teresa is crying.

"It's time to go," Thomas says.

Aris nods. "Into the Swipe, then into the Maze."

Teresa does nothing but wipe away some tears.

Thomas reaches out a hand and Aris shakes it. Then Thomas does the same with the girl he doesn't know.

Then Teresa rushes forward and pulls him into an embrace. She's sobbing, and Thomas realizes that he's also crying. His tears wet her hair as he hugs her tightly.

"You have to go now," Aris says.

Thomas looks at him. Waits. Tries to enjoy this moment with Teresa. His last moment of full memory. They won't be like this again for a very long time.

Teresa looks up at him. "It's going to work. It's all going to work."

"I know," Thomas says. He feels a sadness that makes every last bit of him ache.

Aris opens a door and beckons for Thomas to follow him. Thomas does, but manages to look back at Teresa one last time. Tries to look hopeful.

"See ya tomorrow," he says.

Which is true, and it hurts.

The dream faded, and Thomas fell into the blackest sleep of his life.

CHAPTER 54

Whispers in the dark.

That was what Thomas heard when he began returning to consciousness. Low but harsh, like sandpaper rubbing across his eardrums. He didn't understand any of it. It was so dark it took him a second to realize that his eyes were open.

Something cool and hard pressed against his face. The ground. He hadn't moved since the gas had knocked him out. Shockingly, his head didn't hurt anymore. In fact, nothing did. Instead, a feeling of refreshed euphoria swam through him, almost made him dizzy. Maybe he was just happy to be alive.

He got his hands under himself and pushed up into a sitting position. A look around did nothing—not even the faintest glimmer of light broke up the utter darkness. He wondered what had happened to the green glow of the door that Teresa had shut on him.

Teresa.

His elation drained away. Remembering what she'd done to him. But then . . .

He wasn't dead. Unless the afterlife was just a crappy room of blackness.

He rested for a few minutes, letting his mind wake up and settle before he finally got to his feet and started feeling around. Three cool metal walls with evenly spaced upraised holes. One smooth wall that felt like plastic. He was definitely in that same little room.

He pounded on the door. "Hey! Anybody out there?"

His thoughts started spinning. The memory-dreams, several now—so much to process, so many questions. The things that had first come back to him with the Changing in the Maze were slowly starting to come into focus, solidify. He'd been part of WICKED's plans, part of all this. He and Teresa had been close—best friends, even. All of it had seemed right. Doing these things for the greater good.

Only, Thomas didn't feel so good about it now. All he felt was anger and shame. How could anything justify what they'd done? What WICKED—what *they*—were doing? Though he certainly didn't think of himself this way, he and the others were just kids. Kids! He didn't like himself very much anymore. He wasn't sure when he'd reached this turning point. But something had cracked within him.

And then there was Teresa. How could he ever have felt so much for her?

Something cracked, then hissed, interrupting his line of thinking.

The door started to open, slowly swinging outward. Teresa stood there in the pale light of early morning, her face streaked with tears. As soon as there was enough room, she threw her arms around him, pressing her face against his neck.

"I'm so sorry, Tom," she said; her tears were wet against his skin. "I'm so, so, so sorry. They said they'd kill you if we didn't do everything just like they told us. No matter how horrible. I'm sorry, Tom!"

Thomas couldn't answer, couldn't bring himself to hug back. Betrayal. The sign on Teresa's door, the conversation between the people in his dreams. Pieces were falling into place. For all he knew, she was just trying to trick him again. The betrayal meant he couldn't trust her anymore, and his heart told him he couldn't forgive her.

On some level, he realized that Teresa had kept her initial promise to him after all. She had done those awful things against her will. What she had said in the shack had been true. But he also knew that things could never, never be the same between them.

He finally pushed Teresa away. The sincerity in her blue eyes did little to diminish his lingering doubt. "Uh . . . maybe you should tell me what happened."

"I told you to trust me," she answered. "I told you that bad, bad things would happen to you. But the bad stuff was all an act." She smiled then, and it was so pretty Thomas longed to find a way to forget what she'd done.

"Yeah, but you didn't seem to struggle too much, beating the klunk out of me with a spear and throwing me into a gas chamber." He couldn't hide the mistrust raging in his heart. He glanced at Aris, who looked sheepish, like he'd intruded on a private conversation.

"I'm sorry," the boy said.

"Why didn't you tell me we knew each other before?" Thomas responded. "What . . ." He didn't know what to say.

"It was all an *act,* Tom," Teresa said. "You have to believe us. We were promised from the very beginning that you wouldn't die. That this chamber thing had its own purposes and then it'd be over. I'm so sorry."

Thomas looked back at the still-gaping door. "I think I need some time to process all this." Teresa wanted him to forgive her—for everything to be how it used to be immediately. And instinct told him to hide his bitter feelings, but it was hard.

"What happened in there, anyway?" Teresa asked.

Thomas returned his gaze to her. "How about you talk first, then me. I think I earned that much."

She tried to take his hand but he moved it, pretending he had an itch on his neck. When he saw the flash of hurt cross her face, he felt the slightest bit of vindication.

"Look," she said. "You're right. You deserve an explanation. I think it's okay to tell you everything now—not that we know too much of the *why*."

Aris cleared his throat, an obvious interjection. "But, um, we better do it while walking. Or running. We only have a few hours left. Today is the day."

Those words jarred Thomas completely out of his stupor. He looked down at his watch. Only five and a half hours remained if Aris was right that they'd reached the end of the two weeks—Thomas had kind of lost track himself, not knowing how long he'd been in the chamber. And none of this other stuff mattered at all if they didn't make it to the safe haven. Hopefully Minho and the others had already found it.

"Fine. Let's just forget this for now," he said, then changed the subject. "Is anything different out there? I mean, I saw it in the dark, but—"

"We know," Teresa interrupted. "There's no sign of a building. Nothing. It looks even worse in the daylight. Just forever and ever of flat wasteland. There isn't a tree or a hill, much less any *safe haven*."

Thomas looked at Aris, then back at Teresa. "Then what're we supposed to do? Where do we go?" He thought of Minho and Newt, the Gladers, Brenda and Jorge. "Have you seen any of the others?"

Aris answered. "All the girls from my group are down there, walking north like they're supposed to, already a couple miles out. We spotted your friends at the base of the mountain a mile or two west of here. Can't tell for sure, but looks like no one new is missing, and they're heading in the same direction as the girls."

Relief filled Thomas. His friends had made it—hopefully all of them.

"We gotta get moving," Teresa said. "Just because nothing's there doesn't mean anything. Who knows what WICKED is up to? We just have to do what they told us. Come on."

Thomas had been experiencing a brief moment of wanting to give up, to sit down and forget it all—let whatever was going to happen, happen. But almost as fast as it came out, it disappeared. "Okay, let's go. But you better tell me everything you know."

"I will," she answered. "You guys up for running once we're out of these dead trees?"

Aris nodded, but Thomas rolled his eyes. "*Please*. I'm a Runner."

She raised her eyebrows. "Well, then, we'll just have to see who stops before who."

In answer, Thomas stepped out of the small clearing and into the lifeless forest first, refusing to dwell on the storm of memories and emotions that tried to weigh him down.

The sky didn't lighten much as morning ticked on. Clouds blew in, gray and thick, so thick that Thomas wouldn't have had any idea of the time if it weren't for his watch.

Clouds. Last time that had happened . . .

Maybe this storm wouldn't be so bad. Maybe.

Once they left the dense pack of dead trees, they didn't pause. An obvious trail led toward the valley below, switching back and forth like a jagged scar on the mountain face. Thomas estimated it would take a couple of hours just to get to the bottom—running on the steep, slippery slopes looked like a good way to break an ankle or leg. And if that happened, they'd never make it.

The three agreed they'd hike quickly but safely, then book it once they were on flat land. They started down—Aris, then Thomas, then Teresa. The dark clouds churned above them as wind gusted in seemingly every direction. Just as Aris had said, Thomas could see two separate packs of people in the desert below—his Glader friends, not far from the base of the mountain, then Group B, maybe a mile or two farther out.

Once again Thomas was relieved, and his step felt lighter as he made his way.

After the third switchback, Teresa spoke up from behind him. "So, guess I'll start the story from where we left off."

Thomas just nodded. He couldn't believe how good he felt physically—his stomach miraculously full, the pain from being beaten up gone, fresh air and brisk wind to make him feel alive. He had no idea what was in that gas he'd breathed, but it seemed far from poisonous. Still, his mistrust of Teresa itched at him; he didn't want to be overly nice.

"It all started right when we were talking to each other in the middle of the night—that very first one right after the rescue from the Maze. I was kind of half asleep and then these people were in my room, all dressed funny. Creepy. Baggy jumpsuits and goggles."

"Serious?" Thomas asked over his shoulder. They sounded just like the people he'd seen after being shot.

"Freaked me out—and I tried calling to you, but it suddenly cut out. The telepathy thing, I mean. I don't know how I knew, but it just vanished. From then until now it's only come and gone in spurts."

Then she spoke in his mind. *You can hear me perfectly now, right?*

Yeah. Did you and Aris really talk while we were in the Maze?

Well . . .

She trailed off, and when Thomas looked back at her, she had a worried look on her face.

What's wrong? he asked, turning his attention back to the trail before he did something stupid like trip and go tumbling down the mountain.

I don't wanna go into that yet.

"Go—" He stopped himself before he said it out loud. *Go into what?*

Teresa didn't answer.

Thomas tried as hard as he could to shout inside her mind. *Go into what!*

She stayed silent a few seconds longer before finally answering.

Yeah, he and I have been talking since I first showed up in the Glade. Mostly while I was in that stupid coma.

CHAPTER 55

It took every ounce of Thomas's willpower not to stop and turn toward her. *What? Why didn't you tell me about him back in the Maze?* As if he needed another reason to dislike either of them.

"Why'd you guys stop talking?" Aris suddenly asked. "You yappin' about me in those pretty little heads of yours?" Impossibly, he didn't seem the least bit sinister at all anymore. It was almost as if everything that had happened back in the dead forest had been a creation of Thomas's imagination.

Thomas let out a heavy breath that had been building in his lungs. "I can't believe this. You two've been—" He stopped, realizing that maybe he wasn't so surprised after all. He'd *seen* Aris in the splotchy memories of his most recent dream. He was a part of this, whatever *this* was. And the way they'd acted toward each other in that brief recall seemed to say they were on the same side. *Used* to be, anyway.

"Shuck it," Thomas finally said. "Just keep talking."

"All right," Teresa said. "There's a lot of stuff to explain, so from now on just keep quiet and listen. Got it?"

Thomas's legs were starting to burn from their steady pace on the slope. "Okay, but . . . how do you know when you're talking to me and when you're talking to him? How does that work?"

"It just does. That's like me asking how you know when you're telling your right leg to move and when you're telling your left leg to move. I just . . . know. It's built into my brain somehow."

"We've done it, too, man," Aris said. "Don't you remember?"

"Of course I remember," Thomas muttered, annoyed and frustrated on so many levels. If only he could have everything back—every last memory—he knew the pieces would fall into place and he could just move forward. He couldn't fathom why WICKED felt it was so important to keep their minds clean of memory. And why the occasional leakage lately? Was that on purpose or an accident? A lingering effect of the Changing?

Too many questions. Too many shuck questions, all without answers. "All right," he finally said. "I'll keep my mouth and brain shut. Keep going."

"We can talk about Aris and me later. I don't even remember what we spoke about—I lost almost everything when I woke up. Our comas had to be part of the Variables, so maybe we could communicate just so we wouldn't go crazy. I mean, we *were* part of setting it all up, right?"

"Setting it all up?" Thomas asked. "I don't—"

Teresa reached forward and swatted him on the back. "Thought you were gonna be quiet?"

"Yeah," Thomas grumbled.

"Anyway, these people came into my room dressed in those creepy outfits and my telepathy with you cut off. I was scared and only half awake. Part of me thought it was just a bad nightmare. Then the next thing I knew, they put something over my mouth that smelled horrible and then I passed out. When I woke up I was lying in a bed in a different room and a bunch of people were sitting in chairs on the opposite side of this weird glass wall. I couldn't see it until I touched it—almost like a force field or something."

"Yeah," Thomas said. "We had something like that, too."

"So then they started talking to me. That's when they told me this whole plan of what Aris and I had to do to you—and they expected me to tell him. By, you know, speaking in his mind, even though he was now with your group. Our group. Group A. They took me from my room and sent me to be with Group B; then they told us about the mission to the safe haven, about having the Flare. We were scared, confused, but we had no choice. We went through these underground tunnels until we got to the mountains—we avoided the city altogether. When you and I met in that little building, and then everything that happened from the time we came down to you in the valley with all those weapons—all of that was planned."

Thomas thought about the sketchy memories he'd had in his dreams. Something told him he'd known that a scenario like this might need to happen before he ever went to the Glade and the Maze. He had a hundred questions to ask Teresa, but decided to hold back for a little while longer.

They turned at another switchback; then Teresa continued. "I only know two things for sure. One, they said that if I did anything against their plan they'd kill you. Said they 'had other options,' whatever that means. The second thing I know is that the reason for all this was that you had to truly and absolutely feel betrayed. The whole purpose of what we did to you was to ensure that that happened."

Again Thomas thought of the memories. He and Teresa had both used the word *patterns* right before he left her. What did it mean?

"So?" Teresa asked after they'd walked in silence for a while.

"So . . . what?" Thomas replied.

"So what do you think?"

"That's it? That's your whole explanation? I'm supposed to feel all happy now?"

"Tom, I couldn't take any chances. I was convinced they'd kill you unless I went along. No matter what, in the end you had to feel like I'd completely betrayed you. That's why I put so much into it. But why this was all so important? I have no idea."

Thomas realized suddenly that all this information had started another headache. "Well, you sure were good at it. What about in that building? When you kissed me? And . . . why did Aris need to be involved in all this?"

Teresa grabbed his arm and made him stop and turn to face her. "They had everything calculated. All for the Variables. I don't *know* how it all fits together."

Thomas slowly shook his head. "Well, none of this crap makes any sense to me. And excuse me for feeling a little ticked off."

"Did it work?"

"Huh?"

"For some reason they wanted you betrayed, and it worked. Right?"

Thomas paused, looked into her blue eyes for a long time. "Yeah. It did."

"I'm sorry for what I did. But you're alive, and so am I. And so is Aris."

"Yeah," he repeated. He really didn't feel like talking to her anymore.

"WICKED got what they want, and I got what I want." Teresa looked at Aris, who'd kept walking for a while and now stood down on the next level of the path. "Aris, turn around, face the valley."

"What?" he replied. He looked confused. "Why?"

"Just do it." She didn't have the mean streak in her voice anymore, hadn't since the gas chamber, but if anything, that made Thomas even more suspicious. What was she up to now?

Aris sighed and rolled his eyes, but did what she said, turning his back to them.

Teresa didn't hesitate. She wrapped her arms around Thomas's neck, pulling him in. He didn't have enough will to resist.

They kissed, but nothing stirred inside Thomas. He felt nothing.

CHAPTER 56

The wind intensified, whipping and swirling.

Thunder rumbled in the darkening sky, giving Thomas an excuse to pull away from Teresa. He decided again to hide his hard feelings. Time was running out and they still had a long way to go.

Doing his best acting job, he gave Teresa a smile and said, "Guess I got it—you did a bunch of weird stuff, but you were forced to, and now I'm alive. That's it, right?"

"That's about it."

"Then I'm gonna quit thinking about it. We need to catch up with the others." The best chance he had to make it to the safe haven was to work with Teresa and Aris, so he would. He could think about Teresa and all she'd done later.

"If you say so," she said with a forced smile, as if she sensed that something wasn't quite right. Or maybe she didn't like the prospect of facing the Gladers after what had happened.

"Are you guys done up there?" Aris yelled, still facing the other direction.

"Yes!" Teresa called back. "And don't expect me to ever kiss *you* on the cheek again. I think my lips have a fungus now."

Thomas almost gagged at hearing that. He set off down the mountain again, moving before Teresa tried to hold his hand.

* * *

It took another hour to get to the bottom of the mountain. The slope leveled a bit as they got closer, allowing them to increase their pace. Eventually the switchbacks stopped altogether, and they jogged the last mile or so to the flat and desolate wasteland stretching to the horizon. The air was hot, but the overcast sky and the wind kept it bearable.

Thomas still couldn't get a very good look at the slowly converging Groups A and B up ahead, especially now that he'd lost the bird's-eye view and dust had clouded the air. But both the boys and the girls still moved in their own tight packs, heading north. Even from his vantage point, they appeared to be leaning into the stiffening wind as they walked.

Thomas's eyes stung from the dirt flying through the air. He kept wiping at them, which only made it worse, made the surrounding skin feel raw. The world continued to darken as the clouds thickened in the sky above.

After a quick break to eat and drink—their remaining supplies were dwindling fast—the three of them took a moment to observe the other groups.

"They're just walking up there," Teresa said, pointing ahead with one hand while shielding her eyes from the wind with the other. "Why aren't they running?"

"Because we still have over three hours until the deadline," Aris responded, looking at his watch. "Unless we totally figured wrong, the safe haven should be only a few miles from this side of the mountains. But I don't see anything."

Thomas hated to admit it, but the hope that they were just missing something from a distance had faded away. "By the way they're dragging, they obviously can't see it, either. It must not be there—they don't have anything to run to but more desert."

Aris glanced at the gray-black sky. "Looks ugly up there. What if we get another one of those nice lightning storms?"

"We'd be better off staying in the mountains if that happens," Thomas said. Wouldn't that be a perfect way to end all this, he thought. Burned to a crisp by bolts of electricity while searching for some safe haven that had never been there in the first place.

"Let's just catch up to them," Teresa said. "Then we can figure out what to do." She turned to look at both boys and put her hands on her hips. "You guys ready?"

"Yeah," Thomas said. He was trying not to sink into the pit of panic and worry that threatened to swallow him. There had to be an answer to all this. Had to.

Aris just shrugged in response.

"Then let's run," Teresa said. And before Thomas could answer she was already gone, with Aris close at her heels.

Thomas took a deep breath. For some reason it all reminded him of the first time he'd run out into the Maze with Minho. Which worried him. He exhaled and set off after the other two.

After maybe twenty minutes of running, the wind forcing him to work twice as hard as he'd ever had to in the Maze, Thomas spoke out to Teresa in his mind. *I think I've had some more memories come back to me lately. In my dreams.* He'd been wanting to tell her, but not really in front of Aris. A test, more than anything, to see how she responded to what he'd remembered. See if he could find any clues to her true intentions.

Really? she answered.

He could sense her shock. *Yeah. Weird, random things. Stuff from when I was a little kid. And . . . you were there, too. I had glimpses of how WICKED treated us. A little about right before we went to the Glade.*

She paused before answering, maybe afraid to ask the questions that eventually came to him. *Does any of it help us? Do you remember much of it?*

Most of it. But there wasn't enough there to really mean a whole lot.

What did you see?

Thomas told her about each little segment of memory—or dream—he'd seen over the last couple of weeks. About seeing his mom, about overhearing conversations about surgery, about him and her spying on members of WICKED, hearing things that didn't make a whole lot of sense. About them testing and practicing their telepathy. And, finally, about saying goodbye right before he went to the Glade.

So Aris was there? she asked, but before he could answer, she continued. *Of course, I already knew that. That the three of us were all part of this. But weird about everyone dying, the replacements, all that. What do you think it means?*

I don't know, he answered. *But I feel like if we had the time to just sit and talk about it we could help each other bring it all back.*

Me too. Tom, I'm really sorry. I can tell you're having a hard time forgiving me.

Would you be any different?

No. I kind of accepted it, in a way. That saving you was worth losing what we might've had.

Thomas had no clue how to respond to that.

Not that they could've talked much more even if he wanted to. With the wind howling and the dust and debris flying through the air and the clouds churning and blackening and the distance to the others getting shorter . . .

There just wasn't time.

And so they kept running.

★ ★ ★

The two groups ahead of them eventually met up in the distance. More interesting to Thomas, though, was that it didn't appear to be an accident at all. The girls of Group B had reached a point and stopped; then Minho—Thomas could make him out now and was relieved to see him alive and well—and the Gladers had changed direction to go east to meet them.

And now, just a half-mile away, they all stood around something Thomas couldn't see, packing in a tight circle to look at whatever it was.

What's going on up there? Teresa asked Thomas in his mind.

Don't know, he answered.

The two of them, along with Aris, picked up the pace.

It only took another few minutes across the dusty wind-whipped plain before they reached Groups A and B.

Minho had stepped away from the larger pack of people and stood facing them when they finally made it. His arms were folded, his clothes filthy, his hair greasy, his face still showing signs of his burns. But somehow he was smiling. Thomas couldn't believe how good it felt to see that smirky grin again.

"It's about time you slowpokes caught up with us!" Minho yelled at them.

Thomas stopped right in front of him and doubled over to catch his breath for a few seconds, then straightened. "I thought you'd be fightin' tooth and nail with these girls after what they did to us. To me, anyway."

Minho looked back at the now-mingling group of boys and girls, then returned his gaze to Thomas. "Well, first of all, they have nastier weapons, not to mention bows and arrows. Plus, some chick named Harriet explained everything. We're the ones who should be surprised—

that you're still with them." He gave a nasty glare to Teresa, then Aris. "Never trusted either one of those shuck traitors."

Thomas tried to hide his mixed emotions. "They're on our side. Trust me." And in a twisted, backward way he really was starting to believe it. As sick as it made him feel.

Minho laughed bitterly. "Figured you'd say something like that. Let me guess, it's a long story?"

"Yeah, very long story," Thomas answered, then changed the subject. "Why'd you all stop here? What's everybody looking at?"

Minho stepped to the side, sweeping his arm behind him. "Have a peeky-peek yourself." Then he yelled to the two groups, *"You guys make a path!"*

Several Gladers and girls looked back, then slowly shuffled to the side until a narrow break in the crowd formed. Thomas immediately saw that the object that held everyone's attention was a simple stick poking out of the arid ground. An orange strip of ribbon hung from the top, whipping in the wind. Letters were printed on the thin banner.

Thomas and Teresa exchanged a look; then Thomas pushed ahead for a closer inspection. Even before he got there, he could read the words printed on the ribbon, black on orange.

THE SAFE HAVEN

CHAPTER 57

Despite the wind and the hubbub of people, the world quieted around Thomas for a minute, as if his ears had been stuffed with cotton. He fell to his knees and numbly reached out to touch the flapping orange ribbon. *This* was the safe haven? Not a building, a shelter, *something*?

Then, as quickly as it had disappeared, sound rushed back in, snapping him back to reality. Mostly the rush of wind and the chatter of conversation.

He turned back to Teresa and Minho, who stood side by side, Aris behind them peeking over their shoulders.

Thomas glanced at his watch. "We have over an hour left. Our safe haven is a stick in the ground?" Confusion muddled his mind—he wasn't quite sure what to think or say.

"Wasn't so bad, when you think about it," Minho said. "More than half of us made it here. Looks like even more of the girlie group."

Thomas stood up, trying to control his anger. "The Flare turn you crazy already? Yeah, we got here. Safe and sound. To a *stick*."

Minho scoffed at him. "Dude, they wouldn't send us here for no reason. We made it in the time they gave us. Now we just wait until the clock ticks down and something'll happen."

"That's what worries me," Thomas said.

"Hate to say it," Teresa added, "but I agree with Thomas. After everything they've done to us, it'd be way too easy to have a little sign here, and then they come get us in a nice helicopter as a reward. Something bad's gonna happen."

"Whatever you say, traitor," Minho said, his face hiding none of the hatred he felt for Teresa. "I don't want to hear another word from you." He walked away, angrier than Thomas had ever seen him.

Thomas looked at Teresa, who was visibly taken aback. "You shouldn't be surprised."

She just shrugged. "I'm sick of apologizing. I did what I had to do."

Thomas couldn't believe she was serious. "Whatever. I need to find Newt. I want—"

Before he could finish, Brenda appeared out of the crowd, glancing back and forth between him and Teresa. The wind tore through her long hair, whipping it frenziedly so that she kept pushing it behind her ears only to have it fly out again.

"Brenda," he said. For some reason he felt guilty.

"Hey there," Brenda said, walking up to stand right in front of him and Teresa. "This the girl you were tellin' me about? When you and I were snuggling in that truck?"

"Yeah." The word popped out of Thomas's mouth before he could stop it. "No. I mean . . . yeah."

Teresa held her hand out to Brenda, who shook it. "I'm Teresa."

"Nice to meet you," Brenda replied. "I'm a Crank. I'm slowly going crazy. I keep wanting to chew off my own fingers and randomly kill people. Thomas here promised to save me." Though she was obviously joking, she didn't even crack a smile.

Thomas had to hide a wince. "Funny, Brenda."

"Glad to see you still have a sense of humor about it," Teresa said. But her face could've turned water to ice.

Thomas looked down at his watch. Fifty-five minutes left. "I, um, need to talk to Newt." He turned and quickly walked away before either girl could say anything. He wanted to be as far away from both of them as possible.

Newt was sitting on the ground with Frypan and Minho, all three looking as if they were waiting for the end of the world.

The tearing wind had gained a moisture to it, and the billowing, churning clouds above them had lowered considerably, like a dark fog dropping to swallow the earth. Glimpses of light flashed here and there in the sky, burning patches of purple and orange in the grayness. Thomas hadn't seen an actual lightning bolt yet, but he knew they were coming. The first big storm had begun just like this.

"Hey, Tommy," Newt said when Thomas joined them. He sat down next to his friend and wrapped his arms around his knees. Two simple words with nothing behind them. It was as if Thomas had just gone for a leisurely walk instead of being kidnapped and almost killed.

"Glad to see you guys made it here," Thomas said.

Frypan snorted his usual animal-like bark of a laugh. "Same back at ya. Looks like you had more fun, though. Hangin' with your love goddess. Guess you two kissed and made up?"

"Not exactly," Thomas said. "It wasn't fun."

"Well, what happened?" Minho asked. "How can you trust her after all that?"

Thomas hesitated at first, but he knew he had to tell them everything. And there was no better time than the present. He sucked in a deep breath and started talking. He told them about WICKED's plan for him, the camp, his talk with Group B, the gas chamber. Still none of it made sense, but he felt a little better telling his friends.

"And you forgave that witch?" Minho asked when Thomas finally finished. "I won't. Whatever those shuck WICKED people wanna do, fine by me. Whatever you wanna do, fine by me. But I don't trust her, I don't trust Aris, and I don't like either one of them."

Newt seemed to consider it more deeply. "They went through all that—all that planning and acting—just to make you feel *betrayed*? Doesn't make any bloody sense."

"Tell me about it," Thomas muttered. "And no, I haven't forgiven her. But for now I think we're in the same boat." He looked around—most people were sitting down, staring off into the distance. Not much conversation, and not a whole lot of mingling between the two groups. "What about you guys? How'd you make it here?"

"Found a gap through the mountains," Minho answered. "Had to fight through some Cranks camping in a cave, but other than that, no problems. Food and water's almost out, though. And my feet hurt. And I'm pretty sure another big bolt of shuck lightning's about to come down and make me look like a piece of Frypan's bacon."

"Yeah," Thomas said. He glanced back at the mountains, guessed that all in all they'd probably come about four miles from the base. "Maybe we should bag this whole safe haven thing and try to find shelter." But even as he said it, he knew it wasn't an option. At least not until the time ran out.

"No way," Newt replied. "We didn't come this far to go back now. Let's just hope the buggin' storm holds off a little longer." He looked up at the almost black clouds with a grimace.

The other three Gladers had grown silent. The wind had continued to pick up, and its rushing roars and whips now made it hard to hear each other anyway. Thomas looked at his watch.

Thirty-five minutes. No way this storm would hold for—

"What's that!" Minho shouted, jumping to his feet; he pointed at a spot over Thomas's shoulder.

Thomas turned to look as he stood up, alarm igniting inside him. The terror on Minho's face had been unmistakable.

About thirty feet from the group, a large section of the desert ground was . . . opening. A perfect square—maybe fifteen feet wide—pivoted on a diagonal axis as the dirt-packed side slowly spun away from them and what had lain underneath rose up to replace it. The sound of groaning, twisting steel pierced the air, louder than the roaring wind. Soon the rotating square had fully flipped, and where once had been desert ground now lay a section of black material, with an odd object sitting on top of it.

It was oblong and white with rounded edges. Thomas had seen something just like it before. Several of them, in fact. After they'd escaped the Maze and entered the huge chamber where the Grievers had come from, they'd seen several of these coffinlike containers. He hadn't had much time to think about it then, but seeing it now, he thought those must've been where the Grievers stayed—slept?—when not hunting humans in the Maze.

Before he had time to react, more sections of the desert floor—surrounding their group in a large circle—started to rotate open like dark, gaping jaws.

Dozens of them.

CHAPTER 58

The squeal of metal was deafening as the square sections slowly spun on their axles. Thomas had his hands to his ears, trying to keep the sound out. The others in the group were doing the same. All around them, scattered evenly and fully encircling the area in which they stood, patches of desert ground rotated until they disappeared, each one eventually replaced with a large black square when it finally settled with a loud clank, one of those bulbous white coffins resting on top. At least thirty in all.

The scream of metal rubbing against metal stopped. No one spoke. The wind ripped across the land, blowing dust and dirt in streams across the rounded containers. It made a gritty pinging sound. There was so much of it, it blended into a noise that made Thomas's spine itch; he had to squint to keep stuff out of his eyes. Nothing else had moved since the foreign, almost alien objects had been revealed. There was only that sound and wind and cold and stinging eyes.

Tom? Teresa called to him.

Yeah.

You remember those, right?

Yeah.

You think Grievers are inside?

Thomas realized that was exactly what he thought, but he'd also finally accepted that he could never expect anything. He reasoned it out for a second before he answered. *I don't know. I mean, the Grievers had really moist bodies—it'd be hard on them out here.* It seemed like a stupid thing to say, but he was grasping for anything.

Maybe we're meant to . . . get inside them, she said after a pause. *Maybe they* are *the safe haven, or they'll transport us somewhere.*

Thomas hated the idea, but thought that maybe she was right. He tore his eyes away from the large pods and looked for her. She was already walking toward him. Fortunately, she was alone. He couldn't handle both her and Brenda right then.

"Hey," he said out loud, but the wind seemed to carry the sound away before it even left his mouth. He started to reach out for her hand but then pulled it back, almost forgetting how things had changed. She didn't seem to notice as she walked over to Minho and Newt and nudged both of them in greeting. They turned to face her and Thomas moved closer to conference with them.

"So what do we do?" Minho asked. He gave Teresa an annoyed look like he didn't want her to be any part of the decision making.

Newt answered. "If those things have bloody Grievers in 'em, we best start gettin' ready to fight the shuck buggers."

"What're you guys talking about?"

Thomas turned to see Harriet and Sonya—it'd been Harriet who'd spoken. And Brenda stood right behind them, with Jorge by her side.

"Oh, great," Minho muttered. "The two queens of glorious Group B."

Harriet just acted like she hadn't heard. "I'm assuming you all saw those pods back in your WICKED chamber, too. They had to be where the Grievers charged up or whatever it was they did."

"Yeah," Newt said. "Gotta be that."

In the sky above, thunder crackled and boomed, and those flashes of light grew brighter. The wind tore at everyone's clothes and hair and everything smelled wet but dusty—a strange combination. Thomas checked the time again. "We've only got twenty-five minutes. We're either gonna be fighting Grievers or we need to get inside those big coffins at the right time. Maybe they're the—"

A sharp hiss cut through the air from all directions. The sound pierced Thomas's eardrums and he clamped his hands to the sides of his head again. Movement on the perimeter surrounding them caught his attention, and he watched carefully what was happening with the large white pods.

A line of dark blue light had appeared on one side of each container, then expanded as the top half of the object began to move upward, opening on hinges like the lid of a coffin. It made no sound, at least not enough to be heard over the rushing wind and rumbling thunder. Thomas sensed the Gladers and the others slowly moving closer together, forming a tighter knot. Everyone was trying to get as far away from the pods as possible—and soon they were a coiled pack of bodies encircled by the thirty or so rounded white containers.

The lids continued moving until they'd all swung open and dropped to the ground. Something bulky rested inside each vessel. Thomas couldn't make out much, but from where he stood he couldn't see anything like the odd appendages of the Grievers. Nothing moved, but he knew not to let his guard down.

Teresa? he said to her mind. He didn't dare try talking loudly enough to be heard—but he had to talk to someone or go nuts.

Yeah?

Someone should go take a look. See what's in it. He said it, but he really didn't want to be the one to do it.

Let's go together, she said easily.

She surprised him with her courage. *Sometimes you have the worst ideas,* he responded. He'd tried to make it *feel* sarcastic, but he knew the truth of it far more than he wanted to admit to himself. He was terrified.

"Thomas!" Minho called. The wind, still wild, was drowned out by the approaching thunder and lightning now, cracking and exploding in brilliant displays above them and on the horizon. The storm was about to fully beat down its fury on them.

"What?" Thomas yelled back.

"You, me, and Newt! Let's go check it out!"

Thomas was just about to move when something slipped out of one of the pods. A collective gasp escaped those closest to Thomas, and he turned for a better look. Things were moving in all the pods, things he couldn't quite understand at first. Whatever they were, they were definitely coming out of their oblong homes. Thomas focused on the pod nearest to him, strained his eyes to discern what exactly he was about to face.

A misshapen arm hung over the edge, and its hand dangled a few inches above the ground. On it were four disfigured fingers—stubs of sickly beige flesh—none of them the same length. They wiggled and grasped for something that wasn't there, as if the creature inside was searching to get a grip to pull itself out. The arm was covered with wrinkles and lumps, and there was something completely strange right where what passed for an elbow was located. A perfectly rounded protrusion or growth, maybe four inches in diameter, glowing bright orange.

It looked like the thing had a lightbulb glued to its arm.

The monster continued to emerge. A leg flopped out, its foot a fleshy mass, four knobs of toes wriggling as much as its fingers. And on the knee, another one of those impossible orange spheres of light, seemingly growing right out of its skin.

"What is that thing?" Minho shouted over the noise of the surging storm.

No one answered. Thomas was dazed, staring at the creature—

mesmerized and terrified at the same time. He did finally look away long enough to see that similar monsters were coming out of every pod—all at the same pace—then returned his attention to the closest one.

It had somehow gained purchase enough with its right arm and leg to begin pulling the rest of its body out. Thomas looked on in horror as the abominable thing flopped and wiggled until it lurched over the edge of the open pod and stumbled to the ground. Roughly human-shaped, though at least a couple of feet taller than anyone around Thomas, its body was naked and thick, pockmarked and wrinkled. Most disturbing were more of those bulbous growths, maybe two dozen total, spread over the thing's body and glowing with brilliant orange light. Several on its chest and back. One on each elbow and knee—the bulb on the right knee had busted in a flurry of sparks when the creature landed on the ground—and several sticking out of a big lump of . . . what had to be a head, though it didn't have any eyes, nose, mouth or ears. No hair, either.

The monster got to its feet, swayed a bit as it balanced, then turned to face the group of humans. A quick glance around showed that each pod had delivered its creature, all of them now standing in a circle around the Gladers and Group B.

In unison, the creatures raised their arms until they pointed toward the sky. Then, all at once, thin blades shot out of the tips of their stubby fingers, out of their toes, out of their shoulders. The flashes of lightning in the sky glittered off their surface, sharp and gleaming silver. Though there was no sign of any kind of mouth, a deathly, creepy moan emanated from their bodies—it was a sound Thomas could feel more than hear. And it had to be loud to be heard over the terrible thunder.

Maybe Grievers would've been better, Teresa said inside Thomas's mind.

Well, they're enough alike that it's obvious who created these things, he said back, straining to stay calm.

Minho turned quickly and faced the crowd of still-gaping people surrounding Thomas. "There's about one for each of us! Grab whatever you got for a weapon!"

Almost as if they'd heard the challenge, the lightbulb creatures started moving, walking forward. Their first couple of steps were lumbering, but then they recovered, growing steady and strong and agile. Coming closer with every step.

CHAPTER 59

Teresa handed Thomas a really long knife, almost a sword. He couldn't imagine where she'd been hiding these things, but she now held a short dagger in addition to her spear.

As the lighted giants stepped closer and closer, Minho and Harriet spoke to their respective groups, moving them around, positioning them, their shouts and commands torn away by the wind before Thomas could hear anything. He dared take his eyes off the approaching monsters long enough to look at the sky. Tendrils of lightning forked and arced across the bottom of the dark clouds, which seemed to hang only a few dozen feet above them. The acrid smell of electricity permeated the air.

Thomas looked back down, concentrated on the creature closest to him. Minho and Harriet had been able to get the groups to stand together in an almost perfect circle, facing outward. Teresa stood next to Thomas, and he would've said something to her if he could've thought of anything. He was speechless.

WICKED's latest abominations were only thirty feet away.

Teresa finally elbowed him in the ribs. He looked to see her pointing at one of the creatures, telling Thomas—making sure he knew—that she'd chosen her foe. He nodded, then gestured toward the one he'd been thinking was his all along.

Twenty-five feet away.

Thomas had the sudden thought that it was a mistake to wait for them—that they needed to be spread out more. Minho must've had the same idea.

"Now!" their leader yelled, a bare and distant bark because of the storm's sounds. "Charge them!"

A slew of thoughts spun through Thomas's mind in that instant. Worry for Teresa, despite the changes between them. Worry for Brenda—standing stoically just a few people down the line from him—and regret over how they had barely spoken since being reunited. He imagined her having come all this way only to be killed by a vicious man-made creature. He thought of the Grievers, and his and Chuck and Teresa's charge back in the Maze to get to the Cliff and the Hole, the Gladers fighting and dying for them so they could punch in the code and stop it all.

He thought of all they'd gone through to arrive at this point, once again facing a biotech army sent by WICKED. He wondered what it all meant, whether it was worth trying to survive anymore. The image of Chuck taking that knife for him popped into his head. And that did it. Snapped him out of those nanoseconds of frozen doubt and fear. Screaming at the top of his lungs, he wielded his huge knife with both hands above his head and rushed forward, straight for his monster.

To his left and right, the others also charged, but he ignored them. He had to, forced himself to. If he couldn't take care of his own assignment, worrying about others wouldn't amount to anything.

He closed in. Fifteen feet. Ten feet. Five. The creature had stopped walking, bracing its legs in a fighting stance, hands outstretched, blades pointing directly at Thomas. Those shining orange lights pulsed now, flaring and receding, flaring and receding, as if the hideous thing actually had a heart somewhere inside. It was disturbing to see no face on the monster, but it helped Thomas think of it as nothing more than a machine. Nothing more than a man-made weapon that wanted him dead.

Right before he reached the creature, Thomas made a decision.

He dropped to slide on his knees and shins and swung the swordlike weapon in an arc behind and around him, slamming the blade into the monster's left leg with a full and powerful two-handed thrust. The knife cut an inch into its skin but then clanked against something hard enough to send a jolt shivering up both of Thomas's arms.

The creature didn't move, didn't retract, didn't let out any sort of sound, human or inhuman. Instead it swiped downward with both blade-studded hands where Thomas now knelt before it, his sword embedded in the monster's flesh. Thomas jerked it free and lunged backward just as those blades clattered against each other where his head had been. He fell on his back and scooted away from the creature as it took two steps forward, kicking out with the knives on its feet, barely missing Thomas.

The monster let out a roar this time—a sound almost exactly like the haunted moans of the Grievers—and dropped to the ground, thrashing its arms, trying to impale Thomas. Thomas spun away, rolling three times as he heard metal tips scraping along the dirt-packed ground. He finally took a chance and jumped to his feet, immediately sprinting several yards away before turning around, sword gripped in his hands. The creature was just getting to its own feet, slicing at the air with its stubby bladed fingers.

Thomas sucked in huge gulps of air and could see the others battling in his peripheral vision. Minho jabbing and stabbing with knives in both hands, the monster actually taking steps backward, away from him. Newt scrambling across the ground, the creature he fought lumbering after him, obviously injured. Slowing. Teresa was the closest to him, jumping and dodging and poking her foe with the butt of her spear. Why was she doing that? Her monster seemed to be badly hurt as well.

Thomas pulled his attention back to his own battle. A blur of silver movement made him duck, a wisp of wind in his hair from the swipe of the creature's arm. Thomas spun, crouched close to the ground, stabbing at anything he could as the monster pursued him, barely missing him with several more attacks. Thomas connected with one of the orange bulb growths, smashing it in a flash of sparks; the light died instantly. Knowing his luck had to be running short, he dove toward the ground, tucking and rolling again until he sprang to his feet a couple of yards away.

The creature had paused—at least as long as it had taken Thomas to make his escape move—but now it came after him again. An idea formed in Thomas's mind, and it grew to clarity when he looked back at Teresa's fight, her creature now moving in jilted, slow attacks. She kept after the bulbs, popping them as they exploded in that same display of fireworks. She'd destroyed at least three-fourths of the odd growths.

The bulbs. All he needed to do was destroy the bulbs. Somehow they were linked to the creature's power or life or strength. Could it really be that easy?

A quick glance around the rest of the battlefield showed that a few others had also gotten the idea, but most hadn't, fighting with bloody desperation to hack at limbs, muscles, skin, missing the bulbs entirely. A couple of people already lay on the ground, covered in wounds, lifeless. One boy. One girl.

Thomas changed his whole method. Instead of charging recklessly, he jumped in and took a jab at one of the bulbs on the monster's chest. He missed, slicing into the wrinkled, yellowish skin. The creature swiped at him, but he pulled back just as the very tips of the blades ripped jagged holes in his shirt. Then he thrust again, poking once more at the same bulb. He connected this time, bursting it and sending out a spray of sparks. The creature halted for a full second, then snapped back to battle mode.

Thomas circled the creature, jumping in and back again, poking, jabbing, thrusting.

Pop, pop, pop.

One of the monster's blades sliced across his forearm, leaving a long line of bright red. Thomas went in again. And again. Again.

Pop, pop, pop. Sparks flying, the creature shuddering and jerking with each break.

The pause got a little bit longer with every successful stab. Thomas felt a few more scrapes and slices, but nothing serious. He kept at it, attacking those orange spheres.

Pop, pop, pop.

Every small victory sapped the creature's strength, and it gradually began to visibly slump, though it didn't stop trying to cut Thomas to pieces. Bulb by bulb, each one easier than the one before it, Thomas attacked relentlessly. If only he could quickly finish it off, make it die. Then he could run around and help others. End this thing once and for—

A blinding light flashed behind him, then a sound like the entire universe exploding ripped away his brief moment of exhilaration and hope. A wave of invisible power knocked him over and he fell flat onto his stomach, the sword clattering away from him. The creature fell, too, and a burnt smell singed the air. Thomas rolled onto his side to look, saw a massive black hole in the ground, charred and smoking. A bladed foot and hand from one of the monsters lay on the hole's edge. No sign of the rest of the body.

It'd been a lightning strike. Right behind him. The storm had finally broken.

Even as he had the thought, he looked up to see thick shards of white heat start falling from the black clouds above.

CHAPTER 60

The lightning exploded all around him with deafening cracks of thunder; plumes of dirt flew into the air from every direction. Several people screamed—one was cut off abruptly, a girl. And that burning smell. Overwhelming. The strikes of electricity subsided as quickly as they had begun. But light continued to flash in the clouds, and rain started to pour down in sheets.

Thomas hadn't moved during that first flurry of lightning. There was no reason to think he'd be any safer in another spot than where he lay. But after the onslaught, he scrambled to his feet to look around, see what he could do or where he could run before it happened again.

The creature he'd been fighting was dead, half of its body blackened, the other half gone. Teresa stood over her foe, slamming the butt of her spear down and smashing the last bulb; its sparks died with a hiss. Minho was on the ground, but slowly getting to his feet. Newt stood there, breathing in and out, deep heaving breaths. Frypan doubled over and threw up. Some were lying on the ground; others—like Brenda and Jorge—still fighting the monsters. Thunder boomed all around them and lightning glinted in the rain.

Thomas had to do something. Teresa wasn't too far away; she stood a couple of steps from her dead creature, bent over, hands on her knees.

We have to find shelter! he said in her mind.

How much time do we have left?

Thomas squinted at his watch closely. *Ten minutes.*

We should get inside the pods. She pointed at the closest one, which still lay open like a perfectly cut eggshell, its halves surely full of water by this point.

He liked the idea. *What if we can't close it?*

Got any better plans?

No. He grabbed her hand and started running.

We need to tell the others! she said as they approached the pod.

They'll figure it out. He knew they couldn't wait—more strikes could hit them at any second. They'd all be dead by the time he and Teresa tried to communicate with anyone. He had to trust his friends to save themselves. *Knew* he could trust them.

They reached the pod just as several bolts of electricity came zigzagging down from the sky, striking in blistering explosions all around them. Dirt and rain flew everywhere; Thomas's ears rang. He looked inside the left half of the container, saw nothing but a small pool of dirty water. A horrible smell wafted up from it.

"Hurry!" he yelled as he climbed in.

Teresa followed him. They didn't need to speak to know what to do next. They both got on their knees, then leaned forward to grab the far end of the other half—it had a rubbery lining, easy to grip. Thomas braced his midsection on the lip of the pod, then pulled up, straining with every bit of strength he had left. The other half lifted and swung toward them.

Just as Thomas was repositioning himself to sit, Brenda and Jorge ran up to them. Thomas felt a rush of relief at seeing them okay.

"Is there room for us?" Jorge screamed over the noise of the storm.

"Get in!" Teresa yelled back in answer.

The two of them slipped over the edge and splashed into the large container, a tight fit but manageable. Thomas scooted to the far end to give them more room, holding the cover just barely open—the rain drummed on its outer surface. Once everyone was settled, he and Teresa ducked their heads and let the pod close completely. Other than the hollow thrum of the rain and the distant explosions of lightning and the gasping of breaths, it grew relatively silent. Though Thomas still heard that same ringing in his ears.

He could only hope his other friends had made it safely to pods of their own.

"Thanks for letting us in, *muchacho,*" Jorge said when everyone seemed to have caught their breath.

"Of course," Thomas replied. The darkness inside the container was absolute, but Brenda was right next to him, then Jorge, then Teresa on the far end.

Brenda spoke up. "Thought you might've had second thoughts about bringing us along. Would've been a good chance to get rid of us."

"Please," Thomas muttered. He was too tired to care how it sounded. Everyone had almost died, and they might not be out of the woods yet.

"So is this our safe haven?" Teresa asked.

Thomas clicked the little light button on his watch; they had seven minutes till the time was up. "Right now, I sure hope so. Maybe in a few minutes these shuck squares of land will spin around and drop us into some nice comfy room where we can all live happily ever after. Or not."

Crack!

Thomas yelped—something had slammed into the top of the pod and made the loudest sound he'd ever heard, an earsplitting crash. A small hole—just a sliver of gray light—had appeared in the ceiling of their shelter, beads of water forming and dropping quickly.

"Had to be lightning," Teresa said.

Thomas rubbed his ears, the ringing worse now. "Couple more of those and we'll be right back where we started." His voice sounded hollow.

Another check of the watch. Five minutes. The water *drip-drip-drip*ped into the puddle; that horrible smell lingered; the bells in Thomas's head lessened.

"This isn't quite what I imagined, *hermano,*" Jorge said. "Thought we'd show up here and you'd convince the big bosses to take us in. Give us that cure. Didn't think we'd be holed up in a stinking bathtub waiting to be electrocuted."

"How much longer?" Teresa asked.

Thomas looked. "Three minutes."

Outside, the storm raged, bursts of lightning slamming into the ground, the rain pounding.

Another boom and crack shook the pod, widened the split in the ceiling enough that water began rushing in, splashing all over Brenda and Jorge. Something hissed and steam seeped in as well, the lightning having heated up the outside material.

"We're not gonna last much longer no matter what happens!" Brenda shouted. "It's almost worse sitting here and waiting for it!"

"There's only two minutes left!" Thomas yelled back at her. "Just hold on!"

A sound started up outside. Faint at first, barely discernible over the noises of the storm. A humming. Deep and low. It grew in volume, seemed to vibrate Thomas's whole body.

"What *is* that?" Teresa asked.

"No idea," Thomas answered. "But based on our day, I'm sure it's not good. We just have to last another minute or so."

The sound got louder and deeper. Overwhelming the thunder and rain now. The walls of the pod vibrated. Thomas heard a rushing wind outside, different somehow from what had been blowing all day. Powerful. Almost . . . artificial.

"There's only thirty seconds left," Thomas announced, suddenly having a change of heart. "Maybe you guys are right. Maybe we're missing something important. I . . . I think we should look."

"What?" Jorge responded.

"We need to see what's making that sound. Come on, help me open this back up."

"And if a nice big lightning bolt comes down and fries my butt?"

Thomas put the palms of his hands on the ceiling. "We gotta take a chance! Come on—push!"

"He's right," Teresa said, and she braced her hands to help.

Brenda copied her, and soon Jorge joined them.

"Just about halfway," Thomas said. "Ready?"

After getting a few positive grunts, he said, "One . . . two . . . three!"

They all pushed toward the sky, and their strength ended up being way too much. The lid flipped up and over and crashed to the ground, leaving the pod fully open. Rain pummeled them, flying horizontally, captured by a ferocious wind.

Thomas leaned on the edge of the pod and gaped at what hovered in the air just thirty feet off the ground, lowering rapidly to land. It was huge and round, with flickering lights and burning thrusters of blue flame. It was the same ship that had saved him after he was shot. The Berg.

Thomas glanced at his watch just in time to see the last second tick down. Looked back up.

The Berg touched down on clawlike landing gear and a huge cargo door in its metal belly began to open.

CHAPTER 61

Thomas knew they couldn't waste any more time. No questions, no fear, no bickering. Only action.

"Come on!" he yelled, pulling Brenda's arm as he stepped out of the pod. He slipped and toppled over, landing with a wet *smush* in the mud. He pushed himself up, spitting the slimy stuff out of his mouth and rubbing it from his eyes, and scrambled back to his feet. The rain poured down, thunder cracked from all directions, lightning bolts lit the air in ominous flashes.

Jorge and Teresa had made it out, Brenda helping them. Thomas looked over at the Berg—maybe fifty feet away—its cargo door now fully open, a gaping maw of an entrance to warm light inside. Shadowy forms stood there, holding guns, waiting. They obviously didn't intend to come out and assist anybody onto the safe haven. The *real* safe haven.

"Run!" he screamed, already on the move. He held his knife in front of him, gripped tightly, in case any of those creatures were still alive and looking for a fight.

Teresa and the others kept pace next to him.

The rain-softened ground made it hard to get good traction; Thomas slipped twice, fell down once. Teresa grabbed his shirt and yanked until he was up and running again. Others were around them, making the same dash for the safety of the ship. The darkness of the storm and the veil of rain and brilliant flashes of lightning made it hard to see who was who. No time to worry about it.

From the right side, lumbering around the back end of the plane, a dozen of the bulb creatures appeared; they headed for a spot cutting off Thomas and his friends from the open cargo door. Their blades were slick with rain, some stained crimson. At least half of their creepy glowing bulbs had been busted, and their jerky movements showed it. But they looked as dangerous as ever. And still, the people in the Berg did nothing, only watched.

"Go right through 'em!" Thomas yelled. Minho appeared, along with Newt and a few other Gladers, joining the charge. Harriet and a few of the Group B girls, too. Everyone seemed to understand the plan, as slight as it was: fight off these last few monsters and get out of there.

Maybe for the first time since entering the Glade weeks earlier, Thomas felt no fear. He didn't know if he'd ever feel it again. He didn't know why, but something had changed. Lightning exploded around him, someone screamed, the rain intensified. Wind tore through the air, pelting him with small rocks and drops of water that hurt equally. The creatures swiped their blades through the air, screaming their disturbing roar as they waited for battle. Thomas ran on, knife held above his head.

No fear.

Three feet from the center creature he jumped into the air, kicking forward, both legs held tightly together. He slammed his feet into one of the orange bulbs protruding from the middle of the monster's chest. It burst and sizzled; the creature wailed something hideous and fell backward, slamming to the ground.

Thomas landed in the mud and rolled to the side. Immediately jumped up and danced around the creature, slashing and poking, bursting the glowing growths.

Pop, pop, pop.

Dodging and jumping away from the futile slashes of the creature's blades. Retaliating, stabbing. *Pop, pop, pop.* Only three bulbs were left; it could barely move. Thomas straddled the thing in a burst of confidence and quickly threw down the final vicious thrusts to end it.

The last bulb burst and fizzled out. Dead.

Thomas got up, spun around to see if someone else needed help. Teresa had finished off hers. Minho and Jorge as well. Newt was there, favoring his bad leg, Brenda helping him stab out the remaining bulbs on his foe.

A few seconds later it ended. No creature moved. No orange lights shone. It was over.

Thomas, breathing heavily, looked up at the entrance to the ship, only twenty feet away. Even as he did, its thrusters ignited and the ship started to lift off the ground.

"It's leaving!" Thomas screamed as loudly as he could, pointing frantically at their only means of escape. "Hurry!"

The word had barely escaped his mouth when Teresa grabbed him by the arm, pulling as she ran for the ship. Thomas stumbled, then righted himself, pounding his feet in the mud. He heard the crack of thunder behind them, saw a flash of lightning fill the sky. Another scream. Others beside him, around him, in front of him now, all running. Newt with his limp, Minho next to him, eyeing him to make sure he didn't fall.

The Berg had reached a point three feet off the ground, slowly rising and turning at the same time, ready at any second to shift those thrusters and zip away. A couple of Gladers and three girls reached it first, dove onto the platform of the open cargo door. Still it rose. Others reached it, climbed on, scrambled inside.

Then Thomas made it with Teresa. The open hatch was chest-high now. He jumped and pushed his hands down on the flat metal, arms stiff, stomach pressed against the thick edge. Swung his right leg up, got leverage, rolled his body fully onto the door. The ship, still rising. Others climbing on, reaching to pull others up. Teresa, halfway on, trying to find a handhold.

Thomas reached out and grabbed her hand, pulled her in. She collapsed on top of him, shared a brief look of victory. Then she was off, and both of them approached the edge of the door to see if anyone needed help.

The Berg was now six feet above the ground, starting to tilt. Three people still hung from the edge. Harriet and Newt were pulling a girl in. Minho was helping Aris. But Brenda held on only with her hands, her body dangling as she kicked her feet and tried to pull herself up.

Thomas dropped to his stomach and scooted closer, reached out and grabbed her right arm. Teresa got the other one. The metal of the cargo door was wet and slick; when Thomas pulled on Brenda he started sliding out, but then stopped abruptly. A quick look behind him revealed that Jorge had planted his butt and feet, holding tightly to both Thomas and Teresa.

Thomas looked back at Brenda, started pulling again. With Teresa's help, she finally came over the edge enough for her stomach to gain purchase; it was easy from there. As she crawled on and farther in, Thomas took another look outside at the ground, slowly moving away. Nothing but those horrific creatures, lifeless and wet, full of saggy pockets of flesh that had once been full and brightly lit. A few dead human bodies, but not many, and no one Thomas was close to.

He scooted backward, away from the edge, feeling an immense amount of relief. They'd made it, most of them. They'd made it through Cranks and lightning and hideous monsters. They'd made it. He bumped into Teresa, turned toward her, pulled her in and hugged her tightly, forgetting what had happened for a second. They'd made it.

"Who are these two people?"

Thomas jerked away from Teresa to see who'd shouted—it was a man with short red hair, holding a black pistol pointed at Brenda and Jorge, who sat next to each other, shivering and wet and bruised.

"Somebody answer me!" the man yelled again.

Thomas spoke up before he could think about it. "They helped us get through the city—we wouldn't be here if it weren't for them."

The man snapped his head toward Thomas. "You . . . *picked them up* along the way?"

Thomas nodded, not liking where this was going. "We made a deal with them. Promised they'd get the cure, too. We still have fewer people than we started with."

"Doesn't matter," the man said. "We didn't say you could bring citizens!"

The Berg continued to climb higher in the sky, but the gaping door didn't close. Wind whipped through the wide hole; any one of them could go tumbling to their death if they hit turbulence.

Thomas got to his feet anyway, determined to defend the pact he'd made. "Well, you told us to come here, and we did what we had to do!"

Their gun-toting host paused, seemed to consider this line of reasoning. "Sometimes I forget how little you people understand what's going on. Fine, you can keep one of 'em. The other goes."

Thomas tried not to show the jolt this gave him. "What do you mean . . . the other goes?"

The man clicked something on the gun, then held its end closer to Brenda's head. "We don't have time for this! You have five seconds to choose the one who stays. Don't choose and they both die. One."

"Wait!" Thomas looked at Brenda, at Jorge. They both stared at the floor, said nothing. Their faces pale with fear.

"Two."

Thomas suppressed the rising panic, closed his eyes. There was nothing new here. No, he understood things now. Knew what he had to do.

"Three."

No more fear. No more shock. No more questioning. Take what comes. Play along. Pass the tests. Pass the Trials.

"Four!" The man's face reddened. "Choose right now or they both die!"

Thomas opened his eyes and stepped forward. Then he pointed at Brenda and said the two most foul words to ever pass through his lips.

"Kill *her*."

Because of the odd pronouncement that only one could stay, Thomas thought he understood, thought he knew what would happen. That it was yet another Variable and they'd take whomever he *didn't* choose. But he was wrong.

The man jammed his gun into the waistband of his pants, then reached down and grabbed Brenda's shirt with two hands, yanking the girl to her feet. Without a word, he moved toward open air, taking her with him.

CHAPTER 62

Brenda looked at Thomas with panicked eyes, her face full of pain as the stranger dragged her across the metal floor of the Berg. Toward the hatch and certain death.

When he was halfway there, Thomas acted.

He jumped forward and slammed into the man's knees, tackling him to the floor; the gun clattered on the ground next to him. Brenda fell to the side, but Teresa was there to catch her, pull her back from the dangerous edge of the door. Thomas put his left forearm against the man's throat and reached for the gun with his other hand. His fingers found it, gripped it, pulled it close to him. He jumped up and away and held the pistol with both hands, pointing it at the stranger sprawled on his back.

"No one else dies," Thomas said, breathing heavily, somewhat shocked at himself. "If we haven't done enough to pass your stupid tests, then we fail. The tests are over." As he said it, he wondered if this was *supposed* to happen. But even that didn't matter—he meant every word he'd said. The senseless killing and dying had to end.

The stranger's face softened into the slightest hint of a smile and he sat up and scooted backward until he bumped into the wall. As he did so, the large cargo door began closing, the squeak of its hinges like squealing pigs. No one said anything until it clanked shut, one last rush of wind surging through before it did.

"My name's David," the man said, his voice loud in the new silence, broken only by the low hum of the ship's engines and thrusters. "And don't worry, you're right. It's over. It's all over."

Thomas nodded mockingly. "Yeah, we've heard that before. This time we mean it. We're not going to sit back and let you treat us like rats anymore. We're done."

David took a moment to scan the large cargo hold, maybe seeing whether the others agreed with what Thomas had just said. Thomas didn't dare break his gaze, though. He had to believe that they were all behind him.

Finally, David looked back at Thomas, then slowly got to his feet, raising a hand in conciliation as he did so. Once he was standing, he put both hands in his pockets. "What you don't understand is that everything has gone and will continue to go as planned. But you're right, the Trials are complete. We're taking you to a place of safety—a *real* place of safety. No more tests, no more lies, no more setups. No more pretending."

He paused. "I can only promise one thing. When you hear why we've put you through this, and why it's so important that so many of you survived, you'll understand. I promise you'll understand."

Minho snorted. "That's the biggest bunch of klunk I've ever heard in my life."

Thomas couldn't help but feel a little relief that his friend hadn't lost his fire. "And what about the cure? We were promised. For us and the two who helped us get here. How can we believe anything you tell us?"

"Think what you want for now," David said. "Things will change from here out, and you'll get the cure, just like you were told. As soon as we get back to headquarters. You can keep that gun, by the way—we'll even give you some more, if you'd like. There'll be nothing else for you to fight against, no tests or trials to ignore or refuse. Our Berg will land, you'll see that you're safe and cured, and then you can do what you want. The only thing we'll ever ask you to do again is to listen. Only to listen. I'm sure you're at least intrigued by what's behind all this?"

Thomas wanted to scream at the man but knew it'd serve no point. Instead he answered in as calm a voice as possible. "No more games."

"First sign of trouble," Minho added, "we start fighting. If that means we die, then so be it."

David smiled fully this time. "You know, that's exactly what we predicted you'd do at this point." He motioned with an arm toward a small door at the back of the cargo hold. "Shall we?"

Newt spoke up this time. "What's next on the bloody agenda?"

"Just thought you'd like to eat something, maybe take a shower. Sleep." He started walking around the crowd of Gladers and girls. "It's a very long flight."

Thomas and the others spent a few seconds exchanging glances. But in the end they followed. They really had no other option.

CHAPTER 63

Thomas tried hard not to think about things as the next couple of hours passed.

He'd made a stand, but then all that tension and courage and victory kind of trickled away as the group went through the motions of the most ordinary of activities. Hot food. Cold drinks. Medical attention. Wonderfully long showers. Fresh clothes.

Through it all, Thomas recognized the chance that it was all happening again. That he and the others were being pacified, slowly being led to another shock like the one they'd had when they awakened in the dormitory after being rescued from the Maze. But really, what else was there to do? David and the others on his staff made no threats, did nothing to raise alarm.

Refreshed and full of food, Thomas ended up sitting on a couch that ran along the narrow middle section of the Berg, a vast room full of mismatched drab-colored furniture. He'd been avoiding Teresa, but she came over and sat next to him. He still had a hard time being near her, a hard time talking to her or anyone else. His insides burned with turmoil.

But he put it all away because there was nothing else to do. He didn't know how to fly a Berg and wouldn't know where to go even if he could take it over. They'd go wherever WICKED took them, they'd listen, they'd make their decision.

"What're you thinkin' about?" Teresa finally asked.

Thomas was glad she'd spoken aloud—he wasn't sure he wanted to communicate telepathically with her anymore. "What am I thinking about? Mostly trying not to."

"Yeah. Maybe we should just enjoy the peace and quiet for a while."

Thomas looked at Teresa. She sat next to him as if nothing had changed between them at all. As if they were still best friends. And he couldn't stand it anymore.

"I hate that you're acting like nothing happened."

Teresa looked down. "I'm trying to forget just as much as you probably are. Look, I'm not stupid. I know that we can never be the same. But I still wouldn't change anything. It was the plan and it worked. You're not dead and that's worth it to me. Maybe you'll forgive me someday."

Thomas almost hated her for sounding so reasonable. "Well, all I care about right now is stopping these people. It's not right what they've done to us. It doesn't matter how much I was a part of it. It's wrong."

Teresa stretched out a little so she could rest her head against the arm of the couch. "Come on, Tom. They might've erased our memories, but they didn't remove our brains. We were both part of this, and when they tell us everything—when we remember why we put ourselves through this—we're going to do whatever they tell us to."

Thomas thought about that for a second and realized he couldn't possibly have disagreed more. Maybe at one time he'd felt that way, but not now. Though discussing it with Teresa was the last thing he wanted to do. "Maybe you're right," he murmured.

"When's the last time we slept?" she asked. "I swear I can't remember."

Again with the act that all was well. "I do. For me, anyway. It had something to do with a gas chamber and you whacking me over the head with a big spear."

Teresa stretched. "I can only say sorry so many times. At least you got some rest. I didn't sleep for one second while you were out. I think I've been awake for two full days."

"Poor baby." Thomas yawned. He couldn't help himself—he was tired, too.

"Mmmm?"

He looked over to see her eyes closed, her breathing slowed. She'd fallen asleep just like that. He glanced around at the other Gladers and Group Bs. Most of them were zonked out, also. Except Minho—he was trying to talk to some cute girl, but her eyes were closed. Jorge and Brenda were nowhere to be found—something that struck Thomas as strange, not to mention at least a bit worrisome.

It was then that he realized he missed Brenda terribly, but his own eyelids began to droop, and weariness and fatigue crept in. As he sank deeper into the couch, he decided he'd have time to look for her later. Then he finally gave in and allowed the sweet darkness of unconsciousness to take him.

CHAPTER 64

He awoke, blinked, wiped his eyes and saw nothing but pure white. No shapes, no shadows, no variation, nothing. Just white.

A flicker of panic until he realized he must be dreaming. Strange, but a dream for sure. He could feel his body, feel his fingers against his skin. Feel himself breathing. *Hear* himself breathing. Yet he was surrounded by a complete and seamless world of bright nothing.

Tom.

A voice. *Her* voice. Could she talk to him while he was dreaming? Had she done it before? Yes.

Hey, he responded.

Are you . . . okay? She sounded troubled. No, *felt* troubled.

Huh? Yeah, I'm fine. Why?

Just thought you'd be a little surprised right now.

He felt a stab of confusion. *What are you talking about?*

You're about to understand more. Very soon now.

For the first time, Thomas realized the voice wasn't quite right. There was something off about it.

Tom?

He didn't answer. Fear had crept into his gut. A horrible, sickening, toxic fear.

Tom?

Who . . . who are you? he finally asked, terrified of the answer.

A pause before she answered.

It's me, Tom. It's Brenda. Things are about to get bad for you.

Thomas screamed before he knew what he was doing. He screamed and screamed and screamed until it finally woke him up.

CHAPTER 65

He sat straight up, covered in sweat. Even before he could fully compute his surroundings, before all the information traveled through the nerve wires and cognitive functions of his brain, he knew that everything was wrong. That everything had been taken from him all over again.

He lay on the ground, alone, in a room. The walls, the ceiling, the floor—everything was white. The floor beneath him was spongy, hard and smooth but with enough give to be comfortable. He looked at the walls—they were padded, with large buttoned indentations across them, about four feet apart. Bright light shone down from a rectangle in the ceiling, too high for him to reach. The place had a clean smell to it, like ammonia and soap. Thomas looked down to see that even his clothes had no color: a T-shirt, cotton pants, socks.

A brown desk sat about a dozen feet in front of him. It was the only thing in the entire room that wasn't white. Old and battered and scratched, it had a bare wooden chair pushed into the sitting well on the other side. Behind that was the door, padded like the walls.

Thomas felt a strange calm. Instinct told him he should be on his feet, screaming for help. He should be banging on the door. But he knew that door wouldn't open. He knew no one would listen.

He was in the Box all over again, should've known better than to get his hopes up.

I'm not going to panic, he told himself. It had to be another phase of the Trials, and this time he'd fight to change things—to end it all. It was strange, but just knowing he had a plan, that he'd do whatever it took to find freedom, caused a surprising calm to pass over him.

Teresa? he called out. He knew that at this point she and Aris were his only hope for communication with the outside. *Can you hear me? Aris? You there?*

No one responded. Not Teresa. Not Aris. Not . . . Brenda.

But that had only been a dream. It had to have been. Brenda couldn't be working with WICKED, couldn't be speaking in his mind.

Teresa? he said again, throwing hard mental effort into it. *Aris?*

Nothing.

He stood and walked over to the desk, but two feet in front of it he ran into an invisible wall. A barrier, just like back in the dormitory.

Thomas didn't let the panic rise. Didn't let fear overcome him. He took a deep breath, walked back toward the corner of the room, then sat down and leaned into it. Closed his eyes and relaxed.

Waited. Fell asleep.

Tom? Tom!

He didn't know how many times she said it before he finally responded. *Teresa?* He woke with a jolt, looked around and remembered the white room. *Where are you?*

They put us in another dormitory after the Berg landed. We've been here a few days, just sitting around doing nothing. Tom, what happened to you?

Teresa was worried—scared, even. That much he knew for sure. As for himself, he mostly felt confused. *A few days? What—*

They took you away as soon as the Berg landed. They keep telling us it was too late—that the Flare is too rooted in you. They said you've gotten crazy and violent.

Thomas tried to hold it together, tried not to think about how

WICKED could wipe memories. *Teresa . . . it's just another part of the Trials. They've got me locked up in this white room. But . . . you've been there for* days*? How many?*

Tom, it's been almost a week.

Thomas couldn't respond. Almost wanted to pretend he hadn't heard what Teresa had just said. The fear he'd been holding back began to slowly seep into his chest. Could he trust her? She'd lied to him so much already. And how did he even know this was really her? It was high time to cut off ties with Teresa.

Tom? Teresa called to him again. *What's going on here? I'm really confused.*

Thomas felt a rush of emotion, a burning inside him that almost brought tears to his eyes. He had once considered Teresa his best friend. But it could never be like that again. Now all he felt when he thought of her was anger.

Tom! Why aren't you—

Teresa, listen to me.

Hello? That's what I'm trying to—

No, just . . . listen. Don't say anything else, okay? Just listen to me.

She paused. *Okay.* A quiet, scared voice in his mind.

Thomas couldn't control it anymore. Rage pulsed inside of him. Luckily, he only had to think the words, because he could never have spoken them aloud.

Teresa. Go away.

Tom—

No. Don't say another word. Just . . . leave me alone. And you can tell WICKED that I'm done playing their games. Tell them I'm done!

She waited a few seconds before responding. *Okay.* Another pause. *Okay. Then I just have one thing left to say to you.*

Thomas sighed. *I can't wait.*

She didn't say it right away, and he would've thought she'd left him except that he still felt her presence. Finally, she spoke again.

Tom?

What?

WICKED is good.

And then she was gone.

EPILOGUE

WICKED Memorandum, Date 232.2.13, Time 21:13

TO: My Associates

FROM: Ava Paige, Chancellor

RE: SCORCH TRIALS, Groups A and B

This is not a time to let emotions interfere with the task at hand. Yes, some events have gone in a direction we didn't foresee. Not all is ideal—things have gone wrong—but we've made tremendous progress and have collected many of the needed patterns. I feel a great amount of hope.

I expect all of us to maintain our professional demeanor and remember our purpose. The lives of so many people rest in the hands of so few. This is why it's an especially important time for vigilance and focus.

The days to come are fundamental to this study, and I have every confidence that when we restore their memories, every one of our subjects will be ready for what we plan to ask of them. We still have the Candidates we need. The final pieces will be found and put into place.

The future of the human race outweighs all. Every death and every sacrifice are well worth the ultimate outcome. The end of this monumental effort is coming, and I believe that the process will work. That we'll have our patterns. That we'll have our blueprint. That we'll have our cure.

The Psychs are deliberating even now. When they say the time is right, we'll remove the Swipe and tell our remaining subjects if they are—or are not—immune to the Flare.

That's all for now.

END OF BOOK TWO

ACKNOWLEDGMENTS

I can't really say it better than I did in Book One. To all the same people, especially Lynette, Krista, Michael and Lauren, thank you. You've changed my life forever. Thanks also to all the people at Random House who have worked so hard to make this series a success, including my publicists, Noreen Herits and Emily Pourciau, and all the amazing sales reps out there. I seriously can't believe how incredibly lucky and blessed I am. Thank you. And finally, to my readers: you rock and I love you.

HERE'S A SPECIAL PREVIEW OF BOOK 3 IN THE MAZE RUNNER SERIES.

CHAPTER 2

Thomas had imagined this happening, countless times. What he would do, what he would say. How he'd rush forward and tackle anyone who came in, make a run for it, flee, escape. But these thoughts were almost for amusement more than anything. He knew WICKED wouldn't let something like that happen. No, he'd need to plan out every detail before he made his move.

When it *did* happen—when that door popped open with a slight puffing sound and began to swing wide—Thomas surprised himself by how he reacted. He did nothing. Something told him an invisible barrier had appeared between him and the desk—like back in the dorms after the Maze. The time for action hadn't arrived. Not yet.

He felt only the slightest hint of surprise when the Rat Man walked in—the guy who'd informed the Gladers of the last trial they'd been forced on, through the Scorch. Same long nose, same weasel-like eyes; that greasy hair, combed over an obvious bald spot that took up half his head. Same ridiculous white suit. He looked paler than the last time Thomas had seen him, though, and he was holding a thick folder filled with dozens of crinkled and messily stacked papers in the crook of his arm and dragging a straight-backed chair.

"Good morning, Thomas," he said with a stiff nod. Without waiting for a response, he pulled the door shut, set his chair behind the desk and took a seat. He placed the folder in front of him and opened it, started flipping through pages. When he found what he'd been looking for he stopped and rested his hands on top of everything. Then he flashed a pathetic grin, his eyes finally settling on Thomas.

When Thomas finally spoke, he realized that he hadn't done so in weeks, and his voice came out more like a croak. "It'll only be good if you let me out."

"Yes, yes, I know. No need to worry—you're going to be hearing plenty of positive news today. Trust me."

Thomas thought about that, ashamed that he let it lift his hopes, even for a second. He should know better by now. "*Positive* news? Didn't you choose us because you thought we were intelligent?"

Rat Man remained silent for several seconds before he responded. "Intelligent, yes. Among more important reasons." He paused and studied Thomas before continuing. "Do you think we *enjoy* all this? You think we *enjoy* watching you suffer? It's all been for a purpose, and very soon it will make sense to you." The intensity of his words had built until he'd practically shouted that last word, his face now red.

"Whoa," Thomas said, feeling bolder by the minute. "Slim it nice and calm there, old fella. You look three steps away from a heart attack."

The man stood from his chair and leaned forward on the desk, the veins in his neck standing out in taut cords. He slowly sat back down, took several deep breaths. "You would think that almost four weeks in this white box might humble a boy. But you seem more arrogant than ever."

"So are you going to tell me that I'm not crazy, then? Don't have the Flare, never did?" Thomas couldn't help himself. The anger was rising in him and he felt like he was going to explode. But he forced a calmness into his voice. "That's what kept me sane through all this—deep down I know you lied to Teresa, that this is just another one of your tests. So where do I go next? Gonna send me to the shuck moon? Make me swim across the ocean in my undies?" He smiled for effect.

The Rat Man had been staring at Thomas with blank eyes throughout his rant. "Are you finished?"

"No, I'm not finished. I want you to tell me everything. Now."

"Oh, Thomas." The Rat Man said it quietly, as if delivering sad news to a small child. "We didn't lie to you. You *do* have the Flare."

A cold chill cut through the heat of Thomas's rage. He was sure they'd lied to him before—though Rat Man could just be lying again now. He took a deep breath and shrugged, as if the news was something he heard every day. "Well, even so, I haven't started going crazy yet." At a certain point—after all that time crossing the Scorch, being with Brenda, surrounded by Cranks—he'd come to terms with the fact that he'd catch the virus eventually. But he told himself that for now he was still okay. Still sane. And that was all that mattered at the moment.

Rat Man sighed. "You don't understand. You don't understand what it is that I came in here to tell you."

"Why would I believe a word that comes out of your mouth?"

Thomas realized that he'd stood up, though he had no memory of doing so. His chest lurched with heavy breaths. He had to get control of himself. Rat Man's stare was cold, his eyes black pits. Regardless of whether this man lied to him, Thomas knew he was going to have to hear him out if he ever wanted to leave this white room. He forced his breathing to slow. He waited.

After several seconds of silence, his visitor continued. "I know we've lied to you. Often. We've done some awful things to you and your friends. But it was all part of a plan that you not only agreed to, but helped set in place. We've had to take it all a little farther than we'd hoped in the beginning—there's no doubt about that. However, everything has stayed true to the spirit of what the Creators envisioned—what *you* envisioned in their place after they were . . . purged."

Thomas slowly shook his head; he knew he'd been involved with these people once, somehow, but the concept of putting anyone through what he'd gone through was incomprehensible. "You didn't answer me. How can you possibly expect me to believe anything you say?" He recalled more than he let on, of course. Though the window to his past was caked with grime, revealing little more than splotchy glimpses, he knew he'd worked with WICKED. He knew Teresa had too, and that they'd helped create the Maze. There'd been other flashes of memory.

"Because, Thomas, there's no value in keeping you in the dark," Rat Man said. "Not anymore."

Thomas felt a sudden weariness, like all the strength had

seeped out of him, leaving him with nothing. He sank to the floor with a heavy sigh. He shook his head. "I don't even know what that means."

Rat Man kept talking, but his tone became less detached and clinical and more teacherly. "You are obviously well aware that we have a horrible disease eating the minds of humans worldwide. Everything we've done up to now has been for one purpose and one purpose only—to analyze your brain patterns and build a blueprint from them. The goal is to use this blueprint to develop a cure for the Flare. The lives lost, the pain and suffering—you knew the stakes when this began. We all did. It was all to ensure the survival of the human race. And we're very close. Very, very close."

Memories had come back to Thomas on several occasions. The Changing, the dreams he'd had since, fleeting glimpses here and there, like quick lightning strikes in his mind. And right now, listening to the white-suited man talk, it felt as if he stood a few feet back from a cliff and all the answers were just about to float up from the depths for him to see in their entirety.

But he was still wary. He knew he couldn't trust anything, despite being aware that he'd been a part of it all, had helped design the Maze, had taken over after the original Creators died and kept the program going with new recruits. "I remember enough to be ashamed of myself," he admitted. "But living through this kind of abuse is a lot different than planning it. It's just not right."

Rat Man scratched his nose, shifted in his seat. Something Thomas said had gotten to him. "We'll see what you think at the end of today, Thomas. We shall see. But let me ask this—

are you telling me that the lives of a few aren't worth losing to save countless more?" Again, the man spoke with passion, leaning forward.

Thomas only stared. It was a question he couldn't answer.

The Rat Man might have smiled, but it looked more like a sneer on his face. "Just remember that at one time you did think that, Thomas." He started to collect his papers as if to go but didn't move. "I'm here to tell you that everything is set and our data is almost complete. Once we have the blueprint, you can go boo-hoo with your friends all you want about how *unfair* we've been."

Thomas wanted to cut the man with harsh words. But he held back. "How does torturing us lead to this blueprint you're talking about?"

Rat Man sighed heavily. "Boy, soon you'll remember everything, and I have a feeling you're going to regret a lot. In the meantime, there's something you need to know right now and maybe it'll bring you back to your senses."

"And what's that?" Thomas really had no idea what the man would say.

His visitor stood up, smoothed the wrinkles out of his pants and adjusted his coat. Then he clasped his hands behind his back. "You're *immune* to the Flare, Thomas. The virus lives in every molecule of your body, yet it has no effect on you, nor will it ever."

Thomas swallowed.

"On the outside, in the streets, they call you people Munies," Rat Man continued. "And they really, really hate you."

If you love

THE MAZE RUNNER,

don't miss this sneak peek at the first book in James Dashner's new series, The Mortality Doctrine:

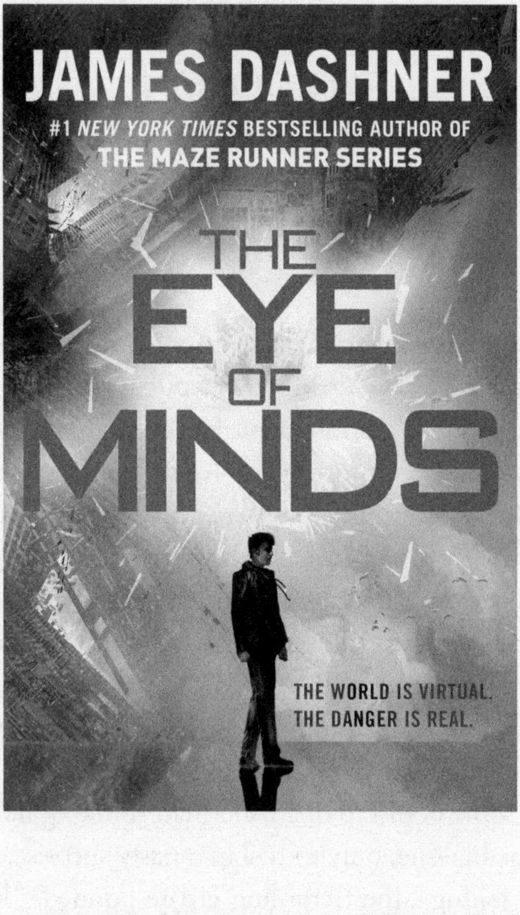

CHAPTER 1

THE COFFIN

1

Michael spoke against the wind, to a girl named Tanya.

"I know it's water down there, but it might as well be concrete. You'll be flat as a pancake the second you hit."

Not the most comforting choice of words when talking to someone who wanted to end her life, but it was certainly the truth. Tanya had just climbed over the railing of the Golden Gate Bridge, cars zooming by on the road, and was leaning back toward the open air, her twitchy hands holding on to a pole wet with mist. Even if somehow Michael could talk her out of jumping, those slippery fingers might get the job done anyway. And then it'd be lights-out. He pictured some poor sap of a fisherman thinking he'd finally caught the big one, only to reel in a nasty surprise.

"Stop joking," the trembling girl responded. "It's not a game—not anymore."

Michael was inside the VirtNet—the Sleep, to people

who went in as often as he did. He was used to seeing scared people there. A lot of them. Yet underneath the fear was usually the *knowing*. Knowing deep down that no matter what was happening in the Sleep, it wasn't real.

Not with Tanya. Tanya was different. At least, her Aura, her computer-simulated counterpart, was. Her Aura had this bat-crazy look of pure terror on her face, and it suddenly gave Michael chills—made him feel like *he* was the one hovering over that long drop to death. And Michael wasn't a big fan of death, fake or not.

"It *is* a game, and you know it," he said louder than he'd wanted to—he didn't want to startle her. But a cold wind had sprung up, and it seemed to grab his words and whisk them down to the bay. "Get back over here and let's talk. We'll both get our Experience Points, and we can go explore the city, get to know each other. Find some crazies to spy on. Maybe even hack some free food from the shops. It'll be good times. And when we're done, we'll find you a Portal, and you can Lift back home. Take a break from the game for a while."

"This has nothing to do with *Lifeblood*!" Tanya screamed at him. The wind pulled at her clothes, and her dark hair fanned out behind her like laundry on a line. "Just go away and leave me alone. I don't want your pretty-boy face to be the last thing I see."

Michael thought of *Lifeblood Deep,* the next level, the goal of all goals. Where everything was a thousand times more real, more advanced, more intense. He was three years away from earning his way inside. Maybe two. But right then he needed to talk this dopey girl out of jumping to her date with the fishes or he'd be sent back to the Suburbs for a week, making *Lifeblood Deep* that much further away.

"Okay, look . . ." He was trying to choose his words carefully, but he'd already made a pretty big mistake and knew it. Going out of character and using the game itself as a reason for her to stop what she was doing meant he'd be docked points big-time. And it was all about the points. But this girl was legitimately starting to scare him. It was that face—pale and sunken, as if she'd already died.

"Just go away!" she yelled. "You don't get it. I'm trapped here. Portals or no Portals. I'm trapped! He won't let me Lift!"

Michael wanted to scream right back at her—she was talking nonsense. A dark part of him wanted to say forget it, tell her she was a loser, let her nosedive. She was being so stubborn—it wasn't like any of it was really happening. *It's just a game.* He had to remind himself of that all the time.

But he couldn't mess this up. He needed the points. "All right. Listen." He took a step back, held his hands up like he was trying to calm a scared animal. "We just met—give it some time. I promise I won't do anything nutty. You wanna jump, I'll let you jump. But at least talk to me. Tell me why."

Tears lined her cheeks; her eyes had gone red and puffy. "Just go away. Please." Her voice had taken on the softness of defeat. "I'm not messing around here. I'm done with this—all of this!"

"Done? Okay, that's fine to be done. But you don't have

to screw it up for me, too, right?" Michael figured maybe it was okay to talk about the game after all, since she was using it as her reason to end it—to check out of the Virtual-Flesh-and-Bones Hotel and never come back. "Seriously. Walk back to the Portal with me, Lift yourself, do it the right way. You're done with the game, you're safe, I get my points. Ain't that the happiest ending you ever heard of?"

"I hate you," she spat. Literally. A spray of misty saliva. "I don't even know you and I hate you. This has nothing to do with *Lifeblood*!"

"Then tell me what it *does* have to do with." He said it kindly, trying to keep his composure. "You've got all day to jump. Just give me a few minutes. Talk to me, Tanya."

She buried her head in the crook of her right arm. "I just can't do it anymore." She whimpered and her shoulders shook, making Michael worry about her grip again. "I can't."

Some people are just weak, he thought, though he wasn't stupid enough to say it.

Lifeblood was by *far* the most popular game in the VirtNet. Yeah, you could go off to some nasty battlefield in the Civil War or fight dragons with a magic sword, fly spaceships, explore the freaky love shacks. But that stuff got old quick. In the end, nothing was more fascinating than bare-bones, dirt-in-your-face, gritty, get-me-out-of-here real life. Nothing. And there were some, like Tanya, who obviously couldn't handle it. Michael sure could. He'd risen up its ranks almost as quickly as legendary gamer Gunner Skale.

"Come on, Tanya," he said. "How can it hurt to talk to me? And if you're going to quit, why would you want to end your last game by killing yourself so violently?"

Her head snapped up and she looked at him with eyes so hard he shivered again.

"Kaine's haunted me for the last time," she said. "He can't just trap me here and use me for an experiment—sic the KillSims on me. I'm gonna rip my Core out."

Those last words changed everything. Michael watched in horror as Tanya tightened her grip on the pole with one hand, then reached up with the other and started digging into her own flesh.

2

Michael forgot the game, forgot the points. The situation had gone from annoying to actual life-and-death. In all his years of playing, he'd never seen someone code out their Core, destroying the barrier device within the Coffin that kept the virtual world and the real world separate in their mind.

"Stop that!" he yelled, one foot already on the railing. "Stop!"

He jumped down onto the catwalk on the outer edge of the bridge and froze. He was just a few feet from her now, and he wanted to avoid any quick movements that might cause her to panic. Holding his hands out, he took a small step toward her.

"Don't do that," Michael said as softly as he could in the biting wind.

Tanya kept digging into her right temple. She'd peeled back pieces of her skin; a stream of blood from the wound quickly covered her hands and the side of her face in red gore. A look of terrifying calmness had come over her, as if she had no concept of what she was doing to herself, though Michael knew well enough that she was busy hacking the code.

"Stop coding for one second!" Michael shouted. "Would you just talk about this before you rip your freaking *Core* out? You know what that means."

"Why do you care so much?" she responded, so quietly that Michael had to read her lips to understand. But at least she'd stopped digging.

Michael just stared. Because she *had* stopped digging and was now reaching inside the torn mass of flesh with her thumb and forefinger. "You just want your Experience Points," she said. Slowly, she pulled out a small metallic chip slick with blood.

"I'll forfeit my points," Michael said, trying to hide his fear and disgust. "I swear. You can't mess around anymore, Tanya. Code that thing back in and come talk to me. It's not too late."

She held up the visual manifestation of the Core, gazed at it with fascination. "Don't you see the irony in all this?" she asked. "If it weren't for my coding skills, I probably wouldn't even know who Kaine was. About his KillSims and his plans for me. But I'm good at it, and because of that . . . *monster,* I just programmed the Core right out of my own head."

"Not your real head. It's still just a simulation, Tanya. It's not too late." Michael couldn't remember a time in his entire life when he'd felt that ill.

She looked at him so sharply that he took a step backward. "I can't take it anymore. I can't take . . . *him* anymore. He can't use me if I'm dead. I'm done."

She curled the Core onto her thumb, then flicked it toward Michael. It flew over his shoulder—he saw flashes of sunlight glint off it as it spun through the air, almost like it was winking at him, saying, *Hey, buddy, you suck at suicide negotiations.* It landed with a *plink* somewhere out in the traffic, where it would be crushed in seconds.

He couldn't believe what he was witnessing. Someone so sophisticated at manipulating code that she could destroy her Core—the device that essentially protected players' brains while they were in the Sleep. Without your Core, your brain wouldn't be able to filter the stimulation of the VirtNet properly. If your Core died in the Sleep, you'd die in the Wake. He didn't know *anyone* who'd seen this before. Two hours earlier he'd been eating stolen bleu chips at the Dan the Man Deli with his best friends. All he wanted now was to be back there, eating turkey on rye, enduring Bryson's jokes about old ladies' underwear and listening to Sarah tell him how awful his latest Sleep haircut was.

"If Kaine comes for *you,*" Tanya said, "tell him that I won in the end. Tell him how brave I was. He can trap people here and steal all the bodies he wants. But not mine."

Michael was done talking. He couldn't take one more word out of this girl's blood-smeared mouth. As quickly as anything he'd ever done in his life, as any character in any game, he jumped toward the pole she clung to.

She screamed, momentarily frozen by his sudden action, but then she let go, actually pushed herself away from the bridge. Michael grabbed for the railing to his left with one hand and reached for her with the other but missed both. His feet hit something solid, then slipped. Arms flailing, he felt nothing but air, and he fell, almost in sync with her.

An incredible shriek escaped his mouth, something he would've been embarrassed about if his only companion wasn't about to lose her life. With her Core coded out, her death would be real.

Michael and Tanya fell toward the harsh gray waters of the bay. Wind tore at their clothes, and Michael's heart felt like it was creeping along the inside of his chest, up his throat. He screamed again. On some level he knew he would hit the water, feel the pain; then he'd be Lifted and wake up back home, safe and sound in his Coffin. But the VirtNet's power was feigned reality, and right now the reality was terror.

Somehow Michael's and Tanya's Auras found each other on that long fall, chest to chest, like tandem skydivers. As the churning surface below rushed toward them, they wrapped their arms around each other, pulling closer together. Michael wanted to scream again but clamped his jaw shut when he saw the complete calmness on her face.

Her eyes bored into Michael's, searched him, and found him, and he broke somewhere on the inside.

JAMES DASHNER was born and raised in Georgia but now lives and writes in the Rocky Mountains. He is the author of the #1 *New York Times* bestselling Maze Runner series: *The Maze Runner, The Scorch Trials, The Death Cure,* and *The Kill Order,* as well as *The Eye of Minds* and *The Rule of Thoughts,* the first two books in the Mortality Doctrine series. To learn more about James and his books, visit jamesdashner.com, follow @jamesdashner on Twitter, and find him on Instagram: dashnerjames.

YOU'VE READ THE BOOK.
NOW SEE THE MOVIE.
BLU-RAY + DVD + DIGITAL HD
THE MAZE RUNNER
LOOK FOR IT ON BLU-RAY™* WITH
A COLLECTIBLE PREQUEL COMIC BOOK
AND MOBILE GAME OFFER!†
ALSO AVAILABLE ON DVD
* Available on 12/16/14.
† While Supplies Last.
PARENTS STRONGLY CAUTIONED
PG-13